JUST BETWEEN US

KU-741-148

Cathy Kelly is the author of five other novels – *Never Too Late*, *She's the One*, *Woman to Woman*, *Someone Like You* and *What She Wants*, all of which were No. 1 bestsellers in Ireland as well as reaching the *Sunday Times* Top Ten. *Someone Like You* was the Parker RNA Romantic Novel of the Year. Cathy Kelly lives in Wicklow with her partner and their dog. Her seventh novel, *Best of Friends*, will be published by Harper-Collins in autumn 2003.

For more information about Cathy Kelly, visit her website at www.cathykelly.com.

Acclaim for Cathy Kelly:

'Cheerful . . . totally believable.'

ROSAMUNDE PILCHER

'. . . Kelly's admirable capacity to make the reader identify, in turn, with each of her female characters. *Just Between Us* is a fast-moving and entertaining account of how appearances rarely match realities and how even if dreams don't come true they're still worth dreaming.'

Irish Independent

'A feel-good tale.' *Woman's Own*

'Plenty of sparky humour.' *The Times*

'A compulsive read' *Women's Weekly*

'Warm and chatty' *Daily Mail*

'That feel-good factor in the form of the loving support of friends and relatives is a particularly endearing trait, spreading warmth and satisfying resolution.'

Publishing News

CATHY KELLY

Just Between Us

INDEX

HarperCollins*Publishers*
77–85 Fulham Palace Road,
Hammersmith, London W6 8JB

www.harpercollins.co.uk

This edition published 2004 for Index Books Limited
3 5 7 9 8 6 4

First published in Great Britain by
HarperCollins*Publishers* 2002

ISBN 0 00 769759 7

Printed and bound in Great Britain by
Mackays of Chatham Ltd, Chatham, Kent

To John, with love

ACKNOWLEDGEMENTS

During the writing of this book, there were times when I seriously thought I wouldn't be able to finish it and toyed with the idea of an abrupt ending that involved everything suddenly working out in the space of two pages, with a classic *Scooby Doo* explanation of how it had all happened, and a final, speedy line such as 'and they all lived happily ever afterwards'.

Anyhow, thanks to lots of love and support from the people in my life, I clambered over the 'I-can't-finish-it/ *Scooby Doo*' hump and finished *Just Between Us*. I think that's what acknowledgements are for: to say a profound thanks to the people who give encouragement, support and who listen patiently to the writer moaning about how awful the whole book is turning out. To other people, acknowledgements probably sound as corny as the acceptance speech at my TV soap awards ceremony, but they're from the heart.

So, from the heart:

Thanks to John, for the sort of love and support that just can't be put into words. To Mum, as always, lots of love from me and Tamsin for everything you do; to Francis and Lucy, the best big brother and little sister in the world; much love to Anne and Dave, and special mentions for my dear nieces and nephew, Laura, Naomi, Emer and Robert. And of course, dear Tamsin.

Thanks to Lisa and Annmarie, whose grown-up namesake appears in this book – with a degree in shopping! Thanks to Stella O'Connell for giving me the name for one of my heroines, thanks to Kate Thompson for advice and kindness, thanks to Margaret, Sarah Hamilton, Marian Keyes and Susan Zaidan for friendship, thanks to Patricia Scanlan for lighting candles, thanks to Srs Vincent and Breeda for prayers, to Sheila O'Flanagan for giving me the notion of Hula Girl. How do you get that off your computer, again? Thanks to Lola Simpson and Siobhan O'Reilly. Thanks to Christine and Simon Calver: for teaching me roulette and getting Bunny in return!

Huge thanks to Ali Gunn at Curtis Brown for endless support and cheering phone calls, also thanks to Carol Jackson and all at CB.

Special thanks and flowers have to go to Rachel Hore, Jennifer Parr and Lynne Drew at HarperCollins, without whom this book would be a pamphlet (although probably easier to read in bed). Thank you all for doing so much for me and for making it such fun. Thanks to the entire team at HarperCollins, who are friends as well as colleagues, starting with dear Moira Reilly and Tony Purdue, the Irish A-team. Thanks to Nick Sayers, Amanda Ridout, Fiona McIntosh, Maxine Hitchcock, Martin Palmer, Jane Harris, John Bond, Victoria Barnsley, Esther Taylor, Venetia Butterfield, Sara Wikner, Anne O'Brien, Lee Motley, Phyllis Acolatse, Mike McQueen, Steve Newell and all the HC team.

Thanks to everyone at HarperCollins Australia for being so wonderful (and letting me in on the yoga class). Thanks to lovely Karen-Maree Griffiths and Louisa Dear for taking care of me, thanks to Christine Farmer, Jim Demetriou, David Lange, Arthur Cavalliotis, John Wilkinson, Michael Mousallem and every one of the team who made me so utterly welcome.

In New York, thanks to Deborah Schneider, also big thanks to my Dutton and Plume family in the US: Carole Baron, Laurie Chittenden, Stephanie Bowe, Lisa Johnson, Brant Janeway and Sarah Melnyk.

Thanks to Joanne, Esther, Larissa, Yvonne, Moria and all my dear ex-colleagues who can never remember any decent gossip when I phone up. Thanks to the wonderful writing sisterhood that includes Martina Devlin, Jane Moore, Colette Caddle, Susan Lewis, Jenny Colgan, and all my writer friends, especially the girls at the RNA who write such wonderful books.

Last but certainly not least, there are two important groups of people to thank: all the lovely booksellers who sell my books and all the marvellous people all over the world who buy them. Thank you.

Finally, Ireland has lots of glorious places with gloriously Irish names, names that probably sound mad to other people but absolutely normal to us. Due to my constant fear of creating characters who coincidentally happen to have the same names as real people who live in the same place as in my book, I like to make up place names. I wrongly thought I'd made up the name Kinvara (don't ask me how) until I was in the supermarket and saw smoked salmon from a real place called Kinvara. Eeek.

And just in case, I asked people did they know of any other Kinvaras.

'Ah, sure there's loads of them,' I was told.

Double eek. Anyway, my Kinvara is my own invention and to make it different, I called it Kinvarra. And ditto Castletown, which is made up and is not one of the scores of Castletowns dotted around the place. Place names aside, I hope you enjoy *Just Between Us*.

JUST BETWEEN US

PROLOGUE: MARCH

Adele looked at the invitation and wondered exactly how much it would cost to print up at least a hundred such creamy, expensive cards. A fortune, she'd bet. It was the embossing that cost so much. And for all that it looked so nice, it was a waste of money.

There were perfectly acceptable invitations available in the newsagent's – ones that you filled in yourself – but clearly, run-of-the-mill invitations weren't good enough for her sister-in-law. But then, Rose had always had notions above her station.

Adele ran a deeply disapproving finger over the extravagant letters.

Rose & Hugh Miller have great pleasure in
inviting Adele Miller to a lunch party to celebrate
their Ruby Wedding Anniversary on Saturday,
April 25th at Meadow Lodge, Kinvarra.

She scanned down to the dress code, which was 'smart casual', whatever *that* meant.

She'd wear one of her knitted suits, as she always did. She might be sixty-five, but she was proud of the fact that she was still trimmer than many women of her age. Maybe a shawl just in case it was cold, because it would only be April, and the party was going to be in a marquee and not in the actual house. Adele hadn't been keen on the idea of a marquee. Talk about a waste of money, not to mention delusions

1

of grandeur. Then Hugh had told her it had been his idea, which had suddenly made the whole plan sound like a great idea after all.

'A big party in the house could destroy the place, what with high heels digging into the wooden floors and red wine on the chairs, you know that, Della my love,' Hugh had said the previous week when he'd popped in on his way back from a meeting with a client in a nearby town. Adele had smiled fondly at her little brother as he tucked into the steak sandwich she'd made for him as a little treat. He was the only person in the world who still called her Della. Not that Adele would have permitted anyone else to call her by a pet name. Even the doctor she'd known for forty years was on pain of death to call her anything but Miss Miller. The cheeky pup of a postman had tried to call her by her first name once, but Adele had soon put a halt to his gallop. She wasn't one for modern ideas of familiarity.

But Hugh could call her any name he liked. Her darling brother could do no wrong.

'You've got to have a party for your fortieth wedding anniversary,' Hugh went on, munching his sandwich appreciatively. Hugh liked his food. He was a big man after all, and handsome, Adele thought, with that six-foot frame and the shock of silver hair. His hair had been an Arctic white-blond once, so he was truly a golden boy. All Adele's friends had been half in love with him all those years ago. If only she'd found a man like her brother, she might have married too, she thought wistfully.

She glanced down at the invitation. 'RSVP' it said. No time like the present.

Her sister-in-law answered on the third ring, sounding out of breath.

'Hi, Adele,' Rose said, 'I was just running the vacuum over the rugs. The place is such a mess.'

Adele thought this was highly unlikely. Her sister-in-law's home, eight miles away on the other side of the sprawling country town of Kinvarra, was always sparkling. And elegant too. Although it irked Adele to admit it, Rose did have fabulous taste. Who else would have thought of knocking down all those internal walls to transform the rather dark reception rooms into a well-proportioned open-plan space? Adele preferred carpets herself, but the pale wooden floors with their muted rugs looked elegantly modern and fresh compared with the conservative dark maroon carpet that graced Adele's more traditional Victorian-style house.

'I got the invitation,' Adele said stiffly.

'Did you like it?' asked Rose. 'Hugh picked it. I feel a bit guilty spending so much, Adele. They've just laid off twenty more people in the tyre factory down the road, you know, and here we are having a big party with a marquee and caterers and flowers ... The poverty action group is in serious need of funds and all this excess doesn't seem right . . .' Her voice trailed off but, in her indignation, Adele didn't notice.

'My brother's an important person in Kinvarra; people would think it odd if he didn't celebrate according to his status,' Adele said stiffly. 'They'd certainly think it was odd if you didn't have a grand party for your ruby anniversary.' Rose seemed to forget that the Miller family were pillars of the community. How would it look if they weren't seen to be doing things properly? People might talk. Adele was deeply against having people talk about the family.

'You're right, Adele,' Rose said lightly. 'I'm getting paranoid in my old age; I worry about the silliest things. I do hope you can make it? Hugh would be devastated if you couldn't. We all would be. It wouldn't be the same without you,' she added kindly.

Adele pursed her lips. This was not going as planned. She hadn't meant to endorse the whole event, certainly not without some reservations. But for Rose to even imply that she, Adele, might miss it! Her darling brother's party. By rights, no arrangements should have been made until she had been consulted. She was the oldest member of the Miller clan, three years older than Hugh. She *should* have been consulted. What if she'd had something planned and couldn't manage the third Saturday in April?

'I must fly, Adele,' Rose was saying in that low, soft, accentless voice of hers. Adele often wondered how Rose had drilled the accent out of her speech. 'I've got another call coming in. Probably the florist. Thank you for calling so early, you are a love. Take care. Bye.'

And she was gone, leaving Adele as highly vexed as she usually was after conversations with her sister-in-law. Florist indeed. Far from florists Rose had been reared. The Miller family had always had lovely flowers in the house, of course. They'd had a maid, for God's sake, when nobody else in the country had one. But Rose came from a tumbledown house on some backroad in Wexford; a house with slates coming off the roof and plumbing out of the Ark. There hadn't been enough money for food in the Riordain house, never mind flowers. Marrying Hugh had been Rose's ticket out of there. Adele glowered at the phone. She had a good mind to phone back and point out that Rose could do the flowers herself and not waste money on a florist. Rose had a knack with flowers. As if in honour of her name, in summer there were always roses all over the place: blowsy yellow ones that matched the buttercup yellow walls and a big china bowl of riotous pink blooms which usually sat on a low, Scandinavian coffee table. All Rose ever did was to carelessly place a handpicked bouquet in a vase and the flowers all fell into place beautifully. She was the same when it came to clothes, thought Adele resentfully. The oldest white shirt looked elegantly informal on Rose Miller because she always had some trick of pinning her dark hair into a soft knot, or of hanging a strand of pearls around her neck, and then she looked instantly right.

Adele had spent years doing her best not to resent Rose. It hadn't been easy, for all that Rose was so kind to her. Kindness, like other people's happiness, could be very hard to deal with. And speaking of happiness, here was more proof of how lucky Rose was. She had a lovely home, three

4

grown-up daughters, Stella, Tara and Holly, who'd never given her an iota of bother, and no financial worries, thanks to dear Hugh.

Hugh, Adele had always felt, was the real reason that Rose had had such a wonderful life. Adele adored her baby brother passionately. He was so clever and kind. He'd plucked Rose from an impoverished background and her dull secretarial job and turned her into a Miller lady. And now Hugh and Rose were celebrating their ruby wedding anniversary, complete with uniformed caterers and florists, the whole nine yards. It was like their wedding all over again, Adele thought bitterly, remembering herself, a drab bridesmaid next to the radiant Rose. All eyes had been on the bride with tiny coral-pink rosebuds pinned into the cloud of her dark hair. Even Colin, Adele's young man, had remarked upon how lovely Rose looked.

'Good old Hugh.' Colin had been frankly envious. 'He's a lucky fellow to be marrying a girl like her.'

Adele had never forgiven Colin for not understanding how much she felt she'd lost Hugh to Rose. She'd spent hours pinning her fair hair up with little hair clips to show off her long neck and had even dabbed on a bit of rouge and Coral Surprise lipstick, angry with herself for giving in to vanity. It had been no good. Rose had glittered like the sun, over-shadowing Adele without even meaning to, and Adele had never, ever been able to forgive her.

Lost in her memories, for a moment Adele let her customary guard down. Her normally stiff back drooped and she sank down onto the arm of a faded old wing chair. If she'd said yes to Colin all those years ago, would she have had a golden life, a family like Hugh and Rose? Colin had been a nice man, sweet and gentle. He simply hadn't measured up when compared to Hugh, though. Nobody could. At the time, measuring up to Hugh had seemed very important, but now it was different. Adele was lonely. The sidelines were cold and she was always on them, watching other people's lives and, somehow, not feeling a part of it all. While Rose had everything. Everything. Why had Lady Luck shone so brightly on Rose, who was only a Miller by marriage, and utterly bypassed Adele?

Even the autumn blight that had savaged Adele's beech hedge had left her sister-in-law's untouched. And Rose had her beloved girls, the golden Miller girls. Those three girls had led charmed lives, Adele felt, and though they'd undoubtedly been indulged by Hugh, it had all turned out so well.

Adele went to the desk where she kept her stamps and notepad, and wrote formally to accept the invitation to the anniversary party. The phone call had been more in the line of information gathering, rather than an actual response. Adele Miller had been brought up properly, and written invitations got a written reply. It was the kind of behaviour that implied breeding, the sort of thing that people who were dragged up in little cottages in the back of beyond didn't understand.

'I would be delighted to attend . . .' wrote Adele, her language as formal as the Queen's. She sighed. Despite everything, she was looking forward to the party, actually. Parties in Hugh's were always fun and a fortieth wedding anniversary was sure to be a splendid affair. She'd get her hair set, of course. Happier at this thought, Adele began to plan.

CHAPTER ONE

The previous December: two weeks before Christmas

Rose Miller hated committees. Which was a bit unfortunate, because she was on three of them. The Kinvarra Charity Committee was the most irritating for the simple reason that its internal wranglings took so much time, there wasn't a moment left to actually raise any money for charity. Discussions about the size of the type on the menus for the annual ladies' lunch, and whether to serve salmon or beef, had taken endless phone calls and two lengthy meetings. If Rose hadn't practically lost her temper, the committee would still be arguing over it.

'Does it really matter what the menus look like or what we eat?' she'd demanded fierily at the final, drawn-out meeting, rising to her feet and making all the other committee ladies clutch their copies of the minutes in shock. Mrs Rose Miller with her dark eyes flashing in anger was not a common sight. A tireless worker for the local charities, she was known for her calm self-possession and for her organisational skills. Tall and strikingly elegant with her trademark upswept hairdo, she was almost regal in her anger. 'We're here to raise money, not waste it. Is this our best effort for the underprivileged of this town? To sit in a cosy hotel bar and slurp our way through urns of coffee and entire boxes of custard creams while we discuss minutiae?'

'Good point,' squeaked Mrs Freidland, the current chair-woman, who'd been stubbornly holding out for flowing script type and seafood chowder followed by beef despite the fact that the majority wanted salmon for the main course and tiger prawns to start. 'We've been wasting far too much time; let's stop arguing and vote.'

Feeling rather shocked at her own outburst, Rose sat down and wondered, as she did every year, why she didn't just resign and take up something less stressful, like hang-gliding or swimming with sharks. But every year she let her name be put forward because, if she wasn't on the committee, no money would be raised at all. And she passionately wanted to help people. A life lived selfishly was a life half lived: that was her credo. The only difficulty was that for some of the other committee members, charity work was more a sign of social status than anything else.

The Church Hospitality Committee only met a couple of times a year and was the least trouble, as it only involved putting together a couple of suppers for inter-church gatherings and, occasionally, a party for a visiting missionary priest.

Rose's third committee, the Kinvarra Motorway Action Group, was halfway up the scale of annoyance. Set up to oppose the proposed new route through Kinvarra's nature park, an area of outstanding beauty around the midlands town, the KMAG committee included a highly efficient local solicitor, several prominent business people and three local politicians. Therefore things got done. But the public meetings were a total nightmare which usually ended up with the committee being instructed to work on at least four wildly differing approaches.

Rose needed a stiff gin and tonic after the KMAG public meetings, although Hugh grinned and told her that in his experience of public meetings, she'd be better off with a stiff drink *before*hand.

As one of Kinvarra's leading legal brains, Hugh was a committee veteran. He'd even served his time as the town's mayor many years before, which he laughingly said had been a lesson to him Not To Get Involved. Rose had a photo of him in his mayoral robes on the mantelpiece: tall, stately and handsome with his immaculately brushed silver hair setting off the high forehead and the benevolent gaze. The camera hadn't picked up the wicked glint in Hugh's eyes that day, a look that said he didn't mind the job but could have done without the mayoral necklace hanging like a cow chain around his neck.

'It's impossible to please even half the people a quarter of the time,' was Hugh's sage advice on committees. 'Everyone goes round in circles for weeks. As for your public meetings, unless someone takes the planners to court, you're wasting your time.'

'We will if we have to,' said Rose heatedly. 'But we must show our solidarity as a community. We don't want to be walked on. Don't you care about the motorway?'

'It won't be anywhere near our house,' Hugh pointed out.

Rose gave up. She found it hard to understand how Hugh could be so pragmatic about important matters. She herself became passionately involved in all her causes, whether they affected her directly or not, but Hugh didn't seem to feel these things as deeply as Rose.

The girls had all taken after their mother. Thirty-eight-year-old Stella, for all she appeared to be a sensible lawyer, working hard to bring up her daughter on her own, hid a romantic soul beneath her sober office suits. Tara, seven years younger, was the same: a debating queen at school and college, she threw herself wholeheartedly into anything she did. She'd fallen in love the same way, marrying computer sales executive Finn Jefferson six months to the day after they met, half-astonishing people who thought that Tara was destined for unconventionality and liable to run off with a rock star if the mood took her.

And as for Holly, the baby of the family at twenty-seven, Rose knew that beneath her youngest daughter's gentle exterior there was a vulnerable, fiercely passionate heart. But while Tara and Stella had the courage to fight for what they believed in, Holly didn't. The secret fear that Rose carried round with her, was that Holly lacked self-confidence because of Rose and because of what she had or hadn't done.

Somehow, Rose felt, she had failed her beloved youngest daughter. But the thought was too painful, and Rose Miller, known for facing all kinds of problems with calm resilience, blocked it out. She wouldn't, couldn't think about it.

Today was the dreaded Kinvarra Charity Committee and as Rose parked her car outside Minnie Wilson's sedate semi-detached house, she had a sudden desire to take off on a mad shopping spree and forget all about the meeting. Instead, she did what was expected of a sensible Kinvarra matron; she checked her lipstick in the mirror, re-pinned a wayward strand of her greying dark hair back into its elegant knot and carried a home-made lemon cake up the path.

'Rose, is that the time? I'm all at sixes and sevens, I'm not a bit organised!' wailed Minnie when she answered the door.

Rose gritted her teeth into a smile and walked in. Minnie had to be at least Rose's age, round the sixty mark, but had the manner of a dizzy young girl and got flustered at the slightest provocation. Minnie was one of the people who'd worried so much about the type size on the charity lunch menus. She'd moved to Kinvarra three years ago when her husband retired and she'd thrown herself so frenetically into local affairs, it felt as if she'd been part of the community for years.

'Don't worry, Minnie, I'll help,' Rose said automatically. 'What do you want me to do?'

'Well . . .' said Minnie anxiously. 'The kettle's boiled but I haven't got the cups out. And look at my hair . . .'

Hang-gliding, definitely. It had to be more fun than this, Rose reflected. 'Why don't you go and fix your hair, Minnie,' she said calmly, 'while I sort out the tea.'

Minnie fluttered off upstairs and Rose grimly thought that the group's chosen charities would be better served if its members all just sent a cheque every year to the charity of their choice. They'd save money spent on endless tea mornings where at least half the time was spent on the process of sorting everyone out with seats, cups and plates of cake.

Rose briskly organised the tea, her mind elsewhere. She often wondered how had she ended up in this life. She'd never wanted to be a pillar of the community and a leading light of every local concern going. When she was eighteen, she'd wanted to work in a modern office in the city, where people addressed her respectfully as Miss Riordain and where a wage packet with the anticipated amount of money was put into her hand every week without fail. The respect and the unchanging wage packet were important. On her father's tiny farm, income fluctuated wildly, resulting in lean times and very lean times. Nobody felt the need to show particular respect to the beautiful and clever daughter of a small farmer and Rose had grown up deeply aware of the nuances of how people treated the daughters of the local doctor and the big landowners. One of her ambitions was to receive such respect. A good, settled job and a pay packet that came every week would give her freedom. She'd got her foot on the ladder all right, with the junior secretarial job in a construction company. Efficient and eager to learn, she'd dedicated herself to self-improvement. She'd battled with an elderly typewriter until her nails broke and she watched the senior secretary for hints on how she should dress. And then she'd met Hugh, the dashing young lawyer friend of the owner's son. Hugh came from a world where people never needed to be told how to dress or which fork to use. But to two people in love, that didn't matter. They were soul mates. Love turned Rose's life plan upside down and within two years she was married with a small daughter.

Occasionally, she wondered what would have happened if she'd said no to Hugh? Maybe she'd be a high-powered businesswoman, having an exciting but selfish life instead of living for others in Kinvarra where her only day-to-day concerns were her charity work, getting the freezer fixed and helping Hugh organise Christmas hampers for the firm's most important clients.

Tonight, his firm was involved in a Christmas fundraiser for the local poverty action group which, with the recent wave of redundancies among the area's big factories, was even more stretched for funds than usual. A black tie gala dinner, it would mean top table stuff and all the Kinvarra glitterati out in force. Rose enjoyed getting dressed up but there were times when she got bored with the inevitable polite conversation at such events. Hugh, on the other hand, never got bored with gala dinners.

She dragged her mind back to the task in hand.

There were seven committee members, so she whipped out seven cups and saucers, because Minnie always made such a big deal about china cups and not mugs. She laid out milk and sugar, cut her lemon cake into slices, and had everything ready by the time Minnie came downstairs.

'Oh, Rose, you're so good,' trilled Minnie when she saw everything. 'I don't know what we'd do without you.'

Rose had been about to say something mundane about how it had been no problem, when she really looked at Minnie. For once, Minnie's girlish complexion ('soap and water every morning!' she claimed) was grey and tired. Her eyes were a telltale watery red. It wasn't mere tiredness, Rose realised. It was something else.

'Are you all right, Minnie?' she asked gently. Minnie looked into the face of the woman she'd been half in awe of ever since she'd moved to Kinvarra. Rose was like some elegant television celebrity; gracious and ladylike, without a hair out of place. She had a look of that poor Jackie Kennedy, God rest her. Minnie had never met any aristocratic types but she knew one when she saw one. Rose Miller came from classy people, Minnie was sure. And she was kind; as friendly to the girl in the pub who served them tea as she was to Celia Freidland, the committee chairwoman.

Minnie had tidied the house extra specially for the meeting mainly because Rose would be there. Rose's husband was a very important man, she had a beautiful house in the most expensive part of town, and she had three lovely girls. Minnie never met Rose without being overwhelmed with a desire to impress her.

'Minnie,' said Rose again. 'Are you sure you're all right? Is there anything wrong?'

Minnie shook her head. 'Nothing,' she said. 'I'm just tired, that's all. Now, the committee will be here any minute.' Her smile was camera-bright. 'I suppose we're all ready?' she added.

'Yes,' Rose said kindly. There was more to it than tiredness, clearly, but if Minnie didn't want to talk, that was her business.

The doorbell pealed and Minnie rushed to answer it, welcoming in her guests as if she hadn't a care in the world.

For once, Rose didn't hurry the committee's ramblings. She was quieter than usual and the meeting meandered on until half five when everyone began making astonished noises at how time had flown and how they had families to feed. Rose left after giving Minnie a meaningful handclasp on the doorstep.

'Please phone me if you need to talk,' she whispered.

As she drove home, Rose couldn't get Minnie Wilson out of her mind. There was something wrong there and Rose longed to be able to do something to help. Poor Minnie. As she speculated on her hostess's misfortune, Rose couldn't help thinking again of her own life and how happily it had turned out.

Adele often said, grudgingly, that Rose was lucky. But Adele was right. She *had been* lucky.

Nobody could be prouder of their daughters than she was of Stella, Tara and Holly. Even if she hadn't been their mother, she'd have thought they were special women. She had a granddaughter she adored, too. Amelia had a great way of staring up at her grandmother with those big, grave eyes and asking things like: 'Granny, will you and Grandad have a baby so I can play with it?'

Stella had roared with laughter when Rose told her about it.

'What did you say?'

'I said we were thinking of getting a puppy and would that do?'

13

'Oh no,' Stella howled. 'She wants a dog more than she wants a baby sister; she won't let you forget that.'

If only, Rose thought, Stella had someone in her life. Tara was blissful with Finn, happier than Rose would have imagined she could be. Seeing her middle daughter so settled, made Rose long for the same happiness for Stella. She'd have given anything to see Stella content. Not that she would ever say that to Stella. But a mother could hope.

And as for Holly: well Holly never told anyone what she wanted. Rose did her best to be there for Holly in the background but her youngest daughter had retreated from life in Kinvarra, and Rose, desperate to help, had to accept it. Perhaps Holly was happy after all. Because you never knew, did you, reflected Rose.

Hugh insisted that Rose should stop worrying about her brood.

'They're modern women, haven't they the lives of Reilly?' he'd say, proud as Punch of his three bright daughters. When the girls came home to Kinvarra, Hugh was always keen to take them into town to lunch or dinner, to 'show them off' as Rose teased him.

'I'm surprised you haven't set up the Daughters Sweepstake Race,' she joked, 'where all the great and good of Kinvarra get their offspring in the race to see who's the best.'

'There's a thought,' he said gravely. 'You're always telling me you're fed up with organising charity dinner dances and cake sales. A sweepstake would be a sure-fire winner.'

Dear Hugh. He'd been blessed with a great sense of humour, for all that he drove Rose mad with his ability to spread chaos all over the house without ever bothering to tidy up. No matter how many times she scolded him, he still left the bathroom looking like someone had been washing the Crufts Best In Breed in it, with at least three soaked towels thrown around and the top off the shower gel so that a trail of sticky gel oozed into the shower tray. But, despite everything, she loved him and he was a wonderful father.

14

There had been bad times, for sure. But Rose had weathered the storms, that was all in the past. She *was* lucky.

The Millers' rambling farmhouse was in darkness when Hugh Miller returned home. Once, Meadow Lodge had been the badly-maintained home of a small farmer with several rackety haybarns, a silage pit positioned right beside the kitchen window and sheep contentedly grazing in the garden, doing their best to fertilise the landscape. When Hugh and Rose had bought it forty years ago, they'd knocked down the crumbling farm buildings, turned the three-acre plot into a decent, sheep-free garden, and had modernised the whole house. Nobody looking at Meadow Lodge now would ever think it had been anything but a gracefully proportioned building with fine big rooms, a huge comfortable family kitchen and gas heating to cope with the winds that sometimes swept down through the midlands and Kinvarra. Rose had filled the house with comfortable couches, luxurious-looking soft furnishings, lots of pictures, lamps that cast a golden glow and plenty of unusual ornaments.

With his arms laden down with his usual consignment of papers and briefcase, Hugh unlocked the front door, shoved it open with his shoulder and turned on the lights in the hall. He wondered where Rose was. It wasn't like her not to be there when he got home. Even if she had one of her meetings on in the evening, she rarely left until he was home and, if they weren't going out, she always had something delicious cooking for him. It was strange, therefore, to find a dark, cold house, especially since it wasn't long before they had to go to the Poverty Action Night dinner.

Dumping his cargo, Hugh threw his big sheepskin coat on the hall chair, dropped his car keys on the hall table not thinking that they might scratch the wood, and went into the big yellow sitting room.

Switching on the overhead light, not bothering to shut the curtains or even switch on one of the Oriental table lamps that Rose liked, Hugh sank down into his armchair, stretched his long legs onto the coffee table because there was nobody there to object, and flicked on the television news.

He was still watching half an hour later when Rose arrived. She switched on the hall lamp and switched off the main light before putting Hugh's keys into the cream glazed pottery bowl where they lived.

Hugh was still glued to the news.

Rose swallowed her irritation when she went into the sitting room and found all the main lights blazing. If opened curtains were the extent of her problems, then she had little to worry about. Silently, she shut the heavy, primrose-yellow curtains and flicked on the lamps, all of which took mere moments. Why did men never do that sort of thing? Did being a hunter-gatherer absolve the whole species from domestic tasks?

'How are you?' asked Hugh absently, without taking his eyes from the box.

'Fine,' said Rose. 'We've got to be out of here in an hour: I'm going to make a cup of tea and then have a shower.'

'Oh I'd love some tea,' said Hugh.

Why didn't you make some, then? Rose thought crossly. She stopped herself snapping just in time. She was grumpy tonight, for some reason. She'd better get a grip on herself. She, above all people, had no excuse for moaning. But as she went into the dark kitchen to boil the kettle, she thought that it was all very well deciding that you were lucky, but Hugh drove her insane sometimes.

She'd just made the tea when the phone rang.

'Hiya, Mum,' said Tara breezily. 'How are you?'

Rose beamed to hear her middle daughter's voice. Tara was one of life's the-glass-is-half-full people and it was impossible to be miserable in her presence. 'Great, Tara love, how are you?'

'Wonderful. Finn and I are just racing out the door to a special film screening but he just got a work phone call, so I thought I'd give you a quick buzz.'

16

'Sounds like an interesting evening,' Rose said, holding the portable phone in one hand and pouring tea into two pottery mugs with the other.

'I wish,' sighed Tara. 'It's a small-budget, black and white and boring thing written by one of *National Hospital's* ex-writers.' *National Hospital* was the television soap which Tara wrote for. 'We've all been press-ganged into going. I'm terrified Finn will doze off in the middle of it.' Tara laughed merrily. 'You know what he's like when he's made to watch anything without either football, car chases or Cameron Diaz in it.'

'Like your father, in other words,' Rose said smiling. She poured the correct amount of milk into Hugh's tea. 'Why do women marry their father?'

'It saves time,' Tara said. 'What have you been up to?'

'The usual. Trip to the supermarket this morning, a charity meeting in the afternoon and the poverty action gala tonight.'

'I hope you're going to be wearing the Miller family emeralds,' joked Tara.

'But of course,' rallied her mother. The Miller family emeralds consisted of old-fashioned earrings and a tiny and very ugly pendant, all of which were in Aunt Adele's keeping. Adele was always dropping heavy hints about leaving them to one of her nieces when she died, but the girls were doing their best not to be remembered.

'Actually,' said Rose, 'I haven't worked out what I'm going to wear and we've got to leave soon.'

'Shame on you,' teased Tara. 'The whole town will be talking if you don't turn up in your glad rags. Do you not have some swanky cut-down-to-the-boobs dress that'll make everyone so astonished they cough up even more money for charity?'

'I'm trying to wean myself off the wanton trollop look,' Rose said gravely. 'Besides which, I don't have the bosom for that type of thing any more.'

'Shame,' laughed Tara. 'I better go then, but can I say hello to Dad?'

With the radar that meant he always knew when his beloved daughters were on the phone, Hugh had already picked up the phone in the hall.

'Hiya, Tara love,' said Hugh happily. 'What mad sexy scenes have you been writing this week to shock us simple television viewers?'

Even Rose, on her way upstairs, could hear Tara's groan of 'Da-ad!'

'She's in great form,' Hugh remarked when he walked into their bedroom a few moments later, pulling off his tie.

'Yes, very happy,' said Rose who was standing in front of the wardrobe mirror attempting to zip up a cream beaded evening dress. 'Will you do me up?' she asked Hugh.

He ambled across the room and threw his tie on the bed.

'Were you talking to Stella today?' he asked as he expertly pulled the zip to the top.

'Not today,' replied his wife. 'She said she was going to have a busy day. And her neck's been at her all week. I might phone her now.'

'Great.' Hugh grinned. He stripped off his clothes quickly, while Rose sat on the edge of the bed and dialled Stella's number. She wedged the receiver in the crook of her neck and began to paint a coat of pearly pale pink on her nails.

'Hello, Amelia,' she said delightedly when the phone was finally answered. 'It's Granny. I thought you and Mummy were out when you didn't answer.'

'Mummy is in the bath. She has a cricket in her neck,' said Amelia gravely, 'and Aunty Hazel gave her blue stuff to put in the bath to get rid of the cricket.'

'Poor Mummy,' said Rose. 'Tell her not to get out of the bath, whatever happens.'

'She's here,' Amelia announced. 'And she's dripping wet bits onto the floor.'

'Sorry darling,' apologised Rose when Stella came on the line. 'I told Amelia not to get you out of the bath.'

18

'It was time I got out,' Stella said. 'I was in danger of falling asleep in there.'

'How's your neck?'

'A bit better,' Stella admitted. 'It started off as a little twinge, or a cricket, as Amelia says, and today it just aches. I can't lift a thing and Amelia has been very good, haven't you, darling?'

In the background, Rose could hear her granddaughter say 'yes' proudly.

'Have you got any of those anti-inflammatories left from the last time?' Rose said worriedly. 'If you're out, remember, you left some here just in case. I'll drop them up tomorrow if you want.' Kinvarra was an hour's drive from Stella's home in Dublin, but Rose never minded the trip.

'That would be lovely, Mum,' Stella said. 'I don't have any tablets left,' she admitted. 'But are you sure you want to drive up? The traffic's sure to be mad this close to Christmas.'

Rose smiled. 'What else are mothers for?' she said simply.

'Can I say hello?' said Hugh.

Rose held up a finger to indicate that she'd be another moment. 'Tell me, what time do you want me there for?' asked Rose. 'If I come up for ten, you can go back to bed and I'll bring Amelia swimming.'

'Oh, Mum, that would be wonderful.' Stella sounded so grateful. 'But I feel so guilty . . .'

'Rubbish. You need a break,' her mother said firmly. 'Here's your father.'

Rose and Hugh changed places.

'I'll come too,' Hugh told Stella. 'Amelia loves swimming with her grandad.'

As he talked to their oldest daughter, Rose hung Hugh's tie on the rack in the wardrobe, then picked up his shirt from the beige carpet and popped it into the laundry basket. The master bedroom was no trouble to tidy. Knowing Hugh's propensity for mess, Rose had furnished it so there was nowhere to put clutter. There was just a king-sized bed

19

with a quilted cinnamon-coloured bedcover, a small boudoir chair in the same fabric, and pale wood bedside cabinets which were adorned with lamps and photos of the girls in wooden frames. Rose kept her scent and make-up in the big cupboard under the washbasin in the adjoining bathroom. The unfussy lines of the room were comforting, in her opinion. Relaxing. Apart from the family photos and the big watercolours of four different varieties of orchid on the walls, there was nothing to distract a person from going to sleep. Hugh had wanted a TV in the room but Rose had put her foot down. Bedrooms were for sleeping in.

Sleep sounded very alluring right now. Rose wished they weren't going out tonight. She'd prefer to get an early night and head off for Stella's early in the morning. Supper on a tray would be lovely.

Hugh said goodbye and hung up.

'Try phoning Holly,' Rose said from the bathroom. She hadn't spoken to Holly for a week, not that this was unusual, but even so, Rose still worried when there'd been no word from her youngest.

'Nobody there,' said Hugh after a moment. 'Her machine isn't on, either. I might buy her one for Christmas. That old thing she has is useless.' He dialled another number. 'Her mobile's off too. Hi, Holly, it's Dad. Remember me? Father-type, silver hair, known you for, oh, twenty-seven years. Just phoning to say hello. Your mother says hello too. I suppose you're out enjoying yourself as usual. Another wild party? Talk to you sometime over the weekend, darling, bye.'

He hung up. 'Holly's terrible at returning phone calls,' he grumbled.

'She's enjoying her life,' Rose said automatically. 'She's entitled to be out having fun and forgetting about us. That's what girls her age do.' Well, she hoped that's what Holly was doing.

'I suppose you're right,' said Hugh.

In the bathroom, he and Rose stepped round each other in the expert dance of people used to forty years of sharing a bathroom. While Rose applied her lipstick in the mirror, Hugh ran water to shave.

In the harsh light of the bathroom, Rose noticed that there seemed to be more wrinkles than ever fanning around her eyes. If she'd religiously slathered eye cream on for years, would it have made a difference? Rose didn't care. She'd do. She left Hugh to his shaving and went back into the bedroom to sort out an evening handbag, and to mentally plan her trip the next day. Then she scooped the dirty clothes from the laundry basket and went downstairs to the kitchen to put on a wash. She felt happier from just talking to her beloved daughters.

Stella had sounded so grateful that Rose was going to drive up and visit, but the reality was that Rose adored seeing Stella and little Amelia and loved being able to help her darling Stella out in some small way. Not that she pushed herself into their lives, no. Letting your children go was the one part of motherhood there was no manual for. Rose did her best not to be a clingy mother. She let her daughters live their own lives, which was why it was doubly wonderful that they wanted her around.

The kitchen in Meadow Lodge was Rose's favourite room in the whole house. Probably, because it hadn't changed much since Stella, Tara and Holly used to sit at the scrubbed pine table moaning as they laboured over maths homework. The walls were still the same duck-egg blue, the floor was still terracotta tiled, with a frayed scarlet kelim beside the shabby two-seater couch, and the cupboards had only changed in that they'd had several more layers of cream paint applied over the years. The child's paintings stuck on the fridge were now Amelia's, while the wall of family photos was crammed with the ever-increasing Miller family gallery. This now included Tara looking sleekly radiant in Amanda Wakeley on her wedding day, the normally camera-shy Holly looking uncomfortable in her graduation dress, and a beautiful black and white portrait of Stella and Amelia, taken by her friend Hazel.

Rose set the washing machine to a warm wash and then looked around for something else to do. This evening wouldn't be too bad, she decided. Talking to the girls had invigorated her. Anyway, there were loads of people who'd love a glamorous night out at a dressy dinner. She was lucky to have such a good social life. She was lucky full stop. People were always telling her so. But then, it was one thing to look as if your life was perfect, it was another thing for it to be so. Looks could be deceptive. Minnie Wilson's was a prime example: bright on the outside, with some sort of hidden misery clearly lurking on the inside. Rose wondered if everybody's life was different behind the facade?

CHAPTER TWO

The following Monday, Stella Miller was also thinking about how appearances mattered as she waited patiently in the jewellers for a salesperson to help her. It was ten days before Christmas, and everyone and their lawyer was shopping for gifts and the streets were heaving with irate shoppers who didn't care if their umbrella took someone else's eye out. The season of goodwill be damned.

Stella had walked in the door of Austyn's Fine Jewellers at precisely the same time as the expensively-dressed couple currently being served but the only available salesman, with an unerring nose for people about to spend bucketloads of cash, had gravitated instantly towards the well-dressed couple, who were looking for an engagement ring.

The woman's coat was cashmere and reeked of money. Stella wryly thought that her coat reeked of nothing but good value, having been a sale bargain two years previously. Still, she didn't mind waiting. Stella had long ago decided that life was easier if she didn't sweat the small stuff.

Leaning against the counter, she watched the engagement ring show unfold in front of her eyes. The salesman's eyes shone with joy as he reached into the shop's main window and let his fingers settle reverently on the pale grey suede cushion. Cushion No 1, resting place of the finest diamond rings in the entire shop.

Carrying it as carefully as if it was a priceless antiquity and he was Indiana Jones, the salesman laid the cushion on the glass counter, discreetly attaching its steel chain to a hook underneath, just in case somebody dared to snatch it and make off with several millions' worth of flawless diamonds.

The customers sighed at the same moment, sighs of relief at finding the perfect engagement ring. They looked thrilled. The salesman allowed himself a sigh too, thinking of the commission.

'Would Madam like to try it on?' he said hopefully.

Stella was close enough to get a really good look at the five rings on their bed of grey suede, each seeking to outdazzle the others. The ring in the centre was her favourite. She'd seen it in the window the week before when she was rushing down the street after meeting a friend for lunch. At the time, there were still at least fourteen shopping days till the holiday, but Stella was one of life's organised people who colour-coded her underwear drawer, rearranged the freezer contents on a monthly basis, and viewed buying Christmas presents any later than the week before the event as reckless.

Her mother adored those prettily painted enamelled pill boxes and Stella wanted to buy her something extra special to say thanks for the weekend when Rose and Hugh had arrived to take Amelia swimming. Rose had brought a basket with organic eggs, freshly baked bread and lots of her special fruit scones, as well as the wonderful anti-inflammatory drugs, which had helped her neck get better. Rose deserved much more than an ordinary pill box and Austyn's had a huge selection: flowered ones, ones with strawberries cunningly painted on; you name it, they had it. Stella imagined that if she'd asked for a pill box with a finely painted dead cockroach on it, they'd have had one.

But it was the diamond ring, sitting fatly on Cushion No 1, that had caught her eye amidst the tinsel-strewn display of pendants and rows of bangles on the day when she didn't have time to stop. Peering in the window and half-thinking that perhaps she should buy a department store gift voucher instead, Stella had spotted it instantly. One luscious marquise-cut diamond surrounded by oval diamond petals, like a wildly expensive flower perched on a fine platinum band. Large but certainly not vulgar; just big enough to proclaim love, devotion and hard cash.

'Try it on, darling,' urged the man, now. The woman beamed at him and stretched out manicured fingers.

The salesman expertly unhooked the ring, all the time thinking of what a bumper year this had been for the shop. They were running out of Rolexes and Patek Philippe watches faster than they could import them; he'd personally sold two sapphire-studded gold necklaces yesterday, and now this: a couple interested in the most beautiful (and expensive) ring on the premises.

In one fluid move, the ring was on the woman's finger. It was exquisite. Stella sighed. Much and all as she adored the costume jewellery she bought for a song in markets and second-hand stalls, there was something irresistibly indulgent about the real stuff.

'Can I help you, Madam?'

She looked up into the eyes of another salesman, who was in a very bad temper because *he* should have been the one serving the diamond-ring hopefuls and would have been if the credit card machine hadn't been taking so long all day.

Stella straightened up, a tall, neat figure in a charcoal woollen coat with a crimson knitted hat adding the only splash of colour to her sober outfit. 'Yes, I'd like to look at some of the enamelled pill boxes,' she said.

With one last wistful look at the fabulous diamond being admired by the besotted couple to her left, she followed the salesman to the back of the store, where a display of enamelled boxes waited.

Within five minutes, Stella had chosen a Victorian-style box and was impatiently waiting for her credit card to be run through the machine by the still-grumpy salesman. She was in a rush because tonight was Amelia's school Nativity play. Stella couldn't wait to see it. Amelia had talked of nothing else for a month, her dark brown eyes shining when she practised her bit which involved shuffling onstage, kneeling at the front of three rows of angels, and singing a carol off-key. Amelia had inherited Stella's tone deafness, but she looked so adorable when she sang that it didn't matter.

Seven years old and cute as a button, Amelia was the image of her mother. In a police line-up, nobody could have failed to notice the similarity between the two, although the younger version had her glossy chestnut hair in pigtails, while her mother's was styled in a chin-length bob. Amelia's heart-shaped little face was graver than Stella's serene oval one, and her huge eyes were watchful, which made people who didn't know her think she was a quiet child. She was anything but. She was simply shy round strangers. But Amelia was perhaps a little more grown-up than most children her age. That was Stella's only regret about divorcing Glenn – his absence and their status as a one-parent family had made little Amelia seem older than her years. Not that Amelia seemed to mind only seeing her daddy a few times a year, but Stella still worried about it.

The night before, Amelia had pranced around the living room in her white glittery angel robes and sang 'Silent Night' in her breathy voice.

'David's dad is going to video-tape it, Mum, and Miss Dennis says she'll get copies for all of us if we give her a tape.'

'We have to get two tapes, then, darling,' Stella had said, hugging Amelia, 'so we can keep one for us and send one to Daddy.'

'OK. Will I sing it again?' Amelia asked.

'Yes, darling.'

The tape might just spark Daddy out of his habitual languor, Stella thought. He really was useless at remembering how important things like Christmas were to kids. Stella had hoped that Glenn's beloved father's sudden death two years previously might have forced him to grow up a bit and remember his responsibilities, but it hadn't. Last year, she'd ended up buying Amelia a gift from Daddy, only to have Daddy turn up on Boxing Day with something else. '*Another* present, Daddy, you are good,' Stella had said between gritted teeth, even though she'd told him she'd bought something for Amelia from him. He was working in the Middle East this year and his present had long since arrived, only because Stella had haunted him with phone calls reminding him to send one. Stella could never comprehend how her ex-husband didn't understand children, seeing as he was such an absolute kid himself. At this rate, Amelia would be a grown-up long before her father.

Stella reminded herself to phone him again and reconfirm the arrangements for their Christmas Day phone call. As long as Amelia wasn't disappointed, that was the main thing. Normally calm about everything else, Stella knew she was perfectly capable of ripping Glenn's intestines out if he upset Amelia.

She glanced at her watch: ten past five. Time she was out of there. Where the hell was the salesman with her credit card receipt? Standing alone, she glanced back at the about-to-be-engaged couple who were still deliberating over the diamond ring.

They didn't look wildly, madly in love, she decided. They looked content, but not candidates for a passionate lunchtime bonk because they simply couldn't wait until evening. Maybe they were *in like*, which was easier than being in love. Less hassle. And a good way to cope with loneliness. Stella had lots of friends who'd do anything to find a good man to be in like with.

I am lucky, Stella thought gratefully, as the salesman appeared with her credit card slip. Without her darling Amelia, she might be one of the lonely people who left the radio on all day so there'd be some noise to come home to. Amelia was everything to her.

She brushed away the brief thought that having a man in her life might be fun. Stella Miller had no time for men – no diamond rings for her. Amelia was her number one priority and that was that.

The wind-chill factor was high and the rain was back

as she rushed out of the jeweller's and up the crowded street, ignoring the rows of over-decorated shop windows showing fabulous party dresses. Sparkly little tops and hip-skimming skirts were not on Stella's shopping list. With her social life, she didn't need clothes like that. Her most important night-time engagement for the festive season was Amelia's play tonight, which was to be followed by a drinks party in the school hall. Stella's work clothes were the dressiest in her wardrobe and she had nothing nicer than the tailored grey suit she was wearing with a cranberry silk shirt.

Thanks to streams of cars driving into the city centre for late-night shopping, the traffic home was astonishingly light and Stella parked the car outside Hazel's house at half past five.

She rarely collected Amelia from Hazel's house without saying a tiny prayer of thanks for having someone so perfect to look after her daughter. Hazel lived one street away from Stella, and she'd been looking after Amelia since she was nine months old. Hazel had started out as a childminder and become a much-loved family friend. To Amelia, Hazel was like another mother, someone who fussed over her, loved her and knew when she was up to mischief. Hazel's own twin daughters were two months older than Amelia and the three little girls played together like sisters, which meant plenty of squabbling and plenty of making up. A former bank manager who'd had her daughters at the age of thirty-eight thanks to IVF, Hazel hadn't needed any encouragement to give up her job to look after her longed-for babies. 'I was waiting for the moment I could dump my business suits and become an earth mother,' she often said ruefully, looking down at her daily uniform of elasticated-waist jeans and a big sweatshirt to hide her spare tyre. She'd certainly thrown herself into the role. Her home was lived-in, comfortable and always smelled wonderfully of home cooking. Hazel even made her own jam.

'You make me feel so guilty,' Stella would wail when

she saw Hazel's line of neat jars filled with jewel-coloured preserve.

'We've four gooseberry bushes, redcurrants and an apple tree,' Hazel would reply. 'I can't waste them.'

Today, when she reached Hazel's house, Stella didn't have the opportunity to ring the doorbell before Amelia raced out, pigtails flying, to open the front door.

'Hi, Mum,' she said eagerly, pretty in flowing angel robes with silver ribbons trailing from her coat-hanger wings. Stella had almost wept making those damn wings. It had taken two nights and three broken nails to finish them.

'Hello Amelia,' Stella said, tweaking a pigtail and kissing her daughter on the forehead. She knew that Hazel didn't allow the children to open the front door themselves but she couldn't bring herself to give out to Amelia for it after such a welcome. 'Are you ready for the play, darling?'

'Yes, Mum. Can I do ballet? Becky and Shona are going to do it and we've got to get the shoes and a dress thing . . .'

'Their class has gone ballet mad,' said Hazel, appearing from the kitchen with a carrot in one hand and a vegetable peeler in the other. She was dressed for the evening in a brown stretchy velvet dress with a bright orange plastic apron thrown over the ensemble to keep it clean. Her russet curls were loose in honour of the event and her pale lashes had been given a speedy sweep of a mascara brush. That was it: Hazel had neither the time nor the inclination for long beauty routines.

'The gymnastics craze is officially over and we're now into tutus and proper pink dance shoes. In a vain attempt to calm them down before the play, Miss Dennis announced that ballet is back on the curriculum in the New Year. I said I was not driving into the city to the dance shop until January.'

Becky thundered out of the kitchen, another angel with golden ribbons in her red curls and gold painted wings hanging lopsidedly from her shoulders. With two little angels, Hazel had had twice as much trouble over making coat-hanger wings as Stella had.

'Mary's mother is going to make her a proper ballet dress,' announced Becky, with the unspoken 'Why can't you, Mum?' hanging in the air.

A small bundle of energy, Becky stomped everywhere like a baby elephant and when she climbed the stairs, it sounded as if the entire top storey of the house was collapsing. 'I want to be a swan princess,' she added firmly.

Hazel and Stella exchanged amused glances over the heads of their children.

'*I'm* going to be a swan princess too,' insisted Amelia.

Becky glared at her crossly.

'You can *all* be swan princesses,' soothed Hazel, ever the peacemaker. 'But we don't want to spend lots of money buying swan princess outfits and ballet shoes if you get fed up with it in a week.'

Both Amelia and Becky looked shocked at the very idea. As if.

'They handed out a note on ballet lessons and I put it in Amelia's schoolbag,' Hazel said.

Stella smiled thanks.

'Look, Mum!' said Amelia, dancing around as if she was already in ballet class. She attempted a creditable prima ballerina spin, holding up her flowing angel skirts as she twirled. 'Look at me, Mummy.'

'No, look at *me*,' insisted Becky, having a go herself and cannoning into Stella.

'I'm sure you'll be a lovely swan princess,' Stella said kindly to Becky.

Amelia, who was at that age when she was keenly aware of the difference between what adults said and what they *meant*, stared up at her mother.

'Right, girls, are we all set for the play?' Stella said quickly.

'Yes!' shrieked the two girls.

'Just give me five more minutes and I'm ready,' Hazel said. 'Shona,' she called.

Another red-headed angel with gold ribbons emerged from the playroom, where she'd obviously been painting herself with glitter glue. The twins weren't identical but both had their mother's wild red hair and her hazel eyes.

'Go upstairs and use the bathroom; we're going in a moment,' Hazel said. 'Wash your hands properly. I'll be up in a moment to check.'

The children thundered upstairs for one final look at themselves in the mirror and a half-hearted bit of hand-washing, while Stella followed Hazel into the homely kitchen. Apart from her two sisters, Stella felt closer to Hazel than any of her other friends. Their lives were totally different, and Stella was thirty-eight to Hazel's forty-five, but they shared the same dry sense of humour. Hazel understood her, Stella felt. Hazel never tried to set Stella up with men, or berated her for not going on dates. She understood, without being told, that Stella was perfectly happy with her life the way it was.

And if Hazel often thought that she'd love her closest friend to have someone special in her life, she kept the thought to herself.

'Do I have time for a quick cup of tea?' Stella asked, flicking the switch on the kettle. 'I've been shopping and I'm shattered.'

'Course, make me one too.' Hazel rapidly chopped up the carrots and added them to an earthenware dish. 'Buy anything nice?'

'A pill box for my mother in Austyn's. I've got everything now,' Stella added with satisfaction. 'I saw this couple buying the most incredible diamond ring: it was enormous. God knows what it cost, but Securicor would need to follow you around permanently if you bought it.'

'Sounds like Hazel's Christmas present,' remarked Hazel's husband, Ivan, as he closed the front door and walked into the kitchen. A tall, wiry man with laughing blue eyes, trendy tortoiseshell glasses and almost no hair at all, Ivan was a building society manager whose first love was his wife and their twins, followed by a lifelong passion for opera. Hazel sometimes grumbled that she was deaf from listening to 'The Ring Cycle' played at full volume, but Stella knew she didn't really mind. She was just as mad about Ivan as he was about her. Affectionate teasing was the glue that held their marriage firmly in place.

'You didn't buy me another huge diamond, sweetie?' inquired Hazel, turning her face up to her husband's for a kiss. 'I've run out of fingers!'

'Sorry, yes.' Ivan did his best to look penitent. 'I'll bring the ring back tomorrow and buy you a tasty red nylon negligee set instead. Any tea left in the pot?'

'I want *pink* nylon, silly. You know I like my clothes to clash with my hair. Ooh, get the biscuits out, Ivan, while you're at it,' Hazel added, as he took a mug from the cupboard. 'We won't be back here before nine and you know school parties: if we get one soggy sausage roll between us, we'll be lucky.'

Stella and Hazel watched as Ivan wolfed down five chocolate biscuits, while they forced themselves to eat only one plain one each.

'How can you eat like that and not put on weight?' Stella marvelled.

Ivan patted his concave stomach. 'Superior genes,' he mumbled with his mouth full.

Hazel took off her apron and threw it calmly at her husband. 'Surely remarks like that are grounds for divorce?' she said to Stella.

'Don't ask me: I'm not a family law specialist,' Stella laughed, used to their banter. 'I'm the property queen.' She headed out of the kitchen, calling over her shoulder: 'Fight amongst yourselves, I'm going to tart up quickly.'

In the small cloakroom under the stairs, Stella took out her brush and began tidying her hair. Although she stared at her reflection in the mirror, she didn't really see herself. Instead, she thought about Ivan and Hazel, and the couple in the jewellers. Stella could live out the rest of her life quite happily without a knuckle-dusting diamond on her ring finger. You didn't miss what you'd never had, as her mother often said. But it *was* possible to miss something you'd grown up with, even if it hadn't been yours exactly. Stella had grown up with parents who adored each other. And she saw true love every day with Ivan and Hazel, who teased each other, had arguments about eardrum-splitting opera, and yet still each worshipped the ground the other walked on. Stella had spent years claiming that love was the last thing on her list, but occasionally, just occasionally, she wished it wasn't.

She came back into the room two minutes later with her cloud of hair swinging from the vigorous brushing she'd given it.

Hazel smiled affectionately at her friend. Stella never bothered with too much make-up either. But then, the difference between them, Hazel knew, was that Stella didn't need it. The huge dark eyes framed by thick lashes dominated her oval face, giving her the serene look of some medieval Madonna, patiently waiting to have her portrait painted. Dark brows winged out in perfect arches above her deep-set eyes. Her straight nose didn't need any careful shading and her creamy skin was good enough to manage without all but a hint of base, which should have made Hazel madly envious. *Her* skin was freckled, red-tinged and needed buckets of concealer. Not that it got it.

Stella had the sort of fine-boned elegance that Hazel, a great admirer of beauty, appreciated, with tiny ankles and wrists which she said she'd inherited from her mother. But Hazel loved Stella far too much to feel jealous of her. Instead, she took pride in her friend's beauty and despaired of Stella ever knowing how lovely she was.

Tonight, Stella had painted her mouth a surprising crimson that matched the rich colour of her satin shirt. She rarely wore such vivid colours and she looked fabulous.

'Get you, missus,' Hazel said.

'Do you think the lipstick's too much?' Stella asked. 'I bought it today but maybe it's overdoing it a bit . . .'

'It's lovely, really sexy,' Hazel insisted. 'I don't know why you don't wear red lippie more often.'

'School parties aren't the right occasions for "sexy",' Stella pointed out. 'Remember last year?'

At the previous Christmas play, the children's teacher had worn a flirty little sequinned dress in honour of the occasion, and had been shocked to be on the receiving end of a jealous outburst from one mother whose husband had a roving eye. Both Stella and Hazel had felt very sorry for sweet, enthusiastic Miss Palmer, a newly qualified teacher, who'd thought she was doing the right thing by wearing her best clubbing outfit. Dancing energetically with the children at the party, Miss Palmer had almost bounced out of her dress, making her very popular with the fathers and not so popular with some of the mothers.

'Simple dress code disaster,' Hazel agreed. 'But there's a difference between a bit of red lipstick and a va-va-voom sequinned dress.' She eyed Stella's grey suit. 'Unless you're planning to rip that off and sing "Jingle Bells" in your knickers?'

'How did you guess?' Stella said deadpan.

'What was wrong with Miss Palmer's dress, anyhow?' demanded Ivan, who was only half-listening to the conversation. 'I don't know why that stupid woman had a go at her. The poor girl looked nice. It's a free country, she can wear what she wants.'

Hazel shot Stella a look that spoke volumes.

Stella tried to explain. 'It was the right dress on the wrong occasion,' she said patiently. 'Imagine if I was going to a party here, for example, and a party at Henry Lawson, the senior partner's house. I couldn't wear the same thing.'

'Why ever not?' demanded Ivan.

Hazel interrupted. 'Because if Stella turned up at Henry Lawson's house wearing a PVC catsuit, Henry would have a coronary and his wife would have one too, from pure rage because she'd be firmly convinced that Stella was a harlot who was after her man.'

'I blame those magazine articles telling women how high the chances are of their husbands having it off with someone

34

he works with,' Stella said. 'They're convinced the office is one big extramarital dating agency where everyone pants with lust. If you're not married, all the wives think you must be after their husbands.'

'Which is hilarious if you look at most of the husbands,' remarked Hazel, who had met Henry at Stella's office. Charming and friendly he might be, but he wasn't hunk material.

Stella grinned. 'I'd love to know what sort of offices they do that kind of research in because, clearly, I've been working in the wrong places all these years. Honestly, if I get a spare moment these days, it's all I can do to rush out to the loo or grab a cup of tea. Chasing the senior partners round their desks would be very far down the list of must-do tasks.'

'Surely not?' Hazel teased. 'There's something about the way Henry's belly swells majestically over his waistband . . . I find him devastating in a sea lion sort of way.'

'You can have him, then,' Stella said kindly.

'I didn't know you had a PVC catsuit, Stel,' Ivan interrupted eagerly. 'Could Hazel borrow it?'

'I'll drop it over tomorrow,' Stella said drily.

They were still laughing a couple of minutes later when both families piled into Hazel's space wagon. Sitting in the back with the children, Stella made sure they were all firmly strapped in and was putting her own seatbelt on when she felt a small cold hand sliding into hers. Amelia looked up at her mother, her face scared and pale in the gleam of the street lights. Stella put her arm round her daughter's shoulders and nuzzled close until she could feel the fake fur of Amelia's anorak hood tickling her face. 'You're going to be wonderful, love,' she whispered. 'You've practised loads of times and you know it off backwards.'

'What if I forget?' said Amelia in a hollow voice.

'You won't forget,' Stella encouraged. 'You're far too clever for that. I know that you know all the words and you're going to be brilliant, and mummies are always right, aren't they?'

Amelia nodded at the logic of this and snuggled closely to her mother for the rest of the journey.

Benton Junior School was blazing with light when they arrived, and there was a line of cars ahead of them as parents pulled up outside the doors to disgorge angels, shepherds, wise men and a few farmyard animals.

'That's not a real sheep, is it?' asked Ivan as they watched a white woolly animal bounce from a car and proceed to lift its leg on the headmistress's prized box tree which was covered with festive golden ribbons.

'That's Mrs Maloney's dog,' said Shona. 'It was in for the rehearsal yesterday. It weed on the stage.'

The children giggled.

'I hope you don't have to kneel in the wet bits,' Ivan said solemnly.

'Uuuughh,' the girls shrieked.

'But you probably will,' he continued, 'and you'll be wet and smelly, and you won't be able to get back in the car but you'll have to run home in your angel clothes in the dark, all smelly and wet and yucky . . .'

Laughing and giggling over wet knees meant that by the time the space wagon reached the door, all performance nerves had gone and Amelia, Shona and Becky were eager to rush in to where scores of children were charging around, squealing at the tops of their voices. Some had glitter on their faces, while others had big Groucho Marx moustaches drawn on. Wings got stuck to other wings and there were several clusters of children yelling as Mrs Maloney, the worn-out music teacher, tried to unattach them. The noise level was pounding, despite the presence of three teachers and several harassed parents.

'Whatever they pay teachers, it's not enough,' Ivan said heavily as he went off to park the car.

'Where will you be sitting, Mummy?' asked Amelia, suddenly anxious again and clutching tightly onto her mother's hand now that they were in the middle of the excited crowd. 'I want to be able to see you.'

'Big hug,' said Stella, crouching down. She held Amelia tightly, breathing in her fresh smells of shampoo and crayons. 'I'll wave to you when you come in so you can see me, I'll be as near the front as I can, I promise.'

'Promise?'

'Cross my heart,' Stella said gravely.

'Quiet children!' boomed a voice and the noise miraculously ceased. Mrs Sanders, the headmistress, had a commanding presence and when she spoke, people hopped to do her bidding. Suddenly, the angels were whisked away into a classroom for a final wing inspection, the shepherds were sent to the cloakrooms for one last pre-show visit, and the parents were told that everything was under control and would they please take their seats.

The hall was almost as noisy as the lobby had been, full of chattering parents and screaming little brothers and sisters who wanted to rush around and fight with other children. Hazel and Stella squeezed into seats halfway down and waited.

'I wonder does Gwyneth Paltrow's mother feel as nervous as this before a show?' Stella said, twisting her handbag strap between shaky fingers.

'Probably not. Don't worry, they're going to be fine,' Hazel said. 'They're all word perfect. My only worry is that Becky will have a row with someone and hit them over the head with her tambourine. She's so headstrong.'

'It's just a phase she's going through,' Stella tried to sound comforting.

'She's been going through that phase since she was a toddler,' Hazel sighed. 'If she's like this at seven, imagine what she'll be like when she's a teenager. You do not know how lucky you are with Amelia; that child is so good. She puts Becky to shame.'

'Shove up and make room, girls.' It was Ivan, shivering from the cold.

Stella moved up a seat and tried to take her mind off her nerves by looking around.

She wasn't the only single parent there, which was a relief, although there seemed to be more couples than normal. There were quite a few lone parents with children in Amelia's class but, as it was Christmas, huge efforts had been made and people who usually only screamed at each other over the phone now sat side by side in icy silence for the sake of their children. Stella didn't miss Glenn for her own sake but on occasions like this, she wondered how much Amelia's heart ached for her dad.

'OK?' asked Hazel, giving her arm a squeeze. 'You're not getting the divorced Mummy guilts again, I hope?'

Dear Hazel. She was so perceptive, Stella thought fondly. She shook her head. 'I'm fine, honestly.'

With a fanfare of trumpets from the school's CD player, the performance began. It started with the babies of the school who trailed on nervously and all started to sing 'Jingle Bells' loudly and in different keys. With the school piano banging out tunes, and the various teachers in the wings urging their pupils on, the performers sang, giggled, sobbed and in one case, screamed their little hearts out. There was one dangerous moment when it looked as if the stable might collapse on top of the Baby Jesus, played by Tiny Tears in an elderly christening robe, but Mrs Sanders leapt onstage in time and pulled the stable backwards, averting the crisis. From halfway down the hall, it was hard to see. Parents kept hopping up and down in their seats to take photos and video footage and Stella was afraid she'd miss seeing Amelia. But when the angels crowded onto the stage, she immediately saw her daughter standing nervously between the beaming twins, and stood up and waved wildly at her. Please see me, she prayed silently as she waved.

'Sit down,' hissed someone behind her but Stella ignored the voice and kept waving.

Under her angel halo, Amelia's expression was tense as she stared out at the unfamiliar sea of faces, the lights shining so brightly on the stage that she couldn't see anything properly ... and then suddenly she saw her mother's frantic waving and everything was all right. Mummy was watching, Mummy was there. A huge smile lit up her little face. She looked at Miss Dennis who was at the front of the stage, ready to encourage her class to sing.

'Ready children?' said Miss Dennis.

Class 5 nodded earnestly and waited, eyes wide with anticipation, for their music to begin before launching into 'Silent Night' as they'd never sung it before.

All around the hall, parents went 'aah' and clutched each other's hands with pride.

Stella felt the tears clouding her eyes as she watched Amelia singing her little heart out. With her big eyes shining like candles, Amelia was the picture of a Botticelli angel. Stella knew she wasn't being biased – Amelia was the prettiest child there, for sure. And the most wonderful.

'Aren't they fantastic, Hazel,' she said tearfully to her friend.

'And the dog hasn't peed on the stage yet,' Hazel remarked.

Stella giggled but never took her eyes off Amelia. She was so very lucky. This mother-love, this was real love. The other sort of love, for a man, just couldn't compete.

CHAPTER THREE

Four days later, Stella's sister, Tara Miller, deeply in love with her husband of six months and deeply nervous about the awards ceremony she was attending, stood in the ladies' room of the ultra posh Manon Hotel and hoisted up her dress for about the tenth time that evening. The problem with wearing a strapless evening gown and boob-enhancing plastic falsies – 'chicken fillets' to the initiated – meant that only industrial adhesive could keep everything in place. Toupee tape didn't have a hope. The ladies' cloakroom at the National Television & Radio Awards was full of famous TV stars, and was not the ideal place for major body repairs; however, Tara had no option but to reach down the front of her silver dress and manhandle each fillet up. 'Built-in bra, my backside,' she muttered at her reflection as she wriggled, hoping everything would fall into place in a vaguely boob-like shape.

'Ooh, Tara,' cooed Sherry DaVinci, floating into view from one of the cubicles, 'that dress is lovely.'

'Thanks,' said Tara faintly, as Sherry squeezed in beside her and unpacked half the Mac range from her Louis Vuitton evening purse. Tara could see why the casting director had been so keen to get Sherry DaVinci to play a sexpot hospital receptionist in the hit television soap opera, *National Hospital*. And it was nothing to do with Sherry's acting ability.

Shoehorned into a clinging, gold, sequinned mini dress, Sherry was a porn-fan's dream, her ample breasts sitting perkily under her chin like two tanned melon halves that threatened to escape at any moment. *She* didn't need chicken fillets, Tara thought ruefully, comparing Sherry's buxomness with her own flat chest.

'Hi, Sherry,' said a fellow soap beauty, smiling at Sherry in passing and ignoring Tara.

Feeling invisible, Tara wondered why the beautiful people weren't given their own loos at glitzy events, so that ordinary, non-beautiful people didn't have to face the perfection of the 'talent' when they were fixing their tights, rearranging falsies and painting gloss on thin lips. Not, Tara reflected, that Sherry was what you'd call talented. But she pulled in the viewers and she was a sweet girl. Her limitations only became obvious when you were a script writer trying to write lines she wouldn't screw up. As a storyline editor and one of the team of contributing writers on *National Hospital*, Tara spent a lot of time writing lines which Sherry then delivered with all the élan of the postman delivering a credit card bill. Which all went to prove that looks weren't everything, as Isadora, Tara's colleague, muttered bitchily every time Sherry fluffed her lines.

Feeling as if she'd better make an effort, Tara investigated the contents of her handbag (black satin, borrowed, no visible logo). Underneath her mobile phone and a notebook and pen in case she had any brilliant ideas for the love triangle storyline she was working on, was a red lipstick, a very elderly concealer and her glasses case.

There had been a pair of tights in there for emergencies but she'd had to break them out after the smoked salmon starter when her watch had twanged a thread on her existing pair.

'Do you want a lend of anything?' asked Sherry, concentrating on applying eyeliner with a professional's touch. She was expertly using a tiny angled brush, Tara saw.

'Er, no thanks,' Tara said. She slicked on a speedy coat of lipstick, and looked critically at herself to inspect the effect. Standing beside Sherry was a mistake. Tara was straight as an ironing board while Sherry was all glowing curves with sparkling gold dust on her silken skin.

Sometimes Tara wondered, in an idle sort of way, what it would be like to be beautiful rather than clever. Her mother, Rose, was beautiful, still beautiful, even in her late fifties. The family teased her about how the Kinvarra postman was besotted with her and how he nearly crashed the post van whenever she appeared. And Stella, her elder sister, was stunning too, with melting dark eyes and a serene, smiling face that made people gravitate towards her. And Holly, who had more hang-ups about her looks than a catwalk full of teenage models, was incredibly pretty in an arrestingly luminous way. But the beauty gene had clearly skipped out when it had come to Tara.

Not that she minded, really. Tara knew she'd been given a gift that made up for not being a head-turner – a brain as sharp as a stiletto and a talent for putting words together. A gift that had brought her here tonight.

She grinned as she thought of her Aunt Adele's mantra at Miller family get-togethers: 'Thank the Lord that Tara's so clever.' Tara knew that this was shorthand for 'It's lucky that Tara doesn't have to rely on her looks.' Her mother used to glare at Aunt Adele whenever Adele said this but it had no effect. Her aunt was one of those people who thought honesty and tactlessness were pretty close to Godliness in the hierarchy of virtue, and felt that speaking her mind was not just important, but compulsory.

But Tara, after a few pointless years of secretly longing to be a beauty, was perfectly content with the way she looked. She'd never be pretty but instead was a combination of quirky and unusual looking, with a sharp little chin, a mischievous full mouth, and a long nose which might have dominated her face were it not for deep-set hazel eyes that glittered with amusement and brilliance. Even beside a raft of golden-haired lovelies, people always noticed Tara's clever, vibrant face. And once they got talking to her, they loved her because she was witty and funny into the bargain.

By the time she'd got to college, Tara had worked out a clever and eccentric look which involved very trendy clothes, short, almost masculine hair and fire-engine red lipstick. It helped that she was tall, so masculine clothes and hair worked on her. Now, at the grand old age of thirty-two and thanks to the confidence that came from having a career she loved, Tara was utterly at home with her looks. Her dark hair was expertly cut and its exquisitely tweaked style owed much to the salon wax she scrunched through the ends each morning. Trendy, dark-rimmed glasses gave definition to her eyes and drew attention away from her nose. She'd toyed with the idea of rhinoplasty for years but Finn had told her she didn't need it.

'I love your nose the way it is,' he'd say, running his finger down it lovingly.

Tara's face softened as she thought of her husband of six months. Darling Finn. Theirs had been the ultimate whirlwind courtship. They'd met a year ago at a party, fell madly in love and got married within six months, confidently telling astonished friends that once you met your soul mate, you knew instantly. Finn was everything Tara wanted in a man: funny, sexy, kind, clever – and drop-dead gorgeous. A rangy man with sleepy, fun-filled eyes, tousled dirty blonde hair and an air of languid sexuality, Finn was genuinely movie-star stunning. People told her he could have been Brad Pitt's stand-in, but a proud Tara retorted that Finn was infinitely better looking.

Even his voice was sexy, automatically reminding her of making slow languorous love even when he was just asking her how much milk she wanted in her coffee.

It would have been lovely to stroll into the ballroom with him on her arm. He looked good in a dinner jacket; but then he'd look good in a sack.

At their wedding, Aunt Adele hadn't failed the Miller family and had pointedly said, at least five times, that she couldn't get over how Tara had netted such a good-looking boy. As if Tara had gone out with a huge fishing rod and reeled in the first gorgeous specimen she saw.

'Your aunt keeps looking at me and shaking her head,' said Finn at the reception. 'Is she shocked that a creative genius like you has married a stupid computer salesman?'

Tara laughed. 'On the contrary, she thinks I've won the lottery. Aunt Adele has been preparing me for spinsterhood for years by reminding me I'm not a great beauty, so she's astonished I nabbed a hunk like yourself and actually got you to marry me within six months of meeting you. And you're anything but stupid.'

Finn pulled her close for another kiss. He couldn't seem to get enough of her. 'Well,' he conceded, his lips brushing her cheek tenderly, 'maybe not that stupid. After all, I've just married a brilliant wife. And a beautiful one, too.'

If only he were here, Tara thought now with a fresh pang of longing. Finn knew how tense she was about things like awards ceremonies, and knew just how important this one was to her. The exact opposite of her; he was laid-back about everything and would have calmed her nerves better than a pint of Rescue Remedy. But tickets to the National Television & Radio Awards were like gold dust and not even all the show's writers had been able to get one. There was no way Tara could have brought Finn with her. She'd phone him quickly, just to say hi, that she missed him. Switching her phone on, Tara dialled rapidly. The phone in the apartment rang out without being answered. She smiled at the thought of Finn rushing across the road to the twenty-four-hour garage to buy something, forgetting to turn the answering machine on. She loved the little things he forgot. They were so endearing. She tried his mobile but it was off too. Idiot. But she was smiling.

'Perfume?' asked Sherry, spraying the contents of a tiny bottle of Gucci Envy down her cleavage.

'Yes please,' said Tara, sorry that she hadn't thought to bring the Coco Mademoiselle that Finn had given her for her birthday. The ballroom was murderously hot and the combination of a spicy main course and too much red wine meant that everyone had red, flushed faces. None of which would look good on television. Tara had a sudden horrified vision of her shiny, lobster-pink face being all that people remembered when the nominations for the soap awards came up.

She took the proffered vial of perfume, sprayed it liberally down her front and gave a final blast to her wrists. 'Sherry, I've changed my mind. Can I borrow some make-up? I think I need it.'

Five minutes later, Tara was expertly revamped. In those few moments in the ladies' she felt as if she'd learned more about Sherry than she had over several months of work. Sherry chatted away about how her mother had helped her shop for the dress she was nearly wearing, and how her whole family were going to meet up the next night when the awards were broadcast in case they spotted Sherry. They never missed an episode of the show, either. They were so proud of her.

'I used to be a beautician, you see,' Sherry said as she dextrously brushed eye shadow onto Tara's lids. 'Mum was worried when I gave it up for drama school.'

'You're brilliant at make up,' Tara said enthusiastically as she admired her newly-sultry eyes, dark and intense thanks to smoky shadows.

'Thanks,' Sherry said happily as she zipped up her bag of tricks.

Tara felt bad that she couldn't say how Sherry was a marvellous actress too, but she hated hypocrisy.

Together, they braved the ballroom. A vast, high-ceilinged room decorated with giant swathes of purple velvet to go with the gilt and purple chairs, it was crammed with every sort of television and radio worker. Actors and presenters rubbed shoulders with writers and producers, all pretending to have a roaring good time because the show was being filmed, and all trotting out the standard remark: 'It's such an honour just to be here: being nominated/winning doesn't matter.' Which was rubbish because it was *all* about winning.

45

The ceremony itself was going to make up ninety-five per cent of the TV show, but nobody wanted to risk glaring sourly at a rival and ending up with *that* broadcast to the world. Or even worse, being included in the inevitable out-takes video which would change hands as soon as the show was over. So the whole place was awash with smiles.

Tara lost Sherry within seconds, as the actress spotted a camera crew and wove her way through the crowds, her shapely hips undulating sexily as she shimmied along. Marilyn Monroe was said to have deliberately had a quarter of an inch taken off the heel of one shoe to give her that sexy lilting walk. Sherry had clearly upped the ante and had taken off an entire inch on one side, leaving her with a hip movement that Tara reckoned a passing bishop would surely declare an occasion of sin.

Weaving her own way through the tables, Tara said hello here and there but didn't stop. She'd worked in television one way or another for nine years and knew loads of the people here: if she stopped, she'd never make it up to her table in its much envied place at the front.

As she passed the *Forsyth and Daughters* table, she nodded at an old work-experience pal of hers who now wrote for the series.

'Good luck,' said Robbie encouragingly. 'I hope you win.'

'You too,' said Tara. Which was true because she hoped he would win. It was unlikely though.

Robbie smiled weakly and Tara passed on, knowing there was nothing she could say to raise his spirits. *Forsyth and Daughters* was a five-year-old show about a family of female lorry drivers and not even ER's Dr Luka Kovac, manfully wielding the cardiac paddles, would be able to bring it back to life. The scripts were tired, the storyline was exhausted and the only option in Tara's opinion was to can the whole series. Robbie and his team hadn't a snowball's chance in Hell of winning anything, while the *National Hospital* team were hot favourites for a whole raft of awards.

A voice on the microphone was asking people to take their seats as Tara reached her place.

National Hospital, as befitting one of the nation's hottest home-grown soaps, had two tables at the ceremony and, now that the empty bottles and the plates had been taken away, they looked bare and untidy with wine stains on the white tablecloths. The actors had been allocated a table close to the stage, while the writers and production people were behind them. There was nobody at the actors' table because, as soon as the meal was officially over, they'd all rushed off to get their photos taken and to work the room. The writers, on the other hand, insisted that they didn't believe in networking and sat getting dug into the wine and trying to out-do each other bitching about rival shows. The truth was that nobody was interested in taking pictures of writers, which galled them. *They* wrote the words, *they* created the canvas on which the actors shone, so why did nobody know who they were?

'Did you hear the one about the bimbo who wanted to be in movies?' muttered Tommy from the depths of his glass, as Tara slipped into her place beside him. Tommy was one of the show's long-timers. 'She went to Hollywood and slept with a writer.'

'Yeah, yeah,' murmured the assembled group, who'd heard it all before.

Isadora, who'd moved so she had a better view of the stage, was now sitting on Tara's other side. Isadora was another one of the storyline editors, writers who shaped the way the show developed and came up with long-range plotlines. She and Tara worked closely together and were great friends.

'You look nice,' said Isadora. 'Have you been beautifying yourself for your acceptance speech?'

Tara laughed. 'Sherry did it. It's good, isn't it?'

'Very.' Isadora was impressed. 'Can she do something for me? I need emergency work. All this red wine has my face looking like blue cheese.'

'Crumbly?' inquired Tommy.

'No, heavily veined,' Isadora replied tartly. 'But still, my veins aren't half as bad as yours, sweetie.'

'Miaow,' Tommy retorted.

The lights went down and there was a frantic dash as people raced back to their seats. The babble of conversation went down to a low hum while the audience waited for the show to begin.

Watching the monitors to the side of the stage, Tara and Isadora could see what the cameras saw. The lenses panned across the room, coming to rest on the big male stars of the day and on the most beautiful of the women, all of whom had nearly killed themselves to wear the most talked about gown of the evening. Slit-to-the-navel, slit-to-the-thigh and slit-in-both-directions dresses were par for the course at these events. The more famous stars didn't bare as much, while the wannabes craved attention and tended to look as if they hadn't enough money to pay for a whole dress.

'Leather is big this year,' Isadora commented, glancing around. 'Look at that woman from that kids' Saturday morning show. That's not a dress; that's a python-skin bikini with a see-through overdress.'

'I dunno why they call it an overdress,' muttered Tommy. 'Doesn't look like overdressing to me.'

'She'd better be careful,' Isadora continued. 'She won't be the darling of the exhausted early morning mums and dads if she wears that type of hot little outfit. They want blue jeans, wacky sweaters, spiky hair and overall purity for their Saturday morning televisual babysitters.'

Silence reigned for a brief moment until the awards' theme music blasted out over the sound system and the show began. Finally, the nerves began to get to Tara. This was an important evening for her. She'd been working on *National Hospital* for three years and in April, she'd been promoted to storyline editor. The youngest person ever to get the job, Tara had had a lot to prove. But she'd done it. Thanks in no small part to her input, the scripts since then had been ratings grabbers. The critics loved the show, the production company loved the show, now, it was time to see if the people who gave out the prestigious Soap of the Year award loved it too. They'd been nominated for the past three years but had been narrowly beaten by *Ardmore Grove*, their nearest rival, every time. If only tonight was the night to claim the prize for *National Hospital*. Tara felt sick with the anxiety of it all.

Across the table, Aaron, the show's director, sat with his beautiful blonde wife. Tara thought of Finn sitting at home waiting for her phone call. Her nerves wouldn't have been nearly as bad if Finn had been beside her, his hand holding hers comfortingly. But only people like Aaron were considered important enough to get two invites to the ceremony.

Onstage, clips were being shown of the best animated films. Tara glanced at her watch. Twenty minutes gone. Although the show wasn't live, it would still run pretty much to time. The soap category was in the first hour but there was ages to go.

The veteran Irish actor on stage was slowly opening the purple envelope for the animation award. He read it out and a table at the back of the ballroom erupted with squeals of joy. Everybody at the *National Hospital* tables smiled. The whole ballroom smiled. They were on camera, after all.

Three more awards trundled by. Winners gravely thanked everyone from their kindergarten teacher to their Pilates coach. The only excitement was when the forty-something Best Actress gave rather an over-enthusiastic kiss to the teenage boy band member presenting her with the award. The audience applauded with delight. At last, somebody behaving badly.

'Give him another Frenchie,' yelled a drunk at the back of the room.

'That's one comment for the cutting room floor,' Tara grinned.

'Were there tongues involved?' demanded Isadora eagerly.

'Not on his part,' Aaron said. 'The poor guy looked scared out of his head.'

'He should be,' Tommy pointed out. 'She eats boys like him for brekkie.'

'Don't be ageist,' snapped Isadora, who was feeling sensitive about arriving at the big four-oh herself. 'Just because she's over forty, she's not a figure of fun, you know. It's perfectly allowable to snog younger men. You're no spring chicken yourself, Tommy, and I bet you wouldn't say no to a big kiss from a teenage starlet.'

'Now, children,' remonstrated Aaron calmly, 'let's not fight. We have to look like we're happy. Save the fighting for the studio.'

Everyone grinned. Tempers often got frayed when they were under pressure at work.

'After the break, we'll be seeing who's the Radio Presenter of the Year, who's the Best Actor, and, which soap has won the Best Soap,' said the MC suavely. The crowd applauded obediently.

The lights went up and the MC added that there'd be a fifteen minute break. Hands went into the air immediately, waving for wine waiters.

Tara thought the break would never end but it did. The Radio Personality of the Year, late-night talk show host Mac Levine, made a very funny speech.

Isadora squeezed Tara's hand under the table so nobody would see how anxious they were.

'Isn't this wonderful?' Isadora said between teeth clenched into a false smile.

'Wonderful.' Tara clenched back. 'Will he ever hurry up before I die.'

And then it was their turn.

A glamorous female singer read out the nominations for Best Soap. There wasn't a sound at their table as clips of the various shows were played. Tara closed her eyes in supplication and then realised how strange and desperate she'd look on film, so she opened them again. The clips were finished and the singer was taking forever to open the envelope. Tara watched French-manicured talons struggling with the paper in agonising slow motion. She could feel her heart rate slowing down to comatose level, please, please let it be us.

'The winner is . . . *National Hospital*.'

'We've won!!' shrieked everybody with one voice. 'We've won.'

Screaming with delight, the occupants of both tables stood up and hugged each other. Tara could barely see with the tears in her eyes.

'Oh, Isadora, we've won, I can't believe it,' she sobbed.

'Come on, Tara, get your butt over here,' said Aaron, his voice cracking. 'We've got to go up and take the prize.'

'What, me?' said Tara, shocked.

'Yes, you and Isadora' he said. 'We can't have everyone on the stage, but you've both got to go up, you've both worked so hard this year.'

Isadora was off like a shot while Tara stumbled over to Aaron. He put an arm around her waist. 'This is your year, Tara.'

'But what about Tommy and everyone else . . . ?' gasped Tara, trying to wipe the tears from her face.

'This is your year, kid,' repeated Aaron. 'Enjoy it.' The entire table of actors and Isadora were already on the stage with the executive producer when Aaron and Tara made it up there.

'Thank you so much!' squealed Sherry, elbows together, boobs shoved up for the cameras. 'Thank you for loving us.'

She was subtly shoved out of the way by the show's female lead, Allegra Armstrong, a deceptively fragile-looking brunette.

'You have no idea what this means to all of us at *National Hospital*,' Allegra said warmly, 'we've worked so hard for this and want to say thanks to all our fans.'

The audience applauded. Allegra was a genuinely loved star and her portrayal of a brilliant surgeon on the show had already garnered her many awards.

'Also, we've got to say thanks to all the wonderful writers without whom we wouldn't have a show,' added heart-throb, Stephen Valli, who played hunky Dr McCambridge. Stephen Valli had also won many awards, at least half of which were for sexiest TV star and the man most women would like to wake up next to. He reached back and put one arm around Isadora and the other round Tara, who blushed. She stared blindly out at the audience. The fierce stage lights meant she could see nothing but darkness and yet she knew that everyone was looking up at the team, and her. It was a strange feeling.

Through the haze, she heard another interval being called.

'Congratulations!' shrieked everyone as the *National Hospital* team clambered off stage.

'My name is Jill McDonnell, I'm with the *Sentinel*. How does it feel to be part of the team responsible for the best soap?' said a woman, suddenly appearing in front of Tara and thrusting a tiny tape recorder in her face.

Tara stumbled on her high heels and had to cling onto Aaron's jacket to stay upright.

'Wonderful,' she bleated, not able to think of anything else to say for the first time in her life.

'Could I set up an interview with you?'

Tara smiled shakily. So this was fame. 'Sure,' she said. 'Phone the office tomorrow and we can fix a time.'

At the table, there were more hugs and champagne appeared.

'I must phone Finn,' Tara said tearfully, feeling the shock waves of emotion finally wash over her. It was still the interval, so she hurried out of the room to find a quiet corner.

The home phone rang out endlessly again and she tried the mobile.

'I'm in the pub with Derry and the lads,' Finn yelled. 'I couldn't cope with sitting at home and not knowing,' he said.

'We won!' said Tara, half-laughing, half-crying.

'Oh my love,' shouted Finn, thrilled. 'Congratulations! I'm so proud of you.'

The final segment of the show was about to begin and Tara rushed back into the ballroom. A tall man with flashing eyes and a wild beard, like a movie version of an old Testament prophet, laid a hand on her arm to speak to her. Tara instantly recognised Mike Hammond, a mega successful producer originally from Galway who'd just worked on a season of Oscar Wilde's plays for the HBO television network in the States.

He never even went to bashes like this; he'd be more at home at the Oscars or the Emmys.

'Congratulations,' he said in a soft Californian-Galway burr. 'I'm Mike Hammond.'

'I know. Tara Miller.' She extended her hand. As if there was anybody there who *didn't* know who he was.

'I hear on the grapevine you're one of the main reasons why *National Hospital* won the award,' he continued.

Tara's eyes were like saucers. Not only did Mike Hammond know who she was, but he'd heard good things about her.

'That's not exactly true,' she said. 'We work as a team. I'm just part of it. There are a lot of contributing writers and a large team of storyline people. You know that writing on that scale has to be team work or the whole thing self-destructs with a clash of egos.'

'Modest too,' commented Mike. 'We should have lunch sometime.'

He reached into his inside pocket and removed a card on which he scribbled a number. 'That's my cellphone number. I'm going to be in the US for a few months but phone me, say in March. We can shoot the breeze, talk about forthcoming projects, whatever.'

'OK,' stammered Tara, taking the card.

'Hi, Mikey,' said a voice and a tall, striking dark-skinned woman came up and laid a proprietary hand on his Armani-clad shoulder.

'Hi, Crystal,' he replied, turning to her.

Tara slipped away, scarcely believing life could be quite

this perfect. Mike Hammond wanted to meet her. The show she worked on had just won a prestigious award. And she was married to the most wonderful man in the world. What more could she want?

CHAPTER FOUR

Twenty-four hours after *National Hospital* won the Best Soap award, Tara still sounded as if she was on a high. She'd loved the congratulatory bouquet of flowers Holly had sent that morning, had spent the whole day pretending to work but being too excited to, and now she and Finn were going out for a celebratory dinner in their favourite restaurant.

'You mean you aren't going to stay in and watch yourself on the ceremony on TV?' teased Holly.

From the phone came the sound of her sister groaning. 'No way! I'm going to tape it instead and maybe one day, I'll be able to bear to look at it.'

'I'm going out too but I'm taping the show,' Holly said, 'so I can make everyone watch it in future and point out my fabulous sister, who was really responsible for *National Hospital* winning.'

Tara was still laughing when she hung up.

Holly, who was running late, rushed back into her bedroom to paint her nails, then sat on the edge of her bed waggling her fingers so the sparkly lilac nail polish would dry more quickly. She still had to wriggle into the instep-destroying boots she'd bought to go with her new black trousers, though she wasn't sure if she'd be able to bend over to zip them up. The Dolce & Gabbana corset, lent at huge risk by Gabriella from the International Design department, was what could euphemistically be called a 'snug' fit. Breathing was difficult, bending over would be impossible.

'It came back because it was too big for one of our best

customers and it's going in the sale in January, but whatever you do, Holly, *don't sweat on it!*' Gabriella had warned the day before. 'And don't smoke!'

'She won't,' promised Bunny, Holly's friend and colleague from the children's department, who'd been the one to wangle the loan of the corset from the fabulously gorgeous Gabriella. Gamine and funky, with cropped blonde hair and a way with clothes that meant her uniform of white shirt and black trousers looked catwalk cool, Bunny was Holly's idol. There was no way Gabriella would have loaned it to her, Holly thought, if Bunny hadn't asked first.

Both Bunny and Holly crossed their fingers regarding the safety of the outfit: strange things regularly happened to Holly, weird and unexplainable things that ruined her clothes. Coffee miraculously leapt out of cups and flung itself at her; drunks on the street crossed perilous traffic to lurch happily against her; perfectly ordinary bits of the footpath reared up to trip her. Therefore, it was entirely possible that some unusual accident would mean the borrowed outfit would get shrunk/covered in bleach/otherwise hideously disfigured in the Bermuda Triangle effect which surrounded Holly. But Gabriella didn't need to know that.

'I know it's a twelve and you need a fourteen, but they look better when they're tight. And it's perfect on you,' sighed Bunny, earlier that day, when Holly had struggled into the corset in a changing room in Lee's Department Store, where they all worked.

The two girls looked in the mirror. In a miracle of wonderful tailoring, the corset had jacked Holly's waist into tiny proportions, giving her a siren-like hourglass figure which she didn't have in real, non-D&G life. Bunny quickly pulled Holly's scrunchie off so that her poker-straight chestnut hair shimmered over her shoulders.

'Now,' said Bunny, delighted with her efforts. 'You look amazing. Those boots make your legs look so long. When you've got my necklace on you'll look perfect.'

'You don't think I look fat, do you?' Holly said anxiously.

She wouldn't have said it if Gabriella was around. Gabriella resembled a very beautiful twig on even more twiglety legs, and fat cells would have blanched at the thought of daring to even touch her.

'*Fat?* Don't be silly.' Bunny shook her head vigorously. 'You look wonderful, Holly. You're going to wow them all tonight.'

School reunions should be banned, Holly muttered, testing a nail to see if it was dry. Ever since Donna had phoned with the exciting news about the ten-year reunion of their class from Kinvarra's Cardinal School, Holly had fretted. For a woman with self-esteem so low it could limbo dance under a two-inch fence, the prospect of meeting the girls she'd been in school with was one filled with terror.

Old schoolmates would want to know what exciting things Holly was doing with her life and what sort of fabulous men she was going out with. 'Er nothing' and 'nobody' would not be adequate answers. On the plus side, at least she'd lost weight since school, but she was never going to be what anyone would call thin. And what was the point of being thinner when she had nothing to show for it?

Donna, her best friend from school, was thrilled at the very notion of a reunion, and had talked excitedly about how lovely it would be to catch up with everyone.

'Just think, our class together again after all these years. I can't imagine some of them as twenty-eight-year-olds: they're stuck in my mind at seventeen. Obviously, I don't mean Lilli and Caroline,' she said. 'I meet them every day at the school gates when I'm dropping Emily off and they're just the same, really. But there are so many girls and I don't really know what they've been up to. So many of them are living in the city or abroad ... It'll be wonderful to see everyone again, won't it?'

'Yes,' bleated Holly.

'I heard that Michelle Martin's coming too, which is a coup for the organising group. Who'd have ever thought that one of our girls would be a big TV star.'

'Donna, she's a news reporter, not Britney Spears,' Holly pointed out, overcoming her anxiety in order to set the record straight. Michelle had been a total nightmare at school: loud, overopinionated and determined to get the shy girls (like Holly and Donna) involved. Anyone who didn't go along with her (Holly and Donna, again) received contemptuous glances which implied that amoebas were more fun. 'We used to hide from her, if you remember.'

'No we didn't.' Donna sounded cheerful. 'Oh it's going to be such fun. You are coming, aren't you, Holly? I know you're madly busy and probably have zillions of glamorous Christmas parties to go to, but this will be fantastic. I know December's two months away but I've already told Mark he'll have to baby-sit because I'm going to stay overnight in Dublin. That's the whole point of having it in a hotel, so there's no awfulness about getting taxis and lifts home.'

Donna still lived in Kinvarra, but many of the school's old girls had moved to the city, which was why a hotel in Dublin had been chosen for the party. Donna was doubly pleased at this. For a start, there'd be no chance of wild misbehaving at a reunion in her home town where gossip spread like wildfire. Secondly, she loved visiting Dublin and this trip would mean a bit of blissful shopping the next day without having to manoeuvre a buggy round too.

'The only problem is what to wear?' mused Donna, before going on to list possible outfits and why they weren't suitable because they were old/unfashionable/too tight on the hips. 'Of course, you won't have that problem, Holly. When you're going out every night like you, you know exactly what to wear. Mark and I never get further than Maria's Diner these days and you can turn up in a sweatshirt covered with baby sick and nobody bats an eyelid.'

After a few more minutes of this, Donna's toddler, Jack, began crying loudly and she had to go.

Holly hung up slowly and smiled ruefully at the very notion of her having a wild life with zillions of glamorous parties to go to and the perfect wardrobe for every occasion.

Dear Donna, she hadn't a clue. She thought anyone who'd escaped the clutches of rural Kinvarra automatically entered some sort of Hollywood-style twilight zone where life was wildly exciting, invitations crammed the mantelpiece and gorgeous men were forever on the phone, demanding to know why you wouldn't go to Rio with them.

Holly had given up trying to explain that being a sales assistant in the children's department in Lee's was short on glamour and actually involved a lot of time in the stock room patiently folding T-shirts for four-year-olds. The only way a man would ever throw himself at her was if one fell down the stairs on the 15A bus when she was on her way up. This had actually happened, although the man in question had been a deeply embarrassed teenager and had practically run off in mortification afterwards. Holly had been bruised for weeks.

And as for going out, Holly was far too quiet to merit inclusion in the Lee's party-animal gang. Parties in general filled her with horror. She became obsessed with what to wear, inevitably ending up in black for its slimming properties, and even more inevitably ending up in the kitchen because of the crippling shyness that overwhelmed her on social occasions. Holly's ideal outing was the pub with Kenny and Joan, who lived in the flat opposite.

She had once explained this to Donna, but Donna would have none of it.

'You're only trying to cheer me up,' she'd insisted. 'There's no point denying it. Exciting things happen in cities, not like in this dump. For God's sake, they nearly declare a state of emergency in Kinvarra when Melanie's Coffee Shop runs out of fudge cake.'

'Kinvarra is a lovely place,' protested Holly.

'If it's that lovely, why did you leave?' demanded Donna, refusing to admit that there was any comparison between the fleshpots of the city and a small, pretty town sixty miles away.

'Ah, you know, I just wanted to travel a bit,' Holly said.

Holly wrote down the date of the reunion in her diary and began a plan of worry. This was similar to a plan of action but involved no actual action and, instead, lots of soul-searching 'how-can-I-get-out-of-it?' moments in the dead of the night. She also wondered how Donna had grown so confident that she was looking forward to this reunion. Marriage and motherhood must be a fiercely powerful combination, Holly decided. Why had nobody put that in a pill? Those pharmaceutical firms were slacking.

At school, she and Donna been drawn to each other by virtue of their quietness. They'd never been part of the reckless but popular gang of girls who cheeked the teachers, knew how to roll joints and went to wild parties with wild boys. Holly would have been struck dumb if faced with either a wild boy or a joint. She and Donna spent their school years in the anonymity of being good girls and Holly would have bet a week's wages that half the girls in the school wouldn't remember either of them now. Except as the skinny girl with the big glasses (Donna) and the plump, shy youngest sister of the Miller trio. The people she'd really like to see were the other anonymous girls, but they were the very people who probably wouldn't turn up. Holly tried to remember them: Brona, who spent all her time in the library and Roberta, a terminally shy girl who was forever drawing pictures in a sketch book and who could never look anyone in the eye.

As the reunion approached, Holly considered coming up with a previous engagement and avoiding it altogether, but then her mother had heard about it (Kinvarra was clearly still a hotbed of gossip where no snippet of information went unrecorded) and had phoned up to make sure she was going.

'Darling, it'll be wonderful,' Rose had said. 'I can still remember Stella's ten-year reunion.' Her mother's voice was wistful. 'She loved it; and to think it's coming up to her twentieth. Time certainly flies. Are you going with Donna?'

'Of course,' Holly said automatically. There was little

point in explaining the difference between going to a reunion when you'd been as adored at school as Stella, and going when you were one of those people that nobody would remember. Or even want to.

'What are you going to wear?' Her mother's voice was suddenly a mite anxious, as if she suspected Holly of going to the party clad in some wild creation.

'Joan's making me a Lycra and leather mini dress,' Holly said, unable to resist the joke. Joan was a fashion student who lived in the flat opposite Holly, and her idea of chic was ripped, heavily graffiti-ed clothes with the words spelt incorrectly. Her mother liked Joan but wasn't so keen on her eyebrow stud. 'Only kidding,' Holly added quickly. 'Something from Lee's, I think.' She crossed her fingers. She was terminally broke, as usual.

'Oh good,' Rose said, relieved. Lee's had a reputation for beautiful, expensive, clothes.

'You're such a label snob, Mum,' teased Holly.

'I am not,' insisted her mother firmly. 'I simply want you to look your best.'

On the other end of the phone, Holly grinned wryly. That made two of them.

By the time the reunion was upon her, Tara, Stella, Bunny, Joan and Kenny were also involved in her nervous state.

'You'll enjoy it, I know you will,' Stella had said sincerely. 'I loved mine, although I know you feel a bit weird at first because everyone looks so different and you've lost that intimacy you used to have.'

Dear Stella, Holly thought fondly. For Stella, school hadn't been a place she'd been eager to escape from.

'And I do understand that school was a difficult time when you were hung up about your figure, Holls, but you're so gorgeous now, that's all in the past.'

That was Stella's encouraging way of telling Holly that she'd moved on from being a shy, overweight girl who wouldn't say boo to a goose in case the goose told her to go on a diet.

'I'm, going to wear one of those sumo fancy dress costumes,' Holly said, 'then whip it off and give them a shock when they see I'm not twenty stone.'

Stella had laughed at that.

Tara was equally supportive when she rang, but more direct: 'Think of what a kick you'll get from turning up looking a million dollars. You and I have certainly improved since school. At my reunion, everyone was stunned when I turned up looking good. Go for hot, Holly. Impress the knickers off them. Make them jealous. I'm sure you've lots of great clubbing gear at home, and you get a staff discount in the store, don't you?'

This was true but Holly didn't use her staff ten per cent to purchase going-out clothes. What was the point if you only went to the pub? Tara believed her younger sister shared the same sort of lively social life she did. Tara was always at parties and glitzy media events. It was part of her job. But although Holly could wisecrack with the same insouciance as her older sister, she could only do it with close friends and family. In company, her wit deserted her and she clammed up.

Naturally, the generous Joan did offer to design an outfit for Holly.

'I can see you in a space-age, semi-Edwardian bondage look; a comment about school in general,' Joan said, sketching on a bit of an old envelope. Somebody had given her a video of the director's cut of Blade Runner and she had got a bit carried away with visions of the future.

'Space-age, semi-Edwardian bondage!' groaned Kenny, who lived with Joan, though not as a couple, as they both constantly informed everyone. Kenny was gay, worked in a designer men's boutique, devoured *Vogue* as his bedtime reading and wished Joan would give up being avant garde so she could worship at the altar of designer Tom Ford, Kenny's greatest idol. They made ideal flatmates because they could argue endlessly about fashion and, together, they could afford the pretty flat with the balcony that neither would be able to afford on their own. 'Holly wants to make all her classmates pea green with envy,' Kenny insisted. 'Not make them laugh at her. Six-stone fourteen-year-old models from Eastern Europe with cheekbones like razors can wear that type of thing but on anybody else, it looks ridiculous. What Holly wants is something . . . ,' Kenny paused dramatically, '*fabulous*. And credit-card droppingly expensive.'

Bunny, practical as ever, had come up with a suitably fabulous outfit which hadn't involved any credit-card action. Holly would never be able to thank her enough. Encased in her borrowed finery – Holly had promised Bunny she wouldn't spoil the effect by telling anyone it wasn't actually hers – even someone as self-critical as Holly had to admit that she looked OK. Well, reasonable. Passable. All she needed to do was not spill anything on herself.

Satisfied that her nails were dry, Holly stood up and took a deep breath before attempting to bend down and put on her boots. After what felt like ages, she zipped them both up and stood up, gulping in air like a deep-sea pearl diver.

She stood in front of the mirror, gave her hair one last brushing, and then picked up her handbag. She'd have killed for a cigarette but Gabriella would go ballistic if the corset came back smelling of Marlboro Lights, so she'd had her last one before she got dressed. How she'd stay off the fags tonight, she didn't know, but she had to. It was a small price to pay. Holly practised her tough-but-sexy look in the mirror again. She even tried her Lauren Bacall, lowered eyes, look (Holly adored Lauren), but gloomily decided that the effect was more Bogie than Bacall. It was time to go. Holly had arranged to meet her friend at the train, take her for a drink, and then travel to the hotel in time for Donna to check in and change. What she hadn't mentioned to Donna was that this plan would make them fashionably late for the reunion. That had been Bunny's suggestion.

'Make an entrance,' Bunny had advised. 'You don't want

to be hanging around aimlessly waiting for the party to get going. Arrive twenty minutes late and you'll look as if you're far too busy to get to things on time.'

Caroline and Lilli had made a cosy corner of the hotel bar their own, with handbags and jackets marking the spot and a double vodka barely diluted with Diet Coke in front of each of them for Dutch courage. The reunion was taking place in an annexed corner of the hotel restaurant, but the committee hadn't been able to arrange a private area of the bar, so Caroline and Lilli had come down early to pick a suitable spot for their gang. Even ten years after they'd left Cardinal School, they still thought of their schoolmates as 'their gang'. Of course, their lives had moved on a lot since then. Caroline had three small children and was a leading light in the Kinvarra Drama Society. Lilli had two little girls and worked part time. Sasha, another gangette, was assistant manager in the local video shop. The other girls, including TV star Michelle, had moved from Kinvarra, and were home rarely, which was why tonight was going to be so exciting: to see how well everyone had done. Lilli and Caroline knew that reunions weren't really about meeting up with old friends – they were about chalking up the successes and failures of their peers.

Lilli consulted her list. 'Twenty-five yeses, three nos and two who didn't reply,' she said. 'That's not a bad tally.'

'I wonder if Michelle's had any work done,' Caroline said, getting stuck into her drink.

'Definitely not,' said Lilli knowledgeably. 'Michelle was always naturally pretty. Her eyebrows are done properly now, that's it. I don't believe in plastic surgery myself.'

'Me neither, of course,' agreed Caroline, who cherished a long-range plan of having her eyes lifted before they got baggy like her elder sister's.

'You shouldn't tamper with nature,' Lilli continued, holding her glass with fingers tipped with rock-hard acrylic nails. 'These don't count,' she added hastily, noticing Caroline's eyes on the acrylic tips. 'You can't have decent nails when you've got small children.'

A lone woman entered the bar, looking round nervously and clutching a small handbag. Short and thin, she was not dressed in the frontline of fashion and her dark, un-styled hair hung limply to her shoulders. Caroline and Lilli surveyed her.

'Brona Reilly,' Lilli whispered to Caroline. 'She hasn't changed a bit.'

'You'd think she'd have made more of an effort for tonight,' Caroline whispered back. She and Lilli had pulled out all the stops and had made a trip to the city to check out wildly expensive, fashionable looks they could copy. They'd both had their hair and make-up done professionally for the night and Caroline, though she hadn't told Lilli, had even had a seaweed wrap in Kinvarra's poshest beauty salon in order to lose a few inches. Her corset-style dress was very unforgiving round the middle.

They pretended they hadn't seen Brona and watched her go hesitantly up to the bar and order a drink. The reunion might have been about meeting people, but it was important that they were the *right* people.

Brona had been one of the people that the girls in Michelle's gang had ignored. Mind you, so had Donna, who was now a friend of theirs. But that was different.

Any mild guilt over how they'd once treated Donna had vanished, because Donna herself didn't seem to remember it. When Caroline, Lilli and Donna had accidentally met up three years ago at the school gates on the children's first day, there hadn't been any bad feeling at all.

'Imagine, three little girls the same age,' Donna had sighed. 'They can go to school and be friends like us.'

Caroline, who was more thoughtful than Lilli, blushed at this, remembering how the more popular girls like herself used to ignore the school mice like Donna except when they wanted to copy their homework. Now that she was a mother herself, Caroline would have personally ripped apart any child who dared to ignore her own beloved Kylie. But Donna clearly had no bad memories of either school or Caroline and Lilli. All was happily forgotten.

'Would you like to have coffee in my house when we drop the girls off?' Caroline had said quickly that day, wanting to make amends.

'That would be lovely,' Donna smiled.

And that had been the start of their friendship. But despite three years of trying to get them together, Donna had never managed to reintroduce them to Holly.

Both Lilli and Caroline were eager to see what Holly looked like now. Her sister was famous and they were keen to see if any of the gloss of Tara Miller had rubbed off on her. Tara was in the papers occasionally, and had been photographed at several high-profile premieres. Consequently, Holly was more interesting than she had been when she was just one of the quiet, mousy girls in school. Fame by association was better than no fame at all.

Donna revealed that Holly lived in a fabulous apartment in Dublin, had a wonderful job in Lee's and partied like mad. She also said that Holly looked like a million dollars. Caroline and Lilli, remembering the plump shy girl with the round, earnest face, wanted to see this for themselves.

Donna was frantic by the time she and Holly pulled up outside the hotel at five past eight. 'We're so late,' she shrieked, leaping out of the cab and thrusting a tenner into Holly's hand. 'Here's my share. I have to check in. We were supposed to be here at half seven, the meal will have started five minutes ago and I've still got to get changed . . .' She fled up the hotel steps into the lobby.

'What's the rush?' said the taxi driver chattily as Holly paid him. 'When God made time, he made plenty of it. And it's Christmas: no party starts on time at Christmas. I'd say you'd be lucky if you get your dinner by ten tonight, never mind by eight.'

Holly smiled at him. 'My sentiments exactly.' Bunny's plan for being late had been a good one. When Holly had picked Donna up from the train station and taken her for a pre-reunion drink, she'd assured her that they'd get a taxi to the party and be there in five minutes. Pre-Christmas traffic, driving rain and the mayhem of late-night shopping combined to make it more like forty minutes.

'Thanks a million,' Holly said, climbing out of the cab and slamming the door. She moved away and realised that her scarf had got stuck. The driver began to drive off.

'Stop!' roared Holly in panic. He slammed on the brakes.

Naturally, her scarf had somehow infiltrated the door locking mechanism and it took five minutes of fervent dragging to disentangle it.

'Thanks again,' she said weakly, holding the frayed ends of the scarf and hoping that she could cut off the destroyed bits. At least it hadn't been the corset.

In the hotel, Donna had checked in and was about to race up to her room to leap into her party dress when Holly appeared. 'Come on!' she yelled at Holly.

While Donna's hysteria mounted as she snagged tights and spilt glitter powder on her dress instead of on her shoulders, Holly sat in a chair by the window and looked out onto the wet streets wondering why she'd come in the first place.

'Let's go.' Donna was ready, still panting from her last-minute rush.

Holly got to her feet, both the corset and her new boots creaking ominously.

She shook back her hair and breathed as deeply as was possible with several hundred pounds' worth of designer corset glued to her.

'I'm ready,' she said.

'That's a fabulous outfit,' grumbled Donna as they went downstairs. 'I hate this old dress. You look great and I look like I've been out milking the cows all day and only stopped ten minutes ago to get dressed.'

'You don't have cows,' pointed out Holly, smiling at Donna's mad logic. 'And you look great.'

'You know what I mean. You have that city gloss about you and I look like a bumpkin.'

'No you don't. And I borrowed this,' Holly confided, breaking her promise to Bunny. 'I was so scared that I'd look awful and the rest of them would think I'd never changed from being boring, fat old Holly Miller.'

'But you look beautiful,' said Donna in astonishment. 'You've looked great for years. Haven't you got a fabulous life and everything? What have you to feel scared about?'

'Are you on drugs?' demanded Holly, mystified as to how her friend had this inaccurate view of her life. 'I don't have a fabulous life, I work in a shop, I live in a flat I can't afford, if I didn't do overtime, I'd never be able to pay the electricity bill and my last date was a disaster.'

'How am I supposed to know these things if you don't tell me?' said Donna crossly.

'I'm sick telling you but you're convinced I'm lying. You seem to think that living away from Kinvarra is like magic dust that transforms your life. It doesn't.'

Donna stopped walking. 'Right, so. We won't mention this, though. I told the girls that you were getting on brilliantly and had men coming out your ears.'

Holly goggled at this. 'You did what?'

'I thought you were having a great time. Ah forget it, we'll say nothing. Caroline and Lilli are great fun, you know,' she added.

'I don't know.' Holly was ready to confide all her fears now that she'd started. 'I never talked to them at school, they looked down on us for being quiet.'

'We were our own worst enemies at school, Holly,' said Donna firmly. 'We should have joined in more. That's why I'm pals with Caroline and Lilli now. I don't want Emily to grow up being all quiet and mousy like us. She plays with Caroline and Lilli's girls and when they're older, they'll look after her. Nobody will call my daughter Speccy.'

So Donna *had* remembered. Holly stared at her friend. 'And all this time I thought you were suffering from selective memory syndrome.'

Donna grinned. 'No, I've just reinvented myself. Like Madonna. I'm making up for lost time. Come on.'

Caroline and Lilli were on their third double each. The bar was humming and they'd been mingling like mad, but there was still no sign of Michelle.

'Stupid bitch,' said Lilli crossly. 'I always said she was unreliable. And where's that Donna?'

'She's here,' crowed Caroline. 'And omigod who's that with her?'

They watched in astonishment as Donna arrived, breathless as usual, accompanied by this tall, voluptuously stunning woman, wearing what looked suspiciously like the original version of Caroline's corset. The woman's dark hair fell gloriously around her shoulders, as glossy as if several catwalk hairdressers had been slaving over it for hours.

She hadn't needed a seaweed wrap to squeeze her body into the corset; like a modern-day Sophia Loren, her figure was a natural hourglass, with a waspy waist that was surely narrower than one of Caroline's thighs. Caroline, who'd put on a stone since her school days, wished she'd stopped her mid-morning Mars bar now.

The dark-haired woman was carrying an exquisite beaded handbag and her necklace was definitely the same one that Posh Spice had been wearing in *Hello!* Confidence oozed out of her like expensive moisturiser out of Estée Lauder radiance pearls.

'It's Holly Miller,' said Lilli, awestruck.

Donna rushed up to her two new best friends, who clambered out of their corner to greet her and Holly. This was true reunion gold. Looking round the room, most people looked almost the same as at school, just with better highlights, real jewellery and more expensive clothes. Pat Wilson had had her long dark hair cut into a bob, Andrea Maguire's red hair was now dyed a startling blonde, and even Babs Grafton had finally had her teeth fixed and sported contacts instead of heavy glasses. But Holly was totally different, like someone who'd just stepped out of one of those six-month make-over things on the telly.

'Holly, I wouldn't have recognised you!' said Lilli, determined to get the upper hand now that she was faced with this much improved Holly.

'Isn't she fabulous looking,' said Donna.

'You look wonderful,' agreed Caroline. 'That's a real designer corset, isn't it?'

'Yes,' said Holly, overcome with the urge to tell them it was borrowed, 'although it isn't . . .'

Donna interrupted before Holly could say 'mine'. 'Wouldn't we all like a staff discount at Lee's.' She gave Holly a prod in the arm and Holly took the hint.

'. . . full price,' Holly amended. 'It wasn't full price. We do get a discount.' She hoped that Lilli and Caroline couldn't tell there was a lie in the midst of all of this. Holly told lies with all the skill of a devout nun.

'Tell us all about yourself,' said Caroline eagerly. 'I'd love to work in Lee's; it must be amazing, all those famous people dropping in and out, trying on Versace evening dresses.'

'I work in the children's department,' Holly said apologetically. 'We stock Baby Dior but we're drawing the line at sticking toddlers into sequinned evening dresses. It's hard to get baby sick out of sequins.'

Everyone roared with laughter and Holly felt herself relax marginally. Normally, she was too nervous to joke round other people.

'Still,' Donna pointed out, 'you get a discount. I must come up and look for an outfit for Emily's First Communion. They have lovely dresses nowadays, not like the terrible frilly things we had to wear. Do you remember mine, Holly? It was awful and my mother put curlers in my hair the night before and it went frizzy and stuck out at angles like I'd been plugged into the mains!'

'I bet mine was worse,' said Lilli, shuddering. 'My grandmother had my mother's old dress put away and she made me wear it. It was all yellowing and too tight. I was a sight!'

And they were off, comparing stories about how awful they'd looked. Holly realised that it wasn't as bad as she'd expected. Lilli and Caroline seemed genuinely interested in her, and they weren't the same arrogant schoolgirls she remembered. Lilli was still capable of being a bit sharp but Holly could cope with that now. And they seemed to think she was funny. Holly knew she'd been funny when she was at school too, it was just that nobody but Donna noticed.

As Michelle hadn't turned up, Holly was certainly the most fashionable and interesting ex-Cardinal girl there that night and Caroline and Lilli attempted to stick with her. Holly would have preferred to talk to the other non-gang girls from school but she didn't see any of them there. She'd met Andrea who used to sit beside her in art class, and Geena Monroe had thrown her arms round Holly and hugged her happily. Caroline's once-great friend, Selina, who'd never even spoken to Holly in school, had been fulsome in her praise of Holly's outfit, necklace and general improvement. But she hadn't seen lovely quiet Brona Reilly who'd sat on her other side in art class, or Munira Shirsat and her best friend, Jan Campbell.

'I think I saw Brona earlier, but a few of the girls didn't reply to the letter,' Caroline said when Holly asked her about Brona, Jan and Munira. 'You'd think they'd want to meet up with everyone again. After all we shared together.'

Holly wondered if the other girls had been so nervous of a reunion that they had deliberately not replied.

'You've heard all about us,' Lilli said, when they were waiting for dessert, 'and we haven't heard a thing about the man in your life.'

'Or should that be *men*?' giggled Caroline, who'd decided that Holly was simply being enigmatic by not talking about herself. That this glamorous woman could be shy never occurred to her, and anyone who looked so amazing must

71

have some gorgeous bloke in the wings. 'Go on,' she urged. 'Tell us.'

'There's nothing to tell,' said Holly.

Donna kicked her under the table. 'What about that guy you were telling me about earlier?'

All Holly could remember was Donna talking about reinventing herself.

'I bet he's a hunk,' said Lilli enviously.

'Look!' sighed Andrea, as waiters converged to place plates of butterscotch mousse, double chocolate cake and Hawaiian Surprise in front of them.

Donna took advantage of the lapse in everyone's concentration to whisper into Holly's ear.

'Make someone up!'

'Why?' Holly hissed back.

'Because I've told them you've got this fabulous life and I don't want you to let me down. We were boring at school, we've got to make up for it now!'

Three spoonfuls into their dessert, attention turned back to Holly. She wished more than anything she could have a cigarette, otherwise she was going to eat all her mousse, and lick the plate, and she couldn't afford to burst out of her outfit.

Caroline, Lilli, Selina and Andrea were waiting eagerly. Donna was smiling, encouragingly. Holly thought of how bad she was at lying, and then thought of how flattering it was that Caroline and Lilli really imagined that she could have a sexy boyfriend.

'Is it someone famous?' demanded Lilli, suddenly suspicious.

'No,' stammered Holly.

Donna gave her another kick under the table and Holly winced. She'd be black and blue tomorrow.

'Well . . .' They all looked at her eagerly. In fact, their entire end of the table was looking at her eagerly. All conversation seemed to have ceased as everyone waited for news of the new, improved Holly Miller's man.

'Go on,' urged Donna.

Holly gulped. For some deranged reason, the only man who came to mind was the current object of Kenny's longing: a male model named Xavier. Hard-bodied, blond-haired and with the face of a pouting archangel, Xavier reeked of sex, although Holly had it on good authority (from a drooling Kenny) that the only sex Xavier was interested in was not the female of the species. Trust her to come up with a fantasy boyfriend who was gay. Kenny would wet himself laughing when he heard.

'Tell us,' demanded Caroline.

Holly proceeded to describe Xavier in each perfect detail, leaving out the vital facts that he was gay and not going out with her. Lying by omission, she knew. What had Kenny said? 'His lower lip is like a big biteable, coral silk throw pillow. Yummy.' Kenny's imagination knew no bounds when he was in lust.

'A throw pillow, imagine. He sounds amazing.' Even Lilli was impressed.

Holly smiled hollowly and took a huge gulp of wine. She'd kill Donna later.

But as Caroline and Lilli began describing their other halves in glowing terms in order to prove that Holly wasn't the only one who could nab a handsome man, Holly began to realise why she'd gone along with Donna and lied. Feminism was a wildly outdated concept to Caroline and Lilli. Having a man was a status symbol to beat all others. Without one, Holly was low caste.

'Hi, Holly,' said a voice.

It was Brona, one of the few girls in school who'd been shyer than she was. Whereas Caroline and Lilli had disdainfully seen Brona as dull and unstylish, Holly's kind eyes saw an old friend whose eyes glittered with a spark of fun.

Holly leapt to her feet and hugged Brona warmly. 'How are you!' she said delightedly, 'it's so lovely to see you. You haven't been here all night, have you? Where were you?'

'At the back of the room, I didn't like to interrupt,' Brona said, sliding mischievous blue eyes in the direction of Caroline and Lilli.

Holly grinned and bore her off to a quiet corner to talk.

'You look completely amazing, Holly,' said Brona in genuine admiration. 'Poor Lilli's eyes are out on stalks with jealousy. How are you?'

After a thoroughly enjoyable half hour, Holly had learned that Brona was working as a locum in Donegal having qualified as a doctor three years before. In her spare time, she painted, went scuba diving and she had just bought a recently-restored fisherman's cottage on the coast. She was utterly happy.

'*Dr* Reilly,' said Holly, impressed. 'Let's go back and tell the gangettes and they'll be wildly impressed.'

Brona grinned. 'Maybe not,' she said. 'I've learned not to want to impress people for the wrong reasons. Whenever I find myself rushing to try and let people see how clever I am, I ask myself: Why would I want to impress them?'

Holly flushed. 'Yeah, you're right,' she said, shame washing over her because that's just what she'd wanted to do: to impress her old classmates. Why had she bothered lying? She was what she was. What was the point of pretending?

'I used to be miserably intimidated by the Carolines and the Lillis when we were in school,' Brona revealed. 'But I'm not quiet any more. Med school knocks that out of you, and I don't feel the need to bother talking to people who once looked down at me.'

'No, you're right, I agree totally,' Holly said.

'I was a bit nervous of coming here tonight, you see,' Brona said, 'and now I have, I'm pleased because it's shown me how much I've changed and become a new, stronger person.'

When Brona left, Holly sat down beside Donna again, feeling like a fraud.

The conversation hadn't moved on from the subject of men.

'You're so lucky, Holly,' Caroline said dreamily. 'I do love being married, but there are times when I wish I was young, free and single like you. I've never had the chance to go out with lots of men and have wild flings . . .'

'I know what you mean,' said Donna, who was quite drunk now. 'It'd be incredible to not be Mummy for a while, and party with gorgeous guys. You can *look* when you're married but that's it.'

'You can look, all right,' giggled Caroline, pointing at the waiter, who was very young and good-looking. 'Holly's the only one of us who can chat him up.'

'Do you know something,' Lilli said thoughtfully, 'he's the image of that guy you used to go out with, Holly. That guy you took to our debs dance. What was his name?'

'Richie!' said Donna, delighted to have remembered the name through the fog of alcohol. 'Whatever happened to him?'

'I have no idea,' said Holly, shuddering. 'It was so long ago I can barely remember what he looked like.' She could, actually, but she didn't want to even think about Richie. He'd been her first boyfriend and the first one to dump her unceremoniously. His image was embedded in her brain as the prototype guy-not-to-trust. Since Richie, Holly's luck with men hadn't improved. She didn't really trust any of them.

'He was cute, that Richie,' Lilli said.

'But not as cute as your new guy sounds,' gushed Caroline.

'We've got to meet this new boyfriend of yours,' Lilli added. 'You'll have to bring him to Kinvarra.'

Holly glued a smile to her face. 'Yeah, sure,' she said.

The children's wear department in Lee's was heaving with pre-Christmas shoppers the following morning, which did nothing for Holly's mild hangover. She hadn't got drunk: you couldn't and keep track of all the lies about a fabulous boyfriend with lips that resembled soft furnishings. But as she hadn't been able to smoke, she'd certainly drunk more than usual – two Bloody Marys followed by a couple of glasses of wine at dinner.

Getting up that morning had been hard and she'd had to hit the snooze button three times before she could haul herself out of bed. She'd only just remembered to grab the bag with the precious corset which she'd sworn she'd return to Gabriella that day.

On her way back down to the basement from her third trip to the loos, she stopped on the staff stairs and had a little rest to revitalise herself. It was ages to her coffee break and she could kill for a sit down and the sugar hit of a chocolate biscuit.

'Miss Miller, good morning,' said a voice behind her.

'Oh, er, good morning Mr Lambert,' Holly said, fumbling frantically in her sleeve for a tissue. She blew her nose loudly so it would look as if she was preparing herself for going onto the shop floor. Trust her to get caught dossing by the store manager. Mr Lambert held the door open and Holly, still bleary-eyed and tired, had to follow him into the children's department. Trying to inject a spring into her step, she walked over to the squashy child-sized purple and orange chairs by the changing rooms where Bunny was trying to convince a ten-year-old boy that he wouldn't face immediate ridicule from his soccer-mad pals if he wore something as boring as a non-football-logo-ed shirt for his baby sister's christening.

From the grateful look on the boy's exhausted father's face, it appeared that Bunny was winning the war.

'You can swap the shirt for anything you like once we're at the restaurant,' the father said eagerly once the despised shirt was wrapped and bagged in the Lee's Department Store's trademark red and gold carrier bag. Thank you,' he added gratefully to Bunny.

'Forget it,' grinned Bunny. 'It's my job.'

Bunny's speciality was small boys, especially when they came attached to good-looking fathers.

'What's your name, so I can ask for you again?' the customer said.

'Bunny.'

The man smiled as if this was a perfectly normal name for a grown-up. Bunny was the only person Holly knew who could carry off a child's pet's name and get away with it.

'My father thought it was cute,' was Bunny's answer that first day, before Holly could even ask why she had such a weird name. 'I'm actually Colleen but nobody ever called me that. Why Holly?' she asked conversationally. 'Are you a Christmas birthday person?'

'July, actually,' Holly replied. 'My mother likes unusual names. My father wanted us all to have traditional names but my mother won. My eldest sister is Stella Verena, I'm Holly Genevieve and my middle sister is Tara Lucretia.'

'After the Borgias, I hope? How cool,' said Bunny. 'Is Tara Lucretia a poisoner type of girl?'

Holly laughed. 'The only person she's ever likely to poison is our Aunt Adele. Tara writes scripts for *National Hospital*.'

'Wow,' said Bunny, impressed. 'You see, that proves my dad's point which is that people with unusual names end up doing out-of-the-ordinary things. Although I think he was hoping for more from me than the kids' department of Lee's.'

Holly soon discovered that, in typical Bunny fashion, this wasn't strictly true.

Bunny had just finished an English degree and was taking a job to finance her year off round the world, when she planned to veg out in India before a stint working as an English language teacher in Japan.

Bunny was one of those people Holly felt utterly comfortable with, and they'd instantly become good friends.

Now Bunny waved off the grateful customer and turned to where Holly was studiously folding sweatshirts on a display. All it took was one person rifling through the clothes for an entire display to look hideously untidy. Miss Jackson, the department head, took a dim view of untidiness even in the war zone that was the pre-Christmas rush.

'Do you mind if I take first coffee break?' Bunny asked. One of the pitfalls of working in the same department was that Bunny and Holly couldn't take their breaks together. There were four of them in children's clothes and there had to be three members of staff on duty at all times.

'Fine,' said Holly, wishing she'd asked first.

'I could kill for a fag.' Bunny started rooting about in the under-till cupboard for her cigarettes and her cardigan. Lee's was strictly non-smoking, so smokers congregated on the rooftop level of the store car park. 'See you in fifteen minutes.'

Fifteen minutes more and Holly could pour herself a huge coffee. She closed her eyes and wished she could learn how to press the stop button when it came to red wine.

'Are you feeling all right, Holly?' inquired Miss Jackson, appearing from the baby wear department.

'Fine, great,' said Holly brightly. She smiled so broadly that her face felt as if it would crack.

Miss Jackson approved of Holly Miller. Diligent and polite to the customers, she was always scrupulously turned out, and never gave a moment's bother, even if she was a little on the quiet side. But then Miss Jackson had seen Holly chatting away nineteen to the dozen with Bunny, so perhaps she was only quiet with management.

'If you have a moment, perhaps we can sort out the fancy dress rails . . .' Miss Jackson began.

'Have you got this in age ten to eleven?' inquired a woman, holding up a pair of boy's trousers.

Saved by a customer. 'Let me check,' smiled Holly, turning her attention to the woman gratefully. Sorting out the fancy dress stuff was a nightmare job at the best of times as customers thought nothing of rampaging through the fairy and wizard costumes like tornadoes when they were looking for a particular size. The last time she'd done it, Holly had absent-mindedly stuck a pair of kitten's ears on her head, forgotten to take them off, and had spent the morning serving customers with fluffy pink and black ears bobbing eccentrically until Miss Jackson had noticed.

As soon as Bunny came back from her break, Holly raced off for hers. Desperate for coffee, she bypassed her usual cigarette-stop in the car park, and made straight for the canteen. This proved to be her undoing.

There was a small clique of the store's party girls in there gossiping about a Christmas drinks they'd all been to. Holly steeled herself for the inevitable queries about her social life. The clique never talked about anything else but parties and men, and they didn't understand why anyone (Holly) didn't share their fascination. Consequently, they thought Holly was a bit stand-offish, not realising that she was simply shy.

She quietly made her way to the coffee machines and poured herself a cup, then, because it would seem rude to go and sit by herself, tentatively sat at the edge of the circle and listened. Pia (ground floor, Clinique counter) was keeping the group enthralled with tales of what happened next, after Tomás, he of the melting foreign accent, had told her she was beautiful enough to be a model.

'It's not as if I haven't heard *that* before,' Pia said without arrogance. She was stunningly beautiful after all. Skin like caramel silk, doe eyes and the grace of a ballerina. Men must surely always be telling her how beautiful she was, Holly thought wistfully.

'But he really *is* a photographer,' Pia went on.

The group were impressed. Men pretending to be photographers in order to chat up Pia was nothing new. One actually turning out to be a photographer was a surprise.

'Which one was he?' inquired Rebecca (ladies' hosiery). 'Not the tall, older guy? I noticed him talking to you but then I went to the mezzanine for a smoke with Leo and we ended up there for ages.'

'The tall one, yes. He's Hungarian,' Pia said dreamily. 'I thought you'd given up smoking, anyway?' she added.

Rebecca grinned. 'You know me: two drinks and I'm scabbing cigarettes from everyone.'

'Oh yes, and what went on in the mezzanine with Leo?'

demanded Fiona (millinery). 'It can't be the same I-never-want-to-see-you-again Leo, can it?'

Rebecca's grin widened. 'Same story as with the cigarettes,' she said wickedly. 'Two drinks and I forget all my good intentions.'

They all laughed.

'I was talking to your Tomás earlier, Pia,' Fiona pointed out. 'He never said he was a photographer.'

'He was probably lying,' Pia said easily.

Fiona, Rebecca and Pia all smiled. Men. What were they like?

'What about you, Holly?' asked Rebecca kindly, dragging Holly into the conversation because it wasn't nice to let her hang on the edge. 'Do anything interesting last night?'

'I was at a school reunion,' Holly said shyly.

The other girls smiled but the languid Pia looked unimpressed. School reunions were very far down her list of exciting events. Real parties involved rock stars, possibly a footballer or two, and at least one gossip column photographer recording the event for posterity.

'I'd never bother going to a school reunion,' said Pia. She eyed Holly speculatively, her cool gaze reminding Holly of Lilli the night before. Pia and Lilli were like sisters under the skin, Holly thought. Both keen to gauge a person's success by the wrong standards.

Holly wished she could say something witty in return but, as usual when faced with people like Pia, words failed her. She smiled weakly, knowing she looked like an idiot.

Fiona began talking about some fabulous new high-heeled boots she'd bought that looked madly expensive even though they weren't. Everyone nodded respectfully at this. Cheap, fashionable stuff that looked expensive was a favourite topic of conversation because none of them were on very good salaries despite their glitzy lifestyles.

'Oh, you won't believe the new shoes I got on Monday.' Rebecca held the floor.

Holly drank her coffee and flicked through the old magazine that somebody had left on her chair. She couldn't concentrate on it because she was wondering why she was such a wimp.

She drained her coffee and got to her feet, her movements graceful. *Say something*, she told herself, *say something*. 'Better go back. See you.' Oh well, it was better than nothing.

She'd just left the canteen when she realised she'd left her cigarettes on the table and doubled back to pick them up. Which was when she overheard them talking about her.

'Do you believe that about a school reunion?' asked Pia in a poor-dear voice. 'I certainly don't. In fact, I don't think she has a social life at all. She's a total oddball, really. She never has a word to say for herself.'

Hovering outside the canteen door, Holly was shocked into immobility.

'She's shy,' protested Rebecca.

'Well, I think she's just rude,' Pia continued dismissively. 'Or stupid. Somebody should tell her. I'd kill myself if I was as dumb as she is.'

'Don't be such a bitch, Pia,' said Rebecca. 'Not everyone's as confident as you.'

'I don't understand shyness,' Pia said haughtily. 'If you stammer, you can get that sorted out. If she's shy, why doesn't she go to classes or something? There's no excuse for that type of thing.'

'Poor thing. And I don't think she ever has a boyfriend. I know, why don't we introduce her to someone?' suggested Rebecca. 'That might give her a bit of a social life.'

'Waste of time.' Pia was scathing.

Outside, Holly's face burned with embarrassment and pain. Blindly, she hurried to the staff stairs, and raced down to the basement and the comfort of the children's wear department. Taking deep breaths to try and stop herself shaking, Holly leaned against the wall hoping that her legs wouldn't let her down. How could they let Pia say such awful things? Grimly, Holly thought of all the things she'd like to say to Pia if only she had the courage. She'd show her. She'd get a bloody fantastic life together and make Pia jealous of her, she would.

Like all the best tear-stained plans of revenge, by evening, Holly's thirst for retribution had vanished and she simply felt miserable and lonely. It was Friday night and as she walked slowly through the streets to catch her bus, she felt convinced that everyone else on the whole planet had exciting pre-Christmas party plans while she was going home alone for a date with Ben and Jerry.

Her mobile buzzed and, for once, she managed to find it in her bulging shoulder bag before the caller had given up.

'Hello?'

'Hi Holly,' said Joan. 'Spill the beans. How did last night go?'

''kay,' said Holly despondently.

'What's wrong?' demanded Joan. 'You sound like Cinderella when the pumpkin coach hits the dust.'

'Nothing's wrong.' Holly couldn't bear to have this conversation in the middle of the street. She might burst into tears, which would undoubtedly give Pia more ammunition for the 'Holly Miller is an anti-social nutcase' theory. Her phone began to crackle. 'The signal's bad here,' she yelled at the phone but it was too late. She'd been cut off. Feeling more wretched than ever, she switched the power off.

Joan and Kenny were both going out that evening, so she wouldn't see them until the morning. She'd tell them about the awful incident in the canteen then. But not now.

Her flat was in a crumbling Victorian monstrosity that had been built onto so many times, the original architect would never have recognised it. It was situated on Windmill Terrace, a long, winding road made up of a strange mix of vandalised old tenements and sprawling Victorian houses which canny property developers were doing up in advance of the area being gentrified. When that happened, Holly's landlord would undoubtedly eject all his tenants out onto

82

the street and sell up. Holly was crossing her fingers that this wouldn't happen until she had saved money for a deposit on a flat of her own, although that prospect was still a long way off. Her current apartment was one of two on the second floor. Across the hall was Joan and Kenny's flat, a much bigger, two-bedroomed establishment with its own miniature balcony, a bathroom with a cracked roll-top bath instead of the shower Holly had, and a kitchen that was never used for anything except making coffee and toast. Kenny and Joan had moved in two years ago, at the same time as Holly, and once they'd discovered that she loved to cook, they turned up at hers at least twice a week looking hungry. Consequently, they pooled the food money and treated their floor like one big flat, with Holly in charge of cooking. Joan, who as a student had the best working hours, did most of the grocery shopping, while Kenny took care of the laundry and ironed. Holly was dangerous with an iron because of her ability to singe holes in all her most precious garments. Anyway, she knew she'd never be able to get knife-edge creases into trousers the way Kenny did.

The walk from the bus stop was cold and she was chilled to the bone by the time she wearily opened her door. She switched on lights and the kettle, hung her heavy winter coat on the door and sighed with relief to be home. It was a tiny flat, but one of Holly's great skills was making a house into a home. With her own special brand of shabby and very cheap chic, she'd transformed the place. All the walls were painted a calming apple white with big colourful prints in distressed white frames grouped on them, and in pride of place stood a big dresser with glass doors which Holly had bought for €20 from a market and had distressed herself. The dresser contained all sorts of treasures: china, books, antique brocade bits and bobs could be seen through the glass, while an embroidered Japanese kimono in saffron silk hung from one knob. Beaded tea lights, an enamelled French lamp and a pretty, carefully-mended chandelier provided the lighting. Two small couches, at least fifth-hand but expertly disguised by two amber velvet throws and a variety of mismatched cushions made of chintzy scraps of fabric, made up the seating arrangements. The single divan bed in her box-like bedroom had a draped canopy that wouldn't have shamed the Empress Josephine and even her clothes hangers were padded floral ones, in colours that went with the rag rugs on her wooden floors.

Her home, unique and utterly individual, expressed her personality in the way she so often was too shy to do herself.

That night, Holly did what she always did when she was upset: she cooked. She slotted Destiny's Child into the CD player, pushed the volume up, poured herself a glass of red wine, lit a cigarette and started cutting up fat juicy tomatoes for her pomodoro sauce. When the sauce was bubbling, she opened her small but perfectly organized freezer and took out a portion of frozen fresh pasta. Purists might have shuddered at the thought of freezing pasta, but it *was* home-made, then frozen into portions for the occasions when she didn't have time to make it fresh. Her pasta machine had been a huge investment but was one of her most prized possessions: there was something infinitely calming about kneading the pasta dough gently and slowly feeding the sheets in and out of the gleaming stainless steel machine. It made her feel grounded, at home, as if endless Italian mamas or her own, Irish one, were looking kindly over her shoulder, helping her and comforting her.

The doorbell rang at half seven and Holly knew who it would be: either Joan or Kenny. She bit her lip, knowing that whichever one of them it was, they would instantly drag the humiliating story out of her.

'Omigod what a day,' groaned Joan, erupting into the room. She was thinner than a pipe cleaner but somehow seemed to take up a lot of space. She was in a purple phase this week, and dressed as befitted a fashion design student: Morticia Addams blue-black hair, an eyebrow stud, dyed purple army fatigues and a hand-painted lilac T-shirt decorated with her version of Japanese calligraphy. Kenny, who, when he wasn't fantasising about Xavier, was cherishing a long-range crush on a handsome Japanese student who lived in a house down the street, was always begging Joan not to wear the T-shirt because he was convinced it said something rude in Japanese. Joan ignored him on the grounds that the Japanese student wasn't gay and wouldn't look twice at Kenny no matter what Joan's T-shirts said. Now she tweaked Holly's cheek, stuck a finger into the tomato sauce to taste it, turned the volume of the CD player up to trouble-with-the-landlord level and threw herself onto Holly's smaller couch, all in a matter of seconds.

'I didn't make enough dinner. I thought you were going out tonight,' said Holly.

'I might be,' hedged Joan, who was sure something was wrong with Holly and was determined to get it out of her. 'What's up?' she inquired. 'You look like you've had a shit day, too.'

'No, why do you think that?' asked Holly.

'Your mouth is all droopy and you look like you might cry any minute,' Joan pointed out. 'So either you're depressed or you've aged very badly in the twenty-four hours since I last saw you, in which case I recommend Botox. What happened, and tell me all about last night's reunion? Did you look a million dollars and did you thump any of the horrible old bitches who used to ignore you?'

'Are you hungry?' asked Holly, only asking the question to avoid having to answer others. Joan was always hungry. Kenny said she had a tapeworm inside her.

'Yes, and what's wrong?'

Holly moved away from the counter which separated the tiny kitchenette from the sitting room. With her back to Joan, she lit up another cigarette. Joan was always nagging her to stop but Holly needed the crutch of smoking, and anyway, if she stopped, she'd just balloon up into a fat girl again. And then she'd be anti-social *and* fat . . .

She stifled a sniff but Joan heard.

'Holly, what's wrong?' said Joan again in a gentle voice.

Faced with her friend's kindness, the whole story came tumbling out: how Holly had felt good because everything had gone well at the reunion, but then how stupid she'd felt for lying about a boyfriend. And then, how utterly hurt she'd been by what Pia had said.

'Stupid bitch!' raged Joan, threatening death, destruction and the reorganisation of Pia's facial features. 'I don't know why you didn't go back and hit her. Did you mention this to Bunny?' Joan and Bunny were on the same wavelength. Both were tough, unafraid of anyone and fiercely protective of Holly.

'No,' said Holly miserably. 'I couldn't tell her. I *am* a mess, Joan. Pia was right.'

Like many sensitive people, all it took was one push and she was down.

'You're not a mess,' screeched Joan furiously.

'When I lied to the people at the reunion, the boyfriend I invented was gay! I can't even lie like normal people.'

'Kenny is cute,' Joan pointed out.

'It wasn't Kenny, I'm dating Xavier.'

Joan grinned. 'Mr Throw-Pillow-Bottom Lip. Holly, love, you *have* to lie at school reunions.' She decided that Holly needed cheering up before her morale could be boosted. 'What else are you supposed to say? Everyone has a fantastic life according to what they say when they meet old enemies. Did you ever hear of anyone at a reunion who said: "I got thrown out of college, was busted for drugs and avoided a jail sentence by doing eight zillion hours of community service, plus I live in a squat, have never had sex and my job involves spending all day saying 'would you like fries with that?'"'

Holly burst out laughing. 'Compared with that, I have a fantastic life and I don't know why I bothered lying.'

'I do,' Joan said, 'you lied, and it was only a teeny, weensy lie, by the way, for the same reason everyone lies – because we're all basically insecure and we want people to think we're wildly successful. Am I right or am I right?'

'Right,' Holly replied hesitantly. 'But that makes me a very shallow person if I give in to that sort of thinking.'

'Everyone does it.' Joan was matter of fact. 'My sister tells people her husband is in the merchandise relocation business when he drives a truck, and my mother tells my grandmother that I dress like this because we have to wear strange clothes in college. It's easier than telling my grandmother to eff off because she's an interfering old cow.'

'That's different,' Holly said. 'I lied because it was easier than admitting that I'm hopeless with men and just can't talk to them. I lied so that all the girls I was in school with wouldn't look at me the way Pia looks at me. She said there was no point in them fixing me up with a man because it would be a waste of time.' Holly looked so downcast that Joan's blood began to come to the boil again. Pia was *so* dead. 'We'll just have to find a fabulously hunky boyfriend for you then, someone who can race into the children's department just before closing and ravage you on top of the Rudolf the red-nosed reindeer pyjamas, and that would show dopey Slut Face Pia.'

'I can't speak from experience but I daresay that type of behaviour would get me fired,' Holly pointed out.

'But at least the girls would know you had a hunky boyfriend.'

'I'd also be jobless.'

'Just an idea.' Joan twiddled a bit of spiky hair thoughtfully.

Holly stabbed out her cigarette and went back to stirring her sauce miserably.

'Enough already,' said Joan, changing the conversation. 'Was everyone at the reunion impressed with your outfit?'

Holly grinned for the first time all day. 'We're talking eyes popping out of heads. They couldn't believe it was chubby little Holly Miller.'

'That's what I call a result. I can't imagine you as a chubby kid,' Joan added. 'You are *so* not fat.'

'Yeah, I know,' Holly mumbled. 'But I was and I still don't feel different, Joan. I still feel like the old me.'

Joan regarded her grimly. 'The problem isn't other people, Holly,' she pronounced, 'it's you. It's in your head.'

The doorbell rang again, a long insistent ring made by somebody keeping an impatient finger on the bell. Only Kenny rang like that. The word 'impatient' failed hopelessly to convey the notion of how much in a hurry Kenny always was.

'Don't mention this to Kenny,' begged Holly as she went to open the door. She couldn't cope with the *two* of them giving out to her all evening for being a neurotic wimp.

'Hello sweeties. Is there enough din dins for me?' inquired Kenny, once he'd hugged Holly and examined the contents of the saucepan bubbling on the stove.

In contrast to Joan's fashion college rig-out, Kenny was beautifully dressed in a charcoal shirt that clung snugly to his slim torso and a pair of elegant grey trousers that looked as though they had been made for him. Gucci and Hugo Boss respectively. Kenny loved labels and could identify any item of clothing at fifty paces. A senior salesman at an exclusive menswear boutique, Kenny was branching out into working as a stylist. His dream was to stop working in the shop altogether and freelance.

Holly thought he could work either side of the camera. He had cropped dark hair with a Richard Gere-esque sprinkling of early grey, and a handsome face with dark stubble. Kenny couldn't cross the road without women looking admiringly at him. Joan's favourite method of teasing him was to sigh and say, 'Isn't it a waste you're gay. Why don't we give it a go? I'm sure all you need is the love of a good woman.'

Kenny's answer to this was to roll his eyes theatrically and shudder: 'Don't go there.'

Holly hunted in the freezer for more pasta. 'There's enough dinner for everyone,' she said.

'Goody.' Kenny bounced onto the couch beside Joan and the two of them looked happily up at Holly, with eager hungry expressions on their faces. They reminded Holly of two kids expectantly watching Mummy cooking. The three of them were certainly a little family unit, she thought ruefully. Although they took turns being Mummy, because there was always one of them in some trauma. Kenny was plunged into gloom roughly every month because his love life never ran smoothly and there was always some gorgeous hunk of a man who wasn't returning his phone calls. Joan's traumatic incidents involved her finances – she spent all her grant on clothes, regularly ran out of rent money and scattered IOUs around like confetti. Holly's problem was herself, which was handy in that it didn't involve outside influences.

'I thought you guys were going out?' Holly said.

'Change of plans,' Kenny said.

'Is there anything good on the telly tonight?' Joan asked, searching in vain for the TV guide.

'Nothing good on a Friday, except Sex and the City on satellite,' Kenny said instantly. Kenny loved TV and read the listings in the paper first, followed by his horoscope, and then the headlines.

From the kitchenette, Holly grinned. She might not know what a wild existence with lots of men was like personally, but she could watch it on TV thanks to the Sex and the City girls. She began to grate some Parmesan reggiano, letting the day's events seep out of her system, while Kenny and Joan argued over the television. What would she do without them?

Ten minutes later, dinner was on the table, served on Holly's auction-house Italian china with the pastel fruit designs. None of it matched, but it was exquisite.

Joan began mopping up sauce messily with a heavily-buttered roll while Kenny fastidiously dipped slivers of unbuttered bread into his.

'Wonderful,' he said. 'Holly, you are talented.'

Holly beamed.

'You've got to forget what happened today,' he continued, having heard a whispered version of the story from Joan while Holly was busy in the kitchen.

Holly stopped beaming. 'You promised not to mention it,' she said to Joan.

'I agree with Joan,' Kenny said, 'Pia is a blot on the landscape but let's not rush into making her suffer. She gets her hair cut by my friend Marco, just you wait till next time she wants her fringe trimmed. Linda Evangelista is the only person I've ever seen who can cope with a one-inch fringe. Huh.'

'But making Pia suffer is not our primary mission,' Kenny added. 'Fun, yes.' He grinned evilly. 'Hilarious, absolutely. But not our primary mission. That,' he paused, 'is to get you a man, Holly dear. It would make all the difference to your life.'

Holly blinked anxiously at him. 'I don't need a man,' she said.

Kenny's smile widened to Cheshire Cat proportions. 'Yes you do,' he said. 'You need to be loved, cherished and adored by some man who spends his whole life telling you how beautiful and wonderful you are. And we're going to help you find him.'

'Is that my Christmas present?' inquired Holly, seeing the funny side.

'Don't talk to me about Christmas,' groaned Joan. 'I haven't bought anything and I'm broke.'

'I'm broke because I *have* bought everything,' Holly added. 'But I'm not really looking forward to Christmas this year because Tara isn't going to be at home in Kinvarra with the rest of the family. She's going to spend it with Finn's parents.'

'The dreaded mother-in-law?' Joan said.

'The very same. For Tara's birthday in September, she bought her a steam iron.'

'Lovely present,' cooed Kenny. 'I hope Tara's buying her something suitably awful for Christmas.'

Holly giggled. 'Tara did mention being tempted to buy a year's supply of constipation pills but she chickened out and bought perfume instead.'

'Well, I've bought nearly everyone's gift, except my mother's,' Kenny added. 'I have my eye on this fabulous Tanner Krolle handbag that she'd just love.'

'Oh, you mean you're not getting a boyfriend for *everyone*,' joked Holly.

Kenny blew her a kiss. 'Only you, Holly, only you.'

CHAPTER FIVE

On the afternoon of Christmas Eve, Tara idly wondered what the rest of her family were up to. Normally, the three Miller girls would be ensconced in the kitchen in Kinvarra, wrapping presents, laughing and joking as they tangled themselves up with Sellotape and shiny paper, with Amelia helping. Christmas wouldn't be quite the same without everyone else, she thought. But then again, she had Finn. Life couldn't always stay the same and if it had, she might never have met him. Noticing the time, she went in search of her husband. While she'd been out buying last-minute bits and pieces, he was supposed to have packed his stuff and all the presents. However, his suitcase lay empty on their bedroom floor and Finn lay sprawled on the bed, fully dressed and loose limbed. One long arm dangled over the side of the bed, almost reaching the floor, the other was flung across the pillow. Tara crept quietly over and gazed down at him. He hadn't shaved that morning, and the combination of stubble and slept-in golden hair should have given him a dissolute appearance. But it didn't. Even unkempt and deeply asleep, her husband shone with inner goodness. It was those long baby-girl eyelashes, Tara decided.

She slipped off her shoes and launched herself onto the bed.

'Wake up!' she roared, as she bounced into position beside her sleeping husband.

'Errgh, what?' groaned Finn, opening his eyes to reveal plenty of red-veined eyeball.

'You were supposed to pack and shave while I was out,' Tara said, crawling up the bed until she was lying on him. 'I needed a rest,' moaned Finn, burying his head under the pillow. 'A few more minutes. It's only lunchtime.'

'It's nearly two thirty and we're supposed to be at your parents' by half three.'

Somehow, they'd been roped into an intimate Jefferson family Christmas when Tara had wanted them to go to Kinvarra instead. But short of faking appendicitis, she knew there was no way out of it. They still had to pack for a three-night stay and the drive would take at least another hour, meaning that unless they left soon, they'd be very late.

'Get up,' she said again. 'You know how awful the traffic is to your parents' place, and today it'll be worse than ever.'

From under the pillow, Finn groaned again. 'We can phone and say we got delayed. Then I can have a snooze.'

Tara whipped the pillow away. 'No way, Finn. Your mother won't blame you if we're late. It'll be my fault. So get out of that bed or I'll go and get the cold sponge.'

'Not the sponge,' pleaded Finn. 'Anything but the sponge.'

Her fingers burrowed under his sweater and she began to tickle relentlessly.

'Stop,' he said weakly. 'I can't cope . . .'

Feeling guilty, she stopped. Finn took advantage of her weakness. In one quick twist, he'd jumped up in the bed and began tickling her, his longer, stronger fingers wickedly insistent.

'No!' squealed Tara as he began tickling her feet. 'Not my feet! No, pig! Stop it!'

'OK.' Too hungover to continue at any event, he rolled off her and they both lay back on the bed, panting.

'Have you packed anything?' Tara inquired.

'I got halfway through and I lay down for a nap,' Finn confided. 'I'm wrecked.'

'That's what happens when you get totally hammered at your office Christmas party,' Tara said smugly. 'I told you that drinking pints wasn't an Olympic sport.'

Finn grinned. 'A man's gotta do what a man's gotta do.'

'Not the day before we go to your parents for Christmas when you leave me to do all the packing,' Tara reproved. 'Get up, lazybones. We've got to be out of here in twenty minutes.'

'Yessir,' saluted Finn, half-heartedly.

Tara began packing quickly, rushing round the flat finding things like her mobile phone charger and her diary. Soon, she promised herself, they'd redecorate.

The bedroom was probably the best room in the two-bedroomed flat as it had the least awful curtains (plain, French blue) and boasted an entire wall of mirror-fronted wardrobes which hid a multitude of sins. Neither Tara nor Finn were tidy people and once the wardrobes were opened, things fell out and had to be carefully jammed back in. In spite of this drawback, they were packed and in the car in thirty minutes. The traffic was, as Tara had predicted, terrible. The Jeffersons lived in a pretty commuter town on the East coast, but the thirty-mile journey from Dublin inevitably took forever.

'Relax,' said Finn as they sat in a four-mile tailback to the toll bridge. 'Mums won't mind.'

Tara managed to keep her mouth shut. Mums or Mrs Gloria Jefferson would mind very much and would undoubtedly take it out on Tara. Just thinking about the next three days made Tara feel sick. She loved her father-in-law, Desmond, because he was funny and kind, like Finn, but Gloria was another matter. Chillier than the faint dusting of snow on the side of the motorway to Naas, Gloria was obsessed with class, money and 'doing the right thing'. The right thing for Christmas, apparently, was a sedate meal out with friends the night before, an intimate family dinner on the day (Tara had previous experience of the great silences at any meal where the guest list was just herself, Finn, Desmond and Gloria), and an afternoon drinks party at the Jeffersons' on Boxing Day where lesser neighbours were invited in to be allowed a glimpse of Gloria's newly-purchased dining room table and twelve, no less, chairs. The *wrong* thing, as far as Tara could make out, was Gloria's beloved only son marrying a television script writer. In her more wicked moments, Tara wished she'd been heavily pregnant when she married Finn, just for the thrill of watching Gloria's deeply shocked face as her daughter-in-law sailed down the aisle in a maternity wedding dress. What a scene that would have made. Tara's inventive mind went into overdrive. Imagine if she'd *had* the baby halfway down the aisle . . .

'She likes you, of course she does,' Finn protested whenever Tara gently pointed out that his mother didn't appear too keen on her. 'She's protective, that's all. And reserved. It was the way she was brought up.'

Unless Gloria had been brought up by Trappist monks, Tara could see no reason for her icy silences. But then, Trappist monks were amiable people and there was no way that Gloria could ever be called amiable. She could be friendly to other people, mind you, just not to Tara, who never ceased to be amazed at how her mother-in-law could simultaneously bestow smiles on Finn, and disdainful glances on her.

There were no beloved ex-girlfriends in the closet to account for this bitchiness, nobody Gloria would have preferred Finn to marry. Tara decided she was simply the sort of woman who viewed all women as rivals one way or the other. Tara might not have been a rival when it came to Mr Jefferson, but she was a rival for Finn's affection. That put her on Gloria's hate list. And boy, could Gloria hate.

It was well after six when they drove in the gate to Four Winds, the Jeffersons' meticulously maintained house. The house was small but even so, it was about three times the size of Tara and Finn's shoebox apartment. Gloria had dropped heavy hints about how the couple would be able to afford a bigger home if only they moved out of the city, nearer to Four Winds. But Tara would prefer to endure constant penny-pinching, not being able to afford much in the way of luxuries and having a bathroom the size of a built-in wardrobe as long as it kept her far away from her mother-in-law.

'We're going to be in trouble,' Finn said gloomily. Even he had decided that his mother would go mad at the lateness of their arrival. Consequently, it was up to Tara to cheer him up.

'We're only going out for a quick meal,' she said, 'I can be changed and ready to go in five minutes.'

'I know,' he said, 'but she won't be pleased. We're going out with the Bailey-Montfords and Mums has a bit of a keep-up-with-the-neighbours thing going with Liz B-M, so everything has to be perfect. Did you bring something dressy to wear tonight?'

'You saw what I packed,' said Tara, startled. 'I don't have anything very dressy with me, not for any day. I thought this was just a relaxed dinner with old family friends. You didn't mention any special significance to this meal.' Tara thought of her suitcase with its selection of casual clothes which she'd imagined were suitable for a family Christmas. She had a couple of sweaters, a white shirt styled like a man's dress shirt, her chinos, jeans for any rambles in the snow with Finn, and an indigo corduroy dress she'd brought to wear for Christmas Day. She was currently wearing black jeans, a black polo neck and her beloved sheepskin coat. Because she'd packed in a hurry, she'd brought far too much but even so, none of this rapidly assembled wardrobe could be described as dressy. 'Why didn't you tell me we'd need to dress up?' she asked.

'I just thought you'd know,' muttered Finn as he parked the car.

'Know what?' Tara was getting angry now. 'I brought the sort of thing I'd wear in Kinvarra for Christmas. It's suitable for there. Are you telling me that your mother is going to be dressed up like a dog's dinner tonight and every night?'

Finn's silence was enough of an answer.

'Great. This is a great start,' Tara said. Another black mark loomed.

'Let's not argue,' begged Finn.

Tara gave him a resigned look. 'You're right,' she said. Anyway, there'd be enough arguing in the Jeffersons' without them being at it too. Gloria could argue at professional level.

Desmond Jefferson opened the door before they could ring the bell. 'Hello Tara, Merry Christmas, hello Finn,' he greeted them. A tall, shy man who looked like an older version of Finn, with the same unruly fair hair and the same kind, handsome face, Desmond Jefferson was often described by friends as 'one of life's gentlemen'. Until his recent retirement, he'd been a civil servant in the Department of Foreign Affairs. His current plan was to spend lots of time in his garden. Tara reckoned he just wanted to stay as far away from Gloria as possible, not that Desmond would ever say so. He was far too kind and liked a quiet life.

She kissed him affectionately on the cheek and handed him a small package. 'A secret present,' she whispered. 'Fudge.'

Desmond smiled. 'Our secret,' he nodded, slipping the package into his trouser pocket.

Like Tara, he adored sweet things but Gloria kept him on a severe diet. There was no adequate excuse for this, Tara knew, because he was perfectly healthy, had no cholesterol problems and went for a four-mile walk every day.

'Mums likes to fuss,' was how Finn explained it.

Mums likes to control, was Tara's personal version.

His mother was in the drawing room waiting for them. She glanced quickly at her watch, and then smiled, as if she hadn't really been clocking the fact that they were very late. She was fifty-nine but looked at least ten years younger, thanks to rigorous dieting, monthly chestnut rinses in the hairdressers' and a painstaking beauty routine. Dressed in a black satin evening dress that was a perfect fit for her tiny body, Gloria should have looked marvellous. But the hardness in her pale blue eyes and the taut disapproval in her jaw ruined the effect.

'Hello, Gloria,' said Tara, 'lovely to see you. Your Christmas tree is nice.' It was horrible, actually. God would strike her down for lying so much.

'Thank you, Tara,' said Gloria in her well-modulated voice. 'So lovely to see you too. Finn,' she added, sweetly reproving. 'You haven't shaved. We're leaving in half an hour.'

Finn's smile didn't falter at the bite in his mother's voice. 'Didn't have time, Mums, too busy with last-minute work,' he lied, putting a pile of gift-wrapped presents under the tree and then giving his mother a hug. Tara never bothered hugging Gloria; she'd tried it once and it had been like embracing a shop-window dummy. 'Just as thin and just as stiff,' Tara had told Stella later. 'She's nothing but a shrew.'

'She's had years being on her best behaviour as a civil servant's wife,' Stella had said kindly. 'I'm sure she really likes you, she's just very formal.'

'Stella, she's the most un-civil person I've ever met. Now when are you going to wise up and turn into an old cynic like me?' Tara laughed. 'You expect the best of everyone.'

'I don't,' protested Stella. 'I hate to see you not getting on with your mother-in-law. She seems nice enough to me, you must give her a chance.'

'She's had six months since the wedding,' Tara replied grimly, 'and there's been no time off for good behaviour.'

'I'll show you to your room,' Gloria said now, rising graciously to her feet. 'If you hadn't been so late, you could have had coffee. Still,' she gave Tara a rather contemptuous glance, 'you're here now.'

Tara said nothing. She knew she wasn't imagining it. Gloria was a cow. As she led them from the room, Tara took a quick look around. The room was beautifully proportioned with big windows and, in daylight, it had a nice view of the trees in the front garden, but Gloria's décor was positively arctic. Pale blue walls, an even colder blue rug and silvery grey armchairs dominated. Even with the heating on at full blast, the effect was cold. It was a million miles away from the comfortable charm of Meadow Lodge, where much of her parents' furniture was beautiful but old and well loved. Everything in the Jeffersons' house was defiantly brand new, as if Gloria consigned everything to the bin in a three-year cycle so she could keep up with the Joneses.

The Christmas tree was worse, decorated with far too few silver bits and pieces because Gloria hated ostentation and thought that less was more. Where were the elderly, much-loved decorations that the family would have had for years? Tara thought of her mother's version of a Christmas tree: a riot of golds and reds, with battered cherubs and some wooden decorations they'd had for thirty years and which one of the family cats had systematically chewed. Rose had even held onto the now faded paper decorations that Tara herself had made when she was about six years old. Gloria would shudder at the sight of that tree.

'I hope you brought your good suit,' Gloria said to Finn as she marched up the stairs to the guest room.

'Yes, Mums,' said Finn.

Behind Gloria's back, Tara stuck her tongue out at her husband, feeling like a naughty schoolgirl following a stern teacher to the head's office.

Finn pinched her bum in return.

'Is this going to be a very formal occasion?' Tara asked innocently, 'because I didn't bring anything suitable.'

Gloria whisked around, her beady eyes slitted down to the size and texture of uncooked lentils. 'It's Liz and Pierre Bailey-Montford,' she said incredulously, as if that fact alone explained why dressing up was a necessity. 'You must remember them from the wedding?'

Tara could remember many things from her wedding, chief among them thinking that she must love Finn very much to marry him when she was getting Gloria as part of the deal. 'Sort of,' she said, deliberately hazy.

'Pierre owns B-M Magnum Furniture!' hissed Gloria, the veneer slipping. 'Their house is two hundred years old. Liz buys all her clothes in Paris.'

That was what was she disliked most about her mother-in-law, Tara reflected: her criteria for assessing people were all wrong.

'So this outfit won't do?' Tara knew she was pushing Gloria to the limit but she couldn't help herself.

Gloria stood by the spare room and let Finn and Tara enter. 'I would have thought that was obvious,' she said venomously.

'We won't be long,' Finn said, interrupting before war broke out. 'Tara has other clothes.'

'Yeah, my lap dancing thong and my feather boa, you old bag,' Tara muttered under her breath as she dumped her bag on the floor.

'Don't wind her up,' pleaded Finn when the door was shut and they were on their own.

Tara sat down on the duvet, which was hysterically floral, as though the fabric designer had accidentally jumbled up two different patterns on one piece of material. It gave her a headache just to look at it.

'I don't wind her up,' she said. 'I simply don't understand why your mother plays games all the time, that's all. If she wanted us to bring formal clothes, all she had to do was telephone and tell us. But no, that would be too easy.' Tara was getting crosser thinking about it. 'Instead, she lets us come and *then* goes overboard with disapproval because I haven't packed a cocktail dress. That's being manipulative, pure and simple. I'm fed up with it.'

'Tara love, please don't get upset.'

Finn sat down beside her and held her. 'Can't we have a nice Christmas, please?'

Tara laid her head against his shoulder, relishing the comfort of being close to his lean, muscular body. Tara never seemed to have time for the gym but Finn went religiously. 'I'd love to do that,' she murmured, 'I'd love our first Christmas as husband and wife to be special, but I don't know how I can cope with your mother, Finn.'

Finn stroked her hair gently. 'Christmas reminds her of Fay, that's all. It's difficult for her.'

Tara sighed. Fay was Gloria's sympathy card. Gloria's younger child and Finn's twenty-seven-year-old sister, Fay had gone off travelling after a huge blow-up with her mother and had refused to talk to Gloria since. Although Tara had never met her, because Fay's dramatic departure had been two years ago which was before Tara and Finn had even met, she sounded like a bit of a free spirit. Fay now lived in California, practised psychic healing and corresponded with Finn and Desmond, but hung up when her mother came on the phone. Clearly, psychic healing could only do so much.

If it had been anyone else, Tara would have felt sorry for a mother who was cut off from her daughter. Tara loved her own mother far too much to ever do such a thing. But knowing Gloria for the past eighteen months, Tara could see why someone would be driven to travelling to the other side of the world to escape her.

'We'll have a nice Christmas,' she reassured Finn.

'Thanks, babe.' He looked so grateful. It was the least she could do. She'd bite her tongue when Gloria was being bitchy.

Tara decided to wear the corduroy dress, plenty of lipstick, and a big, jaw-clenching smile. Gloria, who'd obviously decided to modify her own behaviour, said nothing and the foursome set off in a taxi with Finn and Desmond chatting happily as if they hadn't noticed anything was amiss.

At the restaurant, Tara had to start biting her tongue when she met the others. If Gloria had pulled out all the stops in the dressing up department, she had nothing on Liz Bailey-Montford who was dressed as though *Hello!* were due to photograph her at any minute for a 'lifestyles of the rich and tasteless' piece. Jewels gleamed at ears, wrists, neck and fingers and her silver and black plunging dress was a dizzying combination of sequins and beading. Tara was blinded by the glitter.

There was obviously plenty of one-upmanship between the two supposed best friends because Liz had brought along her daughter and son-in-law as backup and wasted no time telling everyone that Serena was doing a masters in art history and Charles was a tower of strength who worked with his father-in-law in the furniture business.

'I don't know what we'd do without Charles,' Liz said, 'he's *so* capable.'

Charles had a blank, unintelligent face and Tara thought he didn't look as if he was capable of changing a light bulb. But he'd obviously lucked out by marrying Serena who was heiress to the B-M furniture kingdom, so he couldn't be that dumb.

There were lots of double kisses, oodles of 'oh you look *wonderful*, Gloria! Doesn't she, Pierre?' and it took ten minutes for everyone to be seated, according to a table plan, naturally. Tara hated table plans. She liked sitting beside Finn and hated all that rubbish about sticking him as far away from her as possible and putting her beside someone she didn't know.

Pierre, on her right side, appeared tired, while Charles, on her left, looked uninterested until he found out that she worked on *National Hospital*, and then spent the next ten minutes plying her with stupid questions about what the stars were *really* like.

'Theodora, I mean, Sherry,' he said with glazed eyes, 'she's fabulous, isn't she? Is she like that in real life?'

'You mean man-mad?' inquired Tara, bored. 'Men adore her.'

Charles backtracked hastily. 'Oh no, I don't mean that. I just admire good acting.'

'Of course you do.'

The waiter arrived and Gloria and Liz ordered melon and plain fish.

'Thank you,' Gloria said sweetly to the young waiter, who beamed back. 'Can't be too careful,' she added to Liz. 'Melon is the only option. A moment on the lips . . .'

'. . . a lifetime on the hips,' finished Liz and they both giggled.

Tara watched in astonishment. Nobody would recognise her stony mother-in-law in this giggly woman across the table. Talk about street angel, house devil.

'I might have melon too,' said Serena thoughtfully.

'Nonsense!' Gloria was kind but firm. 'You don't need to diet, pet. You've a lovely little figure.'

Despite being seated apart, Liz, Gloria and Serena talked to each other noisily across the round table. Finn and his father were laughing over some story, while Pierre and Charles had livened up enough to argue over the wine. Tara sat silently and watched it all, thinking of the wonderful time Mum, Dad, Stella, Holly and Amelia would be having by now in Kinvarra. Nobody could magic up an air of festivity like Mum, and by now, the house would be filled with the smells of Christmas cooking, with Mum's absolute favourite, Frank Sinatra, belting out love songs from the kitchen. Holly and Stella would be laughing as they stuffed the turkey and Dad would be gleefully sorting out glasses for the traditional Miller Christmas Eve drinks party which always kicked off between half eight and nine. Everyone came to the party; all the close family friends and relatives, half of Kinvarra almost. Mum and Dad had been hosting the party for as long as Tara could remember and it was like the official signal for Christmas to start. Entire families turned up, people were delighted at the opportunity to let their hair down, drink flew around at a fierce rate and such was the spirit of fun that people who'd originally apologised that they could only drop in for a moment would have to be decanted drunkenly into taxis at half eleven before the family went to midnight Mass.

It would all be incredible fun, with no pretensions. Her longing to be there overwhelmed Tara and she felt a lump swell in her throat. It was so easy to forget how important family were until you weren't with them.

She tuned back into the here and now to overhear Serena, Gloria and Liz discussing clothes.

'I love your dress,' Gloria was saying warmly to Serena. 'You can never go wrong with a little black dress and a nice gold necklace.'

Tara glanced over at Serena, who looked quite overshone, despite the LBD, by her flamboyant mother, but who did have a heavy gold necklace hanging from her neck. Tara was not a jewellery person, which was just as well because Finn certainly didn't have the money to shell out on chunky gold stuff. They just about managed the mortgage and the bills on both their salaries: TV script writing wasn't the money-spinner everyone thought it was. That was why Tara longed to get into writing for someone like Mike Hammond. She loved working on *National Hospital*, but if only she could work on a film script or one of the big-budget television adaptations that Mike was involved with, well, she'd be on the road to fame and fortune.

'. . . well,' her mother-in-law was saying, 'these media types don't put the same store on dressing up as we do.' She lowered her voice. 'They're really quite casual, which can be inappropriate on occasion.'

Tara knew exactly who Gloria was referring to. Bitch. Double bitch.

She glared across the table at Finn who seemed oblivious to it all.

'Does Sherry have a boyfriend?' asked Charles, unable to get his mind off her.

'No, rumour has it she's a lesbian,' snapped Tara, although the lie backfired because Charles drooled even more; no doubt at the notion of being sandwiched in bed between the beauteous Sherry and another stunning woman.

Trust him to be one of those blinkered men who saw gay women as some sort of kinky challenge. She'd have to tell him it was a joke. She gave up on Charles and turned to

Pierre, who looked grey in the face and was trying to keep awake.

'Are you looking forward to Christmas?' she asked brightly.

Pierre fixed her with a glassy stare. 'No,' he said and turned back to his wine.

Think of tonight as research, Tara told herself firmly. Writers couldn't write unless they observed. But despite her good intentions, separated from Finn and stuck in conversational limbo with Charles, the evening crawled past.

Pierre came out of himself enough to keep ordering bottles of wine but remained monosyllabic otherwise.

'Poor darling Pierre is worn out,' Liz admitted. 'The pre-Christmas rush has been so busy. What about you, Tara? Do tell us all about the glamorous jet-set life. Do you get to see many stars?'

'Sherry, the girl who plays Theodora, is a lesbian,' interrupted Charles, sounding shocked.

Tara gasped theatrically. 'Charles, you old tease. You know I was joking! She loves men.'

That shut Charles up. She turned to Liz. 'I know them all,' she sighed. 'All the stars. We're like one big, happy family.' Ooops, another lie. The big television stars wouldn't have any time for lowly script editors like herself.

'Really.' Liz leaned big bosoms on the table in her eagerness to hear all. Tara could see the young waiter's eyes popping out of his head as Liz's plunging dress front plunged further still. 'You mean Daniel Anson, from *Anson Interviews*?' Liz named one of the country's biggest chat show hosts. 'You know him?'

Tara nodded. Well, she had stood behind him in the canteen one day; that was almost meeting.

'What's he like?'

Tara thought about the contents of Daniel Anson's tray that day: burger, chips, diet soft drink. He'd thrown his packet of cigarettes and a disposable lighter onto the tray when he was searching for change.

'Very normal,' she said.

'Tell us about Dr McCambridge on *National Hospital.*' Serena looked animated for the first time all night.

'He's handsome,' said Tara truthfully. 'He has that special something that really works on camera . . .'

'Animal magnetism,' growled Serena.

Finn, who knew from Tara that the actor could be hard to work with, smothered a giggle. Tara smiled across at him. She could just about cope with the evening if Finn was with her.

'Welcome back,' she mouthed.

Finn raised his glass to her. He was going to have another hangover in the morning, Tara reflected.

It was just after eleven when the taxi deposited the Jeffersons back at Four Winds.

Tara, exhausted after an evening of trying to be polite under difficult circumstances, wanted nothing more than to fall into bed and cuddle up to Finn. But Finn and his father decided that liqueurs were the order of the day.

'It's less than an hour till twelve, let's stay up and toast in Christmas,' suggested Desmond.

'Great idea.' Finn fell onto the big grey armchair and held out his arms for Tara to sit on his lap. Mindful of Gloria seeing this as another breach of decorum, Tara sat on the side of the chair instead and put an arm round Finn's shoulders.

Gloria disappeared on some errand.

'What would you like, Tara?' asked Desmond, poised over the drinks cabinet.

'Er . . .' Tara didn't know. She generally drank wine and wasn't fond of spirits apart from the odd gin and tonic. 'Baileys?' she hazarded, 'in honour of the Bailey-Montfords? Maybe not.' She grinned to herself. Baileys was creamy and smooth, while the B-Ms were hard to swallow.

She heard a shocked gasp and looked up to find Gloria had reappeared and was staring at her grimly.

'Did I say that out loud?' laughed Tara. She must have drunk more wine than she'd thought. 'Sorry, Gloria.'

'They're nice people,' said Desmond, peacemaking, 'but

it's not easy to be catapulted into a group of people who know each other well. I'm sure you and Finn would have preferred to stay at home.'

He gave Tara a big crystal balloon of Baileys anyway and she took it with a murmured 'thanks', humbled by Desmond's gentle reprimand.

Gloria asked frostily for a crème de menthe, 'very small, please, Desmond,' she said, shooting a poisonous look at Tara and her generous glass.

'I'll get mine, Dad,' volunteered Finn. 'I need to see what you've got.'

Desmond took his brandy over to the other big armchair and Tara watched while her husband fiddled around in the cabinet before pouring himself an enormous glass of Cointreau.

'You'll die in the morning,' she whispered as he sat beside her.

'I need to block out the arguments,' he whispered back, nuzzling her ear. 'Total inebriation is the only way.'

Everybody sat and sipped their drinks in silence.

'This is nice,' said Tara politely, trying to lighten the atmosphere.

'It's a pity you didn't enjoy dinner.' Gloria's tone was glacial.

Tara shrugged. If Gloria wanted to be like that, it was her business.

'Mums and Dad, did I tell you we're going skiing in March?' Finn said.

'No, you didn't. Good for you, son.' Desmond was envious. 'I love skiing.'

'We'd half-planned to go at Christmas,' Finn said, 'but we didn't want to let you down, of course,' he added hastily.

Tara said nothing. She hated these stilted family conversations. In her home, everyone talked nineteen to the dozen about anything and everything. Not like this. It was as if Finn and his father were afraid to say the wrong thing in case they inadvertently upset Gloria.

Still, she glanced at her watch, another interminable forty minutes to go and it was officially Christmas Day, and they could all go to bed.

'I hope it wasn't too much of a sacrifice to give up skiing for Christmas with your father and me.' Gloria's voice dropped plaintively, 'I feel that Christmas is for families.' Her thin face was taut under its perfect layer of base.

'We know that,' Finn said easily. He never displayed even the slightest irritation with his mother. Tara wondered what the secret was.

Gloria sniffed as though she might possibly cry. Tara didn't think tears could squeeze themselves out of the space between Gloria's eye liner and her pinched little eyes.

'I know it's selfish of me, darling, but I love having my family around me at this time of year.' She shot a venomous glance at Tara, who bridled. It was clear that Gloria didn't include Tara in that sentence. Tara glared furiously at her mother-in-law. Then the little demon flicked on in Tara's head.

Rose Miller would have recognised the wicked glint in her daughter's eyes but Gloria carried on regardless.

'As it's your father's first non-working Christmas, I thought the three of us should be together.' Another martyred sigh.

Tara had had enough of her drink and decided she'd like a rapid exit. 'Why doesn't Fay ever come home for Christmas?' she asked innocently.

It was worth it to see the look of horror on Gloria's face. Even Finn looked a bit alarmed. Nobody mentioned Fay in front of his mother.

'We do not speak of Fay,' intoned Gloria icily.

Tara smiled as sympathetically as she could and put her head to one side. 'That's so sad, Gloria. It would be wonderful to forget the past and welcome Fay home. Christmas *is* for families, after all.'

Gloria's face darkened.

'Look at the time,' said Desmond gently, getting to his

feet. 'We should get to bed or we'll be tired tomorrow. Merry Christmas, everyone.'

He hugged Tara and Finn, then put his arm round his wife. 'Come on Gloria dear, time for bed.' He led her from the room and Tara turned in time to see Finn swallowing the last of his Cointreau.

'Another one?' he said, making for the cabinet.

'No,' Tara said, suddenly suffused with guilt. 'Do you need one? Don't you think we've had enough for one night?'

'There's no point blaming that little scene on you having too much to drink,' Finn teased, pouring himself another. 'Anyway, you've certainly found the ideal method of sending my mother to bed quickly.'

'I'm sorry,' Tara apologised. 'I didn't mean to upset your dad.'

Desmond had looked so very sad at the mention of his daughter's name.

Finn sat back with his drink. 'Dad's fine. He talks to Fay too, you know. He can e-mail quite happily from home because Mums never goes near the computer. You're right, though, Fay should come home. She just wants Mums to suffer.'

Tara could identify with that.

'There was no excuse for mentioning her,' she added. 'I feel bad. For your father's sake.' She didn't regret any hurt to Gloria. She'd been asking for it.

'Forget about it.' Finn didn't seem concerned.

She looked at him curiously. 'How come you're so laid-back about it all? Your mother drives me mad, but you never bat an eyelid.'

He shrugged. 'You get used to her. She's highly strung, that's all and a stiff drink helps you deal with her.'

Tara mused silently on the concept of stringing her mother-in-law from somewhere high, then shook her head guiltily. *She* was turning into as bad a bitch as Gloria.

'Anyway, that's what I admire about you,' Finn added.

'You don't pull your punches, Tara. You say what you think.'

Tara had a sudden vision of the ever-tactless Aunt Adele and shuddered. She'd have to watch her tongue or she'd turn into her aunt.

At the same moment in Kinvarra, a very drunk Mrs Freidland was objecting to being given a soft drink.

'I'm having wine,' she said loudly when Stella tried to hand her a tall glass of lemonade.

Not after the bottle and a half I must have served you already, thought Stella. 'We're stopping serving alcohol now, in honour of Christmas Day,' she said gravely. 'We always do at the end of the night.'

'Weally?' Mrs Freidland was fascinated at the very idea. How eccentric these Millers were. Still, it would be rude to argue and she felt very tired all of a sudden. She might just sit down and have a little rest. Or a sleep, even. Rose had lovely, comfy cushions on all her chairs.

Stella helped Mrs Freidland to a chair and peered around the room for Mr Freidland, who had originally said he and his wife would be driving to another party by ten. It was now half eleven. She spotted Mr Freidland in a corner with a glass of something ruby red which was definitely alcoholic.

The Kinvarra taxi men would make a fortune tonight. Rose always pre-booked and the drivers knew she'd make it worth their while with a decent tip.

With Mrs Freidland safely ensconced in a nest of cushions, Stella resumed her trip round the house to make sure that everybody had enough drinks. There were hordes of people, all chatting, laughing and eagerly eating Rose's home-made canapés. Slipping through the crowd, Stella found her mother in the kitchen making coffee. Rose looked as immaculate as ever, her hair swept up and the soft copper colour of her v-necked dress bringing a gentle flush to her face. But Stella noticed that there was a weariness evident in her mother's eyes. Rose had worked very hard to make the party a success, never stopping for so much as a bite to eat or more than a sip of water herself while her guests were there. Everyone else saw Rose Miller gliding through her lovely house, charming everyone and with a kind word to all. They didn't see the heightened activity in the kitchen during the party, or the hectic preparations before.

'You're a bit of a swan, Mum,' Tara would say fondly to her. 'Serene on the surface with your legs going like mad underneath!'

Rose adored that comparison. It was a pity Tara wasn't here tonight, Stella thought. It wasn't the same without her, though Holly was doing the work of two: going round with a tray of food and drinks. And she looked marvellously festive in a slinky black lace dress with a Christmassy red silk flower in her hair and her lips glossed up in poinsettia scarlet.

'Pre-sale,' Holly had revealed delightedly when Stella admired the dress and the way it clung to her sister's curves. 'It was dead cheap because there's a tear under one arm but I've fixed it. You know I don't like things that are very fitted because they show off all the lumps and bumps, but Bunny said it suited me . . .'

'What lumps and bumps?' Stella had demanded. 'I don't think you should be allowed near Dad's friends: they'll all be grabbing you and saying you've turned into a beautiful woman.'

Holly laughed. 'Some hope of that.'

Dear Holly. Stella wished with all her heart that she could give her sister a confidence transplant.

'Should I ask the taxi firm to check on the whereabouts of the cars we've booked?' she asked Rose now.

'That might be an idea,' her mother replied. 'I meant to do it but I got tied up here . . .'

'It's OK, I'll do it.'

'I booked ten taxis for half eleven,' said Rose, 'but they're bound to be a bit late tonight of all nights. Maybe you and

Holly could round up the people who definitely shouldn't be allowed to drive home and steer them in the direction of the hall.'

'Mum looks a bit stressed,' said Stella to Holly as they stood in the hall and waved goodbye to the Freidlands, the Wilsons, and a gang of other happy, swaying people, most of whom had dropped in 'for half an hour' several hours before.

'I know,' Holly said. 'She was fine until she got a phone call an hour ago. She literally went white. To be honest, I thought Tara had been in an accident or something.'

'Who was it?' Stella asked curiously. She'd never even heard the phone ring.

'I don't know. It wasn't anything to do with Tara. She said it was nothing. Probably a wrong number,' she added.

Stella looked worried. 'I hope Mum would tell us if there was anything wrong. But you know how determined she is to cope with everything herself. She's as stubborn as a mule . . .'

'How are my lovely girls?' Their father's best friend, Alastair Devon, came into the hall with Hugh and put an affectionate arm round both Holly and Stella.

'Thank heavens at least there's one guest leaving the premises sober,' said Hugh jovially as he opened the hall door.

'Somebody has to stay sensible,' said Alastair, kissing both Holly and Stella goodbye. 'This rabble have been drinking like there's no tomorrow.'

'I haven't.' Alastair's wife, Angela, who had followed him from the party, sounded insulted.

Her husband grinned and took her hand in his. 'Sorry, darling. There are *two* sensible people in the rabble.'

'What about us?' said Stella, grinning and gesturing at herself and Holly.

Hugh ushered Alastair out the door. 'Get out of here before you get lynched, Alastair. You know we can never say the right thing with women.'

Slowly, the guests went home and the family were left alone. Glasses and crumpled up napkins littered every available surface and Stella sighed at the thought of clearing it all up. Parties were wonderful but the aftermath was not.

'I'll get started here,' Rose said, picking up a tray. 'We don't need to leave for midnight mass for another ten minutes.'

'No, you won't,' said Stella firmly, taking the tray from her mother. 'You have a rest and beautify yourself. I don't have to get ready, so I can do this.' She was staying at home with Amelia who, despite begging to be allowed up with the grown-ups, was fast asleep in bed.

For once, Rose acquiesced. 'Thanks, Stella love.'

'Mummy, is it time?' said a sleepy voice from the doorway. Amelia, eyes crinkled with tiredness, stood there fully dressed in purple corduroy trousers and an embroidered lilac jumper. She must have been awoken by the sounds of people leaving. 'I'm a big girl now, can't I go with you?'

Rose sat with her family in a middle pew of the soaring Kinvarra cathedral and stared at the altar. Amelia leaned against Rose with her eyes half-closed.

'Grown-ups get to go to see Baby Jesus in the crib for the first time,' she'd said miserably earlier. 'Why can't I go? Becky and Shona get to go. I'm not a baby.'

'You'll be too tired,' Stella had said.

'I won't,' Amelia was insistent.

'She wants to,' Rose said, 'why not let her. You can sit beside me, Amelia, and we'll cuddle.'

Amelia had sat wide-eyed and alert beside her grandmother at first but now tiredness was getting to her. Even the thought of seeing the Baby Jesus in his crib couldn't keep her awake and she snuggled into Rose's soft camelhair good coat.

On the other side of Rose sat Holly, who didn't look terribly awake either. Holly leaned in the direction of her father, who sat at the edge of the pew. She adored her father, Rose knew, and was closer to him than she was to Rose. In times of trouble, Holly had always run to Hugh.

From the corner of her eye, Rose could see her husband's proud head, his bearing upright and proper even at midnight. Hugh looked as if he was concentrating totally on the service, although Rose knew from experience that Hugh's mind could be miles away however attentive he looked.

Rose knew that her eyes always gave her away if she didn't pay attention, no matter how carefully she schooled her expression. She stared at the altar and thought about the phone call that had exploded into her Christmas Eve party like a hand grenade.

It was a miracle she'd heard the phone at all, what with the noise of the guests and the sound of Sinatra crooning old hits.

'I'm looking for Hugh,' said the voice on the phone. A woman.

'Well, hold on . . .' Rose had picked up the phone in the hallway so she carried it a few yards so she could look into the living room. She could see Hugh's silver head towering above most of their guests. He was in the middle of a group of people near the piano and she couldn't really interrupt him. She hoped Hugh didn't start a singsong. It always took hours to persuade people to sing and twice as long to shut them up. Nobody would leave until the wee, small hours if the piano got going.

'I'm afraid Hugh can't come to the phone right now,' she said politely. 'Can I take a message?' Even as she said it, Rose thought how odd it was that any caller to their home wouldn't recognise who she was and say 'Hello, Rose.' Unless it was business, of course, and it could hardly be a business call at ten o' clock on Christmas Eve.

'I need to speak to him.' The woman was insistent and there was something else in her voice, something Rose couldn't quite identify.

'We're having a party,' Rose explained, still polite. 'I can't

114

get him for you now. Are you sure you wouldn't like to leave a message? If it's an urgent legal matter, I can give you the number of someone else from Miller and Lowe.' She'd picked up a pen by now, ready to write a message on the notepad, although she couldn't imagine anything so urgent it would require legal assistance right now.

'No message,' the woman said silkily. 'It's not business. Thank you.'

Rose stood listening to the dial tone. She put the receiver back slowly.

Holly was coming downstairs with some coats. 'Are you all right, Mum?' she asked urgently. 'Was that bad news? It's not something wrong with Tara, is it?'

'Nothing like that.' Rose managed a faint smile. 'Just a mistake. Now, I must rush and check the oven.' She flew into the kitchen, shut the door and sat down on the bench seat under the picture window, feeling a cold sweat emerge all over her body. She knew what had been nagging her about the woman's voice, she knew the unidentified ingredient: mockery.

At noon on Christmas Day, Stella and Amelia drove to Adele's house to pick her up for lunch. Amelia, thrilled to have got a bumper haul from Santa, not to mention a pink typewriter from the absent Tara and Finn, could only be torn away from her new possessions with bribery.

'Aunt Adele has your present under her tree and she might forget it if you don't come with me to pick it up,' Stella had said disingenuously.

'Sure, Mum,' said Amelia, instantly getting up from where she was laboriously typing her name for the tenth time. 'What did she get me?'

Rose and Stella's eyes met.

'Something lovely, I'm sure,' Rose reassured her.

Hugh would have gone with them but he'd woken up with a sore throat and was sitting in front of the box with his feet up, being mollycoddled by Holly.

Adele had been at a special carol service the previous evening, which was why she'd missed the drinks party. Now, vexation at having missed the festivities made her sharp-tongued.

'I suppose last night was the big event of the season,' she snapped as soon as Stella and Amelia stepped inside her hall door. 'I'm sure your mother outdid herself, as usual.'

Stella told herself to count to ten. No, she reflected, make that a hundred.

'The party was lovely, Aunt Adele,' she said evenly. 'We missed you.'

Adele harumphed a bit. 'I'll get my handbag,' she said, beetling off. 'The presents are in the living room, Stella. You can manage them, I imagine.'

A Mount Everest of parcels sat on the living room floor. Stella sighed, thinking of dragging them all out to the car. Adele always bought big, un-Christmassy things like frying pans and fake bamboo magazine racks that she liked the look of in catalogues. Over the years, Stella had received two trays specially designed for use in bed and at least three decorative tea towels covered with slogans about the kitchen being the heart of the home.

'Can I open mine now?' whispered Amelia, dropping to her knees to check the labels.

'Better not,' said Stella.

In the car, Adele thawed out a bit but the ice shield went back up when she got to Meadow Lodge and saw the hall table groaning under the weight of a huge bouquet of flowers which one of the previous evening's guests had brought for Rose. Too late, Stella saw Adele reading the card, eyes narrowed as she scanned the message full of praise for Rose and her 'famous Miller hospitality'. Stella thought it was sad that Adele had never been able to get over her jealousy of Rose. Neither of them had sisters; wouldn't it have been wonderful if they had been able to love each other in the way that Stella loved Tara and Holly.

'Poor Hugh, how are you?' Adele sat down beside her

116

brother and held his hand as if he was a Victorian hero on the verge of expiring from consumption.

'Coping, Adele, coping,' said Hugh stoically.

Stella bit her lip as she arranged Adele's presents under the tree. Then, leaving Amelia to bash out more typing, she went into the kitchen.

The smell of cooking was delicious but Rose's normally pristine kitchen was dishevelled, with saucepans, vegetable peelings and various implements all over the place. At least half of the cupboards were wide open and squares of paper towel were strewn on the terracotta tiles where something had spilled. Rose was attempting to wedge a turkey the size of a small ostrich back into the oven.

'That smells incredible, Mum,' said Stella, looking round to see what she could do to help. Her mother was normally so organised and this chaos was unusual. 'Has Dad been helping?' she asked with a grin.

'No.' Her mother shut the oven with a resounding bang and straightened up, sighing as she did so. 'He's in front of the television playing the dying swan and asking for hot lemon and honey drinks.'

There was an uncharacteristic edge to Rose's voice.

'Adele's arrived, so she can look after him,' Stella said easily.

'She's welcome to him,' Rose snapped as she flicked the switch on the kettle.

Stella began wiping up the gunk on the kitchen floor.

'Are you missing Tara?' she asked sympathetically. When her mother didn't reply immediately, Stella answered for her. 'It is strange without her but I suppose we'll have to get used to things being different now that she's married.'

Rose dunked a couple of teabags in two mugs. She missed Tara like hell and resented the notion that bad-tempered Gloria, who didn't appreciate her daughter-in-law, was benefiting from her company. But the lack of Tara was short term, something Rose could live with because she knew that in a few days, she would erupt into Kinvarra like a tidal wave, making everyone laugh and instantly forget about her absence at Christmas. What rankled deep in Rose's heart was the memory of the enigmatic phone call. Painful as the ache of a deep-rooted toothache, it throbbed away maliciously. Rose knew exactly what that phone call had meant.

'Of course I miss Tara.' Rose handed one of the mugs to Stella. 'But it's only natural that she spends time with Finn's parents. I didn't sleep well, to be honest; that's all that's wrong with me.'

'Mum, why didn't you say that?' said Stella, exasperated. 'Holly and I could have cooked dinner and you could have had a rest.'

'Merry Christmas, Rose,' said Adele, sweeping into the room carrying the detritus from Hugh's various sore throat remedies. She sniffed the air, wrinkling her nose doubtfully. 'Turkey? We always had goose at home . . .'

'Yes, it's turkey, Adele,' said Rose, speaking in the calm, measured tones she'd found worked best with Adele. Reacting to one of Adele's snubs was fatal. 'Merry Christmas,' she added. 'But I insist that you don't do a thing. You should relax and enjoy yourself. You're our honoured guest.'

Flattery and a stranglehold of calmness was the key to dealing with prickly members of the family. Rose had learned that the hard way.

'I suppose I *am* tired,' Adele said, taking the bait. 'Last night's carol service was exhausting for all of us in the choir.'

Stella, who thought her aunt sang like a strangulated cat and could only imagine the noise of a choir with Adele in it, smothered a grin.

'Can I get you anything, Aunt Adele?' she asked.

'Tea perhaps, for myself and poor Hugh. He's worn out.' This last remark was directed at Rose and was designed to remind Rose of how Hugh required cosseting far beyond Rose's abilities. But Rose merely nodded and turned back to her cooking. One day, she'd like to tell Adele a few secrets about her precious little brother. That would serve Adele right.

They opened the rest of the presents just before dinner.

Holly loved the set of tiny coffee cups and saucers that Rose had trawled the antique shops for. 'They're beautiful,' she exclaimed, holding up a hand-painted china cup, so delicate that it was almost transparent.

Adele gave Holly a copy of *The Rules* and a contraption for hanging over radiators and drying clothes.

'I told them in the bookshop that I was looking for a present for my unmarried niece and they said that this book would do the trick. It's all about teaching modern girls how to get a man,' Adele said with satisfaction, as Holly leafed through the book in bewilderment.

'Holly doesn't need anyone to teach her how to get a man,' said Stella hotly.

'And it wouldn't do you any harm to have a look at it too, madam,' Adele reproved.

Rose bit her lip so she wouldn't lash out. How *could* Adele?

'Ah now, Della,' said Hugh soothingly, 'modern women don't want men. They have it all tied up and they don't need us any more. Isn't that right, girls?' He put an arm around each of his shocked daughters and squeezed them close. 'Don't mind,' he whispered to Holly. 'She's doing her best.'

Holly smiled bravely. 'Thanks, Aunt Adele,' she said.

Stella blew her sister a kiss and glared at her aunt.

'Holly,' she said, 'I need a hand in the kitchen.'

They scrambled to their feet and hurried out.

'Cigarette?' said Stella.

'I must look very hurt if you're telling me I need a cigarette,' Holly said ruefully.

'Yeah, well, Adele can put her feet in her mouth more easily than anyone else I know. She must have been a contortionist in a previous life. Let's sit in the conservatory. You can smoke, and I'll crack open the wine.'

While Holly sat in the tiny conservatory off the kitchen, Stella opened a bottle of wine that had been cooling in the fridge.

'It always feels weird to smoke in the house,' Holly said,

lighting up. 'I was so used to hanging out my bedroom window and blowing smoke outside.'

'I wish you'd give up,' Stella said gingerly.

'How could I cope with Aunt Adele at Christmas without nicotine?' laughed Holly.

'Wait till I tell Tara what Adele gave you,' said Stella. 'She'll howl.'

'She mightn't howl at all,' pointed out Holly. 'She's probably getting another steam iron or a saucepan from Gloria as we speak.'

'In-laws, yuck,' shuddered Stella. 'That's the problem with marriage – you get saddled with a whole new batch of people.'

'Not my problem,' said her sister.

'Nor mine,' replied Stella thoughtfully.

That night in Four Winds, Tara dragged Finn off to bed halfway through the late-night Christmas film. He'd been snoring for at least the last twenty minutes of *The Untouchables*, although when she woke him, he insisted he was watching the film and that they hadn't seen the best bit yet.

'You were asleep,' she hissed.

'Wuzzn't,' he slurred. 'Oh all right.'

Christmas at the Jeffersons' had been a master class in Cold War tactics. Tara and Finn hadn't emerged until after eleven that morning, which was the first mistake – Tara's naturally. Finn was nursing a hangover and Tara was nursing a grievance over being in Four Winds in the first place. Arriving downstairs to find a prune-faced Gloria on her way out to church without her son and heir, Tara had managed an apology for being up so late.

Gloria was not full of Christian charity on Christ's birthday. 'Good morning, or should I say good afternoon,' she sniped.

'And Happy Christmas to you too, Gloria,' said Tara sweetly.

The present-giving revealed that Gloria had outdone herself in the gift stakes this year, with Tiffany cuff links and an exquisite dress shirt for Finn and a sandwich toaster for Tara.

It had been downhill all the way from then, to the extent that Finn had made sure that the television in the den, the room which backed onto the dining room, was blaring loudly so that the sound of *Chitty Chitty Bang Bang* made up for the lack of conversation at the dinner table.

Making small talk while having one ear cocked for all her favourite tunes from the film, Tara wished she was in the den watching the TV instead.

After dinner, Gloria and Desmond piled on extra sweaters and coats to go for a walk in the December gloom. Finn, snug in the den with Tara and a fresh bottle of red wine, waved them off, saying he was too full of that fabulous dinner to walk anywhere.

'Promise me that we can leave the country next Christmas,' groaned Tara, positioning herself on the couch so that her feet were on Finn's lap. He idly massaged her feet, giving in to a quick tickle now and then.

'The Caribbean?' he suggested.

'We can camp out on the side of a mountain without a tent as long as we're on our own,' Tara said, then regretted being so blunt. 'I didn't mean that,' she added, 'it's just that your mum and I . . .' she tailed off.

'Chill out, love,' said Finn, reaching for his wine glass. 'Christmas is the ultimate endurance test. I don't know why the reality TV people haven't made a game show where they stick a family in one house over Christmas and see how long they last before there's bloodshed over who gets to pull the last cracker.' He tickled her toes, then moved his fingers up to caress her calf. 'I hate Christmas.'

But he shouldn't hate Christmas, Tara reflected. The holiday wasn't an endurance test at Kinvarra. She loved spending it with her family. How sad for Finn that he didn't enjoy it with his family.

The only light relief came when Finn and Desmond dragged

out the box of Trivial Pursuit and inveigled Tara to play with them.

'What about your mother?' Tara murmured to Finn.

'She doesn't like board games,' he replied.

'Count me in,' Tara said loudly and settled down to see how many pieces of pie she could win.

By the time Desmond won, it was time for some of Gloria's sandwiches with coffee and Tara, who thought she'd never be able to face food again, gamely managed two crustless triangles to be polite.

'Do you not like spiced ham sandwiches, then?' demanded Gloria.

Feeling like a foie gras goose, Tara took another sandwich and willed for the day to be over soon. At least tomorrow was the occasion of the drinks party, which meant Gloria would have a whole host of other people to be bitchy to and might forget about Tara.

'I'll tape the rest of *The Untouchables*,' Desmond suggested as Finn and Tara headed for bed.

In their bedroom, Finn flopped onto the bed and began to crawl under the duvet fully dressed. 'I'm wrecked,' he groaned.

'Finn, you've got to take your clothes off,' complained Tara, trying to slip off his shoes.

'I'm too tired,' he said, not helping the undressing process by lying like a giant slug in the bed.

'Cold sponge,' warned Tara.

'Not the sponge,' said Finn, beginning to giggle.

He was still giggling when he sat up and let Tara pull off his shirt.

'I love you, Tara Miller, d'ya know that?' he said, kissing her drunkenly.

'I love you too,' she replied, 'although I don't know why.'

He leaned against her, nuzzling into her shoulder, making murmuring noises.

'Finn, please stand up so we can take your trousers off,' she said.

But Finn was asleep. Sighing, Tara finished undressing her husband and covered him with the duvet. Honestly, he was like an overgrown teenager sometimes. Only a big kid would drink too much at his parents' house and have to be put to bed.

CHAPTER SIX

Stella's fellow solicitor and colleague, Vicki, was insistent that she suffered from SAD. 'Seasonal Affected Disorder,' she repeated for Stella's benefit. 'It means I suffer from depression caused by not enough light. And look,' Vicki gestured out of the office kitchen window where a square of foggy January sky could be seen through the grubby glass, 'look at that weather.'

'It's called winter,' Stella said, taking the milk from the fridge. Full fat, she realised, putting it back and reaching for the skimmed. Why had she eaten all those chocolates over Christmas? Her camel trousers, normally slightly loose, were biting into her belly reproachfully.

'I hate January,' Vicki moaned, pouring hot water onto her low-calorie chocolate drink. A statuesque redhead who was five foot nine in her fishnets, Vicki was always on a diet until about noon, when the thought of nothing but crispbread and low fat yoghurts made her abandon hopes to slither into a size fourteen.

'Join the club,' Stella said with a sigh.

Vicki looked at her friend in surprise. Stella was normally so cheerful. Nothing got her down: not torrential rain when they were rushing back from lunch with no umbrella, not clients from hell who demanded double attention and were late paying their fees, not even Mr McKenna, one of the senior partners and a creep who could put even Vicki off her food for a week with one lascivious leer down her blouse at her 38DDs.

'Do you want to talk about it?' she asked.

Stella shook her head. 'It's just January blues,' she murmured, moving aside to let someone else into the kitchen. A mere cubicle tucked away beside the post room on the ground floor, it was barely big enough for two, never mind three people. Of course, the partners never ventured into it: they had tea and coffee delivered by their assistants whenever they felt like it. Stella, who was the most senior of the conveyancing solicitors, Vicki and another lawyer named Jerry Olson all shared an assistant and, theoretically, could have ordered tea and coffee with abandon. But Lori was run off her feet as it was answering their phones, without making them coffee as well. Or at least, that was Lori's excuse.

They took the lift up to the fourth floor which was where the property department was situated. Property or conveyancing wasn't seen as the sexy part of law: the hot favourite at the moment was the family law department and Lawson, Wilde & McKenna handled many of the highest-profile divorces around. The family law offices were huge. 'Lots of space for exes to scream and hurl things at each other without actually injuring an innocent bystander,' explained Henry Lawson whenever anybody remarked on the vast conference rooms on the second floor.

Conveyancing, which 'earns LW & M *a fortune*' as Vicki said furiously, was relegated to the less prestigious fourth floor, in the grand-looking but unmodernised part of the building where draughty windows, elderly heating and pre-war plumbing reigned.

The fourth-floor conference room was the nicest part of their floor and was decorated in some style with a vast pink-veined marble fireplace, a mahogany table almost big enough to play tennis on, and exotic Indonesian silk wallpaper that had survived decades of cigar smoke. The staff called it the Gin Palace because the maroon-coloured walls made it look like the sort of room where colonial types would have sipped gin slings and moaned about the natives.

'Two calls holding for you, Vicki,' announced Lori cheerfully as they emerged from the lift into the 1930s splendour of the fourth floor. 'I told them you were yakking in the kitchen and would be along later when the mood took you.'

'Ha ha,' said Vicki, who was used to Lori's sense of humour. She picked up her messages with one hand and, holding her coffee in the other, shoved open her office door with one stiletto-ed foot.

'Bad news, Stella,' Lori added, 'Jerry's wife has just phoned. He's been on the bog all night. Dodgy prawn vindaloo. He's got two meetings today and they can't be cancelled. Sorree.'

As the second most senior person in the department, which included five lawyers, three legal executives, a law clerk and a panel of apprentices, Stella merited the biggest office. (The Partner in charge had a large office on the third floor and a golf handicap in single figures.) In return for her big office, Stella also got the flak when anything went wrong and had to juggle appointments when somebody was ill. Jerry had an apprentice named Melvyn working with him for the year, and while Melvyn might be able to keep an eye on things in Jerry's absence, he wasn't qualified to deal with serious issues on his own.

'What time's the first meeting?'

'Half ten. The second one's in the afternoon. I'll get the files for you.'

'Thanks,' said Stella sighing. That was all she needed. It was only half eight and already she was behind. And she was feeling miserable, although she'd lied to Vicki about it being January blues. It was the Missing-Amelia-Blues. Glenn was home from the Middle East and Amelia was staying with him in his mother's house in Cork until Sunday night, five whole days away. It wasn't that Stella begrudged Glenn a week with his daughter, or even that she worried about Amelia when she was there: Glenn's mother, Evelyn, was a marvellous granny and would take the best care of Amelia. It was just that Stella missed her daughter so much.

Her interoffice line buzzed. 'Oh Stella.' It was Lori. 'Forgot to tell you, the plumbing's gone in the ladies' loo. It's like Niagara in there when you flush. I rang Martin in maintenance but he's still on his Christmas holidays. What should I do?'

By ten, Stella had the beginnings of a Grade A headache, not to mention a list of backed-up phone messages as long as her arm. She still hadn't had time to cast her eyes over Jerry's client's file except to glance at the name on the top: Nick Cavaletto. It sounded glamorous but names could be so deceptive. She and Vicki had once laughingly argued over who got a client called Joaquin d'Silva, both instantly thinking of the handsome Spanish dancer Joaquin Cortes, only to find that their Joaquin was many continents away from his namesake in looks. Mr D'Silva had been short, over-hairy and over-friendly, a bit like a dog. Vicki had said she kept waiting for him to lift his leg on the furniture.

'Lori, could you hold my calls for half an hour?' Stella asked.

'Sure.'

Five minutes later, Stella had just scanned through Mr Cavaletto's file and was fast coming to the conclusion that Jerry's handwriting was illegible. Scribbled notes in the margins of the file made no sense whatsoever. The whole thing actually looked quite straightforward, as Mr Cavaletto had power of attorney for his elderly mother and was intending to sell her home for her. The only difficulty appeared to be a problem involving stables which had been built and for which no planning permission had been given. Stella grimaced. She hated planning permission problems. She shut Mr Cavaletto's file briskly. For his sake, she hoped he was on time.

He was early.

Stella's internal line buzzed at twenty-five past ten.

'Mr Cavaletto's here,' breathed Lori in a much more husky voice than usual.

'Put him in the Gin Palace,' Stella said. 'And tell Melvyn he can sit in.'

'Of course,' said Lori, again in that husky voice.

She normally said 'right-oh mate,' in a breezy manner that no amount of discussion about correct behaviour for a legal office could remove. What was with the proper assistant carry on? Stella wondered. Lori must be hoping for a raise.

'Will I order coffee?' Lori added in her new sexy growl.

'Er, yes,' said Stella. Definitely a raise.

The whole place was losing its marbles today.

It was more than five minutes before she left her office to walk to the conference room.

'Coffee's in there,' said Lori. Twenty-something and a vibrant brunette with a liking for va-va-voom clothes, she looked altogether overexcited for some reason. She'd even applied a fresh splash of hot pink lipgloss.

'Thank you,' said Stella, opening the door to the Gin Palace. 'Sorry for keeping you, Mr Cavaletto,' Stella added conversationally, dropping her files onto the polished mahogany. She looked up smiling, her hand extended in a professional manner. And then she realised why Lori was behaving like a cat on a hot tin roof. Mr Cavaletto lived up to the glamorous name and then some, although he was not classically handsome. A big leonine man with grey-streaked dark hair, his clever face had too many crags and hollows in it to ever be called handsome. He had a granite hewn jaw and a firm mouth that gave the impression he was used to getting his own way. But that wasn't it. He was more than the sum of his parts. Presence, charisma, whatever it was, it drifted off him in great waves. Tara might be able to describe him, to capture what it was that made him so attractive. Stella couldn't put it in words.

He'd been staring out the window and now crossed the room swiftly and shook her hand. 'Nick Cavaletto. Thank you for seeing me at such short notice.'

'No problem,' she said, adding, 'I'm Stella Miller.'

Heavy-lidded muddy green eyes, the colour of gleaming Mediterranean olives, locked with hers. Unlike other men, his gaze didn't flicker up and down, quickly assessing her. What Vicki dismissively called the classic man's *'would I or wouldn't I?'* glance. His eyes stayed locked with hers until Stella, feeling that this intense gazing thing had gone on for too long, sat down abruptly.

'Please, take a seat,' she said.

He sat down too, not beside her, thankfully, but in a chair at the top of the table, a few feet away from her.

'Er . . . now I've been looking over your file and er . . .' She opened the file but couldn't seem to lay her hands on the cover sheet. She'd just been looking at it, where the hell was it? Clumsiness swept over her like a rash and she felt her temperature rise rapidly as she fumbled through the pages. It must be the heating. Either that, or the powers that be were pumping hallucinogens through the system, Stella decided wildly. Only that could account for the level of madness on the premises.

'I'm sorry you've been thrown in at the deep end,' Mr Cavaletto said. 'Your receptionist said Jerry was unexpectedly called away . . .'

Stella glanced up to see if Lori had imparted the prawn vindaloo information, but was relieved to see that Mr Cavaletto's craggy face held no amusement.

'Yes, something unavoidable,' she murmured, trying to pull herself together. Well, being glued to the bathroom was probably unavoidable in Jerry's case.

She looked back at her papers, sensing that he was still gazing at her. She wished he'd stop it.

'Now.' She cleared her throat and finally found the cover sheet.

'Shall I pour you some coffee?' he interrupted.

She looked at him.

'It's just that you seem a little harassed and I feel responsible. You could do without having an extra client dropped onto your lap today, I'm sure.' He looked so earnest, so genuinely apologetic, that Stella decided that he wasn't trying to unnerve her. He was just being nice, after all, Stella sighed to herself. She was jumpy today and it wasn't fair to take it out on him.

She sat back in her chair. So much for detoxing. 'I'd love a cup. But I'll get it,' she added, getting up. He was the client after all.

He waved her back into her seat.

'That doesn't seem right,' she said.

'Let's buck convention, shall we?' he said.

'Why not?'

He poured coffee while Stella watched him with interest.

He was tall, which she liked, and she liked the way his hair was carelessly swept back from his high forehead, as if he used an impatient hand to rake it into place far more often than a brush. He wore nice clothes, slightly casual but expensive. And he looked clever, too. Shrewd intelligence burned behind those eyes.

She idly wondered was he married? Then, shocked at herself for even thinking such a bimbo-esque thought, she sat up straighter in her chair.

'Milk and sugar?'

'Just milk, thanks,' she said. Would he chance a hackneyed comment about her being sweet enough already?

He passed the test by saying nothing.

'There's nothing worse than one of those days when you have to take the flak for other people's absences,' he remarked. 'Colleagues imagine that managerial positions mean nothing more than a bigger salary, but it's a hell of a lot more than that.'

'Tell me about it,' said Stella. 'I'm trying to sort out Jerry's client list, my own, and deal with some disaster in the ladies' loo because the maintenance men are out.'

'Maybe I can help with the latter part?' he said.

'Are you a plumber?'

He grinned. 'No, I'm in the engineering business, actually, but I know my way round the u-bend.'

Stella laughed. 'That's better than me. I'll attempt any DIY that involves paint, a hammer or tubs of plaster, but don't ask me about plumbing or electricity. Seriously,' reality reasserted itself, 'I can't ask you to look at the ladies'.'

He got to his feet and made for the door. 'Come on, show me. I might be able to tell you what the problem is.'

Stella followed, feeling surprised and amused.

Lori jerked her head up from her computer keyboard when Nick marched out of the Gin Palace.

'Hello again,' she breathed huskily, batting her recently mascara-ed eyelashes at him.

'Mr Cavaletto needs to visit the ladies' loo,' said Stella gravely.

'What?' demanded Lori in her normal voice.

'You've a problem in there, I hear,' Nick said.

'You mean you're going to fix it?' Lori said, batting furiously again.

Stella grinned. Clearly, Lori was one of those women who went limp at the idea of men who knew what to do with power tools. She'd never made such an effort for the firm's maintenance man, but then, he didn't look like Mr Cavaletto.

'That's wonderful,' Lori said, as she led the way, explaining the problem as solemnly as if she was a doctor describing some hideous illness to a consultant.

Stella followed again, feeling like a third wheel in this adoring little procession.

Nick didn't look like the sort of man who did much plumbing, she thought. Not unless plumbers were going in for fine tweed jackets, of the Milanese palazzo variety.

He reached into his pocket and took out a pair of frameless glasses, which added to the professorial, brain-the-size-of-a-planet effect.

Lori glanced back at Stella and made swooning motions.

Stella glared at her to stop.

Nick crouched down to examine the gushing loo. Both Stella and Lori admired his broad shoulders and the way he stroked his chin thoughtfully.

'It's a leak in the cistern,' he said finally.

131

'You're so clever, we would have never worked that out,' sighed Lori.

Stella began to feel irritated. Just because none of the fourth-floor staff had their plumber's apprentice certificates, didn't mean they were witless little women incapable of changing a light bulb. And why was Lori giving poor Nick Cavaletto the full treatment? Honestly, he was Stella's client. Well, Jerry's really, but Stella was dealing with him. Lori would get eyestrain if she kept batting her eyelashes seductively up at him.

'Do you have a wrench somewhere? I'll close the stopcock, which should solve things until your maintenance men get a chance to look at it,' Nick said, seemingly unaware of the effect his presence was having on Lori.

'There are tools in the maintenance office in the basement,' Lori volunteered, then looked at Stella, as if to say that she certainly wasn't going to leave Mr Cavaletto to trail down to find a wrench when it was far more fun to stay here.

'I have to answer the phones, I can't go,' she announced.

For some reason that she couldn't quite put her finger on, Stella found that she didn't want to leave Lori with Nick. They'd probably be engaged by the time she returned.

'One of the apprentices can go,' replied Stella. She would kill Lori for being so blithely insubordinate but she couldn't say anything in front of Nick.

'Great idea. You better tell them; I have no authority over the apprentices,' Lori added sweetly.

'Right,' said Stella and marched off, furious, to find one.

She dispatched one of the apprentices to look for a wrench and returned to find Lori perched demurely on the edge of her desk, ignoring the phone ringing off the hook.

If Nick thought this was strange, he didn't say anything.

'I'll just wash my hands,' he said. 'In the men's toilet, I don't want to startle anyone.'

'Mm, what a guy,' said Lori when he was gone. 'He can look at my plumbing any time.'

132

'Don't drool, Lori,' said Stella, irritated. 'You'll ruin the carpet. And he's not *that* gorgeous.'

'Hello! Earth to Stella!' said Lori incredulously. 'You *so* need to get your eyes tested.'

'He's too old for you,' Stella added, crossly. 'You're twenty-five.'

'Older men are in,' Lori said in a dreamy voice. 'I've never gone for anyone older than thirty-five before but I could make an exception in his case.'

'He's forty-five if he's a day,' snapped Stella. 'Far too old for you.' She stalked off into the Gin Palace.

'She's quite a character, your receptionist,' Nick commented when he reappeared.

'I suppose you want her phone number,' Stella said sourly.

His gaze caught her by surprise.

'Actually, I'd prefer yours. I'd like to ask you out to dinner tomorrow night.'

Stella sat down quickly on the hard chair, landing painfully on her coccyx. 'Ouch,' she yelped.

'I'm sorry, I didn't mean to startle you. Was that totally out of order?'

'Er, well . . .' Stella stammered.

If only Nick hadn't been looking at her, Stella might have drummed up her standard answer whenever men attempted to chat her up: 'Thanks but no thanks.'

But before Stella the Sensible had a chance to say anything, at the precise moment she'd made her mind up to turn him politely down, in spite of *everything*, he suddenly moved the goalposts. He gazed at her, hopefully. And when Nick Cavaletto's intelligent, warm eyes bored into hers, she'd had no option. Sensible Stella faltered and the long-buried Romantic Stella shoved her out of the way like a shopaholic on sale day.

'I'd love to.' Had she really said that?

His face creased up into a smile. 'I was sure you were going to turn me down.'

To hide how jolted she felt by the entire experience, Stella tried to sound light-hearted. 'I was just about to but you looked so forlorn, I hadn't the heart to say no.'

His craggy face looked even better when he grinned broadly. 'Forlorn? Nobody's ever accused me of that before. But whatever the reason, I'm glad.'

For a full minute, they stared at each other, Stella holding her breath for some bizarre reason. Then Melvyn rushed into the room, stammering apologies for lateness, and Stella instantly picked up a document to give herself something to hide behind in case he picked up on the charged atmosphere.

As business resumed, Stella managed to continue a professional conversation, all the while wondering if she was mad. He was a client. Well, no, he wasn't actually her client and if Jerry hadn't been ill, she never would have met him. But he was a man she knew nothing about, apart from the fact that he needed to sort out a property issue for his elderly mother. He could be married with ten kids for all she knew.

Stella cast a suspicious glance at his left hand. There was no ring but that meant nothing. She'd have to ask.

'Jerry's so very sorry and I'm sure he'll be in for your next appointment,' apologised Melvyn as Nick was leaving.

'That's good,' said Nick, a faint smile hovering about his mouth. 'Prawn vindaloo poisoning can be fatal.'

Stella smothered a snigger. She would *have* to have several words with Lori. So much for saying Jerry had been unavoidably kept out of the office.

'I'll show Mr Cavaletto out,' she added smoothly.

She walked him to the lift, ignoring the looks Lori shot at them.

'Just one question,' Stella said, pitching her voice low so nobody could overhear. 'Are you married?'

'Divorced with two children,' he replied, just as seriously. He held up his left hand. 'Look, no ring.'

'Did you wear one when you were married?' Stella inquired.

Nick threw back his head and laughed. 'No. And did you ever think of becoming a barrister? Your skills at interrogation are wasted here. About dinner, how about Figaro's?'

Stella decided it was time to reassert her independence. Nick was calling all the shots here and she refused to be a pushover. 'Figaro's, I don't think so,' she said. She'd never been to Figaro's but that wasn't the point. Surely there was some modern rule of dating that said only pushovers cooed yes to the first suggestion.

'You pick somewhere you like,' he offered. 'I've been out of the country for so long that I don't know the good spots.'

Stella thought hard, storing away that snippet of information about his time out of the country. The only restaurants she knew were ones suitable for business lunches, girls-only get-togethers or meals with seven-year-olds. It had been a long time since she'd done the eyes-meeting-over-the-candlelight-at-a-table-for-two thing. Years, in fact.

Casting around wildly for an intelligent suggestion, a snippet of something she'd heard about a review of a new restaurant came to mind. Something about The Flying Carpet, a new restaurant on the quays. She hadn't seen the review herself but from the bit of the conversation she remembered, the place sounded good, she was sure of it. 'Mussels to die for' or something.

'The Flying Carpet,' she said confidently. 'At eight.'

'May I pick you up or would you prefer to meet me there?' Nick asked solicitously.

You've already picked me up, Stella thought mischievously.

'I'll meet you there,' she said. 'If there's a problem, I'll phone you. Your number is on the file.' And it was a land line, she remembered. If he was married, he'd instantly give her a mobile number to phone instead. But Nick just nodded in agreement.

'Till tomorrow,' he said.

He turned to go.

'Oh, Mr Cavaletto, you forgot something,' Stella called. 'Yes?'

Stella whispered so her voice wasn't audible to the receptionist. 'Divorced, one daughter. Just so you know.'

Again, the intense green eyes gleamed with amusement. 'Goodbye, Ms Miller, it's been a pleasure.'

A pleasure, thought Stella dreamily as she took the stairs up to the fourth floor. She certainly hoped so. After six years on her own, well, longer really, as you could hardly count the last year with Glenn as actually being with anybody, she was utterly unprepared for the prospect of going on a date. She went back to her office.

'Isn't he lovely?' said Lori dreamily. 'Sort of Sean Connery-esque with a hint of Michael Douglas in there somewhere.'

'You've got to stop reading *Movieline*,' Stella said, biting her lip to stop herself beaming idiotically.

'He was gorgeous, though. Come on, Stella, even you can see that.'

Stella felt a quiver of electricity shoot through her at the thought of Nick's smile. 'I suppose you could call him attractive,' she said.

'Who?' demanded Vicki, appearing at her door. 'Have I missed something?'

'Vicki, can I talk to you for a moment?' Stella asked. She had to tell *someone* and if she told Lori, there was a fair possibility of being stabbed with Lori's trademark silver-ink pen.

Vicki's jaw dropped when she heard the news.

'Lucky you,' she sighed. 'They say that lots of love stories begin at work, but it's never happened to me.' Vicki suddenly looked thoughtful. 'Can we search through Jerry's client list and see if there's anyone else gorgeous coming in today?'

By half twelve, Stella had raced through her workload at twice her normal speed. She felt inspired and excited, as though she'd had ten espressos and no breakfast. She'd been asked out on a date and she'd said yes! What would she wear, what would they talk about . . . ?

Her phone rang and she switched into work mode instantly.

'Hello, Stella?' said a woman's voice. 'It's Jackie Hess.'

Even through the phone lines, Stella could hear her client's anxiety.

Without giving her lawyer a chance to speak, Jackie rattled through her problems.

'If we don't get the contracts signed by tomorrow, I'll lose the new house and I can't do that. I can't. This is a new start for me and I love that house . . .' Her voice rose almost hysterically.

Stella had heard enough. Calming people was one of her many skills, a vital one in the business of legal conveyancing, although nobody had mentioned it in college. There hadn't been any lectures on dealing with real, agitated clients who were splitting up with their husbands and hoping to buy new (smaller) houses in order to start again.

'Jackie,' soothed Stella, 'we'll sort it out, I promise. Please leave it with me.'

Jackie was quiet, as Stella knew she would be. When Stella Miller told you she'd sort everything out, you believed her.

There was something about the low, measured voice that calmed even the most highly-strung client; something about her serene, smiling face with its kind dark eyes that made anxiety seem silly. More than one person had seriously considered taking up yoga after learning that the tranquil Stella was a devotee.

'Are you sure everything will work out . . . ?' Jackie asked more quietly.

'Yes, I'm sure.'

Once Jackie was gone, Stella made a firm decision to stop thinking about Nick Cavaletto. It was ridiculous for a grown woman to get so excited about dinner with a man. This dreaming and staring out the window had to stop. She worked steadily for the next half an hour, making phone calls and trying to sort out Jackie's problems. Jackie had split up with her husband of two years and every time Stella spoke to her, she seemed more shell-shocked than the last, muttering about joint credit union accounts and what were they to do with the oil painting of Venice. Was it Jackie's because her rich old grand-uncle had given it to them as a wedding present or was it joint property? Privately, Stella thought that the distraught Jackie should seek counselling to help her climb out of the dark pit of sudden break-up. She'd hated that painting, she'd told Stella. Yet she was fiercely determined to have it, as if salvaging something that wasn't communal property, could salvage her damaged soul.

Over the years, as she dealt with clients like Jackie, Stella had come to realise that she'd never loved Glenn enough to feel such emotion over their break-up. Teenage sweethearts who'd married when they were ridiculously young, they'd drifted apart. Their over-riding emotion at the break-up had been apathy for each other, and parental worry over Amelia. She wondered what it would be like to love and hate with such passion that splitting up would destroy you.

'Lunch?' said Vicki, peeping round the glass door with her tongue out, her normal signal that starvation was setting in.

'Lunch. Yes, I forgot,' Stella said absent-mindedly.

'How can you forget lunch?' Vicki wailed, shutting the door and perching on the edge of Stella's desk. Then, catching sight of Stella's serene face, she'd grinned. 'You're still living off love, then?'

'It's only a dinner date,' protested Stella. 'I wish I hadn't told you. If you mention it to anyone else I'll kill you.'

'You mean it's a secret?' said Vicki, deadpan. 'I've just e-mailed my 100 closest friends, all the LW & M partners and the Law Society with the news. It's not unethical to sleep with a client, is it? I have such trouble remembering the whole ethics thing . . .'

'We're going to have dinner, Vicki, not rip each other's clothes off over dessert.'

'Pity,' sighed Vicki. 'Mind you, if it was me, I'd go for the actual dessert instead. It's so long since I had sex, I can't remember what it was like, except it was often an anticlimax, which is not something you can say about a double helping of double chocolate roulade with cream.'

'We're going for a sedate meal,' Stella insisted. 'That's all. Anyway, you've been to bed with someone far more recently than me. I'm the poster girl for celibacy since Glenn and I divorced.' Stella knew this wasn't utterly truthful but she wanted to forget the disastrous fling she'd had with an old friend of hers and Glenn's when Amelia had been a toddler. She'd discovered that even when you'd felt like you'd known someone for centuries, they were just as capable of being a sexual predator as a stranger. After a few weeks, he'd dropped her like a hot potato. Burned and humiliated, Stella had never told Vicki about it and she never intended to.

Vicki was in full flood on the subject of her last lover, a fellow lawyer she'd met at a charity ball. 'If you're referring to my encounter with that horrible man from Simpson and Ryan, then forget it. He was a disaster in bed. If he'd wanted to be paid by the hour, I would have wasted my money for fifty-eight minutes.'

Stella groaned. 'You're terrible, Vicki. The poor man would be horrified to hear you.'

'Poor man indeed! He thought he was the last of the red-hot lovers,' said Vicki in outrage. 'That was the problem. He thought I'd be grateful, can you believe it? The louse. His sort think all women over thirty-five should quiver with thanks if a man so much as looks at them, never mind brings them to bed. They reckon we're desperate for any crumb of affection that isn't battery-powered.'

Vicki was getting into her stride on the women-over-thirty-five theme: 'We're on the conveyor belt to single TV dinners and interlock knickers that never come off . . .'

'Vicki, you live with your sister,' interrupted Stella, 'and you know perfectly well that Craig from accounts fancies you rotten but you won't deign to notice him.'

Deflated, Vicki sighed. 'I know but he's six years younger than me. That's the last sign of absolute desperation. Imagine what people would say if I started dating a younger man? It's easier to just sit at home and fantasise about Russell Crowe.'

'Lunch,' said Stella firmly. 'You need your mind taken off men.'

Life conspired against Stella the next day. Jerry was still out sick, leaving Stella to deal with his clients again, which kept her in the office all through lunch when she'd planned to get her hair done. And the lurking demon of pre-menstrual tension paid a visit, bloating her stomach despite her post-Christmas detox.

'Do hormones know when you've got something important happening and deliberately act up?' Stella raged, as she realised she wouldn't be able to wear the burgundy jersey dress she'd planned on because it clingfilmed around her stomach and could only be worn on thin days.

'Yes,' sighed Vicki. 'It's like herpes, which apparently appears on the occasion of any hot date.'

'You have sex on the brain, Vicki,' Stella reproved.

'Don't be so prim and proper,' teased Vicki. 'You don't fancy him for his mind, do you? I bet you're going to wear your best knickers too.'

Stella had to laugh. 'I am, but only because they make me feel good, *not* because there's any vague hope of anybody seeing them.'

As she drove home that evening, she remembered what Vicki had said. Vicki wasn't afraid of the idea of sex, while it terrified Stella. It was five years since she'd felt a man's arms around her; five years since she'd been to bed with anyone. If sex was like riding a bicycle, Stella decided that she'd obviously gone back to using stabilisers.

Going out with a man could, eventually, lead to sex but Stella wasn't sure she was ready for that. Celibacy, by choice or otherwise, was easier, wasn't it?

At home, she washed her hair in an agony of uncertainty. If only she could phone Nick up and cancel the date. Tell him she was washing her hair for the rest of her life.

No, she decided finally. That would be the coward's way out. She'd go out and tell him that it was a mistake, that she was sorry. And she'd pay for dinner. If that wasn't the way to stay in control, she didn't know what was.

The restaurant was empty. So empty that Stella momentarily wondered if she'd got the time wrong. Starkly designed in black and white, there were no tablecloths on the black tables, and no other diners either.

The waitress inside the door fell on her with ill-concealed delight.

'Good evening, lovely to see you, can I take your coat?' she said joyously.

'Yes.' Stella surrendered her coat. 'Miller for two.' Why had she worried over booking?

'Your guest hasn't arrived . . .' began the waitress.

'He has now,' supplied Nick, shutting the door behind him. His eyes were flatteringly appreciative as he looked at Stella, all dressed up in her faithful cranberry red shirt and a long black suede skirt she'd had donkey's years but which was happily back in fashion again.

'Nice to see you,' he said, and leaning forward, he kissed her on the cheek. Stella felt something inside her go 'ping!' with excitement.

'Nice to see you too,' she said and, just as a test, proffered the other cheek for a double kiss. There it was again. Ping!

'You look beautiful,' he said, his eyes caressing her face. Ping, ping, ping!

'Will I show you to your table?' asked the waitress.

Nick shrugged out of his coat, giving Stella a chance to admire him. He'd swapped the casual look for a steely grey suit worn with a pale pink shirt that only the most masculine of men could get away with. Nick got away with it.

'Ready?' He turned around and Stella rapidly averted her eyes, not wanting to be caught staring. But wow, could he fill a suit in all the right places. Nick didn't look as if he needed a detox but then you could never tell with clothes on and . . .

Stella shocked herself. What was she doing thinking about

141

Nick with his clothes off? Vicki was right: she was losing the run of herself. She gave herself a stern talking to while they were led to a table for four at the back of the restaurant. The waitress gave them menus and left them alone in the bare expanse of the restaurant.

'It's odd that we're the only ones here,' whispered Stella, leaning forward.

Nick nodded solemnly but there was a flicker of amusement in his eyes.

'What?' Stella asked.

A smile twitched at the corners of his mouth.

'Tell me,' she demanded.

'If you need any help with the menus, please ask,' said the waitress, appearing beside them. She flitted off again.

'Do you come here often?' Nick asked blandly.

'Never been here before in my life,' Stella said. 'What is it?'

'I wanted to know if this was your favourite restaurant, that's all.'

She was puzzled. 'What's that got to do with the lack of customers?'

A party of six people arrived and the waitress flew to the front desk to usher them in. Despite the increased noise from the new arrivals, Nick still whispered.

'I mentioned to a friend that we were coming here and he told me they'd had a write-up in one of the papers recently.'

She nodded. 'I knew I'd read about it somewhere. Mussels to die for ... Ah.' She got it. 'It wasn't a good review, was it? In fact,' she looked for confirmation in his face, 'it was a Very. Bad. Review, wasn't it?'

'Bad is not the word,' Nick said. 'Horrendous fits the bill more successfully. Apparently, the reviewer had mussels and ended up cancelling his holiday because he was so sick. Mussels you'd die *from* was the tone of the review, I'm afraid.'

The whole situation suddenly struck Stella as hilariously funny. Trying to prove that she was a coolly independent

142

modern woman, she'd inadvertently recommended a restaurant rocked by a food poisoning scandal.

Laughter bubbled up inside her and she bit her lip to stop it erupting. It was no good. She burst into laughter at exactly the same time as Nick. They both roared so loudly that the newly-arrived customers stared at them curiously, interested to see what was so amusing.

'It's not funny for them, but it's hilarious really,' she howled, leaning over the table and clutching her stomach with the intensity of her outburst. 'I knew I'd heard something about this place but I couldn't remember what and I didn't want to say yes to Figaro's instantly because I didn't want you to think . . .'

Their waitress appeared, looking anxious. 'Is . . . is everything all right?' she asked.

'Wonderful,' squawked Stella. 'Joke, that's all.'

Nick composed himself.

'Just another minute, please.'

The waitress drifted off.

'You didn't want me to think you were a pushover,' finished Nick.

Stella grinned. 'Got it in one.'

'We can leave if you want to,' Nick added, 'although I'd prefer to stay now that we're here. It might be hard to get a table anywhere else at such short notice, and our waitress would be so upset if we did leave.'

That did it. Stella smiled at him in admiration. Any man who was so kind would be worth a proper date. She could always say she couldn't see him again at the end.

'I don't think I'd have liked you if you'd wanted to leave,' she admitted. 'The mussels could have been a once off and it would see so mean to leave now, when the dear waitress was so thrilled to see us.'

'I agree. And there's pasta on the menu, anyway, so less chance of fatal illness there.'

Stella erupted again.

'Are you ready to order?' inquired the waitress, once again

materialising out of nowhere. Was she on roller skates? Stella wondered.

'Yes,' smiled Nick.

They ordered quickly – no fish – and agreed on a bottle of claret.

'I am very out of practice at this date thing,' Stella confessed when they were alone after the waitress had served the wine. 'I'm sure that even *saying* that contravenes modern dating standards, but I can't help it. I did all my dating when flares were in, the first time. I've forgotten the rules.'

'I didn't know there were rules,' Nick replied. 'See what I know about women. I thought I had to fill in your dance card, and after fifty dates, we were allowed out without chaperonage as long as I kept one foot on the floor at all times.'

Stella giggled. 'Let's skip a bit. I left my dance card at home, anyway. I think we have to tell each other our histories. That's what they do in those articles in the paper when they set people up on blind dates.'

'I'm afraid I never read that stuff,' Nick said apologetically.

'Men never do. But the theory is simple: we each get five minutes to tell our life stories.'

'Five minutes,' he said. 'I don't know if mine will last that long.'

'I bet,' said Stella in mock cynicism. 'OK then, make it shorter, say . . . twenty words or less. Let's keep it short.'

'Twenty words,' he said thoughtfully. 'OK. You first or me?'

'You,' she said quickly.

'Right. You keep count of the number of words and when I've done twenty, stop me.'

'More than twenty, and I'll leave,' Stella replied solemnly.

'Forty-four, Irish, two daughters, fourteen and nineteen, married for twenty years, worked abroad, ran engineering company, divorced a year ago, head-hunted home. That's more than twenty words, isn't it?' He stopped and his face had a faint weariness about it.

A hard divorce? wondered Stella with intuition. Or something else?

'Sorry,' she apologised. 'That seemed tough for you, I didn't mean it to be.'

'No, you've a right to know who you're having dinner with. Laying your life down in a mere twenty words makes it sound pretty hopeless.'

Stella fiddled with the stem of her wine glass. She wanted to ask why the marriage had broken up but was unsure of venturing into such personal territory. She decided to tell him her story. 'Age: undisclosed.'

He laughed.

'A woman's age, like her weight and dress size, is highly classified information,' Stella said gravely. 'If I tell you any of them, I have to kill you. One daughter, wonderful Amelia, who's seven and absolutely adorable.'

'You're using too many words,' Nick put in.

'Nick.' She fixed him with a stern glance. 'I'm a *lawyer*.'

He laughed again.

'One daughter, Amelia, seven. Lawyer, specialising in property, divorced, erm . . . two fantastic younger sisters, great parents, yoga, perfume bottles, bad at picking restaurants . . .' She broke off.

'That's good.' 'Tell me more about the *perfume bottles* bit.'

'I love those little crystal perfume bottles, the ones with silver tops from ladies' dressing tables a hundred years ago. I have magpie tendencies when it comes to junk like that. And costume jewellery, forties and fifties stuff.'

'What about the fantastic sisters?'

Stella's face always softened when she thought of Holly and Tara. 'Holly's the youngest and she works in the children's department in Lee's. She's so funny, she's brilliant, I worry about her, though.' She didn't know why she'd said that but she felt as if she could say things to Nick. 'Tara,' she continued, 'is a storyline editor for *National Hospital*. She's brilliant too. They just won an award at the television and radio awards.'

'They sound wonderful. Are you a close family?'

'Very. We're like this tight unit. Mum, Dad, me, Holly, Tara, and now Amelia. The Miller clan. It's all down to Mum, really,' Stella added. 'She's an incredible person, very warm and strong. Mum has no time for family squabbles or long-running arguments. She taught us how important family is.'

Nick was quiet.

'What about your family?'

'I've a younger brother, Howard, and an older sister, Paula, and of course my mother. Paula lives in the same village as my mother near Wicklow town and she's looked after her for years. They want to sell both their houses so they can move to a bungalow, which would be easier for my mother to get around. Paula's artistic – she paints – and she hates sorting out legal matters, so my brother and his wife, Clarisse, have always done that side of things. Clarisse feels that now I'm back in the country, I can take over.' His slightly wry smile revealed more than he was saying.

'Clarisse feels put-upon and wants you to shoulder some of the burden?' Stella offered.

'You *are* intuitive,' said Nick, impressed.

Through the meal, they talked about their jobs, places they'd worked and more about their families. Clarisse sounded vaguely like Aunt Adele, Stella reflected. By dessert, they had discussed every relative except their children – and their exes; a glaring omission.

'Tell me about Amelia,' Nick urged.

Stella produced a photo from her wallet. It had been taken the previous summer in Kinvarra, when her parents had held a barbecue for friends and family. Stella's father had hung a low swing from a sycamore tree, and, in the picture, Amelia was sitting on it, colourful in pink and white shorts and T-shirt, laughing into the camera and with her hair swinging in two jaunty pigtails.

'Beautiful, just like her mother,' Nick said examining

146

the photo. 'What about her father? Do you share custody?'

'Nothing that ordinary,' Stella said. 'He works in the oil business and he's abroad all the time. Amelia spends time with him when he's here. She's with him now.' Stella didn't mention how she tried hard not to resent this.

'I split up with my ex husband when Amelia was a baby. There wasn't anybody else, we'd just made an awful mistake. I'd like to say we married too young but I was twenty-eight, old enough to know better,' she added ruefully. 'How about you?'

The silence seemed to go on forever and Stella would have done anything to claw back the words, but finally, Nick spoke.

'Why does any marriage break up?' he said. 'We made a mistake too; it just took twenty years to figure it out. I was seconded to the company's office in Stockholm for four months a couple of years ago and it would have been difficult for Wendy and the kids to come because of school. So we agreed that I'd go and come home as often as I could, which I did, every few weekends. Four months became six months and when I got back for good, we found it impossible to live together again. That sounds terrible,' he said looking at Stella, 'but it's the truth. We even went to counselling for a while. It didn't work. Talking about it made us realise that the only glue keeping us together was the girls. The problem was, Wendy was prepared to put up with that. I knew we couldn't.'

'That must have been tough,' Stella said gently. 'You're not over your divorce, are you?' she added, knowing she was going too far but not being able to stop herself.

His eyebrows shot up. 'Believe me, I am over my divorce. I'm not over the trauma and hurt that went with it. It was the most personally painful thing I've ever experienced and it's with me every day.'

'What about the girls?'

Nick's face lit up.

'Jenna is fourteen and Sara is nineteen. Sara's doing Arts

in college and Jenna's in school; mind you, she looks old enough to be in college. When she's with her friends, they all look about twenty.'

He took out his wallet and extracted a photo of two girls. It looked like a holiday shot. Sara was fair-haired, lanky and smiled up at the camera with her father's warm, intelligent eyes. Jenna was smiling too, but she looked more posed, as if she liked the camera. It certainly liked her. She was incredibly pretty with a heart-shaped face, almond eyes and dimples. Even the glint of the brace on her teeth couldn't dim her teenage beauty.

'How often do you see them?'

'All the time, I couldn't bear not to. But it's caused some problems. Wendy is from Dublin and she never wanted to live in London, but at the time, that was where the work was. After the divorce, she moved back here with the girls. I missed them so much,' he said, 'that when I got an offer of a job here, I jumped.'

Stella was silent. How that must have infuriated his wife. He wouldn't leave London for her, but he could make that sacrifice for their daughters.

'It's been tough,' Nick added, confirming Stella's instincts. 'In so far as any divorce is ever amicable, you could say that ours was. There was nobody else for either of us but it's still hard splitting after twenty years. The hardest part was telling our daughters.' His face was bleak as he spoke.

'We don't have to talk about this if you don't want to,' Stella said hurriedly.

He shrugged. 'We don't have to, but it's a good idea to get to know each other, for, you know, future dates.'

It was Stella's turn to look uncomfortable.

He stared at her. 'I've messed things up, haven't I?' he asked. 'Telling a prospective girlfriend all about the traumas of your divorce is not the way to impress her. I told you I wasn't that clued in about modern dating,' he said.

'Forget it.' Stella wanted to make it better. So what if he wasn't dating material because he had more baggage than a jumbo jet. He was a nice man. 'Let's talk about something else. How about films, the big issues of the day . . .'

'Like politics and religion?' he interrupted, amused.

'I take that bit back,' Stella said, wincing. 'Forget the big issues of the day. I'm fed up discussing politics and religion and you can't talk about either without a row. No, let's go for serious subjects, like which is your favourite James Bond.'

Nick gave her a grateful smile as he leaned forward and poured her more claret.

They were the last to leave the restaurant after a mild tussle over who'd pay the bill.

'Let me,' insisted Stella.

'But I asked you out.'

'No, really, let me.'

The waitress stood patiently to one side while they argued.

'You could always make a run for it so nobody would have to pay,' she suggested.

Both Nick and Stella looked up in surprise.

'Or split the bill,' the waitress added.

They split it and soon found themselves outside on the street where the sky was undecided over whether to send down snow or sleet. A sheet of something white began to fall as they walked along and Stella shivered in the icy wind.

'Let's get out of this for a moment,' Nick suggested. They sheltered in a shop doorway, watching the snow fall onto the wet street and disappear.

'At least it's not sticking,' Stella said, still shivering.

Without saying anything, Nick took off his coat and draped it over both their shoulders so that Stella was warmed by an extra layer. She had to stand close to him so they'd both be covered, and the sensation of being that close to another person felt strangely good. No, she thought, not just another person. Nick. Standing close to Nick felt good and somehow right.

'I don't think it's going to stop,' he said.

'No,' she agreed, pasta and claret churning inside her in

excitement. She couldn't believe she was standing in a doorway with this man; a man she found unbelievably attractive.

'You'll freeze.'

'Body heat's a wonderful thing,' he smiled at her.

Stella smiled back, feeling a little nugget of heat inside her despite the cold. His coat slipped and Nick pulled it back over her, his arm momentarily round her shoulders. She kept staring at him. The arm didn't move, staying wrapped round Stella, who found herself leaning in closer towards him. His mouth was just a few inches above hers and Stella wondered if she was supposed to give him a signal that he could kiss her. Was that how it worked nowadays? Maybe she should have read Aunt Adele's despised copy of *The Rules* to find out. Without waiting for any signal, Nick's mouth lowered onto hers. Then both his arms were around her and they lurched against the doorway, like lovelorn teenagers stealing a forbidden kiss, bodies tight together as the kiss deepened into fierce, hard passion. Tasting the sweetness of his mouth, holding his body tightly, Stella didn't care who saw her. All she wanted was Nick; Nick kissing her face and her throat, murmuring endearments and making tender love to her . . .

Nick broke away first, his olive eyes shining, his breath ragged. 'We haven't had the fifty dances yet and there's no chaperone,' he said.

'You've got one foot on the ground, haven't you?' she replied.

'Yes, just about!'

This time, Stella kissed him and went on kissing him until they were no longer cold and until the snow was swirling around their doorway like a blizzard.

Only when a police car drove carefully down the street, blue light illuminating doorways, did they stop and step onto the street, laughing like kids and holding Nick's coat over their heads.

'I'd hate to see the papers if a respected lawyer and a respected businessman were arrested for obscene behaviour,' chuckled Stella.

'It was only a kiss,' said Nick.

Their eyes met and they both grinned. What a kiss.

He helped her into the first taxi they saw and then took her hand and softly kissed the back of it. Stella smiled at him with affection. From anyone else, such a gesture would have seemed corny but not from Nick.

'I'll phone tomorrow.'

He shut the door and the taxi drove off into the night.

For a brief moment, Stella thought about men and phoning. Everyone from Vicki to Tara said that men promised to phone but rarely did.

It was a game, Vicki insisted miserably. To ring or not to ring.

But sitting in the back of a taxi, feeling the car's heater slowly warm her bones, Stella allowed herself to smile happily. Nick wasn't like that. He'd phone. She knew it.

CHAPTER SEVEN

'Rose, have you seen my waterproof jacket?' Hugh roared up the stairs.

Rose, on her hands and knees on the upstairs landing as she did an emergency sort-out of the airing cupboard, rolled her eyes. She'd left Hugh's waterproof on the kitchen chair nearest the hall door. Unless he was walking round the house with his eyes closed, he couldn't miss it.

'It's in the kitchen,' she yelled back, suppressing the desire to add, 'stupid.'

'Where in the kitchen? I can't see it?'

Rose got creakily to her knees. The cold, damp weather definitely made aching bones worse. If January had been cold and wet, February was proving to be even worse, with gale force Northern winds that made Rose glad of decent heating that kept Meadow Lodge toasty. Braving the great outdoors was another matter, and Rose had decided she wasn't leaving the house that morning without her long-sleeved thermal vest. She knew it was *somewhere* and she'd been searching fruitlessly when Hugh called.

She was halfway down the stairs when Hugh found his waterproof. 'There it is,' he yelled. 'I didn't leave it there,' he added indignantly.

Rose managed not to reply. She walked into the kitchen to find Hugh ready for a Saturday morning walk with his best friend, Alastair. The kitchen, just tidied up by Rose, was a mess again because Hugh had cleaned out his pockets by the bin, brushed the worst of the muck from his walking shoes and made himself a cup of tea, the debris of these three tasks having ruined all her good work.

Hugh spotted Rose's exasperated look in the direction of the mess.

'Oh er . . . sorry about that but I have to rush, love,' he said, dropping a speedy kiss on her cheek. 'I'm meeting Alastair in ten minutes. I'll tidy up when I get back.'

He raced off, leaving Rose crossly thinking that if she had a penny for every time Hugh promised to clean up, she'd be lying on a beach in the Bahamas by now. She tidied up again, went back upstairs to finish ransacking the airing cupboard, then got ready for her trip out with Adele. It was Hugh's birthday in a few weeks and Adele, who'd stopped driving several years previously after a collision with a gatepost, had asked Rose to take her shopping for his present. This was Rose's idea of pure torture but she'd said yes. Charity did, after all, begin at home.

Adele lived in the old Miller family home eight miles on the other side of Kinvarra and Rose never drove there without thanking her lucky stars that she and Hugh had bought their own house when they first got married. She didn't like to imagine what would have happened if they'd ended up living with Adele, without the eight-mile buffer zone.

The old Miller place had once looked so imposing to Rose Riordain, with its hedge-lined drive and its plethora of high-ceilinged Victorian rooms. It had a scullery, for God's sake. But now, compared to some of the big, modern mansions built around the town, the house looked quite ugly. Hugh helped Adele out with the cost of maintaining it, which gave Rose a certain grim satisfaction. She, the poor girl from Wexford whom Adele looked down on, was involved in keeping up the Millers' grand house.

Adele was dressed for Buckingham Palace in her fur coat, tweed suit and a little Russian hat that smelled as if it had spent the past fifty years in a box over a wardrobe. Adele's unforgiving eye skimmed over Rose's tan leather coat, wide-legged Karen Millen trousers and loafers. She said nothing but her expression spoke volumes. Adele believed that middle-aged women should know their place and that included wearing the correct uniform. Rose, with her modern, youthful clothes, refused to conform.

'Adele,' said Rose, embracing her sister-in-law. 'Are you all set?'

'I was expecting you earlier,' Adele said pointedly. It was after ten. Adele had been up for hours. 'You know how bad the traffic gets on Saturdays.'

'We'll be fine,' Rose reassured her. Be nice, she commanded herself. Adele wasn't too good on her feet these days, and was just worried about walking through Kinvarra when it was busy with Saturday shoppers wielding umbrellas and pushing ankle-defying baby buggies.

As they drove into town, Adele reeled off a list of the misfortunes that had befallen her recently, before turning to the knotty question of what everyone was going to buy for her beloved Hugh. Adele herself favoured a nice tie and matching handkerchief which he could wear to his birthday lunch.

'The girls are coming to the lunch, aren't they?' she asked, secretly hoping they weren't and that she could have him all to herself. Well, herself and Rose.

'Of course they're coming,' Rose said, only half concentrating.

'Good. Will Amelia be there too? I'm not sure I approve of children in restaurants,' Adele went on, without waiting for Rose to answer. 'But she's very well behaved. Mind you, she'd probably be better off if Stella had stayed married to Glenn.' Adele hated the fact that a member of the Miller family was divorced. In her day, people stayed together till the bitter end. 'Young people don't have the staying power our generation did.'

Rose gripped the steering wheel in a vice grip. What did Adele know about staying with someone through thick and thin?

She was torn between feeling sorry for her sister-in-law,

whose life was lonely after all, and feeling angry because Adele's tactlessness knew no bounds. Had Adele always been this irritating or was Rose just less able to cope with her? Then another thought occurred to Rose: had loving Hugh been the reason she'd been able to deal so serenely with Adele for so many years?

It was half ten when they'd finally parked and were ready for the shopping marathon. Adele proceeded along the main street at a stately pace that made Rose, used to speed walking everywhere, deeply impatient. First, Adele had to go into the post office to pass the time of day with old Mrs Robinson. This took some time as they had to wait in the longest queue for Mrs Robinson, who processed unemployment benefits and children's allowances with the speed of a two-legged centipede.

Next, they admired the clothes in the window of Madame Irene's and Adele got the chance to tut-tut about the price of things.

'Shocking,' she said, shaking her head so that her curls rattled a bit. 'I remember when you could buy an entire outfit, with a hat, for fifteen shillings. Oh and the hats then, they were proper hats, not like those feathery things that are all the rage now, just three feathers stuck on a comb. Things are different now and more's the pity.'

Adele never remembered the bad things about the good old days before changing social mores and advances in medicine made the world a better place to live. Her sister-in-law, reflected Rose, was in love with the past.

Rose, on the other hand, liked the new order. She still yearned for the sort of clothes she wore when she was young, although she wryly admitted that was probably because she yearned for the sort of figure she had then too. But there were so many positive things about modern life, like the fact that people could be whatever they wanted to be. The iron-clad social structures were a thing of the past.

In McArthur's Men's Shop, Adele enjoyed a heady twenty minutes dallying over the ties before settling on a shirt.

'Hugh's collar size is sixteen,' Rose murmured tactfully when Adele had made the decision and was carrying her prize, in the wrong size, to the till.

'He was always sixteen and a half,' said Adele, triumphant with superior knowledge.

'I know, but he's sixteen now,' Rose said. 'Age diminishes us all,' she said, trying to make a joke about it. She swapped the shirt for the correct size and went off to idly look at the socks.

The Central Hotel for mid-morning tea was the next stop on the tour. Once the premier establishment in Kinvarra, the Central looked as if it had been around since Adam was in short pants. Gracious, ivy-clad and boasting the biggest ballroom for miles around, it had long been the venue for the town's most expensive wedding receptions and had once been *the* place to have dinner. Although she wouldn't have admitted it to anyone, Rose loathed the Central Hotel. She'd never forget the first time she'd been there, the first time she'd met Hugh's family. Now that had been a night to remember. She'd been so unsure of herself then and the hotel reminded her of a time Rose preferred to forget. She'd been so young, so gauche.

Adele's gait slowed down even more as she made the majestic journey up the Central's marble steps and into the foyer, which somehow still looked exactly the same as it had forty years before, despite redecoration since. Rose wondered was there a factory churning out gilt pictures of purple mountains and elegantly faded velvet curtains circa 1950 for selling on to hotels like the Central? They settled themselves into two chintzy armchairs in the drawing room and Rose politely summoned the young waiter.

'Morning tea with scones and real strawberry jam,' Adele told him imperiously when he arrived.

'For two, thank you so much,' added Rose, smiling at the waiter in an attempt to make up for Adele's lack of charm in the ordering department.

Adele waved graciously at an acquaintance of hers, and

then sat back happily in her seat. Two crisp copies of the local paper lay on the table in front of her but Adele didn't pick one up. When she was young, a lady never read a newspaper in public. It was a signal that she wasn't interested in everything around her and young ladies, as her mother used to say, must look interested at all times. The waiter arrived with tea in a silver teapot, china cups and a silver two-tiered cake stand decked with scones. Adele graciously poured tea. All was right with her world.

'This is nice,' said Rose, doing her best. Rose's idea of shopping was a speedy race round the town, gathering up bags of groceries and finishing with a very quick latte in Melanie's Coffee Shop if she was lucky. She sipped her tea slowly and tried not to think of all the jobs she could be doing now. A tea cup clinked in the distance, reminding Rose of another time.

There was a certain smell in the drawing room of the Central Hotel, she realised. A strangely familiar smell that mingled lily of the valley perfume with whatever polish they used on the furniture. If Rose closed her eyes, she could imagine herself back over forty years to that night . . .

As she and Hugh drove to Kinvarra, Rose felt her stomach lurch with nerves. Hugh was eager to show his beloved Rose off to his family, he'd never understand how scared Rose was that his parents would see through her and discover that she didn't come from a suitable background for their only son. Hugh, who adored his beautiful, clever and passionate girlfriend, didn't care where she came from. But the most respected solicitor in Kinvarra and his wife might.

'Dad'll wonder what a girl like you is doing with me,' he said.

Rose laughed.

'My mother can't wait to meet you,' Hugh went on. 'She's fussing over which dress to wear.'

Rose was startled and a little pleased. She hadn't thought that ladies like Mrs Miller would fuss over anything, but it was a good sign that she wasn't the only person suffering from nerves. Maybe this mightn't be too bad.

They both fell quiet as they approached Hugh's home. Rose hated herself for feeling nervous. She was just as good as these people, she was proud of her family and her background, so what had she to be nervous about?

Hugh's parents seemed delighted to meet her, welcoming her enthusiastically to their home. And if Rose noticed that the sedate drawing room was four times the size of the cosy kitchen in her home in Castletown, she didn't let on. Hugh was a carbon copy of his father, Edward; both had the same blond hair and easy charm. His mother, Iris, turned out to be a plump, kind-faced woman with neat grey hair who wore a silk print dress with real pearls shining in her ears. She was warm to her son's nervous young girlfriend, wanting to know all about Rose and wasn't she wonderful to be living in Dublin and working.

'I'm sure your parents worry about you living away from home,' Mrs Miller said. 'We were the same when Hugh went off to college. Young fellows can get into awful trouble but Hugh was never a bother.'

'Iris, you're forgetting that incident with the collapsible umbrella and the number seven bus . . .' Edward Miller chimed in with a grin. 'Only teasing, Hugh. He'll never forgive me, Rose, for teasing him in front of you.'

Everyone laughed and Rose allowed herself to relax. This was going to be fine. The Millers might speak differently to her, and they might have a maid to clean up for them, but they were the same really, with the same worries, and able to joke about the sort of daft things that all families loved.

There was a certain dreamlike quality to the rest of the evening. They drove to dinner in the Central and Rose carried on blithely as if her entire childhood had involved family dinners in such establishments. She was more comfortable with restaurants nowadays, but there was a difference between a meal in the diner on O'Connell Street with stainless steel knives and paper napkins, and this grand affair

158

with silver plate and linen napkins so fine it felt a shame to use them.

Only Adele had shot her envious looks across the table, watching Rose's animated face and her dark eyes glittering with wit and intelligence. Many people looked at Rose that night, admiring the tall, slender figure in the silvery grey shift dress, appreciating her halo of glossy dark hair, wondering who this wide-eyed beauty was. Rose had met girls like Adele, the ones who envied Rose her beauty and watched her jealously. There was no winning with girls like that, Rose thought. Adele was tall, thin rather than slender, and had none of her brother's golden glamour. With her long disapproving face and haughty expression, she was nothing like the other Millers in any way. They were charm itself, while Adele had an air of being frostily convinced of her family's exalted position in life. Rose, aware of Adele's eagle eye on her every time she picked up a piece of cutlery, put on her coolest smile and determined that this girl would not ruin her night.

When she was alone in the spare bedroom after her evening of triumph, Rose sat on the window seat in her elderly pyjamas, hugging her knees to her chest and thinking how much she loved Hugh.

She belonged with him, and nothing, not even the vast differences in their backgrounds, would keep them apart. She was intelligent and spirited, she could learn how to live in this new world, a world far removed from her hard-working background. Money was the only difference. Money and the insulation it brought.

Despite her fears, she'd managed to fit in. The people she'd met all thought she was one of them. Only Adele had looked at her with dislike. Well, she could handle Adele. With her darling Hugh by her side, Rose could handle anything . . .

'Is everything all right, ladies?' asked the waiter.

Rose looked up at him, abruptly wrenched from memories of her nineteen-year-old self. 'Fine,' she said. 'Everything's fine.'

'We could do with more tea,' Adele pointed out. She looked at her sister-in-law for confirmation.

Poor old Adele, Rose thought with a rush of pity. Adele had grown up thinking she had a wonderful, gilded life ahead of her, yet somehow, this fairytale existence hadn't materialised. No retinue of suitors had lined up to marry the self-satisfied Miss Miller. Colin had been the only one who'd been interested and Adele, in her hubris, had seen him off. Now, she was lonely and disappointed because the promise of a lovely life hadn't been fulfilled.

All those years ago, Rose had imagined that her disapproving sister-in-law would be the only fly in the ointment. If only Rose had known then that Adele was harmless and unhappy, and that Hugh was perfectly capable of being the fly all by himself.

CHAPTER EIGHT

Kenny had control of the yoga book. He sat on Holly's couch like a sultan, reading slowly and ordering his subjects with princely brusqueness. It was a cold Sunday afternoon in February and the residents of Windmill Terrace were bored and trying to amuse themselves. To cheer them all up, Holly had suggested trying out her Christmas present from Stella. As Stella was always so calm thanks to her yoga, Holly asked her to recommend a book for novices. Stella had said classes were the way to go for a beginner but had given her a book anyway. After a while spent attempting to work out the moves from the book, Holly reckoned that only a very patient expert could teach her and Joan.

'Now, when you've faced your right leg, inhale and extend your left arm over your head. Reach up and . . .' Kenny quickly flicked to the next page, 'oh yes, don't let your head drop. You're supposed to be one fluid line. Now, *bend* forward from your hips.'

Holly and Joan, barefoot and clad in sweatpants and sloppy sweatshirts, did their best to bend.

'And twist,' Kenny added as an afterthought.

'Twist?' shrieked Joan as she reached the point of no return. 'This can't be good for you.'

'Bend *more*,' ordered Kenny. 'Your left hand is supposed to reach the floor.'

'I thought it was up above my head?' Joan was getting cross now as she tried to swap arms.

'Can we breathe?' gasped Holly.

'You're a right pair of morons,' said Kenny, irritated. 'I told you how to do the breathing in the first place. That's the most important bit of yoga.'

'Show me the book.' Joan hauled herself up off the floor and grabbed the book from Kenny. 'Look,' she said with indignation. 'It says if you're a beginner, you can use a block to rest your hand on in case you can't reach the floor.'

'As the only block round here is in your head,' retorted Kenny, 'I didn't see the point of mentioning it.'

'Can I move now?' Holly was still touching the floor and it was getting very painful. Her leg muscles were on fire and there was a possibility she might collapse.

'Yeah,' said both Kenny and Joan, who were fighting for possession of the book.

'But how?' yelped Holly, just before she fell. The wooden sitting room floor, even with its covering of rag rugs, wasn't much use for cushioning a person after a fall. She rubbed her wrist which ached from unaccustomed effort before examining her right knee, which would probably bruise. 'So much for *Yoga: Starting Out Guide to Inner Peace.*'

'It's Stella's fault. She gave you the book,' Joan accused.

'I think she thought I'd just look at the pictures, not actually do any of it,' grumbled Holly. 'Gimme a look at that position.'

'Why bother,' said Joan. 'We've done ten minutes and it hurts. How can that contribute to inner peace? And Kenny hasn't done anything except order us around.'

'I am already in a state of inner peace,' Kenny said smugly and crossed his legs into an approximation of the lotus position to show them. 'I don't need yoga.'

'You wouldn't know inner peace if it bit you,' snapped Joan. 'You're just pleased because that man chatted you up last night. He wasn't really interested, he preferred me!'

'We were in a gay bar,' shot back Kenny. 'Why would he be interested in you?'

'Maybe he was bi,' Joan said grumpily.

'Or tri,' suggested Kenny evilly. 'Try anything.'

Holly smothered a grin. When Kenny and Joan fought they were like a comedy double act. There was no malice in it: squabbling was like conversation to them and they'd have been astonished if a third party thought they actually meant any harm by their snappy little remarks.

Still grumpy, Joan got up off the couch and marched into Holly's kitchenette where she began opening cupboards in search of chocolate.

It was too cold to dream of venturing outside for a walk and too early in the day to retire to the pub. Holly had got up late that morning and had thrown on scabby grey tracksuit bottoms, a faded navy fleece and yesterday's socks to amble down to the shop for the papers. Once home, she'd flopped on the couch with tea, toast and all the delicious Sunday supplements. She hadn't showered, washed her hair or even put on so much as lip balm. It was that sort of day.

Bored, and arguing like a pair of old tabby cats, Kenny and Joan had arrived just after two, with their newspapers, a family pack of cheese and onion crisps, and a dispute in full flood about whose go it was to wash up.

Kenny, who was as meticulous about washing up as he was about laundry, insisted that he was fed up doing the saucepans when it was Joan's turn. Joan, who thought that saucepans only needed a cursory blast under the tap, argued that she *did* the saucepans and that it was a question of semantics over what constituted washing them correctly.

'If we got a dog, we wouldn't have to scrub dishes at all because it would lick the worst engrained bits off,' Joan remarked, knowing that squeamish Kenny would blanch at the very notion.

'If we put food in the shower, would the dog lick that too?' demanded Kenny, 'because *you* never clean it.'

'You're turning into your mother,' Joan said crossly.

'I am not,' said Kenny. 'Am I, Holly?'

'Don't look at me,' she said. 'I'm not today's referee.'

'I suppose I wouldn't mind turning into my mother,' Kenny said thoughtfully. 'She is amazing, really.' Kenny's mother was a stylish widow who worked part-time in an art gallery and enjoyed a non-stop social life.

'I've never met anyone like you,' groaned Joan. 'Yourself and your mother have this deranged mutual appreciation society going. That's what's wrong with you – your mother spent your whole life telling you you're wonderful.'

Kenny smirked at her. 'That's 'cos I am,' he said sweetly.

'You're very lucky,' said Holly softly.

When all the papers and the crisps had been digested, the boredom and the arguments got worse. There was no joy to be had in watching the soap omnibus because they'd seen all the soaps during the week in the first place.

'I hate Sunday afternoons,' Joan said, when she discovered that there wasn't a sliver of chocolate left anywhere. 'The weekend is almost over and all that's left is miserable old Sunday night and getting up in the morning.'

'We could go for a walk,' suggested Holly.

'And freeze?' said Kenny in outrage. 'Are you mad? If God had meant us to walk in cold weather, he'd have given us fur.'

'I'd never use fur in any of my collections,' Joan said thoughtfully. 'It's cruelty to animals.'

'You made a leather top last month,' Kenny pointed out.

'That was vintage lace with beading and one teeny piece of leather in it,' snapped Joan.

Holly closed her eyes and wished that something would happen to shut them both up. As if on cue, there was an almighty bang outside the door, a hippo-falling-down-the-stairs sort of noise.

The three of them leapt to their feet and ran to investigate.

Kenny wrenched open Holly's door to find three large suitcases and a broken packing case sitting outside, clearly having fallen down the stairs from the upper landing. The suitcases were intact but the packing case had disgorged its filling all over the hall. There was no sign of whoever owned the cases. Kenny leaned over the staircase and looked downstairs. There was nobody there.

'It must be someone new moving in upstairs,' he decided.

'I hope they're nicer than that mad woman who lived up there before,' Joan said, poking around at the packing case to see if she could find anything to identify the owner. 'She was always complaining about my music.'

As Joan's idea of music was club played at tinnitus-inducing volume, Holly could sympathise with the previous upstairs tenant.

'Lots of black clothes,' Holly commented, eyeing the clothes peeking out from the case, 'which means the owner is definitely a woman.'

Both Kenny and Joan groaned.

'Just our luck,' sighed Kenny. 'Why can't anyone gorgeous and male move in?'

Joan pulled out a sweater from the broken case.

'Joan, *don't*,' hissed Holly. 'You can't go through someone else's things!'

'It could have fallen out. Wow, definitely a man!' said Joan, holding up an enormous man's sweater.

'Big man,' said Kenny delightedly.

'Big but not smart enough to stop all his belongings from falling down the stairs,' said a voice.

Holly and Joan jumped guiltily.

A man in his late twenties ambled down the stairs towards them. He had strawberry-blond hair cut very short, a friendly open face with a sprinkling of freckles, long, rueful eyes and enormous shoulders. His mouth was creased up into a huge grin, yet there was something shy about his gaze. He looked, Holly thought, like one of those big, solid men normally found in rugby strip about to run out onto a pitch and thunder into other big, solid men. She could imagine him as a schoolboy sports star, a bit of a hero to younger boys.

'Hello,' said Joan eagerly. 'Are you moving in?'

She and Kenny were both standing to attention: Joan, biting her lips to bring some colour into them, Kenny adopting his model pose of standing slightly sideways to show off his toned physique. Holly, conscious that she looked like a well-fed vagrant in her baggy, horrible old sweat gear and unwashed hair, didn't bother doing anything.

'Yes, Tom Barry,' the giant said, holding out a huge hand to shake.

Up close, he was even bigger, the sort of bloke who'd be useful in a bash-down-a-locked-door situation. But Holly decided he looked too kind and gentle to bash into anything.

'Joan Atwood.'

'And Kenny Erskine.'

Joan and Kenny introduced themselves enthusiastically.

'Nice to meet you,' Tom said.

'This is Holly Miller,' said Kenny, realising that Holly was lurking behind them and being her usual shy self.

Holly, however, was mortally embarrassed at the thought of her unwashed hair. She must look positively rank today.

'Hi,' she said, giving him a little wave from behind the other pair.

'Holly lives here,' said Kenny, 'and Joan and I live opposite.'

'Not,' added Joan quickly, 'that we're a couple.'

'Hell, no,' said Kenny, even more quickly. 'Friends, that's all.'

'Friends,' nodded Joan.

Tom said nothing but smiled down at them all. Holly noticed that his eyes were the colour of faded denim with little yellowy flecks around the irises.

'Is that a Cork accent?' Kenny said in a tone that Holly recognised as coquettish.

Tom nodded.

A man of few words, Holly thought.

'I'm from Clonakilty originally but I've been living in Cork city for years.'

'Ooh, really.' Kenny and Joan looked riveted, as if Tom

had said he'd just arrived in a space ship from another solar system instead of from the other side of the country.

'And you're here to work?' inquired Joan.

'I've just moved from Cork,' Tom said. 'I've got a new job here.'

'Doing what?'

Holly groaned inwardly. They'd be asking him his inside leg measurement next.

'I'm an architect.'

Holly could see Joan standing up straighter with glee. Joan had recently amused herself making a list of her top ten professions for prospective boyfriends. Architects were in the top ten. 'Creative but manly,' said Joan. Firemen were currently top of the list.

'What sort of stuff?' Kenny asked.

'Guys, stop with the third degree,' Holly reprimanded them.

'Sorry,' said Joan. 'Just curious. We must bring you out for a welcoming drink. We do that for all the residents, don't we?'

'Definitely,' agreed Kenny. 'We were just going out to the pub now, in fact. Can you come?'

'Afraid not.' Tom looked genuinely sorry. 'I have a friend coming with the van and the rest of my stuff. But the next time, I'd love to go out for a pint.'

'Goody,' Kenny said.

'Well, bye,' Joan added.

As it looked as if they could stand gawping up at Tom for hours, Holly said a cheery 'goodbye' and dragged the other pair back through her door.

'What a big honey monster,' crooned Kenny. 'I love those big, butch types.'

'Me too,' sighed Joan. 'Which one of us was he looking at? Do you think he's gay?'

'He could be gay, I don't know,' said Kenny. 'There isn't a secret handshake, you know, and it's not always that simple to tell, despite what they say about gaydar. He could be big and butch gay. We really need to have a look in his CD collection. One Barbra Streisand album and I'll know for sure.'

Holly didn't take part in the conversation as she was in the bathroom looking in horror at her greasy, pale face and her greasy, dark hair. Imagine what that guy must have thought when he saw her? She hadn't even had a shower. Just because Sunday was a slobbing around day, didn't mean she had to actually be a slob.

'I am a mess,' she said in disgust, as she wandered back into the living room. 'From now on, I am not leaving this flat unless I have full make-up and decent clothes on. I am going to start a new life of being beautifully groomed.'

'You didn't really leave the flat,' Joan reminded her.

'Even in the flat, then,' Holly said grimly, 'I am going to be beautifully groomed, right!'

'Whatever,' chorused Joan and Kenny and went back to discussing their new neighbour.

Holly shut the bathroom door and turned on the shower so it would warm up. As she stripped off her skuzzy clothes, she cast around for her ideal woman. Stella and her mother always looked immaculate, which made it difficult when Holly went to Kinvarra for increasingly rare weekends. Used to wearing her oldest clothes around the house until it was time to go out, Holly felt she had to make an effort when she was visiting her parents. Not that Rose ever said a word, but Holly was convinced she could feel the faintest glimmer of disapproval emanating from her mother when she appeared in her elderly sweatpants and all-encompassing sweatshirt.

Tara, who favoured jeans and T-shirts for casual wear, said that Holly was imagining it. 'Mum doesn't care what you wear, Holls,' Tara insisted. 'She's just thrilled to see you. Since you started working in Lee's, you never seem to have time to visit Kinvarra. You could turn up in your birthday suit with a line of tattoos down your back, and Mum and Dad would be delighted.'

Holly wasn't so sure. Tara and Stella were different, Rose was so proud of them. Holly tried so hard to make her mother proud of her. She just hoped that one day she'd manage it and Rose would say so. Maybe the weekend of her father's birthday would be the time.

CHAPTER NINE

Stella forced herself to stand beside the huge window and admire the view of Dublin's docklands area from Nick's sixth-floor apartment. A masterpiece of smoky glass and cutting edge architecture, the apartment complex was like a modern hotel, complete with twenty-four-hour concierge and security. The views were spectacular and the rooms were spacious. But what Stella really wanted was to prowl around and look at Nick's things: his furniture, his books, his photos. On her first trip to his home, she longed to know more about him. She needed time to work out exactly what sort of person he was – and what it meant when a man offered to cook dinner on the fourth date.

Vicki said it meant Nick was crazy about Stella and was doing his best to impress her: 'A man offers to cook dinner for you in his apartment and you're trying to analyse it?' Vicki said. 'Are you mad? You're nuts about him, so stop worrying and grab him with both hands.'

Stella was still anxious. 'I can't rush in too quickly,' she confided. 'What if I'm wrong, what if he's not the lovely, kind man I think he is, but some sort of practised seducer who drums up an amazing meal, plies me with wine and then expects to get me into bed?'

'Just say no,' Vicki pointed out prosaically. 'He can't drag you into the bedroom.'

'I didn't say I thought he'd drag me in,' Stella said, 'it's just . . .' She couldn't quite explain that she dearly wanted to be right in her assessment of Nick. But that she was scared of being wrong. He was funny, kind, attractive, he made her feel wonderful inside and he was clearly crazy about her. After their first date, he'd sent her a bouquet of white flowers that was so big that she had to get Vicki to help take them downstairs to her car. On their second date, they'd gone to the theatre and followed it up with a late-night pizza where they'd held hands under the table and gone for long moments with no conversation, as they stared dreamily into each other's eyes. For the third date, they'd gone to the cinema, held hands again and shared a bucket of popcorn. Stella could barely remember what the film had been about.

Nick phoned every day, apologising because he didn't want to interrupt her work but adding that he wanted to hear her voice. She couldn't stop thinking about him and genuinely saw a future for them. Was it too good to be true?

'Fabulous view,' she said, turning round to the kitchen where Nick was getting her a white wine spritzer.

'It's great, isn't it?' Nick said, preoccupied. He'd been like that since she arrived, nipping into the kitchen as soon as he'd opened the door and given Stella a cursory kiss on the cheek. It wasn't like him to be so edgy, a fact that made the knot in Stella's stomach clench even tighter.

She skirted the chocolatey brown divan and wandered idly over to a shelving unit which was crammed with books and papers, all jammed in higgledy-piggledy. His reading matter ranged from political biographies to thrillers, she noted, and there were sailing magazines squashed in too. The mantelpiece was bare but for several brown envelopes from bills and some loose change scattered carelessly. In one corner, moving cartons were still stacked high, proof that Nick hadn't really settled in, despite living in the apartment for several months.

'I know it's a bit of a mess,' he apologised, handing her a glass. 'I haven't had much time to do anything and I'm not good with decoration.'

'It's lovely, really,' Stella said. She liked the rich creams and the dusky browns of the room, although the entire place was too unloved and unlived in for her taste. Glancing around, she spotted a host of photo frames on a low table in the corner. She strained her eyes staring at them but they were too far away for her to see the pictures properly. In the dining part of the room, a very impressive glass and metal table was laid for two with a giant arum lily in a test tube sort of vase as the centrepiece. It was all very beautiful and looked like something from an interior design magazine.

'Sit down, please,' said Nick.

They perched on opposite ends of the divan and Stella felt another sliver of unease. Intuition told her that something wasn't quite right.

'I hope you like duck,' said Nick.

Duck. Stella was surprised. She hadn't pegged Nick as much of a man in the kitchen and had thought they'd probably end up eating something with pasta. That or steak. Men seemed to like cooking steak.

'That sounds very adventurous,' she said politely.

'Er, yes,' he said, fiddling with his tie.

He was nervous, she realised. What was going on? There was something not quite right about tonight. This was either an 'I'm sorry but it's over' dinner or he was planning *something*. But then, why invite her over to say goodbye, why not do it over the phone?

'I'll just check the oven,' Nick leapt to his feet.

Definitely a goodbye dinner, Stella decided. Oh well, she hated being right all the time. It *had* been too good to be true. That explained why Nick was dressed up in collar and tie; formality helped when it came to tough talk. What the hell, she wasn't going to be the perfect guest any more. She got up to examine his photos. All of them were of his two daughters, some from when the girls were children. Jenna made an adorable toddler, with white blonde hair curled around chubby cheeks and an engagingly naughty grin on her face as she was pictured covered in what looked like chocolate spread, with a pot overturned beside her and everything, even her knees, smeared with the stuff.

There were no photos of the girls' mother. Excised from

Nick's life, Stella decided, much the same way she was going to be excised. She felt grief bubble up inside her. She'd been stupid to imagine that they could have a future. Recently-divorced men were looking for freedom from responsibility, not shackling themselves to divorced mothers-of-one as soon as the ink was dry on the divorce lawyer's cheque. She'd been his rebound relationship, nothing more, and now he was trying to extract himself from it.

Perhaps he was heading back to his ex. Perhaps the story about his and Wendy's parting hadn't been strictly the truth. Even Vicki, in the midst of telling Stella to 'go for it', had been sceptical about that part.

'He's said it was an amicable divorce?' Vicki said. 'That's the bit I find hard to believe. That's a contradiction in terms; there is no such thing. Ask Alison in family law if you don't believe me. When you get to know him better, find out if it really was amicable.'

Maybe Wendy had divorced him, and now he was hoping it was all on again, thought Stella miserably.

'Er . . . Stella, could you look at this for me.' Nick interrupted her thoughts. He sounded very anxious.

Stella walked into the pristine kitchen, thinking that Nick must have been slaving away to cook duck and then clear up so efficiently before she got there. But there was no smell of food cooking, which was odd.

'What's the problem?'

Nick pointed to the oven, a gleaming silver and grey double oven affair that Stella would have loved in her kitchen but could never have afforded.

'It's been on for an hour and it's still not hot.' Nick ran an agitated hand through his hair. 'I'm really sorry, Stella, I wanted this to be perfect.'

She bent down and opened one side of the oven. Luke-warm air rushed out. She touched the two foil-wrapped packages inside. Barely warm. The packages looked very professional; too professional almost. She checked the dials and realised that the timer button was lit.

'Did you time it?' she asked.

Incomprehension crossed Nick's face. 'No,' he shrugged, 'I just turned it on like they told me ... Hell,' Nick pulled off his tie and unbuttoned the top of his shirt. 'I wanted to impress you so you wouldn't think I was one of these useless men who can't boil an egg. I wanted you to think I was a New Man. I ordered the entire dinner from this catering company. They bring it over nearly ready and all you have to do is re-heat it. Except the oven ...'

'... was on timer and obviously the timer overrode whatever you did with it,' finished Stella, beaming at him. 'You wanted to impress me,' she said, clicking the oven off. She stood up and put her arms round his neck, leaning close to him. 'I knew something was wrong,' she added. 'You were so edgy, I thought you were going to tell me it was all over.'

'And when there was no smell of cooking,' Nick continued, 'I realised it wasn't heating up ... What did you say?' He looked at her, startled. 'You thought I was going to tell you it was over? Oh Stella,' he groaned, lowering his mouth to hers.

Relief flooded out of Stella as they kissed deeply, and desire flooded in. 'As if I could tell you it's over when I can't concentrate on anything but you,' Nick murmured, his lips trailing from her mouth to her cheekbones, his hands cradling her close to him.

Stella leaned her head back as Nick's mouth slid down to nuzzle her neck. 'Vicki said I should stop analysing things and just enjoy it.'

'Remind me to send Vicki some flowers,' Nick joked. 'Why did you even think I could want to dump you?'

Well, it's all moving so fast.' Stella's firm gaze met Nick's. 'That scares me, Nick, and that would scare most men too.'

'I know it's moving quickly but that shouldn't frighten either of us.' He tucked a strand of Stella's silky dark hair behind her ear. 'I'd never hurt you, Stella. I just want to be with you, I want to talk to you every moment of the day, I want you with me all the time. I can't believe how strongly

I feel after such a short length of time but we can't let that stop us. Why do we have to be cautious? Why can't we just enjoy this and how we feel about each other?'

'I have to be cautious, Nick,' Stella said honestly. 'Because I have to think of Amelia. I don't want her to be injured, and the next step is you becoming a part of her life too, so I have to know that you mean this and that I'm not some rebound fling you're having. Sorry,' she added, seeing a bruised look come into his muddy green eyes. 'But Amelia is everything to me and I have to protect her. And, let's face it, you have your daughters to think about too. Between us, we've enough baggage to start our own suitcase company.'

A smile lifted the corners of his mouth.

'I know what you mean, Stella, but it's probably easier for me in that Jenna and Sara are older than Amelia.'

'Yes,' said Stella slowly, although she wasn't quite so sure about his reasoning when it came to his daughters.

'Just do me one favour,' Nick said. He took her hands in his. 'Don't hold back, don't try not to get involved, please. I've never felt this way about anyone, Stella, this is special. And no, that's not some line I read out of a book on seducing women.'

It was Stella's turn to grin.

'I mean it,' he said. 'I'm falling in love with you, what's wrong with that?'

'Nothing.'

For a moment, they gazed at each other, drinking each other in.

'I think . . .' Stella paused. 'I think I'm falling in love with you too.'

This time, she moved towards him and pulled his head down to hers. Suddenly, the temperature was raised and Stella clung tightly to Nick, her body pushing against his hardness, her lips bruised against his. She knew where she wanted this to end: in his bedroom, where their passion could explode and all the pent-up longing would be exorcised. Her fingers unbuttoned his shirt rapidly, exploring his chest, fingertips brushing sensitively over his skin. She could hear Nick's breathing deepen as he buried his face in her neck, his lips licking and nuzzling as his head moved down to the soft curve of her breast. Stella arched her back, pushing her body closer to his mouth, willing him to reach down inside her silky cardigan and touch her aching breasts.

It was Nick who pulled away first. 'I thought we were going to take this slowly,' he said shakily. 'Because if we don't stop now, I won't be able to stop at all.'

Stella grinned cheekily and buttoned up his shirt. 'You're right. It's hot in here. If we took the duck out of the oven, it might heat up by just being close to us?'

Nick laughed and planted a chaste kiss on her forehead. 'I can rustle up a pretty decent Chinese meal, you know,' he said. He opened a drawer and extracted a laminated take-away menu.

'Cheat.' Stella took off her high heels and opened the fridge. There was cheese, salad stuff, water and lots of orange juice in there. 'We can't waste that duck. Seeing as it's cooked already, how about we have it cold with salad?'

'Brilliant idea.'

'And for future reference, and if we're going to get really comfortable with each other, you'll have to realise that I don't need cordon bleu meals every night. I like to watch TV with a takeaway on my lap and my feet on the coffee table.'

'Sounds good to me,' said Nick happily.

CHAPTER TEN

On the weekend of Hugh's sixty-third birthday, the Miller women came home to celebrate with a big family lunch on Sunday. Stella and Amelia drove from Dublin on Friday night. Tara, Finn and Holly were to come on Saturday, although Holly wasn't staying in Meadow Lodge that night. She was to be dropped off at her friend Donna's house, because Donna had been begging her to stay over for months, but she'd be there for lunch on Sunday.

On Saturday morning, Hugh and Amelia set off on an expedition to investigate the birth of several puppies to Alastair Devon's collie bitch. All of which left Rose and Stella with glorious time on their hands, time they'd decided to spend with a morning shopping.

Melanie's Coffee House was a hotbed of activity on Saturdays. At lunchtime, it got particularly busy with shoppers unable to resist the lure of Melanie's home-made, organic quiches and pizzas, which revitalised even the most shattered customers. Melanie had cannily dumped the hard chairs favoured by the coffee shop's original owners and replaced them with comfortable ones made even more accommodating with fat gingham cushions that matched the sky-blue gingham tablecloths. Coffee at Melanie's was a byword in Kinvarra for putting your feet up after a hard morning. Consequently, by half twelve, the place was usually jam-packed with women proudly wielding bags as proof of their successful morning, and a few weary husbands hoping they'd be allowed to go home soon because they'd cry if they had to lurk embarrassedly outside another changing room.

Rose and Stella had staked their claim early and were sitting at one of the coveted upstairs gallery tables with a view of the bustling main street.

In front of each of them sat a slice of succulent quiche – smoked salmon and feta cheese for Rose and tomato and basil for Stella. Despite the delicious smell wafting up from the pottery plates, neither of them was eating very much.

'It's just a couple of dates,' Stella was saying, vainly trying to fork up some lettuce, 'nothing more. Nick's a nice man and I really like him, but that's all.'

Rose cast a mother's all-seeing eye over her eldest daughter and said nothing. Ever since Stella and Amelia had arrived at Kinvarra for the weekend, Rose had noticed a change in her daughter. Stella's face shone with an inner glow and her eyes were positively luminous, She was dressed differently, too, having abandoned her normal black-trousers-with-shirt weekend wear for a pair of jeans and a tangerine fleecy top that made her look years younger. And nobody could fail to notice the way Stella, when she thought nobody was looking, would smile for no apparent reason.

'I understand,' Rose agreed gravely, somehow keeping the delight out of her voice. 'He's divorced, you're divorced and let's face it, second marriages have a greater chance of ending in divorce.'

Stricken, Stella stared down at her lunch. 'I know all that, of course,' she began. 'It's ridiculous, we shouldn't even see each other again . . .'

She looked up from her plate to find her mother's eyes twinkling.

'Stella, I'm your mother,' Rose said, somewhat unnecessarily. 'Do you really think I can't see that you're wildly in love?'

Flushing, Stella abandoned any pretence of eating. It amazed her how her appetite had vanished in the past two weeks. 'How can it be love when we've only just met? I don't believe in love at first sight.'

'Love at second sight, then?'

This was the question that still haunted Stella. Nobody had been more surprised than she at the speed with which she had fallen for Nick. After six dates, she found herself sitting in her office daydreaming about him living with her and Amelia: cosily happy in Delgany Avenue, sharing family dinners, going for long walks at the weekends, the three of them cuddled up on the couch on Saturday evenings watching television and eating popcorn. Real family life, in other words. But was she living in cloud cuckoo land?

For that reason, she still hadn't introduce him to Amelia, even though she longed to do so. Despite her promise to Nick not to be scared of the intensity of their relationship, she was still anxious.

Rose, who'd been intently watching the play of emotions on Stella's lovely face, gave up on her lunch too. 'You've got to stop being so cautious, Stella,' she said. 'Take a chance on happiness. There are no prizes for never taking risks. Except loneliness.'

'What about Amelia?' protested Stella. 'I have to think about her. I can't afford to risk hurting her by making a mistake with Nick.'

'And what about you?' Rose reached across the table and caught her daughter's hand tightly. 'You know that I love Amelia with all my heart, but I love you too. I don't want to watch you give up a chance of happiness because it might not work out. What's the worst-case scenario here? Nick comes into your lives and after six months, he goes out again. That happens in life. It's already happened to Amelia,' she added gently.

'I know. That's what kills me,' Stella's expression was sad. 'I've already lost Amelia one father, I can't bring another person into her life for them to go away again.'

'Children are tougher than you think,' Rose said firmly. 'You and Glenn handled your break-up very well and there's never been any bitterness between you over Amelia.'

'That's because Glenn's so laid-back he's nearly horizontal. You can't fight with him, it rolls off him,' Stella said. It was true: Glenn's attitude to life in general had hugely helped their access arrangements. 'Shit happens' was his mantra. It used to drive Stella mad when she was married to him but came in useful when they were splitting up, when his philosophy made the issue of who'd care for Amelia very simple. From the 'shit happens' perspective, there was no point arguing over anything. Amelia would live with her mother, and Glenn would go with the flow.

'I sometimes think that I failed Amelia,' Stella insisted. 'You wouldn't have left Dad for anything because of us. I know,' she added hastily, 'that's a crazy thing to even talk about because you adore each other, but you would never have contemplated divorce no matter what. You would have stayed together for me and Tara and Holly. I couldn't do that for Amelia so I've failed her.'

Her mother's expression was unreadable and for an instant, Stella feared she'd offended her.

'Mum, I was just using you and Dad as an example, naturally I didn't mean . . .' she began.

Rose brushed the apology away. 'Don't be silly, darling,' she said lightly, 'I was just thinking, that's all. You haven't failed in the slightest. You did the right thing and Amelia is a wonderful, loving, funny little girl. I'm sure that having a largely absent father has had some effect on her, we can't deny that, but would it be better if you and Glenn were married and hated each other with a vengeance?'

'You're right, I suppose.' A picture of Nick telling her about the pain of his divorce came into Stella's mind. Nick still insisted that his split from Wendy had been amicable, but he'd admitted that the divorce had been his idea and that it had taken a long time, and many arguments, for Wendy to agree with him. His moving back to Ireland, which he'd refused to do during their marriage, had infuriated her. 'At least Glenn and I still get on and we never fought, even when we were married.' Nick said the rows between him and Wendy when they'd been married had been pyrotechnic, particularly in the last year of their marriage. Stella actually couldn't imagine Nick having a raging argument with anyone. He was calmly measured about everything.

'So,' Rose began, 'when are you going to introduce Amelia to Nick?'

Stella laughed. 'I can see why Dad calls you the scourge of the committee ladies. You get straight to the point.'

'It's the only way to do things,' Rose said proudly. 'Hold on for a moment, we're obviously not going to eat any more of this. Will I get us coffee?'

'I'd love some.'

Rose got to her feet gracefully and went to the counter for coffee, her slim figure and elegant bearing that of a woman half her age. And it wasn't only her figure that was young: her mind was as open to new ideas as a twenty-something.

Watching her, Stella thought once again what a remarkable woman her mother was. Rose possessed the uncanny ability to look right into people's hearts and divine what was bothering them. She never judged or moralised. And her advice was always kind, genuine and sensible.

Rose came back with two coffees.

'Right. List the pros and cons of introducing Amelia to Nick.'

Stella stirred one spoon of sugar into her coffee.

'Well, we can imagine the pros. The cons are, they might not get on, Amelia might hate him and the idea of him. She's never had to share me, you know.'

Rose considered this. 'True, but you won't know until you try. There's no point trying to second-guess a seven-year-old. What else?'

'He's not divorced that long,' Stella added. 'He's over it, but he's,' she hesitated while trying to find the right word, 'bruised. The split was very difficult even though they both agreed it was the right thing to do. And he hated leaving his daughters, I think that was the hardest part.'

'Could you love a man who didn't regret hurting his children?' asked Rose sensibly.

'No, you're right. He adores them. He came back to Ireland because he couldn't bear to be away from them, which didn't, I gather, please his ex-wife.' Stella couldn't understand why Wendy was so apparently het up over Nick's decision to move back to Ireland. He was closer to their daughters, and surely the girls' welfare was paramount.

'I'm sure it didn't,' Rose said briskly. 'Darling, just one word of advice: do be careful about demonising this woman. It's a bit like agreeing with a friend about how horrible her husband is when they've had a row, and then having her resent you for what you said when they inevitably make it up. Don't forget that she and Nick were married for twenty years and eventually, one hopes, they'll learn to be friends. You don't want to be nasty about her only to have him resent that later.'

'You're right, Mum,' Stella said automatically. The truth was, she was astonished by how much she disliked the sound of Wendy Cavaletto. In a very un-Stella-like way, she relished hearing about Wendy's outbursts of temper. Of course, it was easier to be the replacement for a bitch than an angel.

She stared out of the window and Rose sipped her coffee, looking around the gallery area in order to leave Stella to her thoughts. In one corner sat Mrs Freidland, and her daughter, both tight-lipped as though holding off on an argument because they were in public.

One of the women who worked in Rose's dentist's office was at another table, sitting with her husband and two teenagers. The woman smiled in recognition and Rose smiled back. She remembered hearing that one of the teenagers had been hospitalised with anorexia not so long ago. Both girls were slender; it was impossible to know which had been ill. The whole family looked light-hearted, as if they hadn't a care in the world. A brave smile was a remarkably good camouflage, she reflected.

'I know I'm panicking,' Stella said. 'I just worry about things, that's all. We've talked about Amelia not liking Nick. What if Nick's daughters don't like me?'

'Everyone loves you,' Rose reassured her briskly. 'Stella, I can't think of a single person who doesn't. It might take time, yes, but you'll win them over. If you and Nick have a future together, you can overcome all these things.'

'You really think so?' asked Stella suddenly, sounding like she used to as a girl when she needed reassurance.

'Absolutely.'

Stella smiled. Her mother was right. Somehow, and she really didn't know how she'd done it, she'd kept a certain distance between her and Nick, just in case. That distance had been her insurance but now it was time to tear up the policy. Live dangerously. Take risks. Nick had asked her if she wanted to go away for a weekend. Anywhere she wanted.

'I was thinking maybe a city break in Europe, would you like that?' he'd asked, his eyes telling her that he knew it was a big step.

She'd said she'd think about it. Sensible Stella, knowing that a weekend away would be a big step towards another destination: the bedroom. The electricity between them was incredible and so far, it had taken all of Stella's self-restraint not to throw her inhibition to the wind and clamber into bed with Nick.

Suddenly, she wanted to phone him and say yes, a weekend away would be fabulous and how about Paris? She'd only been there once, years ago. And why didn't he come to her house next weekend and meet Amelia? There could be no more creeping around. Nick was going to be a part of both their lives. Once she'd made the decision, excitement and a sense of the rightness of her choice, flooded through her.

'Thanks, Mum.' She gave her mother a smile that was full of sweetness. 'You're right.'

At that moment, doubts assailed Rose. Her radar, once so reliable for other people's problems, wasn't as good as it had been. What if she'd given Stella the wrong advice? What if this Nick *was* on the rebound and needed the consolation of gentle, loving Stella to get his confidence back? What would Stella do then, having given him her heart and let him into both her and Amelia's lives? What if the children all hated each other? What if . . .

'You're going to love him, Mum,' Stella said. 'He's very special. He's funny, clever, kind, everything.'

Rose suppressed her fears. 'Is this the man who was just a friend a few minutes ago, the man you'd gone out with on a few friendly dates?'

'That's the one.' Stella grinned.

'When do we get to meet him?'

'Soon.'

'You could bring him to our ruby anniversary party in April,' Rose suggested wickedly, 'and see if your Aunt Adele approves.'

Stella laughed. 'And put him right off me? I'd love to bring him – thank you – but he'll need to be briefed before meeting Adele. But tell me, you're going to organise the party? Tara, Holly and I are supposed to do that for your anniversary and surprise you. We've been talking about it for ages.'

'Your father hates surprises. He's very keen on a big party and has decided that we should arrange it ourselves, so don't feel guilty. He says it's old-fashioned to wait patiently for someone else to do it, and there's nothing he dislikes more than being called old-fashioned. Besides, you three and I would go for a small family gathering, while your father fancies a big mad party where he gets to invite everyone he's ever met.'

'I'll help with the food,' Stella volunteered.

Her mother grinned. 'Don't worry about the food, Daddy Warbucks has decided on caterers and a marquee.'

'Wow,' whistled Stella. 'That's posh.'

'Yes. But your father thinks the more money you spend, the less work you have to do. In fact, it's the other way round. I'll never forget that celebrity Support the Children gala I was involved in. It cost a fortune and I nearly went deranged pulling the whole thing together.'

'It'll be fun, though,' Stella said. 'What a lovely way to celebrate the fact that you've been married for forty years.'

She felt a prickling of tears behind her eyes at the thought of her beloved parents. She was so proud of them.

'Lord, is that the time?' Rose looked at her watch. 'We have to fly. Tara and Finn will be arriving soon and we ought to get home and see what your father and Amelia have been up to.'

That evening, Tara sat on the bed in Stella's old bedroom, engrossed in a book of Amelia's. Amelia herself sat on the stool in front of the mirror while Stella brushed her hair. Tara was supposed to be finding a story to read aloud, but kept getting distracted by other stories as she tried to find the one Amelia wanted, which was a version of 'The Princess and the Pea'. Tara wasn't the only person who was distracted: Stella had phoned Nick with the momentous news about how she'd love to go away with him, and his response hadn't been quite what she'd expected. She mulled over this as she brushed her daughter's hair.

'Ouch,' said Amelia as her mother encountered another tangle and pulled.

'Sorry, pet,' said Stella. 'I know I'm a horrible old mummy who hurts you.'

'Is Mummy mean to you?' inquired Tara.

Amelia giggled and shook her head.

'She is?' said Tara. 'I knew it. Cruel, horrible Mummy. Are you going to stay with me and Uncle Finn when Mummy goes away in a few weeks?'

'Yes,' said Amelia with enthusiasm. 'Can we go to McDonald's and a film like last time?' Amelia had adored her last visit to her aunt which coincided with a weekend conference Stella had been on.

'Definitely. But we can't pick a scary movie,' Tara warned. 'Uncle Finn gets scared very easily.'

Amelia scrunched up her nose and giggled at this.

'You'll have to be very good,' Stella said.

'I'm always good,' Amelia announced with some indignation.

'Saint Amelia,' teased Tara from her position on the bed.

'Done.' Stella smoothed Amelia's hair and planted a kiss on her daughter's forehead.

'Come here and find this story for me,' Tara asked her niece.

Soon Amelia and Tara were curled up against the pillows, with Tara reading aloud. She did all the voices, making Amelia wide-eyed with interest, and making Stella think fondly that her sister was wonderful with kids. And Amelia adored her Uncle Finn who would play endlessly with her and made her scream with a mixture of fear and excitement when he threw her up into the air and caught her expertly.

When the story was finished, Amelia went downstairs to say goodnight to her granny and grandad and the two sisters were left alone.

'I'm glad you're going to Paris,' said Tara, getting off the bed and examining herself in the mirror. She scrunched her hair a bit, making it stand up more than ever. 'You need a bit of romance in your life. Now, if only we could get Holly fixed up.'

'Holly told me that Joan and Kenny are determined to find a man for her,' said Stella. 'Poor Holly can't put them off.'

Tara chuckled. 'Poor Holly is right. I can't think of anything worse than being fixed up by that crazy pair. I don't know how she still hasn't met anyone decent by herself. She's gorgeous and funny, although she's wasted in that dead-end job.' Tara was the only one who recognized that working in Lee's wasn't glamorous and was always urging her little sister to get out of the retail trade and into something else.

'She's different when she's with us than when she's with other people,' Stella explained. 'She really is shy, Tara, you just don't see it because you know her so well.'

'I suppose.' Tara was thoughtful. 'Finn has some cute friends, I could set her up with them.'

'Not that Derry bloke, I hope,' Stella said.

'Hell, no. Derry's a bit wild for our Holly. Anyway, he's going out with a girl for ages now. She's coming to Austria with us next week. There are ten of us going now, but I don't know most of them . . .'

'It sounds great,' sighed Stella. 'I've always wanted to go skiing.'

'Finn says it's great fun and I'll pick it up easily.' Tara sounded dubious.

'You'll be fine.'

'I expect you're right,' said Tara. 'I'll find out on Tuesday. Finn's taking me to the artificial slope after work.'

Stella looked at her sister fondly. Tara had such confidence. Nothing fazed her.

'When Holly comes to lunch tomorrow, I'm going to invite her out with Finn and me one night and set her up with one of his friends,' Tara said decisively.

'Ask her first,' counselled Stella.

'I promise. Now, when are you going to Paris? I'll have to put it in my diary.'

'Probably the weekend after you get back, but I'll confirm when I've spoken to Nick later.'

'I bet he was pleased when you phoned and said yes,' teased Tara.

'He was, but . . .' It had been odd. Nick's tone told her he was thrilled but his words had been oddly formal. When she'd phoned, he said he was in the car with his daughter, Jenna.

'That's great news, can I phone you back later?' he'd said. 'I'm with Jenna and we're just going to meet Sara for a quick bite to eat. I'll phone you tonight, OK?'

Stella, who'd been expecting him to be openly delighted, had said that was fine

'But what?' demanded Tara.

'He couldn't talk, he was with his daughter.'

'So? I don't understand.' Tara understood all right but she didn't like what she was hearing.

'I haven't met his daughters. The divorce was hard for the

187

children,' Stella said. 'Nick doesn't want to rock the boat by introducing me to them until they've got used to the idea of him dating.'

'SOS. Guilty daddy alert!' said Tara. 'If you're his girlfriend, you need to meet his kids and they need to know about you. Put your foot down, Stella. This is important. Either he's divorced or he's not. Is he still pining after his ex?'

'No, definitely no. She sounds like an awful cow,' Stella began, and then remembered what Rose had said earlier about criticising Nick's ex-wife. 'But she's probably just upset over the divorce.'

'Stella,' said Tara, trying to pick her words carefully, 'please don't be so kind and patient with everyone that you get walked on. If you're serious about this guy, he needs to be serious with you and that means meeting his kids. OK?' She hoped she hadn't said too much because Stella was sensitive about being told what to do.

'I know,' Stella said, 'but he hasn't met Amelia yet, so we're both guilty of trying to protect our kids.'

'That's fine,' Tara said, 'as long as him protecting his kids doesn't hurt you. I want to meet this guy and see if he's good enough for you.'

Stella groaned. 'You will, you will. And he is good enough for me. He's wonderful.'

Tara stared speculatively at her sister. 'I hope so, for his sake.'

On Sunday, when Holly heard about Stella's weekend away with Nick, she got into the spirit of things. 'There's this new range of body lotions in the shop,' she said enthusiastically. 'They're called Angel Cake and the best seller is the vanilla one and when you rub it in, it makes your skin incredibly soft and the scent is guaranteed to last for up to ten hours. I'll get you a bottle.'

'But it has to be rubbed in by a nice man,' added Tara, laughing, 'or the guarantee doesn't work.'

It was noon on Sunday and the three sisters were travelling to the restaurant in Stella's car. Amelia had insisted on going with her grandparents and Finn.

'She's trying to convince Dad to get a puppy,' Stella said as she drove down Kinvarra's main street, eyes peeled for a parking space.

'Poor Dad,' grinned Tara. 'He said he might get a dog when he retires but not yet.'

'Amelia can be very persuasive,' Stella pointed out. 'Hazel got a hamster for Shona and Becky, and Amelia keeps making big, sad eyes at me and asking why can't we have one too, and that it would only be small, wouldn't eat much and she'd clean its cage. She did her abused child look last Saturday when we met one of the school mothers outside ballet and Amelia said she was saving all her pocket money for a hamster because I won't buy one for her. Honestly, I was waiting for the child services people to come and take her away.'

The sisters laughed.

'That reminds me of myself,' said Tara. 'I was such a minx when I was a kid. I once told Angela Devon that we never got treats at home and that Mum point-blank refused to give us chocolate or anything nice in our lunchboxes. And you know Mum was always killing herself making sure we had everything we wanted. I still feel bad about that.'

'You were just a kid,' consoled Stella. 'Ooh, parking!' she added, braking suddenly and whipping the car into a space.

The three women walked slowly to the restaurant.

'Have you got the card?' asked Stella.

'Yep.' Holly had found a fabulous card with a picture of a man fishing on the front and inside was a note with details of the fishing rod the three sisters had clubbed together to buy.

'Hope he likes it,' said Stella.

'He'll love it,' said Tara. 'I just wish it was as easy to buy something for their ruby wedding as it was for Dad's birthday. What the hell are we going to get them?'

'We'll think of something,' Stella said confidently. 'It's weeks away.' She looped an arm through each of her sisters'. 'Let's go,' she said, 'and nobody is to mention hamsters, right?'

CHAPTER ELEVEN

When Finn drove up the cobbled drive to Four Winds the following Saturday morning, Tara felt her heart sink. She had at least an hour of Gloria to get through: an hour of barbed comments about *National Hospital* and sarcastic little asides about how lucky her friends were to have grandchildren. The latest news was that Liz B-M's daughter Serena was pregnant, and Gloria was clearly annoyed about being left behind in the game of one-upmanship.

'We're going to have a fabulous holiday,' said Finn encouragingly.

Tara grinned at him. 'Sure we are,' she said. Negotiating lethal ski runs as a first-time skier couldn't be any more treacherous than popping into her mother-in-law's to say goodbye. Tara didn't even know why she and Finn were going to Four Winds in the first place: they were only going to be away for ten days. Surely even Gloria couldn't get withdrawal symptoms from missing her son in that time?

'Do we have to drop in on your mum?' Tara had asked earlier that day when they'd finally packed two suitcases and one big, squashy bag for on the plane. 'Skiing clothes take up so much room,' she added, gasping, as they manhandled the luggage into Finn's silver Volkswagen.

'Yes, we do,' Finn apologised. 'Sorry, she sounded almost tearful on the phone about not seeing me. But we won't be long, and then we'll be on the plane! Wait till you really get into skiing and we have our own skis,' he added, happy in the fantasy of near-professional skiing skill and endless holidays.

Tara was not convinced after her failures at the ski slope on Tuesday. 'That is never going to happen,' she said gloomily, 'not the way I ski.'

'Nonsense, real snow is much more fun than an artificial slope.' Finn pulled Tara's sheepskin hat back and planted a kiss on her forehead. 'You'll love it.'

'I won't if I break something.' Tara was wondering if going to Austria with a gang of ski fanatics was such a good idea. Finn had been skiing several times with Derry, and adored it. Tara had never had much co-ordination. Step aerobics were beyond her and she'd been hopeless at gymnastics at school. She had visions of nine happy people giggling over the gluhwein in their chalet, while she sat miserably in the corner, immobile, with some bit of her itching like mad in an ungainly plaster cast.

'You'll love it,' Finn urged.

'I know I will,' said Tara, resolving to stop being such a moaner. Who cared if she was useless on the slopes anyhow? She'd be away with Finn.

Through some marvellous piece of luck, Gloria was on the phone when they arrived. Tara hoped it was a long, long call.

'Tea or coffee?' said Desmond.

'No, we're fine,' Finn said. 'We haven't got long, Dad.'

Tara picked up a gardening magazine from the table and flicked through it, while Desmond teased Finn about his first skiing trip.

'Tara, if you'd seen him when he came back. He was black and blue and his ankle took months to heal.' Desmond shook his head. 'He said he'd never go skiing again. Only for Derry dragging him off the following year, he never would have.'

'You never told me you hurt yourself skiing,' she laughed at Finn. 'You said you'd been a natural straight off. You liar!'

'A natural?' teased Desmond. 'Natural at falling over. According to Derry, there were four-year-olds with better balance than your husband.'

'But that was my first time,' protested Finn good-humouredly.

'And this is *my* first time.' Tara pointed out. 'You told me I'd have no trouble. I know I'm going to end up falling over the whole time.'

'Yes but you've a nice soft bum to land on if you do,' Finn grinned.

'Thank you,' gasped Tara, pretending to be insulted. 'This is what I have to put up with, Desmond. Insults all the time.'

Finn blew her a kiss. 'She likes it, really, Dad.'

They talked and laughed for half an hour and Tara reflected that when Gloria wasn't present, Four Winds was like a different place.

Finally, Gloria arrived, looking very put out at this interference with her plans.

'That was Liz, I couldn't get her off the phone. You're not leaving yet, are you, darling?'

'We don't have much time, Mums.' Finn looked contrite. 'The plane waits for no man. We'll have to go in less than half an hour.'

'Come out to the kitchen with me while I make coffee,' begged Gloria, 'I need to talk to you.'

And it was nice to see you too, Gloria, thought Tara with irritation as her mother-in-law swept Finn off without so much as a hello in Tara's direction. When they returned some ten minutes later, even Finn's famed easy-going smile looked strained.

'Everything all right?' Tara asked under her breath.

'I'll tell you later,' he replied.

Tara clock-watched through discussions about Liz B-M's prospective grandchild and where the baby was going to be born ('a private hospital, of course'). Next up, was the usual inquisition about Finn's job. Tara was convinced that she was held responsible for Finn not having advanced beyond junior sales manager in the company. In fact, Finn was perfectly happy with his job, particularly since his oldest friend and chief merrymaker, Derry, was his direct boss.

'It's very important to entertain the senior management,' Gloria said, mantra-like. 'I entertained for your father and look where that got him,' she added proudly.

Tara smiled sweetly through this dig. If Gloria thought Tara was going to give up her job so she could devote herself to advancing Finn's career, she could think again. Did Gloria know that women were allowed to vote?

The big hand crawled round to time to go. Tara shot her husband a meaningful look and he nodded.

'We've got to get out of here,' he said apologetically.

Tara hugged her father-in-law goodbye. 'I'll save a space on my cast for you to sign,' she joked.

'Stay for another cup of coffee,' Gloria begged her son. 'Planes never leave on time, I'm sure you don't have to go yet.'

'Our flight's at three,' said Tara coolly. 'We have to leave, Gloria. Sorry.'

It was bad enough that Gloria had insisted on Finn trekking all the way to visit her before they drove back up the motorway to the airport, Tara wasn't going to let her rule the roost entirely.

Finn hugged his mother, who looked tearful.

'Bye,' said Tara breezily. She linked Finn's arm in hers. 'We'll send a postcard.'

'Have fun,' said Desmond.

Gloria said nothing and just stared at them, looking stricken while they got in the car and drove quickly out the gates.

'Your mother is very possessive about you,' ventured Tara when they were safely in the car and back on the motorway.

'I know,' said Finn. 'She's always been like that. It used to drive Fay mad, that's why they fought all the time.'

'She was possessive about Fay too?' Tara could under-

194

stand how a person might want to emigrate if their mother was a clingy, manipulative woman like Gloria.

'No.' Finn sounded melancholy. 'She wasn't like that with Fay at all, just with me. That was what broke Fay's heart. She was fed up with being treated like a second-class citizen.'

To lighten the mood, Tara rubbed Finn's shoulder affectionately. 'Look at all these fascinating things I'm learning about you,' she said.

'Just as well we got married after only six months together, then,' he replied. 'You mightn't have wanted to marry me if you knew all the Jefferson family secrets.'

'I'd have married you no matter what.' She squeezed the hand that rested on the gear shift.

'You're sweet,' he said fondly.

'Yeah, that's me,' agreed Tara, ironically. 'Sweet. Everyone at work says so. "There goes that lovely sweet Tara Miller," they all say.'

Finn laughed. 'That's another black mark in my mother's mind, by the way,' he added. 'My mother disapproves of you not taking the name Jefferson when we got married.'

Tara rolled her eyes. 'If that's all she's got to worry about, then tough bananas. So, what's wrong with her?'

'The usual. Fay. She wants me to ask Fay to phone her. She says I can sort it out and that Fay wouldn't talk to her.'

'That's a cop-out. Why doesn't she just phone Fay herself?' Tara was genuinely perplexed. Gloria was such a strange woman. She could be as sharp as a hypodermic syringe one moment, and behave like a helpless child who needed other people to help her sort out a family rift the next.

'I told you,' repeated Finn. 'My family are weird. You're used to straightforward people, Tara, and we're not straightforward. Where Mums is concerned, there have to be undercurrents and shifting, unvoiced opinions.'

Tara shuddered. She'd hate to come from a family like that. In the Miller family, people said what they thought and no family row would be allowed to last for over two years.

'Mums hopes that I'll square everything with Fay and tell

her that Mums wants her home and wants the row forgotten. Then, she'll talk to Mums and it'll all be over. End of story, everyone's happy. Until the next time.'

'I see,' said Tara. She knew it would hurt Finn if she said what she really thought: that his mother was an arch manipulator. Gloria wanted other people to do her dirty work, so she cajoled poor Finn into listening to her sob over Fay, forcing him to phone his sister and try and heal the rift. Tara was glad that Finn was a strong enough person not to get caught up in his mother's plots. He'd clearly taught himself to switch off and not get involved.

She stroked his cheek. 'Let's forget about all this and have a great holiday.'

The party spirit got underway at the airport. There were five couples going on the trip, including Finn's old school friends Derry, Jake and Ken and their partners, along with a colleague of Jake's and his wife. Tara had met all but Jake's workmate before. The men all knew each other well and the ice was broken when Derry rounded up all the passports at the check in desk and laughed, childishly Tara thought, at the usual Interpol-style passport photos.

'Derry, stop mucking around,' said Kayla, his girlfriend.

Thank God there was someone around to keep an eye on Derry, Tara thought, grinning at the other woman. In her experience of Finn's best friend, he needed constant supervision or he became unbearable.

When they had all checked in, Tara thought a little retail therapy would be in order. But nearly everybody else voted to head straight for the bar. Only Kayla wanted to forgo a drink for a trip to the shops.

'Oh let them at it,' said Kayla. 'You can't shop with a guy hanging round after you.'

She and Tara trailed through the cosmetics hall in companionable silence, stocking up on moisturiser, sun screen and some gorgeous sparkly lip glosses they just had to have. Tara even bought a pair of ski glasses that she thought were very Bond babe.

When she and Kayla finally made it up to the bar, their fellow travellers were drinking champagne.

'Are you all mad?' demanded Tara, counting the bottles. 'They won't let you on the plane if you're drunk.'

'C'mere crosspatch,' laughed Finn, pulling her clumsily onto his knee. 'They won't mind. We're nice, polite drunks.'

With all the happy, slightly tipsy faces looking at her, Tara felt she couldn't say anything. But she was irritated by Finn's behaviour. This was their holiday, not some rowdy stag night. She got off Finn's knee and sat apart from him, ostensibly examining her purchases.

Finn wriggled onto the bench seat beside her. 'We're just having fun, love,' he said, kissing her. 'Relax, Tara. You need a break too. You've been working too hard.'

'Yeah, I suppose,' she said.

Derry shoved a glass of champagne into her hand, spilling a bit on her in the process. 'Here's to skiing!' he said loudly.

She'd never been to a skiing village and didn't know what to expect. But Kitzbuhl fulfilled every dream she'd ever had. The whole medieval town was snow-filled, utterly beautiful, like an illustration from a child's fairytale book.

'Oh, Finn, this is lovely,' Tara sighed, holding his hand as the Snow Tourz bus lurched up the road.

'I knew you were an old romantic at heart,' he said, squeezing back. 'We'll have to go on a sleigh ride.'

'Oh yes!' She leaned over and kissed him tenderly. 'I'd love that, Finn.' Perhaps they could have a second honeymoon after all.

'Can't you keep your hands off each other for five minutes!' yelled a voice from the back.

Tara and Finn dissolved into laughter. Despite their tiredness after the drink and the flight, they were buzzing with excitement. Away from the pressures of work and family, this was going to be their best holiday yet.

The chalet was at one end of the town; a large wooden building that looked quite ample for their party of ten.

'Hope it's as nice inside as out,' Tara whispered to Finn.

'Hope we get a nice room with a big double bed,' he whispered back, 'so I can drag you off there.'

The Snow Tourz rep led the way in and ten weary travellers trailed in behind her, dragging as much of their luggage as they could manage. There was a big hall complete with all sorts of racks, hooks and drying rails for ski clothes.

'So you won't clog up everywhere else,' the rep explained. 'Cool, isn't it?'

Next, she brought them into a big warm room with a very high-tech stove at one end, lots of enormous comfortable couches and chairs, and a big wooden dining table at the other. The table was laid for dinner and the scent of something wonderful was drifting from the kitchen.

'TV, yes!' shouted Derry, throwing himself onto a couch to test it for comfort. 'And we have satellite!'

Next to the dining area was a small, steamy kitchen where a very red-faced young woman was frantically doing things with a catering sized hob and lots of saucepans.

'Meet Midge, your chalet girl,' said the rep.

'Hiya,' said Midge, a chirpy New Zealander with blonde hair in sleek Heidi plaits. 'I got a bit delayed with dinner. Lamb sound good?'

'Yes,' chorused everyone.

The rep handed out keys to every couple, explaining that it was easier to allocate rooms beforehand to save argument. Finn and Tara's room was spacious, with a minuscule en suite bathroom, lots of wardrobe space and a soft Queen-sized bed covered in a blue striped duvet. Photos of picturesque local scenes adorned the walls. The effect was simple and pretty.

'That bed looks good,' said Finn, dropping the luggage wearily and lying on the bed.

'Don't you want any dinner?' asked Tara.

Finn jumped up again. 'Yeah, dinner, drinks and who knows, maybe a little après-ski here in this bed.'

Tara grinned. 'That sounds like my sort of holiday.'

*   *   *

'I ache,' moaned Tara, several days later. 'All over.'

'Poor diddums,' said Finn, dragging off his salopettes wearily. 'I think a few reviving shots of schnapps will soon sort you out.'

'Ugh, no.' Tara couldn't bear the thought of more booze. They'd had far too much again the night before and it had been a miracle she'd been able to get up that morning. The low sunlight bouncing off the snow had made her murderous headache worse and it had been lunchtime before she'd been able to face anything to eat.

'How do you and Derry do it?' she said. 'You drank far more than me.'

'Years of practice, babe,' Finn replied. 'Anyway, we're here on holiday. Getting horrifically drunk is part of the fun.'

'Speak for yourself,' Tara said. 'I'm going to have a long hot shower before dinner and an early night.'

'Come on,' pleaded Finn, 'you can't be a party pooper. We've only got three days left. We've got to paint the town red.'

'Not tonight.' Tara was adamant. 'Can't we stay in just once? We could go to bed early,' she added softly. 'We've been out nearly every night, Finn, well,' she reconsidered, '*you've* been out every night and I've been out most of them, and it's costing us a fortune, not to mention the damage it's doing to our livers.'

'Book me into the Betty Ford when we go home,' he joked, blowing her a kiss. 'We've got to enjoy the rest of the holiday, love, please,' he added in a begging voice. 'Pretty please. I promise we'll have that sleigh ride tomorrow.'

'You said that yesterday.'

'I know, but today flew past. Tomorrow, I promise, you and me on a sleigh ride with that Ronettes song in the background, and sleigh bells going ding ding aling or whatever they do, OK? But tonight, I'm a party animal! We can go to bed early at home any time we want,' he cajoled.

It was no good remonstrating with him. She and Finn

hadn't spent one quiet, romantic evening together. Every night had been a boozing session, and if nobody else wanted to go, Finn and Derry went on their own. Now he and Derry were determined to trawl through the bars yet again, even though nobody else in the group could summon up the energy for another late night. Skiing was so exhausting. Kayla didn't seem to mind Derry heading off without her, but Tara was furious about it. Palming her off with the promise of time alone tomorrow just wasn't good enough, but it was hard to argue when the walls were thin and the others would hear every single word.

She sat grimly opposite Finn at the big dining table and tucked into the goulash that Midge had served with rice. There was much laughing and giggling as they ate, with the local plonk racing up and down the table at speed. Wine wasn't included in the cost of the holiday and trips were made to the supermarket every day to stock up.

Tara drank cranberry juice with her meal. Finn and Derry sat beside each other and shared a rapidly-vanishing bottle of wine, before moving onto the next. Watching Finn wink at her, trying to jolly her out of her bad mood, Tara came to the conclusion that he'd abandoned his plan to go out. He and Derry were clearly partying at home. They *could* have a cosy evening in, she thought, pleased. Maybe they could go to bed early. They'd both been too tired most mornings to even consider making love, and at night they ended up in bed so late that sex was the last thing on their minds. But tonight might be the night. Tara blew a kiss at her husband, who looked relieved to be forgiven.

'I'm so glad you're staying in,' she mouthed across the table when Midge was dishing up a vast bowl of stewed fruit and cream.

'I'm not.' Finn gave her a glassy smile.

Tara was furious and didn't care who heard her. 'You're not going out now, Finn? Can't you stay in for one night?'

Everyone looked nervously up from the table, sensing a full-scale row on the horizon.

'It's a holiday, Tara,' said Derry sarcastically. 'People go out on holidays, you know. That's the whole point.'

'Yeah,' wheedled Finn, 'it's nearly our last day.'

'I'm asking you not to go out tonight.' Tara wasn't sure why this was so important, but it was. She needed Finn to choose between her and his party-animal friend. She'd never wanted to become one of those women who stopped their partners seeing their pals, but this was too much. Her whole holiday had become an awful parody of a lager-lout vacation. She needn't have come at all, for all Finn cared about her presence. His ideal holiday was clearly one with Derry.

'Chill, Tara, why don't you?' said Derry dismissively.

Finn fiddled with his fork and said nothing.

So that was the way he wanted to play it. Tara threw her napkin down on the table and shoved her chair back, staring angrily at her husband. 'You should have gone on holiday with Derry,' she hissed. 'You spend more time with him than you do with me.'

She slammed their bedroom door so hard that the pretty photographs hanging on the wall rattled. She was enraged, but she didn't think she'd have to wait long. Finn would come and say sorry. He wasn't the sulking type and he hated rows. It was damn Derry causing all the trouble. When they got home, Tara vowed, Derry wouldn't be allowed to put a foot inside their home unless he apologised, boss or no boss.

Ten minutes stretched to twenty, while Tara sat on the blue-striped duvet and tried to concentrate on a magazine. Finn didn't appear. Eventually, she threw down the magazine and went back into the big living room. The other five were sitting round the coffee table playing Trivial Pursuit. There was no sign of either Derry or Finn.

'They've gone out,' Kayla said drily. 'I wouldn't wait up. Oh, Finn told me to tell you he'd book your sleigh ride first thing tomorrow morning. He said it'd be romance all the way!'

Tara was too proud to cry in front of them all, but she felt like it. Finn's betrayal hit her like a punch to the solar plexus. She'd asked him not to go out, told him that she wanted to spend time with him. And he had. Publicly.

'Have a drink,' suggested Kayla, proffering a bottle of wine.

Tara shook her head, feeling humiliation and misery welling up in her. 'I'm going to bed.'

It was three when Finn got in and fell into bed beside her, stinking of alcohol and very cold. 'It's freezing out there,' he slurred, trying to cuddle closer to her warm body. His feet were as cold as if they'd just been taken out of the fridge and Tara pulled hers away as soon as they touched them. The bed was too small for sleeping apart, but she managed it.

'Go to sleep, Finn,' she said harshly.

Within minutes, he was snoring loudly. Tara, perched on the edge of the mattress, took longer to drop off. Despite the tiredness from her day's skiing, she lay awake and brooded.

The scent of breakfast woke Tara before her alarm clock. She lay in bed feeling tired after her bad night, wondering why bed seemed so uncomfortable when you couldn't sleep, and so welcoming the morning after. Finn had burrowed down so that his head wasn't visible and there was just a big lump under the duvet to signify his presence. Tara got up without waking him. She wasn't ready for the inevitable apology. In fact, she wasn't sure she wanted to talk to him at all today. In the shower, she let the water stream over her face and hair, trying to clear her woolly head by switching the thermostat as cold as she could bear. Finn wouldn't be able to get up, she knew. He was always the same after a night out. Then he'd apologise, give her some reason for why he'd had so much to drink ('Derry bought another bottle and we couldn't leave it.' 'The waiter just kept filling my glass.') and moan that he'd never drink again. Yeah, right.

Wrapping herself in a towel, she pushed open the bathroom door and stared angrily at the lump in the bed. The others were noisily getting ready for breakfast and her husband groaned as the noise woke him up. Only one foot was apparent, stretched out from under the duvet. Finn had very thin ankles, which was probably why they were so prone to twisting, and she looked at the narrow ankle with its covering of red gold hairs. He had oddly long toes. Tree sloth, she used to tease him. There was something vulnerable about that foot. Tara sighed. It was impossible to stay angry with Finn for too long. But Derry . . . that was another story. The whole thing was Derry's fault. Derry was the one who dragged Finn out all the time. How dare he encourage Finn to behave like an overgrown, boorish schoolboy?

'Hello, am I in trouble?' Finn sounded suitably croaky and hung over. 'I found out where we book the sleigh rides by the way. We can go any time you want.'

Tara shoved his foot out of the way and sat on the bed. 'A very long sleigh ride,' she said ominously. 'And I hope it goes over every bump in town so you feel sorry for last night.'

'I promise.' Finn's hand snaked out from under the duvet and found hers.

CHAPTER TWELVE

By mid-March, Rose decided that planning a grand ruby wedding anniversary was a trial. *Talking* about a huge party with a marquee for hordes of people was one thing. *Organising* it was another. Rose felt like a kindergarten school teacher bringing a stream of three-year-olds for a walk: she simply didn't have enough hands.

Hugh was no help at all but kept saying how much he was looking forward to the party at the end of April.

Then, Rose had discovered just how much it was to hire a marquee. 'It's unbelievably expensive,' she said, feeling stupid for believing a big tent to be a cheap party option. 'Can we afford it?' she asked Hugh, when she showed him her ballpark figure for the entire party, a figure that had made her blanch. Despite Hugh's grandiose plans, the Millers had never been rich people.

'Of course we can afford it,' said Hugh expansively. 'We've got to celebrate this one in style, Rose. Hang the expense.'

Rose had given him a long, thoughtful look that had nothing to do with money. 'We don't have to have a big party, Hugh,' she said. 'There's no need for it.'

'But there is,' Hugh insisted. 'The girls will be thrilled, they love a party. And we have been married forty years, that's quite an achievement. People will expect us to have some sort of bash.'

So a marquee had been ordered, invitations had been chosen and the guest list was one hundred and fifty and rising. Rose knew she'd have to go shopping soon to purchase a special occasion dress because, for your ruby anniversary party, you couldn't turn up in something people had seen before. Normally, Rose loved shopping. The heady feeling of power from a new outfit was better than anything the doctor could prescribe for you. But right now, she couldn't summon up any enthusiasm for it. She hadn't wanted a big party in the first place.

It was partly that the Christmas Eve party had exhausted her. Right now, her idea of the perfect anniversary party was to make an enormous shepherd's pie, bang a couple of apple tarts in the oven, invite the family over, and be done with it. But also, for reasons Rose didn't care to explore, she didn't want a huge public affair where all their friends turned up with big gifts and congratulations, telling her and Hugh how marvellous they were. After the phone call on Christmas Eve, she didn't know if she could cope with that. A big party would be almost tempting fate.

'It'll be wonderful,' Hugh kept insisting. 'I'm really looking forward to it.'

'I'm sure it will,' she replied.

She kept an eye on the arrangements, and got on with her life. She organised a painter and decorator to freshen up the main downstairs rooms. She hosted a book club evening and it coincided nicely with Hugh being in Dublin on business. The evening was a great success and even Minnie Wilson, who seemed to be getting quieter with every passing week, seemed to enjoy herself.

The next book on the club's list was an Anita Shreve novel and, a couple of weeks later, on hearing that Minnie was recovering from flu and was housebound, Rose bought two copies of it, planning to drop the spare into Minnie's that morning. She wouldn't phone, she decided: she'd just drop in casually. It wasn't the polite thing to do but Rose was concerned about Minnie and thought that if only she could get to the bottom of the problem, she could help.

Minnie opened her front door and was astonished to find

Rose Miller there, with a book and a basket of scones. Rose was just as surprised because of Minnie's appearance. She wasn't dressed. Her hair, normally carefully styled in a short bob, was unbrushed and untidy. But it wasn't the combination of dressing gown and messy hair that shocked Rose. It was the flat, miserable look in Minnie's eyes.

'Minnie, I'm so sorry for calling without phoning first,' said Rose. 'I thought you were over the flu, I just wanted to drop this book off.'

'Come in,' said Minnie, her voice as flat as her expression.

'I'll only wait for a moment,' Rose said, shutting the door behind her. 'I'm going into town again later, can I get you any groceries?'

'No. I'm fine.'

'You don't look well, have you seen the doctor?'

'No, I'm fine, really,' Minnie repeated. She sank wearily into an armchair.

Rose sat opposite her, alarm bells ringing in her head. Minnie hadn't even offered to make tea, which was totally out of character. Normally, she rushed around wildly, anxious to provide hospitality. But this dazed, careworn woman didn't have the heart or the energy to dress herself, never mind make tea.

'Is there anything I can do to help?' Rose asked gently.

'No, you are kind but no,' Minnie said. 'I'm just tired. I'm not sleeping and I keep waking up early when I do sleep, that's all. Poor Terence can't get a wink of sleep with me, and he's working so hard at the moment.'

'I see,' said Rose. She did see. For whatever reason, Minnie was clearly suffering from depression. This was no flu, it was something more. 'Maybe if I was to drive you to the doctor,' she suggested.

Minnie shook her head. 'Don't put yourself out, Rose. I'll feel better soon, I always do.'

Rose tried to think of a delicate way to say that Minnie didn't need to wait until she felt better. 'That was the old-fashioned way when you got a bit down,' she said lightly.

'People are wiser nowadays, Minnie. Sometimes your body's chemistry alters and it makes you a bit down, so there are drugs to fix that.'

'I don't believe in drugs, Rose.' Minnie sounded firm.

Rose made tea for them both, although Minnie barely touched hers.

'I'll drop in again tomorrow, will I?' Rose asked, when she'd washed the cups and put the tea things away.

'I don't mind,' said Minnie listlessly.

As Rose drove home, she wasn't thinking about Minnie. Instead, she was remembering the time when depression had enveloped her in a cloud of darkness. It was just after Holly had been born. Rose would never forget the speed and intensity with which the post-natal blues had struck. One moment, she'd been a happy young mother waiting for the birth of her third baby. The next, she was lying in a hospital bed with a screaming Holly beside her, feeling overwhelmed with the futility of life. She'd hoped things would improve when she left hospital but they didn't. It took enormous effort to summon up the energy to change her new daughter. Then, when she'd somehow managed to juggle all the once-familiar baby equipment, she'd try and rest, only for Holly to roar to be changed all over again. And how Holly had cried, endlessly, hour after hour, as if she knew that her mother could barely face looking at her. The elder girls were at school, Hugh was working all the hours that God sent, and even the doctor didn't seem aware of her situation. Anyway, people didn't talk about things like post-natal depression then. Rose had done what she always did and just got on with it. Now, she shuddered when she thought of those dark days.

At home, Rose flicked the button on the answering machine and listened to a litany of messages, nearly all relating to her ruby wedding party.

The caterer had made a mistake on the cost of the corkage: it was to be five per cent more expensive than they'd originally said.

A frantic-sounding woman from the florist's shop begged Mrs Miller to phone to clear up a tiny mess surrounding exactly *which* Saturday the ruby wedding was on. Nothing urgent, just was it the third Saturday in March (hopefully not, she said with a nervous laugh) or the third Saturday in April?

Adele, who was having builders in to do major work on her roof and was staying with Rose and Hugh for the duration, had decided she'd stay in Meadow Lodge for a week instead of just three days. 'I could do with a break,' she said heavily, adding that she'd be there by half ten on Thursday morning. 'Don't worry about me, Rose, I'll look after myself. I don't want any fuss.'

Rose closed her eyes and rubbed her temples to make the dull ache go away. The idea of Adele not wanting any fuss was a contradiction in terms. Adele couldn't make a cup of coffee without fuss. A week-long stay would mean the sort of organisation required for a royal visit. Adele ran her own home like a very spartan hotel with specific hours for every meal and a habit of changing the sheets every day. Seven days of Adele would stretch both the linen cupboard and the washer-dryer to breaking point. That wasn't even mentioning how it would stretch Rose's nerves.

Hugh had phoned to say he had a meeting which might run late and not to bother keeping dinner for him. 'I'll grab a toasted sandwich in the pub before the meeting,' he said, as if he was doing her a big favour. Rose wondered if Hugh ever realised that plans for dinner didn't begin at six in the evening. Oh well, she'd still have to cook the chicken she'd defrosted earlier. They could have it cold the following evening.

The last call was silent. Rose didn't bother to strain to hear some telltale background noise. She made a note to phone the florist and the caterer later, then she wiped the messages from the machine.

The following day, Rose made up her mind. She made a phone call to the doctor's surgery, then drove into Kinvarra quickly, not seeing the beauty of the town as she manoeuvred the car through the busy Wednesday morning traffic.

Today, the mid-week market was set up in St Martin's Square and the parking was particularly bad as everyone and their granny recklessly abandoned their cars at oblique angles in order to buy cheap farm produce. Rose remembered a time when the market had actually sold livestock, but now it was a less rural affair where farmers sold vegetables, eggs, fruit and honey, and where local crafts people set up stalls selling pottery and knick-knacks. Rose quite liked the assorted junk of the bric à brac stalls and often looked to see if there were any old perfume bottles for Stella's growing collection. But today she had a mission that had nothing to do with the market. She'd decided to talk to the doctor and find out what she should do about Minnie Wilson. Rose didn't want to interfere and had never in her life stuck her nose quite so much in anyone's business, but she was too worried about Minnie to do nothing.

She parked in the big supermarket car park and then walked along briskly until she came to one of the town's backstreets where a big redbrick house took pride of place. Rose pushed open the green front door and stepped in as she had done many times before.

'Good morning, Helen,' she said to the receptionist, a girl who'd been in school with Holly. 'I've an appointment with Dr Reshma.'

'I'm afraid Dr Reshma had to go to Dublin urgently,' Helen replied, then whispered, 'his wife's father again. The poor man is still clinging onto life.'

Rose smiled at this proof that Kinvarra still kept its gossipy village mentality, even though the inhabitants bravely insisted that you could live an anonymous life there and that people weren't interested in everybody else's business.

'Dr Collins is away in Galway, so the new doctor is taking Dr Reshma's patients,' Helen added. 'Dr Zeigler. She's very nice.'

Rose hesitated. If she refused to see the nice new doctor,

it would imply that she was one of the town's fuddy duddies who wouldn't have so much as a boil lanced if Dr Reshma or Dr Collins weren't in charge of the lancing. But she'd actually made the appointment with the doctor for advice rather than for any medical reason. She'd hoped that wise Dr Reshma could tell her what to do. She looked quickly round the reception area and saw that it was empty. Most days, there were at least six people waiting. Evidently nobody else wanted to make do with poor Dr Zeigler.

'Of course I'll see the new doctor, Helen,' said Rose.

Helen allowed herself to breathe out with relief. 'I'll show you in,' she beamed, thankful that at least one patient wasn't going to shame Kinvarra by insisting on being sick only on Dr Reshma's time.

Dr Zeigler couldn't have been older than Holly. Maybe twenty-seven at the most, Rose thought as she settled down on the seat beside the doctor's desk. She was freckled, with mousy hair, and if Rose had been asked to guess her profession, she'd have said 'student'.

'What can I do for you, Mrs Miller?' the doctor said.

'I haven't come for any actual treatment,' Rose began.

The doctor's eyebrows moved up a fraction.

'I've come for advice. You see, I think this friend of mine is suffering from depression and I wanted to ask what to do.'

The doctor's expression changed subtly and she moved forwards in her chair, leaning so that she'd halved the distance between them. 'This friend,' she said kindly, 'has she suffered from depression before?'

Rose smiled. 'It's not me. Honestly.'

'Are you sure?'

'Yes. I've never been depressed.' Rose didn't consider this to be a lie, precisely. She'd never told anyone how she'd felt when Holly was a baby and she wasn't going to start now.

'Lucky you.' The young doctor's face was bland.

'This is a friend of mine and I'm worried about her,' Rose said. Without giving Minnie's name, she described her general condition and listlessness. 'Doesn't that sound like depression?' she said.

'It could be,' Dr Zeigler replied. 'But there's very little I can do for her unless she comes to visit me.'

'I suppose.' Rose wished now she'd waited for Dr Reshma, who'd have been more understanding and who would have come up with some plan for meeting Minnie and encouraging her to come to the surgery. This doctor plainly thought Rose was nothing but a well-meaning busybody. Perhaps she thought Rose's actions weren't even well-meaning.

'I've wasted enough of your time,' Rose said, getting up. 'Sorry. I'll try and get my friend to come here.'

'You do that,' Dr Zeigler said and went back to her files.

Rose walked slowly towards the market, feeling useless and a bit stupid. Of course, Minnie had to go to the doctor's herself. What had Rose been thinking? Trying to sort out the world's problems as usual, when she couldn't even sort out her own. She was going to have to make Minnie go to the doctor's. She didn't know how, but she was going to do it, she vowed. As she stopped at the pedestrian lights to cross the road, she realised that she was standing in front of Hugh's office. It was half twelve, early enough to meet Hugh before he left for his customary lunch in The Angler's Rest. Suddenly, Rose wanted to see him and tell him about her morning. Hugh would know the right thing to say. He'd cheer her up, tell her she was wise after all, and point out that young doctors didn't understand the needs of a community the way old Dr Reshma did.

'Mrs Miller!' gasped Hugh's assistant when Rose peeped round the door of her office.

'Hello, Suzanna, I thought I'd surprise Mr Miller by taking him to lunch.'

Suzanna's eyes widened dramatically. 'He's gone already,' she said nervously. 'I'm so sorry you missed him. I'll tell him you called.'

'I could catch up with him,' Rose said. 'Has he gone with a client?'

'No, er yes. Well, yes.'

For a brief moment, Rose wondered if Suzanna was always this hyper. Hugh hated nervy people.

'Never mind,' Rose said, 'tell him I'll see him tonight.'

She set off again, this time determined to take a quick trip round the market in case she spotted something for Stella. Occasionally, she found real gems, like the square bottle with the silver top which Stella had adored.

It was nearly two when she began her walk back to the car, weighed down with a dozen free range eggs from the market and lamb cutlets from the butchers. She'd wandered round the market for ages, and had a cup of coffee and a sandwich with a neighbour she'd bumped into. Feeling guilty for idling round town when the house needed a final tidy up before Adele's visit, Rose took the short cut down a winding street to the car park. At the bottom of the lane was the town's latest restaurant, an intimate little French brasserie set on the corner, with big windows looking out onto the lane and the main street. She and Hugh hadn't been to it yet and Rose looked in the big picture window as she passed, so she could decide if she liked the look of it or not. She'd always liked low lighting in restaurants, especially nowadays, as she joked to the girls. Candlelight was more flattering to older faces than any amount of facelifts.

This restaurant was suitably dark. It looked nice, Rose thought, as she emerged from the lane onto the street beside the shopping centre car park. She stopped to look right and left before crossing the road, then took a sharp, shallow breath as she noticed a couple leaving the restaurant. One of them was Hugh in the grey suit he'd gone off in that morning, and he was smiling down at his female companion in an intimate manner. Rose didn't recognise her, she was petite and red-haired and about ten years her junior. And she was staring up at Rose's husband in a way that suggested their lunchtime conversation had involved more than legal matters. There could be no mistaking that look. Or the one Hugh was giving back. Cautiously, Hugh pecked the woman on the cheek; a careful gesture obviously made so that any observers would think they were friends only. But Rose wasn't any old observer. She'd known Hugh for over forty years and she knew his every nuance intimately. She'd only seen Hugh look at one person in that way: herself.

Some presence of mind made her dash into the shop beside her, not caring that she was hardly the sort of customer that Guyz fashions had in mind. Her hands shook as she pretended to rifle through shirts near the window, while she peered out to see where Hugh and the woman were headed. Hugh must have turned up the lane back to his office, but Rose was perfectly placed to watch the woman walk past Guyz, her every delighted step the movement of a woman who'd just had an expensive lunch with a man she found fascinating. Rose watched until the woman was long gone, then she moved woodenly towards the door. Deep inside her, she'd been expecting this ever since Christmas Eve. It had just been a matter of time.

Somehow, she got to her car and sat in it, shell-shocked, and oblivious to the driver who'd seen her get into the car and wanted her parking space. Eventually, he gave up and drove off to look elsewhere. Rose sat there and stared blankly out of the window.

She'd known about the affairs. There had been three, until now, anyhow. It was hard not to know in a place like Kin-varra. There was always somebody prepared to mention that they'd seen Hugh having dinner with a person they didn't recognise, and . . . well, they'd uncomfortably add that they thought Rose should know. At this point, Rose would smile and say she knew all about it; that Hugh had been at dinner with an old friend of the family and she'd have gone along herself that evening if she hadn't had a cold. Her calm self-possession generally wrong-footed even the most concerned messenger.

Clearly if Rose knew about the tête-à-tête in the restaurant fifty miles from Kinvarra, everything must be above board. And anyhow, who would want to cheat on the lovely Rose Miller?

But Rose had known each time, without the outside information. She wasn't one of those women who lived in a cosy world of their own, the ones who bleated that it was all a big shock. How on earth could they not know, she wondered? She'd known intuitively and knowing was her defence. And her armour. She knew that Hugh would never want to leave the girls because he was devoted to them. It was up to her to protect her children and she had, by saying nothing.

A loud buzzing noise shocked her into alertness. Her mobile phone. Rose had forgotten she had it with her. She still hadn't assimilated this modern convenience into her life. She reached into her handbag, fished out the phone and looked at the name flashing in dark green on the little screen. 'Stella.'

'Hi, Mum,' said her oldest daughter brightly. 'I've got an idea, can you talk?'

'Yes,' said Rose automatically.

'We've had this brilliant idea for you and Dad for your anniversary present. A weekend in Paris! Nick and I will tell you all the wonderful places to go to when we get back but it would be the perfect present from Holly, Tara and me. What do you think?'

Rose laughed mirthlessly. 'Darling, that's a very kind idea but I don't think so.'

'Mum, we'd love to do it for you both; please think about it.'

Rose closed her eyes and searched her confused mind for an excuse. 'Dad's so busy right now, it would be impossible,' she said. 'I don't think we could manage it. Stella, can I phone you back later?' she added lamely.

'Of course, Mum. Call me tonight at home. Bye.'

Rose hit the off button and turned her key in the ignition.

If she was at home, she might be able to think about it all more clearly. She couldn't fall apart in the supermarket car park.

CHAPTER THIRTEEN

It was a month since her father's birthday lunch in Kinvarra and Kenny and Joan's attempts to find a man for Holly had met a hitch: Joan thought that speed dating was the answer and Kenny was opposed to the idea.

'You can't meet an ideal partner at some gimmicky night out,' he insisted. 'We might as well send Holly to a football match and tell her to pick the first person who winks at her.'

'I'd prefer to go to a football match,' said Holly miserably.

But Joan was having none of it, which was how she and Holly ended up in the Purple Mosquito at eight o'clock on a rainy Thursday evening along with thirty-eight other people who'd each handed over €20 to be part of the Purple Mosquito's Speed Dating Extravaganza (free cocktail included).

'Stop shaking,' muttered Joan under her breath.

'How can I stop shaking?' said Holly. 'I'm terrified. I don't know what I'm doing here. I don't like dating, full stop, never mind speed dating.'

The customers were sitting at small tables ranged around the club's minuscule stage and they'd each just been given a card with a number on it, a pencil and piece of A-4 paper. Holly's number was six. She wondered what this meant. She had to go on dates with six men, one after another? She had to go on a date with six men at the same time? She'd been filmed when she entered the club and she'd been judged as rating six out of ten, or worse, six out of 100? Who knew?

'Take deep breaths,' hissed Joan. Joan was number eighteen.

Holly closed her eyes and took a deep breath. With any luck, when she opened her eyes she'd discover this was all a dream and she'd be on her couch at home, with the telly comfortably on in the background and no scary woman stomping around in thigh-high pink suede boots . . .

'Wakey wakey!'

Holly sat bolt upright and opened her eyes. The scary woman in pink suede was still there and staring, well, glaring, at Holly who was sitting near the front, thanks to Joan. Holly would have hidden down the back given a choice.

'I hope we're not boring you,' cooed the woman, insofar as it was possible to coo with half a tonne of panstick welded to her face. Miss Mindy, the evening's compère and the club manager, went for the make-up-as-armour approach. Her maquillage would stop a bullet.

Holly shook her head mutely and Miss Mindy sashayed off to continue explaining the rules.

'She's the ugliest drag queen I've ever seen,' whispered Joan.

'She's not a drag queen,' hissed another voice in disgust. 'She's a woman. Look at those legs. Criminal!'

Despite her nerves, Holly burst into giggles and earned herself another glare from Miss Mindy.

The Purple Mosquito was a cutting-edge club much favoured by trendy fashionistas, models, actors, drag queens and a select crew of men keen to discuss the difficulty of getting sheer tights in extra large. Holly hadn't been keen on the idea in the first place, but to add to the sense of unreality, the speed dating night was packed into the early part of the evening, while Miss Drag De Luxe – a beauty contest for drag queens, no heckling allowed – was the late-night attraction. Consequently, the dating arena was surrounded by drag queens in various stages of make-up-lessness. Holly had never seen so many beautiful, long legs in her life. There was also a lot of PVC clothing and an abundance of flowing, glossy hair straight out of a L'Oréal commercial.

'We've given you each a number and that's to tell you which table to go to first,' said Miss Mindy to the crowd of people who were watching with bated breath. 'We'll bang the first gong and you talk, then when the second gong goes, the woman gets up and goes to the next table but the man stays put. Right?'

The crowd nodded. Apart from a group of rowdy young men at a table clogged with beer bottles, they were all too nervous to speak.

'The girl at number one goes to table number two, and so on. You make notes in your sheet of paper.'

Holly looked anxiously down at her piece of paper.

'And to loosen us all up, the speed dating club will be providing a free cocktail from the list for all the daters.'

This merited a nervous round of applause but Holly knew it would take more than a free cocktail to make her ready for this demented idea. A general anaesthetic might have had a hope.

If only Joan had never noticed the Purple Mosquito's flier stuck to the notice board in college.

'Look,' she'd said brandishing it triumphantly at Holly, 'this sounds brilliant, Holls. Listen to this: "Can't find the one of your dreams and too lazy to chat up another frog? Try the Purple Mosquito's Speed Dating Nite, hosted by Miss Mindy, €20 only. Twenty couples, five minutes each person, and a guaranteed night of fun and frolics. Book early to avoid disappointment. Gay night Tuesday, straight night Thursday."'

'We can't go to that,' Holly said, horrified. Even five minutes talking to someone was too long for her. What would she say to a whole series of men? 'You go, Joan. Count me out.'

'I've rung already and booked, we're both going.'

It was all very well for Joan, who was used to cool clubs and strange people, but Holly knew she was the worst person in the world for a night of talking to strangers.

'I'm not going,' she finally announced to Joan early on

the Thursday evening in question. 'I know you've booked but I'm too nervous.'

Joan looked outraged.

'You're always telling me to stand up for myself,' Holly protested.

'Not to me,' said Joan, shocked. 'You're coming, that's final.'

The Mosquito was all urban cool, with minimalist decor and deeply uncomfortable backless cube seating which looked hip but was actually murderous on the lower back. Still, the whole effect was ultra stylish, Holly thought, looking around. If she hadn't been there for the speed dating thing, she might enjoy herself.

On stage, Miss Mindy banged a gong and Holly jumped in her seat.

'Just testing! Everyone to their tables.'

'Good luck!' said Joan happily as she rushed off eagerly to table eighteen. Holly hastily picked up her shoulder bag and a crash of glass told her she'd managed to knock something off a table.

'It's alright, it was empty,' said a girl at the next table, picking up the remains of a beer bottle from the floor.

'Sorry,' mumbled Holly, her cheeks burning.

A waitress ambled over and surveyed the damage.

'Sorry,' said Holly again.

She turned and somehow banged into the table she and Joan had been sitting at, but just in time, she grabbed the ashtray before it trundled to the floor. 'Sorry,' she said to nobody in particular.

Table six. Where was it? Still bright red, Holly peered round the gloom. In her confusion, she just couldn't see table six. Everyone else seemed to be sitting down in pairs except ... Just in time, she spotted a guy sitting on his own. That had to be six. She rushed forward, slipped between the seats, and landed heavily on the empty chair.

A lurid blue drink with a cocktail umbrella and a giant bit of pineapple in it sat in front of her. Without actually meeting the eyes of the guy opposite, Holly looked up enough to establish that he had a blue cocktail too.

'Is this mine?' she whispered.

'Yeah,' he said.

On stage, Miss Mindy banged the gong enthusiastically. 'The first five minutes have begun!' she shrieked.

All at once, the buzz of frantic conversation began. It sounded like a swarm of locusts droning over a crop field. Holly and her date looked around them in awe, then looked guiltily at each other.

He was pale and freckly and was blinking at a rate that meant he either had a speck of dust lodged in both eyes or was very, very nervous.

He took a huge gulp of his cocktail, looked down at his bit of paper and began to curl the corner up in an obsessive way that Holly recognised as classic shy behaviour. Her stomach lurched in anxiety. He was clearly even shyer than she was and therefore, the onus was on her to talk to him because that was the polite thing to do. But whatever was she going to say? She took a gulp of her drink. It tasted like the sort of thing Joan concocted out of the dregs of bottles when they had no money for decent wine.

'Did you get dragged along by your friends too?' she asked suddenly.

'Yeah.' The look of gratitude on his face made Holly glad she'd forced herself to speak.

'Me too. It was my friend's idea. She's over there.'

They both looked over to where Joan was sitting with a handsome blond guy who was wearing a leather jacket. Joan was gesticulating wildly with one hand and twirling a strand of her black hair with the other, while her date looked raptly on with his mouth open. Holly, who'd seen Joan's technique before, knew that her next move would be to place one hand on the guy's arm, gaze deeply into his eyes and say something along the lines of 'You're incredible, you know that?' This didn't always work but Joan always did it. She'd seen it in a film and firmly believed that it would be successful eventually.

Holly turned back to her date. She better get some information before the gong went. She didn't want Miss Mindy to beat her up for not going along with the rules. Miss Mindy looked like she could stand in for her own bouncers if the need arose.

'What's your name?' Holly asked the guy.

'Ron.'

'I'm Holly. I didn't want to be here either but we can pretend, can't we?' she said lightly. It was quite an experience for her to be the outgoing one in any conversation.

Ron nodded.

Holly wrote his name down.

'What do you do, Ron?' she asked in her newly-acquired chatty voice. She took another slurp of cocktail while she was waiting.

'I'm at college,' he said, looking down at his bit of paper.

Holly waited for him to say what he was studying but he didn't. For a brief moment, she wondered was *she* this difficult to talk to? Did other people cast around wildly for conversational gambits that would work? Making conversation with someone as painfully shy as Ron was hard going.

Holly vowed that would change. Buoyed up by this self-improving decision, she tried again.

'I work in Lee's Department Store,' she said.

Ron kept looking at his bit of paper.

'In the children's department.'

Still no answer.

'What do you study?' she asked in desperation.

The gong banged. Ron still wasn't talking. The time was up.

'Nice to meet you,' said Holly and got up. She brought her drink with her, being very careful not to spill it as she moved to table seven. She needed it.

'Hi,' said her new date. He wasn't bad looking, she realised, dark hair, dark eyes, a nice shirt with a few buttons open to reveal a bit of chest hair, a laid-back attitude to him. He was perhaps two or three years younger than she was. Cute. From table nineteen, Joan gave her a thumbs up signal.

Holly sat down and put her glass on the table carefully. This guy was definitely one of the rowdy gang of students. They were probably out for a night of fun, they weren't seriously looking for dates. Now that she was determined to talk, she could enjoy herself too.

'Hi, I'm Holly. This is a bit of fun, isn't it?' she said brightly, astonished at her own daring.

'I'm Carl and yeah, it's great fun,' said the guy, baring his teeth in a wolfish grin. 'So, you're looking for a man, Holly?'

'What?' said Holly.

'A man, I said are you looking for a man, or are you here for some fun?'

He was drunk, Holly realised.

'Fun, really,' she said. 'My friend and I came here for a laugh.'

'You could have a laugh *and* some fun,' Carl said meaningfully. He reached under the table and gave Holly's leg a suggestive grope.

She drew back in shock and just managed not to spill her drink.

'We're here to talk,' she gasped.

He looked fed up at this. 'Why do all girls want to talk?' he grumbled. 'It's boring. Talk, talk, talk. That's all they do.'

'So what do you study?' asked Holly, determined to interrupt his moan.

'How did you know I'm a student?' Carl demanded.

'You're here with a gang and you all look like students,' she said. 'Don't tell me, you're studying brain surgery.'

'Very funny,' slurred Carl.

Holly beamed back at him. She'd done it. She'd been talkative and she'd made a joke! So, she'd managed it because the people involved were very shy and very drunk, but it was a start.

'God,' Carl said, staring mesmerised at her chest. 'You've a great pair of tits.'

Holly's eyes grew wide. For an instant, she thought of flinging the rest of her cocktail all over his face. But cocktail-throwing was for brave women. Tara would probably do it without a second thought. Joan would possibly land him a punch. She'd done a bit of kick boxing.

But what was the point? Carl was plastered

'If you don't want me to get Miss Mindy over here to tell her what you've just said to me, shut up and be polite!' she said calmly.

It was his turn to widen his eyes. Miss Mindy scared everyone.

'Very sorry,' he said drunkenly.

At the next table on Holly's dating odyssey, the man had disappeared, leaving his piece of paper behind.

'He's gone to the loo,' said Miss Mindy, swooping like a giant flamingo. 'How are you getting on, love?'

Holly looked down at her list. She'd written: *Ron, v quiet. Carl, v drunk.* She had no phone numbers or dates set up, although her boobs had been praised. She didn't know whether Miss Mindy would see this as a negative or a positive reaction.

'Fine,' Holly said. 'I've been getting on fine although it's not what I expected.'

Miss Mindy raised her eyes to heaven. 'The story of my life, love.'

By ten, Holly had met nineteen men (one of the contestants had gone home) and knew for a fact that she hadn't met the love of her life.

The best had been a sturdy guy in his early thirties who worked in a lab and told jokes through the entire five minutes, which was funny, but struck Holly as obsessive shy behaviour under another guise.

'How can you tell you're talking to an extrovert lab researcher?' he asked.

'Don't know.'

223

'He looks at *your* shoes when he's talking to you.'

'You're a panic,' Holly said warmly to him, 'I bet all your friends love you coming out with them and making them laugh.'

He looked sad. 'That's the problem, Holly. I have lots of *friends*, but nothing more, no special someone.'

'How did you get on?' Joan asked her when it was all over.

'It was different,' said Holly diplomatically. After all, Joan had thought it was a great way for a shy woman to meet men.

'But you didn't meet anyone?'

'No. I did get told that I had a great pair of tits, though.'

'Says who?' Joan looked shocked.

'Carl.' Holly pointed him out. 'I was tempted to throw my drink over him.'

'Oh, plastered student boy.' Joan dismissed him. 'Just as well you didn't. It would have been a waste of drink,' she added sagely. 'Listen, I might stay and have a drink with one of the guys I met.'

Holly grinned at her friend. 'Don't tell me, the leather jacket guy. He was nice.'

'Becks. That's not his real name, but he's an ace footballer,' Joan said, looking positively dreamy.

'Go, girl!' said Holly.

'You don't mind walking home on your own, do you?'

'Don't worry about me, I'm a big girl. Literally,' Holly said ruefully. 'No mugger in his right mind would try and steal my handbag.'

When Holly walked up the path to the house half an hour later, their new neighbour, Tom, was dragging a bin liner out the front door ready for the next morning's refuse collection. Even though it was late, he'd obviously just got home from work because he was wearing a shirt and tie, which he'd tugged loose from its knot. He looked different in work clothes; up to now Holly had seen him loping round in jeans and sweatshirts. He looked older and more serious in a collar and tie.

'Hi,' said Holly.

'Hi yourself,' he said, looking pleased to see her. 'How are you?'

Holly thought about it. 'Great. I should be terrible because I've had an awful evening, but I'm not.' She'd made a breakthrough of sorts, after all. She'd made herself face her shyness in the scariest way and she'd managed it.

'That's good,' said Tom.

They walked companionably into the house and up the stairs.

'Do you fancy a cup of coffee?' said Tom suddenly.

'Lovely,' said Holly.

'You can tell me about your awful evening,' he added.

Holly smiled at him. It was funny, really, because she didn't know Tom at all well but she felt comfortable with him. She wasn't shy or tongue-tied in his presence. He was just Tom, the friendly giant who lived upstairs. He didn't know many people and needed new friends. Kenny had brought Tom out for a drink and came back with the news that Tom wasn't gay but was a decent bloke, with a girlfriend back in Cork.

'All the best ones are straight,' Kenny had said mournfully.

Since then, Kenny, Joan and Holly had included Tom in some of their nights out and Holly had found their laid-back new neighbour surprisingly easy to talk to. She didn't need to make an effort to sparkle with Tom.

He pushed open the door to his flat and stood back to let Holly in first. His flat was like Joan and Kenny's: bigger than hers with two bedrooms and a tiny balcony.

'It's nice,' she said, looking around.

Tom had decent furniture, including chairs and a squashy brown leather couch that looked as if it came from Habitat. Everything was very neat and spotlessly clean but it wasn't exactly homey. Holly itched to give it more life.

'Did you have to do much with it?' she said.

'Just a bit of paint. The landlord got very upset when I said I wanted to change a few things. He thought I expected him to pay for it.'

Holly grinned. 'He likes the idea of an investment which doesn't involve any actual investing. The banisters are death traps but he won't replace them. Still, the rent's not too bad.'

Tom went into the kitchenette to make the coffee.

'I own a flat in Cork and I'm renting it out for six months, then I'll make a decision about buying in Dublin.'

Holly wandered happily, admiring a few photos in wooden frames. The biggest one was a shot of a pretty blonde girl with a swathe of blue velvet wrapped artfully around creamy shoulders. Gauzy filters and perfect make-up on the baby-blue eyes made Holly think it was one of those studio shots where women got glamorous make-overs in order to have a set of fabulous photos of themselves for their husbands or boyfriends.

'That's my girlfriend, Caroline,' said Tom, carrying two mugs and a pot of coffee into the room. 'She lives in Cork. She's going to see how I get on here and if everything works out here, she'll move to Dublin too. Caroline's a management consultant and she says she wouldn't have any trouble getting a job here.'

'She looks lovely,' said Holly. 'Next time she's here, you must introduce us to her. We'll all have to go out and she'll be happy knowing that you've got friends here.'

Tom grinned his sweet, even-tempered grin. 'That's great of you. I don't know many people here, for sure. Caroline's very different. She's very independent and if she was in my place, she'd know everyone in the entire area by now and she'd never be home.'

'Opposites attract,' said Holly.

'True.'

They drank their coffee in companionable silence. Holly didn't feel anxious about the lack of conversation. Somehow, there was no need to worry about saying something with Tom, which was comforting.

'Tell me about this awful evening you had.'

He laughed when she told him about the drunken Carl (she left out the comment about her boobs) and about Miss Mindy, who out-dragged the drag queens.

'I'd have liked to stay and watch Miss Drag De Luxe but it wasn't going to start for ages.'

'Were there any guys there you're going to meet again?' Tom looked down into his mug.

'No.' Holly was blithe about it. 'Joan and Kenny have this plan to set me up with a man and this was the first part of the plan. Well, Joan's part. Kenny said it would be a disaster. He's plotting some sort of blind date for me.'

'Do you think blind dates work?' asked Tom.

'Not in my experience,' Holly replied. 'But then my experience is limited to a blind date set up for my debs dance when my friend Donna's brother volunteered a college friend of his.'

In her mind, Holly could still see herself in her cream dress, looking like a meringue on legs because those were her chubby days, with her date for the evening beside her, a short, wiry young man named Liam who could have doubled for a cocktail stick. Together, they looked like the odd couple. Her original date had been Richie, her first love, who'd dumped her just before her debs, leaving her utterly heartbroken.

Somehow, she didn't want to tell Tom about that.

'It wasn't a success,' was all she said.

'Caroline would love somewhere like the Purple Mosquito,' Tom said, adroitly changing the subject. 'She loves nightlife and clubs, I'm a bit of a boring git and like to stay at home more,' he added apologetically.

'That's it. Joan, Kenny and I will bring you both out when Caroline comes to stay,' Holly said firmly. 'We'll paint the town red. Well, pale pink anyway.'

She finished her coffee and got purposefully to her feet. 'I'm off to bed, Tom,' she said. 'Thanks for the coffee.'

'No, thank *you*,' he replied. He opened the front door for her. 'I needed a bit of company.'

'Any time,' she said cheerily, dancing downstairs to her floor. 'Any time.'

He was nice, Holly sighed, as she locked her own flat door. A decent man who clearly loved his girlfriend. Lucky Caroline.

'I told you it wouldn't work out.' Kenny pointed out as he, Holly and Joan trooped out of Windmill Terrace for a Sunday morning brunch in their favourite café down the road. 'You can't expect people to bond in five minutes.'

'*I* met a nice guy,' argued Joan.

'We're not trying to find a nice guy for you,' Kenny said in exasperation. 'We're trying to keep you away from men. You're supposed to be working on your final year collection, not trolloping around like a ho.'

At the gate, the three of them waited for Tom. It was an unusually warm day and the sense of summer shimmered in the air. Holly stuck her sunglasses on, glad that she'd worn a skimpy T-shirt under her denim jacket. Perhaps they could sit at one of the outside tables for their brunch.

'Well, what's your plan, Smarty Pants?' asked Joan, not even bothering to react to being called a ho.

'Sorry I'm late,' said Tom, slamming the front door behind him. 'Overslept.'

'Hi,' said Holly, smiling sweetly up at him. Tom's spiky hair stood up at odd angles where he'd slept on it and he'd obviously thrown himself into his clothes at high speed because he was wearing a sweatshirt that was inside out.

They walked slowly down the road with Kenny and Joan arguing over blind dates versus speed dating.

'They're still trying to set you up, huh?' Tom asked Holly as they meandered along behind the other two.

'Yes, they've run through all their friends and acquaintances and have come up with nothing so far. Coco the Clown is about the only person they *haven't* thought of.'

Tom laughed. 'They should leave you alone. You can't force love.'

'My sentiments exactly,' she murmured, 'but they've got their hearts set on this.'

'You're gorgeous anyhow, you don't need anyone helping you out.'

Holly blushed a deep crimson and said nothing. She wished she knew how to accept compliments. Tom was being kind, that was all. And the nice thing was, he clearly thought Kenny and Joan's attempts to fix Holly up with someone was a bit of fun. He didn't see her as a hopeless case who'd never get a man on her own. This gave her confidence.

At the café, there was one table left outside and Joan and Kenny instantly claimed it, dark glasses and fashionably bored expressions at the ready.

'I'll go in and order,' Holly volunteered. 'What's everyone having?'

When she got back, Kenny was trying to establish how Tom had met Caroline.

'Well, we knew each other for years because we had some of the same friends,' Tom explained, 'I'd noticed her but she didn't really seem to notice me until a gang of us went to the Kilkenny comedy festival and we hit it off. We stayed an extra night in Kilkenny and . . .' He grinned. 'Do you want me to draw you a diagram?'

'Yes,' said Kenny gravely.

'Do you know anyone who met on a blind date?' Joan interrupted.

'No,' admitted Tom.

'My cousin met a man on a blind date and they went out for six years,' Kenny said.

'You mean they're not still going out?' Joan asked.

'No, but that's not the point,' Kenny insisted. 'They'd never have met if someone hadn't set them up.'

'Please, no more blind dating stories,' begged Holly as the coffee arrived.

'OK, truce,' said Kenny. 'I've got two double tickets to a nightclub launch next week. We're going. Would you like to come too, Tom?'

'Sure,' said Tom easily.

'And we can discuss if you have any delectable friends who'd kill to go out with a fabulous girl like Holly,' Kenny continued.

'Kenny!' groaned Holly.

'You're just not meeting the right guys, Holls,' Kenny protested. 'You need to broaden your circle of men friends and you'll meet Mr Right.'

'Yeah, Mr Always Right if he's anything like you,' put in Joan cheekily.

CHAPTER FOURTEEN

Hazel had never seen Stella consumed with such excitement. For her weekend in Paris with Nick at the end of March, Stella had first made an enormous list of possible outfits, covering every eventuality from museum-going to Left-Bank-meandering. Secondly, Stella had actually got her nails manicured, an unheard-of development from a woman who'd never had either the time or the spare cash for trips to beauty salons.

Finally, Stella had drawn up a fail-safe plan regarding Amelia, listing what action Hazel should take if there was any hitch regarding picking up Amelia from school and delivering her into her Aunt Tara's capable hands. The plan ran to two typed pages, a paean to maternal guilt.

'Is there a hair shirt on that holiday clothes list?' Hazel inquired wickedly.

Stella, engrossed in her Taking Care of Amelia plan and nibbling a bit of just-manicured finger, didn't hear her. 'Now, I think that's everything,' she said seriously. 'Will you look and see if I've left anything out?'

It was the evening before Stella and Nick were to leave for Paris. Hazel and Stella were in Hazel's kitchen with a pot of tea brewing, while Amelia, Becky and Shona were sitting in the conservatory beyond the kitchen, pretending to do their homework. They were supposed to be reading, but Hazel could see that they were, in fact, whispering and giggling, casting furtive glances at their mothers occasionally to see if they were in trouble, and scribbling little notes to each other in coloured metallic pens. Metallic pens were big that year and Hazel was fed up trying to scrub the ink out of clothing.

'You don't mind Tara phoning you if she's worried about something, do you?' Stella asked.

'Tara is not going to have anything to worry about,' interrupted Hazel. 'She's perfectly capable of looking after Amelia. In fact, I've a good mind to drop Shona and Becky off with her, and let her take care of them too. They've been moaning all week that their father and I never go away and let them have any fun.'

Stella nodded absently and ran a finger over her list again. She'd included the French hotel phone and fax number, along with Nick's mobile number in case there was any problem. Amelia's doctor's number was there too and the surgery opening times, just in case. Allergies! She'd better write that Amelia wasn't allergic to anything but had had chickenpox.

Hazel watched, shaking her head. The way she was going, Stella would be too entangled in guilt to enjoy the weekend. It was time to be firm.

'Stell, giving birth does not mean you sign a contract stating you will never have fun ever again. Motherhood and weekends away are not mutually exclusive. You're going to Paris for three days, you're not abandoning Amelia by the side of a motorway with a note around her neck saying "Can somebody please look after this seven-year-old."'

'I know, but . . .'

'No buts!' Hazel said loudly. 'Paris in the springtime with a nice man, you have to enjoy yourself.'

Stella allowed herself to smile.

'Besides, Amelia can't wait to spend a weekend with Tara and Finn. She's been talking about it all week.'

'Has she?' said Stella.

'Yes, she'll have a lovely time. It'll be good for her to have a weekend away from you. Children need a break from their parents occasionally.' Hazel cast a quick glance at the threesome in the conservatory where all pretence of home-work had stopped. 'And parents need a break too.'

'You sound like my mother,' Stella pointed out. 'She phoned me yesterday to remind me to pack a nice nightie. "Not one of those oversized T-shirts," she said. You know you're a grown-up when your mother refers to your sex life so blithely,' she added ruefully.

'Your mother is right.' Hazel took Stella's notepad. 'Where's the clothes list? I hope there's sexy undies there too.'

Stella grinned but said nothing. Her mother and Hazel both clearly thought that she was nervous as a kitten at the idea of sharing a bed with Nick Cavaletto. Quite how they'd come to this conclusion, she didn't know, but they were wrong. Once Stella made up her mind to do something, she did it with all her heart. She wasn't planning to leap on top of Nick like a sex-starved maniac as soon as they arrived in their hotel bedroom, but she didn't plan to act the ingénue either. Kissing Nick had reawakened long-forgotten passion in Stella. The week before in Stella's house, when his fingers had moved seductively over the silk of her shirt, to linger on the curve of her breasts, Stella hadn't wanted to stop. But Nick had pulled away gently.

'We should do this properly,' he said, his breath heavy, 'not fumbling on the couch like a couple of kids.'

Stella nodded. When he'd gone, she went through her underwear drawers and found them wanting. The trip to Paris would necessitate a trip to the shops for knickers, and not serviceable plain ones, either.

She knew that if Hazel and Rose could see her newly purchased lingerie, they'd be very surprised indeed.

Amelia was so excited over spending the weekend with her Aunty Tara and Uncle Finn, that Stella was ashamed to admit to feeling slightly jealous. At no point during the packing of her bag had Amelia seemed the slightest bit sad.

'I hope you won't miss Mummy too much,' Stella said anxiously.

'I won't,' said Amelia happily. 'Nick said you and me and him could go somewhere away soon. Not Disneyland. But somewhere with a swimming pool and slides and stuff.' Amelia stuffed her pencil case into the already jammed rucksack.

Stella had to laugh. Her mother had been so right: children were resilient. Stella had agonised over introducing Amelia to Nick and when she had, they'd taken to each other like old friends.

The week after Hugh's birthday lunch in Kinvarra, Stella had gently told Amelia that Mummy had a new friend and she'd like Amelia to meet him.

'He's a special friend and his name is Nick and I hope you're going to like him,' Stella said. 'I like him an awful lot but because you're my special girl, I want you to like him too . . .'

'OK,' said Amelia cheerily.

'He's coming to dinner on Wednesday.'

A thoughtful look came into Amelia's little face and she screwed her nose up questioningly.

This is it, thought Stella tensely, waiting for some poignant question about how could she have anyone else special in her life when she had Amelia? Children were so sensitive, this could be a huge mistake. Should she have introduced the idea of Nick more gently?

'Can I stay up late then?' asked Amelia.

A huge peal of laughter escaped from her mother. Stella scooped Amelia up in a hug. 'Of course you can, just this once.'

On the day that Nick was coming to dinner, Stella and Hazel discussed how Amelia was coping with the introduction of this new figure into her life.

Stella was anxious in case Amelia didn't like the idea of Nick and wasn't saying so.

'Stella, relax,' said Hazel. 'Yes, I know you're fed up with people telling you to relax but honestly, stop worrying. I asked Amelia today about what was happening tonight and she said that a friend of Mummy's was coming, there was going to be cake and she was staying up late. She's harbouring a plan to wear her ballet outfit, by the way, and there's a possibility you might be treated to her version of the Dance of the Sugar Plum Fairy.'

Stella exhaled. 'I know I'm probably worrying too much, but this is so important. I want Amelia to adore Nick and vice versa.'

'Adore might take longer,' Hazel advised, 'so just stick to hoping they get on well tonight. Anyhow, when am I going to meet this marvellous man?'

'If tonight goes well, I'm thinking of having Sunday lunch in a week or so and inviting Mum, Dad, Tara, Finn and Holly to meet Nick. Would you and Ivan come with the girls?'

'Try and keep us away. I'll warn Ivan not to come the heavy-handed male friend who warns Nick not to hurt a hair on your head, etc, etc.'

The two women grinned companionably. 'Poor Nick,' said Stella. 'He's going to have a line of people queuing up to tell him not to hurt me.'

'No, he won't,' soothed Hazel. 'You've chosen him and you're a good judge of character.'

By seven, the chicken salad was crisping in the fridge, the table was ready and Amelia was still in her bedroom beautifying herself. Stella's own beautification had been speedy and consisted of swapping her work clothes for black jeans and a fluffy angora sweater. She didn't want to overdramatise the evening, which was why she'd dressed down and made a simple meal. For Amelia's sake, the cake was her favourite sticky toffee slice, and three indentations in one side were evidence that little fingers had already scraped a bit of toffee icing off.

The door bell rang.

'I'm not ready, Mummy!' yelled Amelia.

'Take your time, darling,' said Stella in amusement.

Nick arrived with flowers, wine and a small silver carrier bag. His arms full, he leaned over and kissed Stella hungrily on the mouth.

'You look wonderful,' he said.

'Right back at you,' she grinned. 'What's in the bag?'

'A present for Amelia.' Nick looked apprehensive. 'I hope you don't think this is bribery and corruption . . .'

'Yes, I do,' said Stella, 'and I love you for it.'

Amelia bounced into the room from her bedroom, her dark eyes wide with interest. She was wearing her white ballet tutu, the plastic tiara Holly had given her for Christmas, and a badly-applied slash of her mother's pink lipstick. She had accessorised the ballet dress with a pair of red and black spotty tights which no longer fitted properly and the battered wand from her beloved purple fairy costume. 'Hello,' she said, looking Nick up and down.

'I'm Nick,' he said, bending down to shake her hand formally. 'I like your outfit.'

Amelia beamed. 'Mummy doesn't like me wearing it all the time,' she confided.' But it goes in the washing machine and everything, so I don't see why.'

Nick nodded as if he was on Amelia's side in all of this. 'Grown-ups have strange ideas about things. Look, I've brought you a present,' he said, holding out the silver carrier bag.

Stella's legs felt wobbly and she had to sit down on the couch. She watched Amelia reach out for the bag, then look briefly at her mother for instructions.

Stella mouthed the word 'yes'.

'What is it?' said Amelia.

Nick grinned. 'A special surprise for a special girl.'

Amelia dropped her wand instantly and plonked herself down on the floor. Nick sat down opposite her and stretched his legs out. 'I can't kneel, I'm too old,' he said.

'Mummy does yoga to keep her young,' Amelia said, intent on dragging her present from the depths of the carrier

236

bag. 'She could teach you.' She pulled out a tissue-wrapped parcel and expertly wrenched the paper away to reveal a small wooden box about eight inches square. Painted peachy pink, the box was like a miniature chest of drawers with a tiny gold key at the top and delicate golden handles on each drawer. 'Ooh,' breathed Amelia in awe.

'It's for secrets,' said Nick. 'You can lock special things away and nobody can open it. The key even has a ribbon on it.'

'It's like a secret treasure box like Barbie would have,' Amelia said. She opened the drawers carefully. Inside, they were lined with satin, ready for her treasures.

'Say thank you,' urged Stella.

'Thank you,' said Amelia, with a rapt expression on her face. 'It's lovely, thank you.'

'What are you going to put in it?' asked Nick.

'Secrets!' said Amelia, clapping her hands delightedly. 'I'll show you my room and where I'm going to put it. Come on.' She got to her feet and led the way.

After that, Amelia treated Nick like her best friend. She wanted to sit beside him at the table, she gave him a running commentary on what they were eating: 'Toffee cake, it's my favourite. Mummy tried to make it but she can't so she has to buy it,' and after dinner, she insisted on sitting between him and Stella on the couch.

'You're very good with her,' Stella said, when she'd finally persuaded Amelia to tidy up her toys before going to bed.

'I've two of my own,' Nick said. 'After two little girls, you get the general idea. She's a lovely child, a credit to you.'

'She is lovely, isn't she?' said Stella proudly.

Stella, smelling of vanilla body lotion and wearing her wildly expensive new underwear under a sedate khaki shirt dress, finished hanging up Amelia's clothes in Tara's spare room. It was Friday afternoon and in a few minutes Nick would be arriving to drive her to the airport for their flight to Paris.

Tara, who'd taken a half-day in order to take care of her niece, was in the kitchen showing Amelia all the goodies she'd bought for the weekend.

Stella could hear her listing all sorts of things that Amelia normally only got for a treat, like Kinder eggs and chocolate-coated cereal.

'No wonder she likes coming here,' joked Stella loudly.

'It's not about food, it's about fun,' retorted Tara, coming into the spare room. 'I could have hung her clothes up.'

'Don't mind me,' said Stella. 'This is my worried mother nobody-does-it-like-me act.'

'Aunty Tara, can I turn the television on?' said Amelia.

'Yes, Amelia,' said Tara. 'You know how, don't you?'

'Know how? She could probably programme your video,' Stella pointed out. 'When the electricity went the other day and the kitchen radio ended up with all the stations de-tuned, Amelia re-tuned them in five minutes.'

'Clever girl,' said Tara approvingly. 'Now, don't worry about her. She'll be fine with us and if there's any emergency, I have all your numbers and I can always phone Mum. Holly's coming over tomorrow after work and we're going to see a film.'

'You *will* phone me if anything happens . . .' Stella began.

'Yes, of course. Just enjoy yourself. And if you get carried away with passion and want to stay in Paris for the week, just phone.' Tara was joking but when she glanced over at her sister, a tiny flush was making its way up Stella's face.

'Stella,' she teased, 'what is it? What are you not telling me?'

'Nothing.'

'Nothing my backside. Is Nick a fantastic lover, is that it?'

'Tara!' hissed Stella. 'Amelia might hear you. And no. Yes. I don't know,' she added in exasperation. 'I didn't want to rush into anything.'

'This is your first time, then?' asked Tara delicately.

'Yes. Should I send an e-mail message tomorrow morning with the gory details or will a text message do?'

'Oh e-mail,' countered Tara, 'you can get more in. Only kidding.'

The entryphone buzzer sounded and Tara rushed to answer it.

'Come on up, Nick,' she said, then added in a low voice, 'I believe you're a hero in the sack.'

'Tara!' shrieked Stella, rushing into the hall to find Tara grinning wickedly. 'I'd hung up before I said the last bit,' she said.

'Bitch,' whispered Stella. 'You have to watch what you say when Amelia's around, you know . . . I don't want her corrupted.'

Tara squeezed her sister's arm. 'Don't worry. Finn and I were due to hold the wife-swapping party this weekend but we pulled out!'

'You're incorrigible,' Stella said, laughing.

'What's the joke?' said Nick when he arrived.

'Don't ask,' said Stella. She kissed him firmly on the mouth.

'You smell lovely,' said Nick, inhaling the creamy scent of vanilla body lotion.

Over Nick's shoulder, Stella could see Tara bite her tongue to stop herself saying something naughty.

'Hi, Nick.' Tara waved at him. At Stella's Sunday lunch party, the two of them had got on like a house on fire. Every one of the Millers had taken to him, in fact. Nick's genuine love for Stella had opened the door for him. Nobody seeing the pair of them together could doubt the intensity of their feelings for each other. Even Rose, who'd been scared for her darling Stella and had been prepared to make her mind up slowly, had adored Nick from the start.

'Hi, Nick,' Amelia rushed out from watching TV and Nick swept her up into his arms.

'How's my princess?' he asked.

'Fine,' she said. 'Auntie Tara's got Kinder eggs for me and I can have them all.'

'What sort of a chicken lays Kinder eggs?' Nick asked, putting her back down.

'No chicken, silly,' giggled Amelia. 'They come from the shops.'

Stella got her coat and her handbag.

'OK,' she said. 'We're ready.' For some reason, she felt tearful. She hated leaving Amelia. They'd been apart so few times since Amelia had been born. She knelt down beside her daughter.

'Bye, Mummy.' Amelia put her trusting little face up to her mother's and kissed her. 'Have fun.'

'I'll miss you.' Stella buried her face in Amelia's hair.

'Me too,' said Amelia. 'But I like it here with Aunty Tara and Uncle Finn, and Aunty Holly's coming too.'

'I know, darling. I'll phone lots of times and if you need me, get Aunty Tara to phone me, won't you?'

'Yup.'

'Come on,' said Nick.

When all the goodbyes had been said, Tara opened the door and Stella walked out, her eyes blurred with tears. Nick held her hand tightly. The last thing she heard before the door closed was Amelia saying: 'Aunty Tara, can we have some chocolate now?'

It was like being fifteen again, Stella thought as they sat together on the plane. At that age, dates had filled the young Stella with wild excitement. Today, over twenty-two years on, the same excitement was bubbling up inside her. Nick clearly felt it too. His hand kept reaching over to touch hers and squeeze it.

'I've never been to Paris with a man,' Stella confided.

'With a Golden Retriever, then?' he asked.

'No, idiot. I came with a school trip when I was in my last year at school and it was hilarious. The teachers were terrified at the idea of keeping this group of kids safe in Gay Paree and we almost had to go to the loos in groups of three. We all wanted to escape and wander round ourselves, but we never managed it. The highlight of the trip was when we had morning coffee in the hotel and these young men tried to chat myself and a friend up.' Stella smiled fondly at the recollection. 'We thought we were the last word in grown-up-ness when that happened. Suddenly, we were experienced, worldly-wise women. This was real life, you see. Having charming men chat us up. Kinvarra seemed a long way away. The teachers were horrified, of course.'

Nick smiled and held onto her hand tightly.

'What would you have done if you'd managed to escape?'

She thought about it. 'All very innocent stuff, really. Gone to see a film, maybe. And I had this very romantic notion of myself in an Audrey Hepburn scarf wafting round Paris and being admired. I wanted to order coffee and sit in a street café looking cool and aloof. The reality was different,' she added. 'We had to wear our school blazers, which would have certainly marked me out as a schoolgirl and, at the time, I was very keen on enormous brass jewellery. My favourite earrings were like satellite dishes, not very Hepburn-esque. And my hair was very long and very bushy, so with wild hair, big earrings and my burgundy school blazer, I wasn't what you'd call the epitome of Parisian chic.'

'I bet you looked wonderful,' Nick said. 'We could relive the experience and you could pretend you're an earnest schoolgirl who's managed to throw off her teachers.'

It sounded like a marvellous idea.

'Can I pose in a café wearing my sunglasses?' she begged.

'Only if you tie your hair back in a scarf and pretend to be in a film,' Nick said.

'Let's,' said Stella enthusiastically.

They began to draw up a mental plan of sightseeing and it was clear that Nick had been to the French capital many times. But Stella deliberately didn't ask him about how often he'd been there and who with. The answer would surely involve Wendy, and Stella felt strongly that hearing about her might break the spell.

The problem with romance at their age, she reflected, was that you were never the first to do anything. You were never the first person to go to Paris with them, or the first person

241

to walk on a rain-soaked beach. She knew it was childish, but Stella felt a certain sense of loss at not being the first to do things like that with Nick.

Still, she resolved not to think about it. They were together now. Stella wanted the past to stay in the past. Surely that couldn't be too difficult?

Their elegant little boutique hotel reminded Stella of Holly's interior decoration.

'Shabby chic,' she whispered to Nick as they stood in the faded lobby beside a giant armoire that was genuinely rather than deliberately distressed.

'I've never stayed here before but I was told it's unusual and very elegant,' Nick said. 'I thought we should go somewhere neither of us had ever been before.'

Her smile was grateful. He *did* understand how the ghosts of past relationships could be hard to live with. This was new, this was *theirs*, Stella thought delightedly. No past lovers would loom up in the middle of the night to taunt her.

Their room was just as pretty as the lobby, a vision of sea-green muslin with prints of Fragonard paintings on the walls, spindly white furniture and violets in painted pots. Dominating the room, however, was a huge bed big enough for an orgy, complete with an elaborate canopy and enough flowing muslin to drape an elephant.

'Lovely room,' said Stella, skirting the bed with all its meanings, to look into the bathroom.

'Great view,' agreed Nick, also avoiding the bed to stare out of the louvred window at the spires of Paris.

The female receptionist who'd shown them to the room looked worried. 'You don't like the bed?' she said, perplexed. Everyone loved the bed in this room. It was the first thing people mentioned. What was wrong with this couple?

Nick's eyes met Stella's across the expanse of the bed.

'We love it,' Stella said firmly, controlling the urge to giggle. 'It's the best bit of the room.'

Satisfied, the receptionist left.

'The best bit?' said Nick, grinning.

Stella's gaze was even. 'Possibly the best bit,' she said.

'Only possibly?' Nick crossed the room to stand beside her. He took off his raincoat and threw it on a chair.

'I can't be more sure until I test it out,' Stella said, unbuttoning her coat. She threw it on top of Nick's.

'Research, you mean?'

She nodded.

A knock on the door signalled the porter with their bags.

'I'm glad we were still dressed when he got here,' Stella said when the porter had departed, having left their luggage carefully on the rack.

'I'd say he's seen things that would make our hair turn,' Nick said cheerfully. 'This is Paris after all. A couple standing tamely beside a bed, dressed or otherwise, must be very dull to him.'

'Dull?' inquired Stella. 'Are you saying we're dull? We've got to put a stop to that. Phone down this instant and order champagne, strawberries and a mirror for over the bed.'

Nick grinned at her and gently pulled her close.

'We don't need champagne.' He undid one button on her shirt dress. 'Or strawberries.' He undid two more buttons. 'Or a mirror on the ceiling.' He opened the dress and his hands slid round her waist.

Stella felt profoundly grateful for having bought her new, sexy underwear, because she didn't think she'd have felt as sexual if she'd been wearing her standard cotton knickers and plain, firm control bra. These lacy, silken garments made her feel like a different woman, a sensual, beautiful woman. Yes, underwear did help.

Very soon, she wasn't thinking about underwear any more because the passion she'd been damping down for months came rushing to the fore. Nick's body was close to hers, he was as turned on as she was, there was a hugely inviting bed at their backs and they were, after all, in Paris.

'I've waited a long time for this,' murmured Stella, when

Nick's lips were buried against her neck and his hands were cupping her breasts in their covering of lace.

'That's supposed to be my line,' he said.

'I'm an equal opportunities sort of person,' Stella said, arching her back as Nick unhooked her bra and took a nipple sweetly in his mouth.

Stella, who'd thought she'd forgotten what lovemaking could be, discovered that she'd never really forgotten. It was perfectly natural to caress Nick and undress him, natural for him to peel down her silky pants so she could sit straddled across him on the bed, feeling his hands caressing her fiercely and his mouth on hers. Then, she couldn't think straight because she felt herself go liquid with desire and she wanted him inside her. Then he was, holding her closely with his powerful arms, their bodies locked together in wild sexual tension, driving her to an exquisite orgasm that made her shriek out in pleasure and astonishment. Even some strange flapping noise going on outside the window couldn't stem the blissful release that throbbed through her body as she came. When Nick's body stiffened in her arms and he moaned softly, she clung to him, willing his orgasm to be as good as hers. At last, they lay panting on the sheets, still tangled together, too shattered even to move apart.

'I think we frightened the pigeons,' said Nick, wiping away the beads of perspiration from Stella's upper lip.

'Was that what the noise was?' She felt the laugh grow deep in her belly and rumble up into her chest. 'I can't believe we frightened the pigeons.'

Nick rolled her over until she was lying on his chest gazing down at him. 'Actually, you frightened the pigeons,' he said gravely.

'It wasn't me,' she giggled.

'Yes it was,' he said, kissing her again. 'We'll probably be thrown out of the hotel, you know.'

Stella rested her head against his chest, glorying in the sensation of his body close to hers. She'd had sex before. She knew what that felt like, but this, this utter transporta-

244

tion with someone she loved, this was something else. This felt perfectly right. Nick's body fitted hers perfectly.

As they lay spent, her face nuzzled up to his big shoulder, Stella felt a protective love so intense that it startled even her. She would kill for this man. She loved him, cared for him, wanted to take care of him and, in turn, be taken care of by him.

His hands caressed her back, idly massaging her muscles, moving from her shoulder blades down to the base of her spine. Then his fingers splayed down further, cupping her bottom gently in a way that was suddenly intensely erotic. Stella, who'd been worn out a few minutes before, found her body responding.

'Since we're going to be thrown out soon, should we have another go?' she whispered, moving slightly to test if Nick was getting as turned on as she was.

'Oh yes,' he murmured. 'Definitely.'

The pigeons didn't make quite as much noise the second time.

Stella, curled up beside Nick and ready to fall asleep, decided that they must have got used to it.

CHAPTER FIFTEEN

Tara had a cramp in her leg from standing patiently behind the cameraman. She was also boiling hot because the powerful studio lights kept sound stage seven at tropical heat, even on a chillier-than-usual late March day. The make-up department went through horrendous amounts of translucent powder toning down glistening faces.

Rotating her ankle to deal with the cramp, Tara stared intently at the set but her mind was elsewhere. Professionally, she was on a high since Mike Hammond had phoned her and mentioned that a friend of his with a small production company was trying to get a low-budget Irish movie off the ground and needed a reliable, and cheap, hand with the script he was writing.

'Script polishing,' Mike had said, 'that's what we're looking for.'

It wasn't exactly the A-list Hollywood stuff she'd dreamed of, but Tara had been delighted. The script doctoring was something she could do in her spare time and if it worked, she was sure Mike would come up with something more concrete for her. This was an audition of sorts. Mike owned a tiny share in this friend's production company and if her work was good enough, she knew Mike would be impressed. The second subject taking her mind off her job was Finn. Apart from the past weekend when they'd been taking care of Amelia, he was socialising every second night and, in her darker moments, Tara wondered if there was someone else in his life. That could be the only explanation for both the late nights with the boys and the endless evenings when he was out with clients, yet when Finn crept into bed beside her, hugging her and telling her that he loved her, Tara knew instinctively that he wasn't lying. So what was wrong?

Sighing, she turned her attention back to the set where Sherry DaVinci, boobs jacked up to her chin in a strawberry-pink V-necked dress that was highly unsuitable for working as a receptionist in a doctor's office, was confronting the lantern-jawed Dr Jack McCambridge, her boss and serial womaniser.

Theodora, Sherry's character, was the only person in the country who hadn't realised that the handsome Dr McCambridge was engaged to be married and was, therefore, going to dump her before rushing up the aisle with the virginal and rich daughter of the chief surgeon. Their frantic weekends in a country hotel had meant nothing to him. Although being used as a location for the nation's most popular soap had done wonders for the hotel's business.

'You pig!' hissed Theodora, bosom heaving, flecks of mascara flying as she emoted with all the skill of four months of drama college. 'You absolute pig!'

Tara had wanted her to call him a bastard, but *National Hospital* went out before the nine o'clock watershed. Bad language was not an option. As the scriptwriters liked to joke, aliens could come down and perform quasi-sexual experiments on the entire cast for ten episodes and nobody would bat an eyelid. But let one character utter an expletive and *National Hospital* would be at the centre of a controversy over corrupting the nation's youth with profanity.

'Theodora, stop shouting, someone will hear,' said Dr McCambridge testily.

Tara watched in approval. Unlike poor Sherry, Jack could act.

He sounded exactly like a charmer who was trying to perform damage limitation, a dangerous charmer who could possibly turn nasty. Millions of women tuned in at eight p.m. twice a week to see how dangerous Dr Jack could get and to watch him stripped to the waist in the surgical scrub room where lots of the show's action took place. Male TV critics complained that the surgery rate would be higher if the show's chief heart-throb didn't spend so long stripping off. Female TV critics had been known to express the opinion that there wasn't half enough of Dr Jack with his shirt off. Even the revelation that he got his chest waxed hadn't put Dr Jack's fans off.

On the set, the emotional temperature was rising.

'But Jack,' wailed Theodora. 'How could you do this to me?'

'Grow up, Theodora,' he snapped back. 'You knew what this was about. Don't kid yourself that you didn't. We had a bit of fun, that was all.' He let his dark eyes rove over her full figure. 'I had fun,' he said evilly, 'didn't you?'

At this point, Theodora's eyes were supposed to brim with tears. Tara, who couldn't resist liking Sherry since the awards, had decided that the vampish receptionist should suddenly reveal her more vulnerable side.

'Perhaps the problem with Sherry is that she has a problem playing such a bitch on screen,' Tara had said at the storyline meeting. People had shrugged their shoulders. Most of the writers felt that Sherry's problem was acting full stop but they let Tara run with her idea. It was therefore important to her that Sherry could pull the sympathy card off.

On camera, Sherry's eyelids fluttered.

Tara scrunched up her own eyes, as if to stimulate tears of her own in sympathy with the character. But Sherry appeared to be tearless. She narrowed her eyes a bit but couldn't produce anything. Tara sighed.

'It wasn't supposed to be fun, it was supposed to be love,' she said finally.

Tara winced at every word. It was official. Sherry simply couldn't act. No wonder all the show's other actors, many of them charismatic stage stars who'd done everything from Pinter to the Bard, were annoyed to see someone as talentless as Sherry on the show.

Dr Jack moved closer to Theodora/Sherry and took her pointed little chin in one big hand.

'I don't do love,' he growled.

Staring at the scene, Tara felt an answering growl deep in her solar plexus. Dr Jack could do that to a woman, even when the woman in question knew what he was going to say because she'd written his lines. Off camera, Dr Jack was the sort of person Tara avoided. On camera, he was droolingly delectable with enough sexual charisma for a dozen men.

'You don't mean that,' said Theodora woodenly.

'Yes I do.' And Dr Jack, an expert soap star after ten years on the job and two technical rehearsals that morning, swept around and exited, leaving Theodora to sink to her desk and pretend to sob.

'Cut!' yelled the director.

Everyone on sound stage seven sighed with relief. The last scene of the day was finally in the can and everyone could pack up and go home, albeit an hour later than usual.

Dr Jack, aka Stephen Valli, stalked angrily off the set muttering about working with amateurs and how he should have never given up theatre.

Everybody ignored him.

Tara looked at her watch. Ten past six, time to go home to Finn. Maybe they could have a heart-to-heart discussion and get a few things out in the open. She knew that Finn had to entertain clients, but his job seemed to be taking over their lives. When they'd got married, Tara hadn't thought there'd be quite so many late nights. 'The computer industry's in a bit of a recession,' he'd said when she'd lost her temper the last time. 'This is my job, Tara. I don't complain about your hours or the times you're up late glued to the laptop, do I?'

He never complained, she had to admit that. If she had to work late, Finn was happy to phone Derry and head off for a 'quick pint down the local'. But then he didn't come back for hours and when she finally switched off her laptop, she ended up alone again.

Finn obviously didn't understand that things were different now that they were married; he wasn't the single man about town any more. It was up to her to make him understand. Tonight, she decided, she'd get a Chinese takeaway, his favourite, and they'd have a talk.

Tara smiled to herself, relieved to have sorted this out in her mind and relieved the day's shooting was over. There was only one more scene to shoot the following morning and the episode would be finished. The scene involved other actors and, even though Tara had written it, she wouldn't be needed on set because it didn't involve Theodora and there was no possibility of having to rewrite anything because the actress fumbled her lines.

Normally, the writers didn't spend too much time on set: instead, they sat in their office writing scripts and discussing things like the ratings and how they were going to get rid of Theodora. So far, the ideas included suicide (unlikely as Sherry wouldn't be able to fake abject misery) and leaving to visit her sister in Boston (this was an in joke as six people so far in the programme's ten-year history had gone to visit their sister in America). Dr Jack/Stephen had popped his head round the door the previous day and suggested that he shoot Theodora. 'I'd like that,' he said grimly. 'It could be a crime of passion.'

'You'd have to go to jail and we can't do without you,' said the story editor.

'I could dump the body in the canal and nobody would know,' Stephen replied.

Everyone in the room had laughed. They'd already had a body in the canal in the Christmas episode three years ago. Two bodies in the canal would be pushing it.

Tara was grinning at the thought as she left the set and walked slowly up to the control room for a few words with Aaron, the director. But Sherry got there before her and managed to accost Aaron just as he was nipping out of the room.

'What did you think?' Her bosom still heaving in full-on

Theodora mode, Sherry stood in front of Aaron and blinked appealingly. A great bear of a man with a gruff manner and a gentle heart behind it, Aaron regarded the pretty girl who'd brought the show buckets of publicity. Tara had known directors whose savage sarcasm could strip paint and it was a joy to work with one who genuinely considered people's feelings before he spoke. Standing behind Sherry, she smiled at Aaron and hoped he'd stay true to form and wouldn't say anything awful. Sherry was sweet, after all.

'Too much anger in your passion, darling,' Aaron said finally.

Sherry had to think about this for a moment. 'Is that good or bad?' she asked.

When Sherry had gone, Aaron and Tara walked back to the *National Hospital* production offices.

'I've heard your name mentioned in connection with the TV film of the Paton Smyth book,' Aaron remarked.

Tara was astonished. 'Where did you hear that?' she demanded. Mike Hammond had only phoned her two days previously. He'd told her the film was hush-hush.

'I have my sources,' said Aaron. 'I don't hear everything but when my best scriptwriter and top storyline editor is moving on to something bigger and better, I keep my ears to the ground.'

Tara decided to be honest with Aaron. She owed him that. 'I'd tell you if they asked me to do something big, Aaron. Mike called me. We met at the awards and he said he was interested in talking to me sometime. Now he's rung and suggested I might be interested in polishing this script. It just needs tweaking, he says. It's a low-budget flick and it might never get made because they haven't got the financing sorted out yet. Writing a real film script is just a pipe dream,' she added lamely.

'Not for you, Tara,' Aaron said seriously. 'You're good, better than good. You don't need me to tell you that. And I've always known you're ambitious, don't forget.'

They reached the tiny office kitchen and Aaron paused in

front of the coffee machine. 'I knew you wouldn't end up with us forever, that you'd want to move on to something different. You high-fliers don't sit still for long.'

Tara patted Aaron's arm affectionately. He'd been such a good mentor, always ready to listen to her ideas even when she'd been a novice scriptwriter and the most junior on the *National Hospital* team. He'd been the one who told her she could really write, the one who said that coaxing a performance out of the most wooden actor was much easier when Tara Miller had written the lines.

'I'm not rushing off anywhere just yet, I promise. I'd tell you if I was, so don't advertise my job. Deal?' Tara added.

'Deal,' he agreed. 'Look at this,' he added in disgust, pouring a stream of pale muddy liquid into a mug. 'What's with this fake coffee stuff? Can't we have real coffee round here?'

Tara left him to it. Glancing at her watch, she wondered what the rush hour traffic would be like.

'Hey Tara, coming to the pub?'

It was a contingent of the show's writers, all intent on their customary last-Tuesday-of-the-month trip to the pub. Not that this was the only trip to the pub every month by any means, but this was payday, the only firm date in their diaries. Other sessions were more spontaneous.

'You haven't been over to the pub for ages,' complained Lisa, an avowed party animal.

'Do we smell or something?' demanded Ralph, the oldest writer in the team, who was just as mad for partying as Lisa and had a sharp tongue.

'I'm sorry, Ralph,' Tara said in mock distress, 'but we thought it would be kinder to let you drink on your own instead of leave cans of deodorant around the office to give you the hint. BO is a terrible thing.'

'Funny ha ha,' said Ralph. 'So, are you coming for a drink or not?'

'Yeah, I'll meet you over there; save me a bar stool,' Tara said, wishing she'd managed to avoid them because she genuinely didn't want to spend any time in the pub. Her weekends with Finn revolved around pubs. Still, she hadn't been out with the team for weeks and a lame excuse would not do.

'And you can tell us all about this hot new script you're working on,' said Lisa coyly. 'Is it Spielberg or Coppola who's interested?'

Tara laughed outright at that. 'Is nothing a secret in this damn place?'

'No,' said Tommy, who was an inveterate gossip with a nose like Lassie when it came to scandal. 'We know who's been sleeping with Dr Jack while the real Mrs Jack is away having her eyes de-bagged in a clinic in London, and we know which nymphet from publicity is having after-hours trysts with her female boss.'

'Tommy, are you sure that you sent your CV to the right place?' inquired Tara. 'This is *National Hospital*, not the *National Enquirer*.'

The other three were laughing as they departed, with Ralph threatening dire repercussions if Tara did not arrive at the pub in ten minutes.

Still smiling from the encounter, Tara went to her partitioned cube in the writers' office and phoned home, hanging up when she got the answering machine. Of course Finn wouldn't be back yet. Then she phoned his mobile. Another machine.

'Hi, I'm going for a quick drink with Aaron and the team. I won't be long. Bye.'

As she hung up, Tara thought back to the days before she'd met Finn; when going out with the team was the focal point of her social life. They'd had some wild nights back then when anyone going home before one in the morning was considered a party pooper. Clearly, the gang thought that love and marriage had turned Tara into the ultimate party pooper. She, the girl who'd taught them the tequila forfeit game; who could clear a dance floor with her hysterical River Dance impersonation. After nine months of marriage, she still hadn't made it back to the tequila game. Finn, as they all guessed, was the answer. Ralph regularly teased

253

her about Finn's resemblance to Brad Pitt and never lost an opportunity to enquire about what he called 'the love of the century'.

Tara, used to constant ribbing and aware that Ralph's bark was worse than his bite, rarely bothered replying. She was intuitive enough to realise that Ralph's remarks stemmed from jealousy: to him, she and Finn must have looked like a sickeningly perfect couple.

But ... well ... it wasn't perfect, not quite perfect.

Determined not to give in to introspection, she applied her signature bright scarlet lipstick without needing a mirror. Tara knew the contours of her mouth well enough without having to actually look at it. Bright lipstick was the ultimate mask: enough Ruby Woo and she looked sparky and happy. She dumped her briefcase in her car and walked across the carpark and over the road to Browns, the *National Hospital* local. In the pub, the TV people had divided into two very separate teams. Near the door sat a group of actors, all looking different from their soap personas. Even though she'd worked in TV for years, Tara was still astonished at how actors could transform themselves. The woman who played Staff Nurse Mo was virtually unrecognisable in real life. Mo wore buttoned-up-to-the-neck uniforms and looked permanently stern, while the actress floated around with rippling blonde hair, a rosebud pout and flowing skirts.

The actors nodded at Tara and she smiled back as she walked towards the group of writers who were plonked in the darkest section of the pub.

'We're going for the body in the canal,' yelled Tommy.

Tara grinned ruefully. 'As long as I don't have to write it.'

'Drink?' asked Lisa.

'Mineral water,' Tara said tightly.

'Have a real drink and get a taxi home,' urged Tommy. 'Let your hair down.'

Tara shook her head and took her water.

'Right, now spill the beans,' said Lisa, pulling her stool

up beside Tara's so they could have a quiet conversation. 'What's the exact story with this film script?'

'It's supposed to be confidential for a start,' Tara pointed out with a grin, 'so don't tell everyone. Basically, I've been asked to look at this script with a view to polishing it, that's all. And I want to know where you found out about it?'

Lisa grinned. 'Now that would be telling.'

The apartment was silent when Tara got home at nine, carrying her briefcase and the bag of groceries she'd picked up at the supermarket on the corner.

'Finn!' she called, dropping her briefcase beside the spindly-legged hall table. Her voice echoed in the silence of the wooden-floored hall. Tara liked the idea of wooden floors but they certainly magnified noise.

Tara didn't bother calling out to her husband twice. He must still be out. So much for her cosy chat over a Chinese takeaway. She was too hungry to wait for Finn, so she put some fresh pasta on to cook and went into the bedroom to strip off her work clothes.

Within two minutes, she was back in the kitchen, barefoot and dressed in a sloppy black sweater and jeans.

She stirred some supermarket sauce onto the pasta, took half from the saucepan, and went into the living room with her plate.

The late-night news was almost over when she heard Finn at the door. He never fumbled with his key, no matter what time he got home. Tara couldn't understand it. She wondered did he practise when she wasn't there: eyes closed or even eyes crossed as he slid the key in the lock, again and again to make sure he was perfect at it.

'Hiya, honey,' he called. 'How's my baby?'

To the untrained ear, Finn's voice sounded light-hearted and perhaps a bit tired. A normal 'I've-had-a-hard-day-at-the-office' sort of voice.

But Tara knew exactly what her husband's precise tone of voice signified: drunk. Honestly, she thought angrily. That job was killing him. He'd have a liver like a prune soon. This had to stop.

'Hello.' Finn appeared, still immaculate, his tie as perfectly tied as it had been that morning. Tara wondered how he did that, too. When she drank too much, she ended up looking dishevelled, with her hair in that dragged-through-a-bush-backwards state.

'Sorry I'm late. Work. Have you eaten?' Finn leaned over to brush his lips against her cheek and Tara caught the familiar sweet smell of alcohol. 'I shared chicken wings and chips with the guys,' Finn continued.

'Finn, why didn't you tell me if you had to go out tonight?'

Finn's face slipped into its beguiling hangdog look. 'Sorry babe, I couldn't get out of it and when I got your message on my phone, I knew you'd be out late and it was all right.'

'It wasn't all right,' she protested. 'I came home early and had to spend another bloody evening alone. You're married to your damn job.'

'Oh, honey.' He flopped onto the seat beside her and rested his head on her shoulder, almost childlike. 'Don't be cross,' he wheedled. 'You know how tough things are for the company right now. We're way off target for this quarter; we're in serious trouble. You know I didn't want to go out but I've got to back up Derry. As the boss, he carries the can. I just couldn't let him down.'

Tara sighed. 'You're lucky that I'm such a softie,' she said. 'I bet the other guys' wives don't let them off as easily.'

'No, but you're a wonderful, understanding person,' said Finn, burrowing in close to her. He kissed her neck softly.

'Go away you big boozy pig,' said Tara, but he knew she was joking.

'I think I'll get some milk, might settle my stomach,' Finn said off-handedly.

'OK,' said Tara, 'get me some too. And then bed, right?'

'Yes, mistress,' he teased.

*   *   *

In the kitchen, Finn went about his regular routine. He noisily opened the fridge and took out a carton of milk. Pouring half a glass, he listened carefully in case Tara decided to come into the kitchen. The wooden floors were wonderful for hearing her approach. When he was satisfied that she was still watching the television, he opened the drinks cupboard quietly and reached carefully into the back. Hidden behind a half-empty gin bottle, the usual selection of mixers and two boxes of unopened brandy (Finn felt that having unopened drink fooled everyone), was the bottle of diet tonic water. Or at least, the label said it was diet tonic. It was vodka, topped up by Finn every few days with a bottle bought specially. The vodka bottle was then hidden in his briefcase ready to be dumped somewhere else. The moment his fingers touched the tonic bottle, he felt a sudden giddy relief. He snatched it quickly and poured a shot into the trendy chrome measure someone had bought them as part of a chrome cocktail shaker set. In one swift move, he downed the spirit, not even gagging as the raw liquid hit his throat. One more, for the road, he decided. He downed another shot. Maybe he could do with some more in his milk. Just in case. He didn't want to get into bed and suddenly need another drink when he couldn't nip out and get one. Finn didn't like going to bed without a decent hit inside him. At night, he really wanted to be someplace else, somewhere there were no feelings. He wanted to be perfectly numb. Only then, when his brain was nicely fuzzy, did he actually like himself. Not that anyone else ever guessed about the howling loneliness inside. He hid it too well. The real Finn was useless, ineffectual, unlovable. If Tara ever knew what sort of a person he really was, she couldn't love him.

The following morning, Finn lay in bed, willing the fog in his head to disappear and hoping that the nausea wouldn't be too bad when he sat up. Some mornings, he was unable to get up for ages because one wrong move, and he'd have to rush for the toilet bowl and heave his guts up. This morning, he lay quietly, listening to the sounds of Tara in the ensuite shower. He could tell exactly where she was in her morning routine just by listening carefully. Once she was out of the shower, he had perhaps ten minutes' grace before she'd open the bathroom door, made up and still in her dressing gown, ready to run the hairdryer over her short hair before she got dressed That precious ten minutes meant he could rush into the other bathroom and puke, if necessary, without her knowing. He could also have his first painkiller cocktail of the day, two painkillers fizzing in a glass of orange juice to slake the murderous hangover.

Finn knew other people who liked a drink and who didn't get hangovers, but he wasn't one of them.

Today, he tested himself by sitting gingerly up in the bed. Not too bad. Not puking time, definitely. Hey, it was almost like not having a hangover at all, he congratulated himself. He must have been very restrained the night before.

He made it to the kitchen, popped his painkillers in a glass and put the coffee on, which was his sole gesture towards breakfast. By the time he got back to the bedroom, Tara was drying her hair in front of the mirror so conversation wasn't required. Great.

Finn leapt in the shower and did his best to scrub away the scent of last night's bender. One of the lads in work insisted that people could smell the drink off a person when they'd been drinking heavily the night before, but Finn was convinced that this notion was wrong. With enough Eternity for Men, he smelled irresistible, he was sure of it.

Tara was finishing both the paper and her toast and coffee when Finn finally emerged, shaved, sweet-smelling and clad in a very sharp grey suit. Despite her uneasy feeling that something was going badly wrong, Tara smiled in appreciation of her handsome husband. He had that effect on her. She loved his strong face with the boyish smile, she adored running her fingers through the fair hair that he tried to keep cut short to stop it flopping over his forehead. She liked the way his eyes appeared intensely blue when his skin was faintly tanned. He still had the last vestiges of his skiing tan and it suited him.

Tara thought of all the things she'd planned to say the night before, and decided that now wasn't the time or the place. 'Hi, lazybones,' she said. 'I am going to buy you the loudest alarm clock I can find; you are hopeless at getting out of bed.'

'Lucky you're such a hard worker,' Finn teased in return. He felt relief flood through him. In the mornings, he always wondered how drunk he'd appeared the night before. He didn't want Tara to know, he didn't want to hurt her. She mightn't understand that he just liked a drink now and then. Not everyone did but he did. It didn't mean anything. So he watched carefully for any sign that she was worried about his drinking. Today, things were fine. Phew. They were out to a party tonight and he decided he'd go easy on the booze. He wouldn't drink, not a single glass. That would impress her.

Tara shut the dishwasher door and it slammed.

Finn winced. The tablets didn't work as well as they used to.

She leaned over and kissed him goodbye. 'Watch out for strange women,' she said, as she always did.

'I'm married to the strangest one around,' he replied happily.

When she was gone, Finn relaxed. He finished his coffee and poured another one. With another cup, he'd be able to face the day.

CHAPTER SIXTEEN

Snow White. Now *there* was a stepmother from hell, thought Stella idly that same morning as she switched on her computer. It was ten to eight, and the office was mercifully quiet. That was the way Stella liked it, the time when she could work without the phone ringing off the hook.

No, Stella decided as she clicked on her computer desktop calendar, stepmothers still on her mind, Cinderella's stepmother was more relevant to her personal story. At least she hadn't tried to murder her stepdaughter like Snow White's evil stepmom. Although Cinderella's mother by marriage was definitely a candidate for charges of child abuse. *Your Honour, the defendant wilfully differentiated between her two daughters, the Ugly Sisters, and her husband's daughter, poor Cinders. He could do nothing to help, being, as he was, blinded by his second wife's sexual power!*

Stella grinned wryly at the thought of Nick being blinded by her sexual power. He was crazy about her, she knew that. But blinded? Not quite.

Still, that was the myth behind the fairy story of the stepmom. Stella thought about the two real stepmothers she knew personally. One was the stepmum to three very young children and the chief worry appeared to be making a small house expand to fit an influx of extra children every second weekend. The other had married the long-divorced father of grown-up children, many years after he and their mother had split. The stepmother had adult children of her own as well, and from a distance, it all seemed remarkably civilised and friendly. There didn't *appear* to be any problems there, but Stella had to admit that she'd never asked. Perhaps under the surface was a simmering cauldron of hate with the step-siblings locked in an eternal battle with each other and with their step-parents.

And now it was her turn: Stella Miller, wicked stepmum-in-waiting.

With a desk full of legal documents in front of her and the first of the day's skinny lattes in her hand, Stella didn't feel she quite fell into the Cinderella/Snow White Evil Step-mum mould. For a start, she didn't have the waspy waist that all classic fairytale evil female characters had. And her hair wasn't coal black and sculptured but prone to frizziness. Stella was a slave to anything in the chemists' with the words 'sleek' on it.

But there could be problems ahead. Stella sipped her latte absently. She and Nick had been going out for three months and she hadn't met Nick's kids yet. According to *The Art of Step*, this was a fatal mistake. One of many fatal mistakes, in fact, because she and Nick had apparently done everything wrong. If there was an award for Most Inept Modern Couple, they'd win it hands down because they'd fallen blindly in love and hadn't thought of the consequences.

Nick insisted that Jenna and Sara would adore Stella. 'They're not babies,' he'd said firmly. 'They know the score.'

The score, Stella reflected, sounded reasonable to herself and Nick, but what if it didn't make as much sense to a nineteen-year-old in her first year of college, and to a four-teen-year-old who sounded like Daddy's pet?

She knew that her friends had found it hard to fathom how she and Nick had fallen in love so quickly. Their relationship hadn't been a gradual slide into love: there had been this intense, instant bond and after their second date, there was really no option for them to be apart. But try explaining that to anyone else, especially teenage daughters.

Stella wasn't an expert at teenagers. Amelia was only seven, and it felt like a zillion years since Stella herself had experienced teenagerdom. Surely modern teenagers were much more mature and sophisticated. They'd deal with Daddy's new girlfriend, wouldn't they?

Unfortunately, the book hadn't cheered her up on this point.

The first rule of stepfamilies was to gently introduce your children to the new squeeze before any life-changing decisions were made. This was vital. No, VITAL. In big letters. The stepfamily book didn't discuss what would happen if you did make life-changing decisions without telling the various children first, but the implication was that serious misery would follow. Nick and Stella hadn't planned any huge decisions. Not yet. But she suspected that everything might not be plain sailing for a while. Reading between the lines of the things Nick told her, his ex-wife, Wendy, was in denial over her divorce. She phoned Nick over every little problem, from flat tyres to trouble with the fuse box, and expected him to drop everything to rush to her aid. How would she take the news that her ex had a serious new relationship? That would be bound to hurt. Would that sense of hurt make her suddenly change her mind about an amicable split and start using her daughters as ammunition? Nick saw none of these possibilities but Stella saw them all.

She stopped scrolling through her diary for a moment. Should they slow it all down, for Jenna and Sara's sake? What if Nick's girls couldn't face a new woman in his life, a woman who couldn't imagine life without him and who was already daydreaming of the day they lived together?

'Hi Stel, did you go home at all last night?' asked Vicki, appearing at the door with her briefcase. 'Or do you have a bed in there?'

'I left at six, you slacker,' Stella joked back.

'That's practically a half-day for you. I remember when you used to stay in the office until half seven on Monday nights,' sighed Vicki. 'But now that you have the delectable Nick to go home to . . .'

'I only stayed until half seven on Mondays because that

was Amelia's swimming lesson night,' Stella retorted. 'And the delectable Nick doesn't live with me.' He had his own key, though, she thought happily.

'Yet,' said Vicki, batting her eyelashes dramatically in the manner of a silent movie star, 'he might as well move in, he's there all the time.'

'He isn't,' protested Stella.

'Vicki grinned. 'Give it time,' she said with a knowing smirk. I'll see you for lunch?'

Stella workĕd flat out all morning, pausing only to grab another cup of coffee after her noon meeting. She took the coffee back to her desk and decided that a five-minute break was in order.

Vicki was buried under a mountain of paperwork.

'Sorry to interrupt, but have you still got that gift catalogue?' Stella asked. 'I've got to look for an anniversary present for Mum and Dad. The party's in two weeks and we still haven't got anything. Tara and Holly will kill me because I'm in charge of getting it.'

'Hold on,' said Vicki, delving into the drawer where she kept her supply of magazines, spare tights and tampons for emergency use.

She handed Stella a fat luxury gifts catalogue.

Back in her office, Stella flicked through the catalogue rapidly, past endless pages of murderously expensive cutlery, and several displays of sickeningly twee figurines. Who bought this stuff? she wondered as she looked at a particularly hideous carriage clock that was a disastrous fusion of Louis XIV and Liberace. She knew the answer: people desperate for fortieth anniversary presents. When there wasn't anything the anniversary couple needed, the only option was something straight from such a catalogue.

Presents like that came complete with an unspoken: '*Yes, we know it's awful but it cost lots of money and that's the whole point, right?*'

Only this present was for her parents and Stella didn't want to buy a soulless canteen of cutlery or an ugly clock.

She wanted to buy something special, the perfect gift that reflected her love for them – and their love for each other. These days there weren't many couples who'd lasted forty years together. Her marriage hadn't.

But forty years of Nick, she thought dreamily, that would be wonderful. She dragged herself back to the task in hand. Reaching the ruby anniversary was one hell of an achievement and was why Hugh and Rose Miller's present had to be perfect. Stella turned a page and came upon a section where the Liberace/Louis XIV fusion thing had resulted in a selection of statues of Greek goddesses with lots of gilt embellishment on their flowing robes and way too much bare bosoms. Sighing, Stella threw the catalogue in her desk drawer and wished her mother had agreed to the holiday.

Stella and Tara had thought it was the best idea they'd ever had; that their combined anniversary gift would be a week in Paris.

'No, I wouldn't hear of it, Stella, although you're wonderful girls and I'm so proud of you all for even thinking of it,' Rose had said.

Dear Mum, Stella smiled. She was always thinking of other people. Rose Miller was the sort of mum who pretended she wasn't hungry if too many people turned up for dinner and who wouldn't dream of buying herself so much as a new pair of tights if she could possibly spend the money on any of her three daughters or her husband. Her daughters adored her. There *had* to be a perfect anniversary present out there.

Vicki stuck her head round the door. 'Lunch?'

'Give me one minute,' Stella replied and began to tidy her desk. She was ready to leave when the phone rang and a sense of duty made her pick it up.

'I hoped I'd catch you,' Nick said. 'They work you too hard. You never get to go to lunch on time.'

'Pot, kettle and black,' retorted Stella. 'Rearrange these words into a simple sentence.'

'Point taken,' he said ruefully. 'I'm going out for a sand-

264

wich later. This is just a quick call to say three things. One, I'm definitely cooking dinner tonight.'

Stella smiled. 'Two lessons and you're already an expert,' she teased. Nick had barely known how to turn an oven on until Stella had given him a crash course in cooking. Twenty years of marriage to a brilliant cook meant he could hardly make a cup of coffee without consulting a recipe book.

'I'm a fast learner,' he replied. 'Roast chicken sound OK to you?'

This time, she couldn't stop herself laughing. Roast chicken was the only thing he could cook. She planned to teach him a couple of other menu options one day.

'Roast chicken would be lovely. What are the two other things?'

'I was talking to Wendy earlier about bringing Jenna and Sara out at the weekend. It's Jenna's birthday on Friday and she's having a party, but I wanted to do something with her. And,' he hesitated, 'I told Wendy that I wanted the girls to meet you and that I'd have a big talk with them about it tomorrow night.'

'How did she take it?' asked Stella anxiously.

'Not bad, she seemed OK. She didn't say much but that's good, right?'

'Well, yes,' said Stella slowly.

'Last but not least, my brother phoned and he and Clarisse want us to go to dinner with them next week.'

Stella grimaced. Nick's caustic sister-in-law was definitely one of the clouds on their horizon. Howard was a sweetheart. But Clarisse was another kettle of fish.

Stella had met her only once and it had not been fun. The two couples had bumped into each other in a hotel lobby and Clarisse had looked at Stella the way an exterminator would inspect a cockroach. Stella was not used to people looking at her like that, with ... with disgust, she realised in shock. Afterwards, an embarrassed Nick explained that Clarisse was very friendly with Wendy.

'Ah,' said Stella, suddenly understanding why Clarisse's

face had frozen when Nick had artlessly introduced Stella by putting a protective arm around her shoulders. During the few minutes the four of them had been together, Clarisse hadn't addressed a single word to Stella. An entire dinner with Clarisse was not something Stella looked forward to.

'It won't be so bad, Stella,' Nick said, knowing exactly what she was thinking. 'Clarisse will love you when she gets to know you.'

Stella raised her eyes to heaven. Men, they were so innocent, really. Nick hadn't a clue when it came to personal relationships. Emotional intelligence was the key and Nick, for all his brilliance as a businessman, had none. He honestly believed that his sister-in-law would roll over like a playful kitten as soon as she got to know Stella. In his rose-tinted view, the two women would be bestest friends in months. Stella knew that they'd be sending out for gas heaters in Hell before Clarisse did anything but curl her lip at the sight of Nick's girlfriend.

'I didn't set a date for dinner, mind you,' Nick was saying, 'I said we'd need to check your diary but Howard thinks they're free next Thursday.'

'Great,' Stella said, wincing. She'd bet anything that Clarisse had organised dinner to either inspect Stella at close quarters – or to frighten her off.

'I'll bring the ingredients for dinner tonight and see you at half six, then?'

'Great. Love you,' she said.

'Love you,' he replied.

As she hung up, the sense of unease that had been dogging Stella all day returned. It was nothing to do with another evening of roast chicken, with Nick opening the oven door every ten minutes to 'check if it's done'. It was the thought of his blind innocence when it came to his sister-in-law. If he could be so sure that she'd like Stella, when Stella knew this was highly unlikely, then he could be wrong about other important things. Like how his Jenna and Sara would react to their father's new partner, and how their mother would react, too.

Luigi's was jam-packed, with at least half of the tables taken up by lawyers from Lawson, Wilde & McKenna. Stella smiled at a few people and sank onto a banquette beside Vicki, who was already deep in *Hello!* and crostini smothered in garlicky tomatoes.

'What's up?' Vicki asked, shutting the magazine, even though she was in the middle of a very juicy article about the Monaco royal family. 'You haven't had a bust-up with the love of your life?'

'No,' said Stella, unable to stop the moony look crossing her face. 'He's still fabulous. His sister-in-law is the fly in the ointment. We're going out to dinner with her on Thursday next.' She didn't mention the worry about the children. It seemed disloyal to Nick to talk about this most private thing, even with her dear friend.

'The sister-in-law? The one who looks like Gary Oldman in his ancient Dracula make-up?'

Stella erupted with laughter. 'You're evil, Vicki, you know that?'

'*You* were the one who told me she had this sort of stretched face as if the plastic surgery had gone wrong,' protested Vicki.

'I never mentioned Dracula,' Stella pointed out, deeply embarrassed by the way she'd described Clarisse to Vicki. It wasn't like her to be so bitchy but she'd felt so upset by the other woman's reaction to her, and painting Clarisse in unflattering terms had somehow got the rage out of her system.

'No, but you described her so well, I moved a step on. A disapproving hen's bum mouth and skin-stretched-tautly-over-cheekbones, you said. Dracula, I thought. Reminds me of Dracula.'

Stella winced. 'Don't,' she begged. 'I should never have said that. I'm turning into a horrible cow, just the sort of person I hate.'

'Are you ready to order?' asked the waitress.

'Lots of garlic, I think,' Vicki murmured under her breath.

Stella asked Vicki's opinion on anniversary presents, explaining that the Paris week was off. 'Mum says Dad doesn't have the time,' Stella said, 'but she never actually asked him. I keep thinking that maybe I should phone him at work and ask him what he thinks. He might be madly keen to go to Paris with Mum. I can see them walking hand in hand through the old quarter. Oh well, if they can't go, they can't go. I must ring Holly and Tara to sort out a trip into town to buy something.'

'Imagine being that in love after forty years,' sighed Vicki. 'It's wonderful.'

'I know,' Stella said. 'But you have to find the right person. That's rare. My parents have these friends, people I've known since I was a child, and I'm amazed at how they stay married at all. When this couple turn up at my parents' house for dinner it's like the Cold War: all icy glances and contemptuous remarks. It's horrible. Why do they bother staying together?'

'You only think it's horrible because your mum and dad are so happily married,' Vicki pointed out equably. 'You were lucky, dearie. The Cold War is the norm. My parents fought so much it's a miracle they didn't murder each other. I used to think that happy families was another bit of Disney propaganda and that open warfare was standard relationship behaviour. That must be why I'm so hopeless with men,' she added.

'What do you mean "hopeless"?' chided Stella. 'You floated into the office on cloud nine last week after that date with Craig.'

'Yes, I suppose I did,' twinkled Vicki. 'He is cute, for a younger guy. I don't want to get too serious though.' She grinned. 'What are we like? This time last year we thought all men were pigs.' She waved her fork at Stella. 'The romance fairy has seriously affected our judgement.'

Stella laughed at the idea as the waitress laid two plates

in front of them. Vicki's eyes lit up at the sight of her thin-crust pizza, glistening with extra cheese. 'Who needs the romance fairy when the mozzarella fairy is alive and well?' she said, digging in.

After lunch, they walked slowly back to the office, enjoying the fine day.

'I hope it stays fine at the weekend,' Vicki said. 'I'm going to Wexford with the girls and you know me, if I plan a weekend away, a tropical rainstorm is bound to hit. What are you up to?'

'Clearing out the spare room,' Stella replied. 'There's so much junk in there and I began to think that if Nick and I did move in together...' She ignored Vicki's big grin. '*If* Nick moves in with me and his kids come to stay, they'll need a room. Not that it's very big, mind you. His ex has bought this huge, detached house on a third of an acre.'

They'd reached the glass and steel revolving doors of Lawson, Wilde & McKenna. Vicki looked at her colleague. They'd known each other for eight years, had joined the company at the same time. Stella had been a good friend to Vicki during the time when Vicki's wheelchair-bound mother was slowly dying, the years when Vicki had no life outside the office and her work as a carer. Vicki had been there for Stella when she'd split up with Glenn, when Amelia was only a baby, and both money and childcare arrangements had been hell. They'd come through the hard years together and now Vicki was thrilled that her friend had found love. She was worried about her too.

'Stella,' she said now, 'it might not be a bed of roses, you know, the whole children bit.'

Stella gave Vicki her sunny, warm smile. It lit up her face, made her dark eyes dance, and transformed her from an attractive woman into a stunning one. 'Come on, Vicki,' she said, 'if I can deal with the Machiavellian politics in this office, I can certainly deal with Nick's children.'

Vicki nodded and went through the revolving doors. She ignored her sense of foreboding. Vicki's brother had stepchildren and it had taken years before they'd all settled down into a proper family. Years. But then, it was probably different when the step-parent was a woman, and a mother to boot. Stella could manage it, sure she could.

Miles away, in her big kitchen with its antique pine and gleaming professional-sized oven, Wendy Cavaletto sat at the table and cried. Her tears were of misery and fury mingled. It was such a shock to find that Nick had somebody else in his life. He'd said there was nobody else when they'd divorced and Wendy herself had known that it was all over between them. Yet now he had this other woman and it was so soon, so soon that it had shocked her. Not even a year since they'd been divorced. It was the ultimate insult for him to find somebody else so quickly. The pig, the bastard. *How dare he!* Still sobbing, she stalked past the granite-topped island unit to the saucepan rack and began slamming saucepans around. Here she was, planning meals for his children, worrying about every aspect of their lives, when he was off with another woman. He was probably swanning round in restaurants, having a marvellous time while she tried to cope with two nightmarish teenagers, one who sulked non-stop and another who didn't know how to pick up her dirty socks off the floor. Fury rose in Wendy's throat like bile. She wanted to hit Nick, she wanted to kill him. With an absence of her ex-husband to hit, she picked up the nearest weapon and fired it viciously at the floor. Her biggest copper-bottomed saucepan made one hell of a noise as it clattered onto the terracotta tiles. Wendy wished it was Nick's head. He'd hurt her and she wanted to hurt him. How could he find another woman to love so quickly? Where was the period of mourning for their marriage?

This was even worse than when he'd told her he was moving back to Ireland. Wendy remembered the years when she'd begged him to move home with her. But no, Nick's career had come first and he'd insisted that they live in the UK. And then as soon as they were no longer married, he moved back to Ireland. Not for her, no. For their daughters. Wendy had wept tears of rage at that. It was as if her power over Nick had gone forever. She was at the end of the queue and the girls were at the top, with this new woman.

She wouldn't make it easy for him. No way. He could rot in hell for all she cared. *She* was the mother of his children. Surely she deserved some respect and Nick's flaunting a new girlfriend so soon was not respect.

'Have you been talking to your father?' she snapped at Jenna when her younger daughter slouched into the kitchen, still in her pyjamas from that morning.

'He phoned me earlier,' Jenna said. 'Said he wanted to talk to me about something tomorrow night.' She sounded gloomy. Her mother was clearly in a nark, which was nothing new since the divorce. Jenna hated her dad and mum living apart even though you were the odd one out in her school in London if your parents were married. But Jenna wouldn't mind being the odd one out if it meant her parents getting back together again.

'You used to complain they were always fighting,' her friend Maya pointed out when Jenna said she hated the split. 'Mine were the same. Now there's no fighting and you get twice as many presents!'

Maya was right about the fights. Jenna remembered the arguments, and how the anger and tension seemed to linger in the air for days. She could hear them yell at each other about not involving the children, but honestly, did they think she was deaf? When he'd gone, her Mum had said 'good riddance, he should have gone years ago'. But she still didn't seem happy. They'd moved back to Ireland, which Jenna had really hated because it meant leaving behind all her friends. And then Dad had moved back too, which was great, although that made Mum even more furious for some reason. She kept going on about how she'd finally seen what he thought of her and how she was second best to her own children.

Sara didn't seem to mind: she loved going to Trinity College, because of some guy she was going out with. And Jenna was the one who got stuck at home with Mum. Sometimes Mum was happy and hugged Jenna, saying this was the best move of their life and that they were going to make it work. Other times she sat and watched telly all night, ready to leap on Jenna if she said the wrong thing.

Jenna wanted to know when things were going to improve, the way Maya insisted they would. There were no rows now, but the atmosphere was somehow worse. It was like being in the park before a thunderstorm; scary and electric. Dad had never shouted or yelled, not like Mum. He calmed things down. Worst of all, she missed her dad more than anything. He'd said that the divorce didn't mean he was leaving the girls, but Jenna felt as if she had lost him. He was her dad and he wasn't there any more.

'I'll tell you a bit of news about your father, shall I?' said Wendy tearfully, banging the kettle down on its stand.

Jenna noticed the slug trails of tears down her mother's face.

'Your father has a new girlfriend, he's really serious about her and he wants you to meet her. Did he not tell you that? I don't suppose he thinks he has to tell us anything. We're not important any more. Well, I know *I'm* not important but he should have told you.'

Jenna felt the pain like a stabbing sensation in her chest. Dad hadn't told them about any girlfriend. How could he not have told Jenna? She was his best girl, his pal. He loved Sara too, but she, Jenna, was his special girl because Sara was grown-up almost and never there. And now he had someone else in his life, someone he must love more than her.

Her mother was still talking, her voice tight with anger. 'I hope he realises how this makes me feel,' she was saying. 'He didn't waste time getting my replacement, did he? She's got a kid, too, some single mother looking for a fool to pay the bills, no doubt.'

Jenna was no longer listening to her mother's tirade

because the pain in her chest had got worse. Dad with another girl, maybe he'd bring her to the cinema. Maybe he wouldn't care about Jenna ever again, he'd have someone else. He'd said they'd go on holiday to France this year and do Euro Disney, Jenna had always wanted to see it, she didn't care if it was for kids, she loved that stuff. She had a snow globe with the Disney castle in it from when she was small. Dad had bought it for her and she loved it.

'I'm not seeing him,' she said fiercely, shoving her chair back from the table. 'I don't want anything to do with him again.' She ran to her room, threw herself on her bed and let the tears come. How could he do this to her? He loved her to bits, he'd said so the day he left. That would never change, nothing would stop him loving her. But he was wrong, it had changed. He'd lied to her. She hated him.

The scent of barbecuing food filled Stella's nostrils as she walked slowly up Delgany Terrace that evening with Amelia chatting happily alongside her. She'd driven home from the office in record time and decided to walk to Hazel's and enjoy the evening air. It was balmy for early April, just warm enough to sit outside. Perhaps she should buy a barbecue, she thought idly. No, perhaps *they* should buy one. She and Nick. It was strange thinking like a couple again. It had been so long since there had been anybody but herself and Amelia. Nick might be good with a barbecue. Men liked that type of cooking. Stella had often gone to neighbours' barbecues and drank wine with the women, while their children played and a couple of husbands wielded big metal implements and made a big deal about cremating a few steaks. It was one of the few occasions that Stella had felt a wistfulness for a male presence in her life. Barbecues had always had that effect on her. Not that she longed for burnt food, but the whole idea of the family unit around the barbecue had always reminded her of family life, with mother, father and kids, not like her own life with Amelia.

The barbecues when she'd been a child had been wonderful.

Her mother was the party queen. Entertaining had been a huge part of life in Kinvarra.

She had been lucky, Stella reflected, growing up with such a loving family background. She, Tara and Holly hadn't appreciated just how lucky they'd been or that other families weren't so happy.

'Mum, for my birthday, can I have a new bike?' Amelia began. Her birthday was over three months away, but they had this conversation at least twice a week.

'What about the dolls' house?' asked Stella, smiling.

'I'd like a dolls' house but I'd like a bike more and I can get a dolls' house from Santa, can't I?'

Stella grinned. 'You have this all planned out, haven't you!'

They reached their house, a redbrick terraced cottage that looked quite small from the street but which stretched out behind into a comfortable, if compact, home. In the seven years Stella had been living there, she'd transformed it so that the cottage now boasted a large living room, with a small galley kitchen off it. The kitchen led to a neat little conservatory which Stella had installed, and the back garden was a tiny white-walled courtyard complete with rambling roses and lots of plants in painted tubs. Originally, the cottage had just included two bedrooms and a compact bathroom on the ground floor but a previous owner had cleverly created a third guest bedroom out of the attic space. That was the bedroom Stella planned to clear out for Nick's daughters.

Stella took off her high shoes as soon as she stepped inside her front door. Picking them up, she went into her bedroom to get ready for Nick, while Amelia scooted off to her own room to dump her school things. Stella had taught Amelia not to leave things lying around, partly because she was tidy by nature and partly because in such a small house, junk cluttered the place instantly. It had worked: Stella had often noticed her daughter tut-tutting when Becky and Shona scattered belongings around in Hazel's.

'Look at this mess,' Amelia had said crossly one day, hands on hips, imitating her mother perfectly. Hazel and Stella had to hide in the kitchen and stuff their hands in their mouths to stop themselves laughing out loud.

'I wonder where she picked *that* up?' Hazel said wickedly.

'Out of the mouths of babes,' Stella added, shaking her head. 'It just shows, you can never forget they're listening.'

Stella hung up her jacket but left on her pink skirt and white cotton shell top. In the bathroom, she brushed her hair and took a look in the mirror, wincing at the sight of mascara smudged under her eyes. Wetting a finger, she rubbed it away, knowing that such treatment didn't do anything for her wrinkles. And there were definitely more wrinkles these days. She gently pulled the skin around her eyes taut, trying to imagine what she'd look like after an eye lift. Would plastic surgery be worth it? Stella wasn't sure, but she wished Nick had met her when her face was smooth and unlined. Until she was thirty-five, her skin had been perfect without the slightest effort on her part. Her women friends had told her she was lucky not to be plagued with PMT spots, dry patches or pores the size of dinner plates. But suddenly, almost as soon as the ink was dry on her thirty-fifth birthday cards, everything in her face had gone downhill at the speed of an avalanche. Now her dark eyes had a fan of tiny lines around them and she needed to draw a firm line around her mouth to make sure the lipstick stayed put and didn't bleed.

Still, she wasn't too bad. Age meant her cheekbones were more pronounced, giving her face a sculpted air it had never had as a full-faced twenty-something. Being on the road to forty had its compensations. She spritzed herself with perfume and then went to phone Holly and Tara to discuss the ruby wedding present conundrum. Neither of them was home yet, so she left messages and had only just put the phone down when she heard Nick's key in the door.

'Hello,' he said loudly from the hall.

Stella rushed out like a schoolgirl. He came into the sitting

275

room looking tired, the dark circles under his eyes more pronounced than usual 'He's got that lived-in look,' Tara had pronounced after their first meeting in Stella's for Sunday lunch. Tara loved to get people's descriptions right instantly. Part of being a scriptwriter, Stella knew. She couldn't pass a stranger in a phone box without writing a mental précis.

'Lived in, but sexy,' she'd added approvingly. 'You lucky thing. I'm dead jealous.'

Stella had grinned proudly, knowing that Tara, with the gorgeous Finn in tow, was only kidding about the jealousy.

'Hi, Stella, hi, Amelia,' said Nick, dropping his briefcase and several shopping bags onto the floor.

Smiling, Stella went towards him but Amelia got there first. Now dressed in a lurid purple dressing-up fairy costume that her Aunt Holly had got her the Christmas before, Amelia danced up to Nick and did her twirl. 'Isn't that good, isn't it?' she demanded.

'Perfect,' said Nick. 'You're a fairy ballerina, then?'

'No, a swan princess,' Amelia corrected. 'We had ballet today and the teacher said I was very good.'

'You need someone to lift you up to do proper ballet,' Nick pointed out. He lifted her up by the waist and she pointed her toes as he bounced her along, her feet barely touching the floor in an imitation of a *pas de chat*.

'Stella, you should have dancing music on the CD player,' Nick reproved, his eyes shining as he met Stella's.

'Yessir,' she said, saluting. Nothing could have made her happier than the way Nick and Amelia got on with each other.

'*I'll* do it,' said Amelia eagerly, keen to make the entire ballet experience more realistic.

Nick put her down and she rushed off to the sound system to look for CDs with pictures of ballerinas on them. Nick smiled at Stella and moved forward to hold her. They fitted together perfectly, her body just the right height for his, her head able to rest perfectly against his shoulder. At five eight,

Stella was a tall woman and Nick was four inches taller than her, tall enough for her to wear high heels with him.

'You wouldn't be threatened if I wore platform shoes and was taller than you, would you?' she teased once.

'I'm too old to feel threatened,' he replied truthfully.

That was the lovely thing about Nick. She knew that some women's partners were made uneasy by clever women but not Nick. He was proud of her. He loved her cleverness just as much as he loved her kindness.

'How are you?' he murmured now, content to hold her close and let the stresses and strains of the day wash away from both of them.

'Better now,' she murmured back, breathing in the familiar scent of his body, his cologne and his jacket. She loved that Nick-smell that lingered on the pillows when he'd gone: a hint of vanilla from his cologne and the smell of him.

'Did you remember to buy a free-range chicken?' she asked, still leaning against him dreamily.

'You old romantic, you,' he replied. 'Should I have got one with giblets or one without?'

'Stop talking dirty to me,' she said, giggling. She planted a kiss on his cheek and made to move away to start work on the chicken, but Nick held her firm. 'Do giblets turn you on?' he asked, a glint in his eyes. 'If only I'd known that, I wouldn't have bothered with chocolates and flowers.'

His mouth, smiling, came down upon hers and they kissed as new lovers kiss, softly at first and then deepening, eyes closed and sighing. Finally, they drew apart.

'I'm ravenous,' he confessed. 'Can you roast a chicken quickly?'

'No. But I could carve it up, slice the breast and we could make a speedy stir-fry?'

They ate their dinner of stir-fry chicken in the conservatory and afterwards, Stella got Amelia ready for bed.

When Amelia was dressed in fresh flowery cotton pyjamas, Stella realised that the bottoms were now at least two inches above Amelia's ankles.

'You're getting so big,' she sighed.

'I know,' said Amelia proudly. 'Hazel says I'm going to be tall, not a little fairy like Becky.'

Stella smiled at the thought of Becky as any sort of fairy.

'Mummy, Becky isn't as good at ballet as me,' Amelia announced.

'Don't say things like that, Amelia,' Stella said, absent-mindedly. 'That's very unkind. Becky is your friend.' She picked up her daughter's discarded clothes for the laundry basket, thinking that it only seemed like yesterday when Amelia was a tiny baby, snuggled in Babygrows.

Amelia's bottom lip wobbled, a sure sign that she was tired.

'I know you didn't mean to be unkind,' Stella said, back-tracking. 'I'm sure Becky will be good too if you help her. Now, what story do you want tonight?'

When Amelia's light was out, Stella and Nick sat down on the low russet sofa and talked about the holiday they'd been planning and their days at work. Stella skirted cautiously round the subject that had been niggling at her all day. 'I've been thinking about the girls. Your girls,' she said finally. 'It may take them some time to get used to the idea that you've got somebody new in your life.'

'Kids adapt,' Nick said easily. He looked so content that Stella almost didn't have the heart to ruin it for him. But she had to. These girls would be her stepchildren, give or take a wedding ring. There were two families to be carefully joined together and she and Nick needed to talk about this.

'It might not be that straightforward,' she said carefully. She looked up at Nick. His face was still happy. 'They may find it hard to deal with, you know ... me and you being together so soon after the divorce. Just because your marriage is legally over, doesn't mean it's over in the eyes of your kids. I've been reading this book on divorce and stepfamilies and it can take a long time for kids to get over the trauma of a split.' Stella paused. 'Their mother might find it hard to deal with too, and that will affect how they feel about us,' she added. 'People don't just get over a divorce that quickly . . .'

Nick's mouth set in that uncompromising line. 'Wendy will have to learn to live with it, then, won't she?' he said, the content look vanishing to be replaced by a taut expression.

Stella bit her lip. This was not going as planned. 'Jenna and Sara live with their mother. They'll be thinking of how this affects her too. We can't bulldoze them into meeting me or accepting the new situation . . .'

'Amelia's perfectly happy, she's much younger and she can deal with it,' Nick said.

'Yes, but she's not recovering from her parents' break-up,' Stella pointed out. 'Amelia has never known a time when Glenn and I lived together. She's used to seeing Mummy and Daddy separately. That's normal for her so you're not replacing him. Yes,' she added quickly, 'I know I'm not replacing the girls' mother, but they might see it that way. You're only just divorced and it all happened so fast, Nick, remember that. You've said yourself that both girls want nothing more than for you two to get back together again. I'll be like the one obstacle to that happening, they could hate me.' There. She'd said it: what she was most frightened of.

'They're not children, Stella,' Nick said quickly. 'You don't know them yet. Sara's the smartest girl in the world. She's genuinely brilliant, she always was, even when she was little. And Jenna's just as bright, all her teachers say so. They're smart. They'll get it.' He moved closer and stroked her arm lovingly. 'It will work out, you'll see.'

Stella thought of her book on stepfamilies. Brains were not seen as a get-out clause when it came to family strife. Nothing was. No matter how bright the children were, dealing with a stepfamily caused friction.

Small children were the way to run stepfamilies, as far as she could see. Little ones were less likely to throw wobblies when confronted with new mummies and daddies. Older children took sides and fright. Nick just didn't seem to understand this. But then, they were his daughters. He knew them, he knew what he was talking about.

Nick left at ten. 'I wish you didn't have to go,' Stella blurted out as they hugged goodbye at the front door. She knew it was crazy to say this when she'd pointed out to Nick that it might confuse Amelia to have Nick stay over. He'd never stayed the whole night – they made love, quietly, and then Nick would leave.

'One day, I won't be going anywhere,' he murmured, his face buried in the silk of her hair.

'I know.' Stella snuggled closer, wanting one more hug before he left.

She was constantly astonished by how much she wanted to wake up with him every day, to fall into bed wearily every night, doing the mundane things like setting the alarm clock and groaning when it went off next day; Stella longed for that normality because she'd be sharing it with Nick.

'I'll call you in the morning, OK?' He walked halfway down the path, then turned abruptly and came back to kiss her again. 'Love you.'

'Love you too,' she said.

She watched until his car had disappeared at the end of the street. It was funny how her life had felt complete with just her and Amelia until she'd met Nick. Now, she was incomplete without him. It was both a wonderful and a scary feeling. Wonderful: because she loved him, and scary: because she was no longer in control. The self-sufficient unit of herself and Amelia was no longer enough. Stella needed Nick. She'd taught herself not to need anyone after Glenn. Independence was safer. And now she was back relying on someone. She didn't allow herself to think of what it would be like if it all went wrong.

She locked up and checked on Amelia before getting ready for bed. Finally, she slipped under the pure white covers and sank back against the pillows. Bliss. Her bedroom was the most feminine room in the house, complete with a kidney-shaped dressing table dressed with a white frilly skirt, and a faded floral bedroom chair with girlish, embroidered cushions. People who knew only the businesslike, efficient Stella Miller would have been astonished to see her feminine bower with its junk-shop crystal perfume bottles and padded satin hangers in peachy pinks and soft lilacs.

Her bedside table was dominated by a cluster of framed photos showing Amelia and the rest of the family, all laughing and smiling for the camera. Her favourite was one of the three generations of Miller women: her mother, her sisters, herself, and Amelia, looking impish on her grandmother's lap. Dear Mum. Stella stared fondly at her mother's lovely face. Rose Miller steered clear of beauty salons, and had her hair trimmed only a few times a year. Yet her warm face shone with beauty, of both the inner and the outer kind. Love, decided Stella. True love gave you that glow.

'Night, Mum,' said Stella, switching off the light.

CHAPTER SEVENTEEN

A week later, Tara strode into the children's department of Lee's, looking like she'd just stepped off the catwalk in her red leather biker's jacket, lean black trousers and wedged boots, and with a Prada shopper hanging off her shoulder. Holly, who'd been waiting for her eagerly all afternoon, waved hello.

'It's my sister,' she said to Bunny, who was in a daze re-folding a gigantic pile of identical white T-shirts.

'Tara Lucretia, the Borgia sister,' said Bunny delightedly, eager to leave T-shirt folding behind. 'How nice to meet you finally! I've heard all about you.'

Tara grinned. 'Are you sure you don't want to hear my side?' she asked.

Holly laughed. 'I only say nice things about you,' she insisted. 'I never mentioned all the terrible things you did to me as a kid!'

'She told me *everything*,' said Bunny in a grim voice.

Tara's throaty laugh could be heard rippling all over the children's floor. Bunny joined in, wondering how two such different women could be sisters. It was as if the feisty, strong Tara had somehow got self-confidence enough for two, while Holly had none.

'I've heard all about you too,' said Tara to Bunny. 'Are you one of the wild gang she goes off partying with?'

Bunny didn't hesitate. 'Sure,' she said. 'Mad party girls, that's us.' Beside her, she could feel Holly breathe more easily with relief.

'Right, are you ready to go?' Tara said, looking at her watch. 'It's just four o'clock, Stella said she'd meet us at a quarter past, which gives us two hours before the shops close. If we can't find a present by then, I give up.'

Holly collected her handbag from the cupboard under the register and nipped over to say goodbye to Miss Jackson, with whom she'd arranged to leave early.

Bunny stayed chatting to Tara.

'You're looking for an anniversary present, aren't you?' Bunny said. 'I hate that sort of shopping. My mother is impossible to buy for.'

'We're very lucky,' said Tara, her strong features softening. 'Mum is such a pet, she genuinely doesn't care what we give her. She'll love it no matter what. But we want to get something really special, she deserves it. They deserve it,' Tara amended.

Bunny looked at her thoughtfully. Two strange revelations in one meeting. First, Tara clearly and incorrectly believed Holly was a wild thing who was never at home. And two, Tara adored their mother while Holly never spoke about her. She talked about Tara, Stella and Amelia all the time. Bunny could have written a thesis on Tara's career and Holly was forever putting away little bits and pieces from Lee's for Amelia, saying that Stella would just love that appliquéd T-shirt or that her niece looked so adorable in blue. But of Mum and Dad, nothing. Curious.

'See you tomorrow, Bunny,' said Holly, coming back. She slipped an arm though her older sister's arm and they headed off to the escalators.

'I want all those T-shirts folded when I get back,' warned Tara as she went.

'Yessir,' joked Bunny. She turned back to the messy mound. 'Yessir,' she said again wearily. It was easier said than done.

Tara insisted on a detour into the china department. 'Stella is keen on some big ornament type of thing,' she said as she stalked through dinner service displays, casting disparaging glances at fussy floral designs. 'I still think a weekend away is the best idea but if we have to look at ugly vases, we have to.'

Holly wandered over to the silver flatware because she had a horror of upending a display of wildly expensive dishes. She'd never forgotten the time she'd cannoned into a table of special offer soup bowls in the supermarket and had broken pounds' worth. 'This could be an idea,' she suggested, holding up a spoon from an elegantly old-fashioned canteen of cutlery.

'Too traditional,' said Tara. 'For someone else but not for Mum and Dad. It's got to be special. Do you know what I mean?'

'Special,' mused Holly, looking at some oddly-shaped salt and pepper canisters that fitted together. They were weird.

'Proof of a lasting love from their daughters,' added Tara, as if she was reciting from a soppy card. 'You know what I mean.'

'Yeah.'

'Those salt and pepper things are awful.'

They left Lee's and tried the expensive gift shop that sold Waterford Crystal, where they'd agreed to meet Stella. Tara preferred the modern designs to the more traditional ones, while Holly loved the dainty old-fashioned goblets which she knew would look lovely glinting behind the glass of her cherished armoire. But she was careful not to pick things up.

The problem, Tara decided, was that their parents had loads of crystal.

'What are we going to get?' she wailed.

'Not so easy now, is it?' teased Stella, appearing from the shop entrance, looking miles more glam than usual in a duck-egg blue macintosh with her dark hair tumbling lustrously around her face. Since meeting Nick, Stella's wardrobe had livened up considerably and she'd abandoned her sober suits for more flattering and more colourful clothes.

'I never said buying the anniversary present would be

easy,' retorted Tara, hugging her sister hello. 'I just said I refused to put money to some horrible gilt and enamel clock that looks like it came from a bordello.'

'You have too much imagination, that's your problem,' Stella laughed. 'Nobody else thought that clock looked like it came from a bordello.' She hugged Holly.

'You look lovely, Holls,' she said. And it was true: Holly had a light in her eyes that Stella hadn't seen for a long time. A sort of happy glint.

'What's responsible for this gleam in your eyes?'

'Nothing,' Holly grinned, thinking of Tom. It was nice to have a new friend, someone she felt she could be completely herself with. Since Tom had moved in, he'd become an important part of Holly, Joan and Kenny's lives, d'Artagnan to their three musketeers. She knew he could never be anything more to her because he was in love with Caroline, but it was nice having him as a friend all the same. 'If there's a glint in my eyes, it's exhaustion,' she joked now. 'Anyway, I can hardly compete with you two for glamour. I'm still in my boring work clothes. It's you pair who are all glammed up. That's a new mac, isn't it?'

Stella blushed. 'Nick bought it for me.'

'Nice,' commented Tara. 'Does he have any brothers? I could do with a few new things in my wardrobe.'

'He does have a brother but I daresay Finn would object if you went off with another man purely to boost your closets,' laughed Stella.

'Hardly,' grumbled Tara. 'I'm not sure he'd notice at the moment.'

Holly and Stella shot surprised glances at each other. Tara never moaned about Finn, never.

'What about this?' Tara asked, looking at a crystal clock.

'I'd break it the first time I walked past it,' said Holly. 'Can we not go to one of the antique shops? There's a lovely one I like. It's too expensive for me normally,' she added, 'but they have beautiful pieces. We might see something there, something one-off and special.'

285

'Lead the way,' Tara said.

And then they found it, the perfect present. All three of them loved the golden-hued nineteenth-century oil painting of rolling, verdant hills with a pretty village nestled in the valley.

'It was a brilliant idea to come here, Holls,' said Tara when the painting had been paid for and delivery instructions had been given. Tara was going to bring it to Kinvarra on the morning of the anniversary and Stella was going to buy a suitable card.

'I love this shop.' Holly ran an admiring finger over a pair of jade fire dogs. 'I could decorate my entire flat from here.'

'Will you decorate mine first,' begged Tara. 'If we don't do something with it soon, I'll move out. Right, are we ready to go? My car's in the garage, Stella, so I'll come with you.'

They were all going back to Stella's for dinner and, after a quick detour into the local grocery store for extra bread, they arrived at Delgany Terrace.

Holly volunteered to go to Hazel's house to collect her beloved Amelia, while Stella and Tara sorted out food.

'Is Nick coming tonight?' asked Tara as she watched her sister laying out five places at the table.

Stella looked up from her task in surprise. 'No, this is for Finn. He's invited too, I did tell you, didn't I? I'd hardly invite you for dinner and not mention poor Finn.'

Tara busied herself getting wine glasses from the cupboard. 'I meant to say, he probably won't be able to come until much later. He's going to pick me up though.'

'That's a pity,' Stella said, trying to keep her voice bland as she removed one setting and arranged the others symmetrically. She wondered if she should ask was everything all right. It had been very strange the way Tara had given out about Finn earlier. When they'd got engaged with such speed, Stella had tried to gently advise Tara that she didn't need to rush into marriage, that if they truly loved each other, they could spend time getting to know each other. Tara had been furious, saying Finn was perfect, she loved him and as she knew this for sure, why bother wasting time? Since then, she'd never said one negative thing about him. Not one.

'It's some work thing, you know,' Tara added quickly, before Stella got the chance to say anything. 'They're trying to win this big contract and Finn's busy night and day.'

'Hello!' sang Amelia, rushing in with her artwork for the day followed by Holly with Amelia's schoolbag. 'Mum, I'm starving!' the little girl said, plonking herself down at the table.

'Hello, you too,' said Tara, kissing her niece on the forehead. 'Does Hazel not feed you at all?'

'Only biscuits,' said Amelia dismissively. 'Oh, and soup.'

'Organic, homemade soup with wholewheat bread, also homemade,' put in Stella. 'She's a deprived child. Did you wash your hands, deprived child?'

Amelia nodded, big eyes fixed on the dish of vegetable lasagne that Stella was carrying to the table.

The three sisters laughed.

'She takes after me,' said Tara. 'I was always ravenous as a kid.'

'I remember,' commented Stella. 'If I left a chocolate bar down for two minutes, you'd gobble it up.' She hoped that she'd have a chance to talk to Holly privately so she could mention her worries about Tara. But there was never a chance.

Despite this, dinner was lively with Amelia chatting happily once she'd eaten a big portion of lasagne. The grown-ups drank a bottle of Chablis, hoovered up their own lasagne and finished a big bowl of Greek salad. Amelia, who was in charge of desserts, got a tub of ice cream from the freezer and Holly helped her dish it out.

'Did Mummy get into trouble ever?' she wanted to know tonight. Amelia was fascinated by the idea of her mother as a child and when she got her aunts together, she demanded stories of Stella.

Normally, Tara loved concocting stories of Stella's mischief but she didn't seem to have the heart for it this evening.

'Your mummy was never in trouble,' she said. 'I was always in trouble but then, that's me. Nothing changes.' She gave a little ironic laugh and alarm bells began to ring in her sisters' heads.

They waited until Amelia was in bed before they began to investigate.

'When Finn comes, can you drop me home too?' asked Holly.

'Sure,' said Tara. She was flopped out on the couch flicking through the television channels with the zapper, cradling her wine glass with her other hand.

Holly dropped down beside her and Stella took the armchair.

'Is everything OK between you and Finn?' Stella asked gently.

'Everything's fine, Finn is fine,' Tara said brusquely.

Both Stella and Holly glanced at her.

'You sure?' asked Holly.

'He's fine, right?' Tara's voice was shrill. 'He's just busy,' she added more quietly. 'Honestly, there are bound to be teething problems in a new marriage.'

Holly and Stella looked at each other again. Stella had a sinking feeling in her guts. Was there something wrong between Finn and Tara?

'Stop doing that!' Tara said angrily. 'It's like being out with Aunt Adele with you pair exchanging "I told you so" looks every five minutes.'

'We're not,' said Stella calmly. 'Don't fly off the handle, Tara. What's wrong?'

'Nothing.' Tara slammed her wine glass down on the big chest Stella used as a coffee table and stormed off to the bathroom. Holly got up to follow her but Stella stopped her with a gentle hand. 'No, leave her. She'll tell us when she's ready.'

'What do you think it is?' said Holly, sitting down again. 'I thought she and Finn were so happy.'

Stella shrugged helplessly. 'It could be a row, that's all. I hope that's all it is, anyhow. You know how Tara hates rows, she's too impetuous to cope with them and every argument is like WW2 to her. It'll blow over.' At least, she hoped it would.

Holly wasn't so sure.

When Tara emerged from the bathroom, Holly was telling Stella a wildly hilarious version of the speed dating night. Tara, looking relieved to be off the rack and mildly apologetic for her outburst, sat down.

'Sorry,' she murmured.

'For what?' said Stella and Holly in unison.

All three laughed.

'So then,' Holly continued her story, 'he said I had fabulous tits.'

'Who said that?' demanded Tara.

'This prince among men I met at the speed dating in the Purple Mosquito. We had five minutes of conversation and that's the bit I remember most.'

'I'd have thrown my drink over him!' said Tara, outraged at the very idea of anyone insulting her sister. 'Who is he? It's not too late to throw a drink over him now.'

Holly giggled. 'That is just what I thought you'd do. I sat looking at him and thought that you'd fling your drink over him and that Joan would throw a punch at him. I told him I'd get Miss Mindy over to give out to him.'

'Miss Mindy?'

By the time Holly had retold the whole story, making it clear that Miss Mindy was no idle threat, it was after ten. 'I'm worn out,' she said. 'I think I'll head off soon.'

'Off to meet up with one of your speed dating boys?' asked Stella wickedly.

'I told you I wasn't going out with anyone,' Holly explained earnestly. She didn't add that there was only one man on the horizon she had any interest in, and that he was taken. 'Unfortunately, Joan and Kenny are determined to set me up with somebody, but I'm not keen on blind dates. Especially not with friends of Finn's,' she added pointedly to Tara.

Tara's grin was weak. 'Yeah, well Finn's mates aren't exactly prize specimens. I promise I won't set you up with any of them.'

'They must be keeping him very late, poor dear,' Stella said, clearing up the glasses. 'Why don't you phone him and if he can't pick you two up, I'll phone for a taxi.'

'Sure.'

Tara got her mobile from her bag and phoned Finn's. It went straight to his answering service. She clicked 'off' furiously, then realised that Holly, still comfortable on the couch, was waiting to see what he'd say. Shame washed over Tara. Finn had promised he'd be at Stella's for dinner. Then, when the work function came up, he'd promised that he'd be there by half nine to pick her up. Now it was nearly a quarter past ten and he was still out, his wife forgotten.

Tara turned away, the way she often did when she was out and wanted a modicum of privacy while she was on her phone.

'Hi, Love,' she said into the dead phone. 'Yeah, yeah. Well it can't be helped. I'll tell Stella you're sorry. Bye.'

She turned back to face her sister. Holly's lovely face was alight with understanding, and the guilt at deceiving her grabbed Tara like a vice grip.

'Don't worry, babes,' Holly said. 'We'll get taxis. Poor Finn, he must be fed up with all these late nights.'

'Yeah.' Tara's voice was hollow. 'Totally fed up.'

Holly waved the taxi containing Tara off into the night and went upstairs to her flat where she found a big message stuck onto her door with Sellotape.

Having drinks – come in!!! Select gathering and impromptu party, party! Kenny had written in his sloping hand.

Holly smiled. She didn't need a message taped to her door

to tell her that there was a mini-party going on in Kenny and Joan's: the music was enough of an indicator. Ricky Martin or Madonna at high volume meant Kenny was entertaining because he adored Madonna and felt that Ricky's early Spanish albums were the height of cocktail party sophistication, and delectably smoochy into the bargain. Tonight, Ricky's husky Latin vocal filled the second floor.

Holly threw her coat and handbag onto the couch and glanced briefly at her reflection in the hall mirror. Her make-up was almost gone and her hair was windswept. On a thousand other nights, she'd wandered in next door without so much as combing her hair but for once, and without really knowing why, she decided to bother. She stripped off her white work shirt and plain bra and exchanged them for a lacy bra and a slinky black chiffon shirt. Instant revamp. In the bathroom, she brushed her hair until it shone and rapidly repaired her make-up the way Gabriella did: a sweep of eyeliner and lashings of mascara to pep up tired eyes, then glossy pink on her lips. Three minutes and she was done.

The others would probably laugh at her. When Tom had begun joining her, Joan and Kenny on their trips to the local pub in the evenings, Kenny had mortified Holly by announcing that she was trying to reform her normal, at-home slobby image in order to impress him.

'Kenny!' Holly had wailed.

'It's all right, love, Tom's one of us,' Kenny had said comfortingly. 'The terrible trio has become the queer quartet.'

'Speak for yourself,' joked Joan.

Holly had done her best to explain that she wasn't trying to impress *anyone* but that she thought it was about time she made more of an effort even when she was at home.

'I dress up for work, so I should dress up here too,' she explained. 'I'm fed up with looking like a tramp when I'm not working.'

'Quite right,' said Kenny approvingly. 'If only we can

get Joan to tart herself up at the weekends, we'll be very respectable.'

The door to Kenny and Joan's was unlocked and Holly pushed it open, announcing loudly that there'd been no need to tell her they were having a party.

'Sweetums, welcome. We were going to phone and tell you to come home early!' said Kenny gleefully, wrapping one arm round Holly and holding onto a full bottle of wine with the other. He was happily drunk.

Raul, Kenny's new boyfriend, was sitting on the floor with Joan, who was making an almighty mess with several bottles of liqueurs, a fork, a bowl of mashed-up bananas and a lemon that looked ten years old.

'Joan and Raul are making cocktails,' said Kenny, shooting Raul an adoring look.

'Banana surprise!' said Joan.

'I hate bananas,' said Raul mournfully as he attempted to cut the lemon up with a blunt knife.

Holly laughed. Raul was quite unlike Kenny's normal male-model-type boyfriends in that he didn't possess a six-pack, had dirty blond hair instead of the jet-black that Kenny liked, and had no visible cheekbones. Kenny adored cheekbones. Raul's flatmate, Anto, was crouched in front of the TV fanatically playing PlayStation 2 and making grunting noises.

Sprawled on the couch, clad in his usual denims and a marl grey T-shirt that showed off his rugby-player's body and looking reassuringly normal in the midst of the chaos, was Tom. Unlike the others, he was stone cold sober and gratifyingly pleased to see her.

'There's beer if you'd like,' said Tom, making room for her on the two-seater couch. 'Or Coke.'

'Coke,' said Holly, stepping over Joan and Raul's messy cocktail bar to sit beside him. The couch was too small for Tom and anyone else, but Holly didn't mind being squashed up beside him.

Tom snapped the ring pull on a can of Coke and handed it to Holly, who couldn't help but blush. 'Thanks.'

'Shit!' yelled Anto as his game went wrong.

'Banana cocktail!' said Joan triumphantly, holding up a glass jug of murky yellow sludge.

'I am not drinking that,' said Kenny, pouring himself another glass of wine. He was dancing happily by himself, doing little Ricky moves around the room as he swayed with his eyes closed. Only a drunken sixth sense stopped him falling over the furniture.

'I don't care if you don't wanna drink it,' hiccuped Joan, dividing the sludge with great difficulty between two glasses. It was more solid than liquid. 'Ready, Raul?' she said, handing him one glass. 'One, two, *three!*'

They downed their cocktails in one gulp and Raul made retching noises immediately afterwards. 'I told you I hate bananas!' he moaned.

Holly and Tom watched them with amusement. 'Kenny got a styling job today,' Tom revealed. 'That's why we're celebrating.'

'Ah,' said Holly. 'I did think it was a bit weird to be having this drink-fest on a weeknight. I can see I'll have to come in tomorrow morning to drag them all out of bed for work.'

'You do look after them, don't you?' said Tom.

'We look after each other,' Holly said. 'They're sort of like a second family to me, like a brother and sister to be honest.'

'You've got two sisters, though, haven't you?'

'Yes. I was with them tonight. They're marvellous. I mean, Kenny and Joan don't replace them, they're just . . . extra,' she finished. 'And my sisters are older than me, so I look up to them and want them to approve of me but with this pair,' she gestured to Kenny and Joan, 'they see me utterly as I am. There's no compulsion to be approved of. Does that make sense?'

'Absolutely.' Tom looked thoughtful. 'They say where you come in the family can have a huge effect on your personality,' he said. 'Caroline's a great believer in that. She's a middle child; she says that's why she's tough and ambitious.'

'Wow, is she tough and ambitious?'

He grinned ruefully. 'Very. I don't think it would have mattered where in the family Caroline was born, she'd have succeeded.'

'How about you? Are you the baby of the family or the middle?' Holly asked.

'Eldest of four. Very sensible, organised and boring, I'm afraid.'

'No, you're not,' protested Holly, patting him affectionately on one huge shoulder. 'You're reliable, what's wrong with that?'

'It's not very exciting,' Tom smiled.

'Excitement is over-rated,' Holly insisted. 'My eldest sister, Stella, is reliable and sensible and she's wonderful. She's the sort of person I'd go to in a crisis. Actually,' she grinned, 'Caroline's theory *does* fit because Tara, who's the middle sister, is ambitious and tough in her own way.'

'And you, as the baby, are supposed to be wildly indulged and spoilt rotten by your parents?' Tom queried.

It was Holly's turn to grin ruefully. 'Not really,' she said. 'My parents are very busy people, my mother does a lot for charity and has firm ideas about spoiling children. Besides, I think my parents were hoping for a boy and they got me instead.'

'You don't mean that, do you?' Tom's kind face was anxious.

'No, not in a bad way,' Holly said quickly. 'But I know my mum would have liked a boy. She even had the name picked out. Emlyn Hector. My mother likes unusual names.' Holly paused, instantly sorry she'd mentioned it. Even Kenny and Joan didn't know about that. Holly had buried it so far inside her that nobody knew. But Tom had that way of making her tell him things. He was easy to talk to, easy to confide in. 'I'm sorry . . .' she began.

'Don't be.' Tom's hand held hers tightly, telling her he understood and that she didn't need to say anything else.

'My parents are great, honestly . . .' Holly tried again but Tom silenced her with a gentle finger to her lips.

'Don't apologise. Families make mistakes too, you know,' he said. 'Your mum and dad can be saints on earth, and still screw things up occasionally, and you're not a bad person for noticing. Unconditional love doesn't mean you can't tell when your family do the wrong thing.'

Holly felt as if she couldn't speak. It was like opening a door she'd been terrified to open for years. The emotion she endlessly suppressed over little Emlyn Hector bubbled up inside her. She never criticised her family, never said a word against her mother. It was like a forbidden thought, punishable by expulsion from the Miller family. And now she was being told that it was all right to think those awful, disloyal thoughts.

'I know,' she whispered, so quietly that Tom had to lean close to even hear her. 'I never told anyone before.'

'Don't be sorry just because you told me,' he whispered, his face close to hers, his breath warm against her face.

'Please, don't mention this,' Holly begged.

In reply, Tom laid his mouth against her temple and gave her the softest kiss. Holly wouldn't have thought that such a big person could be so gentle.

'You can always talk to me,' he murmured.

Holly leaned against him, weak now from the emotion of her revelation. Tom put a strong arm around her and it was so comforting to lean there, her eyes closed, feeling a strange peace from having even spoken those forbidden words out loud.

'Holly!' roared Joan crossly. 'Tell Kenny to change the CD. He won't and I am bloody fed up with bloody Ricky bloody Martin!'

The flat was dark when Tara pushed open the front door.

'Hi, honey, I'm home,' she said bitterly. She went into the kitchen and opened the drinks cupboard with a great wrench. Brandy was the first thing she saw. She hated brandy. Next was gin. No, she decided. Wine would do nicely. They never kept chilled white wine in the fridge the way people did in magazine features. Tara had read loads of those 'what's in your fridge' celebrity articles where people always had lots of rocket salad, quail's eggs and Moët, but strangely, no mouldy old Philadelphia cheese or lettuce that had practically swapped DNA with the fridge from being stuck to the crisper compartment for so long. She and Finn were not spare bottle of white in the fridge people. They were lucky if they were 'up to date carton of milk' people. Finn was crap at remembering basic groceries as Tara knew to her cost. She *loathed* black coffee. At the back of the drinks cabinet, she found a bottle of white wine and opened it, poured a glass and stuck an ice cube in on top. Tough titty to the wine aficionados, she thought grimly, drinking half the glass in one fell swoop. She refilled it, then took glass and bottle into the sitting room, switched on the TV and waited.

The bottle was nearly empty when Finn came home.

'Hi, honey,' he said, eyes only slightly glazed, when he peered round the corner of the sitting room door. 'Sorry I'm late. What have you been up to?'

'I was at Stella's,' said Tara evenly, turning back to the television. She didn't want to look at him. She watched the television as if her life depended on it, her back ramrod-straight with tension. She wasn't paying any attention to the TV because her head was crammed with furious words that she wanted to scream at him. It was a mistake to argue when they'd both been drinking, she knew that, but reason had long since left the building.

Tara turned on him. 'Where the hell were you?' she hissed. 'You were supposed to pick me up from Stella's.'

'Oh shit.' Finn stayed in the doorway, as if scared to come in.

'I'm really sorry, honey, I just forgot. It was Bill's fault because . . .'

'Stop blaming other people!' Even Tara was astonished by her roar of fury.

For a second, there was silence. Then she found her voice again. 'You let me down in front of my sisters, you humiliated me! I had to lie and pretend you were working late so I wouldn't look like some idiot whose husband couldn't even be bothered to phone her!'

Finn stayed in the doorway, wincing at every word. 'I'm really sorry,' he repeated mantra-like. 'Really sorry.'

'Sorry isn't good enough!' howled Tara. 'You're late every second night with work and you're pissed half the time.' She glared at him, waiting for him to say something about it being work and how he couldn't help it. But he said nothing, he just looked at her with a strange, almost scared look in his eyes.

'I'm fed up with it, do you hear, fed up! You better get your act together, Finn, or I'm leaving.' She lurched to her feet. 'And you can sleep in the spare room tonight!'

She hadn't thought she'd be able to sleep but the combination of tiredness and too much booze sent her into a heavy sleep only for her to wake, hot and sweating, at five a.m. She lay in the double bed, exhausted and headachy and waited for morning to come.

While she waited, she thought. And as she thought, something clicked into place in her mind. Like the feeling she got when writing a scene in work and one word eluded her, buzzing round her subconscious but not coming to the fore. It was always the simplest word. Something from a schoolroom spelling test. Today's word was alcohol. Booze. Drink. Liquor.

As dawn slowly lit up the room, creeping in past the unlined blue curtains, reality came crashing into Tara's mind. It wasn't that Finn liked constant partying; he liked constant drinking. Booze flowed through their lives like tap water. It was always there. Finn wouldn't have dreamed of an evening at home without something alcoholic to drink. Meals out involved several aperitifs, wine and something in the liqueur department. They never met friends over coffee: pubs were the preferred meeting place. In crisis, without crisis, whatever. There was only once constant: Finn drank.

Tara looked at the clock. Ten to six. Too early to wake Finn? No.

Tara had never been good at waiting. She had to do it now. She thrust back the duvet and got up, not even bothering to pull her dressing gown on over her flimsy T-shirt. She stormed into the spare room where Finn lay snoring in the bed. His clothes were carefully laid on the exercise bike he'd had in his previous flat. Boxes of possessions were lined up all over the place, some opened with their contents spilling out after one of Tara's manic searches for something vital.

'Wake up!' she shouted.

Finn sat up in shock, his hair standing on end like a punk's. 'Whassup?' he said.

'I know,' she said, 'I know what's wrong.'

Through the veil of sleep, Finn's eyes looked suddenly wary. 'Sorry about last night,' he said. 'I know you're fed up with me working late . . .'

He got no further. Tara leaned over him and there was fury and menace in her face. 'It's nothing to do with you working late. It's to do with you drinking.'

Finn slumped back to his pillow. 'What about it?' he said flatly.

'You're drinking every day, Finn. Every day and every night.'

'It's work,' he said. 'I can't socialise and do my job properly if I don't.'

'You mean you can't go out without having a drink?' Tara's face was fierce. 'I know plenty of people who can. I can. It doesn't bother me.'

'Well, bully for you,' Finn said bitterly.

'You've got to stop. This is destroying us. You're never home at night and when you do get home, you're plastered. The only time I see you sober is in the morning and then you're hungover.' The truth of this hit her forcefully. Breakfast really was the only time when she was guaranteed that there'd be no tell-tale scent of alcohol on his breath. The fierceness vanished from her face, leaving a vulnerable look of pain. 'Why, Finn?'

The rapid change of attack seemed to affect Finn more than her full-scale anger had. He buried his face in his hands and watching him, Tara sank onto the bed, all the fight suddenly gone out of her.

'Why? What are you trying to escape from? Is it me?' She looked so lost and forlorn, so utterly devastated.

Finn grabbed her and held her so tightly that it hurt.

'It's not you, Tara. It's never you. I love you, I'm crazy about you,' he said hoarsely. 'I just forget to say stop when I'm out, that's all. You know me, life and soul of the party. I just needed a kick up the bum to remind me that life isn't all a party.'

'Are you sure that's all?' Clinging to him, feeling his heart pumping through the thin cotton of his faded T-shirt, Tara wanted to be reassured that everything was all right.

'Of course I'm sure. Listen, I'll stop drinking for a month, will that convince you? Not a drop shall pass my lips. I don't need it, all I need is you.'

She half-laughed, half-sobbed. 'Good, I'm glad to hear it.'

'Oh, Tara,' Finn buried his face in her shoulder, kissing the soft place where her neck curved and her collarbone began. 'I do love you, so much, you don't know how much.' He slid his fingers under her T-shirt, his touch tantalising her flesh.

He could make her melt by touching her, his skilled fingers stroking her gently, sending desire quivering through her body. Just looking at his face, sleepy-eyed with lust for her, was enough to make her want him. Nobody had ever looked like that at Tara before: nobody had ever made love to her the way Finn did. His technique had blown her off her feet when they'd first met, this movie star man who could make her gasp with pleasure. Finn's hands reached the curve of her buttocks, clasping her close to him, caressing gently with his fingers slipping inside the soft cotton of her panties.

'I love you too,' she said crying. And then he pulled her

T-shirt off and she dragged his off and they were wrapped around each other on the spare room bed, kissing fiercely, passionately, as if the force of their love was a physical thing and could protect them from every harm.

CHAPTER EIGHTEEN

It was the worst week in the world to be suffering from serious hair shock. The following Saturday, Stella was meeting Nick's daughters for the first time and she'd just had the haircut from hell. There was no other way to describe it. Feeling absurdly naked, she reached up to touch her ears, vulnerable to the world now that her shoulder-length dark hair had been shorn to frightening proportions. There wasn't a strand of hair on her head that measured longer than five inches.

The swinging, glossy mane had been cut up around her ears in an approximation of the style that made Christy Turlington look gamine and chic. On Stella, it had gone terribly wrong. The shocked face in the hairdresser's mirror looked like a stranger: Olive Oyl on a bad hair day. Even worse, it was all her own fault. The cut was lovely. It just didn't suit her.

Cristalle in the salon opposite the office cut her hair every two months, had done so for six years. Reliable and possibly a bit stick-in-the-mud, Cristalle was never going to be swept up to do hair at any avant-garde catwalk show in New York but she suited Stella. Until today, when Stella had decided on a change in honour of meeting Nick's daughters for the first time. She also had a longing to look glamorously different for the anniversary party in Kinvarra the following week. She'd booked an appointment in a different salon, feeling wild and daring, imagining herself with one of those wash-and-go styles which require no painstaking blow-drying or even a brush, for that matter.

Seated in a high-tech salon staffed with trendy people, armfuls of glossy magazines on her lap and a cappuccino in front of her, she'd uttered the fatal words: 'I'm not sure what I want: something completely different. Do what you like!' Idiot!

Stella wondered how the law hadn't caught up with hairdressing and made it illegal to say such things to a hairstylist you didn't know. Subsection 4 of the Penal Hairdressing Code could cover it. The hairdresser would have to ensure that the client had taken the proper professional advice before agreeing to 'something different' or uttering the inflammatory 'do what you like'. Two independent witnesses would be required, one of whom would have to be a best friend like Vicki and therefore licensed to say: 'Short hair with your jaw line? I don't think so.'

'It really suits you,' said the stylist, showing Stella the back of her hair with a second mirror. The back was just as bad. Worse, it revealed that her natural hairline went so low down the nape of her neck as to qualify her for primate status.

'Oh, it's lovely,' cooed the colourist, walking by.

'Wonderful, fantastic cut,' said another hairdresser.

Stella knew she was destroyed. When every member of staff queued up to tell you how lovely your haircut was, you were either a dead ringer for Nicole Kidman or you looked like you used to when your mother cut your hair with the aid of a pudding bowl. There was nothing she could say. It was her own fault. Knowing the law backwards was of no benefit when you'd given the stylist carte blanche. She should never have got so immersed in her magazines. If only she'd looked up from those hints on how to transform your wardrobe with accessories, she'd have realised that short hair was very definitely not her. And how had she never noticed her strong jaw before? You needed dainty little heart-shaped faces to carry off such severe hair.

Outside, having over-tipped out of guilt, Stella walked slowly back to the office, self-consciously touching her shorn hair every few minutes, as if smoothing it down could make it grow more quickly.

If only there was a wig shop on the way back to the office, she'd have bought a wig. But there wasn't. Instead, there were acres of plate-glass windows where Stella could catch horrified glimpses of her reflection.

The receptionist in Lawson, Wilde & McKenna was too well trained to be honest. 'Your hair is . . . lovely,' she said, blinking rapidly. A sure sign of lying. Stella slunk off to the lift, praying that she would meet no-one she knew until she'd had another look at herself in the loo mirror.

Vicki was such a bad liar that she'd given up trying years ago. She looked up from Lori's desk to see Stella trying to sneak surreptitiously into her office. 'Jeez, your hair! What happened, Stella?'

Stella bit her lip. 'I said I wanted something different,' she muttered.

'Different?' said Lori. 'Did she use a lawnmower?' Lori was still sulking over Stella's annexing of the most gorgeous man she'd seen in years.

'Don't,' begged Stella. 'It's awful, I know. Whatever am I going to do? It's the anniversary party in a week and I'm meeting Nick's daughters for the first time on Sunday. This is absolutely the worst time for this to happen. I look like a complete idiot.'

'Lots of make-up and hair wax,' said Vicki firmly, 'that's what we need. We've got to make it look intentional.'

'Short hair is fashionable,' added Lori, trying to make up for the lawnmower joke.

'It is on people like my sister, Tara. She can carry it off. She's trendy, she's younger than me and she doesn't have a jaw like a shot-putter,' wailed Stella.

It was like waiting for the President, Stella decided, when she'd peered out the window for the fifth time in twenty minutes because she'd heard a car door slam. She'd have some camomile tea and forget that Nick was coming with

Jenna and Sara for their first ever visit. She was pouring boiling water on a camomile tea bag when she heard the front door opening. Determined to be calm and unfussed, even though her heart was beating double time, Stella added honey, stirred her cup carefully and smoothed her hair down again.

'Hello,' said Nick's voice. Tense, definitely, Stella thought. And a bit odd. He normally said 'Hello, Stella.'

Still holding her teacup, partly as defence, she walked into the living room to meet Nick's daughters. Nick stood awkwardly in the room with just one girl. She had to be Jenna, Stella realised, but Jenna had just had her fifteenth birthday and this unbelievably adult girl-woman looked as if she was at least nineteen. The photo Nick had shown Stella all those months ago did not do her justice.

Slender as a model and very pretty, she had long fair hair, a disdainful grey gaze and a lipglossed mouth that was set in a firm line of dislike. She wore hip-hugging jeans, a T-shirt that showed off her tanned, flat stomach and a lot of make-up. Stella couldn't help staring.

'Jenna, this is Stella,' Nick said, still awkward. 'Sara will be coming later. Some college thing came up.'

'Hello, Jenna, welcome.' Stella moved forwards, unsure, in the face of this adult creature, if she was to shake hands or air kiss both sides.

Jenna took matters into her own hands. She leaned back as if she couldn't bear Stella to touch her and the disdainful gaze hardened into insolence.

'Well,' said Nick, falsely jovial and deliberately ignoring Jenna's rudeness in not replying, 'isn't this nice?'

'I'm having camomile tea,' said Stella. 'Would you like me to make you some or would you like juice?'

'No.'

Stella noted the absence of the word 'thanks' but said nothing. Instead, she watched as Jenna scanned the room. The corners of the glistening lips turned up faintly, as she smirked at everything she saw. She clearly wasn't impressed with the museum prints that Stella had framed cheaply herself and she literally looked down her nose at the big old couch with the rich brocade throw that hid a multitude of ancient sins. None of this comfortable, lived-in furniture could compare with the interior-decorated grandeur of her own home, her haughty expression said.

Stella felt her long-planned welcoming smile shrink. Loving her new-found family, Nick's family, suddenly seemed like a much tougher task than she'd thought.

'Stella made lunch for us all,' Nick said, putting an arm around Jenna.

'I'm not hungry.' Jenna stared defiantly at Stella, as if daring her to say something sharp in return.

'That's fine,' Stella said evenly, thinking of the feast laid out on the kitchen table. 'We can eat later.'

'I won't want to eat later.' Still that defiant stare.

Stella picked up her cup of tea and took a sip, more to reassure herself than for any other reason.

'Hey, Stella has that Macy Gray CD you like. You do like Macy, don't you?' said Nick. He flicked through Stella's CD collection rapidly, found the CD in question and put it into the player. Stella watched Jenna watching her father. She was evidently shocked at his familiarity with everything to do with Stella. He knew what CDs she had; he was comfortable enough in Stella's home to put music on without asking. Stella could see this knowledge shaking Jenna's notion of how friendly Nick and Stella were.

The music started. Nick stood between his girlfriend and his daughter and smiled earnestly, as though goodwill alone would break down the barriers.

Stella decided she'd have to take matters into her own hands. Don't be afraid to touch the sensitive issues, *The Art of Step* counselled.

'I have a daughter,' Stella said. 'She's seven, her name's Amelia. I'd love you to meet her but I thought it might be easier if you and I met without her first, because I can understand that this is hard for you.'

Jenna's little face moved from defiance to sneering. 'Hard for me?' she said. 'You don't know what's hard for me. You don't know anything about me. I don't want to be here today. I don't want to know about your stupid daughter . . .'

This was too much for Stella. Amelia was sacrosanct. 'Don't you dare be so rude to me. This is my home, I won't tolerate such rudeness.'

'I don't want to be in your home!' screeched Jenna, switching to tears in an instant.

'Sweetheart, don't get upset.' Nick pulled Jenna towards him and cradled her in his arms like a baby as she sobbed.

Shaking with rage and impotence, Stella stood and watched.

'Hush, darling,' soothed Nick.

Suddenly, Jenna pulled away from him and rushed for the door.

'I'm sorry,' said Nick, before going after her.

Stella sank to the couch, her legs weak, and listened to Macy Gray's husky helium voice fill the room.

It was five minutes before Nick returned, alone.

'Darling,' whispered Nick.

Oh, she was *darling* now, was she? Stella glared at him.

'Jenna's upset. I'm going to bring her out for a while, let her get used to the idea. Maybe buy her something.'

'Buy her something?' hissed Stella back. 'As a reward for bad behaviour? That's not the sort of advice they give in parenting classes.' She knew she was being sarcastic but she didn't care.

'Come on, Stella, this is tough on the poor kid. She's had a lot to take in today. It can't be easy for her.'

'And what about me?' Stella wanted to ask, but she couldn't, because Nick had already rushed back to his daughter. Through the window, Stella watched him get into the car, say something to make Jenna smile up at him, and then drive off.

Stella didn't know which of them she was angriest with.

306

Nick: for allowing his badly brought up daughter to be so rude. Or Jenna: for the gratuitous rudeness. She was grateful that she'd decided to drop Amelia at Hazel's just in case the meeting didn't go as planned. If Amelia had been exposed to such naked hatred, Stella was sure she'd have thrown Jenna out.

'How's it going?' asked Hazel eagerly half an hour later when Stella arrived to pick up Amelia.

'You choose the word,' said Stella grimly. 'Awful, terrible, catastrophic, rude!'

'That bad?' winced Hazel. 'Is it too early for a glass of wine?'

'Oh no,' said Stella. 'It's not too early at all. What I don't understand,' she said, sitting on the edge of a chair, too taut to sit back and relax, 'is why none of Nick's bloody family seem to like me. His sister-in-law, the horrible Clarisse, cancelled our dinner, ostensibly because she was sick but I know it's because she just didn't want me in her house. Now Jenna's being unbelievably rude.' Feeling childish, she blinked back tears.

Hazel changed her mind and got out the big wine glasses instead of the small ones.

'Where are the girls?' asked Stella, suddenly startled to realise that in her rage, she hadn't looked for Amelia or the twins.

'Ivan took them swimming,' said Hazel. 'They should be back any time now.' She poured a glass of white wine for Stella. 'Biscuits?'

'Only if you've got double, double chocolate chip.'

Two glasses of wine, four biscuits and an hour of Hazel's down-to-earth advice later, Stella and Amelia walked back home hand in hand.

'Did Jenna and Sara see my room?' said Amelia excitedly. 'I want to show them myself.' She chattered away nineteen to the dozen about Jenna and Sara, while Stella felt herself tense up again. In Amelia's innocent eyes, these two girls were going to be like big sisters.

'Mum, don't squeeze my hand so tight,' complained Amelia.

'Sorry, pet,' said Stella, loosening her grip.

She began to pray silently. Please let Jenna and Sara be kind to little Amelia. It wasn't her fault.

At home, there was a message on the answering machine to say that Nick would be back by six with Jenna, and that Sara might make her own way there earlier.

Stella thought of Hazel's advice: 'Plod along with a smile on your face and take no offence at anything.'

'Only a robot could smile at that girl's antics,' Stella had said mournfully.

'It must be difficult for her, Stel,' said Hazel. 'And difficult for Nick, too. She's his little girl and he's trying not to hurt her, that's all.'

'*I* haven't hurt her,' protested Stella. 'Her parents split up before I even met Nick but she wants to take it out on me.'

'Yeah, but kids can be irrational. You know that.'

'Kid? Jenna Cavaletto isn't a kid: she's a spoilt brat.'

'Stel, calm down. You want this to work, don't you? So learn to deal with it. Just think of how you turn the other cheek when someone cuts you up in traffic or whatever. That doesn't get to you.'

'This is different,' Stella tried to explain. 'When somebody cuts you up in the car, or when they bang their trolley into yours in the supermarket, they don't know you. It's not personal. This is. If you'd seen the way that girl looked down her nose at my home . . .' Stella could feel her blood boil at the very thought of it.

'She's a kid and you're an adult. Do some yoga, that'll help.'

When Amelia was half watching television and half playing with Barbie, Stella changed out of the shift dress she'd worn to meet the girls, and pulled on an old T-shirt and loose leggings. She set up her mat in her bedroom and slipped automatically into her first position. Normally, she'd barely started before the relief would begin to flood through her but today, calm eluded her. Instead of being able to tune out her problems, the silence magnified them and Jenna's insolent little face filled her mind no matter how hard she tried.

Finally, Stella gave up. Yoga had brought her through her split with Glenn and the years when there was always some financial worry to stop her sleeping. Stella often claimed that there was nothing yoga couldn't fix. Not today.

Still in her yoga clothes, she walked into the living room to sit beside Amelia when, for the second time that day, she heard Nick's key in the lock. This time, Stella didn't feel excited. She felt sick to the stomach.

'Hello!' cried Amelia excitedly, bouncing up happily as Nick appeared with Jenna and Sara.

'Hello, Amelia,' said Nick, picking her up.

From her position on the couch, Stella watched the girls' expressions. Sara, a tall slightly scruffy girl with dark hair and Nick's incredible eyes, smiled awkwardly and said 'hello'.

Jenna's jaw tightened as she watched her father hugging Amelia, but she too said 'hello'.

Progress, thought Stella with relief.

'Hello, Sara,' she said, getting up and extending a hand. Sara flushed and said, 'Nice to meet you.'

'How about we start again, Jenna?' Stella said, turning to the younger girl. She was smiling but her voice was firm. The olive branch was a cast-iron one.

Jenna took her time but said 'OK' in a tight little voice.

'Wonderful,' boomed Nick heartily.

They all looked at him.

'I haven't done anything in the way of dinner because I didn't know what time you'd be home,' said Stella in even tones.

She could see Jenna wince at the word 'home'. That was a mistake. She had to make an effort. Jenna was a child after all, albeit a precocious one. 'I had salad ready earlier,' she continued, 'we can eat that.'

'Great,' said Nick.

'Amelia, you can help me,' Stella said. She didn't want her daughter left to Jenna's tender mercies.

During dinner, Jenna spoke in monosyllables but at least she was polite. Nick talked enough for four people while Stella got on quite well with Sara who was plainly a little shy, but didn't seem to have a problem with the concept of her father's new girlfriend.

She told Stella about college and seemed good-humoured when Nick teased her about her boyfriend there.

'Is this serious? Should I start saving for the big white wedding?' he joked.

'Dad, get real,' she laughed. 'I wouldn't start saving just yet.'

Nick laughed over-loudly and even Stella managed a little chuckle, but it was hard to act merry when all the time she was aware of Jenna watching fiercely from under her lashes, ready to pounce.

Amelia helped Stella tidy away the dishes. Neither Jenna nor Sara moved a muscle. What sort of woman would bring up her daughters with such bad manners? Stella thought grimly as she worked. When she was a teenager, Rose would have killed her if she'd sat at a table in someone else's house and hadn't lifted a finger to help.

Amelia was eager to show off the glazed apricot tart that Stella had slaved over.

'Mummy made this,' said Amelia artlessly to Nick, carefully carrying the tart to the table.

'Mummy's very good to make something this nice,' said Nick fondly.

Stella held her breath, waiting for the terrifying moment when Jenna would snap at Nick's affectionate use of the word 'Mummy'. But nothing happened.

Finally, Stella began to relax. Nick must have given Jenna a good talking to earlier. She was behaving.

'This is great,' said Sara with her mouth full.

Stella smiled, grateful for this crumb of praise.

Jenna refused any tart but Stella didn't mind. Jenna was obviously highly conscious about what she ate.

'Dad, I've got to go,' Sara said when she'd finished her coffee. 'I'm meeting some people in town.'

'We should all go,' Nick agreed instantly.

'Can I use your bathroom?' Sara asked politely.

'I'll show you where it is,' said Amelia.

'I'm just going to turn on CNN and pick up the headlines,' Nick said, also rising from the table.

Stella and Jenna were left alone in deafening silence. Stella thought of her own reputation for being cool, calm and in control of any situation, and here she was speechless in the presence of a defiant teenager. For Nick's sake, she wanted to make an effort at conversation but suddenly the stresses of the day washed over her. She was too tired. It would be easier to smile, tidy up and wave them all off into the sunset with the first, difficult visit over.

Jenna had other ideas. When Stella got up from her seat and began collecting up empty plates, Jenna spoke.

'I don't know what you think you're doing, but it won't work,' she hissed. 'You're ruining everything. My mother hates you, don't you know that. She loves Dad properly. But you're ruining it all, you bitch.'

Stella stepped back as if she'd been hit. The venom in Jenna's voice shocked her as much as the words. How could Jenna loathe her so much? Stella had done nothing but love Nick. She'd been absolutely prepared to love his children, too, no matter how hard that was. And even though she guessed that Jenna's insults were parroted from her mother, the nastiness shocked Stella to the core.

'Dad's ready to go,' announced Sara.

'Great,' said Jenna brightly, hopping up from her chair. 'See you.'

There was nothing Stella could do but mouth goodbye.

311

CHAPTER NINETEEN

With a week to go to Rose and Hugh's ruby wedding party, Tara felt very unpartyish. Her mind just wasn't on her work as she sat in her cubicle and failed to find any intelligent way of writing the scene in question. During the storyline meeting, it had sounded easy. *National Hospital*'s hard-nosed administrator, an unsympathetic character with the improbable name of January Vincent, had just discovered that her elderly mother was dying of cancer. In a pivotal scene with her regular adversary, the deeply caring Dr Burke, January had to let her guard slip and reveal that she and her mother had a turbulent relationship and hadn't seen each other for four years. Needless to say, the argument which had caused the split had to be January's fault.

The scene had to achieve three aims: to help explain why January had grown into such a bitch, to make the viewers long for the scene when she had to meet her mother, and naturally, to show her the error of her ways.

Viewers liked nasty characters to get their just desserts. And January was deeply nasty, unlike the woman who played her, a gentle soul named Alison.

Normally, Tara loved writing for Alison, who was a marvellous actress, but today, the muse was not around. In fact, Tara reflected, the muse had stomped off the premises altogether.

The tangled plotlines of *National Hospital* kept vanishing from her mind and the only storyline being played out in Tara's head was of her own life, with Finn the main character. He hadn't had a drink in over a week and Tara felt that she should be delighted with this. But something flickering in the dim recesses of her brain told her this particular scene was far from over. That was the terrifying thing.

Nothing was normal in the Miller/Jefferson household. Finn was outwardly buoyant and merry, as if he didn't miss alcohol at all. While Tara tried to be blithe, all the time watching and waiting for the moment when he'd arrive home with the tell-tale scent of booze on his breath. It was like waiting idly for the tidal wave to crash to shore.

Tara kept thinking of the big party in Kinvarra and the effect that all the boozing would have on Finn. Would he be able to resist or would he fall off the wagon spectacularly?

''Lo,' said a grumpy voice as Isadora, clad all in khaki combat gear like some glamorous commando, appeared and threw herself onto a chair. She looked in a foul temper. That makes two of us, Tara said to herself.

'What's up with you?' she asked.

'Reverse badger,' Isadora said, pointing to her hair.

Tara was familiar with Isadora's unusual turn of phrase but this was new to her. 'Explain, pliz?'

'Badgers are black with a white stripe; my hair is blonde with a big dark stripe down the middle where my roots need doing.' Isadora rummaged in her jacket for her cigarettes. 'I haven't time for an appointment at the hairdresser's and I look a mess. I know,' she groaned as she lit up, 'smoking is the work of the devil and my arteries are probably clogged up like the toll bridge road at rush hour. I've heard it all before but I don't care. I need my emotional crutch, specially when my roots are bad.'

'Did I say anything?' demanded Tara, annoyed

'No,' admitted Isadora, 'but you had that *look* on your face.' She settled back into the chair and inhaled deeply. 'How's your great script for the we're-not-worthy Mike Hammond?'

Another sore point. Since meeting Mike and agreeing to polish up the script for his friend's movie, Tara hadn't re-written a single word. Not one. Her ability to write had vanished full stop and, faced with a script that required sandblasting as opposed to polishing, she felt like a complete novice. Time was of the essence with the script, and Tara was afraid she'd have to phone Mike up and tell him she couldn't do it.

She gave up on the scene between January and Dr Burke. 'Don't ask,' she said, clicking 'save' on the computer. That done, she shoved her chair back, stuck her feet up on the desk and held a hand out in the direction of Isadora's packet of cigarettes. 'Can I have one?'

Isadora was startled out of her usual nonchalance.

'A cigarette?'

'No, a lobotomy,' said Tara in exasperation. 'Yes, of course a cigarette.'

'You've spent years telling me not to smoke.' Isadora looked outraged.

'You're not the only one who can do with an emotional crutch.' As soon as she'd said it, Tara was sorry. She didn't want to talk about why she was depressed and mentioning that she needed an emotional crutch would be like a red rag to a bull where Isadora was concerned. Today however, Isadora didn't bite. She handed over a cigarette and flicked her lighter on. Tara sucked the cigarette inexpertly and asked herself what it would be like to be addicted to cigarettes. Or anything.

She'd had the odd cigarette socially when she was in her college but had never longed for a fag as soon as she opened her eyes, which was what people like Isadora and Holly did. Tara had spent years trying to get her younger sister to give up, although Holly, a pushover in most arguments, held firm.

'It doesn't suit you,' muttered Isadora, gesturing at Tara's cigarette. 'You look like it's your first time behind the bike shed.'

Tara felt vaguely insulted. 'Are you telling me I'm a boring old square?'

'No, just that you don't suit smoking. Sorry.'

Tara took a few more exploratory puffs until she felt nauseated and dropped the half-smoked cigarette into a polystyrene cup of cold coffee. Try as she might, she couldn't imagine what it would be like to be a slave to those little white sticks. She knew they were deadly, but strangely, they didn't seem as deadly as alcohol. Did smoking destroy marriages in the same way that Finn's drinking was slowly destroying theirs?

'Have you ever tried to give up?' she asked suddenly, wanting to understand what it was all about.

Isadora winced. 'For ten years, I had only one New Year's resolution: to stop smoking. By dinner on New Year's Day, I was deranged with bad temper. Whoever was living with me at the time would practically force a fag into my hand and tell me to shut up and light up. What can a girl do?'

'When people give up, are they always smokers who have just managed to stay off them, or do they become ex-smokers?'

Isadora grinned. 'You'd have to ask someone who's managed to give them up for longer than eighteen hours and four minutes.'

'Right. But if you really wanted to,' Tara insisted, 'could you do it?' She wasn't thinking of cigarettes: she was thinking of Finn. She wanted to *understand*. 'Is it the craving that gets to you in the end? Do you think that if people really want to give up things they're addicted to, that they can? Or is it deeper than that?'

Through a veil of smoke, Isadora gazed at her friend. 'Why do you ask?' she said. 'Oh, don't tell me, you're dreaming up an addiction storyline. Is it going to be fags, drink or drugs and who have you lined up to get the poisoned chalice?'

Tara laughed and picked up a notebook. 'You know me so well,' she said ruefully. Her mind was racing, trying to think of which character she could suddenly land with an addiction. She didn't want even Isadora to know what she was really thinking. She wasn't ready to open up the pain. 'I saw this documentary on a rehab clinic,' she stalled, 'and

I've been playing around with the idea. I don't know who's the right person for it but we need to spice up things.'

Isadora's eyes narrowed.

'It was just a thought,' Tara added lamely, cursing herself for saying something so stupid. Both she and Isadora firmly believed that the best storylines were character-driven rather than issue-driven. Blindly saying she had an issue but no idea who to pin it on just wasn't the way she worked. 'Actually, I must be tired,' she added lightly, 'because that really was a crap idea.'

'Addiction isn't a crap idea,' Isadora countered, dropping her cigarette in the cold coffee. 'It's one of the few issues you can drop in and out, and we haven't had a major addict story for ages; not since Billie and the prescription drug one.' Another fag was lit up and Isadora leaned back in her chair thoughtfully. 'Which doctor should we make a slave to the bottle?' she grinned. 'You know they say you're not an alcoholic unless you drink more than your doctor.'

Tara looked at her stonily.

'We could use that line,' Isadora mused. 'The idea has to be introduced gradually, though. We can't rush it on this one. Nobody suddenly starts drinking like a fish.'

Somehow, Tara managed to look interested without betraying the battering her heart was getting. Isadora grabbed a pen and pad from Tara's desk and began scribbling notes. 'Alcoholism is a slow builder, we need that sense of pace.'

'What needs a sense of pace?' Tommy, the show's senior storyline editor, pulled up a chair and sat down.

'Tara's got an idea for an addiction storyline,' Isadora announced enthusiastically.

Tara knew what a snowball felt like when it started rolling down the hill.

'It was just an idea out of thin air,' she said. The story conference had been the day before and she hadn't mentioned it then. Some of the editors felt immediately threatened if any idea materialised without it having been discussed to death at the conference. 'I saw a documentary on addiction the other day . . .'

'What channel was that on?' Tommy looked interested. 'Maybe we could get a copy of it?'

'I think it was on satellite, I forget to be honest, but it was last week maybe,' Tara lied hastily. 'It wasn't a good programme but the idea stuck in my head.'

By the time the subject had been thrashed out by Tommy and Isadora, Tara's brain was addled with the idea of addiction.

'Brilliant idea,' Tommy said approvingly to her. 'We needed a shake-up for Dr Carlisle and this is definitely it. You should write it, seeing as it's your idea.'

'Slow build, that's vital,' repeated Isadora.

'Yeah, to get that sense of impending doom and only the audience know what's coming.'

Isadora nodded. 'And Carole, his wife, doesn't pick up on it because of the problems she's got with the sexual harassment case.'

'Great,' said Tara weakly.

When Isadora and Tommy had gone, she punched a key on her computer to rescue it from screensaver-dom. The word game which automatically appeared onscreen when the screensaver had been on for over ten minutes, came into view. Tara loved the conundrum game and had to limit herself to playing it for five minutes a day. Now, she exited it with one hard key stroke and stared at the monitor blindly. How dumb could any one person get? Finn was an alcoholic and she must have been an utter idiot not to have noticed until now. Nobody slipped from being a social drinker to being an alcoholic in a few short months. There were signs, warning signs, and Tara must have seen them. She and Finn had been together for nearly eighteen months, married for nearly a year. Had he always drunk this much and had she been too blinded by love to notice? Or, even worse, had it only started since they were married because their marriage was the reason he drank?

Everyone would think she was an idiot to have noticed only now. And they'd tell her to get out. Mum, Dad, Stella and Holly – they loved Finn but none of them would want her tethered to an alcoholic for life.

Aaron popped his head round her cubicle. 'Tara, Scott Irving's here. We're introducing everyone to him in the conference room. Want to come?'

Yes,' said Tara quickly. Scott Irving was Aaron's latest wunderkind, a hot young writer he'd swiped from a rival channel. Ordinarily, Tara might have experienced a moment of jealousy that her mentor was bringing in another young writer. But she was too preoccupied to care.

She followed Aaron along the grey-carpeted corridor to the conference room. There was something comforting about the combination of Aaron and the familiarity of the office. Surely nothing life-shattering could happen in this ordinary, everyday world? Finn might not be an alcoholic after all. Other people would have noticed, wouldn't they? Finn wouldn't be able to do his job. His colleagues would phone up, frantic that he'd drunk several bottles of vodka or something.

People just didn't become alcoholics suddenly, she told herself. She was worrying too much.

In the conference room, the executive producer, whom the writers secretly called Godzilla because he was so thick-skinned, was opening champagne to celebrate a triple whammy: superb ratings, the arrival of a fading Irish movie star in a cameo role and the poaching of Scott Irving from TV222. The room was full and noisy with the customary laughs and wicked remarks about Godzilla, who wasn't as loved as he'd have liked. Playing jokes on Godzilla was an office sport and he still hadn't discovered who'd changed his mobile phone ring tone to the sound of a female porn star faking orgasm. Ralph was heading the leader board on the Godzilla-jokes for that one, although Tommy had apparently planned something wicked to do with Godzilla's office chair and superglue.

Tara slipped in and leaned against the back wall beside Isadora, letting herself finally relax.

'He's a bit of all right, isn't he?' said Isadora, gesturing to the tall lean man at the top of the room with God and Aaron. 'I like that Byronic smoulder.'

Tara glanced up and saw that the new writer did indeed have enough physical charms to be on the other side of the TV cameras. Pale-skinned enough to be an Anne Rice hero, his coal-black hair and heavy five o'clock shadow gave him a tortured-artist air.

'You're incorrigible,' Tara whispered to Isadora. 'What happened to the gorgeous Michael?'

'I dumped him,' Isadora said, eyes on Scott. 'Three weeks was long enough.'

Tara laughed out loud. Situation normal.

CHAPTER TWENTY

Her parents' big anniversary bash was just three days away when Holly gave her own party, a select birthday dinner for Tom. It had been her idea, although Kenny had taken it a step further and suggested making it a surprise and having it on Tom's thirty-first birthday itself, which was a Thursday, instead of the day after.

'He might have arranged something with his friends for that day,' said Holly hesitantly when Joan and Kenny began brainstorming exactly how to inveigle Tom down to the pub, and then get him home in time for a surprise meal.

'*We're* his friends!' Joan said, as if that was patently obvious. 'Sure, he spends all his time with us.'

This was true. Tom went along with the three of them on their trips to the pub at the weekend, and on their forays to the Purple Mosquito, which, since the triumph of the speed dating night, was Joan's favourite spot.

'Imagine; so many men, so little time,' she sighed. 'I'm turning into a man magnet.'

'Fridge magnet, more like,' said Kenny. His fling with Raul was off and he was grumpy.

Holly found it fun going out with Tom along. She was never shy in his presence and when Kenny and Joan flitted off like social butterflies to talk to their enormous raft of acquaintances, Tom kept Holly company. It was nice to have someone to talk to instead of sitting on her own, pretending to look as if she was enjoying herself.

Tom, in turn, had brought the three of them hill-walking

320

(not a huge success with either Joan or Kenny) and they'd all been out on a boat owned by a colleague of his (much more successful, although Kenny's prized vintage Gaultier boating jacket turned out to be useless for keeping the cold out on the high seas. Tom had lent Kenny a windcheater and he'd spent the rest of the trip looking like a child in a grown-up's clothing and moaning, 'I can't believe I'm actually wearing chain store clothes' in a weak voice.)

Now, Holly tasted the sauce one last time. The subtle flavours of ginger, lemon grass and chicken all mingled together brilliantly. She smiled to herself with childish delight.

The flat was decked out in candles and balloons. Joan had done the blowing up, which she said was her aerobic exercise for the week. Holly had decked herself out in her best, slimming jeans and a daringly low-cut antique lace top in a glowing old gold. It was going to be a fantastic evening.

Joan had been in favour of a huge party, complete with flashing disco lights and a proper DJ. But because nobody had the funds, they reached a compromise: a small dinner for Tom, Holly, Kenny and Joan, followed by some wildness down at the Mosquito with the usual crowd.

It was all to be a big surprise, with Kenny and Joan charged with meeting Tom after work and dragging him off to the pub. They then had to get him home at eight on the nail.

The venue for the dinner was Holly's flat because she was cooking, and she'd gone to great lengths to set the table beautifully, with her prettiest dishes, and Moroccan tea glasses containing candles lighting the whole place.

Joan had made a huge birthday card and Kenny had supplied the present: a soft-as-kitten-fur cashmere jumper which was from his shop's winter line and therefore, out of date and, with staff discount, a quarter of the original price.

'It's beautiful,' said Holly reverently when she saw it. She imagined it on Tom; the sleek charcoal fabric flattering his big frame. He could do with some new clothes. He clearly never spent a penny on fashion and lived in comfortably worn sweatshirts and faded jeans, occasionally putting on a suit for important meetings.

Kenny had tried to style Tom, but he'd laughingly resisted saying: 'There's no place for Gucci shoes on building sites, Kenny. I'm an architect, not a fashion plate.'

Holly turned off the telly and switched on some music. It was five to eight and she was ready. Well, maybe she'd just add a bit more lippy and brush her hair again. Her face was becomingly flushed in the mirror and she couldn't suppress a small smile of excitement. She had a present for Tom too, a private one she hadn't told the others about. It was a book on Le Corbusier, an architect apparently, someone she'd never heard of until she did a bit of research. The man in the bookshop had said that Tom would love it.

'He's a lucky fella,' the man had added, giving Holly a grin as he keyed in the exorbitantly-priced book.

Holly had blushed and knocked over a display of *The Little Book of Serenity* in her embarrassment. 'He's just a friend,' she muttered, now an interesting puce colour.

'Oh right so,' said the man. 'I hope there's a few of you clubbing together to buy this. It's a hell of a present.'

'Y . . . yes, a few of us friends are buying it,' stammered Holly.

The book was wrapped, tied with a blue ribbon and was now stored under Holly's bed, waiting for the right moment to give it to Tom without anybody else noticing.

The doorbell rang lustily and Holly threw the lipstick into the cosmetic bag on the sink and rushed to open the door.

'Happy Birthday!' she said joyfully.

Tom looked stunned.

'Surprise!' carolled Kenny and Joan, pushing him into the hall.

Holly put her arms around Tom and gave him a shy kiss on the cheek. It was his birthday after all.

'Holly . . . I didn't expect this,' said Tom. 'I had no idea . . .'

'But what a lovely idea it is!' From behind Joan, appeared

a petite blonde girl, wrapped up in a tiny denim jacket that could have easily fitted a child. Holly's heart fell into her boots.

'I'm Caroline, Tom's girlfriend and I've heard all about all of you. It's lovely to meet you.' She wrapped her arms round Tom and snuggled close like a tiny woodland elf-type-creature snuggling into a tree. Holly felt like ape woman by comparison. Suddenly, her most slimming jeans didn't feel very slimming at all and the lace top with its low front made her feel like a raddled old slapper compared to this fresh-faced little sprite.

'I'm ravenous,' said Joan, moving the party into the sitting room. 'Let's eat. There's enough for Caroline, isn't there, Holly?'

'I don't eat much,' said Caroline sweetly. She even had dimples, Holly noticed. Dimples, a heart-shaped face and a sweet little rosebud mouth. 'I hope I'm not barging in, but I came up from Cork to surprise Tom on his birthday. It's lovely that you're taking care of him like this!'

She beamed at them all and perched herself on the two-seater couch, patting the cushion beside her for Tom. He sat down obediently. Holly gazed at the newcomer. Caroline didn't look as if she thought there was any real possibility of anyone thinking she'd barged in. Caroline looked as though she felt she belonged anywhere she liked.

'Holly, this is wonderful,' Tom was saying.

Holly gave him the automatic smile perfected at years of Miller family Christmas parties.

'You're so good to have cooked,' he added.

'It's your birthday,' she said quickly, 'we couldn't let you celebrate on your own.'

Kenny opened wine and the sparkling apple juice Holly currently adored, Joan cranked the stereo up a few notches, and the party continued happily, while Holly went back to the kitchenette and did some utterly unnecessary stirring. 'It'll be a few minutes more,' she lied. Everything was ready. It was she who needed a few moments to recover. From her position behind the breakfast bar, she watched Tom and Caroline. They looked so happy together; Tom, the big, comforting protector and Caroline, the petite, jewel-like apple of his eye.

Caroline was telling the company about her drive up to Dublin and how she'd got a flat tyre outside Fermoy, 'but this absolutely sweet guy in a Porsche stopped and helped me fix it!' She squeezed Tom's arm. 'You know how hopeless I am at things like that,' she said. 'Give me a business in trouble, and I can turn it around in a flash. Ask me to change a light bulb and forget it!'

Everyone laughed, Tom most of all.

Watching them, Holly felt a stab of pain so intense that for a moment, she wondered had the underwire of her cheap black bra escaped to dig into her chest. But even as she discreetly checked, she knew that wasn't the answer. The pain went deeper than that.

She'd been stupid to even think that Tom could like her. He had a girlfriend, for God's sake. A tiny little princess of a thing, so what would he want with her? She didn't have a car with tyres to change but if she did, nobody would ever screech to a halt beside her to help change it. They'd drive by, Holly thought miserably, expecting such a fine heifer of a girl to be able to lift the car up without the aid of a jack.

'Right, dinner's ready,' she said heartily. 'Everyone sit down and I'll dish up.'

Caroline squeezed in between Tom and Joan, exclaiming with delight at Holly's pretty mismatched china and stealing a bit of tomato and fennel bread from Tom's plate after refusing any herself.

'I don't eat much wheat normally,' she revealed, as Holly put flatware and plates in front of her.

No wheat from now on, vowed Holly. That was the secret, clearly.

'How about you, Joan?' inquired Caroline. 'You're very slim. Do you eat wheat?'

Joan, halfway through spreading a divot of butter on a lump of bread, grinned.

'There's nothing she doesn't eat,' said Kenny. 'I have to nail the furniture down in case she takes a bite out of the coffee table.'

Caroline's delighted peal of laughter rang out. 'That's soo funny,' she said, grabbing Tom's arm and squeezing.

'I don't know what you're talking about diets for, you hardly have to diet,' Joan pointed out, with her mouth full.

Caroline raised her eyes heavenwards. 'I'm so small,' she sighed. 'If I go a pound above seven and a half stone, it really shows.'

Holly's mouth opened. Seven and a half stone. Her left leg probably weighed that.

'I have one cabbage soup day a week when I think thin thoughts,' Caroline proclaimed.

Thin thoughts. Holly wondered how you did that. The cabbage soup bit sounded awful but she might be able to manage thin thoughts.

She brought the serving dish to the table and she began to spoon out the ginger and lemon grass chicken she'd slaved over.

'This looks and smells fabulous, Holly,' said Kenny, inhaling deeply.

'Yes, thank you,' said Tom, leaning across the table to touch Holly's hand.

'To Tom,' said Caroline suddenly, picking up her wine glass. 'Happy Birthday, darling.'

They all raised their glasses. Caroline stood up and kissed Tom fully on the mouth.

Holly, who'd planned to stick to apple juice all night because she didn't want to get all silly in front of Tom, took a huge slug of wine and then reached for the bread. Giving up wheat would have to wait, while her thin thoughts were being blocked out by jealous ones.

Kenny handed her the butter and caught her eye. His expression was sympathetic as he blew her a kiss.

Holly smiled gratefully. She might have lost Tom but she still had her little family.

Caroline was the life and soul of the party. She laughed at every word Joan or Kenny said, clutched Tom's arm so often that Holly was sure he'd be bruised, and she nibbled at her dinner in the manner of a rabbit shyly nibbling a lettuce leaf.

Although she'd been ravenous earlier, Holly found that she had no appetite after all and pushed her food around her plate.

Having exhausted the subject of diets, Caroline was now talking about how much she loved management consultancy and the challenges of taking on a fresh company every few months.

'People can underestimate a woman like myself,' she said gravely. 'They think that because I'm small and blonde, I'm some sort of pushover.' A deliciously impish grin lifted the corners of her pretty mouth. 'That's a mistake they don't make twice.'

Joan was fascinated by the idea of this. 'What do you wear?' she asked. 'Pinstripe men's suits, kipper ties and spats, to make the point that you're a tough chick but on the edge of fashion?'

'No way!' said Caroline. 'I'd never wear trousers to work. And I always wear heels. Just because I'm a woman working in a man's world, doesn't mean I have to compromise my femininity.'

Joan looked blank. 'I'm not into skirts myself. I don't actually have one,' she said. 'I'm not a skirty person.'

Caroline shrugged. 'We're all different. You have your look – cool and hip. I adore that T-shirt.'

Joan looked proudly down at her latest creation, an incursion into smocking brought bang up to date with Joan's peculiar graffiti skills and with a line of pearls sewn on in homage to Chanel. It was acid green on the front and a dark purple on the back.

'It's very me,' Joan said. 'I'm doing ten of them for this

designer boutique in Castle Market and if they sell, the boutique will buy more.'

'You see,' said Caroline, 'you have a unique style. So do I.'

She glanced at Holly, who waited to hear what her unique style was. Caroline nibbled another bit of her dinner. 'This is fabulous, Holly,' she said. 'You obviously love cooking.'

Holly had another big gulp of wine.

By eleven, they were on their way to the Mosquito, to squeals of delight from Caroline who said she'd heard all about it. She'd even run up to Tom's flat to change, appearing five minutes later in a teeny little blue floral slip dress with her denim jacket over the top. The fact that she looked even better in a dress didn't upset Holly half as much as the knowledge that *of course* Caroline would be staying with Tom, sleeping beside him, giggling with him over breakfast. Holly fastened a big smile to her face and led the way to the club. She had done no make-up repair work: what was the point in having your lips painted cherry-blossom pink when your heart was breaking.

Miss Mindy was on the door. She was having a pillar box-red night and was wearing the biggest, reddest Lurex minidress Holly had ever seen. Her feet were jammed into red wedge sandals the size of tugboats.

'Hey, girlfriend,' she said to Holly. The rest of the crew trooped into the club. 'How've you been?'

'Fine,' said Holly.

'You look tired. Working too hard, huh?'

'No,' said Holly. 'Just miserable.'

'Man trouble,' guessed Miss Mindy shrewdly.

Holly didn't bother lying. Miss Mindy was the sort of person who saw through lies. 'Yes. I was looking for a guy and the one I liked was under my nose all along.'

'The big fella with the hands like hams?'

'That's the one.'

'He'd be a great bouncer,' sighed Miss Mindy, who was suffering from staffing problems.

'He's very gentle,' protested Holly.

Miss Mindy's panstick cracked as she smiled. 'All the best ones are,' she said. 'That's the sort of fella I like too: giant on the outside, pussy cat on the inside. Is the little blonde in the denim with him?'

Holly nodded miserably.

'Why do these lads always go for little cutesy bimbo types?' Miss Mindy cast a derogatory eye towards where Caroline could be seen perched on a bar stool with her legs crossed demurely, for all the world like a poster of a '40s cigarette girl. All she needed were the bows on her shoes.

'When I was your age, I wanted to be one of those little girl types,' Miss Mindy added. 'But I was six foot one and I had a stronger right hook than most of the men I knew. Men don't like being towered over. They prefer to have their protective instinct activated. Us big girls don't stand a chance. Well, I don't. You do, girlfriend. You're a beaut.' She patted Holly's cheek affectionately. 'Hopefully that big lummox will see what he's missing and dump the little blonde.'

Holly gave Miss Mindy a hug and went into the club, cheered up. OK, so it wasn't all that hopeful that Miss Mindy clearly bracketed herself and Holly in the big-girls-lonely-hearts club, but at least she'd been kind and she seemed to understand the whole unrequited love thing. People were a constant surprise, Holly decided. Under her make-up shell, Miss Mindy was a bit of a pussy cat herself.

The party rolled on, with assorted pals turning up and wandering off. Holly, who'd decided that drinking wasn't the answer, nursed glass after glass of mineral water and kept as far away from Tom and Caroline as possible without looking rude. It wasn't hard. The group were sitting in a corner around a big, low table, with Tom and Caroline on one side, and Holly on the other.

Caroline took to the party atmosphere with relish. For a teeny little thing, she could certainly put the vodka away, shovelling in Cosmopolitans like there was no tomorrow.

She was soon clinging to Tom like a cute drunken rag doll.

On her last stagger to the loos, she'd tied her hair up in a topknot, which Joan was now looking at with contempt.

'What is she like?' Joan demanded. Joan had drunk a lot of Cosmopolitans too but to no great effect. 'Pebbles, that's it. She's like Pebbles from *The Flintstones*.'

Holly hid her giggles behind her hand. 'Shush, Tom will hear.'

She felt guilty to be laughing at Tom's girlfriend, but it made her feel a bit better.

'I mean,' Joan sounded grim, 'she asked me why I didn't have my own flat and why you, me and Kenny hang around together. She said did we think we were recreating *Friends*? She's lucky I didn't kick box her top knot into oblivion.'

Across from them, Caroline appeared to have fallen asleep.

'I think I'll take her home,' Tom said loudly, so they'd hear him over the music.

Holly, saved from having to hug him goodbye by virtue of the fact that she was hemmed into her seat by several of Kenny's friends, waved in a friendly manner. 'Bye,' she said cheerfully. 'Hope you had a nice birthday.'

'I did.' Tom stood up and seemed to be thinking how he could get past the gaggle of people to reach Holly.

She was relieved when he changed his mind and helped Caroline to her feet.

When they were gone, Holly allowed her face to betray her lack of party spirit.

'Do you want to go home?' Kenny asked, flopping down beside her.

'Yes, but can we wait a few moments?' she asked.

'Give Tom a chance to get a taxi,' Kenny said, nodding.

Joan was keen to stay, so Kenny and Holly set off home on their own.

In the taxi, Holly stared out the window silently.

'It wasn't quite the night we'd planned,' Kenny remarked.

'No.'

'What did you think of Caroline?' he asked.

'You certainly liked her,' Holly said, feeling angry with herself that this fact hurt so much.

'Actually, sweetie, I didn't,' Kenny said, surprising her. 'I tried to like her for Tom's sake but I'm not keen on those tough cookie women.'

'She's not a tough cookie, she's feminine,' said Holly, who longed to be petite, blonde, and able to fit into a size eight slip dress.

Kenny shuddered.

'Don't be fooled, Holly. She's as tough as old boots under that cute-little-me act. Femininity isn't just a weapon to women like her: it's a cruise missile and if she aims it at you, watch out. She's not the sort of girl I'd have expected from Tom,' he mused. 'I noticed she was very edgy round you,' he added.

'Round me?' Holly laughed. 'I don't think so.'

'No, really, she was. She kept looking at you, Holls. I see things, you know.'

At home, Holly undressed and folded her slimming jeans carefully. They looked so big when she held them up. Caroline's whole body could probably fit in one of the legs. Holly put them at the bottom of the wardrobe with all the other never to be worn again clothes. She was stupid to have thought she looked nice in them, and stupid to have thought she had a hope in hell with Tom.

What had she to offer in comparison to Caroline? Tom was a professional and he clearly wanted a girlfriend who matched his achievements: someone gorgeous *and* successful. Someone other men admired too. Holly pulled on her favourite navy slobby tracksuit bottoms and slumped down in front of the telly. She was too wound up to sleep.

Channel-hopping until she found a black and white film, Holly curled up with a bar of chocolate. At least chocolate never let you down. She was alone again, and she still had the ruby wedding to get through on Saturday.

CHAPTER TWENTY-ONE

The last Saturday in April dawned without a cloud in the sky. The gleaming white marquee shone in the early morning sun and the scent of bluebells from Rose's garden mingled with the scent of freshly cut grass. When Adele woke at six, Meadow Lodge was silent despite having more inhabitants than usual. Stella and Amelia had driven down from Dublin on Friday evening, arriving in time for a quick, and very casual, Adele had thought, supper. Sausage casserole must be a modern invention, she sniffed. Adele herself had been stationed in Meadow Lodge since Thursday in preparation for the party, although there didn't seem to be much preparation involved. Rose had blithely assured Adele that caterers, florists and marquee people were doing the hard work and all she and Adele had to do was turn up with their hair done. Hugh had taken Friday off to do a few last-minute chores around the house, like cutting the grass, and Adele had enjoyed spending some time with him. He'd nipped off to meet his old pal, Alastair, in the afternoon, so Adele had taken it upon herself to oversee the erection of the marquee. She hadn't been able to find any fault with either the inside or the outside of the marquee. Not that she hadn't tried. When the marquee staff began to erect the giant structure she had watched intently, determined to winkle out the person who was doing a shoddy job and to admonish them. But there had been no shoddy work. The team had worked at great speed and efficiency and they'd been relentlessly cheerful, waving and smiling at her every time she made her stately progress in their direction.

The two men working on the flooring were the worst.

'Suppose you're going to be dancing the night away on this, Missus, are you?' asked one of them cheekily.

Adele had given him one of her hard stares. 'I don't want any impertinence out of you, young man,' she'd snapped and marched off in high dudgeon.

Rose had been typically laid-back about the whole thing when Adele found her sitting at the kitchen table, wearing jeans for heaven's sake. Adele thought jeans were for young people.

'There's no point in my hanging around and watching every move they make, Adele,' Rose had said, looking up from the list of acceptances which she was using to work out a loose seating plan. 'I don't know the first thing about setting up marquees. When it's finished and the tables and chairs are in, then I'll go out and have a look.'

'Well, if that's the way you feel about it,' Adele had said, miffed. 'I can do the seating plan. I'm good at things like that.'

Rose looked uncomfortable. 'Actually, Adele, it's easier if I do it because there are lots of people coming who you don't know, and you won't know who you can put them next to.'

Adele would have liked to have stormed out of the room but she didn't. Instead, she poured herself a cup of tea from the pot (rude of Rose to have made some and not called her) and sat heavily down beside her sister-in-law. She'd just keep an eye on the seating plan, in case Rose got it terribly wrong.

Now it was the morning of the party, and Adele had a headache. She got dressed and went downstairs to find Rose and Amelia having breakfast happily.

'Good morning, Aunt Adele,' Amelia said gravely.

Adele glanced at her grand-niece suspiciously. There had been a long conversation about manners the previous evening and Adele had impressed upon Amelia the need to say 'Good morning,' and 'Good evening,' instead of 'Hi.' But there was no mischievous glint in Amelia's eyes to say she was teasing. Dear little thing just needed to be told how to speak properly. Children liked a firm hand, Adele felt.

'Did you sleep well?' asked Rose, rapidly tidying up the table and wiping away toast crumbs.

'Tolerably, I suppose,' Adele began, planning on explaining how she'd woken up at five and how that bed was past its best because she couldn't get comfortable in it.

'Good,' Rose said briskly, cutting the conversation off. 'Now Amelia, what next? There are lambs in the field at the end of the lane. Would you like to look at them?'

'Lambs, yes!' breathed Amelia.

Adele got a cup and saucer for her morning coffee and listened to little Amelia talking nineteen to the dozen about how she was going to have lots of animals when she grew up. 'And not just goldfish,' she added firmly. 'Goldfish end up floating and have to be flushed away. Becky flushed her one away but Shona buried hers. Mine are still alive but Mummy says we can have a funeral if they die. I thought Goldie died last month but he got better only he was a different colour,' she added, looking up at Rose. 'Can that happen?'

Around her Granny, Amelia was a lively little imp, those dark eyes gleaming with mischief and fun. Children and animals loved Rose; they were instinctively drawn to her.

In Adele's company, Amelia wasn't the same. Instead, she was a formal little girl on her best behaviour.

'We'll see you later, Adele,' Rose said, leaving with Amelia for their foray into the world of lambs.

Imagine going off out on the day of a big party in your home. Adele was scandalised at the idea. There were things to oversee and Rose was swanning off with her granddaughter as if she didn't have some 200 people about to descend upon her in a few hours.

Of course, Rose could have delegated some of the responsibility to Adele. But oh no, that would never do for Madam Rose. She didn't understand family and how Adele longed to be involved. Adele let the familiar feelings of hurt swell up inside her until her headache got much worse. That was it: she was telling Hugh all about Rose's cavalier treatment.

Tara stretched luxuriously in the bed, feeling rested after a fantastic night's sleep. She was sure that her good humour had something to do with the fact that Finn hadn't had a drink since their row. Last night was the first Friday night in ages when they'd spent the evening without a drop of alcohol. It hadn't bothered Tara in the slightest. She was just as happy drinking mineral water with her dinner. And Finn had said the same.

'It's good for us,' he'd insisted, holding out his glass for a fill-up of water.

They'd gorged themselves on chocolate afterwards. Finn's sweet tooth was working overtime and he kept bringing home family-sized bars of milk chocolate.

Finn appeared at the door with coffee, orange juice and toast on a tray.

'Breakfast in bed, milady.'

'Fantastic,' said Tara, grinning at him. Normally, she needed a cattle prod to get Finn out of bed in the mornings. Today, he was up earlier than she was.

He put the tray on her knees and settled himself carefully beside her, taking a piece of buttered toast and biting hungrily.

'Eat up,' he said with his mouth full, 'it'll probably be hours before we get fed at your mum and dad's.'

'The food sounds wonderful,' Tara pointed out. 'Mum read the menu out to me and there's all sorts of fish, lamb and cold beef for the carnivores, and some incredible-sounding strawberry dessert.'

She munched some toast thoughtfully.

'Finn, please don't drink today? For me?' Tara hoped that begging Finn would work. Today, of all days, she couldn't cope if he got terribly drunk and made a fool of himself and her.

'You don't even have to ask,' Finn said, sounding angrily offended. 'I'm hardly going to fall into a bottle of vodka in front of your parents, am I?'

Tara bit her lip to hold the words back.

'I drink socially and sometimes, I forget to say stop, that's all,' Finn continued. 'You don't have to treat me like a child.'

'OK, OK,' she said, anything to keep the peace.

'I haven't had a drink for nearly two weeks.' His eyes were angry now, flashing with fury.

'Forget I said it,' Tara said rapidly. 'I'm sorry.'

'So you should be.' Finn got off the bed so quickly that the tray wobbled and spilled coffee all over the duvet. Tara cursed and grabbed a tissue to mop up the excess, hoping this wasn't a symbol of how the day was going to pan out.

Holly scanned the guest list in disbelief.

'I thought I'd better warn you,' Stella said apologetically. They were sitting on the small patio outside the back door of the house in Kinvarra with the morning sun on their faces. Holly was chain smoking.

'Richie Murdoch,' she said as she found the name in question. 'How the hell could she have invited Richie Murdoch?'

'His mother's sprained her ankle and he's driving her.'

Holly's sweet face was flushed with remembered anger and hurt. 'The guy is a complete scumbag. I mean, doesn't she know I asked him to go to my debs dance and he said yes until the last minute and then turned me down to go off with another girl?' Holly felt outrage remembering this and even more outrage that it seemed to have escaped her mother's notice. The humiliation of being dumped by a guy just before the important school graduation dance had never left her. If it hadn't been for Donna fixing her up with a blind date, she wouldn't have been able to go. As it was, the blind date had hardly been what she'd describe as a roaring success, but it spared her the shame of appearing on her own.

'You never told her,' Stella said gently. 'Mum doesn't have a clue. You just told her Richie and you had fallen out. I never understood why you did that.'

Holly dropped her cigarette to the ground and flattened it with her boot. For the first time in her life, she wanted to be openly angry with her mother.

'Mum wouldn't have understood,' she said, shaking a new cigarette from her pack and lighting up.

'You can't say that,' Stella pointed out. 'Mum's great, she's always interested in us and she always got involved with everything. She'd have gone round to Richie's house and given him a piece of her mind if she'd known.'

'I told Dad,' Holly recalled. 'Dad said he was a little shit and did I want him to break both his legs?'

They both laughed at this vision of their genial, law-abiding father even saying such a thing.

'Daddy's pet,' teased Stella gently, trying to cheer her sister up.

'I just don't understand how Mum could ask Richie and not even mention it to me,' Holly said. 'She must have wondered why we split up so quickly. I mean, *you* weren't even living at home then and *you* knew something was wrong,' she added hotly. 'Mum hadn't a clue. How interested is that?'

'Hi, girls, we're home,' said Rose, her voice coming from the hall. 'Where are you two?'

Holly leapt to her feet and thrust the guest list into her sister's hand. 'I'm too angry to talk to her,' she said and rushed off into the shrubbery.

Stella stared after her sister, feeling strangely confused and unsettled by their conversation. Stella had always felt backed up by the strength of her family bonds. It unnerved her to find that her vision of the Miller family unit wasn't shared by all concerned.

Holly smoked two more cigarettes as she walked furiously around the garden and thought back to those awful teenage years.

She'd been crazy about Richie Murdoch. She'd known him since she was fourteen but had never even imagined that cool Richie, one of Kinvarra's most popular guys, he with the Kawasaki motorbike all the other lads envied, would be interested in her. Painfully shy and even more painfully aware of her plump figure, Holly had barely even spoken to her hero and was content to watch him from afar. Then he'd asked her to dance at a rugby club dance. Nobody had been more surprised than Holly. It had been the start of a three-month relationship, a glorious time for Holly where she finally felt as if she belonged. She'd been on top of the world with her first boyfriend until a week before her debs when Richie had told her in a phone call that it was off.

Heartbroken didn't quite describe how she felt. His action was more than simply ending their relationship, it was a hideous rejection.

Now, with a bit of experience of men behind her, Holly could look back and realise that they were hardly Romeo and Juliet. The conversation had always been limited. Richie only wanted to talk about his bike, while Holly had listened adoringly.

As grown-ups, they wouldn't have lasted five minutes together. But that wasn't the point. The point was: he'd dumped her cruelly and callously, and her mother hadn't even noticed.

Holly stubbed out the cigarette and didn't pick up the butt to dispose of it carefully later. She didn't care. She wouldn't be the good, quiet Holly any more. She wanted to feel angry with her mother and she wanted Rose to notice. Now that Holly's anger had finally erupted, she found that it had a life of its own.

*   *   *

'Do you like it?' Hugh looked anxiously at Rose's face. She was staring down at the red leather jewellery box which contained an antique charm bracelet, with a fine heart-shaped padlock.

'It's rose gold,' Hugh said. 'I thought you'd like that.'

Rose tore her eyes away from the present. It was such a thoughtful gift, just the sort of thing she loved. 'It's beautiful,' she said. Still holding the box, she put her arms around her husband and held him tightly. They'd decided that they wouldn't buy each other presents because the party was costing so much, and now Hugh had gone and broken his promise and bought her this lovely bracelet. Rose wished that she'd got him something in return.

'Oh Rosie, Rosie,' said Hugh, his face buried in her cloud of dark hair. 'Forty years. Who'd have thought it, eh?'

'Not your mother, that's for certain,' Rose joked, wiping away tears with a tissue. There were only two hours to go before the party and she didn't want to be all red-eyed. But emotions swamped her. It was like their wedding day all over again, yet this time, they had their three daughters with them. And Amelia. Those forty years had produced so much.

'Don't cry, love.' Hugh took the tissue from her hand and began carefully dabbing her eyes. 'You don't want to smudge all that careful make-up. Adele will think we've been rowing and she'll march up to give you a talking to.'

Rose managed to laugh. 'God forbid,' she said. She could do without Adele on one of her poor-Hugh missions. 'I'm not sad, Hugh,' she added with a hiccup. 'It's an emotional day.'

'For me too,' he said. 'I never thought you'd stick with me for forty years. I thought if I could hold onto you for forty days, I'd be lucky! Are you going to put it on?'

Rose took the bracelet out of the box and sat down on the end of their bed. The room smelled of flowers. The florists had brought so many that Rose had taken some upstairs to decorate their bedroom and a mass of freesias in a vase on the window sill spread their glorious scent everywhere.

'Let me.' Hugh sat down beside her and reached for the bracelet. He opened the clasp and slipped the bracelet over Rose's slender wrist, snapping it shut firmly. Then he turned the little padlock over so that Rose could see what was engraved on the back.

'R & H 40 years.'

'I know it's corny . . .' he said with a grin.

'It's not corny at all,' Rose said softly. She held the bracelet closer so she could see it more clearly. 'I love it. It's the nicest present you've ever given me.'

'Better than the girls?'

'I had something to do with them myself,' Rose laughed. 'You weren't the one who had an emergency caesarean with Holly!'

'True.' He kissed her hand with an old-fashioned flourish, then got up. He looked handsome in a new grey suit with a silver grey shirt and a yellow silk tie. To Rose's eyes, he didn't look much different from the strong, blond-haired man who whisked her down the aisle forty years before. Only the fine lines on his face and the thinning hair revealed that he wouldn't see sixty again.

'I'm off to meet Alastair in the golf club for a drink. I'll be back within the hour.'

'Be sure you are,' she warned with a glint in her eyes. 'Or I'll drive down to the club and drag you out myself!'

When he was gone, she changed out of the jeans and white fitted blouse she'd worn all morning, and slipped on her dressing gown. It was noon, so she had exactly two hours before the guests were due to arrive. She was going to soak in a relaxing bath and get ready in luxurious slowness. Stella was overseeing the caterers, Amelia and Holly had gone for a walk, Tara had phoned to say that she and Finn would be arriving at about half one. Adele was lying down with a headache. The whole family was accounted for. Nobody needed Rose. She could close the bathroom door and forget

339

about everyone but herself for a few hedonistic moments. When the bubbles were a foamy mass and the bath was nearly full, Rose turned off the taps and lowered herself in. Her hair was covered with a shower cap and she'd rolled up a small towel as a pillow. Sitting back in comfort, she closed her eyes and allowed herself to remember forty years before. Her mother in her lemon-yellow suit, bought at great expense in Dublin and costing more than all of the other clothes in Anna Riordain's entire wardrobe put together.

'I'm not letting my only daughter down on her wedding day,' Anna had said proudly when she showed Rose the suit and the little cloche hat with the silk flowers. 'Your father's good suit is a bit shiny in places so if you don't think it's suitable, tell me. We'll get him another one, we'll manage.'

There were tears in Rose's eyes again as she thought of her mother's fierce pride. In their quiet way, the Riordains would bankrupt themselves so that Rose could walk up the aisle with her head held high. Rose, who knew that Hugh's mother would be decked out in a dress ordered from London, had never loved her mother more than on that day.

The phone rang. Rose sat abruptly up in the bath and hoped somebody else would answer it. Still it rang.

'For God's sake!' Rose hauled her aching bones out of her lovely hot bath and dragged a towel round herself. Into the bedroom she marched and lifted the phone crossly.

'Hello!'

There was silence on the other end of the line, just the faint sound of somebody breathing.

'There's a law against nuisance phone calls, you know,' Rose said angrily, knowing she was dripping onto the carpet.

'I'm not the nuisance, you are!' shrieked a woman's voice.

'What are you talking about?' demanded Rose, perplexed.

'Ask your husband, Mr Ruby Anniversary,' said the caller in anguished tones and hung up.

Still clad only in a now very damp bath towel, Rose ran from the room and ran downstairs to the hall phone which boasted the latest in technology. Caller ID was the way of the future, the young telecoms engineer had explained earnestly when he installed the new phone and told Rose how she'd be able to see who was phoning her and get the numbers of people who'd rung. The booklet that explained all this technology was still on the hall table for further reference, although Rose knew it wouldn't be long before it joined all the other unlooked-at reference books that were kept 'just in case' in the odds and ends drawer in the kitchen. Rose flicked through the booklet, found the page on recalling the numbers of callers, picked up the high-tech portable phone and pressed two buttons. The distant phone began to ring. Rose walked slowly upstairs, somehow knowing that she didn't want to have this conversation where other people could hear her.

'Yes,' said a tearful voice on the other end of the phone.

Rose shut the bedroom door and locked it. 'This is Rose Miller,' she said simply. 'You phoned me. I wanted to know why.'

The woman sniffled. 'Don't you know?' she said.

Rose sat down on the bed where the leather jewellery box that had contained Hugh's gift still lay. 'No,' she said. 'You'll have to tell me.'

'I'm sorry, I shouldn't have rung. It just got to me.'

'Please tell me,' Rose said, even though she knew.

'I'm sure you're a nice woman . . . I didn't mean anything by it.'

'Is it Hugh?'

'I know he said he'd never leave you but I couldn't cope today . . . It's so hard,' the woman broke down into great sobs. 'You must understand.'

Rose wanted to know more but couldn't face it. Yet.

'Please forgive me . . .' the woman wailed. Normally, Rose was the expert at saying the right thing and helping people in pain. But comforting her husband's mistress was a step

341

too far. She pushed the 'end call' button and dropped the phone onto the bed beside the jewellery box.

She sat there for a long time, thinking, then began to dress mechanically. Adele envied her, this unknown woman envied her. What precisely had she done that made all these people envy her?

It was five past two and Adele was ready for the party. Hugh had gone out to greet a few early guests but there was no sign of Rose. Honestly, where was the woman?

As she heard a noise on the stairs, Adele looked up. She could hear laughing and joking, and knew it was her three nieces. They were always like that when they were together. How ever had Rose managed to rear three girls who got on so well? More good luck.

'Aunt Adele, what are you doing in here?' asked Stella warmly, eyes shining as the sisters appeared in the hall, decked out in their party finery. Stella was elegant in a dusky pink printed dress, Tara was striking in a sleek red outfit, and Holly was clad in some dark brown dress that reached her ankles and did nothing for her. Stella linked her arm through her aunt's. Stella was the most like Rose, Adele thought. She had the same kind face as her mother's, the same shining dark eyes and the same cloud of dark hair. But she'd got her hair cut short for some reason and it was terrible, really terrible. Adele was about to say so but thought better of it.

'We should be outside, Aunt Adele; the guests are due any minute and Dad wants us all ready to greet them,' pointed out Tara. Adele was never sure who Tara resembled but she certainly didn't like Tara's boyish haircut and those terrible rectangular glasses with the black frames.

Adele's resolve cracked. 'Why don't you get nice gold-rimmed glasses,' she found herself saying. 'They're so much more flattering, Tara.'

Her niece smiled tightly. 'Finn picked them out for me, Aunt Adele,' she said.

Adele's face softened. Finn was such a great lad.

'Are you not wearing anything brighter?' Adele asked, turning her eagle eye to Holly. 'You'll die with the heat in that dark thing. It's a warm day.'

'It's a Ghost dress, it's very light,' interrupted Stella, before Holly could say a word. 'I think it's lovely, Holly.'

'Me too,' said Tara.

The four of them proceeded out the patio doors and walked the few yards to the marquee, whereupon Adele slipped her arm from Stella's and sailed forward like a stately galleon in her lilac two-piece. Behind her, the three sisters exchanged resigned grins.

'How many years in jail would you get for aunt-ricide?' inquired Tara, gazing after their aunt.

'Tara, you're terrible,' said Stella, laughing. 'It would break Dad's heart if anything happened to Adele. He loves her, you know.'

'I'd love her too if she didn't say such awful things,' protested Tara. 'Gold-rimmed glasses indeed. Finn didn't pick these glasses, actually, but I knew she'd shut up if I said he did. She honestly thinks he can do no wrong.'

'At least you've got a husband to do no wrong,' pointed out Holly gloomily. 'She already told me this morning that I'd have a much better chance of getting a boyfriend if I wore more conservative clothes. And now she's slagging off my dress.' Holly couldn't quite hide how much these remarks had hurt her.

'Silly cow,' said Tara crossly. 'Anyway, Mum will probably murder her before the day is out.'

Stella looked at her in surprise. Their mother practically never lost her temper, particularly with Aunt Adele, which showed remarkable restraint, Stella always thought.

Tara explained herself. 'I overheard her telling Mum that Dad is looking very tired and Mum should stop him working himself into the ground. Mum said 'It's none of your business, Adele,' in a very hard voice. I've never heard her speak to Adele like that before, although it certainly shut her up, mind you.'

'Don't you just love family parties,' Holly murmured wryly. 'Fun for all the family: a big row.'

'Cheer up, Holly,' said Stella, giving her youngest sister an affectionate hug. 'This is going to be great.'

Stella didn't noticed Holly's resigned face. Instead, she'd turned happily to Tara. 'It's a pity Finn couldn't get here until later. I've got to say, that company really works the poor man's guts out. I know he hates horse racing and imagine them forcing him to go to that corporate clients' day out when he'd something else on.'

Tara smiled but said nothing. She could hardly say that there was no corporate day out but that she and Finn had rowed and that Finn insisted on driving down by himself as he didn't want to get 'stuck' in Kinvarra all the next day. Incredibly, Stella hadn't noticed that Tara was in any way upset. Her sister was usually so astute but since she'd met Nick, she was on a different planet. Planet Lurve. Whatever the oxygen:nitrogen ratio was there, it had stopped Stella from noticing anything except Amelia and her beloved Nick. Not that Tara wasn't delirious that Stella had finally found love. Far from it. But with Stella eating, sleeping and breathing Nick Cavaletto, her sisterly radar was out of action. Since that night in Stella's, when Finn hadn't arrived to collect Tara, she'd longed to confide in Stella but her pride got in the way and she didn't know how to broach the subject.

The three sisters reached the marquee. Their father was holding court with a few early guests with Aunt Adele in attendance but their mother was nowhere to be seen. At one end of the marquee stood the buffet tables clad in linen and decorated with lots of flowers. Huge piles of plates, cutlery, glasses and napkins were waiting, along with the giant stainless steel burners for the hot food. An enormous banner fluttered along one wall: *Congratulations Rose and Hugh on your Ruby Wedding Anniversary.*'

'Isn't this lovely,' sighed Stella, thinking, as she always was these days, of Nick. She was so lucky to have found him. It was meant to be. Two people with bad marriages behind them, ready to leap into a wonderful new life together. All she needed to do was learn how to deal with Jenna. Time was the important factor. All Jenna needed was time to get used to the idea of her father and Stella as a couple. Then, everything would fall into place. In her heart, Stella sent up a silent prayer that this might happen. Then, everything would be perfect.

Holly faltered at the entrance to the marquee, trying to work out where would be the best place to stand in case Richie Murdoch and his mother turned up. Beside Tara might be a good idea. Tara would make her feel strong and give her the courage to say one brief hello to the scumbag and then ignore him. On her own, Holly knew she'd cave in and smile cravenly at him, pretending she'd forgotten how he'd humiliated her.

'Tara.' She grabbed her sister's arm. 'Did you hear Richie Murdoch's coming?'

Tara looked astonished. 'Who invited that low life?'

'Mum did,' said Holly.

Her sister said nothing for a moment, then linked her arm through Holly's. 'Don't worry, we'll take him on as a twosome, right?'

'Right,' said Holly gratefully.

Tara wished her own men problems could be solved as easily. Holly might be scanning the horizon for her horrible ex, but Tara was scanning it for her husband's car. Finn had been so very angry earlier. Who knew what he'd do? He might not even turn up. Or, he might turn up jarred, having driven the car down drunk. Tara didn't quite know which was worse.

By three, the road outside the house was thronged with cars, the waiters were sweating in the April sun from running round with bottles of wine and champagne, the partygoers were having a whale of a time, and the three Miller girls were on high alert. Something was wrong and for once, it wasn't the men in their lives.

Nick had arrived at twenty past two, bearing a bottle of Cristalle for the anniversary couple, and a bouquet of white roses for Rose herself, who was still closeted in her bedroom with the door locked. He didn't need to be looked after, he told Stella, after giving her a passionate kiss. He'd be fine on his own. He understood that she had to circulate.

Richie Murdoch hadn't turned up, to Holly's passionate relief. His mother had been driven by someone Holly didn't recognise, a man in an awful suit, and Holly had given them both a wide berth, not wanting to so much as talk to a member of the Murdoch clan. Tara had been keeping her eyes peeled on the gate in case Finn did turn up pissed and attempted to park where he normally parked in Kinvarra, right in front of the house, which was now decorated with tables and pretty parasols. But there had been no sign of him. His mobile was turned off and she had visions of him crashing the car in a drunken haze and killing himself and some poor innocent in another car. *She'd* kill him if he turned up drunk after driving from Dublin.

But the real problem was Rose. When she hadn't appeared by half two, Stella had run upstairs to see what was wrong.

'Mum,' she'd called, tapping softly on her parents' bedroom door. 'Can I come in? Are you OK?'

'I've an awful migraine,' Rose had replied. 'I'm just going to lie here with the curtains closed for a few minutes more.'

'Oh you poor love,' commiserated Stella. 'Can I get you anything?' As she spoke, she turned the handle of the door and was amazed to find it was locked. This discovery made her momentarily speechless.

'No, I'm fine, Stella.'

'Are you sure, Mum?' Her mother was not one for locked doors. In Kinvarra, everyone wandered in and out of rooms and none of the girls had ever locked the door of the bathroom the three of them had shared: they just yelled 'I'm in here!' when footsteps approached.

'Yes,' Rose said lightly. 'I'll be down presently.'

Stella went downstairs and smiled with utter brilliance at all the guests as if her beaming face would make people forget the fact that the hostess hadn't appeared.

'Where's Mum?' It was Tara, clutching a glass of juice and shading her eyes with her hand to see if Finn was on the horizon.

'Locked in her room with a headache,' said Stella shortly.

The sisters exchanged anxious glances.

'We'd better tell Dad,' said Tara.

'No.' Stella didn't know why but she didn't want their father to know. 'Let's not ruin things for him, we'll tell Holly. Mum probably just needs a rest. The stress of organising this must have told on her.'

Upstairs in the bedroom she shared with Hugh, Rose lay on the bed surrounded by the detritus of Hugh's home filing cupboards. His diaries for the past ten years – Hugh had a thing about keeping diaries – were also strewn on the bed. She had spent at least an hour going through them all and had realised that Hugh's legal brain had come up with some sort of code for his activities. Being Hugh, however, it wasn't much of a code and Rose had soon cracked it. On the day Rose had spotted him emerging nervously from a restaurant with his red-haired little friend, he'd supposedly been at a 'Moriarty case review'. There were quite a few Moriarty case reviews listed over the years, which either meant that Miller & Lowe derived massive income from this unsettled case, one she'd actually never heard of. Or, that Moriarty didn't exist, which seemed far more likely. His mobile phone bills – itemised – had also helped. Some of the numbers were unfamiliar to her, so she phoned them. One turned out to be his assistant's voice mail. Another got the answering machine at Alastair Devon's house. Rose hung up rapidly, feeling stupid. She should have recognised that number. Maybe she was being foolish. But when she examined a third number, it was the same one as identified on her phone's caller ID earlier.

She hadn't seen Hugh since he'd given her the bracelet.

When he'd come home from his drink in the golf club with Alastair, and tried to get into the bedroom, he'd swallowed the story about her migraine hook, line and sinker.

'Fine, dear, I'm ready anyhow. I'll do a last-minute check on everything,' he'd said from outside the door, sounding far too pleased with himself.

If he knew *anything* about her, Rose thought with rising fury, he'd know that she'd never had a migraine in her life.

She took her new dress from the wardrobe and looked at it objectively.

Lacey, doyenne of Kinvarra's designer boutique, had only produced two outfits on the day Rose had visited to look for her party dress.

'That floaty muck would look terrible on you,' said Lacey dismissively, gesturing at an entire rail of ethereal floaty, mother-of-the-bride rig-outs. 'I've got two things that would suit you.'

That was what made Lacey such a good saleswoman, Rose thought. There was no faffing around trying on tonnes of unsuitable clothes so that by the twentieth outfit, the customer would be in utter despair and buy the thing that looked least horrible on her. Lacey cut out the faffing about and the despair. From her shop-full of stock, she had picked out two dresses for Rose and they both looked perfect on her. Rose went for the amber raw silk shift dress with a matching short jacket. It was timeless. French chic mixed with Hollywood glamour.

'Fantastic,' was all Lacey said when Rose stood in the shop, looking elegant and almost regal. The soft amber colour suited her skin tones; as she aged she could no longer take the bright colours she'd worn in her youth.

Now, Rose dressed and examined herself in the bathroom mirror. Apart from her pallor, she looked every inch the successful wife of the town's top lawyer. The betrayed wife. Rose couldn't face looking at herself any more and went back into the bedroom.

She knew she shouldn't have gone ahead with this day,

knew it was asking for trouble. Some 200 guests were arriving to celebrate the fortieth wedding anniversary of Hugh and Rose Miller when both Rose and Hugh knew that their marriage wasn't of the fairy-tale variety.

Then the realisation reached her with such a jolt that it was almost physical, like being hit in the solar plexus. Rose had to sit down on the bed, winded. It wasn't just her and Hugh who knew. God knew how many other people knew. The women he'd slept with over the years certainly knew. She'd thought there were three but there might have been more. And surely some of his friends knew too? He'd always been so close to Alastair Devon. There was no way Alastair didn't know. They'd been best friends for thirty years, he and Angela had been close to Rose and Hugh all that time, and even though the two women had built up an enduring friendship, the real bond was between the men. What would Alastair have done for Hugh: given him an alibi; told him he was stupid to risk it all? Encouraged him to leave Rose?

The anger was slow to burn. For years, Rose had carried this secret with her. She'd told no-one. Not her mother, dear Anna who'd died thinking that her beloved Rose was the happiest woman in Christendom. Nor her daughters, whom she didn't want to hurt with the information. She never wanted to diminish their father in their eyes. That would be true bitterness and would only be for her own pleasure. So she'd misled well-meaning friends who'd thought they'd seen something and had kept her silence, hoping that in so doing, she would hold the Miller family together. But at what price?

Even Hugh was experiencing a moment's worry. The marquee was getting fuller with every moment and people were keen to see Rose. There was only so many times Hugh could blithely say, 'Oh Rose, she's just checking something with the caterers, she'll be here any minute.'

Stella, Tara and Holly had jaw strain from smiling as if

nothing was wrong. Only Aunt Adele seemed oblivious to any tension and had set up camp near a few like-minded old friends and was reminiscing about the old days; how young people had terrible haircuts now and wasn't it an awful pity that gloves had gone out of style. There was nobody the same age as Amelia, but she'd made friends with a chubby-faced toddler and was playing at being a grown-up and leading him round gravely, helping him over steps and stopping him eating the roses.

'Naughty boy, they'll make you sick,' she could be heard saying sternly every time one of his fat little hands headed for a clump of petals. 'I'll get you some orange juice instead.'

'Mum says she's ready and will be down in five minutes,' Tara reported after her most recent trip upstairs. 'But she still won't let me in.'

'I'm worried about her,' said Stella. 'This is so unlike her.'

The jazz band Hugh had specially wanted struck up a tune. They were booked to play until half six. People's feet tapped on the wooden marquee floor.

Holly emerged from the kitchen. 'The caterers say can we make a decision on the hot food now. They're ready to go and if they cool it and reheat, the stroganoff will toughen up and taste like old boots.'

The sisters stared at each other. Stella went back upstairs but stopped when she heard her parents' door open.

'She's coming,' hissed Stella, rapidly retracing her steps.

At that moment, Finn walked up to where they were standing, perfectly sober and beautifully dressed in a grey linen suit and open-necked shirt the same sky blue as his eyes. He kissed Tara on the mouth deliberately so that she'd know he hadn't been drinking.

'See,' he whispered, 'I haven't touched a drop. Happy now?'

'Hello, Finn,' said Rose, wafting down the stairs gracefully, looking far too bright-eyed and elegant to have been confined to her room for the past two hours with a migraine. Her cheeks were healthily flushed, she'd glossed her lips with a rosy pink and not one dark hair was out of place. She kissed each of her daughters on the cheek, then headed for the kitchen. 'I'll just check the food and I'll be right out.' She whirled round to smile wickedly at the four of them. 'I promise, this time.'

The sisters began to relax. Stella took a glass of wine and found Nick.

'Crisis over,' she murmured. 'Mum's headache is better.'

'She certainly looks great,' said Nick, watching Rose emerge from the house and make for the marquee. He adored Rose and thought she was funny, wise and strong. She'd welcomed him into the family with great kindness.

'Yes, she does look great,' Stella replied. 'I'm just afraid she's tired herself out with this party. Mum's so vital that it's easy to forget that she's not as young as she used to be.'

'She's certainly enjoying herself now,' Nick pointed out, as Rose was surrounded by well-wishers.

If anyone had been watching carefully, they'd have noticed that Rose deliberately stayed away from her husband as she circulated. It was done subtly. Rose could see Hugh's silver head towering over most of the guests, so she moved away from him, greeting, hugging, kissing and thanking people, but always aware of where her husband was and somehow, managing to be somewhere else.

Everyone was thrilled to be there. It was a happy day, they all told Rose, 'proof that true love really does last forever and makes a strong marriage' said one neighbour with a fondness for romantic novels and two unaccustomed glasses of champagne down her. When Alastair Devon and his wife Angela appeared in front of her, Alastair beaming at Rose happily, Rose felt her fixed smile harden.

She kissed Angela and stared up at Alastair with a stony gaze.

Alastair blinked nervously. Rose looked angry with him for some reason. He racked his brains for what he'd done wrong, but it was too late, Rose was talking to Angela, ignoring him.

If anybody thought it was odd that the happy couple weren't standing together, nobody mentioned it. When the food was finally being served and the buffet queue wound untidily around the tables, Rose nipped back to the house. The dining room table was laden down with gift-wrapped packages. Rose had specifically asked people not to bring gifts, but they hadn't listened. They wanted to do something nice for the Millers to celebrate this special day.

'Whatever was wrong with you?'

Rose turned to face her sister-in-law.

'Hugh was worried,' continued Adele, running a finger over the dining room table to check for dust. 'Really, Rose, it's not the done thing to let your guests arrive without being there to greet them –'

'Adele,' interrupted Rose, '*please* don't fight with me today.'

'I'm not fighting,' harrumphed Adele. 'I'm only saying . . .'

'Don't say anything, for my sake.'

'It's for your sake I'm doing it,' Adele protested.

'No, it's not.' Rose did her best to keep her voice even but it was hard to disguise the tremor. 'You're doing it for Hugh because you want everything to be perfect for Hugh, don't you? I wanted everything to be perfect for him too but it wasn't perfect enough, evidently. He needed someone else.'

She saw Adele's eyes widen.

'Lots of someone elses,' Rose added.

Adele's hand was at her breast now, as she clutched the lapel of her suit in horror. For the first time in years, words didn't flow automatically. She held onto the back of a dining room chair for support. 'How can you say such terrible things?' she cried.

'Because it's true.'

'I don't believe it,' Adele said fervently. 'Not Hugh; he idolises you, always has.' For once, the jealousy wasn't there. Adele was simply stating a truth. Hugh loved Rose. He would never cheat on her. Yet Rose looked so . . . so sure.

'I'm going to see Hugh now,' announced Adele. 'This is all some silly misunderstanding, some woman who's got a crush on him. They were the same with my poor father, women could never resist him. My mother ignored them, stupid women. I'm sure Hugh's done his best to deal with this but you've got the wrong end of the stick.'

'Don't say anything, Adele,' Rose said softly. 'Let's wait till later, we've guests here.'

'Of course. I wouldn't dream of it.' Reminded of her social duties, Adele stopped in her tracks but she still looked shaken.

'Why don't you sit down here, Adele, and I'll get you a glass of port.' Adele rarely drank but was fond of port.

'Thanks, Rose.'

With Adele breathing deeply on a dining room chair, Rose hurried to the drinks cupboard in the other room, feeling guilty for what she was doing. She couldn't go through with this. It would hurt too many people: the girls, Adele. It wasn't fair on them. Hugh had never been any different. She was just hurt because she thought all those other women were in the past, that he had finally got over it and was content with her. She poured a glass of port for Adele and considered pouring one for herself, but no, she needed to be stone cold sober. Alcohol would only make her more emotional.

Holly had taken a walk round the garden to have a final cigarette before lunch. She was just on her way back to the marquee when she was stopped by the guy who'd driven Mrs Murdoch to the party. He was smiling broadly at her, in a remember-me sort of way. Holly smiled back and racked her brains for his identity.

'Hi, Holly, you're looking a million dollars, and I don't mean all green and crinkly,' he said with a lascivious wink.

The voice did it. Holly's mouth fell into an oval. *This* was Richie Murdoch? Where was the devil-may-care charm, the sparkling eyes and the buckets of sex appeal? Had she imagined all that? Because her mental image of Richie bore no resemblance to this guy with his smug, avaricious face and a tight haircut which revealed a bull neck.

'Speechless, eh?' said Richie, still looking delighted with himself. 'You always were quiet but wow, look at you now, babe.'

While Richie's gaze travelled unashamedly from her head to her toes, Holly smothered the impulse to giggle out loud with relief. She could barely believe that she'd ever fancied him, motorbike or no motorbike. And as for that suit. Chalk-stripe suits were always on the tightrope of fashion and could look very classy or, as in Richie's case, very tacky. All he needed was a huge pinkie ring to complete the effect.

'How have you been, Richie?' she asked.

'Great, just great. Business is top,' he boasted, making a gesture with both hands to prove this. A pinkie ring glinted in the sun. 'I'm in import/export,' he elaborated. 'Doing well. *Very well.*'

'You don't have the motorbike any more?' Holly said, for lack of something else to say.

'Hell, no.' He was shocked. 'Got the latest Jag. So,' he moved closer to her. 'Are you going to be around for a while? We could go out maybe, I'll show you how fast the Jag goes from nought to sixty, eh?'

'No thanks,' said Holly gravely. 'Speed kills. I've got to go, Richie. Bye.'

She hurried back to her seat in the marquee. Had Richie really changed beyond all recognition? Or, had he always been awful and, because she was lost in her first romance, she'd just never realised it?

Rose stood at the main entrance and watched the guests enjoying themselves. Most people were seated and eating. The jazz band were purring their way through a Cole Porter medley. Rose loved Cole Porter, both for the melodies and for the memories.

Hugh stood waiting for her, arms outstretched, an expansive smile on his face. She could see the family already seated at their table, with places waiting for Hugh, herself and Adele. Hugh had a microphone in his hand.

'Welcome my darling lady wife,' he said to roars of applause.

The band stopped playing, ready to leap into song whenever Hugh ended whatever clever speech he'd worked out on the back of an envelope.

'It's a very special day for myself and Rose,' he began, 'the anniversary of our wedding, one of the most important days of my life.'

Hugh smiled at Rose and put an arm round her, drawing her close.

The crowd sighed happily. Wasn't this lovely?

At one of the front tables, Alastair Devon was still a bit anxious. Rose didn't look herself, he could tell. He'd known her for nearly thirty years and although her face looked outwardly serene, she had a mad look in her eyes. Women got like that, Alastair knew. The change. Stupid name, that. It wasn't a change, it was a bloody cataclysm. But Rose must have gone through all of that already, surely? So what could be wrong with her?

Tara and Finn were sitting as far apart as it's possible to sit when you're actually seated beside someone. Finn was still not drinking and he'd barely touched the Thai chicken he'd piled his plate with. Tara had taken some shellfish and salad, but couldn't eat either. Her fingers beat a tattoo on the tablecloth as she watched her parents.

Stella and Nick were seated next to Tara. Amelia was standing between them, leaning against her mother who had one arm round Amelia's waist. Nick was holding Stella's other hand, stroking her fingers with his thumb as they watched Hugh address the crowd.

Holly sat at the bit of the table nearest the edge of the marquee. She was smoking surreptitiously, holding the cigarette down near the tent flap and turning away from everyone to take a lengthy drag every few moments. Imagine meeting Richie Murdoch again after all these years. Imagine not feeling anything but dislike for him.

'As you all know, I wouldn't be where I am today without Rose,' Hugh continued. 'She's been my rock, my centre, the centre of our family. And it's thanks to Rose that our lovely daughters, and granddaughter, are here today.'

Amelia grinned, delighted to be included.

Holly threw down her fag and stamped it out hurriedly. Maybe they'd have to get up and stand beside their parents in front of all these people. Her triumph with Richie notwith-standing, Holly quivered with nerves at the very idea.

'I want to pay tribute to Stella, Tara, Holly and little Amelia,' continued Hugh.

Everyone clapped.

'But,' Hugh shut them all up by talking even more loudly into the microphone, 'the jewel in the crown is Rose.'

Alastair must have helped him write the speech, Rose thought, still smiling. Hugh would have never thought of that 'jewel' nonsense on his own.

'I'm sure you'll agree with me on that.' Cue more clapping.

'I want to . . .'

Rose had heard enough.

Smiling, she leaned over and gently took the microphone from Hugh's hands. 'It's my day too, darling,' she said, eyes glittering.

Hugh relinquished the mike and kissed her hand in a courtly fashion.

The crowd clapped happily again.

Rose surveyed her audience, who were beaming up at her, their faces full of goodwill. She hated hurting them too but it had to be done.

First things first. She went over to Amelia.

'Darling, would you go into the house and talk to Aunt Adele for a few minutes?'

Amelia nodded and ran off. Stella looked at her mother curiously, but Rose just smiled benignly and waited until Amelia was out of sight to begin.

'At our wedding forty years ago, I didn't have the opportunity to make a speech,' she said. 'Brides didn't make speeches in those days, even though that will sound very odd to the younger women here.' She spotted plenty of women grinning.

Rose moved away from Hugh and walked down the marquee, looking comfortable, like some skilled chat show host who could charm a crowd, marvelled Tara. 'In those days,' Rose said chattily, 'marriage was seen as the be all and end all for women. Even if you were lucky enough to go to university, it was to keep you busy until you got yourself a husband. That was women's lot.' She laughed. 'God help our sense.'

Alastair wasn't the only man in the place who felt a frisson of anxiety at the way this speech was going. At the top of the marquee, Hugh himself experienced a smidgen of unease. This wasn't very Rose-like.

'When I married Hugh,' went on his wife, still in that same conversational tone, 'I didn't expect a fairy tale. I came from a small farming community and marriage was often as not a matter of two people joining together to face the world, to earn a living from the land and, hopefully, raise a few children as well.' She turned and looked lovingly at her daughters.

'My daughters are the love of my life,' she said, 'my proudest accomplishment, if it's fair to say that adult human beings who have found their own way in the world could be called my accomplishment. But, I brought them into the world, even if I was knocked out for Holly's birth.' She sent a smile of such extraordinary sweetness to Holly that Holly made a little noise of recognition, like a small animal in pain.

Rose carried on. 'That's what marriage became for me: my daughters. They were my life. And it's all down to Hugh.' The crowd smiled again, thinking that this was back on slightly more familiar territory.

'Yes,' Rose paused and sent another smile, this one chilly, up to her husband, who blanched. 'I told you I didn't expect

357

the fairy tale but I didn't expect Hugh.' If she hadn't turned away from Hugh, she'd have seen him go even paler. 'That's why I feel that it's unfair to invite all of you lovely people here to celebrate a ruby anniversary when in fact, there's nothing to celebrate.'

The whole room held its breath in shock.

'Hugh has been unfaithful to me throughout our entire marriage. I stayed with him because well, girls,' she smiled at a group of her charity committee friends who were sitting, shell-shocked, to her left, 'that's what women of our genera-tion do. We stay. We knit sweaters. We raise money for famine victims and for sick children. We carefully cook stews with the cheaper cuts of meat. We vacuum. But not any more.'

Stella's hand dropped limply from Nick's. She couldn't believe it. Finn broke the Cold War to squeeze Tara's knee in sympathy, but she seemed oblivious to it and just stared, open-mouthed, at her mother.

Holly, with tears glittering in her eyes, pulled an empty glass towards her to act as an ashtray and lit up openly.

There wasn't a sound in the marquee.

'Rose,' croaked Hugh. 'Please stop.'

'Why?' she asked in her clear voice, still amplified by the microphone. 'You wanted this party, even though I told you I felt it was a mistake. You wanted to parade our marriage when I knew it was hypocritical. And look, you haven't denied it in front of our friends.'

Alastair leapt to his feet to do something and Rose shot him a look that could fell a lion. Alastair sank down into his chair again.

'I'm leaving you, Hugh,' she said.

'Oh my God,' whispered Stella, leaning against Nick for comfort.

'We must do something,' said Tara, who'd been stunned into immobility.

Rose waved encouragingly at the band, who were just as dumbfounded as everyone else. She didn't notice Minnie

Wilson, who was staring at her heroine in utter shock. 'The party is continuing and maybe some music might be nice,' Rose said. There were a few wrong notes and suddenly the marquee was filled with the strains of The Girl from Ipanema. There was no other noise.

Rose handed the microphone to Hugh and walked towards the house. Stella and Tara shot after her. The buzz of astonished conversation began to drone loudly with aghast guests saying 'I can't believe it!

'Aren't you going too?' Finn asked Holly.

She shot him a sideways glance. 'In a minute,' she said. Her earlier anger at Rose was gone. It was as if somebody had punched her in the stomach and winded her. She felt wicked and ungrateful for ever feeling angry with her mother. Her mother had been hurt too, just like Holly had been.

Finn waved at one of the waiters, who'd just come back into the marquee with bottles of wine and who had clearly missed Rose's bombshell.

The waiter filled Holly's glass with white wine.

'Red for me,' said Finn happily, holding up a fresh glass. 'After a shock like that, we all deserve a little drink to steady our nerves.'

'Mum, talk to us.' Stella and Tara rushed after Rose into the house but Hugh got there before them.

'Girls,' he begged, 'let me talk to your mother.'

'Dad,' said Stella, her dark eyes awash with tears, 'what's going on?'

'I don't know,' he hedged, 'let me talk to her.'

He followed Rose up to their bedroom, leaving the sisters alone. Stella sank down onto the bottom step of the stairs. Her legs felt too weak to support her.

'What can have happened?' she said. 'I don't understand.'

Tara sat down beside her and put a comforting arm round her sister's shoulder. 'Neither do I.'

* * *

'What's going on?' Hugh demanded, as he shut the bedroom door with a resounding bang.

'You know exactly what's going on,' answered Rose calmly, opening a drawer and taking out a neatly folded pile of clothes. She put the clothes on the bed and did the same with another drawer. 'I'm fed up with playing second best to your women. I'm fed up with your womanising. I'm fed up, full stop. But tell me, precisely how many have there been over the years, Hugh? Don't lie to me because I know, I've always known.'

The blood drained from Hugh's face.

'Did you really think I was that stupid?' she said. 'I knew you so well that I could tell instantly the moment you fancied someone. The doctor's wife all those years ago when Stella was a baby, was she the first? I always thought she was. And other people told me, you know. They'd say *I saw Hugh with somebody at dinner* and they'd wait for me to look shocked or deny it, but I brazened it out, Hugh. I didn't want to be humiliated.' She glared at him, despite her intention to remain coolly calm.

'Rose,' said Hugh weakly, 'don't do this. I can explain.'

'It's too late for explanations,' she replied, moving to her wardrobe and surveying the contents. 'I genuinely thought it was all over, that you no longer had other women or brought them out to discreet lunches or dinners. But your latest phoned me. She says she knows you'll never leave me but that it still hurts. Poor dear. I know how it feels. It still hurts me, Hugh.'

Rose wasn't even angry any more. At least, not with anyone else. She was angry with herself for having put up with it all for so long.

She began taking clothes from the wardrobe, carefully smoothing skirts and trousers so there were no creases in them as she folded. She was probably bringing too much but where she was going, it was better to be prepared for any eventuality.

'What are you doing?' For the first time, Hugh realised that Rose had two big suitcases on the floor.

'Packing. Leaving you.'

'Oh, Rose, you can't do that.' Suddenly it was Hugh who was sinking onto the bed in shock, all the fight gone out of him like a punctured balloon.

She looked at her husband with a tinge of sympathy.

'Hugh, what do you expect me to do?'

He hung his head in his hands. 'I love you, Rose. Don't leave me, please.'

'I should have left you years ago, Hugh. I stayed for the children. I could cope with a certain degree of humiliation for them but not any more.'

'I was discreet,' cried Hugh in anguish.

'Not discreet enough,' she shot back. 'I, personally, spotted you coming out of *Monsieur's* earlier this year. 'The redhead. Is she the current popsie?'

'No, there hasn't been anyone for years. I was friends with her once and her husband died and she wanted to meet me again . . .'

'She thought you could take up where you left off? How convenient. You should offer a service to widows. A valued customer service.'

'Rose, stop it.' Hugh looked genuinely pained.

'You're right, that was below the belt, Hugh. I need to get away from here,' she added, still packing.

'Where will you go?'

'I'm not telling you, Hugh. I don't want you following me there and begging me to come home. We need time apart.'

Hugh picked up the jewellery box which still lay on the bed even though Rose had carefully tidied away the incriminating diaries and the phone bills. She'd used them to prove to herself that she wasn't going mad. She didn't need them any more.

'Why now, on our ruby wedding anniversary, why today of all days?' he asked weakly, looking at the box he'd given her with such happiness earlier.

Rose looked him in the eye. 'To humiliate you,' she said. 'So you'd know what it feels like.'

'I never knew it would hurt you so much.' He gazed up at her sorrowfully. 'You must believe that. I didn't think you knew and I thought, well, what you didn't know, didn't harm you.'

'I daresay that's the difference between men and women,' Rose remarked. 'Men believe that a casual fling won't hurt the relationship and that she'll never find out. Women know that even the most careless affair has the capability to deliver a mortal blow. It's my fault too, you know,' she added. 'I should have confronted you all those years ago and told you how I felt.'

'Why didn't you?' he said, almost crying.

'I didn't think you'd choose me.' Rose finished one case and snapped the lid shut.

'It's over, Hugh. I'm going. You ought to go out and say goodbye to the guests. Somebody has to. Oh, and you may need to explain matters to Adele. Send the girls in, could you please?'

Mutely, Hugh did as he was told. He knew that there was no point in saying anything more to Rose. She had made up her mind. Rose's steely determination was one of the things he'd been drawn to forty years before.

Rose and Holly were the only members of the Miller family who weren't white faced when Hugh opened the door and let the three sisters in.

'Dad?' asked Tara, grabbing her father's arm. 'What's happened? It's not true, is it?'

Hugh looked her in the eye. 'I'm sorry, girls, I'm so sorry.'

Tara gasped and rushed over to her mother. 'Oh, Mum,' she said, hoarsely, hugging her tightly.

Stella sat beside them and laid her hand on Rose's knee. Holly perched on the end of the bed and patted Tara's back.

Seeing this tableau of feminine solidarity, Hugh bit back a sob and left them. This was all his doing. His ego. His hubris.

'I'm sure you all think I've made a mess of everything, don't you?' Rose said. 'You're probably convinced I've gone stark, raving mad but I haven't. I feel . . .' she searched for the word, 'empowered. Isn't that the word?' she asked Tara, who was still too weepy to respond in any intelligent way. 'I didn't want to hurt you three but I have done, and I'm sorry for that. I was just so angry and I hope you can understand why I had to do it.'

'Tell us why,' said Stella, who didn't understand at all.

Rose chose her words carefully. She didn't want to overdramatise things or make the girls hate Hugh.

'Your father and I need some time apart,' she said. 'Well, I need time apart from your father. He was unfaithful to me and it hurt. But I was culpable too,' she added. 'I never told him that I knew about the other women. I wanted to believe that men were different and could have meaningless flings . . .'

'Why didn't you tell us?' demanded Tara furiously. 'How could you have let him away with it? If Finn was unfaithful to me, I'd stab him and *then* leave!'

'You're young, darling,' said Rose, stroking Tara's tear-stained cheek. 'It's different when you've got children and it's different for women of my generation. I never wanted to split up the family or create waves.' She made a wry face. 'I thought it was the wisest thing to do, but I've changed my mind. Something happened and I was so angry with your father for being a hypocrite. And,' Rose was ashamed to admit it, 'I wanted to hurt him publicly.'

'But why now?' begged Stella. 'Why today?'

'Today seemed right,' her mother replied. 'I'd had enough of the hypocrisy and when I came out and heard your father's speech, I just flipped.'

'You didn't mean it, though, did you?' Tara said frantically. 'You're not really leaving Dad.'

'I am.' Rose was determined and even pleading from her daughters wouldn't change her mind. She was doing this for *her*.

'Where are you going to go?' It was the first time Holly had spoken.

Rose leaned across and touched Holly's fingers. 'To my Aunt Freddie's. I phoned her and she's expecting me.'

'Is that why she didn't come today, because you knew you were going to do this?' asked Tara.

'Not at all. I asked Freddie but she couldn't come. She mentioned something about a bed-pushing charity event she was involved in to raise funds for the hospital.'

'Freddie and bed-pushing,' said Tara, brightening up. 'That's a howl. She must be seventy-five if she's a day. I hope she was *in* the bed and not one of the pushers.'

The four of them grinned.

'Knowing Freddie,' said Rose, 'she was pushing, all right.'

She got off the bed. 'I have to finish packing,' she said.

'You're really going?' Stella asked.

'Yes.' Rose was firm. 'I'm doing this for me, girls, please understand. I need time to myself and this is the only way I can think of doing it.'

'But you could stay with me or Tara or Holly,' protested Stella. 'You don't have to go all the way to Aunt Freddie's.'

'You have your own lives and I'm not going to land in on top of you and disrupt things,' Rose pointed out. 'I'd love to spend a few weeks with Freddie. I haven't spent much time in Castletown since I left there forty years ago. Your father was never very keen on going there,' she added bitterly. Her husband had always been reluctant to visit Rose's hometown. He hadn't minded spending the day there but never wanted to stay in Rose's parents' small, pristine cottage. It was too much of a contrast to the big Miller family home, Rose reckoned.

'Can we come and visit?' asked Tara.

'Of course. I'd prefer if your father didn't know where I am, although it's entirely your decision whether to tell him or not.'

Her daughters watched silently as she finished packing.

'I've got my mobile too,' she added. 'I'm not going to the far side of the moon.'

They kept watching, reminding Rose of their childish selves when they'd watched her every move with big, dark eyes. 'I promise I'm not having a breakdown,' she insisted. 'I'm just doing something wild and unpredictable to shake up my life. Aren't mothers allowed do things like that, even at my age?'

'Yes, of course you are,' said Stella wearily. 'It's just a shock. And I don't know what to say to Amelia.'

'That's why I made her come into the house,' Rose said. 'I didn't want her to hear. We'll tell her I'm going on a holiday on my own.'

'But when are you coming back?' asked Tara.

'I don't know.'

The caterers had never seen a party disperse so quickly. Within half an hour of Rose's announcement, the marquee was empty, with half-filled plates lying on the tables amid empty glasses and congratulations cards never handed over. There was a lot of food untouched and Stella, whom everyone seemed to feel should be in charge in the absence of Rose, couldn't think what to do with it. The freezer in Kinvarra would never hold it all and the family would be eating cake for a month if they took it.

The head caterer mentioned a friend who worked with homeless groups and said that the huge untouched vats of food could be a Saturday night feast for some of the people who lived rough. Satisfied that at least somebody would benefit from the debacle, the Miller women sat in their parents' kitchen and waited for whatever was going to happen next.

Their father had disappeared. Holly had looked for him in the garden but there was no sign of Hugh anywhere. He wasn't answering his phone.

'I hope he's all right,' said Holly anxiously. 'Maybe he's with Uncle Alastair.' She found the Devons' number and phoned but the answering machine was on.

Aunt Adele sat beside Tara at the kitchen table and stared blankly into space.

'Would you like a cup of tea, Aunt Adele?' asked Stella kindly. Adele seemed to be taking this particularly badly. Incredibly, she hadn't lost her temper the way Stella had expected she would. Instead, she kept saying that she must talk to Rose.

'Rose needs me,' she said in a weak voice.

Stella, who didn't think her mother would appreciate a visit from Adele, explained that Rose was packing for a few days away and wanted to be on her own.

Now she placed a cup and saucer in front of Adele and gave her a slice of fruit cake.

'We've got to keep our strength up,' said Stella, attempting some false jollity.

'Hi, girls, how are things?' It was Nick, arriving back after a trip with Amelia into Kinvarra for ice cream. He and Stella had thought it best if Amelia was out of the house.

'I'm going out for a cigarette,' said Holly, getting up and heading for the back door.

Nick took her place. 'Any news?' he asked Stella.

She shook her head. Nick reached over and took her hand in his, giving it a comforting squeeze that said he was there for her.

Tara watched them for a moment, then got up to look for Finn.

She found him in one of the armchairs in the living room, watching Sky Sports. At his elbow was one of Rose's occasional tables upon which rested a glass of brandy. The bottle was beside it.

Finn looked up warily when Tara entered the room.

'What's the situation?' he asked carefully.

Tara stared at the bottle of brandy. 'I'd say it was situation normal, wouldn't you?' she said caustically.

'After a day like this, you need a drink . . .' began Finn.

'On a day like this? Surely you mean *on any day*? You might have laid off the booze for once . . .'

'For once!' yelled Finn, getting to his feet. 'I haven't had a drink all week. I'm fed up with it.'

They stood facing each other like pit bulls about to go for the kill. The pent-up emotion of the day had spilled out of Tara and she felt as if she could very easily hit Finn. All she wanted was some support from her husband, the sort of support that Nick was providing for Stella. But Finn couldn't provide it, because he'd sought solace in the bottom of a glass. He would never change, she felt it in her heart and in her bones. She would never be able to lean on him while he was leaning on alcohol.

'Why did I marry you in the first place?' she asked. 'I didn't know you at all.'

'No, you didn't,' he hissed back. He looked around for his car keys but Tara was too fast for him. She swiped them from the coffee table.

'Just because you want to kill yourself, there's no need to kill anyone else,' she said.

Finn flushed. 'I wouldn't have driven far,' he said. 'Just to the hotel beyond Kinvarra.'

'That's too far,' Tara said. 'Driven too far, hah. That's ironic. That's what you've done to me.'

Finn stormed out of the house. There wasn't anywhere he could go, Tara decided. She had his keys and he'd left his jacket on the couch. She checked quickly. His wallet was in the pocket and all he'd have in his trouser pockets was loose change. He couldn't come to much harm.

'Girls, I'm going.' Rose stood in the hall with two suitcases beside her. She also had a small bag and her handbag. 'Could someone put these in the car for me?' she asked.

Nick put the cases in the boot of Rose's car. The three sisters, Adele and Amelia stood outside the front door and watched.

Rose bent down to talk to her granddaughter. 'Now Amelia, love, I'm going on a small holiday and you'll have to come and visit me, won't you?'

'What about Grandad? Why isn't he going with you?' asked Amelia.

Rose hugged her. Out of the mouths of babes, she thought bitterly.

'Grandad has to work so he's staying here. But we both love you, that's the important thing, isn't it?'

Amelia's huge chocolate brown eyes were concerned. Rose kissed her on the forehead and straightened up.

'Take care, Adele,' she said, her lips barely brushing her sister-in-law's dry cheek.

'Rose, don't go,' said Adele. She was pleading. 'Hugh didn't mean it, I know. He would never have hurt you. You can't do this to him.'

'It's not your decision, Adele,' said Rose quietly. 'You can't save him this time.'

She hugged Nick. He was like family. She knew he'd be a tower of strength to Stella.

She looked around for Finn.

'He's gone for a walk,' said Tara quickly.

Rose reached out and took her middle daughter's hands in hers. 'Say goodbye to him for me. And don't be upset, Tara. I have to do this.'

'I know,' murmured Tara, although she didn't. The whole world was changing in front of her eyes and there was nothing she could do about it. 'I wish you'd let me come with you.'

'Darling, I've got to do this on my own,' replied her mother.

Stella put her arms about both Rose and Tara. 'Phone us when you get to Freddie's.'

'Of course.'

Finally, Rose came to Holly who stood with tears in her eyes.

'I'm sorry,' said Rose. She hugged Holly tightly, then got into the car quickly as if she mightn't be able to leave them if she thought about it at all.

They watched her drive off in silence. Amelia held onto her mother's hand.

Adele could feel an ache in her throat, a strange feeling

she couldn't quite identify. She turned to walk in and Nick offered her his arm. They went in, leaving two generations of Miller women staring into the distance.

CHAPTER TWENTY-TWO

The engine didn't sound right even to Rose's non-mechanical ears. She drove fast along the main road to Castletown and listened to the engine roar even when her foot hadn't increased the pressure on the accelerator. Damn car. Hugh's garage were good with it, she'd get him to drive it there ... The knowledge that Hugh wouldn't bring her car to the garage because she'd left him, hit her anew. She'd just left Hugh. After forty years. A vision of his shocked, bewildered face came to her and she had to slow down because her eyes misted over and her heart began to race in panic.

There was a farm gate set in from the road and Rose pulled in and switched off the engine. She forced herself to breathe deeply until the dreadful shuddering was gone and her heartbeat had slowed.

Hugh hadn't watched her drive away from Kinvarra; only the girls, Amelia, Adele and Nick had waved from the house, all of them trying to behave as if this was an ordinary trip and she would be back in a few days, rested and happy.

Rose herself had gone along with the cheerful facade, and she'd felt just as if she was heading off for a relaxing holiday. Until now. In her entire ordered existence, she'd never behaved like this and, now that she'd actually done it, the shock was setting in.

A watery sun was low in the sky and the evening was growing cooler, but Rose wound down the window to let some air into the car. The harsh scent of wild elder hit her nostrils, along with the fresh, sharp tang of the wild onions that grew abundantly in the long grasses beside the gate. In the distance, she could hear cows calling plaintively to be milked and the clock tower in Castletown sounded the hour in seven muffled, echoing rings. Rose had been driving for an hour and three quarters and Castletown was just over the crest of the next hill. She'd told Freddie she'd be there before half six but there was no feeling for having to rush on. Rose's normal impeccable timekeeping had vanished now that she was back home. She let herself breathe in the scents of her youth, knowing that Freddie was vague about time and wouldn't raise an eyebrow no matter what time she arrived at. That was partly why she'd chosen to stay with Freddie. Her mother's younger sister was exactly the sort of person to run to when you'd just left your husband after forty years of marriage. Unconventional and without a judgmental bone in her body, Freddie would not ask too many questions.

She had asked practically nothing when Rose had phoned earlier.

'Course you can stay,' she'd said cheerfully. 'It's lucky you caught me, in fact. We've got this charity bed-push starting in an hour and I must be there. Will you want dinner or is this problem making you too sad to eat?'

Despite everything, Rose had burst into laughter at this. It was classic Freddie.

Slightly cheered up at the thought of seeing her aunt, Rose started the car and set off to Castletown.

A pretty seaside town with two miles of glorious beach and a reputation as a quiet spot for a holiday home, Castletown's main street was quiet when Rose drove down it. Despite its old-fashioned air, the town had changed hugely since Rose herself had lived there forty years before. Then, it had been pretty but with an air of shabbiness. The Grand Hotel in the centre had sported a cracked facade that seemed to say the whole of Castletown had seen better times, while the shop fronts, though spotlessly clean, had been dull and old. Now, the hotel had been revamped with an enormous extension for weddings, and a sports complex out the back. Carriage lamps and pretty Virginia creeper completed the picture out the front. The small shops beside the hotel boasted old-fashioned signs that were far too shiny and perfect to be really old. The tiny grocery shop where Rose herself had worked for one summer had trebled in size and turned into a convenience store, with big signs in the window proclaiming that fresh bread and lottery tickets were available inside.

She kept driving, past the road down to the beach where she and Hugh had walked all those years ago when he'd come to meet her parents for the first time. Rose didn't want to remember that. She clenched her jaw and took a right turn at a T-junction, heading up a winding hill that wound round behind the town. At the crest of the hill, she turned left down a tiny lane to a cottage surrounded by trees.

Freddie met her at the gate.

'Welcome, Rose!' she said cheerfully and loudly, so her voice could be heard above the barking of three wildly excited dogs. A white-muzzled Jack Russell, an equally white-muzzled black mongrel with sad eyes, and a fawn-coloured sheltie collie who quivered with nerves, all clustered around Rose.

The two women embraced, then Freddie effortlessly picked up the hold-all Rose had thrown on the passenger seat.

'The kettle is boiled if you want tea and the man from the drink shop has just delivered, so I've got blue gin too.'

She beamed at her niece and Rose, feeling utterly welcome and suddenly near to tears, beamed shakily back.

'It's lovely to be here,' she said.

'About time you came home for a visit,' Freddie said.

Rose estimated she must be at least in her late seventies, perhaps early eighties. But whatever words you'd use to describe Freddie Maguire, old-age-pensioner wouldn't be the first to mind. Lively and eccentric would be more accurate, Rose decided.

Freddie's face was brown from the outdoors and covered with a patina of fine lines, like a beautiful but very old vase crisscrossed with many delicate cracks. Her hair was snow white, luxuriant and flowed back from a widow's peak. Rose could recall black and white family photos of Freddie as a young, vibrant woman when the rippling, wild hair had been jet-black and she'd stood tall and slender, gazing firmly into the camera. Only the eyes remained the same: a wise and curious sea-green, they were the eyes of a young woman.

She was still slender but the slim waist had thickened with age. Her hands too were aged, with tendons standing out like ropes under the fine skin. But she didn't stoop when she walked, and she still marched along at a sprightly pace, as Rose found when Freddie set off towards the cottage swinging Rose's bag. The dogs followed her.

'I must introduce you to the girls,' Freddie said when they got to the front door. 'This little imp of a terrier is Pig,' she said. 'This lady is Mildred.' The black dog looked mournfully up at Rose. 'And this little darling is Prinny, who was abandoned and needs constant reassurance.' The sheltie gazed up at her mistress with anxious, darting eyes as if to prove the point. 'Come on in and welcome to Nettle Cottage. It's called that because nettles remind me of myself: astringent but very good in hot water,' added Freddie with a glint in her eyes.

Nettle Cottage was like the cottage Rose had grown up in. On the outside, anyhow. On the inside, the resemblance vanished. Rose's family home had been very much in the traditional mould, with pale painted walls, a big range in one corner, and the sort of comfortable but unfussy furniture that was suitable for people who worked on a farm. Freddie's cottage was done up like a Tudor dwelling, with black beams, open brickwork, brass hangings all over the place and an open fire in front of which the three dogs' beanbags had pride of place. Books, photos and knickknacks lined the walls, along with prints of Klimt and Tamara de Lempicka paintings. In a glass cabinet were crammed lots of books.

Rose peered in to see everything from de Beauvoir to the entire works of Anaïs Nin.

'I keep the racier ones in there,' said Freddie airily.

The guest bedroom was at the back of the house with a view of a big, wild flower-filled meadow. The flower theme was reflected inside. One wall was painted with a stunning mural of the meadow.

'I had this darling little Spanish girl staying for a while and she painted that instead of paying rent,' Freddie said, sitting on the bed to admire it. 'There's only one bathroom, I'm afraid, and the shower is a bit bonky so I just have baths. Haven't got round to fixing it. I'll get the drinks, right, and we can talk about what might be nice for dinner.' With a quick smile, she was gone, her retinue of dogs with her. Rose looked around the small, cosy room. There was a high, old-fashioned bed with sheets and a white quilted bedcover instead of a duvet. Pine bookcases were filled with books, still more paintings covered three of the walls, and a gleaming Art Deco wardrobe stood in one corner. By the bed was a selection of fresh candles in a variety of containers. Usually a stickler for instant unpacking, she didn't even consider going out to the car to get her suitcases. She didn't want to be on her own for however long unpacking would take. She didn't want the company of her own tangled thoughts. She threw her handbag on the bed and went out to the sitting room.

'I'm having a gin and Dubonnet,' said Freddie, without looking round from a bamboo table laid out with every drink imaginable. 'I always say if it was good enough for the dear old Queen Mum, it's good enough for me.'

'One for me too,' said Rose, who rarely drank anything other than a little wine and the occasional gin and tonic.

Freddie handed Rose a highball glass. 'That'll put hair on your chest, Rose,' she said.

Rose took a sip and her eyes watered.

'Too strong?' said Freddie worriedly. 'I forget sometimes. Not everyone likes a strong one.'

She spooned some ice into Rose's glass, then sat down with her own. The dogs, who'd been watching her every move, finally settled comfortably onto their beanbags, noses happily on paws, content now that their restless mistress had finally stopped. Freddie tasted her drink, smiled, and then lit up a long dark cigarette.

'I only have four or five a day now,' she said. 'I know it's bad for me. So's the booze but you can't kill a bad thing.' She twinkled irrepressibly at Rose.

'Now, Rose, you can stay as long as you like and I don't want to know what it's all about. You can keep your counsel. I can't imagine you've come back to Castletown for the first time in years without there being a damn good reason but if there's one thing I've learned in my life, it's that busybodies are a right pain in the backside. Are you hungry? Do you fancy dinner?' At the word 'dinner', all three dogs sat up instantly, tails wagging.

'Not you, sweeties,' crooned Freddie. 'You'll get fat if you have anything else today. They're such gannets when it comes to food,' she added to Rose. 'There's a lovely Indian restaurant ten miles away and they do takeaway . . .'

'I've walked out on Hugh because he'd been unfaithful,' blurted out Rose.

'Well, I'm sure that was absolutely the right thing to do,' Freddie said, not a hair out of place. 'Men are like puppies. A bit of rolled up newspaper tapped on their nose soon housetrains them.'

The dogs, none of whom looked as though Freddie had even waved a bit of rolled up newspaper in their direction once, watched her adoringly. 'Do you think you'll go back to him or is it for good?'

Rose had a bigger sip of her drink. Freddie was disconcertingly direct. There was no palaver about 'how awful, poor you but have you thought this out properly?' Nor did she gasp at the notion of forty years of marriage coming to an end.

'I don't know,' Rose said honestly.

Prinny leaned her long fawn-coloured nose against Rose's legs and she leaned down to stroke the little dog. 'It was a spur of the moment thing. Everybody else is horrified and wants us back together.'

'Everybody else isn't as old as I am,' Freddie pointed out. 'When you get to eighty, you're entitled to think for yourself and be as mad as a bicycle.'

'That's not age,' pointed out Rose. 'You were like that years ago.'

'I suppose I was,' Freddie smiled. 'I've never been one for monogamy. I've had lots of lovers. I never wanted to settle down with any one of them, well,' she paused, her mind years and miles away. 'I did once, but he was married.'

Rose stiffened and Freddie noticed.

'Rose, my dear, I didn't rush off and drag him from the bosom of his family. I know you're feeling a bit sensitive about extramarital affairs but it's not like that. He was unhappily married but it wasn't like now, people didn't leave. That was fifty years ago and we decided it was easier to part. Some people aren't good at monogamy, and others think a bit of spice makes life more fun.'

'I don't,' said Rose sadly.

'And Hugh did.'

Rose nodded.

'When you and Hugh got married, I wondered how it would go.' Freddie drained her glass and got up to make another drink. 'Your mother and father were so happy together, I wondered how any mortal man could possibly match up. And,' Freddie paused, 'he was from a different world from us. Your mother was always half thrilled you'd got out of Castletown and half scared that you'd set your sights too high with the Millers.'

For a second, Rose bridled at the notion that she wasn't good enough for the Miller family. Then she sank further back into the chair. Freddie was right. The world might have moved on from class divisions but forty years ago, those divisions might have been marked in stone. A poor farmer's daughter and the college-going son of a prosperous solicitor were miles apart.

'How are the girls?' asked Freddie, changing the subject easily.

They feasted on Indian food and the dogs were outraged when Freddie refused to let them have any titbits.

'Too rich and spicy for you,' she insisted as they sat, shiny-eyed with anticipation, around the table.

Edith Piaf played softly in the background. Freddie didn't have a television. She read the news in the papers, she said, and she hated looking at wars on the news.

By ten, Rose was wilting. The combination of the intense stress of the day, and two of Freddie's gin and Dubonnets had worn her out.

'I think I'll go to bed,' she said, getting to her feet.

'Good idea,' said Freddie. 'We've a busy day tomorrow. Tomorrow's my day for meals on wheels for the elderly,' she added without a hint of irony.

Why would she, thought Rose. Until Freddie became elderly, why not?

'You'll be a great help,' Freddie continued. 'The clutch in the van is slipping and it's great to have help. You're supposed to do the meals in pairs but I'm always on my own. We'll have great fun.'

Rose, who had envisioned the following day as more a meander through old memories, nodded.

'Night, Freddie.'

She prepared for bed in the small, deep blue bathroom and used some of Freddie's carrot moisturiser because she'd mysteriously forgotten her own. An old glass-fronted cabinet hung on the bathroom wall and inside were all sorts of interesting mementoes, including some pretty silver cigarette cases, a tiny enamelled medal and a very old, empty bottle of Chanel No 5. Rose wondered who had given it to Freddie and why it was so precious that it had been kept when the scent had long since vanished. Had it been a gift from the married lover fifty years before?

In her bedroom, she changed into a nightie and slipped between the cool cotton sheets. The bed was as hard as the hob of hell and Rose felt like the Princess and the Pea as she tried to get comfortable. But suddenly sleep came and despite the hard boards beneath the mattress, she slept deeply and dreamlessly.

'Tea,' announced Freddie, arriving in the room the next morning with her retinue of dogs making a tap-dancing racket as their claws clicked on the tiled floor.

Rose sat up in bed, unsure of where she was until Freddie opened the curtains and sunlight streamed into the room, illuminating the floral mural on the wall opposite the bed.

'Did you sleep?'

'Really well, actually.' Rose took the mug of tea and sat back against the pillows, revelling in the luxury of being brought tea in bed. Freddie's tea was the colour of peanut butter or 'strong enough for a duck to trot across,' as she said herself. But today, it was revivingly sweet and familiar. Rose remembered her mother loving strong tea too, real tea, not tea bags.

'What time is it?' she asked.

'Half six. Later than I usually get up. On Sundays, I bring the girls for a bit of a jaunt round the Sally Woods, then go for breakfast in O'Malley's and then on to help with the meals on wheels dinner.'

Rose, who was many years younger, wondered how her aunt managed this punishing schedule. Her idea of a relaxing Sunday involved breakfast, Mass in the cathedral, and home to peruse the newspapers at her leisure.

'Are you on for a walk?' Freddie looked very keen.

'Yes,' said Rose decisively. In for a penny, in for a pound.

The bit of a jaunt round the Sally Woods turned out to be an energetic three-mile hike up a tiny road, then up a very steep hill to a beautiful glade of willow trees and back. The dogs bounced around delightedly, burying their noses in tufts of grass and running into streams before dancing

378

out again and shaking their fur. Rose's mental clock kept tuning in to Kinvarra time. Now, she and Hugh would be sitting in the kitchen, listening to the Sunday morning news and eating breakfast: toast for Rose, porridge for Hugh.

A cluster of wild bluebells made her think how lovely they'd look on the kitchen table, before she remembered she wasn't in Kinvarra.

'Let it go, Rose,' advised Freddie gently, seeing Rose's face cloaked in the pain of remembering. 'Enjoy your time here. You haven't burned your bridges yet, you can still go back. So relax.'

Rose, unable to speak, nodded. She would do that, she would. She'd do her best to forget about the pain of the past twenty-four hours. This was to be her healing time and she wanted to enjoy it.

'Some bluebells would look nice in the bathroom,' she said, bending to pick a few of the fragile stems.

Freddie grinned. 'Yes, they would.'

CHAPTER TWENTY-THREE

For once, Holly didn't cook. Instead, she made a big pot of coffee and put it in front of Stella and Tara with a packet of chocolate biscuits in case anyone was hungry. Stella, who tended to comfort eat when she was upset, took two biscuits. Tara took a cup of black coffee without sugar. She wouldn't be able to force a biscuit down.

Unusually, neither of them noticed the newest addition to Holly's apartment: a foot-high stone angel that Tom had brought her from a building he was working on. The angel was cracked and would be of no use to an architectural salvage company, but Tom had known that Holly would love it.

'It's beautiful. How did you guess I liked angels?' she gasped with delight when he'd carried it into the flat. She ran her fingers over the angel's radiant upturned little face and through the carefully carved curls, loving the feeling of the smooth stone. One wing was very chipped but Holly didn't care. It was the most beautiful thing anyone had ever given her.

'Lucky guess,' said Tom, beaming.

Holly touched her angel for luck before she sat down on the small couch and faced her sisters. It was a Miller sister council meeting to discuss what they were going to do with their parents.

It was Tuesday evening, three days after the cataclysmic events of the ruby wedding anniversary. In those three days, the sisters had spoken to their mother several times by phone.

380

She'd sounded calm and convinced she'd done the right thing. She'd also said she was enjoying the relative calm of Castletown.

'Freddie's always on the go and there are people dropping in to the cottage at all hours, but, because they're not here to see me, it's strangely relaxing,' Rose said.

Their father was another matter.

He had gone to pieces. Alastair Devon was on the phone every day telling Stella that Hugh was a broken man and begging one of the girls to move back to Kinvarra and take care of him. Stella, torn between loyalty to her mother and concern for her father, and not sure how she'd manage to put her life on hold to return to Kinvarra, had mentioned this to Hugh. He'd said he wouldn't dream of it.

'It's my bed,' he said in a faint voice that seemed a pale comparison of his usual booming tones. 'I have to lie on it. I'm just so sorry for all the hurt.'

'We've got to make them see sense,' Stella said now, taking another chocolate biscuit. Of the three of them, she was the most shocked by their parents' split. In one fell swoop, Hugh and Rose's supposedly deliriously happy marriage had been proved to be a sham. At night, Stella found herself going back over events in her childhood, trying to remember if she'd just imagined the happiness. Every seemingly 'perfect' moment was suspect and her blind acceptance of this happy family image made her even doubt her own judgement. How could she not have seen what was going on?

'What I don't understand,' said Tara, putting down her empty cup and refilling it, 'is how we never knew. Well, me and Stella, anyway.'

'You should have told us, Holly,' said Stella for what seemed to Holly like the millionth time. On Saturday night, the three girls had sat up and talked for hours. Holly had given Stella and Tara the second shock of the day when she revealed that she'd known about their father's dalliances, or rather, about one of them.

'I knew years ago,' she'd said, almost apologetically. She hated telling them.

The others gasped. 'You knew?' said Tara, astonished.

Holly shrugged.

'But why didn't you tell us or Mum?'

There was no easy way for Holly to answer that question. Her loyalties were slightly different from Stella and Tara's. She'd always adored her father. Hearing him murmuring endearments on the phone to a woman clearly not her mother had shocked her sixteen-year-old soul, but she still loved him. She didn't want him to split up with her mother, which was what happened when people went off and had affairs. So Holly had kept the secret to herself. She'd never had any evidence of any other affairs, but even so, she'd always known that she hadn't been mistaken in what she'd heard.

'How could I tell you?' Holly demanded now, taking a chocolate biscuit herself. *'By the way, guys, Mum and Dad aren't happily married after all.* You wouldn't have believed me. And when I was older, I assumed you'd known all along; that it was only me who didn't. You're both closer to Mum. I thought I was the only one who wasn't in on the secret.'

'Why didn't she tell us?' Tara was maudlin. 'We could have talked to Dad and made him see sense. We still can . . .'

'Maybe if Dad stopped being defeatist and went to Aunt Freddie's to see Mum,' added Stella hopefully.

Holly stared at her sisters in exasperation. 'We can't fix it, it's not ours to fix,' she said fiercely. 'To think everyone tells me *I'm* the naive one.'

'Yeah, you're right,' admitted Tara.

Tara felt this great weariness that everything in her life was falling apart. Finn hadn't apologised for what he'd said in Kinvarra. He hadn't been drinking since, although the atmosphere was as tense as if he was sinking a bottle of brandy a night. She felt powerless to say anything. Her ability to deal with life had vanished along with her conviction that her parents adored each other. Everything felt upside down. She knew that as a grown-up, she should be able to deal with this because after all, lots of people's parents split up. But it just wasn't that easy.

Stella finished the biscuit and promised herself she wouldn't have another one. Holly was right. They couldn't fix Hugh and Rose's marriage any more, she thought wryly, than Jenna could make Wendy and Nick Cavaletto love each other. At least she was one step closer to understanding her stepdaughter. When the chips were down, she and Jenna had reacted in exactly the same way: clinging blindly to the belief that they could make it all better.

'If we're all agreed that it's not up to us to get them back together, we should take it in turns to see Mum and Dad, so they know we love them and we aren't taking sides,' said Holly decisively. 'And to make sure that Dad's all right. Somebody's got to show him how to use the washing machine.'

Tara and Stella looked at their little sister in admiration. This was a new side to Holly they'd never seen before. She was taking the initiative and doing the right thing. Both Tara and Stella were aware that their initial instincts hadn't been anywhere near as clear-headed as Holly's.

'I'll take Saturday off and go to Dad's on Friday night,' Holly said decisively. Both of her sisters flinched at the use of the word 'Dad's.' It was as if Kinvarra wasn't their family home any more, but was part of some complicated separated family set up. The magic that had surrounded Meadow Lodge in their minds had disappeared.

'I suppose you're right,' Stella said. 'That's all we can do: wait, be supportive and hope they come to their senses.'

When Stella and Tara had gone, Holly didn't bother tidying the cups away. Instead, she put a much-loved Ella Fitzgerald CD on and lay on the couch. As Ella's soft voice warmed her heart, Holly thought about her sisters' reaction to their parents' split. Both Tara and Stella wanted to do something. Holly had never entertained such an idea. Was she being realistic or was she a bad daughter for not moving heaven and earth to get them back together?

Joan stuck her head round the door. 'Council of war over?' she asked.

Holly grinned, glad of the distraction. 'Yeah. Come on in.'

'Oh, biscuits,' said Joan joyfully, swooping on the unfinished pack on the coffee table. She wolfed two in thirty seconds, and took a third for good measure.

Joan was working hard on her final year collection and working all night was par for the course. She was also consuming lots of coffee and high-energy snacks, neither of which were doing anything for her skin. She was pale and a fat spot lurked miserably under the skin on her forehead, waiting to appear at the most inconvenient moment possible.

'Will I make you a fruit smoothie?' asked Holly kindly.

'Go on,' sighed Joan. 'Anything to stop me eating chocolate biscuits.'

While Holly chopped up fruit and whizzed it around in her blender with some orange juice, Joan lay back on the couch with her eyes closed.

'Here you are.' Holly sat on the edge of the couch and handed Joan the smoothie. She really must make a pot of chicken soup for Joan to heat up when she worked all night. Chicken soup cured all ills. 'How's the collection going?' she asked tentatively.

Joan rubbed her eyes before she took a sip of the pulped fruit drink. 'Not bad but I've got two weeks of work to do and only one week to do it in.'

'If you want any help, ask,' said Holly. 'You know I don't mind and I know I'm not as good as you, but . . .'

'You're miles better than me,' interrupted Joan. 'If I could appliqué and embroider as well as you, I'd be much faster. Actually, I've got a vest top that needs beading and it would be great if you could do it for me. I've traced the design on with tailor's chalk, it's a sunflower thing, really simple.'

'No problem,' said Holly, happy to be able to help. 'I'll start now. There's never anything good on the box on Tuesday evenings, I'd love something to do.'

'Whoa, girl, you're not doing it tonight,' said Joan enigmatically. She finished the drink. 'We're going out. There's a great gig on in the Olympia. You know Fiona from my year? Well, her brother is the guitarist in the support band and we're going to watch them. You on for that?'

'I thought Fiona's brother was in a metal band?' said Holly suspiciously, preferring the idea of a quiet evening in with some beading to a night of eardrum-bashing metal in the company of hundreds of head-bangers.

'I've got earplugs for both of us,' Joan smiled winningly. 'Say you'll come. There's going to be a crowd from college, Kenny and Tom are going to come too.'

'Count me in,' said Holly quickly.

The four of them got a taxi and Kenny made them all laugh with a story of his latest fashion shoot where it had taken three hours to get everything right, including lighting, and then, just as the photographer was ready to start, the electricity had gone. His first shoots had gone so well that two photographers had passed on his name to fashion editors and Kenny was now working as a stylist at least twice a week.

'You're not going to be too busy to style my collection in the end of year show, are you?' asked Joan.

Kenny adopted his outraged fashionista expression: eyebrows raised, lips pouting, wrist limp. 'Darling, I'm up to my tonsils but I'll try and squeeze you into my organiser,' he lisped. 'Seriously,' he dropped the camp stylist act and grinned at his flatmate, 'do you think I'd miss your show, you big dope? Course I'll do the styling. You don't have to ask.'

Outside the Olympia, Joan's friends congregated, most of them clearly fashion mavens from their achingly trendy clothes. Kenny, who was one of them, was welcomed into the pack with open arms and even Holly, who was wearing one of Joan's graffiti-ed T-shirts over jeans, felt that for once, she fitted in.

The madly chattering group surged in the doors and Holly found herself at the back of the crowd beside Tom.

'How's Caroline?' asked Holly. She found it was easier to talk about Caroline first, rather than to wait for Tom to mention her. Whenever he said her name, Holly felt that pinprick of pain in her heart, so she'd come to the conclusion that attack was the best form of defence. Consequently, she cheerily asked what Caroline was up to, how the job was going, when was she coming to Dublin next, all in a chatty, friendly voice that, she hoped, gave no hint of the ache behind the questions.

'Fine, she's working away like a demon,' Tom responded. 'She's all fired up about buying a new car. She's had a test drive in just about everything that moves and she's got her eye on this BMW coupé.'

'Wow,' said Holly, imagining Caroline with her blonde hair flying in the breeze, attracting wildly envious glances from male drivers as she whizzed along. You couldn't get the same effect with a double-decker bus, Holly knew, although her hair did fly sometimes when the bus driver let it rip on one of the bus corridors.

'How are you?' asked Tom. 'I haven't seen much of you, lately. How's your angel?'

'Lovely, thanks. She's beautiful. I've just been busy, you know. I applied for a job in the interior department, I mean, I haven't got it or anything, I just thought it would be nice for a change . . .' Holly added lamely, thinking how hopeless she sounded. Tom's girlfriend was a business woman with her own flat and a sports car in her sights, and she was telling him about her own tiny career leap from the basement in Lee's to the third floor. Whoopee. 'Sorry, didn't mean to drone on.'

'You're not droning on, I want to hear all about it,' said Tom softly.

'Holly!' squealed a voice.

Joan appeared from the throng, dragging a tall guy by one arm. The guy was laughing but he wasn't resisting too much.

'Holly,' said Joan triumphantly, 'this is Fiona's other brother, Vic, not the one in the band. He said he'd love to meet you.'

Holly smiled nervously.

'Nice to meet you too,' she said.

The guy moved easily beside her, conveniently ignoring Tom. He wasn't as tall as Tom, Holly noticed. She'd found herself comparing all men to Tom these days, but Vic still managed to be attractive in an intense way. He didn't look as if he could possibly be related to Fiona, because she was pale and freckled with features straight off a Discover Ireland poster, while he was sloe-eyed with slanting cheekbones, sallow skin and shaggy, uncombed dark hair.

'Victor Dunne,' he said, shaking her hand, 'known to all and sundry as Vic.'

'Holly Miller,' she said, blushing. 'And this is Tom Barry.'

'Hi, Tom.' Vic flashed a smile at Tom and turned back to Holly.

Taking the hint, Tom followed Joan, leaving Vic and Holly on their own.

'Don't go . . .' began Holly, but Tom had disappeared down the foyer steps towards Kenny.

'I saw you before, actually, in the Purple Mosquito a few weeks ago,' Vic said. 'You were talking to that guy, Tom. I thought he was your boyfriend.'

'No, he's a friend,' Holly said quietly, still scanning the people ahead for Tom. He must have got his ticket and gone in. She felt embarrassed at how he'd rushed off. Why had he done that?

'Fiona mentioned it to Joan, who said he's just a guy from the same flat complex so, I thought I'd come over and talk to you,' Vic continued. They'd reached the ticket desk.

'Two please,' said Vic, holding his credit card out to the teller.

'There's no need to buy my ticket,' said Holly, who hadn't really been paying attention and was now astonished at the notion of a man voluntarily buying her ticket.

'You can get me a drink in the interval,' said Vic, giving her a sloe-eyed grin.

'Thanks,' stammered Holly. He really was attractive. 'You know,' she added, looking at him curiously, 'you don't look a bit like Fiona.'

'We're all adopted,' he replied.

'Oh, sorry, I didn't mean . . .' She went pink again at this new faux pas, her arm jerked convulsively and a heap of leaflets advertising a series of comedy nights went flying onto the carpet. Both Vic and Holly bent to pick them up, their heads coming within an inch of banging.

'Sorry,' repeated Holly, thinking she should just get a tape recorder with her voice saying 'sorry' on it and she wouldn't have to talk at all.

'I don't mind people noticing we look different, honestly,' Vic chatted away as he briskly gathered up the scattered leaflets. 'A lot of people notice because we genuinely look nothing like each other. Sandy, our other brother, has green eyes and white blond hair.'

'That must make for great family group photos,' Holly said admiringly.

'You said it,' said Vic easily. 'Let me tell you about Fiona's twenty-first birthday . . .' And he was off. As Holly soon discovered, Vic was easy to talk to. A junior doctor in a busy city accident and emergency department, he was accustomed to talking to anyone and everyone and could get conversation out of a stone. He also hated silence and could keep up a stream of hilarious remarks for hours on end. All Holly had to do was listen and stop herself from laughing too much.

By the interval, neither Holly nor Vic had paid much attention to the band his brother was playing in.

'We should watch a bit,' suggested Holly guiltily, as they stood down the back of the Olympia, drinking gin and tonics from plastic cups and talking loudly so they could hear each other above the thumping bass guitar.

Vic screwed his expressive face up in fake horror. 'Holy shit, no. I've been listening to Sandy for years. The band practise in our garage when Mum and Dad are away and I could sing most of the songs myself. Besides, I've seen people half deaf from being too near to the amps. We're much better down here where our ears are safe.'

Holly found that she was enjoying herself and the evening raced by. It was easy to talk to men when you weren't interested in them. That was the secret, she realised. After all these years of feeling shy, she'd finally arrived at the truth. When a guy talked to her like a normal person, her shyness vanished. But the ones she liked made her tongue-tied. Even Tom, her dear friend and a man she could have chatted to for years, had been affected by this horrible syndrome. Until she'd realised she was crazy about Tom, she could chat to him easily. Once the sisterly feelings went, so did the conversation.

She could see Tom towering over the heads of most of the concert-goers, his fair hair glinting in the lights from the stage. He looked around but obviously couldn't see her because when she waved, his gaze went past her and he turned away without waving back. Holly's heart gave a resigned little thump. She knew she had to get over Tom. He loved Caroline. There was no hope for stupid Holly. She might as well forget about him and get on with her life.

Vic, wildly indiscreet and onto the story of his previous night in A & E, was trying to make her laugh.

'So this woman came in with abdominal pain and said she thought it was post-natal pains and that they could be dangerous, couldn't they? So I said how long since she'd had the baby, and she said 'five years'. He stopped suddenly. 'I'm not boring you, am I?' he asked.

Holly laughed out loud at the thought of anyone asking *her* that question.

'That's my line, normally,' she teased.

'You?' Vic reached out and gently pulled one of her lustrous dark curls straight. When he let it go, it bounced back like a spring. 'I can't see you boring anybody, Holly. You are so not boring. You haven't an ounce of boringness in your whole body. You are the least boringest person I have ever encountered in my entire boring life, and I know about boring because I personally . . .'

'Stop it,' laughed Holly. 'I'm not going to buy you any more gin if you keep this up.'

Vic grinned broadly. 'It's not gin,' he said indignantly. 'It's love.'

'I said stop!' Holly thought he was a howl. 'I've always known that doctors were mad but you take the biscuit. My sister writes for *National Hospital* and the doctors in that all come across as deranged. Now I see the scriptwriters don't know the half of it.' Usually, mentioning Tara's job enthralled listeners and they demanded details, wanting to know what the stars were *like* and how did they make all those mad story lines up? But Vic wasn't even vaguely interested.

'Junior doctors have to be deranged,' he joked, 'it's part of the job. First the Hippocratic Oath, then the Deranged Oath. No, seriously, to get back to you, Holly, I am entranced by your non-boringness. Will you come out with me sometime? On a date?'

'Vic,' said Holly, 'you are sweet.'

'I don't want to be sweet,' he protested, 'I want to be He-Man to your Shee-La Queen of the Jungle or whatever her name was. Go on, will you come on a date with me? I promise not to be deranged. It'll be fun, although it'll have to be on Friday because I'm on shift for the next four days.'

He looked so keen, and so interested in her. After yearning in vain for Tom, there was something infinitely comforting to Holly about a man who did like her. Even if she actually wasn't interested in him. Vic was good-looking but he wasn't her type. Still, it might be fun. She cast Tom resolutely out of her mind.

'As friends,' Holly said. 'We'll go out as friends.'

Vic growled and banged his chest like Tarzan. 'Me He-Man, you Shee-La.'

'Is he annoying you?' asked Fiona, coming out of the bar with a tray of drinks.

'No,' said Holly, still laughing. 'Not at all.'

For once, Joan didn't have the energy to go clubbing. 'Bed, I need my bed,' she moaned as a slightly depleted crowd reconvened outside the Olympia after the gig to discuss further plans.

'Me too,' said Holly.

'Three-in-a-bed!' sighed Vic, rolling his eyes. 'Will I be able for it?'

Everyone laughed, except Tom, who was noticeably stony-faced.

'No three-in-a-bed romps for you, my boy,' said Holly sternly. 'Go home and get some sleep yourself. We don't want you killing anyone tomorrow due to lack of sleep.'

'I'll do my best, ma'am,' said Vic, saluting. 'Your wish is my command. But,' he added in a stage whisper, 'if the three-in-a-bed thing should come up, I can be at your place in fifteen minutes, twenty max. I'll bring my stethoscope and my white coat, OK?'

Happily tanked up on beer, everyone roared with laughter again.

'I'll call you,' promised Vic, blowing kisses in Holly's direction.

Kenny hailed a taxi and shoved Joan in. Holly clambered in after her, still giggling over Vic's antics, and Tom got in last, bending almost double to avoid knocking his head on the roof.

'Vic's a panic, isn't he?' said Joan, leaning against Kenny and closing her eyes. 'Fiona says he's totally brilliant and utterly mad, which is quite something coming from her because she's the maddest of our whole year.'

'Go to sleep, Joan,' groaned Kenny, closing his eyes too. 'I'm exhausted and I can't believe I spent the evening listening to those awful bands. What is it about straight men and crap music?' he grumbled. 'I mean, I have to be up at half six to be in the studio by seven thirty.'

Silence reigned. An uncomfortable silence, Holly thought in alarm. Both Joan and Kenny were snoozing, while Tom sat on the bucket seat and stared grimly out the window. The seat was far too small for his big frame and he looked like a giant on a child's seat.

'Did you've a nice time?' she asked.

'Fine,' said Tom, still looking out the window.

Holly nibbled a bit of fingernail. He must be missing Caroline. 'I suppose you wish Caroline was here,' she said kindly.

Tom dragged his gaze away from the fascinating spectacle of a traffic island with nobody standing on it.

'She hates that sort of music,' he said shortly.

'Oh.'

He stared back at the traffic island. The lights changed and the taxi lurched off.

'Well, she'll be up from Cork soon, won't she?' Holly was doing her best to be chatty. 'And when she gets the MG convertible thingy, she'll be able to whizz up. It'll eat up the miles.'

'Coupé,' said Tom.

'Sorry, coupé,' said Holly. 'I know I'm stupid, you'd think I didn't know the difference between a coupé and a convertible.' It was her turn to look out the window. She hadn't a clue about the difference between a coupé and a convertible. She'd thought they were the same. The roof came off, didn't it? Obviously she was wrong about this, more proof of how Caroline was Ms Trendy, On-The-Ball person while she was Ms Gobshite, Never-Owned-A-Car and Never-Likely-To person. Shit, she didn't care.

'I can't drive,' she said recklessly. 'I can't afford to buy a car in the first place.' She glared at Tom. Just because he was going out with perfect bloody Caroline, didn't mean he had to get the hump with her.

Tom looked at her for a moment, then went back to the window.

Holly rooted around in her handbag and found her mints. She took one out and began crunching it crossly. Men. Pains in the backside, that's all they were.

CHAPTER TWENTY-FOUR

Tara's 'must do' list was growing longer. First it was just: *buy binbags, dishwasher stuff, dandruff shampoo, FOOD, phone bank about standing order problem, get birthday present for Isadora, phone Dad to see how he is*. Then her credit card bill came and added another 'must do' to the list – a call-credit-card-people-and-complain job.

She opened the bill on the way to work when she was sitting in the car in a tailback at least a mile long with no sign of ever moving again. The new skincare range was going to be on the bill, she reflected. She should never have gone into the chemist when she was feeling grey-faced and old. Beauty counter experts had some sort of special radar for people experiencing hate-themselves days. The experts instantly spotted the said miserable person and convinced them that gorgeous pots of wildly expensive creams were the solution. Tara, despite knowing that it was going to be an expensive month because her car insurance was due, had succumbed to the power of the gorgeous pots. Now she wished she hadn't. She scanned down the list of purchases. The skincare range was there in all its glory and she told herself firmly that shopping was not to be considered an acceptable form of therapy. They didn't have the funds for luxuries.

Then, she noticed a huge debit that just had to be a mistake. Money taken from a cash machine. Well that was wrong for a start. Tara never used her credit card to take money from the hole in the wall – the interest knocked in straight away and it would be cheaper to rip up a couple of tenners than borrow money that way. Honestly, first the bank messed up the mortgage payment which resulted in a snorter of a letter from the building society about how they were going to nail somebody's kneecaps to the floor if the money wasn't paid pronto. Now this.

Phone bank went to the top of the *must do* list.

In work, there were messages from Stella, from Lenny in publicity about a reporter who wanted to spend the day on the set, and a please-call-someone-in-the-bank.

'What's up?' asked Scott Irving, peering into Tara's cubicle. He leaned his jean-clad hips against her desk and smiled at her over his cup of coffee. Scott's smile was one of those slow-burn ones that made women pull their stomachs in. Tara tried to suppress the desire to check her reflection in her darkened computer screen.

'Fine,' she said. She *had* put lipstick on, hadn't she?

'Fancy lunch later?'

Tara smiled with genuine pleasure. 'I'd love to,' she said.

Scott treated her to another slow-burn smile that reached places most smiles couldn't. 'See you at one, then.'

Tara sat at her desk with her messages in her hand and tried to assimilate what had just happened. She'd said yes instinctively but was that a mistake?

'Lunch?' asked Isadora innocently on her way to her desk with a coffee in her hand.

'I, er . . . well . . .' said Tara, suddenly feeling embarrassed by the idea of telling Isadora that she was going out with Scott. It was only lunch after all, they worked together and had to discuss work and stuff, but people might read the wrong thing into it . . .

'You're a crap liar, Miller, you know that.' Isadora gave a lascivious wink. 'I heard you get asked out on a lunch date already. I was a step behind Mr Irving.'

'It's not a date,' insisted Tara, going puce. 'It's work.'

'If it's about work, how come he's never asked *me* out to lunch?' countered Isadora.

'That's because you insist that men take you to fancy, expensive restaurants,' Tara said, recovering quickly. 'Us married women are cheap dates.'

'So it's a toasted cheese and tomato sandwich in the pub?'

'Yes,' Tara said. 'Anyway, it's work, I told you. I'm a happily married woman. I can't refuse to go out with people I work with just because they're good-looking, can I?'

Isadora didn't have to reply: her expression said it all. Yeah right.

Tara decided to quickly run through her personal calls before she got down to work. Stella must have been sitting on the phone because she answered her private line on the first ring. She sounded uncharacteristically tense.

'Hi, Tara, just thought I'd update you about Dad. He's been leaving the answering machine on all the time, as you know, but I phoned Angela Devon first thing this morning and she said Dad was OK. She's making him dinner tonight, although he says he's not much company and he might not come. He and Alastair went out last night and Alastair said Dad cried in front of him.'

'Oh God,' said Tara horrified. It was like imagining Superman in tears.

'I know. I think that's why he won't talk to us: he's afraid he'll break down.'

'This is terrible.' Tara rested her forehead on one hand. 'I wish there was something we could do.'

'There's nothing we can do,' Stella answered bleakly. 'All Dad wants is for Mum to come home and she won't. I said that myself and Amelia would visit her this weekend but she says no, she needs to be on her own.'

'That's not like Mum. She'd climb the Himalayas with one foot in plaster to spend five minutes with Amelia.'

'She says maybe next weekend.'

'What about Dad?' asked Tara, doodling small, dark shapes on a bit of paper.

'Well, as Holly told us, she's definitely going down tomorrow night to spend the weekend with him. Originally, he insisted that she get on with her life and not visit him, but she talked him into it.'

'Good for Holly. She's the only one of us who seems to be dealing with this.'

'Forewarned is forearmed,' Stella murmured.

Next on Tara's list was the bank. The misery curdling inside her at what was happening to her family coalesced into pure bad temper. So the bank thought they could cancel the direct debit that paid the mortgage, did they? And their credit card division thought they could screw up her statement, adding in non-existent transactions willy-nilly and hoping she wouldn't notice? Well, they couldn't dare do such things and they were about to experience Tara Miller in full fury. She might be impotent about a lot of things in life but not with regards to the bank. She dialled the number, fingers stabbing the telephone buttons furiously.

Ten minutes later, she put the phone down and the only thing stabbing was the pain throbbing in her temples. A softly-spoken but firm assistant manager had taken the wind out of Tara's sails. The mortgage hadn't been paid because there weren't enough funds in Tara and Finn's joint account. The reasons for this were several withdrawals from the account by Mr Jefferson's bank card. The assistant manager had understood that Tara was shocked by all of this. The couple's tiny savings account hadn't been touched but as they weren't the sort of people who managed to save, there wasn't much in there. The bank suggested a meeting to talk about what could be done.

Tara said she had to make one more phone call first. The credit card people confirmed her suspicions: the large withdrawal had been made one weekend at the bank machine nearest to the flat, the machine Finn and she used.

On the A-4 pad on her desk, Tara had scrawled the pitiable amounts left in the account. She added the credit card bill, made a rough guess at the electricity, phone, heating and grocery bills for the next month. Then, she added her salary and Finn's. Like a straining waistband that wouldn't meet, the two figures were far apart. She and Finn never saved money and just scraped by each month. With the mortgage money blown, they were in trouble. If they didn't eat for three months, sat in the dark and never turned on the water heater, there was a vague hope of paying the bills. Otherwise, they were up to their eyeballs in debt.

Tara could have coped with debt if it hadn't been for how they'd fallen into it. Finn hadn't bought anything with the money he'd siphoned out of their accounts. He didn't have a spectacular new designer suit and he hadn't splashed out on a better car. Tara knew what he'd done with the money: he'd drunk it. Generous to a fault, there was nobody keener to buy people drinks than Finn. And when he was happily drunk himself, he'd buy drinks for an entire pub. Their mortgage had been squandered at the bottom of a bottle.

She phoned Scott to cancel lunch: there was no way she could sit and talk companionably with anyone right now.

'I'm sorry, Scott,' she said, 'I'm having family problems right now and I'd be very bad company.'

He was very understanding. 'No problem, Tara,' he said easily. 'We can do it some other time.' Then, he hesitated. 'Do you want to talk about it?'

'Nah,' she said, trying to sound light-hearted. 'Other people's family problems are boring, aren't they?'

'No,' said Scott softly.

'Well, bye.' Tara hung up quickly. At this precise moment, she didn't have time for idle office flirtation.

Her final call was to Finn's mobile which was, as ever, switched to voicemail. As she waited to leave her message, she grimly wondered how he ever did business when he never answered his phone. 'Finn, we need to talk about money. The mortgage hasn't been paid because there isn't enough in the account. Phone me back, it's urgent.'

Despite Tara leaving two more messages, Finn never called. Tara's ever-increasing rage meant she could barely work and at five on the nail, she left the office and went home to wait for her husband. As she waited, she thought back over the past year. When they were first married, she'd genuinely thought they were so happy. Life held such promise. She adored Finn, she thought she still did, although it was buried deep inside her now.

How had she not noticed what he was like? She cast her mind back, wondering was there some specific time when everything had changed.

Before they'd got married, Finn didn't appear to drink any more than anyone else but he was drunker, faster. She remembered that weekends revolved around a visit to the pub. There was no day where wine wasn't opened. All the signs had been there but she hadn't noticed them. Maybe it was because her husband was a far cry from the archetypal abusive drunk. He was still the same Finn: charming, funny, loving. Just slightly changed, slightly out of it when he drank. Finn was never aggressive or even raised his voice. But the drunk Finn was different from the sober version. The drunk Finn was anaesthetised to become a robot, a creature who smiled and talked but was a million miles away. Tara hated this interloper.

When eleven came and there was still no sign of Finn, she gave up and went to bed to spend a restless night. The next morning, she showered and dressed quickly, wanting to be dressed before she checked if Finn was crashed out in the spare bedroom. There was a dull ache in the base of her neck, from hours of tossing and turning in hot sheets. When she was ready, she made herself a quick cup of coffee and then opened the spare room door. He was awake, his eyes wary despite the welcoming smile on his face.

'I got in late, I thought I'd sleep here so I wouldn't wake you,' he said, as if he was bestowing some great favour.

Tara just stared back at him. How could he lie there and act so nonchalantly?

'Why didn't you come home last night?'

'I told you yesterday,' he said, 'a work thing with clients. We've nearly netted that big cleaning company contract. It's a huge franchise and they're going to buy a lot of computers for their outlets all over the country.'

Seeing Tara's lip curl, he added: 'You've got to network to stay ahead of the game. Going out and buttering people up over dinner is part of my job.'

That was Finn's standard response to any comments about his socialising. Tara had thought of getting the phrase chiselled into one of the apartment's walls.

'Hey, some of the lads were talking about a trip to Cork at the weekend.' Finn looked over at Tara hopefully. 'You know, a gang of us could go and stay in some really nice place. Nice dinners, a bit of clubbing. It'd be a blast. You'd love it.'

The tension in her neck spilled over into migraine alert. Tara reached up to massage her neck before the pain made its inevitable journey up to behind her eyes.

'We can't afford a weekend away,' she said. 'We're broke, Finn. The mortgage hasn't been paid.'

'Never mind,' said Finn good-humouredly. 'The lads will have to do without us in Cork.' He got out of bed, stretching his arms up to the ceiling and yawning.

Tara flipped.

'Don't you realise what I just said, Finn?' she shrieked. 'We're broke and the mortgage hasn't been paid because you've been cleaning out our account. You even took money from my credit card.'

'I was going to tell you about that,' he said guiltily. 'It's just that I needed some cash and I had none, but don't worry about the mortgage,' he added. 'I'm due my bonus any day now, it's going to cover everything.' He was smiling now, like a child. 'We could go to Cork for the weekend, in fact. You just need to be cool about the money because it's coming, and we can have a fantastic time. The bonus will be in the account in a few days and that'll clear all the bills. You know I'd never mess up our mortgage payments or anything, Tara. I just miscalculated, that's all.'

He reached out tentatively and touched her arm. 'Don't

be angry with me, love, please. I'll buy you a top-notch present when the money comes in, I promise.'

Tara jerked her arm away from him. He just didn't get it, did he?

'It's not about the money, Finn,' she said, 'and a present won't solve things. The problem is that you took money from our account without mentioning it to me, and I bet you anything I know what you needed the money for. Booze. You *promised* me you'd stop, you promised you'd cut down but you haven't, have you?'

'Course I've cut down,' Finn said sharply. 'I don't have a drink problem, if that's what you're implying. I have to socialise for work. You're just uptight because of your parents splitting up.'

'That's not it and you know it!' she shouted back at him.

'Yes it is,' Finn said wearily. 'You can't cope with the fact that everything in the Miller garden isn't rosy. Well, face up to it, Tara. Family life isn't all fun and games and picnics. We didn't all have an idyllic childhood, you know. You've got to get on with life and forget about the past.'

Tara wanted to scream that her parents weren't the problem, that it was Finn and his bloody selfishness that upset her, but the words didn't come. Instead, she thought of her father's betrayal of the family and how she, Tara, had loved him almost more than her mother and now she'd been proved wrong. He wasn't the man she'd thought he was. He'd hurt them all for nothing. She'd chosen the wrong daddy and now she'd chosen the wrong husband.

Tara wasn't the sort of person who cried. But in the five days since the disastrous ruby wedding, she'd felt the threat of tears welling up inside her. She'd fought them off furiously, refusing to give in, but now they flooded out. Finn watched in amazement as Tara silently started to cry. She didn't sob or howl. She barely moved, but still the tears rushed down her cheeks.

'Tara, love, don't cry, please.' He wrapped himself around

her, holding her tightly in his arms. 'We can get through this, we love each other. That's all we need, isn't it?'

It was nice being held and having her tears gently wiped away as if she was a child again. Like a child, Tara didn't try to stop crying. She simply let the misery wash over her, draining away the pain, she hoped. She didn't want to hurt like this but she couldn't help it: the hurt was just there, deep inside her.

'I love you, Tara, you know that, please say you know that.' Finn stroked her tenderly. 'I know I'm hard to live with but I'll try, honestly I'll try. Will you give me another chance?

With his arms encircling her and feeling his heart beating close to hers, Tara said yes. 'I love you,' she said through the muffled veil of tears. 'I want to be with you, I don't want to be alone.' She couldn't bear to be alone now. All the things she'd planned to say to Finn had vanished from her mind. She wanted the comfort of him holding her because if he wasn't there, she might have to think about it all.

'You won't be,' Finn said reassuringly. 'I'm here, love, I'm here.'

Tara wiped her face with her sleeve and buried her face in her husband's shoulder again. Everything would work out, wouldn't it?

CHAPTER TWENTY-FIVE

Holly sipped her takeaway latte gratefully as she joined the last few stragglers in the queue for the Kinvarra train. She'd been sure she'd be too late for the half six train because she'd missed two buses to Kingsbridge Station and had ended up leaping in a taxi and promising the driver a big tip if he got her there on time.

Miraculously, the taxi had slipped through the worst of the traffic and got her there with ten minutes to spare, long enough to buy a ticket, a magazine and a latte. Even more incredibly, she got what had to be the last seat on the train. She hoisted her hold-all onto the luggage rack, managing not to hit anyone while doing it, and then flopped onto the seat and relaxed.

She hadn't even got round to the magazine crossword when the train pulled into the tiny station at Kinvarra forty minutes later. Holly got off to see her father waiting patiently behind the barrier, waving the way he'd waved so many times over the years when he'd picked her up from the station. With a shock, she realised that he'd aged years in the past week. His face was lined and drawn, and his usual beaming smile was absent. He stooped, as if the mental anguish was physically weighing him down.

'Hi, Dad,' said Holly, desperately trying to hide how shocked she was by his appearance.

His answer was to enfold her in his arms so tightly it hurt.

'Hello, Holly,' he mumbled. 'It's so nice to see you, so nice.'

Holly thought he was going to cry there and then.

'Come on, Dad,' she said, taking his hand in hers and heading briskly for the station door. 'I'm starving, why don't we go out to eat?'

'Do we have to go out?' asked Hugh plaintively. 'I thought we could stay at home. Angela sent Alastair over with a stew. They're trying to feed me up.'

He could certainly do with feeding up, Holly thought worriedly. Her father's tall frame had always allowed him to carry a few extra pounds round his middle without making him look even vaguely overweight. But there wasn't an extra ounce of flesh on his frame now.

'A huge steak and lots of fat, greasy chips, that's what you need,' Holly said. 'I hate stew, even Angela's!'

They went to Maria's Diner, ordered steak for Hugh, Maria's special seafood pizza for Holly and two glasses of red wine. When the wine came, Hugh didn't touch it. He gazed into space beyond Holly as if he didn't even see her.

She chatted idly about her week in work, how it looked as if she might be moving out of children's wear, possibly to interiors, and how she'd really love to be in international fashion, but that was a bit unlikely because she didn't have any experience in that department. Normally, Hugh would indignantly point out that international fashion would be lucky to get someone of her calibre, that she was clearly the brightest person in the entire department store and she ought to realise how skilled she was. Tonight, he just nodded blankly and made 'um' noises as if he was listening, but he was miles away. Holly ploughed on.

She told him about the plans for Joan's show, which was in ten days and promised to be a wildly glamorous social occasion, complete with real models and television cameras. She told him that Stella and Tara were worried about him, but didn't mention that she'd spoken to her mother the previous night.

Rose hadn't said a single word about Hugh.

'I don't want to talk about your father,' she'd said firmly

when Holly had phoned. 'Tell me all your news.' So Tara had, and in return, heard all about Freddie's wonderful house, the dogs, and how Rose was cooking for meals on wheels. It was as if Rose was away on some marvellous holiday with a return date all planned, so there was no need to talk about it. Holly was an expert at not mentioning tricky subjects, so she listened to her mother's holiday diary and said nothing.

The food arrived and Holly dug into her pizza. Her father didn't even pick up his fork.

'Dad, you've got to eat,' she said quietly. 'It's not doing you any good to starve yourself. You'll get ill.'

He raised tortured eyes to hers. 'I don't care,' he said listlessly.

'You won't get Mum back like this.'

'Your mother isn't coming back to me. I know that for sure. She never does anything by half measures. She's left and she's gone for good.'

'How can you be so defeatist?' Holly asked. 'Perhaps Mum is waiting for you to talk to her. You know she's staying with Aunt Freddie?'

'Stella told me. But it doesn't make any difference. She could be staying down the road or she could be in the North Pole for all it matters because she won't see me. She left me a letter, you know.' His face was grey with misery. 'She said she didn't want me to think I could follow her and sort it all out, because there was nothing to sort out. Our marriage was over and she naturally wanted a divorce. She said she should have done it years ago, that she hated me for humiliating her and she hated herself even worse for letting me do it. *I hope you're suffering as much as I suffered.* Those were her exact words. I've read it over and over.'

Suddenly, Holly didn't feel hungry any more.

She could understand why her father kept staring into space dismally. They left after eating little of their food.

'Was the meal all right?' asked the waitress anxiously.

'Lovely, it was lovely,' said Holly. 'We weren't as hungry as we'd thought.'

They drove home with the radio loud to cover up the gaping silence. Holly thought about her mother. The woman who'd written such a hard, angry letter didn't sound like Rose.

It was sad to see this new side to her mother, this hard edge of anger in that normally calm and lovely facade. Holly had grown up with everyone wistfully saying that Rose was a truly marvellous person, so much so that Holly had felt disloyal for ever thinking that she wished her mother loved her as much as she seemed to love everyone else. When she'd heard about how her parents had longed for their third child to be a boy, Holly had decided that this was the root of the problem. It wasn't that Rose didn't love Holly, she told herself, just that her mother had hoped for a son.

As Hugh negotiated the familiar bends and twists on the way to Meadow Lodge, Holly was filled with the desire to ask him about this forbidden subject that burned in her heart. She glanced at him, noticing the way his knuckles were white from clenching the steering wheel. He didn't need her angst right now. He had enough to deal with.

'All right, Dad?' she squeezed his shoulder affectionately.

He nodded, not saying anything. Holly thought she saw the glint of tears in his eyes but she couldn't be sure.

The next day was glorious, with not a cloud in the sky and the scent of summer in the air even though it was only early May. Holly jollied her father along enough to get him out for a walk with Alastair and Angela.

'We can't stay stuck in the house all weekend and a walk will do us both good,' she said, hurrying round before they left to collect the bits and bobs they needed like her lip screen and a baseball hat to protect Hugh's head from the sun.

He took the baseball hat meekly and put it on. 'A walk will do us good,' he repeated blankly.

Alastair seemed pathetically pleased that Holly was talking to him.

'Stella's been so very cool with me on the phone,' he said

mournfully as the four of them made their way along a lakeside path in Kinvarra's huge nature reserve observed by several odd black and white ducks who were clearly hoping that somebody in the party had brought along a few crumbs of bread. 'She seems to blame me more than your father.'

Holly patted Alastair's hand. 'She'll get over it, Alastair. She wants to blame someone and Dad is too shattered to blame him.'

'You're getting very wise in your old age, Holly,' said Angela fondly.

'Am I?' Holly looked pleased. 'Stella was always the wise one.'

'And you were the one who underestimated herself,' Angela replied. The two women slowed down, letting the men walk on ahead. 'Your father has always thought the world of you: I'm glad you're sticking by him. I know it's not easy but he needs you.'

There was one question Holly had to ask.

'Did you know?'

Angela shook her head vehemently. 'No, I didn't have a clue. I'd have told Rose if I did. Believe me, I nearly killed Alastair for keeping it a secret from me. All the modern marriage guidance experts tell you we need our little secrets and our own private space, but I'm of the old school. I like to think I'm the map-maker of every crevice of Alastair's mind,' she added firmly. 'Well, it's too late now but if I had known, I'd have done something, told Hugh to sort himself out and not risk everything.' She sighed.

Holly believed her. Angela hadn't known but *she* had. She plucked up the courage to tell Angela, in preparation for when she'd have to tell Rose.

'The thing is, Angela, well, I knew Dad had been seeing someone else. Do you think Mum will be angry with me?'

'You did?' said Angela, startled. 'When did you find out?'

'When I was sixteen or seventeen. I didn't know for sure, but I guessed.'

Angela looked so astonished that Holly was sorry she'd

said anything. 'He was just talking to someone on the phone and it sounded so . . . so intimate. But it didn't upset me or anything.' Oh no, that sounded weird, as if she didn't care about the thought of her father cheating on her mother. Holly tried to remedy matters.

'It's just that I loved Dad so much and I was never as close to Mum as Stella and Tara were. That's not Mum's fault or anything,' she added loyally.

Holly, anxiously trying to make sure that Angela understood that none of this was Rose's fault, didn't notice Angela stare sadly at the most-loved of her three adopted nieces.

She and Alastair had never been blessed with children of their own. Oh there were godchildren and nieces and nephews, but none wholly theirs. Perhaps because of that, the Miller girls had been like surrogate children to them, Tara and Holly in particular. Stella had been a grave, self-reliant little girl of eight or nine when the Devons and the Millers had first met, a mini version of Rose with the same calm dark eyes and an air of self-possession. She'd adored her mother too much to spend time in the Devons' house with Hugh when he dropped over to see Alastair. But Tara, an engaging tomboy, had loved joining Hugh and Alastair on their days fishing and had grown up feeling utterly at home with Aunty Angela and Uncle Alastair. Angela loved Tara's madcap sense of fun and sparky humour, and would have done anything for dear, kind Stella, but her heart belonged to the shy, insecure Holly.

As she'd watched Holly grow up, Angela had often felt troubled by the hairline crack she detected in Holly and Rose's relationship, a flaw so fine that almost nobody else appeared to notice it.

'Your Mum loves you, Holly, she won't be angry with you. You didn't want to hurt her by telling her the truth.'

'Do you really think so?' Holly looked so pathetically anxious that Angela felt an unaccustomed stab of irritation towards her friend, Rose. Fine, so Rose had stormed off in high dudgeon over Hugh's affairs. His carry-on had been shocking any way you looked at it and Angela had told him so in no uncertain terms. But Rose wasn't the only injured party in the Miller family. Somehow, in the mess that had grown out of Hugh and Rose's very separate lives, and allied to what had clearly been Rose's post-natal depression when she'd had Holly, little Holly was the one who'd suffered. It was high time Rose realised that, Angela decided.

'They'll work it out, you know,' she said, linking arms with Holly. 'Your mum will come back, I'm sure of it.'

'Just because that's what we all want, doesn't mean it will happen,' Holly pointed out. 'They have to sort it out for themselves.' She watched her father walking in the distance with Alastair. Rose would survive, Holly knew. Her mother was a strong person. But without Rose, would Hugh manage?

CHAPTER TWENTY-SIX

Vicki rummaged around in her handbag and pulled out a bulging, clear plastic make-up bag. From the middle of a jumble of tubes, pencils and compacts, she extracted a giant brush and a black compact.

'Bronzer,' she said. 'You need it, Stella.'

'Thanks.' Stella looked at her wan face in the compact mirror. There were mauve circles haunting the thin skin under her eyes. She felt as if she was ageing at double speed. 'You don't have the equipment for a blood transfusion in there, do you?'

Vicki smiled but didn't laugh. 'You look terrible, babe. Like you haven't slept in weeks.'

Stella didn't need anyone to tell her that. She could see it for herself. She did her best with the bronzing brush, sweeping it round her face in big generous strokes the way they did on fashion programmes. 'It's nothing to do with sleeping. I'm out like a light when I get into bed, I sleep the sleep of the dead. The problems start when I wake up.'

'Your mum and dad?'

Stella snapped the compact shut. What was the point of bronzer. 'More my dad than Mum. She's doing fine and says she's too busy to come to Dublin to spend some time with myself and Amelia, although I think that's so she can avoid talking about their split and what happens next. Dad's falling to pieces and my mother won't talk to him.'

'Difficult being piggy in the middle,' said Vicki.

'That's only the half of it,' Stella added grimly. 'Problem

two is Jenna. She is the rudest child I have ever met in my life. Nick and I took herself and Amelia to the cinema the other night and she was utterly obnoxious to me.'

'Is the problem Nick's ex-wife?' asked Vicki. 'Is she poisoning Jenna against you.'

Stella sighed. 'That's the thing, Nick says she isn't. He says that Wendy is fine about us and is totally reasonable about Jenna and Sara spending time here. But she doesn't seem to want to let Nick go, does that make sense? She phones Nick night and day about Jenna's latest exploits. It's like Wendy has this finely-tuned telepathic sense and she rings exactly when we're going somewhere or doing something. As soon as I put dinner on the table, bam, she's on the phone. It's not that he shouldn't be involved with her, it's just that . . .' Stella paused, 'she's always there and I think Nick's kidding himself about how she's dealt with everything.'

Stella couldn't explain the infuriation of watching their meal cool and congeal on the table while Nick talked to his ex-wife, made 'sorry' gestures to Stella and agreed to talk to Jenna. No matter how much he praised the food afterwards, Stella was grimly convinced it was now inedible. Nick would eat more heartily than usual to make up for it, while Stella sat there with her shoulders tense and her jaw set rigidly. She'd come to hate Nick's phone ringing. The very noise made her stomach lurch.

'Does she always phone about Jenna?' demanded Vicki.

'Pretty much, yes. I don't phone Amelia's father over every problem. I know it's different because Glenn's not really part of our lives but it drives me mad that Wendy is supposed to be this intelligent woman and yet all of a sudden, she can't deal with anything without phoning Nick up. He says she's fine about the divorce and wants them both to get on with their lives, but,' she paused, 'it doesn't seem that way to me. She wants him in her life, she's not going to let him go.'

'When did she start this?' asked Vicki shrewdly.

'When Nick told the girls we'd discussed living together.'

'Maybe she thought there was some hope for them getting back together until that happened,' said Vicki. 'This is her knee-jerk reaction. She can't help it.'

'Why?' asked Stella in exasperation. 'They're divorced, they both agreed to get divorced, it's over. Why can't she get on with her own life? When Glenn and I split up, *I* had to get on with my life. I didn't phone him every day asking him how to programme the video.'

'You're not the sort of person to go to pieces, Stella,' Vicki pointed out. 'You're one of life's copers. That's what you do. And besides, you and Glenn weren't married that long. Nick and Wendy were married twenty years and it's obviously hard for her to come to terms with the fact that it is over. When she got married, there was no divorce in this country, and people expected marriage to be for life. That could take some getting used to. It's a whole life change.'

'Fine,' said Stella in a brittle tone. 'But I don't see why I'm getting all the grief. They were apart before Nick met me. If Wendy got on with her life, then perhaps Jenna wouldn't be so vile to me. I'm convinced that Jenna believes that if I wasn't around, her parents would be back together again and that's not fair. I didn't split up their marriage: they did that themselves.'

'Calm down,' said Vicki. Stella was worrying her. She never normally lost her cool like this. 'It'll work out in the end.'

'I'm glad you think so. But the odds are definitely against us, particularly if we decided to get married. They did this research and it seems that when men divorce, sixty per cent of them remarry. Out of that group, sixty per cent of the second marriages fail.'

Vicki worked the figures out in her head. 'So out of a hundred men, you end up with twenty-four who are happily married for the second time.'

'That's not all.' Stella's face was grim. 'The first five to seven years of a remarriage are as bad as the year following a divorce. In other words, hell on earth.'

'Time is a great healer,' ventured Vicki. 'Anyway, you never told me you'd talked about getting married.'

'We have,' Stella revealed, 'but I don't know if that's much of an idea seeing as how Jenna hates the sight of me. Another seven years of this and I'll be on every anti-depressant known to woman. Nick's not much better. He tries to hide it, but he's deeply stressed about how Jenna reacts to me, and it is affecting our relationship. But he still thinks we can work it all out. We're going away for a weekend together, the five of us.'

Vicki winced. 'Jesus,' she said.

'My sentiments exactly.' She sighed. 'We must have been out of our minds to even mention moving in together to Nick's kids. Until then, there was a sensation of living at the foot of a volcano. Now, it's as if somebody's put a nuclear bomb in the crater.'

Amelia was excited about the weekend. She'd spent hours packing and unpacking her belongings, and the purple denim backpack Stella had told her to bring with her books and toys was disembowelled at least twice a day. Now, it was ready, full to the brim, and with odd bulges from Barbie's pointed feet and the lump that was Casper, the grey furry toy rabbit Stella had brought her from Paris.

Stella hadn't deliberated so long about her own wardrobe. She'd packed to match her mood: dark.

They were going to Moon's Hotel, a big holiday complex on the coast. Moon's was a watchword for family holidays and Stella could remember many friends of hers heading off there with a carload of kids for weekends of tennis, swimming and with the possibility of a romantic dinner for two courtesy of the hotel's nanny service. Stella had always felt mildly jealous of those people. Families. Moon's was a place for families, where dads brought the kids swimming and let mum have a facial in the hotel spa.

Ironically, now that she was going there with a ready-made family, she wished she wasn't. If only it had been just her, Nick and Amelia, she'd have been so happy. In the two weeks since her parents' devastating split, Stella had been stressed out of her head and a few days holiday seemed just what she needed. But not this sort of holiday.

When Nick arrived outside the house with Sara and Jenna already installed in the car, Stella tried to ignore the sinking feeling in her stomach at the thought of a weekend with everyone on their best behaviour, except Jenna, who would be on her usual child-of-Satan behaviour.

But Jenna had clearly been bribed with something or other. First, she got out of the front of the car and climbed in the back so that Stella could sit in the front. Secondly, she was civil.

'Hello, Stella, hello, Amelia,' she said when Stella opened the back door for Amelia.

'Hello, Jenna,' said Stella cautiously. 'Why don't you sit in the middle, Amelia, as you're the smallest.'

Amelia climbed carefully over Jenna and plonked down beside Sara, who was curled up on the other side, eyes half-closed. She wore her customary jeans and a hoodie, and her dark hair was unruly.

'Hi, Sara. How are you?' asked Stella.

'Wrecked,' came the reply. 'We had exams today. I was up all night studying.'

Stella stifled a grin. She'd burned the midnight oil herself when she was at college.

'Five in the morning was the toughest time to stay awake,' she remarked, getting into the front seat. 'Tiredness hits you and you want to crawl into bed, but there's no point because you'd never wake up and when you did, you'd be like a zombie.'

'You pulled all-nighters, too?' said Sara, surprised.

'Doesn't everyone?' Stella laughed. 'But if you do a couple of them, you soon learn to get your study done long before the exams. It's easier than facing a whole night awake propped up with coffee.'

'You said it!' Sara made a cushion from a jumper, wedged it into a corner and closed her eyes. 'Wake me when we're there.'

Outside, Nick slammed the boot.

'All set?' he said, sliding into the driver's seat. He put a hand on Stella's and gave her a warm smile.

'All set,' she replied, determined not to worry about Jenna's reaction to his affectionate action. Stella had got so used to modifying her behaviour around Jenna that she was almost reluctant to hold Nick's hand in public.

'It's going to be a great weekend,' Nick said, driving off.

Stella crossed her fingers.

Spending a lazy Saturday morning being pampered in the hotel spa had made Stella feel languorous and almost her usual serene self.

'Have everything done,' advised Nick the night before when Stella had examined the brochure and debated the wisdom of having a facial, back massage or manicure. 'Sara will be in bed until lunchtime and I'll bring Amelia and Jenna out for the morning. Then, we can try out the pool. You enjoy yourself.'

'Jenna won't be interested in water slides and messing around in the pool,' Stella pointed out.

'You'd be surprised,' said Nick.

Filled with a sense of wellbeing after her back massage, Stella got back to their room to find a message from Nick telling her that he and the girls had returned from their jaunt into the town, and had now gone to the pool. Still in the hotel dressing gown, Stella made her way down to the sports complex. There was one pool dedicated to adults who wanted to swim laps in peace, and a larger one with slides for kids or anyone who wanted to whizz down into the water at high speed. To one side were tables grouped around a poolside café where parents could sit and watch their offspring cavort. Stella kept her eyes peeled, half-expecting to see Jenna perched in the café, watching the youngsters enjoying themselves with a disdainful look on her face.

But there she was, standing in the pool and yelling at the top of her voice as Nick and Amelia climbed the slide to the top.

'Face down,' she was yelling. 'Dad, you've got to come face down this time.'

'No way,' he yelled back.

Stella could see Amelia giggling at the thought.

'Coward!' yelled Jenna. 'Amelia, make him come face down!'

With her blonde hair slicked down her back and her face wet and devoid of make-up, she looked like a child for the first time since Stella had met her. A happy child.

Stella sat down by the café and ordered a mineral water. She sat there for ages, watching the other three laughing and splashing about until finally, Amelia noticed her.

'Mummy!' She doggy paddled over. 'I went down the slide, Mum!'

'I saw you, you were very brave.'

'Jenna went down on her front!' Amelia said. 'She says water goes up your nose.'

Jenna's face closed off and the guarded, adult expression returned. For the first time in ages, Stella felt a sliver of sympathy for the girl. Nick was right: Jenna was still a child and she hadn't been able to deal with her parents' break-up. Stella thought of how she had reacted to Hugh and Rose's abrupt split. The very idea still knocked her for six. If it was hard to deal with that at the age of thirty-eight, how much harder could it be for Jenna?

Nick hauled himself out of the pool.

'C'mon, Jenna,' he said, holding a hand down for his daughter. 'Time for refreshment.'

Stella pulled up another chair for Jenna while Nick went to the counter to order drinks.

'Are you having fun, Jenna?' Stella asked, forgetting herself enough to put a hand on the girl's shoulder. Jenna shrugged it off as if Stella's hand was burning hot.

416

'Sorry,' Stella said automatically. Then she stopped. Why should she say sorry? She was trying to be kind. 'Jenna, we have to get along. It would be easier on everyone if you made a bit of an effort.'

'Why?' demanded Jenna, hatred burning out of her eyes. And she turned and ran off.

Amelia turned to her mother with big, grave eyes. 'Why doesn't Jenna like you, Mummy?'

Stella had answers for most of Amelia's questions, even ones about how next door's terrier had got the four puppies in her tummy and why the puppies knew how to drink their mummy's milk when they didn't have their eyes opened yet. But she didn't know how to answer this one.

Amelia answered for her. 'Is it because you're not her mummy?'

Stella bit her lip. 'Noo,' she said. 'It's hard to explain, darling. I'll do my best when we get home, is that OK?'

'I'm sorry,' said Stella, when Nick returned. 'My fault, I tried to be nice to her.'

Nick's face slipped into what Stella silently called 'the look'. It came over his features so regularly now, a tautening of the jaw along with a sorrowful and helpless look in his eyes.

She caught his hand and held it tightly, willing the look to disappear.

'I better go and talk to her,' he said.

'Yes, of course,' said Stella automatically.

She watched him go, noticing how his tall frame looked weighed down because of the way his shoulders were uncharacteristically slumped, then turned to Amelia with a big grin fastened on her face.

'What will we do now?' she said brightly. 'You choose.'

Amelia chose more swimming, followed by a walk in the town which led mother and daughter past a shop that had an entire section devoted to sparkly pens, cute lurid pink and purple notebooks and pencil cases decorated with marabou, sequins and feathers.

'Why do I get the impression that you were here earlier?' inquired Stella, smiling as Amelia headed straight for the pen department.

'We were, but Nick said we should get back to the hotel and Jenna said we'd come back later on our own and buy things. She said she'd come with me and it would be all right because she's a teenager. That's almost as good as being a grown-up.' Amelia pottered away and Stella idly looked at the fridge magnets. Normally, these wise little gems made her laugh. But she didn't feel like laughing. She tried to work out what she *did* feel like. Then the word came to her: failure. She felt as if she'd failed. She'd found the man of her dreams and he came, like she did herself, with a certain amount of emotional baggage. Instead of being able to make it all work, she had made the whole situation worse. Faced with a fifteen-year-old girl's implacable hatred, she hadn't been able to accept that Jenna was entitled to her opinion. Accustomed to being liked and loved by everyone and accustomed to being treated with respect, Stella had not known how to deal with such naked hostility. The result was a disaster. She was stressed, Nick was even more stressed, and their dreams of a blissful united family looked a million miles away.

'I think I like this one best,' announced Amelia, holding up a silver pen with a pink hula girl on the top.

'That's lovely,' said Stella. She bent down beside Amelia and kissed her fiercely on the cheek. 'I love you, Amelia.'

Amelia's beaming smile was her reward. 'Love you too, Mummy.' She held up a miniature notebook decorated with cartoon kittens. 'Can I have this too?'

Worn out by her busy day, Amelia was happy to flop in front of the cartoon channel in the small adjoining room of their family suite. When they'd checked in, there had been an option of having a family suite with two rooms joining onto the master bedroom instead of one. Stella was glad she'd said no. Sara and Jenna shared a room opposite.

There was no sign of Nick so Stella assumed he was with

the girls. Satisfied that Amelia was happy, she sat down on the bed and phoned her mother.

There was no answering machine in Nettle Cottage.

'Freddie doesn't believe in them,' Rose had told Stella. 'She says that if anybody wants to speak to her that urgently, they'll keep trying.' After seventeen rings, Stella hung up and tried her mother's mobile, not really expecting anything. Rose had seemed only too happy to fall in with Freddie's *mañana* attitude to telecommunications and rarely switched her mobile phone on.

'I'm afraid I can't come to the phone right now but please leave me a message,' said Rose in calm, low tones.

Hearing her mother's voice made tears prick behind Stella's eyes. She hung up abruptly. What message could she leave?

I wish you and Dad were back together, because then it would feel as if some part of my life was still normal. And I could tell you all my problems instead of bottling them up because your problems are bigger than mine.

She devoured the mini-bar chocolate-coated nuts and then opened a small bottle of white wine to drink in the bath.

'How are you getting on?' she asked, peeping her head round the door to look at Amelia who was glued to the TV.

'OK.'

'I'm going to have a bath, Amelia, and then we're going to get ready for dinner.'

But Amelia was back in thrall to the television.

The bubbles were up to her neck and her wine was almost gone when Nick arrived. He leaned down and kissed her tenderly.

'Will I wash your back?'

'Lovely.'

Resting her head on her knees, Stella closed her eyes and let Nick use a sponge to gently massage soap into her back.

'That's lovely,' she murmured. 'It's a pity you can't get in too,' she added. With Amelia next door, she wouldn't dream of it.

'Tonight.' Nick planted a kiss on the nape of her neck.

'After dinner, when everyone's in bed,' he said, 'then I'll let you wash my back.'

'Not just your back, surely?' Stella countered wickedly.

'No,' he agreed, moving the sponge lower to rub rhythmically at the base of her spine. 'Not just my back.'

'Mummy, can I have some chocolate from your fridge?' came Amelia's voice.

Nick's hand moved out of the water rapidly.

'No, darling, we're going down to dinner in a few minutes. Do you want to change into your blue dress or will I do it for you?'

'I will,' said Amelia grumpily.

Nick rinsed the soap from Stella's back. 'Are you having a good weekend?' he asked.

'Yes,' she replied, eyes shining up at him. 'It's still hard with Jenna. Is she ever going to learn to deal with me?'

'I don't know, Stella.' Nick put the lid on the loo and sat down. 'I'm doing my best but she is so set against the idea of my being with anyone but her mother.'

Stella stood up in the bath, soapy water streaming from her body. She wrapped herself in a huge bath towel from the heated rack. 'Can't you tell her that's the way it is . . .' She broke off. What she wanted to say was why couldn't Nick explain to Jenna that he loved Stella and wanted her treated with respect. She tried again, determined to be careful not to hurt him.

'Kids need to be told things, Nick.'

'Amelia is eight. She listens to you, every word you say is important to her,' Nick said tautly. 'One day, that will change, Stella. She'll look at you differently, she'll do the exact opposite of whatever you tell her to do, she'll be a pre-teen and then a teenager. You can't tell kids what to do when they get to Jenna's age; they don't obey orders.'

'I'm not saying you have to order her,' Stella said wearily, 'I'd just like her to be a bit nicer to me.' Even saying it sounded pathetic, like a child in the playground whining that another child wasn't friendly to her.

'Stella, I'm doing my best,' Nick said. 'It's not going to happen overnight, right? You're going to have to live with it for now.'

He strode into the bedroom and Stella sighed. Another magical moment shattered.

Nick sat in a chair and watched the news channel as Stella dressed in silence. As she struggled to zip up her long suede skirt, Stella grimaced. Even her waist was betraying her. Her parents were in mid-life crisis, her stepdaughter hated her and she was getting fat. Life was just too good.

'How about we drop in to Granny and Aunt Paula on the way back home?' Nick had been talking in that cheery voice all day Sunday.

Sara and Amelia were the only ones who seemed to be responding to it. Jenna was monosyllabic in the back of the car, staring gloomily out of the window as soon as they'd set out from Moon's hotel.

Stella was reading the Sunday supplements in the front seat, to the astonishment of Sara who said she didn't know anyone who could read in a car.

'Mum gets ill if she reads in the car. She can't read on trains either,' Jenna had added loudly.

Stella gritted her teeth and managed to stop herself asking if Mummy could read at all. She hated herself for being so childish but Jenna brought out the worst in her.

'I'd love to see Granny but I've got to be back by six,' Sara pointed out. 'I'm going out tonight.'

'With the love of your life?' teased her father.

'A gang of us are going out for a pizza because we don't have another exam until Wednesday, and you can't study all the time,' Sara said. 'Isn't that right, Stella? Too much studying is bad for you.'

Sara was sweet, Stella thought fondly. She made such an effort to keep the atmosphere relaxed.

'You're absolutely right, Sara,' she replied. 'All work and no play makes Jack a dull boy.'

'Is that what happened to you?' muttered Jenna under her breath.

Stella stiffened.

'Shut up,' she heard Sara hiss. 'Don't be such a bitch.'

Stella stared at the page she was reading as if it was the most fascinating thing she'd ever seen. She wouldn't betray how much she was hurting. Nick couldn't have heard Jenna's comment or he'd have said something, wouldn't he?

'I don't think we'll have time to visit Granny's then,' Nick said presently. 'We'd only have time for a pit stop and you know your Gran, she likes long visits.'

'She has a cat called Lady, doesn't she?' asked Amelia.

'You've been to my gran's house?' asked Jenna sharply.

'We had butterfly cakes and Lady sat on my lap,' Amelia revealed.

'Do you like cats?' asked Sara quickly.

'Yes, I'd love a kitten and a puppy and a rabbit.' Amelia longed for a menagerie.

Jenna said nothing for the rest of the trip, even when they stopped for coffee. It was nearly five when they arrived at Wendy's house. Stella hadn't wanted to be with Nick when he dropped the girls off but as Sara was going out, and Stella's home was at least twenty minutes further on, it seemed most sensible to arrange things this way. Stella's curiosity to see Nick's ex-wife's home just about balanced out her nerves at having to go there.

Set in a pretty coastal suburb, all the houses in Athens Valley estate were detached. Halfway along the main road into the estate, Nick turned right into a shrub-lined driveway. 'White Elms' said the wooden sign on the granite gatepost. To Stella's eyes, White Elms was huge, three times the size of her terraced place in Delgany Avenue. It probably had five bedrooms and certainly more than one bathroom. A twinge of jealousy sparked inside her and she instantly felt angry with herself for giving in to childish emotions. It was ridiculous to feel any envy for this big house. After all, Wendy only had the house because she and Nick had split up. Despite her lovely home, her marriage had broken down and she was struggling with a difficult teenager. She deserved Stella's sympathy. And yet, Stella still felt shocked. Although she knew that Nick was comfortably off, she didn't think he was really wealthy. But then divorce was expensive. Obviously, Wendy had bought this big house with her settlement. Get a grip, Stella, she told herself. Don't be so childish.

Jenna clambered out quickly without so much as a goodbye.

Sara gave Amelia a little kiss on the cheek. 'Bye, Amelia,' she said. 'Be good.'

Stella turned back in time to see her daughter's little face glow with pleasure.

'I will,' she said happily.

'Bye, Stella,' Sara said. 'Thanks for the weekend.'

'No, thank you.' Stella was serious. Without Sara making an effort, the whole weekend would have been even more nightmarish, if possible.

'Won't be long,' Nick said to her.

When they were gone, Stella switched the radio from the rock station that Nick had tuned to for the girls' benefit and found something more soothing.

'Mummy, I want to go to the bathroom,' said Amelia plaintively.

Oh no, that was all she needed.

'You'll have to wait, darling.'

'Why, Mummy?'

'Because Nick's coming and we're in a rush,' Stella said. If Amelia wet herself, they were not walking up to Wendy Cavaletto's house and asking to use her bathroom.

'But, Mummy,' wailed Amelia.

'Look, here's Nick,' said her mother with relief as Nick hurried out.

'Sorry about that,' he said. 'Wendy wanted me to have a look at Jenna's computer.'

Stella smiled but her fingers dug into the sides of the passenger seat.

'Did you have a nice weekend, Amelia?' he asked.

'Yeah,' said Amelia, twirling her new pen with the hula girl on top.

At least that makes one of us who enjoyed it, Stella thought grimly.

CHAPTER TWENTY-SEVEN

Kenny was all fired up over styling Joan's first big show.

'Native American is the look I see,' he said. 'Sleek black hair with a sheen to it, plaits and long ponytails, and the make-up has to be Apache princess.'

Holly, who was in charge of writing down Kenny's creative nuances, jotted it all down.

'Not too out-there,' requested Joan, who was sitting cross-legged on the floor arranging and re-arranging Polaroid photos of her collection, as she worked out which order she'd show it in. Each graduate could show from eight to twelve pieces and Joan, who'd worked intensively on her collection, was going for the maximum, which meant twelve models and twelve different, but cohesive, looks.

'I don't want to detract from the clothes,' Joan insisted. 'This show isn't about hair and make-up. Some of the most influential fashion buyers in the country will be there. I want them to notice my clothes, I want to grab them by the nuts.'

Holly giggled. Kenny nodded. 'Absolutely, I agree. But the make-up and hair have to be strong.' He picked up one of the Polaroids. 'I love your new look,' he said. 'I was worried about the funky, graffiti and pearls T-shirt thing, because that sort of stuff doesn't last.'

He handed the Polaroid to Holly, who had been just as surprised as Kenny to see the proof of Joan's new fashion direction. Some of her collection did feature her trademark off-the-wall designs, but seventy per cent was made up of exquisitely cut and very wearable clothes; from floaty chiffon dresses to a couple of business suits with a very Joan-esque twist of interesting linings and handmade buttons.

'I know,' Joan said. 'The T-shirts and the graffiti stuff are for a diffusion collection. That's the way to make money.' Joan hadn't learned the lesson of avant garde designers for nothing. 'But tailoring and cut are where it's at. If I'm famous for nothing more than graffiti, then someone will come along with something better and I'll be yesterday's news. I need staying power and that's about real designs for real people.'

'I love this new stuff,' Holly said enthusiastically. 'I'd wear everything here.'

'That's good 'coz I want you to be a model in the show,' Joan said absent-mindedly.

Holly's mouth dropped open.

'Me? Don't be silly. You've got models from the agencies. The college are paying for them, aren't they?'

'I want you too,' insisted Joan.

'I can't,' bleated Holly. 'I can't dress up and walk up and down in front of all those people.' She'd die first. There was just no way she was going to do it, no way, no matter how much Joan begged.

'Please, Holly. I'm getting my mother to model too. Real people is the theme of my show. Six foot models can make a sack look good but I want all the buyers to see that my clothes work on everyone. Please say you'll do it?'

'Yes, Holls, you'll be gorgeous,' Kenny added. 'What'll she be wearing?'

'The wedding dress.'

'Wedding dress?' said Holly faintly.

'Valkyrie warrior wedding dress,' corrected Joan lovingly, extracting the Polaroid in question for Kenny and Holly to admire. 'I haven't shown you this one before. It's a surprise.'

'You can say that again,' said Holly.

Photographed on a tailor's dummy, the dress looked extraordinary: white chiffon with a pleated bodice hand-beaded with seed pearls. The beading made up swirls and whorls in a pattern that reminded Holly of the decoration on Viking longboats. A plait of fabric over one shoulder held up a flowing train, on which the beading was done with silver beads.

'I've got a headpiece too; a skull cap with beading. You'd have to wear your hair in a long plait or maybe two plaits,' Joan said.

'Fantastic,' murmured Kenny.

'It's beautiful, Joan,' said Holly, 'but the answer is still no.'

'Ah, come on.'

'I'm really sorry, Joan, I can't.' Holly was apologetic. 'I love you and I'd do anything for you but I can't do this.'

'All you have to do is walk down the runway,' protested Joan. 'You'll look amazing, I was thinking of you when I designed the dress. It's got to be worn by someone who's tall and dark and . . .'

'. . . big,' blurted out Holly.

Joan and Kenny regarded her crossly.

'I wasn't going to say "big",' pointed out Joan. 'You're not big. You're a normal woman. In fact, better than normal. Most normal women would kill for a waist like yours. I don't have a waist at all,' Joan added, looking down at herself. 'I'm the same all the way down . . .'

'I can't,' repeated Holly.

'You don't have to,' Kenny said, shooting Joan a look. 'Don't bully her, Joan.'

'It was just an idea,' grumbled Joan. She stared at the photo. 'I could ask my cousin. She's tall but she has short hair.'

'I can sort out a wig,' suggested Kenny.

Holly smiled at him gratefully. She might have been getting over her horrific shyness but marching down a catwalk really was a step too far.

Backstage at the fashion college final year show was nothing like Holly had imagined it to be. She'd had a mental picture of beautiful people squealing with delight and air-kissing

427

each other, in between wafting around in stunning outfits. Instead, there was an air of determined efficiency and everything was on such a tight schedule that there wasn't time for such frivolities as air-kissing or wafting.

Racks of garments encased in see-through plastic divided up the room, and beside each rack were the designer's friends/stylists with checklists at the ready. The models' names were on each outfit, with corresponding shoes and accessories underneath.

The models themselves were sitting at the mirrored section which had been set up in the middle of the room, some in huge rollers, others leaning back in make-up chairs, their exquisite faces immobile, like beautiful blank canvasses ready for the make-up artist to paint on.

Bottles of mineral water and packs of cigarettes accompanied them everywhere.

Joan was very calm, thanks to a huge vodka and orange from Fiona.

Her mother and her cousin, Lizzie, were not calm. Faced with a phalanx of professional models in flesh-coloured G-strings with every rib showing, like so many elegant greyhounds, Mrs Ursula Atwood and Lizzie wanted to back out of modelling.

'You can't,' insisted Joan, not thinking for a moment that either of her relatives would desert her in her hour of need.

'I can,' shrieked her mother. 'I thought it'd be all normal people, not wall-to-wall models and us two like a pair of stray elephants.' Ursula clutched her big pink towelling dressing gown tightly around her in a manner that suggested it was not coming off.

Lizzie, who was wearing a violently green kimono of Joan's, nodded in agreement. 'I'm not doing it either,' she said, brave now that Aunt Ursula had put her foot down. Joan hadn't explained things properly at all. She'd let on that this was some sort of happy family event where well-meaning relatives helped out by marching up and down a school hall, like the charity fashion show Lizzie had been to where nobody minded that one of the amateur models had fallen off her stilettos. Instead, this was a professional event with real models, real hairdressers, a real audience – and two normal people who would stand out like sore thumbs. There was no way Lizzie was going to parade up and down like Two Ton Tessie in front of all those skinny beautiful people.

'There's only half an hour 'till it begins,' said Kenny, who *was* anxious about the show. Joan might be anaesthetised with vodka but he, being a professional, wouldn't dream of touching anything other than still mineral water until it was all over. And he could tell that Lizzie and Ursula were deadly serious about not modelling, which meant that he and Joan had a big problem.

'Mum,' said Joan, 'go on, put the dress on. It looks lovely on you.'

'No,' insisted Ursula. 'I won't. In fact, I'm going out to sit with your father. I'm not making a show of myself here. I only said I'd do it because you said I'd meet that lovely Merrill Anderson from the telly.'

She dived behind the rail of clothes and emerged a minute later wearing her blouse and plaid skirt.

'Mum!' said Joan, as the penny finally dropped. 'You can't mean it?'

'I can.' With that Ursula marched towards the door that led into the audience.

'Go after her,' Kenny hissed at Holly. 'Make her change her mind. Coax her.'

Holly ran after Joan's mother.

'Mrs Atwood,' she said, dodging between people and rails of clothes.

Ursula passed the door and was in the auditorium with the speed of a sprinter. Holly rushed after her and finally caught up as Ursula sat down beside Joan's father.

'Holly, love, I can't do it,' said Ursula. 'I know she'll be angry with me but there must be models there who can fill in. I can't do it, honestly I can't.'

'Me neither,' said Lizzie, flopping into the seat beside Holly.

'But there's nobody who can take your place,' beseeched Holly.

'You do it, then!' said Lizzie tearfully.

There was no point saying anything else. Feeling that she'd failed utterly, Holly made her way back to the stage door.

'Hiya, Holly,' said a voice. It was Tom, seated at the back with Caroline perched beside him. In honour of the event, Tom was wearing the cashmere sweater they'd bought him for his birthday. Caroline looked as if she'd rampaged through Lee's designer section like a hurricane, bought every expensive designer label item she could find, and was now wearing them all at the same time. Her ensemble included a Burberry raincoat, Chloé sunglasses perched on top of her head like a hairband, a Louis Vuitton handbag, a giant Miu Miu belt and a gaudily-coloured Moschino jacket. All together, the combination was a little hysterical.

Kenny himself had overseen Holly's outfit, which was standard fashion hag black from head to elegant toe. A wool Joseph skirt, chiffon Whistles blouse and LK Bennett kitten heels. Beside her, Caroline looked like an expensively-decked-out Christmas tree.

'Hello, Tom, hi, Caroline,' Holly said.

'You're going backstage;' sighed Caroline. 'That must be fascinating. I said to Joan that I'd love to be backstage just to see what it was like, but she said it was only designers and their assistants for security reasons.'

Holly nodded gravely at this whopping big lie. At least ten of Joan and Kenny's friends had flitted backstage to bestow good luck hugs and squeal with delight at the clothes. Joan still hadn't forgiven Caroline for that crack about the three flatmates trying to recreate *Friends*.

Holly perched on the chair in front of them.

'Is everything going OK?' asked Tom. 'Only I saw Joan's mother legging it out from the back. Isn't she modelling for Joan?'

'Last-minute nerves,' Holly said, not wanting to be disloyal to Joan. Then she felt bad for not telling Tom the truth. He was her friend, but she didn't want Caroline to know anything was wrong.

'Tom says you were asked to model and you said no,' Caroline went on. 'You must be mad. I'd adore to be up there on the stage.'

Holly gazed at her. Caroline really was excruciating. Her vocabulary was limited to one word: me.

'Being the centre of attention isn't my scene,' Holly said lightly.

'Now, tell me about the party afterwards.' Caroline was all business. She wasn't really interested in Holly's opinions. 'It's in the Happy Bunny Bar on Clarendon Street, right?'

Holly nodded and got to her feet. 'I better go back.'

'You see,' said Caroline urgently, 'I want to make sure everyone is there because we've got an announcement to make tonight.'

'An announcement?' Holly asked.

'Not now, Caro,' said Tom uncomfortably.

'But yes, now. I can't keep it all to myself!' Caroline beamed at Holly and held out her left hand, on which sparkled a dainty sapphire which suited her tiny fingers. Holly's first instinct was to gasp but she smothered it and managed to say 'Ooh, how lovely,' instead.

'I knew you'd be pleased,' said Caroline smugly. She splayed her fingers and admired her ring. Holly watched her, wondering how somebody as decent as Tom could ever want to become engaged to Caroline. Love clearly *was* blind.

'Congratulations to both of you,' Holly said, backing away. She couldn't give Caroline a hug, she just couldn't. It would be hypocritical. 'I must rush.'

She fled to the safety of backstage where Kenny and Joan were tearing their hair out over the lack of tall, normally-built women to model two vital parts of Joan's collection.

'The wedding dress looks like a rag on Ivanka,' screeched Joan, as she tried to pin her Valkyrie dress on a etiolated girl with mahogany plaits and the face of a angel. Ivanka looked like a child in her big sister's dress. 'The whole show is ruined.' Joan looked desolate.

'It'll fit me, won't it?' said Holly.

Joan and Kenny looked up like dogs hearing the rattle of the can opener.

'Strip,' ordered Kenny.

Within minutes, there was a graceful ballet going on around Holly. Her hair was being sleeked down and plaited by the hairdresser, while Joan made a few last-minute alterations to the wedding dress because Lizzie wasn't as slim as Holly. The make-up artist stood on a chair and worked on Holly's eyes, painting feathery little strokes with her sable brushes, making Holly's dark eyes appear huge and exotically Eastern. They were barely finished when Joan unhooked the wedding dress and Kenny handed over the evening dress that Ursula had been going to wear. It was too big.

'There's nothing I can do,' Joan said hopelessly.

'Beg your mother,' said Kenny.

The show's compère, a handsome singer who strenuously denied that he was gay, appeared. Merrill Anderson was forty, looked thirty thanks to so much Botox he hadn't smiled in ten years, and was a huge hit with ladies unfamiliar with the sly sniggering of the gossip columns.

Kenny knew Merrill from the shop. Nobody was fussier over the cut of a jacket or the shape of a shirt collar than Merrill. Kenny batted his eyelashes. 'Merrill, you look divine. We have one teensy, weensy problem and you might be able to help. One of our models is having second thoughts. Could you coax her onstage?'

Ten minutes before the show began, the buzz began like a slow burning fire. It started when the music began to pulse from the speakers. Suddenly, backstage came alive. Last-minute Marlboros were lit, pulses began to race and Holly, clad in her dress and afraid to touch anything in case she somehow spilled something on herself, felt her whole body tremble with nerves. The fit of bravery that had come over her as a result of hearing that Caroline and Tom were engaged had receded somewhat. But she couldn't back out now.

'He's a lovely man, that Merrill,' sighed Ursula, now dressed in the midnight blue and silver evening dress and enjoying an emergency vodka. 'If I wasn't happily married, I'd go for him in a big way. He told me he preferred mature women, you know.'

'Mrs Atwood, can I have some of your drink?' asked Holly.

Fear of spilling was overcome by fear of modelling.

'Sure, have this one,' said Ursula, handing over a full glass that had been sitting on the make-up table. 'It's Joan's. She's had enough.'

Holly gulped the whole glass quickly, spilling none of it despite her trembling hands.

Fiona rushed past, her hair standing up like a brush because she'd run her fingers through it so many times. 'Vic's here and I told him you're modelling,' she told Holly. 'He says good luck!'

A huge round of applause told them that Merrill had gone onstage.

Everyone backstage watched the big TV monitor where the show was being relayed. The college's communications department were having a blast producing and filming the show. Merrill rattled on about the prizes for the top three designers, lauded the show's sponsors, and laboriously thanked the judges.

'Winning this award will be the start of a fabulous career for one lucky designer, a guaranteed one-year-contract with the Walton Street Design Centre. In fact,' Merrill smiled at the ladies in the audience, 'this could very well be the most important night in the life of our designers!'

'Is he trying to make us all even more nervous?' groaned Joan.

Holly reached out and squeezed Joan's hand. Merrill announced the first designer and the show proper began.

The first model set out onto the catwalk and Holly gulped with the knowledge that soon, very soon, she'd be going out there. Thirty minutes of applause and speedy changes later, the assembled models were clad in Joan's clothes. They all looked incredible, Holly thought, forgetting for a moment what she had to do.

As the person modelling the wedding dress, she would go last.

'Bottoms up,' grinned Ursula, swaying past in her midnight dress, perfectly able to face the crowd now that she'd been chatted up by the host and had plenty of vodka inside her.

'And introducing Joan Atwood's collection,' announced Merrill.

The first model stepped out.

Holly's turn was coming. The penultimate model set out and Holly was poised at the entrance to the catwalk, with the show co-ordinator's hand firmly pressed in the small of her back.

'Off you go,' said the co-ordinator, increasing the pressure. Terrified, Holly walked out, unsteadily at first, staring blindly over the sea of faces. Then, it happened: she became aware of the collective goodwill of the audience. In the crowd were her friends, and Joan and Kenny's friends, all wishing her well and crossing fingers so she'd walk happily down the catwalk, not tripping or stumbling. They wanted Holly and Joan to do well. The strength of their goodwill was like a palpable force. Holly felt it wash over her, comforting her and giving her confidence.

Suddenly, she felt sure-footed and light as a feather. Swaying her hips in time to the Shakira track that Joan had chosen, she sashayed down the ramp, a smile dancing at the corners of her mouth. She held the skirt with one hand, swishing it gently, making sure everybody was getting the benefit of this luscious dress. She was doing this for Joan, her dear friend.

Her smile deepened as she reached the judges, and she stopped, gazing confidently out at the audience, letting them know that this dress was making her feel wonderful. She was the bride, happy on this special day. Then, with a flick of her wrist and a wiggle of her hips, Holly turned and let the dress ripple out behind her. Still walking proudly, she made the return journey, conscious that her every move had to be perfect to show the dress to its best advantage. At the end, she shot them another triumphant bridal smile over her shoulder and she was gone.

'Holly, you were incredible!' Joan hugged her first, followed by Kenny who was tearful.

'I've never seen anything like it!' he shrieked. 'You were born to model! I've known you for nearly four years and it was like watching this beautiful stranger, I never knew you had it in you!!'

She was laughing and talking, telling them she'd been scared but then it had been all right, and then there was no time because Joan's collection had to head back down the ramp altogether. One by one the models strode past onto the runway and as they passed Holly backstage, they smiled at her and made thumbs up signs because she'd been like a professional; she was one of them.

'Well done,' smiled Ivanka as she swayed past Holly.

'You were great,' said another.

'You're next,' said the show co-ordinator but Holly didn't need the push this time. She stepped out, following the gorgeous procession. The first model had reached the end of the catwalk and stopped, clapping and waiting. Holly stood triumphantly at the back. For the first time ever, Holly Miller felt that she too was gorgeous. Then Joan appeared from backstage and grabbed Holly's hand, leading her past the line of models to accompany her down the catwalk as she received her acclaim as the designer of this fabulous collection. The audience went wild. Joan had to win, Holly thought.

In the crowd, Holly could see people. She saw Joan's family clapping wildly, she saw Vic on his feet yelling congratulations, she could see Tom's head at the back and he was clapping vigorously too. She felt a surge of pride that she'd been involved in this wonderful evening.

The Happy Bunny club was heaving. Joan was surrounded as soon as she stepped into the club, with well wishers hugging her and telling her they were thrilled she'd won. Joan brandished the glass trophy in one hand, and a rapidly-disappearing bottle of champagne in the other. Vic led Holly in through the throng, not letting her go for a moment. Some people recognised Holly and they hugged her too.

'That dress was fabulous,' they sighed. 'You were the star of the show but we won't be able to afford Joan's clothes now.'

'Do you get to keep the dress?' asked someone else.

Holly laughed. 'No,' she said.

'Yes, she is keeping it,' said Vic proudly. 'She's going to marry me and she's wearing that dress. All those other girls are going to be bridesmaids too, which should please whoever I pick to be best man.'

Holly laughed even louder.

Joan's father, Andy, was at the bar with Ursula, who was still wearing her midnight blue evening dress. 'I'm the designer's mother so I get to keep it,' Ursula told everyone grandly.

Joan's father ordered champagne and Ursula interrupted to tell the barman that they wanted a big bottle.

'A whatchmacallit bottle,' she said, drunk on her success and Fiona's quadruple-strength vodka and orange.

'I think she means a magnum,' said Andy.

'Magnum! That's it,' said Ursula happily. 'God, I loved Magnum. That Tom Selleck, phoar.'

'Don't ask your mother to model again,' Andy begged his

daughter. 'I cringe when I think of what the photos will look like.'

Several press photographers had turned up to take photos of the winning designer and her clothes. Faced with the usual line-up of beautiful, slender models, they'd been fascinated by the real-life, voluptuous glamour of Holly. Joan had insisted on being photographed only with Holly and her mother. This fresh chance of fame had gone to Ursula's head.

The magnum disappeared like a shot. Vic managed to get two glasses for him and Holly.

'I suppose you'll be off to Hollywood now that you're famous,' he teased.

'Tickets are booked and everything,' she said, keeping the joke going.

'Does that mean we're not going out any more?' Vic looked more serious now.

Holly decided that the light-hearted approach was best. 'Vic,' she said cheerily, 'we're not going out. We're friends, remember?' True to his word, Vic had seemed happy enough to keep things on a friendly footing when they'd gone out for a Chinese meal a few days earlier. Holly had been ready to tell him that she wanted to keep it like that in case he wanted to progress things, but he'd said nothing and had been marvellous company.

'I like being your friend, Holly,' Vic said now, sounding serious for once. 'But I'd like to be more than that . . .'

Holly felt her skin flush up; the first sign of embarrassment. What was she going to say?

'You were fabulous tonight. Have you ever thought about being a model?'

A tall, eccentric-looking woman with raspberry-coloured hair stood beside them, gazing intently at Holly.

'Cassiopeia Alexander,' said the woman, armfuls of gold bracelets jangling. 'Fashion director at Heavenly Style Plus. We're new to the market, a magazine for plus-sized women. You're a bit thin for us, we specialise in size sixteen or over, but we could make an exception in your case. Those curves are very now and a decent twelve to fourteen looks best in photos.'

Both Holly and Vic looked blank. It was the raspberry hair that did it. Holly wondered what sort of hairdresser would do that for you and Vic wondered if it was poisonous.

'No?'

'Well, probably no,' said Holly, blushing some more. 'Tonight was the exception, I'm not very good at standing up in front of strangers.'

'Photographic modelling isn't about standing up in front of strangers,' insisted Cassiopeia. 'There's six people in the room, max. You'd love it; you're a natural . . . You sure can walk the walk,' she told Holly. 'Here, take my card. Call me if you change your mind.' And she swept off.

'What about that hair,' said Vic in awe.

'I know,' whispered Holly. 'Do you think she's for real?'

Together they examined the card, which was expensively cream with black letters on one side and gold on the other. 'Looks good to me,' said Vic.

'We've told everyone we're engaged!' squeaked Caroline, dancing up behind Holly with Tom following loyally. 'They wouldn't let me use the club loudspeaker to announce it, so I've just told everyone myself!'

'Told them what?' inquired Vic.

'That we're engaged.' Caroline's hand shot out in a Pavlovian reaction and Vic dutifully admired the ring.

'So when's the big day?' he asked.

Caroline began to tell him.

'You were great,' said Tom in an undertone to Holly.

'Thanks.' She looked at the floor, anything rather than look at his face.

'What made you do it? I didn't think wild horses could get you on a catwalk.'

Holly's mind rushed through possible answers because saying that she'd been spurred on by the shock of his engagement would sound very odd indeed.

'Er . . . Joan needed me,' she mumbled.

'You're a good friend, Holly,' he said, taking her hand and holding it.

Holly dragged her gaze from her shoes and looked into Tom's earnest, kind face. It was like he was trying to tell her something, but what? Then it came to her: Tom's message was surely along the lines of *'Sorry you fancy me but I don't fancy you back. Please don't be upset.'*

It would be too shaming to have Tom think that. She forced herself to hold her head high. If she could parade up and down in a fashion show, she could be brave now in defeat.

'I'm delighted you and Caroline are engaged,' she said, trying to make her eyes sparkle so they wouldn't betray her sadness. 'You deserve to be happy.'

She didn't wait for a reply but quickly pulled her hand from his and tapped Vic on the shoulder.

'We should be going now, Vic. To the other party . . .' she added meaningfully.

'Of course,' said Vic, skilfully taking his cue. 'The other party. Yes, gotta go.'

Holly bestowed her best modelling smile on Caroline.

'Hope you both have a nice evening,' she said. 'And congratulations again.'

Vic was taller than Holly and together they made an imposing couple as they sailed through the club, stopping only to say goodbye to Joan, her family and Kenny.

'You're my best mate,' snuffled Joan tipsily as she grabbed Holly and hugged her. 'And you too,' she added, spying Kenny and dragging him into the circle.

Holly and Kenny laughed as Joan pulled them even tighter.

'Friends forever,' muttered Joan.

'You bet,' said Holly.

'Holly! There you are,' said an excited voice. The threesome parted and to Holly's utter surprise, the person who appeared wildly pleased to see her was Pia from work.

'Holly,' repeated Pia excitedly as if they were bosom pals

reunited after an eternity apart, instead of people who disliked each other intensely. 'How great to see you. You were wonderful. You must meet my friends. I love your clothes,' Pia added cravenly to Joan, who was trying to work out who this interloper was.

Holly prayed she wouldn't remember. Joan had promised death and facial reconstruction the last time she'd thought about Pia. From the look on Kenny's face, it was obvious he knew exactly who it was.

'Hi,' said Holly, leading Pia away before Kenny recommended the Linda Evangelista fringe. 'I didn't know you were going to be here.'

'I didn't know you were going to model,' said Pia breathlessly. 'You should have told me. I'd have got everyone from work to come.'

A flash of raspberry red hair descended and Cassiopeia clutched Holly's shoulder tightly as she flitted past. 'Don't forget me, Holly, promise?'

'I promise,' Holly said politely.

'You know her?' said Pia, impressed. How had she never realised it before? Holly Miller knew *everyone* from fashion mag movers and shakers to the country's newest, hottest designers. To think that she, Pia, had made the mistake of ignoring Holly when they could have been best friends?

'God, you were fabulous,' added Pia with renewed flattery. She shot assessing eyes over Holly's outfit, clocking the filmy chiffon blouse that looked ultra chic worn with the very trendy woollen skirt. Out of her work outfit and with the gloss of all these famous friends on her, Holly looked great. 'You were like a professional model up there.'

'Yes, wasn't she,' said Vic, stepping in to rescue Holly because she had that trapped look in her eyes.

Vic looked at his best in low lighting situations when his exotic dark looks appeared even more exotic and when the semi-dark hid the inevitable junior doctor bags under his eyes. Tonight, he was dressed to the nines in his only suit (Steve McQueen style from Oxfam) and looked as though he'd languidly stepped off Concorde moments before. Pia was definitely impressed.

'Sorry, but we've got to go,' Vic said, gently leading Holly away by the hand.

Holly waved at Pia, who smiled back brightly and yelled 'See you tomorrow!'

'Who was that?' asked Vic, somehow managing to part the crowds so they could sail through.

'A woman who never bothers talking to me normally,' Holly explained.

'Star fucker,' said Vic sagely.

Holly giggled at this accurate analysis of Pia.

'Have you said goodbye to everyone and their granny?' he inquired.

'I think so,' Holly replied, taking one last look back, still half-hoping that Tom would rush over and tell her the engagement was all a mistake. But he didn't.

Holly's last sight as she and Vic left, hand in hand, was of Tom standing on the mezzanine at the back of the club, watching her. What was wrong with him, she wondered as she ran out onto the street with Vic.

'I'm glad you thought the same as me about leaving when that obnoxious Caroline began whining on about her engagement,' Vic said, still holding Holly's hand as they walked up Clarendon Street. 'Save me from women like that. What is it about women and weddings, anyhow?'

'Don't ask me,' said Holly glumly.

Vic invited her back to his place for a nightcap.

'I'm afraid it'll really be only coffee,' he added ruefully. 'I'm on early shift tomorrow so I've had my champagne quota.'

'OK,' said Holly, not really thinking about it. 'Coffee would be nice.'

Vic's place was a tiny modern apartment in the city centre. He obviously hadn't been living there long because the miniature hallway wasn't so much decorated as littered with books.

While Vic made coffee, Holly sat on his couch thinking about Tom and Caroline.

'Well,' Vic sat down beside her with one hand resting easily on the back of the couch, just inches away from her.

Holly sipped her coffee and Vic casually let his arm slip onto her shoulders. She put her cup down. She knew what he was doing and she didn't stop him. Encouraged, Vic pulled her close and kissed her. Almost experimentally, Holly kissed back. It felt good to be kissed, it felt warm and tender. Holly wanted to feel loved and when she moved closer to him, Vic pulled her onto his lap and started caressing her shoulders and her breasts through her clothes while his mouth moved softly over her face and neck. As though she was watching from a distance, Holly wondered was this what she wanted. She couldn't tell, not really, not with the excitement of the night behind her and several drinks inside her. Vic ran his hands over her body with practised ease. Holly giggled. He must be good with bodies because he saw naked ones every day.

'What's so funny?' he asked, nuzzling her shoulder.

'Nothing,' she said.

Before she knew it, her top was off and so was Vic's. His hands were trying to undo her bra and Holly desperately asked herself if this was right. She wanted to exorcise Tom, but she knew that it wasn't Vic's lips she wanted kissing her flesh, it wasn't his fingers she wanted caressing her; it was Tom's. She closed her eyes and, feeling like the most horrible person on the earth, let herself imagine that the man holding her was Tom.

'Oh Holly,' moaned Vic. 'I want you so much.'

She opened her eyes.

'Vic, we can't do this, not like this, not yet. I'm sorry.'

Sitting up, she pulled her top from the coffee table and dragged it on.

'I'm sorry,' Vic apologised. 'I didn't mean to offend you, honestly, it's just that I'm crazy about you.'

'I think I should go home,' she said, standing up.

'Sure.' Vic stood up too. 'It's just that you'll have a hell of a time getting a taxi now. You can stay the night if you'd like. I'll take the couch and I'll drop you home in the morning. I'm on early, remember.'

She could see the wisdom of this.

'OK, but I'll take the couch. You've got to save lives tomorrow,' she joked.

'I didn't upset you or anything, did I?' he asked. 'I didn't mean to, I thought you wanted to as much as I did . . .'

'Don't be silly,' she said. 'This is all too soon for me, that's all.' As soon as she'd said it, Holly hated herself for lying to Vic. But she couldn't face telling him the truth there and then.

Holly woke up next morning feeling worse than she thought it was possible to feel. Tom was engaged to Caroline; he'd made his choice and he hadn't chosen her. And in her attempts to exorcise him from her mind, Holly had messed around with a kind, decent man who didn't deserve to be used as a distraction. She was a bad, horrible person and she was deeply ashamed of herself.

Vic dropped her home on his way into work. When his alarm clock had gone off loudly at a quarter to six, Holly was relieved that the twenty-minute gap between the alarm and when Vic had to leave meant that there was no time for any early morning conversation. She would have found that particularly hard to bear, because she knew she had only one thing to say to Vic.

'The only good thing about going to work at half six in the morning is that there's no traffic,' he said, kissing her goodbye when he'd stopped the car outside her apartment.

Holly did her best to return his kiss but felt like a traitor as she did so. If last night had proved anything, it was that the feelings she had for Vic would never be love. She felt ashamed of how she'd treated him.

'Talk to you later,' she said breezily, climbing out of the car. She ran up the steps to the front door and then turned and waved. Vic sat and waited until she was inside. Shutting the door quietly, Holly leaned against it and closed her eyes. Why did you do that? Why?

She went up to the second floor and was just about to insert her key in her front door when she heard footsteps on the stairs above.

The key was upside down and she hastily twisted it the right way round, shoved it in and pushed . . .

'Helloo, Holly,' said Caroline chirpily. 'It must have been a good party if you're only coming home now, you naughty girl.'

Holly turned round. Caroline, clad in a baby blue velour tracksuit and ostentatiously stretching her calf muscles, was clearly ready to go out jogging. Tom, whom Holly had never seen go jogging, was behind her, looking uncomfortable. If Caroline was all matching perfection, with her blonde hair in girlish pigtails, Tom looked dishevelled in a sloppy T-shirt and jogging pants that looked as if he usually used them as a dishcloth.

'Hi, Tom,' said Holly. She wouldn't blush. She was entitled to stay out all night if she wanted to. She was young, free and single. And she'd tell them so too! 'Yeah,' she said, feigning exhaustion, 'it was a great night. And the party was good too,' she added.

'We left early and watched Moulin Rouge,' said Caroline, her sweet expression implying that this type of coupley behaviour was far preferable to single-girl screwing around town.

Holly thought of how much she'd have preferred to be sitting snuggled up to Tom watching a video.

'Nice,' she said, managing a smile that Hermesetas could market. 'Well, bye.'

Holly shut the door behind her and for the second time in a few moments, found herself asking herself why she'd done something so clearly stupid. She should have said nothing, or else said they'd been out all night at a club. She didn't want Tom to think badly of her. But he would. He knew she'd only known Vic a short time and he'd believe she'd gone to bed with him. And he'd never think nicely of Holly ever again . . . At that, Holly sank to her knees in her tiny hall and burst into tears. How could one of the best nights of her life have turned into one of the worst?

CHAPTER TWENTY-EIGHT

At the party to celebrate *National Hospital*'s highest ever ratings, the Dom Perignon flowed like water. Godzilla, the executive producer, had decided uncharacteristically to push the boat out and brought the entire team – writers, crew and actors – out for a night of expensive partying. Partners were not invited, which was even better, according to some of the partygoers.

Tara had not felt in the mood for celebrating. Despite all Finn's assurances to the contrary, his bonus still hadn't appeared. He seemed unconcerned about this, insisting that 'it'll happen, Tara. Loosen up.'

Tara didn't want to loosen up. She still felt humiliated after her encounter with the bank when they'd agreed to up her overdraft for six months to cope with the financial crisis. Tara had come out of that meeting feeling like a schoolgirl who'd just been rebuked. Under the circumstances, a party was the last thing she felt like but Isadora had persuaded her to get dressed up and come.

'It'll do you good to get your glad rags on and stop behaving like an old curmudgeon,' she'd told Tara briskly.

So Tara had gone for the full monty, just to show that she still could.

And even Isadora had been surprised to see her friend clad in high-heeled sandals and a breathtaking jersey sheath dress, held up by straps as thin as a spider web which kept falling provocatively off her shoulders.

'Wow, what did Finn think when he saw you leaving the flat dressed like that?' Isadora had asked.

'He wasn't home,' replied Tara in a flat little voice. Finn had reacted to news of Tara's party by saying he might just go out with Derry and the lads himself. Tara didn't like to think what that meant.

'Just as well Finn wasn't home,' said Tommy chauvinistically. 'No man in his right mind would let a gorgeous creature like you out of the house in that outfit.'

Tommy wasn't the only one who commented favourably on Tara's outfit.

'Nice dress, Miller,' remarked Scott Irving, wicked dark eyes sliding over her body appreciatively. 'I might have to bring you up for a dance later.'

'If I dance, the dress will fall off,' Tara joked, to hide how jolted she was by Scott's obvious admiration.

'Dance, dance,' yelled Scott and Tommy in unison.

By the time the party got to the nightclub, Tara was worn out with the emotional stress of the past weeks. She had drunk two glasses of champagne but it had failed to inject some fizz into her. She was wondering whether it would be very rude to slope off home when Scott appeared beside her and plonked himself down on the squashy leather couch beside her. Tara perked up.

'You look great, Tara.' Scott put an affectionate arm around her waist and held on, and somehow it wasn't affectionate at all. It was something else: a signal as subtle as a silver bullet. Tara didn't know which was most astonishing: that Scott was behaving in this way or that she could feel herself responding. Her breath quickened and she looked at him, eyes widened, lips parted.

Scott's expression was just as friendly as ever but as the conversation rolled on around them, his arm stayed round her waist. Aware of how it must look, she moved slightly so his arm dropped to the couch, just inches away from her body.

She turned to Tommy, who was on her left telling some convoluted story about the Oscars, but all the time she was aware of Scott beside her.

He was hugely magnetic and since he'd been working as a writer on *National Hospital*, the number of female staff who found they had to walk past his cubicle on a daily basis had quadrupled.

Tara, mired in the pain of her marriage, had managed not to notice Scott since the day he'd asked her out to lunch. But he wasn't the sort of man who liked remaining unnoticed. He'd deliberately sought her out on many occasions, sat beside her at the daily meetings and bumped into her by the coffee machine more times than was purely coincidental. He'd done everything but say 'are you avoiding me?', a question Tara would have found difficult to answer truthfully.

Tommy's meandering story came to its confused conclusion, and Tara found herself, almost unwillingly, turning back to Scott. She watched him for a moment, taking in the wild dark hair, the pale, unshaven skin and the dissolute but utterly exciting expression on his mobile face. She tuned into his conversation. He, Aaron and Lisa were talking business.

As though he knew she'd tuned in, he patted her knee but kept facing the other two. Tara leaned closer as the waitress arrived with more champagne. Tara refused a glass: she'd had enough. When Aaron was busy signing for the wine, Scott turned back to Tara.

'Having fun?' he asked, coal-black eyes roaming over her flushed face.

She nodded.

His eyes glittered, as if a thought had just come into his head. 'Hey, what are you up to at the weekend?'

Tara shrugged. 'Same old, same old.'

I'm going to London for a few days, want to come?'

He wasn't joking.

Tara was astonished at how much she wanted to go.

'I, I can't,' she said automatically.

'Can't or don't want to?' whispered Scott.

'I'm a happily married woman,' she said lightly.

'So?'

His look contained such naked sexuality that Tara gulped nervously. Normally, she'd have laughed this off but Scott was too serious to be laughed off. And suddenly Tara found she didn't want to.

She bent her head closer to his. 'We can't do this, Scott.'

'Why not?' His head was beside hers. Nobody could hear what they were saying although Tara wondered if people could hear the machine-gun pumping of her heart.

'You're amazing, Tara,' he murmured. He reached out and let his arm encircle her waist again. 'So slim,' he said admiringly.

'People will see,' she said.

'So?'

'Is that your word for the night?' she asked, looking up at him curiously. He was so different from Finn, like a negative image. Finn was fair and golden, while Scott was dark and definitely dangerous. Devilish to Finn's angel. But then, Finn was no angel. The thought pierced Tara's bruised heart. She wondered where he was now? In some bar with Derry, drinking another mortgage instalment? She should never have let him go out. She should have confronted him about his drinking.

'You've got that sad look on your face again.' Scott's grey eyes burned into hers. 'What is it?'

'Nothing.'

'Nothing you want to talk about, you mean?'

'That's it.'

'Still family problems, huh?'

She could feel Scott's fingers splayed over her back, moving softly, a gentle massage on her muscles. What would it feel like to have those fingers splayed over naked skin, touching and massaging?

'I'll be right back,' she said, getting abruptly to her feet. She bashed knees with Tommy getting out past him, the more difficult exit. But she didn't want to pass Scott in case he held onto her. If he had, she knew she mightn't have been capable of tearing herself away.

Away from the group, she walked quickly in the direction of the women's room so her dramatic exit wouldn't look too weird. Once out of sight, she stopped and leaned over a balcony, staring down at the normal people laughing and having fun on the level below. She didn't know how to have fun any more. She was so wired up with nerves and anxiety that a little light flirtation had sent her over the edge. Scott had only been joking with her, surely . . .

'I wondered where you'd gone in such a hurry.' It was him, his body inches away from hers. She hadn't even seen him walk up to her. More proof of devilry.

'Are you following me?' she asked lightly.

He nodded. Then he leaned down and kissed her. Tara watched his face, watched his eyes closed and his expression transported by kissing her. She tried to remember seeing Finn's face the same way, then she closed her eyes and let her mouth move with Scott's, their tongues probing fiercely. And then Tara's fingers were grasping Scott's head as though she could pull him physically closer to her by force. Scott moved away first.

'Come back to my place,' he said, his breath ragged.

Tara shook her head.

'Please,' he urged. The grey eyes roamed longingly over her face. He reached his hand up and the fleshy pad of his thumb caressed the softness of her lower lip. Despite herself, Tara closed her eyes and leaned towards the caress, her mouth opening to lick his thumb and pull it inside the soft cavern of her mouth, sucking and biting.

'Please,' he said again.

Why not, she asked herself. Why ever not? The sexual attraction she felt for Scott was like a monster deep inside herself, demanding and urging. And would anyone blame her for giving in to the temptation, would anyone blame her if they knew what her life was like?

Tara opened her eyes as Scott gently removed his hand. 'Nobody must know,' she said fiercely.

He nodded.

'I'll go first,' she added.

She went to the women's room and avoided looking at herself in the mirror. She didn't want to have to look hard into her own eyes and ask herself what she was doing. Back at the group, she reached in and pulled her coat from the couch. Scott was sitting there, talking to Aaron again, not even looking her way.

'I'm going, everyone,' she said. 'Headache.'

She waved goodbye to them all, trying not to let her eyes linger on Scott.

'Do you want me to walk you out?' asked Aaron.

'I'm fine.' She shot him a weak, headachey smile. 'You stay. I'll grab a taxi.'

The huge bar was pulsing with excitement as Tara walked down the stairs, clutching her small bag and her coat, her mind racing. She wove her way through the crowds, and at the door, she slipped her coat on. A taxi stood outside on the pavement, letting two women out. A third was paying the driver. Tara pushed through the door and hopped in. The driver nodded at her in his mirror, telling her he'd be with her as soon as his passengers had paid. She sat back in the seat and closed her eyes. She'd tell him to drive her home. She'd be home in no time and all this madness would be forgotten. What had she been thinking?

Her eyes jerked open with the opening of the cab door. Scott leapt in beside her, eyes glittering, pupils huge.

'Where to, love?' asked the driver.

'Fordham Road, Killiney,' said Scott, his eyes locked with Tara's. 'My place,' he added softly.

Suddenly Scott's mouth was hard on Tara's, his arms tight around her waist and hers wrapped around him. The taxi driver drove off into the night.

Even before she opened her eyes, Tara knew she wasn't in her own bed. The pillows felt different and the scent of fabric conditioner was a strong launderette one, not the subtle one she liked. She moved slowly, feeling her muscles ache strangely as she hauled herself up in the bed. Then she opened her eyes. The room came instantly into focus in the dawn light. Teal-blue walls, framed film posters and one huge expanse of wall covered with the sort of blinds that weren't conducive to long lie-ins. The views in Scott's apartment were incredible and the windows were floor to ceiling to take advantage of this fact. Tara remembered standing on the balcony the night before, staring out at the breathtaking view of the sea. Scott had produced a bottle of champagne from the fridge when they'd got to his apartment, and they'd stood in the chill night air, drinking slowly and talking. That had been her last chance to say that coming there had been a mistake and she was leaving. She hadn't taken it. Scott had shivered and pulled her and the champagne inside, shutting the balcony doors and leading the way into his big, minimalist bedroom with the huge bed that would have taken up the entire living room in Tara and Finn's cramped flat.

It could have been a hotel bedroom, Tara thought now, propping herself up and looking around. Apart from the film posters – *Giant* and *Cat on a Hot Tin Roof* – it was impersonal. The show apartment, in fact.

She let her gaze settle on Scott. He slept with the duvet thrust down to waist level, arms splayed out, his lean body lying at an angle across the bed. Last night, she'd made love to that body and it had made love to her, had held her, kissed her, entered her, tensed in orgasm with her. And now it looked like a stranger's body. She could remember the passion and the way they'd made love like they were making war, with ferocity and wildness. She could remember leaning back in Scott's arms after the first time, feeling the ice cold of his champagne glass against her nipples, laughing as she'd told him she'd never had sex like that before, that she'd never felt such abandoned arousal.

How could she have said that? It wasn't true. Nobody ever made her feel the way Finn did. Their lovemaking could be wildly passionate, and then exquisitely tender. That was what she loved about him. And she'd betrayed him doubly, by sleeping with someone else and by saying that the adulterous sex was the best ever.

Tara lay there in Scott's bed and felt the breath leave her body in one, long shuddering gasp. What had she done? As quietly as she could, she slipped from the bed and tiptoed across the American Oak floor to the en-suite.

She'd avoided looking at herself the night before but now her eyes stared out at her, eyes that shone dully. How could Finn look into those eyes and not know? He'd know because she wasn't home, anyhow. She looked at her watch. It was ten to six in the morning. Even if he'd been pissed the night before, Finn was capable of adding two and two and coming to the correct conclusion.

Tara pulled off a piece of loo roll and wet it to scrub the make-up from her eyes. They were still sooty with the remains of mascara when she was finished, but it was an improvement. She rinsed her face with Scott's soap and debated whether or not to use his toothbrush. It was funny, she thought wryly, that she'd shared every centimetre of his body the night before, glorying in every part of him, and now she wondered if he'd mind her using his toothbrush.

She used it anyway. Then ran his comb through her hair. Her face was pale but she looked reasonable. Or she would until she put on her sexy black dress and high heels. She might as well get 'dirty stop-out' embroidered on the back of her fitted leather jacket.

She dressed in the living room, and was ready to leave in five minutes. All she needed was some water to make her feel more human after last night's excesses. She knew why she'd drunk more champagne in Scott's: to numb herself from what she was about to do. Well, she was paying for it now, in spades.

Scott's fridge contained nothing but wine, beer and orange juice. Tara poured herself a glass of juice and drank it standing up by the sink.

'Leaving so soon?'

She almost dropped the glass.

'Yes.'

Scott stood at the bedroom door, naked and sleepy, but his expression was hard.

'I'm sorry, Scott. I have to go.'

'I don't mind you going, I hate the way you're doing it,' he said evenly, walking towards her.

'I shouldn't have come here last night,' Tara said.

'So much for "no regrets", huh?' He stood beside her, close enough to touch but he didn't and Tara was struck again by how powerfully attractive he was, even tired and unshaven. It would have been easy to put her arms around him and let herself be taken back to bed for more earth-shattering sex and intense orgasms. But she couldn't.

Last night, she'd clicked off the switch that connected her brain with her conscience. Now, she couldn't. It had been reconnected and Finn's face was hovering in her head.

'I love my husband,' she said.

'Don't tell me you were drunk and didn't know what you were doing, Tara,' he said angrily. 'You weren't in the slightest bit drunk when we left the nightclub; you wanted me as much as I wanted you. What happened wasn't a mistake, the way we were together wasn't a mistake. You can't fuck like that if you don't mean it.'

Tara didn't flinch at his words. 'I didn't say I didn't mean it,' she answered, looking him straight in the eye. 'But I love my husband and I have to go. I made a mistake, I can't give you what you want. We can't have a relationship.'

She could see the hurt in his face when she said that.

'How do you know what I want?' he demanded.

Tara shrugged. 'If you wanted a one-night stand, you'd be happy for me to get out of here as quickly as possible.'

'Suddenly you know a lot about me.' His gaze was harsh and uncompromising. 'I don't do one-night stands.'

'Neither do I,' she shot back, stung.

'Looks like you just did,' he said coldly.

'Scott, I can't do this . . .' she began. 'I'm married and I love Finn.'

'Even though he's destroying you?'

Tara closed her eyes. The only hazy part of the night before was when Scott had asked her about Finn and she wasn't sure what she'd said. She must have told him enough. Too much, in fact.

'I'm sorry, Scott,' she said. She put her glass down and walked past him. Scott didn't make any attempt to stop her. It was only when she was standing outside the building that it occurred to her that she should have phoned a taxi.

Her high heels weren't the most comfortable for walking in but Tara marched briskly on, ignoring the ache in her feet. She didn't notice the pain, all she could think about was what she was going to say to Finn.

It took at least fifteen rings before Isadora answered the phone.

'Isadora, it's Tara.'

'Tara, hi,' said Isadora blearily. 'What time is it? What's wrong?'

'Did Finn phone you last night?'

'No. Why?' Isadora sounded awake now. Awake and suspicious.

'I wasn't at home last night.'

'Scott?'

'Inspector Poirot strikes again,' said Tara wryly.

'Well, the sexual tension was buzzing off the pair of you all night,' Isadora pointed out. 'I did speculate that you were up to something when you rushed off with a headache with Scott rushing after you.'

'Subtle, huh?'

'As a brick. So, I'm your alibi,' Isadora added briskly.

'Would you mind?' Tara held her breath as she waited for her friend's response.

'Of course not.'

'Thanks. I'm sorry to do this to you, it's not fair,' Tara

said. She felt close to tears. Not only had she betrayed Finn, but, in her attempts to cover it up, she was telling someone else. She thought of how hurtful this would be if he ever found out: the husband being the last to know.

'Where are you?'

'Somewhere in Killiney. Have you got any taxi phone numbers handy?'

'Sure. And come here,' Isadora suggested. 'Alibis work best when there's a grain of truth in them.'

'Yeah,' said Tara sadly.

She was grateful that her friend didn't ask for any sordid details. With one look at Tara's pale face, Isadora ushered her in, sat her down at the breakfast bar in the kitchen and poured a cup of strong, sweet tea.

'Do you want to shower and change into something of mine?' asked Isadora. Her own hair was wet from the shower and she was wearing a silky dressing gown in a very un-Isadora-ish shade of feminine pink.

Tara nodded. 'What have I done, Izzy?' she said miserably. She held onto her cup with both hands and stared into the dark brown depths.

'You went to bed with someone you fancied. You didn't run amok with an AK47 and murder anyone.'

'It feels like I did.'

Isadora lit up a cigarette. 'Tara, I know you're not happy for some reason and I haven't interfered and asked why. I figured you'd tell me if you wanted to but I guess something's wrong between you and Finn. Otherwise, you wouldn't have gone off with Scott. My advice, for what it's worth, is forget about what happened with Scott and see if you can sort things out with Finn.'

'But what if Finn finds out?' said Tara hollowly.

'He's not going to find out. Have a shower, borrow some clothes and come to work with me. Then phone Finn and tell him we went clubbing and you stayed here. He'll believe you.'

'I'm no good at lying, Isadora.'

Isadora poured more tea into both cups. 'I'll teach you.'

In the shower, Tara scrubbed herself with strawberry shower gel, trying to wash away the memory of Scott's caresses. Then she stood for ages with her eyes closed and let the water stream over her face, flattening her hair against her skull. When the water began to cool, she got out and wrapped herself in a big towel. She was clean but she still felt dirty.

'Phone,' yelled Isadora from outside the bathroom. 'It's Finn,' she added when a white-faced Tara opened the door. 'Just as well you came here.'

Dripping wet, Tara picked up the receiver. 'Hi,' she said.

'You might have phoned,' Finn said harshly. 'I was worried.'

'Sorry, we went clubbing . . .'

'So I believe. If you managed to get home to Isadora's, why couldn't you get a taxi to bring you home. Or,' he added viciously, 'are you trying to punish me because I went out too?'

'No, I was drunk, that's all. I wanted to crash out somewhere and Isadora said I could stay.' Tara began to shiver and it wasn't from the cold.

'Whatever,' he snapped.

'I'll see you tonight,' Tara said but Finn had hung up.

At work, Tara and Isadora passed Scott in the corridor.

'Hello, Scott,' said Tara, fixing him with her clear gaze.

'Hi,' he said brusquely.

'That wasn't too bad, was it?' whispered Isadora as they parted to go to their desks.

'That was easy,' murmured Tara, untruthfully. It had been a battle to look Scott in the eye. But what really worried her was seeing Finn. If the message of guilt in her eyes didn't give her away, then the livid love bite on her neck might. Isadora's camouflage make-up had hidden it for the moment. She couldn't spend the next week hiding it.

* * *

457

Finn was at home when Tara reached the flat at seven that evening. Don't rush home early, Isadora had advised. 'That's like proof of having done something wrong. Be your usual, bolshy self.'

Tara wondered where Isadora had picked up all these Adultery: The Easy Way tips. But she didn't say anything. In her position, she couldn't afford to sit on the moral high ground.

'Hi,' she yelled when she arrived home and plonked her briefcase on the floor. She threw her leather jacket on the overladen hall chair as usual. Acting as normal as possible was vital but why then did her every move seem like that of a particularly clumsy actress in an amateur play?

As usual, she walked into the living room where Finn was watching the news. Once, they'd have hugged when they met up at the end of the day, but lately, the frostiness in their relationship meant that the hug had bitten the dust.

Tara sat down on their only armchair, forcing herself to sink lazily into it rather than sit on the edge and wait for Finn to grill her.

'Well?' he said caustically. 'Don't I merit an explanation?'

'I gave you one,' said Tara, her heart thumping. 'We were dancing and I stayed over in Isadora's.'

'Why not come home?'

Be your usual, bolshy self, Isadora's voice echoed in her head.

'Because I was drunk and angry and I needed a night off!' she yelled.

'Fine!' he yelled back. He got to his feet and stomped from the room. The next noise she heard was of the front door slamming. Tara closed her eyes in relief. She didn't know how long she'd have been able to keep up the normality charade.

She was a bad actress and for the first time in her life, she began to appreciate the difficulties of playing someone else. Tonight, she was playing the old Tara Miller, the pre-sleeping with a colleague version. And as far as she was concerned, every gesture and every sentence screamed *'Fake'*.

*   *   *

When Finn came in at two in the morning, Tara closed her eyes and pretended to be asleep. It was hard, lying there and not moving a muscle, but she did it. The bedside clock read a quarter to three before Finn's breathing had evened out into the regular breaths of someone who was asleep. Only then could Tara move and stretch her cramped muscles. She turned onto her back and lay gazing up at the ceiling. If only she could turn the clock back to somewhere around eleven o'clock last night. She'd never have kissed Scott, never have allowed him into her taxi, never gone willingly to his bed. But she had done all those things and they couldn't be undone.

CHAPTER TWENTY-NINE

The wave of Mediterranean weather that had hit the sunny south east at the beginning of May, continued into June. At Nettle Cottage, this meant that the three dogs didn't like to leave the cool of the house and spent their days lying on the cool stone floor of the kitchen, only moving to slobber some more water up from their bowls. Rose, who adored the heat, didn't mind how high the temperature got. Her olive skin was lightly tanned from sitting outside the cottage on a deckchair, reading her way through Freddie's collection of novels, with bees buzzing lazily in the herbaceous border beside her. The mock-orange blossom on the other side of the garden was losing its bloom, but she could still smell the heady scent drifting around her.

At night, she left her bedroom window open and she loved the sense this gave her of being close to nature. In Meadow Lodge, her bedroom was on the first floor and she never heard the crickets singing wildly outside, or the foxes barking at night.

She'd been in Castletown for five weeks now and in some ways, it felt as if she'd never lived anywhere else. There was a restful routine to her days with Freddie. For a start, formality was not part of her aunt's life. Freddie dressed unconventionally in clothes that looked as though she'd found them in a chest marked 'Second World War Fashions'. When she entertained, guests had to be prepared to take pot luck. The meal could involve one of Freddie's famous Moroccan stews or might mean phoning the takeaway if she hadn't had time to cook. The only definite appointments in any week were Freddie's work with the meals on wheels people, and her poker nights. Rose was invited along to everything Freddie went to, but if she couldn't go, Freddie never minded in the slightest.

For the first time in forty years, Rose felt as if she could do what she liked, when she liked. The sense of personal freedom was dizzying. She didn't have to be the respectable Mrs Hugh Miller any more. She could race down the lane on Freddie's elderly High Nellie bicycle with her skirt tucked into her knickers if she felt like it. She could throw on her oldest linen skirt and a T-shirt, slip her feet into dusty old sandals, and never bother about her appearance from morning to night. The people she met through meals on wheels were delighted to see cheery faces appearing at lunchtime; they didn't care whether Rose had great wefts of dog hair on her skirt or hadn't bothered with lipstick. If she didn't feel like answering the phone, she didn't, and if she had had the inclination to walk through Castletown at four in the morning, she could have.

This morning, she was clad in a pair of Freddie's ancient khaki shorts and a short-sleeved blouse so she wouldn't get too hot as she cleaned up the camp bed. Stella and Amelia were coming to stay for the weekend and, as there wasn't much room, Freddie had hit upon the idea of dragging out the camp bed for Amelia.

'Stella can sleep with you and there's loads of room for the camp bed to fit in your room so Amelia can be with you and her mum,' Freddie said enthusiastically.

Unfortunately, the camp bed was past its best. Rose had hosed it to death outside the cottage back door but it still looked grim, creaky and far too decrepit to hold even little Amelia without collapsing under the weight.

Rose gave up and went to find Freddie, who was sitting in the front garden under an sun umbrella, reading the newspaper and drinking diet lemonade.

'It's too far gone, Freddie,' Rose said. 'I'll have to go into town to see if I can buy a little foldaway bed of some sort.'

'Get cakes, will you,' asked Freddie. 'We've eaten all the biscuits and I'm peckish.'

Rose had just turned to go into the house and change, when she noticed a taxi struggling up the laneway.

'Who could that be, I wonder?' she said out loud.

Nettle Cottage was situated on a quiet lane where there was little traffic and Freddie could accurately predict what was going on around her just by looking at the cars trundling up and down the lane.

Freddie put down the paper to have a good look. 'We didn't invite anyone and forget about it, did we?' she inquired thoughtfully. 'I can't remember, anyhow, but you never know.'

Rose grinned at this proof of her aunt's laissez-faire attitude to guests. Freddie was not the type for rushing round with the vacuum when people were due. She was more likely to brush Prinny's luxuriant golden fur carefully so she'd 'look her best for the visitors'.

The taxi pulled up outside the cottage gates and Rose watched in astonishment as Adele Miller climbed out. The taxi driver took a vast suitcase out of the boot and hauled it up to the cottage, with Adele following, taking careful steps in her low-heeled court shoes. Wearing one of her infamous knit suits with yellowing pearls at her neck, Adele looked somewhat out of place amid the relaxed bohemian atmosphere of Nettle Cottage.

At the sound of visitors, the dogs rushed out of the house, barking wildly and dancing round both Adele and the taxi driver.

'Adele,' said Rose weakly. 'What are you doing here?'

'I've come to stay. I hope that's all right,' Adele said. 'I was afraid to phone in case you put me off.'

The driver dropped the cases and headed back down to his car.

'Thank you,' said Freddie, seeing as no-one else was bothered with talking to the poor man. 'Long time no see, Adele,' she added cheerily.

'Hello, Freddie,' said Adele, sinking onto the seat beside Freddie and fanning herself with her hand. 'I'm not intruding, am I?'

'Not at all,' said Freddie. 'You're welcome but you might have to sleep on the floor. We're all out of beds.'

When Adele's case had been dragged into the house and she'd been shown where the bathroom was, Rose boiled the kettle and went out to apologise quietly to Freddie.

'I had no idea she was coming,' Rose said. 'I honestly don't know what she's here for.'

'Don't worry.' Freddie was sanguine. 'We can manage. We'll have to buy two camp beds, that's all. She can sleep with you and Stella can have one of the camp beds . . .'

'No way,' hissed Rose. 'I'm too old to start sleeping with people I've never slept with before. Adele can have a camp bed or, if she doesn't like that, we can fix her up with a room in one of the hotels.'

'Not with this heatwave, you won't. I doubt if there's a hotel or a bed and breakfast round here that isn't full to bursting.'

Rose closed her eyes briefly.

'Don't worry,' Freddie repeated. 'We'll manage.'

'You don't know what Adele's like,' Rose whispered. 'She's very particular about sheets and what sort of bed she sleeps on. She's not an easy guest.'

Freddie's sea-green eyes twinkled. 'We'll soon knock that out of her.'

Rose began to make tea for Adele, her mind racing. Why had Adele come and interrupted her idyll? Rose had done her very best not to think about Hugh. She'd somehow blanked the whole painful memory of the party from her mind, and any time she thought of that awful phone call and the anguished voice of the anonymous woman, she forced herself to think of something else. And now Adele had come and brought all the pain into sharp relief.

Rose laid the tea things and a jug of water on the cast-iron table in the garden and moved the sun umbrella so that the table was shaded. Freddie pulled her deckchair over but said no to tea; she was too hot. Rose agreed and took some iced water herself.

'Thank you, Rose. I could do with some tea.' Adele emerged from the house and sat down at the table. It was a very old piece of garden furniture and in Meadow Lodge, it wouldn't have been let out in public without being sanded down and repainted every year. In Nettle Cottage, it was left to peel elegantly. Indeed, Rose had spent many a therapeutic hour peeling off strips of black paint while gazing out at the sea beyond the roofs and spires of Castletown.

She poured tea for Adele and proffered a plate of very plain biscuits.

The dogs, sensing that the new visitor would have no truck with wet, questing doggy noses, sat a respectful distance from Adele and kept their eyes peeled for titbits.

'How are you, Freddie?' asked Adele politely.

'Great,' sighed Freddie. 'Enjoying the sun. You picked a great weekend to come, Adele. The fair's on tonight and all day tomorrow. Tonight, the history society are re-enacting the Viking years on the village green and tomorrow, there's a gymkhana, and the children's fancy dress.'

'Lovely,' said Adele weakly. She took a biscuit and the dogs leaned forward as one.

'Girls!' warned Freddie.

They all leaned back again. Freddie got to her feet. 'I'll bring them for a quick walk and let you two talk in private. Come on, girls,' she called. The dogs, with one longing look back at the plate of biscuits, galloped after her.

'Does she walk far?' asked Adele, watching Freddie stride off up the lane at a cracking pace.

'Probably only a mile or so in this heat,' Rose said. 'The dogs aren't able to walk too far when it's hot.' She sipped her glass of water and waited for the lecture. *Hugh needs you, people in Kinvarra are talking. Isn't it time you came to your senses and came home?*

'I suppose you're wondering why I'm here,' Adele said.

'The thought had crossed my mind,' Rose replied politely. 'I wanted to show my support.'

If Adele had said that she wanted to run off and join the navy, Rose couldn't have been more surprised. 'Why?' she said finally.

'I'm so angry about what Hugh has done. I knew that women liked him but I never thought he'd do anything other than flirt mildly with them. My father was the same; women loved him and it was mutual, I can tell you. But I thought that's all it was, Rose. Flirting. I would never have believed it of my own brother. If only I'd known, I could have done something . . .'

'Adele,' sighed Rose, 'you're not responsible for Hugh. He's a big boy, he makes his own mistakes.'

'But such mistakes! I can't forgive him, Rose, I've tried but I can't. That's why I'm here,' Adele added hotly. 'To show Hugh what a terrible thing he's done and that I'm on your side!'

Rose was more touched than she could say. She knew that Adele adored Hugh. For Adele to publicly choose between them was a huge sacrifice.

She reached out and touched her sister-in-law's arm briefly, a moving gesture between two women who were not affectionate towards each other. 'Thank you,' she said, 'that's lovely of you.' She paused before asking: 'How is he?' It was strange to ask after Hugh as though he were a stranger. All her life it had been the other way round: Adele and everyone else asked *her* how Hugh was.

'Sad and sorry,' Adele replied. 'He really is sorry but, as I told him, that's no good now. He should have thought of that in the first place and not cry to me when the milk is spilt.'

Rose grinned to herself. Trust Adele to come up with an apt homily. If Hugh's leg had fallen off, Adele would have had something moralising to say about being especially thankful for the one he had left.

'Adele, I have to go shopping,' said Rose. 'Stella and

465

Amelia are coming this evening and I've got to purchase a couple of camp beds.'

Adele's eyebrows arched. 'Camp beds?' she said in a Lady Bracknell voice.

Rose smothered a grin. Adele might have defrosted a bit but she hadn't changed *that* much.

'This is a two-roomed cottage, Adele, two rooms with two beds and this weekend there will be five people staying. So somebody's going to be on a camp bed.'

Rose knew she couldn't put Adele on a camp bed. 'You can share with me. Stella and Amelia can have the camp beds. Or you can have a camp bed yourself. Either way, you won't have either a room or a bathroom to yourself. And Freddie's linen cupboard doesn't run to changing the sheets every day, either.'

Adele sniffed. 'I suppose that will have to do,' she said. 'I can rough it.'

'Don't let Freddie hear you saying that,' laughed Rose.

It was still so hot that Rose decided to leave her shorts on and change her shirt into one with sleeves to protect her shoulders from the midday sun. Adele's concession to the heat was to extract a straw sunhat from her suitcase.

'Normally, you'd be scandalised by my wearing shorts,' Rose commented as they got into Rose's car.

'You're lucky you have the figure for shorts,' said Adele. 'I wish I did.'

By the time they'd found the camping shop, and bought one foldaway bed and one child's blow-up bed, both women were tired and hungry.

'Let's go into Molloy's for lunch,' said Rose impulsively. 'They do lovely seafood salads.' Ordinarily, she'd have never suggested taking her sister-in-law into a pub but she had a strong sense that things were changed between her and Adele. Some ancient barrier had been broken down and the rules were different.

'Why not?' said Adele.

The owner of Molloy's had styled his pub-restaurant on

the harbour restaurants of his native Sydney and in summer, the huge wooden terrace area was jammed with people wanting to enjoy gigantic plates of seafood overlooking the curving Castletown Bay. Rose and Adele nabbed one of the last seats on the furthest-out terrace and sat with the sea breeze cooling them.

'It's very hot,' said Adele, watching enviously as Rose eased her bare feet out of her sandals and rested them on the lowest bar of the wooden rail surrounding the terrace.

'Why don't you take your cardigan off? And your tights,' said Rose.

'I couldn't,' said Adele, who never dared go without tights except when she was at home. 'I've only got a camisole under this,' she added.

'Yes you could, Adele,' said Rose. 'Nobody's watching.'

Sixty-five years of conditioning fought for supremacy in Adele's mind. She scanned the other diners. There were families with toddlers plonked in high chairs, happily covered in tomato ketchup and waving chips. A group of twenty-something men and women were decked out in tiny T-shirts and denim cut-offs. To Rose's left was an enormous party of tourists from hotter climes, all bronzed and looking pleased at this seventy degree Fahrenheit proof that Ireland was more than a country of mist and rain. They were all ages and sizes, yet nobody seemed worried about wearing shorts with varicose veins and chubby knees showing.

Adele got up and made her way to the ladies' room. She returned with her tights in her handbag and her knit cardigan draped around her shoulders.

'Isn't that better?' said Rose.

They feasted on Molloy's famous crab platters and then took a gentle stroll down the beach in their bare feet, sandals dangling from their hands.

'If all of Kinvarra could see us now,' laughed Rose ruefully. 'The two Miller ladies ambling along on the sand in bare feet.'

Adele looked alarmed at this. It was one thing to throw caution to the wind in a place where nobody knew you, quite another to do so and tempt fate by imagining some Kinvarra resident observing such reckless behaviour. Still, she'd forgotten how wonderful grains of sand could feel between the toes. The beach was hot to walk upon but at the edge of the water, the sliding wet sand was cool and gritty, slithering away when she walked on it.

'Hugh would enjoy this,' Adele remarked thoughtlessly.

'Do me a favour, Adele. Don't talk about Hugh. Please. I need time and peace, give me that, please.' Rose kept walking, her eyes on the misty blue horizon. In the shimmering distance, she could see a yacht, a sleek racer basking in the sun. Hugh loved boats, although it was years since they'd cruised the Shannon in one of those solid cruisers. Rose could remember the two of them setting off for a weekend, with nothing more taxing to do than negotiate the cruiser into tiny, sun-dappled harbours and meander along to some pretty pub for delicious, home-cooked food. It all came back to Hugh, really. She thought about him all the time, without any help from Adele. You couldn't spend forty years of your life with one person and then cut the cord, never looking back. Rose spent hours looking back. Even in this wonderful, obligation-free life she was living, there were many quiet moments where introspection was inescapable. If Hugh was cast in the part of poor Lot, she would have turned into a pillar of salt many times.

Adele walked on in silence. She didn't notice the pretty opalescent shells washed up on the beach. It would take more than taking her tights off to make Adele the sort of person who collected seashells.

Rose spotted a booth selling ice cream.

'What do you think, Della?' she asked. 'Would you like an ice cream?'

Adele smiled at the affectionate use of her childhood name. 'Why not,' she said.

*   *   *

The beds were set up by seven, and Freddie had concocted a simple meal based on salad, garlic bread and an omelette, which was ready to be cooked when Stella and Amelia arrived. While they waited, the three women sat outside in the golden evening, enjoying the evening sun. One of Freddie's precious vinyl records played in the background, sending the gentle rhythms of Hoagy Carmichael spinning out into the evening air. A bowl of stuffed olives and a jug of Freddie's Singapore Sling sat on the cast-iron table. Prinny lay panting across Rose's feet, while Pig and Mildred had thrown themselves down beside Freddie.

'The Viking evening doesn't start till eight,' Freddie remarked, 'so we should see some of it.'

'I'm surprised you're not involved,' Adele said tartly.

'Oh they asked me, but two years ago, we did Irish folklore and I was Queen Maeve and the trouble that white bull caused. The problem with these re-enactments is always the animals.'

Adele looked astonished. Rose grinned and took another olive.

'Look,' she cried suddenly, getting to her feet. The dogs jumped up too. 'They're coming!'

Amelia chattered wildly for the first ten minutes after she and Stella arrived, telling Granny that she'd got a hamster named Dimples, that she'd been to Moon's and gone on the big water slide, and that for Becky and Shona's birthday, Aunty Hazel had got a bouncy castle in the back garden. Shona fell off and bumped her head but Amelia didn't.

'I've missed you,' said Stella, holding her mother tightly. 'You've no idea how much I've missed you.'

'We've gone a month without seeing each other before,' said Rose, trying to hide how guilty and shocked she felt at the heartfelt plea in her daughter's voice.

'Yes, but that was different,' Stella said, her face still buried in Rose's shoulder. 'I knew you were there with Dad, this is different country, isn't it? Everything's changed.'

'We've been in touch every few days,' Rose protested,

remorse overwhelming her. She'd thought that Stella would understand her desire to get away from everything and sort out how she felt. And normally, although they spoke on the phone a lot, they didn't live in each other's pockets. Rose despised those mothers who demanded that their city-dwelling children trek obediently home every second week-end, refusing to believe that they had their own lives in another place. Rose had thought she'd made the right choice by avoiding all those pitfalls, but now it seemed as if she'd been mistaken.

Adele had been in the shadows and at that instant, Stella noticed her.

'Aunt Adele, hello, what are you doing here?' she asked stiffly.

'Adele's come to offer support,' Rose said quickly.

Stella looked just as surprised as Rose had been but she rallied quickly. 'That's nice,' she said.

Amelia loved Freddie's cottage and was delighted with the sleeping arrangements, especially her blow-up bouncy bed. Most of all, she adored the dogs, who returned the favour and clustered happily around her. Freddie knocked out the omelette at high speed so that the entire party would get to see some of the Viking show.

'It's history coming alive,' she told a wide-eyed Amelia, who was even more thrilled that she was going to be allowed to stay up late.

Stella was very quiet, so Rose found herself overcompensating in the conversation department, chattering on about the meals on wheels and how she'd toned up from walking so much with the dogs.

When the meal was finished, they walked down the lane to the Viking show. Amelia skipped on ahead, while Freddie slowed her pace to walk with Adele, leaving Rose and Stella in the middle of the party.

'You seem so happy here,' Stella said. 'You've made this life for yourself and,' she hesitated before voicing her fears, 'I can't help but feel that we're not a part of it.'

'Don't say that,' said Rose, stung. 'My being here isn't a rejection of you, Stella, it's just me reclaiming my life.'

'I know. I'm sorry, I really am.' Stella clung onto Rose's hand as they walked. 'I'm being selfish. You have a right to your life. I shouldn't have said that. I do want you to be happy, Mum. I just need to feel that Amelia and I are still a part of it. Tara and Holly feel the same.' This wasn't absolutely true. Tara, who seemed very distant and pre-occupied lately, a fact which worried her older sister, had said how depressing it was that the family seemed to have splintered.

'It's like a death in the family,' she'd told Stella on the phone the night before. 'Everything's changed, Mum's changed, and it's horrible.'

Holly, however, didn't seem as concerned and was more worried about their father. She hadn't mentioned feeling left out because Rose appeared content in her new, family-free life. Stella had put this down to Holly's guilt at having known about Hugh's affair and not telling their mother.

'You'll always be the biggest part of my life,' Rose said shakily. 'I'm your mother and I'm so proud of all of you. But . . .' She struggled to put what she felt into words. 'This isn't about the family. It's about your father and me. It's about me deciding what to do next, and it's easier to do it away from everyone. You must understand, Stella. If I stayed with you, surrounded by the memories of myself and your father, I'd be drawn back into our marriage, without having actually made any decisions about whether I wanted that or not. I know you think it's selfish of me being here but, I have to be a bit selfish. Can you understand that?'

They'd reached the enormous field behind the tiny Norman chapel and rowdy noises could be heard coming from beyond the hedge.

'I do. I suppose I hadn't thought of it like that before,' Stella said quietly. 'You were never selfish; that's why you didn't leave Dad, isn't it?'

Rose nodded. 'Selfish isn't supposed to be an option for mothers, as you know.'

Amelia was waiting for them to catch up. Rose and Stella each caught one of the little girl's hands and they swung her in the way she'd loved when she was a toddler.

'Mummy, Auntie Freddie says there's a horse thing on tomorrow. Can we go to that too?' Amelia asked.

Over her daughter's shining dark head, Stella's eyes met Rose's. 'Whatever you want, pet.'

Saturday had a holiday air to it. The gymkhana was a huge success and by evening they were all almost too tired to visit one of Freddie's neighbours who was hosting a huge barbecue. Amelia found two little girls of similar age to play with, leaving the grown-ups to enjoy the food and the chance of a sit-down with paper cups of sangria.

'My feet are killing me,' Adele groaned, lowering herself into one of the mismatched chairs in the neighbour's enormous back garden.

'Mine too,' said Freddie, sinking into the chair beside Adele's.

Rose was too restless to sit and prowled the garden, investigating the tiny herb garden at the end. On the other side of the dry stone wall was a field where sheep stood chewing contentedly. Stella came to find her.

'Isn't this lovely,' said Rose.

'Beautiful,' agreed Stella, perching on the stone wall. 'It's very calming here. Like the city is a million miles away and none of the stupid things you worry about really matter.'

'What stupid things would those be?' Rose asked, sitting beside her daughter.

Stella sighed. 'Life, the universe, you know.'

'I don't. Is it Nick?' Rose prompted. 'I thought you were very happy.'

'We *were*,' Stella replied. 'It's all become so complicated. Jenna hates me, and I mean that. It's not dislike, it's sheer hate, which is kind of hard to cope with. She's also behaving badly at school and Nick's ex clearly blames Nick for that. Nick *and* me, actually. I can just imagine what she's thinking: *If Nick had never met that woman, Jenna wouldn't be behaving like a monster, etc, etc. She's only a kid and how can she cope with her father's new life.* I feel like public enemy number one.'

Rose, who knew when to hold her tongue, said nothing.

'I wouldn't mind,' Stella continued, 'but Nick doesn't stand up to Jenna when she's behaving badly, which makes her worse. It's like he's deaf when she's making these horrible comments under her breath. He doesn't stand up for me.' It sounded so petulant saying it, but Stella couldn't help herself. Jenna's behaviour wiped out the calm, rational adult in her and brought out the furious screaming child instead.

'Poor you,' said Rose. 'I remember when you told me about Nick for the first time, you had a premonition this might happen.'

'Yeah, I've heard all the stepmom stories but I really thought I could handle it. I honestly didn't think it was going to be this bad. Sara is a lovely girl, she's funny and friendly, and she's really sweet to Amelia. But the other one . . . she's a nightmare child.'

'You must understand that Jenna's life has changed and the only person she can see to blame for that is you.'

'That's irrational,' snapped Stella.

'People aren't rational, children especially so. She is still a child,' Rose said. 'You have to be calm when you deal with her, let her see that her bad behaviour gets no rewards or no added attention. But you have to remain adult in all of this. And, even more importantly, you can't blame Nick for his daughter's behaviour.'

'Mum, I don't want you to be wise and see everybody else's point of view, I want you to be on my side!' Stella said heatedly.

'It's because I *am* on your side that I'm being wise.' Her mother stared at Stella. 'There's no benefit in my saying

"God, Jenna's a brat and Nick doesn't deserve you." Where will that get us? Nowhere. Listen, Stella, you have a good, strong relationship with Nick. It's worth fighting for. Jenna will learn to live with you eventually, and Nick's ex-wife will learn how to let go and live her own life. It's going to take time and patience, but it will be worth it. When you've got something special, it's worth fighting for it.'

Stella was silent. She didn't want to mention the one other gloomy factor lingering over her and Nick: the shock of Rose and Hugh's split. Seen through the prism of her parents' troubles, Stella's relationship with Nick appeared on shakier ground. If Rose and Hugh could separate, then what hope was there for Nick and her with all their complicated problems? How long would it last before everything, inevitably, went wrong? And was there any point in love at all if you just got hurt in the end?

'I suppose you're right,' she said. 'But it's hard to be love's middle-aged dream when you're always waiting for the next explosion. Nick and I do have something special, but ... it's so hard dealing with Jenna's hate all the time. I thought I could make her love me, I honestly thought we could be sort of a family ... Still, let's not talk about it any more. What I actually wanted to talk to you about was Tara. I'm worried about her.'

'Worried, why?' asked Rose, jerking her hand up from toying with the leaves of a fragrant thyme bush.

'I think there's something wrong with her and Finn. Not,' Stella added hurriedly, 'that she's said anything. But a few months ago, I got the feeling that all wasn't well. And on the night of the ruby wedding, they rowed and Finn stormed off. She wouldn't say what it was and now acts as if everything is perfect. You know Tara, she'd never tell you in a million years. But, I just know something's not quite right.'

Rose crumpled a sprig of thyme in her fingers absent-mindedly.

'She hasn't mentioned anything to me,' Rose said. 'But then, she wouldn't, would she? Not now.' She gave a bitter

474

little laugh. 'I've been so busy thinking about myself, that I've neglected the rest of you.'

'No you haven't.'

'I should talk to her,' Rose said, 'get her to come here for the weekend. She might be able to act as if everything's fine over the phone, but she wouldn't be able to do it with me in person. How's Holly?' she asked tentatively.

'Seems fine,' said Stella. 'She modelled at Joan's fashion show and never told us, the minx. I'd have loved to have gone to see her. I was thrilled to hear she'd done it, though, it might give her some confidence. Honestly, she's so gorgeous and talented, and she thinks she's anything but. It kills me to see her undervaluing herself; don't you agree?'

Rose felt the weight of guilt over Holly crush her. She could barely reply. She cast her mind back over the last month, when Stella and Tara had phoned regularly, anxiety in their voices. Holly had phoned too, but on those occasions when she'd reached only Rose's mobile phone answering service, she'd left a message but hadn't phoned back. When Rose had rung Holly's flat to return the call, the answering machine was always on. It was the same with her mobile phone. Rose couldn't suppress the thought that Holly didn't want to be contacted.

'Do you think that Holly might come down and stay too, when Tara comes?' Rose asked now.

'I'm sure she'd love to,' Stella said brightly.

Everyone except Freddie was tearful on Sunday afternoon. Rose, still crushed from feeling she'd let her daughters down by running away to stay with Freddie, hugged Stella as if they would never see each other again.

'I wish you'd talked to me about Dad,' Stella said quietly.

'I'm sorry, I just can't. Not yet,' Rose replied. 'Promise me you'll phone often and tell me about Nick.'

'Promise.'

'Granny, when will I see you again?' asked Amelia.

'Soon. I won't be here forever,' Rose said, 'Aunt Freddie's

going to throw me out sometime, so I'll come to stay with you.'

'Will you bring Prinny, Mildred and Pig?' Amelia wanted to know.

Even Adele laughed at this.

'Goodbye, Rose, take care,' she said, giving her sister-in-law the warmest hug they'd ever exchanged. 'If you're going to stay here, perhaps I could come again?'

'If I stay here, of course,' Rose said.

CHAPTER THIRTY

The following Friday evening, Joan, Kenny and Holly sat on the small balcony in the bigger flat and talked about the letter.

It was from SallyYvette Inc in New York and had been folded and unfolded so many times, it was beginning to resemble a piece of origami. Joan looked at it at least every ten minutes, just to remind herself that it wasn't a dream and that SYInc were actually asking her to join their design team in Manhattan in September.

'Me, they're asking me,' she said reverently, opening the precious letter again and running her fingers over the type as if some of the New York high fashion magic would enter her veins by osmosis.

'It's fantastic,' said Holly, for the hundredth time. She did her best to inject wild delight into her voice but it was hard. She adored Joan and was as proud as any parent that Joan's talent had been recognised. But the letter meant one thing: the beginning of the end of the terrible threesome's flat-sharing days. Holly knew that she, Joan and Kenny would never lose their close friendship but once Joan left, things wouldn't ever be quite the same again.

The three of them had their feet up on the iron railings and their faces to the sun as they caught the last few rays of a torrid June day. The street below them was busy with people heading off out for the evening. The man at number seventy-one was cutting his grass and the scent mingled with the heady smell of Kenny's prized, though somewhat stunted, herb pot which sat on the balcony in all weathers. This misshapen terracotta pot was designed with holes at odd places and was supposed to be perfect for growing herbs. The basil had long since died an unnatural death but the parsley was flourishing and the lavender ('Lavender's not a herb, is it?' Joan had asked the day he got it) was rampantly fragrant.

Holly was eating crisps, holding her bottle of fruit juice between her thighs, and trying to tell herself she had no right to feel miserable when Joan was getting this marvellous career chance.

'We'll miss you,' said Kenny mournfully. Kenny had taken the news worst. After an *Absolutely Fabulous* explosion of 'Sweetie, that's *fabulous*!', he'd realised that Joan would be leaving. 'Who'll forget to clean the shower now?' he asked, reaching out for a handful from Holly's bumper bag of cheese and onion crisps. 'Who'll take my avocado and cucumber face mask from the fridge and smear it on their toast? Who's going to put my Prada nylon T into the boil wash in the launderette?'

Holly giggled.

'Don't be sad,' begged Joan.

'We're not,' said Holly quickly. 'We're thrilled for you, we're just being selfish pigs and thinking of how lucky New York is going to be because you'll be there and we'll be here being lonely without you.'

'You can visit.'

Kenny perked up. 'There's this rumour of a designer outlet in the garment district where you can buy Calvin Klein pieces before they hit the stores. It could just be one of those urban myths, but imagine . . .' his voice trailed off dreamily, lost in a vision of exquisite shirts and sharply-tailored suits with him inside them.

'We'll find it, wherever it is,' promised Joan fiercely, as if this mission was the search for the Holy Grail. 'I'll track it down, right?'

Holly was floored by guilt. All poor Joan wanted was for

her two best friends to be happy for her, and there they were, whingeing like a couple of spoilt brats.

'We should make plans,' she said. 'A plan for your leaving party and a plan for when we come and visit you.'

Joan's eyes glittered suspiciously. Noticing this, Holly surged on. Joan never cried.

'In fact, we could help you find a flat in New York on the Internet.'

'No,' shrieked Kenny, 'we could go over with you for a long weekend and help. Feck the net.'

'Yes,' said Joan joyously. 'You'll both come, for more than a long weekend, right? You could come altogether!'

'Why not?' shrieked Kenny.

Holly thought of how she had nothing planned for the next hundred years. She also thought of Tom and how he and Caroline were up to their eyeballs planning the wedding of the century. Caroline drove up to Dublin every weekend now, clinging to Tom and insisting on honorary membership of their foursome, to the irritation of both Kenny and Joan. Holly never said anything when Joan complained about Caroline and her fake-friendship.

'I hate that woman, do you know that? She's so bloody plastic,' Joan raged. 'When she's sweet to me, I know she doesn't mean it. She's working out how useful I could be to her in the future. Well, if she thinks I'm designing her bloody wedding dress, she can get stuffed.'

'New York sounds great,' Holly said now. 'But how can we afford it?'

They all looked out over the balcony reflectively. Finances were always a problem. The landlord had put the rent up and Holly was doing as much overtime as she could to cope with the increase. Kenny was saving for a car, which would be invaluable for his styling work. Joan would have her ticket paid for, according to the letter from SYInc. 'I wonder will they send me first class?' she mused.

'Probably,' said Kenny. 'You'll fly first class and me and Holly will fly no class.'

'Is that on the wings?' joked Holly.

'No, with the suitcases. And it's BYOS too. Bring Your Own Sandwiches,' he added.

'If I get a first-class ticket, we could swap it for three economy ones,' Joan said.

'I always said you were a creative genius,' beamed Kenny, clinking his can of Sprite with Joan's bottled water.

The next evening Holly, shattered after a particularly busy day in Lee's, was on her knees sorting through her laundry. Both Kenny and Joan were out, the television schedule for Saturday was dire and Holly decided that she might as well celebrate her exciting single girl lifestyle by spending the evening in the launderette. To add an edge of untrammelled decadence, she planned to buy a magazine and some chocolate on the way there. Who said career girls don't have thrilling lives, she reflected wryly as she made neat piles of dark stuff, white stuff and things that had to be handwashed. The handwash stuff joined the permanently-growing pile in a basket. Tomorrow, Holly vowed, she would do it. The laundry had been heaped into two bags when the doorbell went. The landlord? Joan looking for a loan of some money? Holly went through the possibilities as she walked to the door.

Tom stood outside, looking uncomfortable. This wasn't new. Since the morning after Joan's fashion show triumph, he always looked uncomfortable when he met Holly. She knew that she probably looked the same. Their easy camaraderie had vanished the instant Tom had seen her returning home after the night with Vic. Now they muttered hello and went through the motions; politely saying things like 'how are you?' and even worse, 'how's work?' like strangers who meet at the same bus stop for years. Because Kenny, Joan and Caroline each talked enough for ten people, nobody really noticed the huge, yawning gaps in the conversation between Holly and Tom.

Holly leaned against the door jamb. 'Hi,' she said, noticing that he had something in his hand.

'Hi.' He followed her gaze and held up the something. It was a small envelope and he offered it to her. 'We're having an engagement party next week and this is your invitation.'

'Oh, thanks.' Holly took it. 'Er, do you want to come in?'

He nodded.

Holly led the way in and sat down. At least she hadn't got as far as pulling on something slobby and comfortable to schlep to the laundry, and was still wearing a chic work shirt and well tailored black trousers. Tom perched on the other couch but he didn't sit back and relax. He kept looking at the envelope in Holly's hands. She wasn't sure if he wanted her to open it or not, but she did anyway.

Trust Caroline, she thought, as she stared at the formal invitation which invited 'Holly & guest' to a party in a city-centre hotel in ten days time. The '& guest' bit really irritated Holly. She could imagine Caroline filling that in with a certain relish. Poor Holly, she hadn't any significant other to bring with her, so she could bring a *guest,* the unattached woman's face-saving device.

'I sort of imagined you'd have a party in Cork rather than Dublin,' Holly remarked.

'Caroline's moving to Dublin next month. She thought it would be a good way to start her life up here with a party,' Tom explained.

'Oh.' Holly wondered how many of Tom and Caroline's friends would be devoted enough to make the six-hour round trip from Cork and back for a mid-week party.

As if Tom could read her mind, he said: 'A lot of the Cork crowd probably won't be able to come, but Caroline says we've enough new friends here.'

Holly felt a certain sympathy for Caroline's old friends, ruthlessly consigned to the bottom of the pile as she went in search of new ones. She cast around for something else to say. 'Is it going to be a big party, then?'

A flash of irritation crossed Tom's face, so fleeting that Holly thought she must have imagined it. 'You know Caroline, she likes to make a splash. She's trying to get Vic's brother's band to play.'

At the mention of Vic's name, Holly cringed inwardly. Tom wouldn't know how things had ended with Vic: Holly still squirmed when she thought of that.

Suddenly, she was too weary to spend any more time having a wooden conversation with a man she'd cared for from afar. Tom belonged to someone else anyhow, and he obviously disapproved of what he believed to be her whirlwind relationship with Vic. Holly had had just about as much of other people's disapproval as she could cope with. She stood up. 'I've got to go out, Tom,' she said apologetically. 'Sorry about that.'

'Oh yeah.' He got up quickly. 'Me too.'

'Yeah,' Holly glanced at her watch. 'Time flies and all that.'

'Yeah.' A brief smile flashed across his face. 'So you can come to the party? With Vic?'

Somehow, Holly managed to fix a noncommittal look on her face. 'I'm sure I'll be able to,' was all she said.

When Tom was gone, her enthusiasm for the launderette had vanished. But it had to be done. Holly pulled her denim jacket on, grabbed her wallet and the washing, and set out.

Soapy Susi's was virtually empty, apart from one gloomy looking man in a shabby suit who'd clearly had a bad day at the office. Holly averted her eyes from his miserable face. She stuck her washing in the giant tubs and wished she had enough money to afford the service wash all the time. Or a washing machine of her own. It had been lovely when Kenny wasn't too busy for laundry duty: he liked doing the washing. Holly made herself comfortable on an old vinyl chair, carefully opened the foil wrapping on her chocolate bar and flicked to the first page of her magazine.

She was deep in an article on celebrity break-ups when the door of Soapy Susi's squeaked open. She didn't look up. Eye contact was fatal in the launderette. With no diversion (you couldn't count the wonky television set high up on one wall and permanently tuned to the shopping channel), it was easy to get embroiled in a two-hour conversation with a complete nutter. Holly's Bermuda Triangle effect meant that if a weirdo of any variety was in the vicinity, they would somehow detect her presence and rush, open-armed, to find her. Her most disastrous encounter had happened the previous month when she'd been there with Joan. The sweet, confused, elderly man in yellow paisley pyjamas *hadn't* lost his way and wandered in by mistake. No. He'd been a flasher who'd gleefully flashed the whole of Soapy Susi's clientele just as a well-intentioned Holly was asking him if he knew where he was and could she phone anyone to come and pick him up. Joan had laughed so much, she'd sounded like a hyena.

'I thought he might be lost and we should phone the police or someone,' said a bewildered Holly when Pyjama Man had legged it out the door before any of the astonished customers could get a hold of him.

'We could phone the police, all right,' screeched Joan between hyena noises, 'but they might say we're wasting their time over a flasher wielding nothing more than a cocktail sausage.'

Holly had learned her lesson. Eyes down and don't get involved: that was her new motto.

She turned the page, still nibbling her chocolate. Holly could make one chocolate bar last ten minutes as she savoured every forbidden sliver. *What's Your Love Match?* screamed the headline at the top of a feature on horoscopes and picking the perfect partner. Holly instantly looked up what sort of man liked Cancerians. Her ideal partner would be *strong, kind and able to nudge gentle, shy Cancerians out of their shell. Your ideal mate understands that even though you appear reserved, you're still passionate and wild under that gentle exterior.*

Holly popped the last square of chocolate into her mouth, scanning to see if Cancerians were compatible with Taureans,

Tom's sign, when somebody loomed over her. On lunatic-alert, she jerked her head up to see Tom himself, holding an empty sports bag.

'I'm glad I'm not the only one with thrilling Saturday night plans,' he said ruefully, grinning at her. He sat down beside Holly, stretched out his long legs, and leaned back in the vinyl chair.

Holly couldn't resist seeing the funny side of it. 'Wait till nine, then this place comes alive,' she said. 'You have no idea . . . Man, it's hot. There's dancing, occasionally nudity, and the shopping channel gets really interesting.'

'Fancy that,' said Tom, still grinning. 'Tell me about the nudity bit. You mean people come in and strip down to their underwear, like that old Levi's ad?'

Holly had a sudden vision of Pyjama Man and she started to laugh.

'You wouldn't believe it if I told you,' she said.

'Try me.'

He laughed at the story, but not as heartily as Joan had. 'You must have been upset,' he said, probing gently.

'Well, not really. If Joan hadn't been with me, I'd have cried. But she laughed so much that it sort of made it funny.'

'Good for Joan.'

'You see, normally, I'm on my own when these mad things happen. It's the magnetic effect; I attract strange people.'

'Don't be silly.' Tom looked irritated that Holly would think this of herself.

'No, it's true,' she said. 'I am magnetic in a bad sense. Some women have an aura that makes men swoon at their feet. I have an aura that makes drunks chase me.'

'Come on,' laughed Tom. 'You're joking. They don't.'

'They do,' insisted Holly. 'On the bus, drunk people always sit beside me. Even in work, there's this wino called Rasher who sleeps outside the store and if the security man turns his back, Rasher rushes in and he always comes to me!'

'That's because he knows you're kind and that you care,'

484

Tom pointed out. 'I bet nobody else in Lee's even knows his name.'

'Well, no. Security know his name because they have to make him leave. I mean, all I do is talk to him when I pass him.'

'See, you're kind and the world's lonely, sad people can sense that.'

Holly's inappropriate blushing mechanism went into action.

Tom, noticing, changed the subject. 'What are you reading?'

The blush moved from plain old crimson to an interesting shade of magenta. 'Er . . . nothing,' mumbled Holly. She didn't want Tom to see her poring over an article on finding her ideal date via their star sign. Men thought horoscopes were daft. In fact, the only man she'd ever known who was into horoscopes was Kenny, who was more in touch with his feminine side than most men. But Tom had gently taken the magazine from her and was reading, fascinated.

'What's your sign?' he asked.

'Cancer. Because I'm crabby,' she added jokily.

'There are lots of words to describe you, Holly, but crabby wouldn't be one of them.' Tom kept reading. 'I'm Taurus,' he said.

'Really?' she said innocently.

She watched him read and it looked as if he was reading the piece on Cancerians. But he couldn't be, unless Caroline was one too.

'What's Caroline's sign?' she asked.

'Leo,' he answered shortly.

Extrovert, passionate, memorable, driven to success. People noticed Leos, in Holly's opinion. And Caroline was certainly all those things, she just wasn't very nice. Holly wished Tom had picked a nicer Leo, a kind, genuine one. Caroline was too hard-edged for him. But then, what did she know? Holly stopped reading over Tom's shoulder. It was nice sitting talking, almost like they used to talk before Caroline had daintily crash-landed into Holly's life.

Tom flicked a couple of pages.

'Oh, *Brainbox or Bimbo: Test Your Brain Power*. We've got to do this, Holly,' he said enthusiastically.

Whatever she'd planned for the evening, Holly had never expected that she'd be sitting in a launderette with Tom, arguing good-humouredly over the answers in a quiz. It took them ages to finish it and there was a definite squabble over the spatial relations bit.

Then, they turned to the puzzle page, and ended up with the crossword. At intervals, they both checked their laundry. The time flew. They were still struggling with the group term for larks when Holly noticed that her tumble dryer had stopped. For the first time ever, she wished she could spend longer in the laundry.

She got up and began unloading the machine, folding everything carefully, anything to delay. When she had finished, she smiled at Tom. 'I suppose I should go,' she said.

'You could wait for me, mine will be finished soon,' he said.

Holly hesitated and glanced at her watch, more because she didn't want to look too puppy-dog eager than for any other reason, but somehow Tom misinterpreted this gesture.

'Sorry,' he said. 'It's getting late. You should go. Say hello to Vic for me.'

Holly was horrified. He thought she was meeting Vic. She opened her mouth to say that she and Vic weren't seeing each other any more, but would that sound worse? Like she was a total floozy and bedded Vic after three weeks only to dump him a week later. These thoughts raced through her mind at record speed. What could she say?

Tom resolved the issue by handing her the magazine. 'Thanks for keeping me company,' he said. 'It was fun.' That guarded look was back in his eyes.

'Yes, it was,' said Holly dully. She took the magazine, shouldered her bags of washing, and went out into the night. If only Tom knew.

She walked slowly up the street and replayed her mental Vic: The End video.

Feeling cowardly, she'd managed to avoid Vic's phone calls for two days. Finally, he'd turned up to pick her up after work in Lee's.

'He's cute,' Bunny said to Holly as Vic wandered round children's wear. She hadn't seen Vic before, having been on holiday at the time of Joan's fashion show.

'He is cute,' agreed Holly, 'but I just don't fancy him.'

'Does he know that?'

Holly sighed heavily. 'No, I have to tell him tonight.'

She and Vic sat in a juice bar waiting for their drinks, strawberry surprise (Holly) and a wheatgrass shot (Vic).

In all her twenty-seven years, Holly had never dumped anyone. She'd always been the dumpee and simply didn't know how to handle things from the other side. The dumpee bit their bottom lip, became fascinated with their cuticles, and managed to hold the tears back when they nodded that *'Yes, you're right. We're not suited, we need some space, of course we can still be friends.'*

She'd thought *that* was bad, but being on the other side was worse. For the past two days, she'd gone through every permutation and combination of saying 'I like you as a friend but not as a boyfriend.' Now, all those carefully-chosen words deserted her.

'I'm sorry, Vic,' she blurted out. 'I just don't . . . I can't . . . em, I don't think we're right for one another.'

Vic took this remarkably well, but then, he hadn't been the brightest guy in his year in med school for nothing.

'It's Tom Barry, huh?'

Holly felt six inches tall.

'I'm sorry,' she said, hanging her head. 'I'm not involved with him or anything.'

'But you are crazy about him?' Vic said shrewdly. 'I'd almost prefer if there was someone else,' he said. 'Otherwise, it means that I'm such a hideous bore that you can't bear to be with me. And I did always have an inkling that you liked Tom more than you let on.'

Holly felt a mist of tears shimmer over her eyes.

Their juices arrived and Vic knocked back his shot in one. 'Yeuch, this stuff is vile.'

'It takes a while to get used to wheatgrass,' snuffled Holly.

Vic took their bill from the table top. 'I'll pay this and go,' he said.

Holly shook her head and reached out to take the bill from him. Her wrist caught the top of her untouched juice drink and knocked it all over the table. Quick as a shot, Vic grabbed a wedge of napkins from the counter and soaked up the sea of shocking pink.

'Sorry,' said Holly tearfully. 'Sorry about *everything* . . .'

'Don't get upset,' Vic said gently, hunkering down beside her chair. He handed her a napkin to wipe a glob of strawberry juice from her hand. His kindness made her feel even more upset and her snuffles threatened to turn into full-blown sobs.

'Don't cry. You're a pretty special person, Holly. It's a pity I'm not your sort of guy. But, hey?' He shrugged. 'You win some, you lose some. Nobody died here today, right?'

She nodded, wiping her eyes with the napkin.

Vic got to his feet and smiled down at her. 'See you around.'

And he was gone. Holly had sat there for ages, hating herself. Vic was such a lovely, decent man. Why couldn't she love him? Or was she destined to always hanker for what she couldn't have?

The laundry felt like it was growing heavier every second, and Holly was grateful when she reached home. She left the bags in the hall and immediately turned the TV on. She didn't care what sort of rubbish was on, she'd watch it. Tonight, she didn't want to be alone with her thoughts.

CHAPTER THIRTY-ONE

'So tell me, what sort of *research* do you do?' The reporter blinked at Tara from behind discreet gold-framed glasses, her tape recorder at the ready, her every gesture earnestly probing. 'Do you get inside the minds of your characters? How difficult is it to write about subjects like, oh, say euthanasia or adultery? Those have been fabulous storylines, by the way. And is it true that there's a big alcoholism storyline coming up?'

Tara did her best to wipe the look of misery off her face. It wasn't the poor reporter's fault that *National Hospital*'s recent storylines could have been plucked from Tara's personal life and whacked up on screen without any rewriting whatsoever. The guilt about going to bed with Scott Irving grew inside her like an abscess, getting bigger and more painful with every day. When she stared at her computer screen, she could see Finn's face. Every sentence she wrote made her think of him. Every scene seemed to have some resonance with her guilt. And it felt as if everyone and everything were conspiring to make her feel worse.

Bea, newly-hired junior features writer with women's magazine *Style,* allowed her gaze to flicker past Tara's preoccupied face. Everything was so interesting on the set. People rushed around all the time, with mobile phones and headsets, talking and gesturing, discussing camera angles, dragging huge cables around. Bea could barely believe she was spending the whole day on the *National Hospital* story and she'd been promised access to all areas, which included watching some of the show being filmed. She hoped she might get to interview that gorgeous Dr McCambridge who really was her favourite but there was no sign of him anywhere . . .

Tara dragged herself back to the task in hand. Aaron had specifically asked her to talk to Bea. On the set, they were about to film a pivotal scene where one of the main characters owned up to an affair with a colleague. She was a junior doctor and originally Tara had wondered, given the workload of real junior doctors, how the hell the poor woman would have the energy to have sex with her husband, never mind an extra-marital fling. These days, Tara tried very hard not to think about the concept of extramarital flings full stop.

'Research is key,' Tara heard herself saying. She hated the word *key*. It was real middle-management gobbledegook and just using it was proof that her thought processes were as scrambled as satellite TV signals. 'All the writers sit around and brainstorm when we're working on a particular storyline. We bounce ideas off each other. It doesn't work as well when you're sitting at home on your own. Working with the team is what makes it happen.'

Bea was fascinated, holding her tiny tape recorder under Tara's nose as if Tara was revealing the meaning of life, plus how to get rid of cellulite.

'But where do the ideas come from?' asked Bea, eyes flicking down to the huge list of questions that she'd spent the previous night thinking up. 'Like the scene today with Dr Kavanagh. I'm a huge fan and I've been watching those episodes where you know her husband is going to find out and she's doing her best to cover it up. Oh, it's so real. You really get into her heart and see how awful she feels. It must be difficult to get inside someone's head like that?'

Tara managed a thoughtful expression, as if she was mulling over the precise way to answer all these knotty questions. It would certainly make for an interesting article if she said '*Yes, I know all about adultery because I just cheated on my husband with one of the scriptwriters. I'm talking about*

Scott Irving, who's pretty hunky and goes like a train but now he's not talking to me, which means the atmosphere on set is icy and uncomfortable. And my husband suspects, so he's not talking to me either, which certainly helps my understanding of the subject. So yes, personal experience heightens your ability to write about something . . .' Instead, she shrugged. 'I didn't write today's scene,' she said. 'I've been working on a different storyline, the one about Tony Carlisle.'

'She could have kicked herself as soon as she said it. The Tony Carlisle story was about a consultant's descent into alcoholism, which really was her specialised subject. Now, Bea would want to know what sort of research she'd done on that and as soon as Tara thought about Finn, she would cry, she knew she would.

'Oh, there's Dr McCambridge,' whispered Bea excitedly, the interview forgotten. 'I love him. Is he nice or is he too starry and grand to speak to normal people? I'd love to talk to him but he's probably fed up with being interviewed.' She looked eagerly at Tara with shiny, star-struck eyes.

'Not at all,' lied Tara. Saved by the bell. 'He loves reporters.' She waved at Stephen who came over at high speed once he spotted the tape recorder.

Up close, Stephen was even more heartbreakingly attractive than he was onscreen and Bea reacted the way they all did: she blushed, broke out into a cold sweat and reached a shaking hand out towards his.

'Hi,' said Stephen, sinking into a chair. 'Honestly, what a bloody disaster. I told the PA I had to get away early today to go to the dentist and now I check and I'm shooting till eight!'

Tara smothered a smile. If Stephen went to the dentist as often as he said he did, he'd have teeth of solid gold. She reckoned he just wanted to doss off early because it was opening night for a Pinter play. At least half the cast had already pleaded medical emergencies, babysitting problems and ill relatives in order to get home early.

'Do you always work that late?' asked Bea, the hand holding the tape recorder still a bit shaky as she held it closer to Stephen's handsome face. 'I thought acting on a show like this would involve more regular hours, even if it's not quite nine to five.'

'I wish! The director is a bloody slave-driver!' snapped Stephen before starting off on his tried and tested rant about long hours, low pay, zero rehearsal time, the lack of respect for soap actors, and reams of new lines to learn every day.

'Not to mention no time off for other projects,' he added grimly, referring to a lucrative role in a French film that had been shot in Connemara the previous winter. It would have paid his tax bill too.

'If I was to tell you what goes on behind the scenes, you wouldn't believe it,' Stephen added maliciously.

Tara felt a moment's guilt. The publicity person who'd been taking care of Bea had vanished, and would no doubt be furious that Stephen had been allowed to speak to her unchaperoned. He might have been the star of the show and become hugely successful because of it, but Stephen was one of those people who like to feel aggrieved over something. He never realised that he was far more powerful and privileged than many of the cast.

'Very little rehearsal time, shooting scenes back to back so you never get a change to work on a scene,' he listed off his grievances, 'and as for storylines. Huh. Lately, I've been stuck with the storylines from hell.' He glared crossly at Tara. 'Like the love scenes with that stupid Sherry DaVinci. My character would never *look* at an idiot like her.'

He sounded so furious that Bea gulped and edged back in her seat.

'Stephen.' Armed with a clipboard and a radio mike, the production assistant smiled over at Stephen, hoping she wasn't interrupting anything or she'd get a tongue-lashing.

Without so much as saying goodbye to Bea or Tara, Stephen stomped off.

'He wasn't quite like I imagined,' Bea whispered.

'He's the exception,' Tara said, taking pity on her. 'Most of the actors and actresses on the show are fantastic people. I must introduce you to Allegra Armstrong, she loves working on *National Hospital* and she's a real professional, as well as being lovely. You'll really like her.'

'Thanks,' murmured Bea.

'You see, Stephen's very vocal about the down side of acting,' continued Tara, 'although he does have a point. Acting in a soap is a tough job but because everyone sees the actors looking glam in press interviews, nobody cottons onto the difficult parts. It's actually quite a small cast, and they work very long hours to shoot three episodes a week. They get a couple of days to learn their lines, then they've got to come out here and perform. The technical rehearsals are really for the benefit of the crew, so nobody's waiting to see if the actor has a scene right or not. And then they're totally at the mercy of the viewers. Most of their contracts are only renewed every season, and if a character gets bad feedback, they're out. Imagine being constantly under that sort of pressure.'

'I never thought of it that way,' said Bea, frantically writing notes in case her recorder packed up at this vital point. 'You sounded a bit critical there, Tara. Don't you like working here?'

In the distance, Tara could see Scott Irving pop his head round a partition.

She didn't answer the question immediately, concentrating on watching him. He was clearly searching for Aaron.

She sunk down in her seat, not wanting that laser gaze to rest on her. Scott would stare with such naked dislike that Tara frequently wilted under his gaze. Not that she made this obvious. She stared back defiantly, giving him her toughest 'You're confusing me with somebody who gives a shit!' look.

'Of course I do,' she said automatically. 'I love it. We all do.'

'I'll have to go, Bea,' she said, looking round for someone

to off-load the reporter onto. 'Oh gosh, have I asked you everything?' Bea riffled through her notes and checked her list of questions.

'Tell me about the National TV awards – the team won one. Was that the highlight of your career?'

Tara remembered that night so many months ago, a time when her life had been on track, when she'd had a marriage, when she hadn't known that Finn was drinking himself to death, when her parents lived happily together like normal parents, when she wasn't an adulterous bitch. It seemed like a million years ago.

'Fantastic,' she said woodenly. 'It was a fantastic night, definitely the highlight.'

Finn's car was there when Tara got home, which was unusual these days. Since the night of Godzilla's infamous party, Finn had been coming home later and later. Suffused with guilt and terrified he'd guessed her terrible secret, Tara felt she could say nothing to him. It was checkmate. She tiptoed around without mentioning his drinking, ready to endure anything as penance for betraying him. As long as he never found out, she could cope. In time, they'd confront the problem of Finn's drinking but only when Tara's own demons were laid to rest. If they ever were.

'Hi,' she said, letting herself into the apartment. She dumped her briefcase, kicked off her shoes and reached under the hall table for the comfy espadrilles she liked to wear as slippers in the summer.

'Hi.' Finn was in the kitchen eating breakfast cereal, which was probably one of the few things left to eat in the house.

Tara picked a blackening banana out of the fruit bowl and peeled it, vowing to visit the supermarket at the weekend. They were out of so many household staples it would be easier to say what they weren't out of.

'We should talk,' he said. 'About us.'

Tara's toes curled in her espadrilles. 'What do you mean?' she asked, stalling for time.

'I mean, we should talk about our marriage and what's left of it.' Finn took another spoonful of cereal.

'What do you mean by that?' Tara asked again.

Finn finished the cereal and dumped the bowl in the sink. He faced her. 'Have. Some. Respect. For. My. Intelligence,' he said slowly.

Adrenaline coursed through Tara's body as the fight-or-flight reaction kicked in.

'Even now, you're denying that there's something wrong, Tara. I thought you were smarter than that. There's no point lying. I *know* you slept with somebody. I don't know who,' Finn added, 'but I know you did it. In fact, I don't really give a fuck who it was because I don't care any more.'

Tara hadn't known that she was capable of experiencing such fear. Her heart plummeted deep into her solar plexus. She opened her mouth to speak but all that emerged was a guttural gasp of shock.

'I was waiting for you to tell me, you see,' Finn went on. He leaned back against the sink with his arms folded, observing her coldly. The easy warmth in his expression was gone, along with the sleepy-eyed sensuality and the faint turn-up at the corner of his beautiful mouth. Finn wasn't smiling any more. 'Call me stupid, but I had this vague notion that our marriage meant something to you and that you'd come clean about whatever happened. You were under strain, we were experiencing problems, whatever. We could have moved on, Tara. I'd have forgiven you, I loved you.'

Tara could only stare at him mutely, shame burning inside her. Then, the tense of his sentence kicked in. *Loved*. He'd said loved. Not love.

'You were different afterwards,' he went on. 'The next evening when you came home, I knew instantly you'd fucked someone else. Did you think I wouldn't notice?'

Tara longed to rush over and throw her arms round him, cradling him close so that his head could dip to kiss her face and she could taste the sweetness of his lips gently against hers. She could make it better if she did that, she knew she could. Finn couldn't resist her.

'The love bite on your neck was a dead giveaway too.'

She thought of her feeble attempts at camouflage.

'Finn, listen . . .' she began.

'No, I won't,' he exploded. 'I would have listened a few weeks ago but not now. It's over, Tara. We should never have married each other. We barely knew each other. What the hell were we thinking of?'

'We loved each other,' gasped Tara, 'that's why we got married. It doesn't have to be over, Finn. We can get counselling, talk to someone, get all the problems out in the open.'

'Spare me the counselling shit,' he snapped. 'I can't think of anything worse than laying our bloody misery out for some head-wrecker to analyse. My head's wrecked enough as it is, I don't need it further screwed up trying to sort out our *relationship issues*. Go on your own. I won't be around to watch.'

'No!' she yelled, rushing to him and putting her arms round him. 'We can sort it out, Finn, we love each other and that's all you need, right?' She was babbling now, her loving words tumbling out any old way instead of in the careful sentences that would show Finn that she adored him.

'Forget the dramatics, Tara. This isn't an episode of your show. It's real life and it's over.' With uncharacteristic roughness, he shrugged her off him.

'Don't go,' she wailed. But he was gone anyway and the next thing she heard was the front door slamming. At least he hadn't taken anything with him, Tara reasoned with herself. He'd be back, she knew it, and then she could make everything all right. She'd tell him that she'd felt lost and alone because of his drinking, but that they could deal with that. She'd been stressed, she'd acted out of character, she loved him and no matter how much he hated what she'd done, she hated it more. And she hated herself.

Still working out what she'd say, she made her way slowly

into the living room but stopped at the door. Something was wrong, where was all their stuff? The stereo, the CDs, the black leather recliner that Finn loved even though it was old and the leather was paper-thin in places: all gone.

Blindly, she rushed into their bedroom. The wardrobe doors were open and Finn's side was cleared out. The only things left were the shirts she'd bought him, hanging forlornly in the empty space. His clock radio was gone, along with all his books, magazines and photos. He must have done it today while she was at work.

Walking shakily like an invalid on her feet for the first time in ages, Tara returned to the living room and numbly surveyed what was left. She'd spent months remarking that they had too much stuff between them and that the apartment would benefit from a ruthless clean out. Well, it was certainly cleaned out now. Tara sank onto the couch.

Finn was gone for good and it was all her fault.

CHAPTER THIRTY-TWO

The weather in Castletown had changed. As if Mother Nature had decided to reflect Rose's darkening mood, the sun sulked and sent clouds out in her place. Storms wracked the east coast, dispatching punishing winds and torrential rain to keep the locals and holidaymakers indoors.

Rose sat at the window in Nettle Cottage for the third day in a row and watched colossal waves topped with dancing white caps in the distance. There were no boats beyond the shelter of the harbour, not with gale force warnings on every weather forecast.

'I hate the rain,' remarked Freddie, pulling on an elaborate dog-walking-in-the-rain costume that included a strange-looking oilskin that Sherlock Holmes might have liked.

'It's depressing, all right,' agreed Rose, still staring blankly into the middle distance. She'd felt so happy to see Stella and Amelia, but now, that happiness had vanished and all that was left was a lingering sense that she'd let everyone down. Tara, Holly, even Adele. They all needed her and she'd swanned off and left them. It wasn't as if she hadn't known about Hugh for years. She had. She'd just chosen now to make her anger public and they'd all been innocent victims caught in the crossfire.

'Come on, Rose,' urged Freddie, jamming a hat firmly down on her snow-white head. 'Come for a walk with me. It'll do you good to get out. You've been stuck in the house since Sunday apart from yesterday's meals on wheels.'

'No,' said Rose. 'I'm not in the mood.'

'Suit yourself,' said Freddie easily.

She was gone an hour and when she returned, wet and windswept with three happy, muddy dogs, Rose didn't appear to have moved a muscle.

Freddie said nothing but took herself off to the bathroom for a boiling hot bath to ease her aching muscles. Her left ankle twinged where she'd put her foot down on an unsteady piece of bank by the stream and it had collapsed under her. The ankle had hurt when she walked on it, and now, after the long trek home, it felt ominously bigger than the other ankle.

In the bath, it seized up altogether and it took all of Freddie's strength to haul herself out. Sitting in an ungainly heap on the cotton bath rug, naked, wet and with a throbbing ankle, even the indefatigable Freddie felt a frisson of fear for the future. She would not give up her enormous roll-top bath for some old-lady shower thing with a sit-up bath. She'd die first. She might be getting older but she wasn't an invalid. After a few minutes rest where she'd given herself a stern talking to for such miserable thoughts, she hobbled out of the bathroom, wrapped in her Chinese silk dressing gown.

'Rose,' she said, wincing at the pain, 'I don't suppose you'd have a look at my ankle. I seem to have twisted it.'

Rose jumped up in concern. 'Freddie, what did you do to it?' she asked, helping her aunt to the couch.

'Sort of twisted it by the stream,' Freddie said, as Rose helped her swing both legs onto the couch.

'That looks very swollen and painful,' Rose said worriedly. 'I'd better call the doctor.'

'Nonsense,' declared Freddie. 'There's not a thing wrong with it that a rest and some arnica won't cure.'

'You're overruled,' said Rose firmly. Freddie looked mutinous at this attempt to impinge upon her independence, so Rose sweetened the pill. 'Besides,' she said airily, picking up the phone, 'the sooner your ankle heals, the sooner you'll be back walking the dogs again. They're never entirely happy walking with just me, you know. They keep looking back to see where you are.'

Freddie grinned and relaxed back against the cushions. 'That's a classic piece of manipulation,' she said, 'but as it was so expertly done, I won't complain.'

The doctor arrived late that afternoon. He strapped Freddie's ankle up, gave her painkillers and drugs to take any inflammation down, and told her to stay off it for as long as possible. He also checked her blood pressure and chest.

'Fit as a fiddle,' he remarked, putting his stethoscope back in his bag. 'Freddie, you're living proof that lots of wine, fresh air and not worrying are the secret to a long life.' His eyes narrowed. 'Have you stopped smoking those cigarillos yet?'

'No,' said Freddie defiantly.

The doctor laughed and Rose joined in. 'My other patients all lie when I ask them things like that, but you're always brutally honest.'

'I have a couple every day and they haven't killed me yet,' Freddie pointed out.

The doctor refused a cup of tea because he was on his way to the Albertine Nursing Home, which was on the far side of Castletown.

'They do such wonderful work there,' he said, 'and they've lost another care worker this week. Without volunteers, I don't know how they're going to stay open. The staff are fully stretched as it is. I don't know what'll happen to all the patients if they have to close.'

'Blast this ankle,' said Freddie furiously. 'If I wasn't laid up, I could help.' Her eyes lit up. 'But if you got me some sort of crutch, I could hobble around . . .'

'You'll do no such thing,' said Rose. 'You'll rest until your ankle's better. I'll help. I've no experience of nursing homes, but I can make beds and that sort of thing,' she said to the doctor. 'Would that be any good?'

Both he and Freddie looked delighted at this offer.

'You'd be perfect,' he said. 'I'll phone the matron and get her to call you. In the meantime, you rest up, Madam,' he said to Freddie.

It was nice to be looking after someone again, Rose thought on Thursday morning as she made breakfast for Freddie. Under normal circumstances, Freddie required absolutely no looking after and prided herself on fierce independence.

'You're a natural at this,' Freddie said as Rose laid a tray on her lap.

'At making scrambled eggs?' laughed Rose.

'No, looking after people. You need people to look after,' Freddie said. 'It's the motherly instinct.'

'I suppose I do.' Rose finished her own coffee and got ready for dog-walking duties. Then, she was off to do the meals on wheels run on her own. Being busy was invigorating, she decided. She'd forgotten how good it felt to feel in charge of a host of things, things that would fall down like a house of cards if she wasn't around. In Kinvarra, she'd been running the house, taking care of Hugh and taking responsibility for her various charities. Here, she'd had no real responsibilities at all.

Freddie, on the other hand, couldn't conceal her growing impatience at being stuck on the couch with her ankle up. By the time Rose came back from meals on wheels and the supermarket, Freddie was bored rigid.

'I hate this!' she groaned. 'Lying on a couch reading is no fun unless you're *not* supposed to be doing it. And I can't do anything.'

Rose, with many years of rearing small fractious children behind her, racked her brains for something to occupy her aunt.

'Your box of photos!' she said, in triumph. 'You said you've been meaning to date and sort them into albums for years.'

Freddie brightened.

'I'll rush down to the town and see if I can buy some

albums,' Rose volunteered. Before she went, she found the big dusty box which Freddie had stored on top of her wardrobe for decades. She settled the box on a low table beside the couch so that Freddie wouldn't have to move to go through the photos.

'When I get back, I'll get dinner started. I bought some lovely lamb pieces and you can tell me how you'd like them. I'll help with the photos then.'

Freddie didn't answer, already lost in sheaves of sepia-toned memories.

In Castletown, Rose met the doctor who wanted to know if Freddie was managing to keep off her ankle. Then, she bumped into a posse of her aunt's poker friends who promised they'd be up on Friday night for a game.

When she got home, Freddie had abandoned the couch and was sitting at the dining room table with her hoarded photos spread all around. Her strapped-up ankle was resting on one of the dining chairs.

'Look, Rose, pictures of Anna. I thought I'd lost these ones.'

Rose leaned over the table and looked at three tiny black and white photos of her mother. She looked younger than Rose could ever remember seeing, her dark hair girlishly loose, her figure slight and youthful.

'I've let her down,' Rose said, unable to take her eyes from the photo.

'In what way?' Freddie asked idly.

'By not staying married. I did my best to keep it going, Freddie. Mother was so happy when I married Hugh, it was what she'd always wanted, to see me move up in the world.'

Freddie took off her glasses and rubbed the bridge of her nose where the glasses had made an indentation. 'I still don't understand why you stayed with Hugh. If you knew he'd had affairs with these women, why didn't you confront him? Because you did mind, didn't you?'

'Of course I minded,' said Rose. 'I adored Hugh, I was devastated when I found out the first time but who could

I talk to? Who could I tell? Adele? Hugh's mother? My mother?'

'Why didn't you confront him?'

'I don't know.'

'Pride, Rose. Pride kept you from saying anything. You didn't want to admit that there was anything wrong in the Miller paradise. You clearly got all the pride out of your system when you flipped at your ruby wedding and gave the locals something to think about. Now you've got to continue the work.'

Rose began to feel irritated at this attack on her. She hadn't cheated on anyone. Hugh was the person at fault here. 'You said you wouldn't get involved,' she said.

'No, I decided not to until you were ready for some straight talking,' Freddie said. 'Now, you're ready. Go back to Hugh and talk to him, for God's sake. Even if you kill each other within five minutes, at least you'll have faced up to it. You can't run away forever, Rose.'

'I'm not running away,' protested Rose.

'You are. You ran away from your past, you know. You could never reconcile your new life with your old one, I could see that.'

Rose stared at Freddie, shocked now.

Freddie spoke sensibly and kindly, the way she always did, but the words still hurt.

'Rose, you have to heal yourself before you can move on,' Freddie continued. 'I know this is painful, but let's keep going. You never confronted Hugh because you didn't want his family to think that you'd failed somehow, and you had to prove that you were just as good as them. And, Rose,' Freddie was gentle, 'you never seemed to realise that you were always just as good as the Millers.'

The truth of her words were like little chinks of light in Rose's mind. She had done her best to prove that everything in her life was perfect; it was her defence. She'd done it when Holly had been born and Rose had somehow kept her misery and depression to herself. Nobody must know. There could be no visible cracks in Rose's life. Because of that, the misery lingered for years and poor Holly had suffered. Rose's pride had hurt her darling baby.

'Anna was happy because you didn't have to work your fingers to the bone like she did,' Freddie went on. 'She was proud of what she'd done, that was an achievement to her, getting you out of the poverty our family had grown up with. But you felt ashamed of having left, didn't you?'

'Yes and no,' said Rose thoughtfully. 'It was just that I never felt I quite belonged anywhere.' She remembered how her mother had insisted she stay on at school when most others of her age had long since given up. Anna Riordain had given birth to three children and had seen one of them die as a baby. Stoic in the face of this tragedy, Anna was determined that nothing would touch Rose and her brother, James. Six years older, James had grown up with a plan to emigrate to Australia, and when he was just seventeen, he had. Bereft of her beloved son, Anna set her sights high for her only daughter.

Rose could have helped out on the farm as a teenager; indeed, most young girls left school in their early teens to work on the land. Not Rose. 'Lady muck, aren't ya?' the other local children yelled at her when she returned to school year after year, while they gave up their books to help their fathers.

'Don't mind them,' Anna would say proudly to Rose. 'You'll do well for yourself and they won't be laughing then.'

When the headmaster told Anna that Rose was his prize pupil and that she should go to the convent fifteen miles away if she was to fulfil her potential, Anna started piece work, knitting jumpers for the big tourist shops and their stream of wealthy customers who wanted hand-knit Irish sweaters. Ruining her eyes with bad lighting and complex stitches, Anna made enough money for Rose's school uniform and her books.

She'd been paid buttons for her work, Rose thought bitterly. But that work had given Rose the education that allowed her to enter a different world.

'I know you won't like me saying this, Rose, but you are partly to blame for what went wrong with yourself and Hugh.'

'Me?'

'Yes. You should have put a stop to it years ago or else left him. Hugh loved you but he was always a bit of a charmer.'

'That's ridiculous. It wasn't my job to police him,' Rose said heatedly.

'True. But you could have told him that he had a choice: you and your family or other women. Not both.' Freddie's expression was noncommittal and she went back to sorting through the old photos.

There was silence in the room after that, with just the ticking of Freddie's old clock breaking the silence. Glancing at Freddie, Rose saw that she didn't seem the slightest put out by the exchange of views. She was quite comfortable working on her photos and stroking Pig's ears every few moments when she leaned her furry head back against Freddie's knee specifically for that purpose. There was nothing wrong, in Freddie's eyes, with saying what you thought. Not saying what you thought was a far greater crime.

Maybe this was why she'd been so eager to forget about Castletown, Rose thought grimly. Both sides of her family were such combative people. Her mother had been the same, a blunt talker. Her mother, she realised with startling clarity, wouldn't have put up with infidelity. She'd have held her family together by putting her foot down. But then, Rose's father would never have dreamed of straying. Not like Hugh. The injustice of it all struck Rose. Freddie couldn't blame her, Hugh had been the one who'd failed.

'Hugh hurt me, he should regret it and be sorry for it!'

'You're not a plaster saint, Rose Riordain,' said Freddie

sternly. 'Haven't you ever done anything you regretted, that you felt sorry for?'

Freddie was the grand inquisitor now. 'Holly.' Even to her own ears, Rose's voice was faint. 'I let Holly down.'

'How?'

'I went through post-natal depression when she was a baby and it took me a long time to come out of it – years maybe.' Rose closed her eyes against the pain of remembering. 'I could barely manage to look at her and then, she grew up and she knew. I know she knew. She wasn't like the other girls. Stella and Tara couldn't wait to see me, to hug me and tell me everything but Holly was so self-contained, so distant, as if she knew I hadn't loved her properly when she was a baby and couldn't forgive me.'

'If you don't mind me saying so, that's ridiculous,' said Freddie briskly. 'She didn't know, she just sensed that you were different towards her. Children aren't stupid. You were different to her and she reacted to that. She's still reacting, I daresay. She was always the quiet one, watchful and silent. Gauging the world.'

'It's still my fault,' said Rose, crying now.

'Well, all you have to do is make it up to her. It's up to you to go back and make amends.'

'How?'

'Tell her about it, be honest.'

'I nearly told someone about it a few months ago,' Rose said slowly. 'A friend of mine, Minnie, she's obviously depressed and I tried to get help for her but I wouldn't let myself do the one thing that might have really helped. I couldn't tell her I'd gone through crippling depression and that it was possible to come out the other side.'

'How is she now?' asked Freddie.

'I don't know,' admitted Rose. 'I haven't phoned her since I've been here.' Suddenly, she grinned. 'You know, Freddie, all that's left is for you to tell me I'm the Weakest Link.'

Freddie looked puzzled.

'Never mind,' said Rose. 'It means that I'm suitably chastened.'

'That wasn't my intention,' Freddie said honestly. 'I love you, Rose, and I want you to be happy.'

'I know.' Rose leaned over and patted her aunt's arm. 'I suppose I have to walk these three hounds before dinner.'

At the word 'walk', Mildred, Prinny and Pig looked up expectantly.

'Come on, girls,' said Rose. She changed her shoes and headed out into the evening. She was looking forward to some time on her own. She had a lot to think about. So much of what Freddie had said had the painful ring of truth to it. She was right about meeting Hugh. Rose had to face him. As she hiked up the hill behind the house, with the dogs rushing delightedly in front of her, she made a decision: she'd stay with Freddie until her ankle was fully healed. Then, Rose would go home.

CHAPTER THIRTY-THREE

Tara negotiated the heavy traffic on the M50 roundabout with her mind only half on the job. At least she didn't have the radio to contend with. Since Finn had left, she hadn't been able to listen to the radio. Every song seemed to be about love and heartbreak, and Tara couldn't cope with any of it. Even the funkiest dance tracks reminded her of some night out with Finn.

She realised she was in the wrong lane and tried to move over, receiving an irate blast on the horn from another driver.

'Sorry,' she waved a hand apologetically. Sorry for everything, sorry for living.

In her early days as a scriptwriter, Tara had written a script about someone who'd disappeared into thin air. Not vanished like a magician, but vanished in every other sense. At the time, Tara had thought it was a stupid storyline. People just didn't disappear, she'd pointed out to Isadora.

Now, she knew that they could and did. To all intents and purposes, Finn had vanished on Monday night. It was now Thursday afternoon, nearly three terrifying days since she'd seen him. He hadn't been in work, a fact which was clearly infuriating Derry, his boss, when Tara had humiliated herself by phoning the office.

And he hadn't gone home to Four Winds and his parents, which Tara had discovered by clandestine means. She'd phoned the Jeffersons' several times until Desmond answered instead of Gloria, then casually asked if she and Finn could take Desmond and Gloria out to dinner at the weekend.

'That would be wonderful but I'll have to check with the War Office,' joked Desmond in his usual gentle way.

On the other end of the phone, Tara had gone white. Obviously Finn wasn't with his parents, so where was he?

'Desmond, I haven't been telling you the truth. Finn and I have argued and he's left me – I don't know where he is. I thought he might be with you and Gloria.'

'Oh Tara,' was all Desmond could say sorrowfully.

That had been yesterday. Today, she was driving out to Four Winds to talk to her father-in-law to find out if there was anywhere else Finn might be. Gloria would be out and Tara fervently hoped that Desmond hadn't mentioned this to her. She couldn't ask, naturally. It was Desmond's business what he told his wife.

Nobody at *National Hospital* knew what had happened either. Not even Isadora. Distraught, Tara had gone in to work as usual on Tuesday but looked so wild-eyed and white-faced that everyone assumed she was ill.

'Don't come in here if you've got the flu,' said Tommy in horror as he met a ghostly Tara in the script room for the early morning meeting. 'We don't all want to catch it.'

'You look terrible,' Aaron agreed. 'You should go home.'

Tara had taken the chance and left before she could bump into Isadora. Her closest friend would know that whatever ailed Tara, it wasn't flu. Since then, she'd called in sick every day and sat numbly at home, waiting by the phone in between trying Finn's mobile. She could no longer leave messages for him. The message service told her crisply that his message box was full. Was it full because he wasn't listening to and deleting her tearful pleadings for him to come back? Or was it full because he hadn't heard any of his messages, and was lying in the crumpled wreck of his car, injured and unable to phone for help? These were the thoughts that raced through Tara's mind endlessly.

Seeing Four Winds basking in the afternoon sunlight made the pain in her heart more intense. She'd never driven here without Finn beside her, laughing and joking, trying to cheer her up before seeing his mother. She'd give anything to turn the clock back so he could be beside her again. How differently she'd do things then.

Desmond came out to meet her. He looked so like Finn that Tara had to force herself not to cry. They embraced.

'I've been in the shed working on some cuttings,' Desmond said. 'Would you like to see them?'

Tara had never been in her father-in-law's inner sanctum before, so she said yes. Once inside, she could see why he preferred working in the shed to spending time in Gloria's frosty domain. There was a worn old armchair with lots of springs sticking out of the back, and a big workbench with pots, plants and all manner of garden equipment. To Tara's inexperienced eyes, it didn't look as if Desmond had been doing much in the gardening department. She moved that day's newspaper crossword from a stool and sat down.

'No, please take the armchair,' insisted Desmond gallantly.

'I'm fine,' Tara said. She waited for him to ask her what this was all about but he didn't, and it occurred to Tara that there were many similarities between her husband and his father. Finn never wanted to discuss problems either. Or at least he hadn't, until that last awful night.

'Finn and I rowed on Monday night and it was bad. He said he was leaving me.' Tara felt deeply ashamed to be saying this to Finn's father. 'We'd been having problems but this was my fault,' she admitted. 'I haven't heard from him since. He hasn't been in to work, his mobile is turned off. Even Derry doesn't know where he is, and I know that for a fact because Derry's furious with Finn for missing some important meeting. I just thought you'd know where he'd go,' she finished lamely.

'I wish I could help, Tara,' said Desmond. 'But I can't.'

His expression was one of sympathy rather than condemnation, which made Tara feel even guiltier. She didn't deserve Desmond's kindness. She'd cheated on his son, she deserved his disgust.

'There must be somewhere he'd go, somewhere from childhood, some place I don't know about,' she said, desperate for any help. 'I've tried all his friends, everyone, and nobody has a clue. Would he tell Gloria where he was going?'

Desmond's smile was wry and more than a little bitter. 'She's the last person he'd tell,' he said. 'I thought you'd know that.'

Well, no,' said Tara. 'I don't really know anything about Finn's relationship with his mother at all. I just know that she loves him . . .'

'Oh she loves him, all right. Too much,' said Desmond. He got up and began fiddling round with some of the black pots on his workbench. 'Gloria's always been intensely involved in everything surrounding Finn but she's like that, you know. She gets worked up about things. Finn and I are old hands at defusing her and keeping the peace when she gets wound up but it's not always easy. It's been harder since he married you,' Desmond added, almost apologetically. 'I know you can't have failed to notice that she resents you.'

There was silence for a few moments as Tara digested this information.

'I'd always thought that Finn got on well with his mother, that he handled her . . . intensity well.'

Desmond sighed. 'I don't think so, dear. He blanks it out really, that's how he handles it. And since Fay went, it's been worse.' He turned around suddenly, cheered up as if he'd just cracked a particularly difficult cryptic clue in his crossword. 'That's it. Talk to Fay. She might know. He tells her things.'

Tara felt unbelievably sad to think that her husband told things to his sister, who lived thousands of miles and many time zones away, and said so little to her, the woman who'd shared his bed and his life. Why had she never probed him for details of his relationship with Gloria? It was clear that Gloria adored her son with an obsessive zeal that went over and above normal mother-son relationships. Tara, with all her expertise at human relationships thanks to her work as a soap writer, had completely failed to see that this might affect Finn. She'd blithely accepted his cheery remarks that people 'got used to' Gloria. She remembered Christmas, before she'd realised that his drinking was out of hand, when he'd deliberately kept himself in a state of comfortable drunkenness to cope with the holiday. She should have known then. How had she missed all the signs? Was she so in love with the physical aspect of Finn that she'd failed to look any deeper?

'You don't want Gloria to know that Finn has disappeared, I presume,' said Tara.

'Hell no.' Desmond looked alarmed. 'Finn will be fine. He's resilient. He obviously needs time on his own. When he was a kid, before we moved here, he used to hide in the attic. It wasn't easy to get up there and he'd have to climb up onto the tank in the airing cupboard to get up where the water pipes ran into the attic, but he'd manage it. He liked peace.'

'So you could say he's run away before?' Tara was clutching at straws.

'Ask Fay.' Desmond tore a piece of paper from the bottom of the newspaper and wrote an e-mail address on it. 'You'll like Fay,' he said. 'She's a great girl.' He looked dreamy-eyed and Tara felt overcome with pity for this lovely man who'd seen his daughter flee to the other side of the world, all because of his bitter, jealous wife.

Tara kissed Desmond on the cheek. She wanted to be long gone before Gloria came home on her broomstick.

Dear Fay,
You don't know me but hopefully, you've heard of me. I'm Tara Miller, Finn's wife. I know you're probably wondering why I'm writing to you for the first time but I'm desperate. Finn and I have rowed and he's left me. That was three days ago and I have heard nothing

since, which is so unlike your brother. He doesn't hold
grudges.

He hasn't been to work and he's not with your parents.
(Your father knows what's happened – he gave me your
e-mail address – but your mother doesn't.) Please, if you
can think of any place Finn might have gone to, tell me. Or
if he's been in touch with you.

I am so scared. I don't know what could have happened
to him and I keep imagining the worst. I've rung all the
hospitals and even the police, but because he walked out
on me and because he's an adult, they don't consider it a
missing person case.

Sorry for bothering you but I am desperate.

Tara Miller.

Tara reread the e-mail. It was not up to her usual standard,
but who cared? She pressed 'send'. All she had to do now
was wait.

She couldn't relax and logged onto her e-mail account
every half hour to see if a message had come through. Finally,
at half eleven, after an evening of flicking desultorily through
the TV channels, she gave up. Fay could be away, out at
work, anything. She might not want to respond to Tara; she
might be fed up of family hassles. Wasn't that why she'd
emigrated in the first place?

In bed, Tara fell into an uneasy sleep where she dreamed of
being on a sun-swept desert island. She was running through
sand, trying to find Finn but he was always a few steps ahead
of her, and her legs didn't seem to work. She screamed Finn's
name but he didn't turn round. 'Finn!'

Tara's own scream woke her up. Her heart was pounding
and she was sunburn hot. Flicking on her bedside lamp to
banish the demons of the night, she looked at the time. Half
three. That was half six in the evening in California, or was
it half seven? She logged on and there, winking at her, was
a message from Fay Jefferson. It had been sent half an hour
ago.

Hi, Tara,

Nice to meet you, Sister-in-law. Sorry it's because of this. Do you mind me asking what you argued about? I don't want to get into your personal lives but I think I can guess what part of the problem is. Finn and I have talked about it many times. By the way, Finn hasn't been in touch with me but if he does, I will tell him to get in touch with you. I have to say that normally, he's not the one to run away. That's my job.

Adios,

Fay.

Still shaking from her dream, Tara typed rapidly.

Fay, are you still there? Can I phone you? Please?

Tara.

She didn't disconnect the line and stayed near the computer, waiting. Seven minutes later, a single-line message arrived with a phone number.

'Thank you, Fay, thank you,' said Tara joyfully as she dialled.

Her sister-in-law answered on the third ring. 'Hi, Tara, say it's late for you, isn't it?' Fay's Irish accent had mellowed into a soft Californian purr but Tara could still hear traces of Finn's husky voice in there.

'Hi,' she said and burst into tears. 'You sound like your brother.'

'He's done a lot of things but he doesn't usually make women cry,' Fay said gently.

'No, that's my fault,' said Tara.

'Why?' asked Fay.

Tara told her, the real version, not the sanitised 'we rowed and he left' one. It never occurred to her not to tell the truth. She was desperate and this total stranger, Finn's sister, was the only chance she had left.

'That's not what I expected,' Fay said finally. 'I guessed it was something to do with Finn's alcoholism.'

Tara's sharp intake of breath was audible. 'His alcoholism?' she said.

'Ri-ight.' Fay drew the word out into two syllables. 'He hasn't talked to you about it?'

'Never, but I know. I've been so worried and every time we talk about it, he says he doesn't have a problem but he does and oh, Fay, it's been hell.' Tara began to cry again, this time silently.

'Tell me.'

Tara wiped her eyes with the back of her hand. 'When we first got married, I thought the problem was his job and all the schmoozing the sales team had to do,' she said, her voice thick from crying. 'It seemed as if Finn was always out late and home drunk. He was never bad tempered or anything when he drank, just different.' She tried to find the right words to explain his distant state, the way he was still Finn but somehow different, as if he wanted to be miles away. 'I began to hate him saying he had to entertain clients or anything with Derry.'

'Oh, Derry, yeah.' Fay laughed but there was no mirth in it. 'I remember him.'

'I hate Derry,' Tara said tonelessly. 'He's a heavy drinker and even if Finn was going out for one pint of beer and he was with Derry, it ended up with them getting plastered. Then, Finn spent money from the bank account and we couldn't pay the mortgage.'

'What did you do?'

'I confronted him. I was furious. He said it would be fine, he had this bonus coming, but it didn't, and he kept drinking and I was so angry . . .' Tara had been standing up and now she slumped onto the remaining armchair in the room. 'That's when I slept with this man I worked with. That's not an excuse, Fay. Just because Finn drinks doesn't mean I have to hop into bed with other guys.'

'But you wanted to pay him back, didn't you?'

Tara sighed. 'Fay, if this is psychic healing, you are an expert at it.'

Her sister-in-law's chuckle was deep. 'I'm not a psychic healer, I just said that to irritate my mother. I'm a fitness instructor. I had an arts degree from home and that didn't help much in the job market, so I retrained.'

'You don't get on with her,' Tara remarked.

'You could say that,' Fay said sardonically. 'Finn and I have very different relationships with her. She and I didn't get on but she adored Finn. He was always so sweet, he tried to get her off my back by being extra nice to her so she'd be happy and cut me some slack. You know, he'd say, "Mum, you look tired. Why don't you have a rest and Fay and I will clean up," and she'd be all "Finn, darling, you're so good" and she'd go upstairs and lie down or paint her nails and everyone would be happy because she wasn't around.'

Tara had to ask: 'Do you think that he drinks because of that, because of your mother and your childhood?' She wanted there to be a reason because then, it could be fixed.

'That reminds me of the joke written on a bathroom stall door: "*My mother made me an alcoholic.*" And written underneath in different writing is: "*If I get her the wool, will she make me one too?*" Nobody makes anybody an alcoholic, Tara,' said Fay firmly. 'What happens to you in life can probably push you down that path, but it's a cop-out to say another person forces you into it. Now, I'm not standing up for my mother here. She's quite a piece of work.'

Tara agreed with that. Gloria was a strange woman, and yet her daughter was warm and friendly. Tara realised that even the way Fay spoke felt so familiar that Tara didn't think twice about having this bizarre and deeply personal conversation with her.

'I've read that scientists are still juggling the nature versus nurture effect of alcoholism, like is it genetic or is it learned behaviour. But to be fair, my mother didn't hand Finn a bottle and say "finish this, kid". He did that himself and he's the only person to blame. Finn's been drinking for a long time,' Fay continued. 'He's two years older than I am and I noticed it for the first time when he was, I don't know, perhaps nineteen. He never drank for fun, he drank to get really out of it. We all tried to get served in bars then, it was the classic teenage rebellion thing. We were adults, we could handle our beer, yeah right. But Finn drank differently, even then. I didn't realise what it meant until I was in college and I did psychology in the first year. We had this lecture about alcoholism and it sort of clicked. Everything the lecturer said reminded me of my brother. Drinking is his coping mechanism.'

Tara felt so incredibly sad hearing this. It took a phone call to the other side of the world to tell her things she should have known about her husband.

'Finn's known he's had a problem for years,' Fay went on. 'He and I discuss it but nobody else does. My mother would never admit that he has any flaws and Dad, well Dad hates hassle.

'When Finn phoned last year and said he was getting married, I didn't like to ask him if you knew. He said he was drinking but it was under control.'

Tara sat in miserable silence. It all made so much sense; how had she never noticed before? 'Why didn't I realise at the beginning?' she said. 'I could have helped.'

'Finn doesn't fit into the Photofit of your typical drunk. He doesn't hang around street corners and stumble off the sidewalk. He's clever, he's kind, *he functions*. How would you know?'

'I should have,' insisted Tara. 'I love him.'

'You've got to ask yourself can you still love him, knowing this?'

'Of course I can. But where is he?'

'Did you try phoning the rehabilitation clinics? He might have booked himself into one.'

'Do you think that's possible?' Tara felt a glimmer of hope.

'He probably feels he's lost you, that he's reached the end of the line, so the only way of winning you back is sorting out the problem.'

'But *he* left *me*,' Tara pointed out. 'Not the other way round.'

'Had he been drinking that night?'

Tara didn't know.

'Let's keep our fingers crossed that he's in rehab. If he is, he'll need you when he gets out.'

'I'll be there,' Tara said, her voice cracking.

'I've got to go, Tara,' Fay said. 'I'm on late shift tonight at the health club. Keep in touch, won't you?'

'Yes, and thanks for everything.'

As she hung up. Tara tried to imagine what she'd do if either Stella or Holly were alcoholics. She'd have dragged them into a clinic and kept them there until they were better. Fay appeared to know all about Finn and yet she'd never forced him to do anything about it. Then again, didn't they say that was the problem with addiction: you couldn't force anyone to do anything. They had to want to do it. Tara felt so ignorant about the whole subject. She should have bought a book on alcoholism or something. Then it hit her: the Internet. Of course. She didn't need a book. She got on-line and began to search.

She sat up into the night reading on-line about families and partners of alcoholics. The facts of the stories were often different on the surface, but underneath, they all shared the same thread of pain from living with an alcoholic. There were wives and husbands who'd divorced their drinking spouse, having been pushed to the limit too many times, and who told of how it was an uphill battle recovering from what they'd been through. There were adult children of alcoholics who, years after their drinking parent was dead, still had nightmares about what it meant when Daddy or Mummy came home with that familiar glitter in their eyes and the miasma of alcohol in the air.

And there were the good stories, where people came on-line to give hope that there could be life after the bottle.

'I was married to two people, the kind man I loved and the bitter, cruel man he became when he was drunk,' wrote one woman. 'For years I lived with both until I'd had enough and threw him out of our home, for my sake and for our children's sake. Only then did he face up to what he'd done. Now my husband is back, not the drinking one, the kind, decent one. He's been back for four years and not a day goes by but I don't praise the Lord for giving him back to us. It can be done, I promise.'

Tara felt a lump in her throat as she read each account. These real stories were more poignant than anything she could have written.

If only she could get a second chance with Finn. But that was out of her hands now. All she could do was hope he'd done the positive thing and gone for treatment. Until she knew otherwise, she had to get on with living her life.

CHAPTER THIRTY-FOUR

'Remind me again why we're going to this party?' grumbled Joan, fiddling with her newly-dyed coal-black hair, now cut in a sharp modern crop. In preparation for her trip to New York, she'd revamped her personal style and was getting used to wearing pieces from her tailored collection. She still wore her funky graffiti T-shirts but worked hard to make her more outrageous clothes look good with mainstream pieces.

'I want to be successful and being too weird won't work on Seventh Avenue,' she told Kenny and Holly when they expressed amazement at this new look. Tonight, she was dressed in a sleek charcoal pinafore dress with a clinging, filament-thin white net shirt with cotton collar and cuffs underneath. Genuine 'Forties stack heels and a classic YSL evening bag from a vintage shop completed the look. Somehow the outfit was the epitome of French chic with a very modern twist.

'We're going to this party because we love Tom and have to support him in his hour of need,' said Kenny, who didn't need to fiddle with his outfit because he knew that his Diet-Coke man cream linen suit was exquisite. 'And we're hoping that Caroline will fall for some of the top totty I've arranged to crash the party, thus leaving dear Tom alone.' He didn't add 'alone for Holly'. He and Joan might think that Tom would be perfect for their Holly but they said nothing. Holly had been bruised enough as it was. 'Besides, the only other option is to find a witch and put a hex on Caroline, and they haven't opened up a branch of Witches Я Us in Dublin yet,' Kenny continued irrepressibly.

It was the Thursday evening of Tom and Caroline's grand engagement party and Joan and Kenny were in Holly's apartment waiting for her to emerge from the bedroom.

'Holls, what are you doing in there?' yelled Joan. 'I want to get to the party and meet Kenny's model boys.'

In a daring move, Kenny had phoned Caroline and mentioned that he'd be working on a shoot on the day of the party. 'I'll be working with four of the most delectable male models in the country. Could I ask a huge favour and take them along? They'd love your party.'

Predictably, Caroline had jumped at the chance.

'Jennifer Lopez is in the ha'penny place compared to Caroline when it comes to ego,' Kenny sighed. 'Honestly, I've organised rent-a-crowd and she genuinely believes the country's top male models are wetting themselves to go to her little bash.'

In her bedroom, Holly stared at herself in the mirror. She couldn't go out in this dress. It was Caroline's night and there was an unwritten rule about upstaging the bride, wasn't there? Vintage shopping with Joan, she'd come upon a red Hervé Léger dress, a marvellous construction which worked like a fabulous foundation garment, squeezing Holly's hourglass figure into even more Jessica Rabbit proportions. Holly wouldn't have tried something so daring on except Joan wanted to see it modelled so she could croon over the brilliance of Léger. Once it was on, even the manageress of the shop had come to admire the effect. After that, Joan insisted that Holly buy it.

Now Holly decided that she just didn't have the nerve for so much va-va voom. This was a dress to be tried on when she needed cheering up, because it did make her look fabulous, but she just wasn't the sort of person who could actually set foot outside the flat wearing it. People would look at her in a dress like that.

'We hope you're not taking that dress off?' Joan stood at the bedroom door.

'Oh good, you're ready,' said Kenny, popping his head into the room. 'Let's go.'

'I don't know . . .' said Holly miserably.

They grabbed her and propelled her out the bedroom door. Joan rushed back and picked up Holly's evening bag. 'Jesus, Holly, what are you like? You look wicked.'

The two fashion mavens examined Holly critically.

'A teeny bit more lip gloss,' said Kenny. 'Otherwise, it's perfect.'

Joan opened the front door and they trooped down the stairs. Holly fiddled with her dress, hoisting it up so that it covered her boobs a bit more.

'Caroline will die when she sees you,' crowed Joan happily.

At that, Holly stopped. She didn't want Caroline to die at the sight of her in full battle dress. Because that's what it would look like; the desperate, embittered woman who'd lost and who was giving it everything she'd got one last time. Caroline knew damn well that Holly liked Tom, even if he seemed oblivious to it. And Holly would compound matters by making a fool of herself in this dress; a dress that screeched 'Look what you're missing!' She might as well paint a banner with that legend on it.

She didn't want that air of desperation to be Tom's last vision of her. She wanted to be cool and calm, and as happy for the engaged couple as she could: it was bad karma to be anything else. And after tonight, she'd never see them again. Tom and Caroline were moving out into a bigger flat. Holly knew she'd be invited to the wedding but she wouldn't go. Tonight was bad enough. Tonight, she would be graceful and hopefully nobody would notice that she was being graceful in defeat.

'I've forgotten to turn the . . . er . . . television off,' she improvised and dashed upstairs. 'Keep walking, I'll be with you in a moment.'

In her flat, Holly ripped off the dress and threw it on the bed. She pulled a sleekly-fitting ebony trouser suit out of the wardrobe along with a white wrap shirt. Dressing quickly, she swapped the original strappy sandals for chic black mules and changed her sparkly evening bag for a simple leather one. The woman in the mirror looked classy and businesslike, and the outfit looked enough like she'd rushed home from work without time to change. It didn't say she'd tried too hard.

'What the hell . . . ?' said Joan when Holly joined them outside the gate, where they were waving for a taxi.

'Leave her alone,' chided Kenny. 'Holly knows what she's doing.'

At the hotel, a big sign in the lobby announced that the Jacob anniversary party was in the Sackville Room, the O'Connor wedding reception was in the Hill of Tara Room, and the Barry/Davis engagement party was in the Cuchulainn Room.

'It's all a bit historical for a hotel that's only ten years old,' remarked Kenny. All three names were important ones in Irish history and mythology.

'I suppose tourists love getting in touch with the old Ireland,' said Joan. A thought struck her: 'God, do you suppose I'll have to learn all sorts of Irish history when I go to New York? When my aunt came home from Philadelphia years ago, she went out of her mind that I didn't know any old Irish songs or any of that stuff. She thought I'd be able to speak Irish too and you know all I can say in Irish is "Can I have permission to leave class to go to the loo, Miss?" '

'Stop worrying,' laughed Kenny. 'Nobody's going to expect you to start spouting guff about leprechaun legends. Anyway, you'll probably get all homesick when you're there and start buying Irish folk music and getting maudlin on Paddy's Day, sobbing about the Auld Sod.'

'Will not. I'm a club music girl and the only reason I like Paddy's Day is because it's a bank holiday.'

'But you must know some Irish history,' Kenny went on.

'I wasn't good at history, so what?' said Joan crossly. 'We weren't all the teacher's pet at school.'

'Are you two going to argue all night or are we actually going into this party?' demanded Holly.

'Right, I'll go first,' said Joan. 'You pair come after me, talking as if you're having the most fabulous conversation on the planet and haven't noticed you're here at all yet.'

'Will we talk about Irish history?' said Kenny innocently, and Holly burst out laughing. Thus, the first impression that the other guests had of the threesome was of beautifully dressed, elegant people who were having a marvellous time, thanks to their own scintillating company.

'That wasn't too hard, was it?' murmured Joan, nudging the small group in the direction of the bar.

'Should we go and say hello to Tom and Caroline first?' asked Holly anxiously. She could have quite happily done without seeing either of the blissfully-happy affianced couple but she knew it would have to happen.

'No, they can come to us,' Joan said and began ordering drinks.

Holly looked around surreptitiously.

The room, decorated in expensive ivy wallpaper for the mystic Ireland effect, was big enough for around two hundred people, and had a stage at one end. A lurid pink 'Congratulations Tom and Caroline' banner hung above the stage. Scores of pink, heart-shaped balloons were dotted around, clashing wildly with the riotous wallpaper.

'Can you see any of my guys?' said Kenny, craning his neck.

'No, they're probably all in the bathroom making frantic calls on their mobiles to find a cooler party to go to,' Joan said.

'They're doing this for me,' Kenny pointed out, 'and they won't leave until they've made dear Caroline see that she's making a huge mistake by settling down when there are so many handsome men in the world who fancy her rotten.'

'I wouldn't bank on it,' Joan said, eyes widening.

Holly and Kenny followed her gaze to where a crowd of people had parted, revealing a petite blonde woman in a spray-on red dress. It was Caroline, smiling smugly like a cat who'd just consumed a pint of double cream. Her dress was not unlike Holly's discarded one as it revealed lots of flesh and had a devastatingly deep plunge neckline, combined with a more subtle gash up one thigh. But while Holly had the curves to carry off such a siren's outfit, Caroline did not. Her tiny pert breasts and boyish hips, perfect for her trademark slip dresses, were lost in the dress.

'I can't believe she's wearing that,' said Joan pityingly. 'That is so not her style.'

Holly sent up a grateful prayer that she'd changed out of her own little red number. Beside each other, she and Caroline would have looked like Little and Large. Or worse: the lo-cal and full-fat versions.

It was obvious that Caroline didn't have any doubts about her outfit and she sailed triumphantly over to the trio.

'I'm sooo pleased you're here!!' she squealed, hands flapping excitedly. 'Isn't this exciting! Do you like my dress?' she added to Joan, clearly still keen to butter the designer up over the as yet unresolved matter of her wedding dress. 'It's Versace.'

'Last season and a copy,' murmured Kenny sotto voce into Holly's ear.

She gave him a tiny slap on the wrist. 'Don't be mean.'

'What do you think of my wonderful balloons?' gushed Caroline. 'I should have had red to go with my dress, but I prefer pink. It's more womantic,' she added, lisping prettily.

Holly hoped that Joan wouldn't start to make sick noises at Caroline's baby talk. Joan's bullshit-ometer was very sensitive.

'Where's Tom?' Holly asked.

'Over there somewhere,' Caroline said, distracted as a gaggle of newly arrived women in party sequins waved gaily at her.

'Talk to you later!' shrieked Caroline. She tottered off in her high heels to greet the newcomers, screaming, 'I'm sooo pleased you're all here!'

Behind the new arrivals stood three of the most handsome men Holly had ever seen in her life. All casually clad in worn jeans with their hair fashionably tousled, they had the careless elegance of people so beautiful that what they wore didn't matter. One bore more than a slight resemblance to Brad Pitt, reminding Holly of her brother-in-law. Finn had that same effortless way of walking, a sexy stroll that said he had all the time in the world. They spotted Kenny and drifted sexily over. In contrast to their languid beauty, close up they all seemed excitable and almost boyish in their enthusiasm. They hugged Kenny and shook hands with the girls.

'Lovely to meet you.'

'Oh, you're Joan and Holly!'

'We've heard all about you.'

Soon, the six of them were laughing and giggling like they'd all known each other for years. Kenny pointed out the betrothed couple to the boys.

'He's divine,' sighed Brad Pitt, whose real name was Napier.

Holly giggled into her orange juice. Kenny winked at her.

'Nape's a diesel,' Kenny whispered.

Holly looked bewildered.

'He runs on different fuel.'

She got it.

When Tom walked over to say hello to them, with Caroline holding his hand firmly, it looked as if Kenny's cunning plan was going to backfire. The two straight models ignored Caroline, while Napier smouldered away at Tom.

'Caroline, you must meet Napier, Denzil and Kurt,' said Kenny firmly, shoving Napier away from Tom and towards Caroline.

'Hello, boys,' simpered Caroline. Imagine, real models at her party. Moving to Dublin was going to work out after all.

Tom slipped his hand from hers and moved closer to Holly.

'Thanks for coming,' said Tom. 'You look nice.'

Holly looked down at her businesslike suit. 'It's a bit formal for tonight,' she said apologetically. 'Sorry.'

'No, it's lovely. You always look . . .' Tom stopped mid-sentence, as if realising it was inappropriate to talk to her like that. 'lovely,' he said finally, 'you always look lovely.'

'Right back at you,' she said. He was in the cashmere sweater she, Kenny and Joan had bought him for that fateful birthday; the night when Caroline had appeared on the scene, dashing hopes Holly hadn't even known she'd had. She thought of the expensive book on that famous architect she'd bought as a private present for Tom. It was still under her bed, still tied up with ribbon, like a parcel of hopes and dreams.

'This is the sweater you gave me,' he said.

'Yes,' said Holly. What was the point of feigning ignorance. She remembered everything Tom wore and what he'd said to her when he wore it.

'Kenny tells me you've got a new flat; one of those posh ones in Glasnevin,' she said.

He nodded. 'Caroline's madly keen to have a house-warming before we get the wooden floor down.'

'You're turning into a party animal,' she teased gently. 'Engagement parties, house-warmings, the wedding . . . So, when are you moving out of Windmill Terrace?

'Next week.'

'That soon?' She looked down into her glass. Just another week, then, and Tom would be out of her life for good. It was better that way.

'I hope we can all keep in touch,' he said, 'you, Kenny, Joan, me. The Purple Mosquito gang.'

It was all too much for Holly. She couldn't bear to be just another name on Tom and Caroline's Rolodex, a memory of the days in Windmill Terrace. She could picture Caroline introducing her: *This is Holly who used to live in the cutest flat below Tom's. Yes, remember when he moved to Dublin first and lived in this crummy house, before I moved too.*

Well, Holly was Tom's neighbour, one of a trio of marvellous mad people. Joan Atwood, the designer, was one of them actually.' Then Caroline would whisper that Holly used to have a crush on Tom. *'Sweet girl, sobbed at our wedding, you know. Bless.'*

'Tom, I'm sorry, I have to go. Have a lovely party.' Holly thrust her glass into his hand and, without taking in the astonished look on his face, rushed out of the room into the lobby. She didn't wait to see if either Kenny or Joan had noticed her abrupt flight. They'd figure out roughly what had happened. Out the hotel door and down the street she ran, dodging pedestrians; anything to get away from Tom.

In her haste to get away, she didn't look back. If she had, she'd have seen Tom fighting past party guests as he tried to follow her. But when Tom made it to the street, Holly was long gone.

When she was far enough away, she slowed down to a gentle walk. She never wanted to see him again. It hurt too much. There was no point agonising over 'if only'. If only she'd told him how she felt in the early days; if only he'd had the chance to say that he liked her as a friend and nothing more, then perhaps she'd have got over him. But the endless hoping that he'd recognise her love, recognise that she, not Caroline, was the right woman for him, that had been torture. Holly speeded up. She'd made the decision to walk out of his life. He wasn't walking out of hers, *she* was walking out of *his*. She was powerful and strong. She was going to get over Tom Barry.

CHAPTER THIRTY-FIVE

Clarisse and Wendy Cavaletto sat in the hotel restaurant and perused the lunch menu. Wendy wasn't hungry and would have preferred a sandwich somewhere local but Clarisse was very keen on being seen in all the right places, and insisted that the Michelin-starred restaurant in the Manon Hotel was just such a place.

'Wendy, you can't hide away. You've got to get out and meet people,' insisted Clarisse on the phone.

Wendy wasn't sure how meeting her ex-sister-in-law for lunch constituted meeting 'people' but decided it was part of some grand plan of Clarisse's to get her name in the gossip columns. Clarisse had a not-very-secret desire to be one of the country's society people and had made frantic, albeit so far unsuccessful, efforts during the summer racing season to win 'best dressed lady' prizes at Leopardstown, Fairyhouse and the Galway races.

'I haven't been hiding away,' Wendy had pointed out. 'I've joined the amateur dramatic group and the gym.'

'That's not what I meant,' Clarisse said impatiently. 'You need to be seen at the right places.'

Now that they were there, sitting in a balcony area where they were highly visible, Wendy regretted not holding out for that quiet sandwich. The Manon Hotel was full of what Clarisse assured her were movers and shakers, and Wendy didn't fancy the prospect of breaking down in tears in front of such people. This was a possibility because Clarisse had news of Her, Nick's new woman, and Wendy found herself ludicrously emotional when it came to her ex-husband. After several last-minute cancellations over the past few months, Clarisse had finally entertained Nick and Stella to dinner and was now bristling with information.

'A glass of champagne, I think,' said Clarisse when the waitress came to take their order.

'Not for me,' said Wendy. 'I've got the car.'

'Nonsense,' her sister-in-law retorted. 'One glass won't kill you. We'll hit the shops afterwards so it'll be hours before you're driving. Isn't this fun?'

'Yes,' said Wendy, faking a smile. Clarisse was doing her best, but she was a poor substitute for Belinda, Wendy's best friend in London. Belinda was the sort of person who'd know exactly how to buoy Wendy up. Having lunch in a pretentious, expensive hotel would not have been on the agenda. Sometimes, Wendy found herself wishing that she hadn't moved away from London.

Her support system was there, in a city she'd spent years trying to get out of. Now that she had, she almost regretted it. Ireland wasn't like she'd expected. It had selfishly moved on. While she'd kept the old Ireland alive in her heart, it had changed into this new modern European country she didn't recognise. After twenty years away, she knew nobody and felt she didn't fit in.

Her sister lived in the States and her parents were dead. Her circle of old friends had all moved on and she was left with Clarisse.

It was tough relying on someone like her sister-in-law for support. Clarisse had a way of telling you things with her own idiosyncratic twist, a sort of spin. She didn't just give you the facts, she gave her interpretation of them too, which was why Wendy wasn't entirely sure she wanted to hear about Nick's new girlfriend from her.

They both managed a bit of idle chat about nothing until they had their champagne. Thus fortified, Clarisse began.

'Well, I wasn't that impressed, I can tell you. She obviously doesn't spend much money on clothes. She had this linen skirt on and it was at least five years old. I had one like it but I've long since thrown it out. And her hair, well. What a disaster. She has one of those short, unforgiving haircuts.' Clarissse shuddered.

Wendy felt slightly cheered up by this, cheered up enough to ask: 'Is she good-looking?'

'Not bad, if you like that sort of thing. Dark haired and not much make-up. Blonde would suit her better.' Clarisse touched her own expensively streaked mane. Both she and Wendy were blonde. Clarisse couldn't understand why everybody wasn't blonde. Bleach hid the grey and was so much more flattering, she felt. 'And I think she looks her age.'

Wendy desperately wanted to know what that age was. She'd managed not to ask Nick during that shaming phone call where she'd screamed at him and told him he was a bastard for finding someone new so quickly and she hoped he'd drop dead.

Clarisse didn't disappoint. 'She's younger than him, late thirties I'd say, although she could do more with herself. I can't see her as the sort who spends a moment in the beautician's.'

Wendy digested this, not sure if she was happy or sad that her ex-husband was with a woman who could do more with herself. It shouldn't matter what sort of a woman he went out with, but somehow, it did. It was as if his new choice of mate was a direct reflection on Wendy herself. A younger and ambitious girlfriend implied that Wendy lacked those very attributes. Which was nearly as humiliating as the speed with which Nick had apparently got over the divorce and found Her.

'What did Howard think?' asked Wendy. She'd always been fond of Nick's brother, although they didn't have much in common. He was a tax inspector, a subject Wendy found terminally boring.

'Well, you know Howard.' Clarisse's expression signified that she knew Howard too well and, in fact, was fed up with knowing him. 'He likes the oddest people. The three of them were talking all night, gabbling away about the planning tribunals and offshore accounts.'

Their salads arrived.

'I'll tell you one thing though,' said Clarisse, spearing a sliver of chicken, 'I have a feeling about her. I told Howard when they were gone: "Mark my words," I said, "they're going out more than three months."'

Wendy stared at her. 'What do you mean?'

'Well, it's a bit convenient, isn't it? He and you split up, he rushes back home and suddenly, there's this new woman on the scene. I'd call that a bit quick, wouldn't you?' Clarisse looked archly at her former sister-in-law. 'I hope you don't think I'm interfering, Wendy, but I wanted to mark your card. I have a suspicion that Nick isn't being totally honest with you about Stella.'

Wendy dropped her fork with a clatter, not caring if the noise startled all the lunching movers and shakers. She gulped down her champagne and stared grimly at Clarisse.

'I'm not saying anything for definite,' Clarisse went on, waving a be-ringed hand in the direction of the waitress for service. 'I just thought you ought to know.'

Wendy needed another glass of champagne. To hell with the car. She'd leave it in the car park.

'The other interesting thing,' Clarisse was getting into her stride now, 'is when I asked how she was getting on with the girls. Well, you could have cut the atmosphere with a knife. She smiled, yes, but you could see she wasn't smiling inside. Oh no. Nick just sat there and he looked grey. That's it,' Clarisse said triumphantly, 'that's your trump card, Wendy. The girls don't like her and Nick would never stay with anyone if the girls don't get on with her. He'd do anything for Sara and Jenna. You could have him back with a snap of your fingers.'

A bottle of the house champagne arrived.

'We're divorced,' said Wendy weakly. 'He's my ex-husband.'

'Piffle,' said Clarisse dismissively. 'You can get married again. People do it all the time. Just a blip until you came to your senses. Nick and you had a fine marriage and let me tell you,' she waggled a witchy finger across the table, 'there aren't too many single men waiting around for women of our age. Nick's a catch, that's why Ms Never Been to the Beautician's snapped him up so quickly.'

Wendy sipped her champagne. It was lonely on her own. And dealing with Jenna was becoming more and more difficult. Together in the house, they snapped at each other from morning to night with no Nick to calm things down and jolly Jenna out of her sulks.

The part of Wendy's mind that had accepted the irretrievable demise of their marriage simply shut down. They could do it for the children's sakes. Wendy could have coped with staying together for the children in the first place: that was what women did, wasn't it? Only Nick had said it was no good any more, that it had been over for years and they both knew it. And she'd known he was telling the truth, then. But now . . .

Clarisse was right: Nick adored their daughters. He'd do anything for them. Sara was old enough to cope on her own but Jenna needed stability.

'Have some more champagne,' said Clarisse, reaching over with the bottle.

'Don't mind if I do,' said Wendy.

'You see,' Clarisse went on, 'if I were you, Wendy, love, *not* that I want to put my oar in or anything, but if I were you, I'd let that woman see that the children come first with Nick. Let her see where Nick's loyalties lie. That'll take the wind out of her sails.'

Clarisse, who'd taken an instant dislike to Stella Miller, sat back in satisfaction. She'd seen through Stella instantly. Women like her were just after other women's husbands. Clarisse knew the type. They waited until there was a chink in a good marriage and then bam! They were in there with their big eyes and their firm bodies. They were a danger to decent women, Clarisse decided firmly. She didn't want Howard getting any ideas from the likes of her.

'He does adore the girls,' said Wendy tearfully.

'There you are, then,' said Clarisse. She raised her glass. 'To the future,' she said.

Stella loved having Nick pottering round the galley kitchen with her. Not that he was up to taking over any of the major culinary tasks unless it involved putting a chicken in the oven, but he was eager to peel, slice and chop, and he never seemed to mind emptying the dishwasher, a task Stella hated. This was what family life was all about, Stella thought happily, as she gently poached pears for the Roquefort, pear and fig salad she was working on. It was a glorious Sunday at noon and they were getting ready for a buffet-style Sunday lunch in Stella's tiny courtyard garden.

She and Nick had given it a fresh coat of white paint the previous week and now it was like a glorious, Moroccan-inspired sun trap, with clematis-covered walls. Prettily coloured pots clustered in the corners, while hanging baskets added vibrant colour.

Amelia was setting up her toys outside in the courtyard, in preparation for the arrival of Shona and Becky. Hazel, Ivan and the twins were due in half an hour, along with Vicki and the current love of her life, Craig from work.

'What can I do next?' asked Nick, leaning over her shoulder as she poached the pears. He nuzzled her neck and wrapped his arms tightly round her waist.

Stella forgot about poaching for a moment and leaned back against him, loving the feeling of his strong body wrapped around hers.

He'd stayed over the night before and the three of them had enjoyed a pizza. When Amelia was in bed, Stella and Nick had lain together on the couch and watched an old movie on the TV, blissfully happy until it was time for bed. That had been even more blissful. Their lovemaking had been intense and the relaxed atmosphere of the evening had vanished, to be replaced by fervent, very physical sex, where each one's fierce passion had matched the other's.

Their bodies slick with sweat, they'd come together, hungry for each other until finally, they'd climaxed fiercely.

'Better than a sleeping pill any day,' Stella had murmured, as she curled up beside him, her eyes already closing.

Now she felt sexy and loved, her muscles aching pleasurably from their acrobatics and aware of her lover's body close beside hers. Sex definitely made her feel sexier, Stella thought, groaning with pleasure as Nick's hands cupped her breasts and rubbed her nipples into exquisite peaks through her black vest top.

'Stop or we won't be having poached pears, we'll be having mashed pears,' she murmured. God, but he knew how to turn her on.

The sound of Amelia calling 'Mum' from the garden made them part, laughing.

'Then stop tempting me with that little skimpy top thing,' Nick retorted. 'As you're tied up, I'll go and see what Amelia wants.'

Stella watched them through the window. Amelia was pointing at a bug which had landed on her dolls. Nick picked it up and carefully removed it, before coming back and crouching down beside Amelia to listen to her plans for a dolls' tea party.

Stella tested the pears, thinking how lucky she'd been to find Nick.

He'd given her confidence in so many ways: confidence in her looks for one. Not that Stella had ever seen herself as ugly, but she'd always been restrained in her demeanour, wearing clothes that would have suited an older woman just as well, never giving in to the impulse to be young and daft. These days she bought jaunty modern tops, which she wore with comfortable jeans. She'd dumped her neutral lipsticks for rich glossy colours, and she wore all her vintage jewellery, instead of leaving it to look beautiful in her bedroom.

The sense of renewed confidence had included entertaining. Suddenly, it was fun to invite people over to lunch and dinner, and the new, improved Stella didn't worry too much about the menu either. She flicked through her cookbooks, whisking up home-made pizza with salad and her own, fabulous bruschetta. She roasted huge garlic and lemon scented chickens, gently cooked baby vegetables, and dredged potato wedges in rosemary and spices. Today, she was serving a glorious buffet where less work and more conversation was to be the order of the day. She wasn't worried that she only had four matching wine glasses and there would be six adult guests. They had enough glasses to go round, nobody would mind in the slightest.

Nick's mobile phone rang.

'Nick, phone!' she called, grabbing it from the counter top and handing it to him through the patio doors.

'Hi, Jenna,' he said warmly, stepping into the kitchen.

Stella scooped the pears out of the poaching liquid and arranged them in a dish. Next, she began to top them with cheese ready to be grilled. Fresh figs and scrolls of Parma ham in a mixed leaf salad with some dressing would finish it off.

Nick had gone into the living room to talk. The radio *was* loud, Stella acknowledged. It wasn't that Nick didn't like to talk to his daughter in front of her. Still, Stella couldn't resist straining to overhear the conversation. She held her breath too and a little knot of tension crunched into place in her gut.

'Of course I can come, darling. Don't worry. Tell Mum not to worry, either.'

Alarm bells jangled in Stella's head. He couldn't mean that he was going to see Jenna and Wendy now. Jenna and Sara were going to an afternoon open-air gig in the Phoenix Park, which was why they'd cancelled their usual Sunday visit with Nick. That had given Stella the chance to organise this impromptu lunch. She didn't usually plan anything with Nick on Sundays because it was one of his days with the girls. But now that Stella had planned something, Jenna had changed her mind. Impotent fury raged through Stella.

Nick's face said sorry before he had a chance to get the words out.

'It's Jenna,' he said. 'Wendy's car battery is dead and she can't drive them to the concert. There are four of them going, so I said I'd drop over and drive them.'

'Now?'

Nick grimaced. 'Yes, now. Sorry, Stella, but she begged me.'

'What's wrong with the bus or a taxi?' Stella asked tartly.

'They'll be late for the concert if they try either of those. You know what buses and taxis are like on Sundays. Listen, I won't be long.'

'You won't be here to help me; you won't be here to entertain everyone, even though it's supposed to be our lunch.' Stella could feel the blood thumping angrily through her arteries. 'Why couldn't you have said no to Jenna? This is important to me.'

'It's only a lunch,' he said in placatory tones.

At this, all Stella's much-vaunted patience drained away.

Nick tried to drop a forgive-me kiss onto her forehead but she was in no mood for kisses.

'Only a lunch?' she shrieked. 'It's not only a lunch. I invited my friends to come here and spend time with us, not me, *us*. And you have to go before they even arrive because your daughter can't bear to be late to a concert and demands that you drive her instead of getting the bus like normal teenagers.'

This outburst from his gentle, calm Stella shocked Nick. 'It's not like that,' he protested.

'That's exactly what it's like,' she shot back. 'I can see precisely where I stand in your life, Nick. Way down the food chain, a long way below Jenna and Sara. No wonder Jenna doesn't show me any respect – *you* don't show me any respect! She knows that all she has to do is click her fingers and you jump, regardless of what I want. That's what you've taught her, Nick, and I'm fed up with it.'

Nick listened silently to the tirade.

'Do you know what's the worst thing?' Stella added. 'I'm beginning to understand how Wendy felt – sidelined by Jenna and Sara.'

'Please don't say that, Stella,' he begged. 'You know how much I love you. This is something I have to do. Don't make it into a big choice: you or my daughters.'

'I've never asked you to choose,' Stella said bleakly. 'Never. I understand what it's like to love a child, I'd never expect you to give that up for me. But you can love me *and* your daughters. All I'm asking for is respect from you and your family but Jenna will never respect me because you let her away with it; you've chosen to ignore her behaviour because you're consumed with guilt over the divorce, and the person who gets hurt is me. So there *is* a choice in all of this.' Stella stared at him. 'And you've clearly made your decision. I've been too stupid to realise it up to now.' She whirled around and began pointlessly re-chopping the fresh basil she'd already chopped.

'I won't be long, I'll be back before you know it,' Nick said. 'We'll talk about it then, please?'

She didn't reply. Normally, Nick never so much as went out to buy a newspaper without kissing her goodbye tenderly. Today, she knew she couldn't look at him again without screaming with all the pent-up rage that had curdled inside her for so long.

She listened to the sound of him picking up his car keys, then the front door shut and Stella burst into tears. The whole day was ruined and she knew who was to blame.

An hour later, nobody would have known that Stella had spent ten minutes crying in the bathroom where Amelia wouldn't see her. The only tell-tale sign was the fact that Stella's face was more made-up than usual, with heavier foundation to hide any tear stains and a smoky blast of Cabaret-style eyeliner to camouflage redness. Amelia didn't notice that her mother had changed from her strappy top into a long flowing linen shirt that covered her as successfully as a Bedouin tent. Stella couldn't bear to go on wearing the little top that Nick had admired so, she felt foolish in it. Her linen shirt was pre-Nick, pre-historic really.

'Hazel, Ivan, come in!' said Stella brightly when she answered the door to her guests. 'Hello, Shona and Becky.' She kissed both little girls, then hugged their parents.

'You look very cool,' said Hazel as she shut the door. 'I've never seen you wear that before. Is it a kaftan?'

The doorbell rang merrily again. On the doorstep stood Vicki, Craig and a big bouquet of flowers.

'Hello,' said Vicki. 'It's only us.'

Stella greeted them effusively, and had to stop herself getting teary-eyed at the beautiful bouquet. Vicki was such a generous person. She wouldn't dream of visiting a friend without bearing gifts.

'You shouldn't have, Vicki,' Stella said, 'but I'm glad you did. They're lovely.'

'You deserve them after doing all the cooking,' Vicki grinned. 'I'm famished, so I hope you've made buckets of whatever it is. I'm taking a day off my diet.'

Craig followed her, carrying a bottle of wine. Craig's two-year pursuit of Vicki had finally paid off. Cheeky-faced with a mop of sandy hair and a quick-fire sense of humour, he was the perfect match for Vicki, whom he adored.

Stella led the way through to the courtyard and when the new paint job and the carefully-laid mosaic table with its pretty dishes and orange gerbera flower arrangement had been admired, Vicki plonked herself down on a chair, closed her eyes to the sun and basked. 'I love eating outdoors,' she sighed. 'This is a wonderful idea, Stella. Thank you.'

Ivan and Craig sat down, while the twins and Amelia disappeared into the house on some errand of mischief. They spent all of their time in the twins' house, so it was doubly exciting for the three of them to be together in Amelia's home and she was keen to show them her newest treasures.

'Drinks, everyone?' asked Stella.

When Stella hurried back inside to get the mineral water and wine, Hazel followed.

'Nick's not here yet?' she asked, admiring the platters of food in the fridge when Stella opened it.

'Oh, he was called away on a work thing,' said Stella airily. 'The office alarm went off and he went in. He shouldn't be long.'

Much and all as she hated lying to dear Hazel, Stella couldn't bear to feel her friend's inevitable pity if she revealed exactly where Nick had gone and why. It was bad enough that Stella now knew Nick would choose his daughters over her, every time. She didn't want her friends to know it too. A woman could only take so much humiliation.

'On a Sunday? What a pain,' commiserated Hazel. 'Wow, that looks incredible,' she added as Stella lifted her pears and cheese combination and placed the dish under the grill.

Stella handed the wine and a bottle of mineral water to her friend. 'Would you pour?' she asked. 'I've got to stay here.'

She went through the motions of finishing off the lunch preparations, and overheard Ivan ask when Nick was coming.

'Oh, he got called in to work,' Hazel replied.

'Poor lamb, he'll miss all the food,' said Vicki sympathetically. 'What is it about work – just when you've planned something wonderful, work messes it up.'

They talked of other things and by the time Stella emerged with two platters, the conversation had moved on to soccer.

In every respect, it was a perfect lazy lunch. Stella carried out her mini stereo so that the three children could listen to the pop music they loved. The sun shone all afternoon and there was much angling of the big sun parasol so that people could stay out of the burning heat. The buzz of happy chatter was loud and Stella was determined to act the hostess with the mostest, cheerily filling glasses, chatting nineteen to the dozen, jumping up from her seat to bring out a gorgeous strawberry meringue and fresh fruit for dessert. But, all the time, she was listening anxiously for the phone. Had Nick taken her outburst to heart, she wondered? Had he decided not to bother coming back at all?

'Please, no more,' groaned Ivan, when he'd had two portions of meringue and was leaning back in his chair patting his belly.

'It's time we went home,' Hazel said regretfully. 'It's after three and I have a tonne of clothes to iron. It's a pity Nick couldn't get back. Did he phone?'

'He left a message on the machine,' Stella lied. 'He's stuck there, I'm afraid. Pity.'

She whisked around, piling up used plates and cutlery.

'I'll help,' said Hazel.

'Not at all.' Stella flashed her best camera smile. 'You go on, Hazel, and I'll see you in the morning.'

When they were gone, Stella returned to the courtyard. Craig and Amelia were having a discussion about worm farms.

'Can we look for worms in the pots, Mum?' asked Amelia, keen to start her own farm now that she'd had it explained to her.

'Under the clematis is probably better,' said Stella. 'Just be careful.'

She sat beside Vicki, put her feet up on an empty chair and poured herself a glass of sparkling water.

'What's wrong?' asked Vicki.

'Nothing.'

'And I'm the Queen of Sheba.' Vicki fixed her friend with a quizzical glare. 'Spill, girlfriend.'

Stella spilled, quietly so that Amelia and Craig wouldn't overhear.

'And he hasn't rung since.' She ended the story and helped herself to the last sliver of meringue.

'What are you going to do?'

541

Stella shrugged. 'I don't know. I'm trying not to think about it. I'm scared I said too much.'

'There's no such thing as saying too much,' Vicki pointed out. 'Keeping it all to yourself is the problem. You were right to tell him the truth. I know he loves the kids, but today was hardly a life or death scenario. He could have said he wasn't able to come but he'd pick them up after the concert or something.'

'Yeah.' Stella grimly shovelled more meringue into her mouth. She'd been too busy rushing round being the merry hostess to eat much. Now she was hungry. Nick *could* have said he wasn't able to pick Jenna and Sara up. 'I'm not asking him to choose between me and the girls. I'd never do that. I'm a parent myself, I understand what having children is about but . . .' She sighed. 'I want Nick to see that he can love me *and* the girls, it doesn't have to be one or the other. We could make it work.'

'He's a good guy, though,' Vicki said. 'He loves you, you know that. You've got to deal with this, together.'

Stella nodded wearily. She wished Rose was around so they could talk about it all. Without Rose, she felt strangely rudderless. Rose had said it would all take time, but Stella was weary of waiting for that time to pass.

'But it's odd that Nick hasn't rung or come back,' Vicki said.

'I know. I'm half-afraid something's happened to him.' Stella glanced at her watch. The big hand was on its way to four. It had been hours since he'd left and she felt suddenly nauseous at the notion that Nick might have been involved in a hideous car accident, and the last thing she'd said to him was horrible. She pushed the melting meringue away. 'I'll phone his mobile.'

'Hold on. What if he just hasn't phoned you: what are you going to say then?'

'That we can work it out,' Stella said as she rushed indoors. To her astonishment, the light on the answering machine was winking at her. With the noise of everyone talking and the music blaring, she hadn't heard the phone ring. Because of that, she hadn't even glanced over at it when she walking through the living room to say goodbye to Hazel and Ivan. Oh no, anything could have happened and she hadn't noticed the damn message light. Anxiously, she listened to the message.

'Stella, hi.' Pause. 'I'm outside the concert with the girls and one of their friends hasn't turned up, so they've got an extra ticket. They really want me to go with them. I'll go for the first hour or so and then I'll be over to you, OK? It's hardly my sort of music,' Nick added wryly. 'But I thought it might improve things with Jenna. She just needs to know I love her and then things will be fine, I promise. She's insecure, that's the problem. I should be with you by three. Hope the party's going well. Bye. Love you,' he added.

To Stella's ears, the *Love you* sounded like an afterthought.

She didn't cry this time. Instead, she phoned Nick's mobile, got his message service and left a short, sharp message: 'Its ten to four, the party's over and I'm going out. I'll be out all evening. Don't bother coming over.'

Her face was still flaming when she marched down the galley kitchen and into the courtyard.

Craig had given up on the worm search and now sat with Vicki's feet and legs stretched out on his lap. He was giving her bare feet a slow massage. Vicki moaned orgasmically and sank further back in her chair. 'He's wonderful at this,' she said to Stella.

Craig grinned. 'She wouldn't let me touch her feet at first but now,' he looked adoringly up at his girlfriend, 'she loves it.'

'I refuse to get out of bed in the morning without a toe job,' confirmed Vicki, wriggling languorously.

Stella felt a tight ball of temper settle in her skull. She should have a man here massaging her toes and helping her clear up this almighty mess of a party. Instead, she was sitting like one of the ugly sisters, on her own and with nobody to massage any part of her.

'Did you get talking to him?' Vicki asked.

'Yes and no,' said Stella with gritted teeth. 'He rang earlier and left a message to say he's going to the first hour of the concert with the girls, and he'd be over later. By now, in fact.' Her bright smile was dangerous.

Vicki sighed. 'We should go,' she said. 'So you can go out.'

'Are we going out, Mum?' asked Amelia.

'Yes,' said Stella, brushing earth from her daughter's once-spotless pink T-shirt. 'We're going to the cinema.'

'Yay!!' yelled Amelia. 'Is Nick coming?'

'No.'

Vicki, Craig and Amelia helped Stella carry the dirty dishes indoors, where she left them piled on the draining board waiting to be put in the dishwasher.

'That's fine, Craig, you can leave it,' she said when Craig attempted to put things in the dishwasher. 'I'll do it later. We're in a rush, I just want to get the stuff in.'

What she wanted to do was get out of Delgany Avenue as fast as possible before Nick arrived. She didn't trust herself to see him because she was so angry. Who knew what she'd say if he arrived? The neighbours wouldn't have to turn on their TVs to catch up on the soaps: they could just hang out their windows and listen to the catastrophic row coming from Stella Miller's.

Vicki and Craig left, with Vicki kissing Stella goodbye and whispering 'Phone me later,' into her friend's ear.

Five minutes after that, Amelia and Stella were walking rapidly up the road to the Sandymount train station. There was a huge cinema complex in Dun Laoghaire, just twenty minutes away on the DART train. Amelia was delighted with this unexpected treat and wanted to know what film they were going to see.

Stella didn't know. She hadn't even checked the newspaper to see what was on and when. At worst, they'd have to wait an hour for a suitable movie and there were lots of things they could do in the interim, like walk on the pier and watch the yachts. Stella took out her mobile, got the phone number of the cinema from directories, and dialled the film listing line. There were two animated films showing and luckily, Amelia hadn't seen one of them yet. It started in forty-five minutes and Stella booked two seats. It would be at least half eight before they were home, long enough for Nick to get the message.

On the train home, sated by the excitement of the day, the film and too much popcorn, Amelia leaned against her mother and dozed. Even the thrill of watching the scenery speeding by couldn't keep her awake, and Stella felt guilty for keeping Amelia out so late. Her temper still hadn't abated. Watching the film, she'd seen nothing but a blur, her mind running through exactly what she'd say to Nick when she saw him. And she had to face him. Running away and hiding wasn't Stella's style. If he phoned later, she'd tell him to come over. If they had to break up, she'd do it face to face.

The sound of a thunderstorm woke Stella early on Monday morning. She sat up groggily in bed, not sure what the noise was. Then another loud crack punctured the air. Rain drummed against the windows, sounding as if it desperately wanted to come in. Stella peered at the clock. Half five. Exhausted by a restless night, she slumped back against the pillows and wondered if there was a hope she might go back to sleep. She didn't have to be up until seven.

But her mind was racing too much for sleep to be a possibility. She gave it another ten minutes, willing herself to drift off into nothingness, but it wouldn't come.

'Shit.' Wrenching the duvet off, she got out of bed and pulled her dressing gown on. The storm had taken the heat out of the air and it was cooler than it had been for days. Stella walked into the kitchen, thankful that she'd tidied up the night before. Facing a pile of unwashed dishes with rock-hard congealed food would not have been a good beginning to the day. Then again, the day was doomed from the start, she thought grimly. Her conversation with Nick the night before had made that inevitable.

She found her favourite rich coffee beans, ground them and made a pot. She usually only made fresh coffee at the weekend. There was never time in her normal morning routine of rush cubed. With a fat mug of coffee in her hands, she sat in her favourite chair in the tiny conservatory and stared out into her courtyard where the rain was lashing the clematis to shreds. An mini regiment of worms were stretching their way across the patio stones, their pink bodies shiny and elongated on their great trek. Why did worms only travel in rain? Did they believe that humans stayed inside on wet days and they wouldn't get squished by shoes and car tyres? Or were they trying to escape their avian adversaries, hoping that the aerodynamics of wet feathers ruled out flying in the rain?

Stella smiled ruefully. Amelia had only caught one worm captive the day before and now here were scores of them.

Curling her feet up under her, Stella sipped her coffee until the view receded and the picture in her mind was of Nick's face. How was she going to get through the day without him?

Nick had left two messages the evening before. Both calm and a little sad, asking her to phone him. She hadn't. Then, she was sorting out Amelia's school uniform for the morning when the phone rang. Before Stella had a chance to say 'Don't pick up . . .' Amelia had answered it.

'We went to see a film and I had popcorn and Mummy didn't,' gabbled Amelia.

Smiling, Stella reached for the phone.

'Bye, Mummy's here.'

'Hello, Stella,' said Nick.

'Hello.' Unaccountably, now that she was talking to him, she felt like crying, for all her previous internal conversations where she'd raged furiously at him. Her anger was gone, leaving only a miserable sense that their wonderful relationship had reached breaking point.

'I'd like to come over . . .'

Stella's heart leapt.

'. . . but I can't. Jenna's staying with me. She and Wendy had a row this evening and . . . well, it ended badly. So Jenna came here. Lucky I was in.'

Wasn't it, thought Stella bitterly. But her temper didn't flare again.

'I know you're angry,' he said.

'No, I'm not angry. I'm resigned, resigned to our relationship not working out because I'm making all the effort and you're not making any,' Stella said. She knew this wasn't totally fair but she didn't care. Hadn't Nick heard a word she'd said that morning?

'That's not true, Stella.' Nick sounded downhearted. 'I love you, I'd do anything for you, but today was difficult.'

'How do you think it was for me?' she asked. 'You let me down today, Nick. That was bad enough but instead of coming back and trying to sort it out, you stayed away.'

'I've just got divorced, Stella,' he said in exasperation. 'I'm trying to rebuild bridges with Jenna and Sara. It's not easy. I thought today would be good for the girls.'

'Even though you knew I expected you here for lunch?' Stella was calm now.

'I thought you'd understand.'

'Yeah, good old Stella, understanding Stella. Do you know what happens to people who always understand? They get walked on, Nick. I can't afford to let you walk on me and Amelia. We can't be second best forever.'

'That's below the belt. I'd do anything for Amelia and you're not second best.'

'That's funny, because that's just how I feel.' She wanted him to understand, so she gave it one last try. 'I love you, Nick, and it's wonderful the way that you get on so well with Amelia. I've always been ready to love Sara and Jenna, they're part of you, of course I want to love them. Sara's a wonderful girl, I'm so fond of her. But I've never had the chance with Jenna, she won't let me, she won't meet me halfway. And,' she paused for a moment, 'she'll never meet me halfway until she knows that you and I have a solid relationship. Can you understand that?'

There was a voice in the background. Stella could hear Nick's hand cover the receiver so that when he spoke next, it was muffled but she could make out what he was saying.

'Just a moment, honey. I won't be long.'

This time, the tears burned in Stella's eyes. They couldn't even break up like normal people. Jenna had to be involved.

She reached for the tissues on the coffee table, holding the phone away from her ear as she wiped her eyes.

'Stella, hello?' said Nick.

'I have to go, Nick,' she said quickly. 'I have to think. I'm sure you do too. Perhaps we've made a big mistake.'

There was silence on the other end of the line.

'I'll talk to you later in the week.'

He made no effort to change her mind.

'Good night, Nick,' she said, balling the tissue in her hand.

'Good night.' His tone was cold.

Stella hung up and, for the second time that day, burst into tears.

Now, in the early Monday morning light, Stella rocked back and forth on her chair, still clutching her cooling coffee. Had she made a huge mistake? That thought had kept her awake long into the night and her dreams had been tortured, restless ones where she woke every half hour, soaked in sweat and burning up.

Her mind flickered back to the last time she'd lain on her bed with her skin slick with perspiration. Had it really only been Saturday night when she and Nick had made such wonderful love? It felt like a thousand years ago.

The fear grabbed her again. Had she driven away the only man she could ever love because her dreams of happy families didn't happen fast enough? Or had she done the right thing, and said goodbye to someone who had too much unfinished business to ever truly love her?

That was the horrible thing: Stella just didn't know. There

were no definites in life, not like in the law where rules made sense and you knew where you were with them. In life, the rules made no sense whatsoever.

CHAPTER THIRTY-SIX

Rose stood in the ladies' room in Lee's and examined herself in the mirror. Her clothes were fine: a cream linen shirt and chocolate palazzo pants would take you anywhere. It was the look on her face that was the matter. There were lines of tension in her jaw and Rose decided that she looked as if she was en route to the dentist for two hours of root canal without an anaesthetic. This wouldn't do. Rose rubbed her temples to dissipate some of the tension and tried some deep breathing. She knew that Holly would get a surprise when she realised that her mother had driven to visit her unannounced, and Rose didn't want to frighten her by looking as if somebody had died and she'd come to break the news.

Going to see Holly had been a last-minute decision. Rose had spent days mulling over what Freddie had said to her. Strangely enough, Rose found she wasn't dwelling on Freddie's remarks about herself and Hugh. Rose understood the dynamics of their relationship well enough to see that Freddie had been speaking the truth. What did occupy her mind endlessly was the thought of how she'd failed Holly and how she might just mend the crack between them if she told Holly the truth of what had happened when she was a baby. Holly deserved to know. Freddie had been right about that as well: the time for running away from unpalatable things was past. Freddie had said she'd be fine on her own all day, but Rose, fearing Freddie would hop up and damage her still-fragile ankle, had asked some of her aunt's friends to pop into Nettle Cottage during the day.

'I'm not a child, Rose,' Freddie had said mildly when she heard of these convoluted arrangements.

'Humour me, Freddie,' begged Rose. 'That way I can go to Dublin to visit Holly with a clear conscience.'

Now Rose slicked on some lipstick and, after one final look in the mirror, walked out into the store. She'd been there so rarely, she realised as she walked through the bed linens and kitchen department. It was a beautiful department store and yet, since Holly had gone to work there, Rose could count on one hand the number of times she'd visited.

The store had changed a lot since her last visit. Now it was spacious and airy, rather like an elegant loft apartment where you could buy beautiful things. It didn't resemble the dark, cluttered department stores of Rose's youth. She walked into the international design department, which was where she knew that Holly longed to work. Rose didn't feel intimidated by elegant assistants eyeing her up from behind the Yves St Laurent racks. Rose had long perfected the art of looking as if she belonged. But she felt a pang of guilt that her dear Holly had no such ability. Holly had inherited Rose's effortless sense of style but was wracked with self-doubt and insecurity. And was that Rose's fault? She ran her fingers over a rack of filmy chiffon garments in natural shades and mentally shuddered at the price, before moving on to touch exquisitely folded jeans, each pair delicately touched with crescents of silver embroidery.

'Do you need any help?' asked one of the assistants. She was pretty and nicely turned out in a white wrap shirt and black pants, but she was nothing to Holly, Rose thought. And Holly would have asked if she wanted help in a more genuine way. This girl looked as if she was longing for her break and fervently hoped nobody would require any assistance until it was over.

'No, thank you,' said Rose smoothly, gliding off.

She made her way down to the basement. The children's department was busy and Rose was able to stand near the escalator and watch her daughter at work. She and another girl, one with cropped blonde hair, were both at the cash register. Holly was carefully folding up a selection of little garments while the other girl was processing a credit card for a customer. Holly looked relaxed and happy, confident in her work, Rose realised with pleasure. Here, it seemed, her shy youngest daughter was at home. The customer began walking away with her carrier bags and Rose approached the cash register.

'Mum.' There was utter astonishment in Holly's face.

'Hello, love, I was up doing some shopping and I thought I'd surprise you,' said Rose.

'You have. Mum, this is Bunny, my friend. Bunny, this is my mother.'

'Hello, Mrs Miller,' said Bunny. 'I've got to say, you two really look alike.'

She gazed from mother to daughter. Holly's wide-spaced eyes were shyer than her mother's, but otherwise, they were the image of each other.

Rose beamed. 'Thank you for the compliment,' she said. 'I don't suppose we could have lunch, Holly?'

'I'm not due to go for another half an hour,' Holly said, looking at Bunny who nodded, 'but Bunny will cover for me.'

'They've really changed the store,' remarked Rose as the two of them took the escalator to the ground floor. 'I haven't been here for so long, I hardly recognised the place.'

'You need to visit more often,' Holly replied lightly.

They walked out of the store and Holly led the way to a small coffee shop. 'Is there something wrong, Mum?' she asked as they sat down at a tiny table in the window.

Rose sighed. 'I deserve that,' she said. 'If I came to see you more often, you wouldn't automatically assume there was some tragedy if I do turn up.'

'That's not what I meant,' Holly said quickly. 'It's just . . .'

'That I never come to see you. I'm sorry. That's why I'm here: to sort out this problem between the two of us.'

Holly's eyes grew wary. 'What problem?'

'Holly, we know it exists and it's my fault. I want to make it right.'

'D'yawanna order?' A gum-chewing waitress stood over them, boredom dripping from every pore.

Rose could see that Holly was too startled to speak. 'Two tuna sandwiches on brown?' She looked to Holly for approval. Holly smiled weakly.

'Two mineral waters, one still, one sparkling,' continued Rose. 'Thank you.'

'D'wanteaorcoffee?'

'Not now,' said Rose firmly.

The waitress shuffled off.

'Is tuna fish all right for you?' Rose asked.

Holly smiled again. Rose didn't know how she was going to do this but she had to. She ploughed on: 'I'm making amends, you see. Freddie and I were talking about your father and I was so angry for what he'd done and then Freddie, quite rightly, asked me if I'd ever hurt anyone. She was trying to show me that we all make mistakes but we have to move on. And,' Rose found she couldn't bear to look into her daughter's huge dark eyes any more and she stared down at her hands which she realised she was clasping and unclasping. 'I said I'd hurt you because of the post-natal depression I went through when you were born.'

'What? I never knew you had that.' Holly was incredulous. 'Nobody told me.'

'Nobody knew,' Rose admitted. 'It was my big secret but it affected you and I never told you. I'm so sorry, love.'

She reached across the table and held Holly's unprotesting hands.

She could see the tears swell up in her daughter's eyes, could see Holly battling with them so they wouldn't fall.

'I thought it was because you'd wanted a little boy instead of me,' she said finally.

'Never,' cried Rose. 'I was so happy to have you. Midway through the pregnancy, the doctor told us you were a boy at first, but that wasn't it at all. Oh, Holly, it's so hard to explain. It was nothing to do with you, the problem was me.'

'Tell me, then. We have lots of time,' said Holly.

Rose cast her mind back twenty-eight years.

She'd been so excited in the early stages of pregnancy but towards the end, Rose had felt so tired all the time. Stella was a self-reliant little girl of nine, but Tara was a demanding five-year-old who needed a lot of attention and who didn't understand that her heavily-pregnant mother wasn't able to rush around after her. By the time the baby was due, Rose thought she'd never give birth. Instead of being eager for her baby to be born, as she had been with Stella and Tara, she was eager for the whole procedure to be over. But even that proved to be complicated. After an agonising thirty-three-hour labour, Holly was born by caesarean.

Rose could still remember lying exhausted in the hospital bed, feeling that dull ache deep in her belly and the rush of nausea from the morphine. A screaming Holly lay beside her in the hospital cot and the kind, rushed-off-their-feet nurses didn't have time to do more than pick Holly up and place her gently in Rose's arms.

'You've two other little girls, haven't you? So you're an old hand at this,' they smiled at Rose.

The pain and the misery overwhelmed Rose and she felt as if she couldn't possibly cope with this new baby, a baby who never seemed to stop crying. How could such a tiny creature make so much noise? Surely Stella and Tara hadn't cried so much? Glancing round the ward, she saw other mothers joyfully holding their new-born babies and Rose envied them for their happiness and their ability to cope.

The trail of delighted family members who visited all adored little Holly and told Rose, by now forcing herself to smile, how lucky she was. If only she felt lucky.

Everything would be better when she was home from hospital, she told herself. Being stuck in a busy ward and listening to other crying children, that was the problem. In the comfort of her own home, both she and Holly would settle. But when she got home, things got worse. Hugh did his best and Angela was great for taking care of Tara and Stella so that Rose had time to spend on Holly. But nothing Rose did seemed to help her new baby settle down, and exhaustion and misery engulfed Rose like a tidal wave of darkness. She told nobody how she felt because how could she? Covering up this shameful secret seemed to be the only option. What sort of person felt a sinking misery in her heart when she heard her baby cry? What type of mother wanted it all to go away so she could crawl into her bed until the despair and unhappiness receded?

She felt an unnatural mother, as if nobody else had ever felt that way. How could she not love Holly? What was wrong with her?

'Looking back, I don't know why I kept it to myself,' Rose said quietly. 'I think Angela guessed but I pushed her away. I refused to let anyone in, I didn't want anyone to know that I'd gone through this. Pride is a terrible thing.'

'You were depressed,' cried Holly, 'you weren't up to making decisions. Don't be so hard on yourself.'

Dear Holly, she was so kind and forgiving, Rose thought. 'Pride was part of it in the years after,' she said. 'If only I'd told you what I'd gone through, then you might have understood. I felt such huge guilt that I wasn't a very good mother for probably the first nine months of your life. And when you were a teenager and we weren't getting on, I felt as if it was all my fault for how I'd behaved when you were a baby. I thought you somehow knew and blamed me.'

'That wasn't it,' Holly admitted. 'I honestly thought you'd wanted a boy instead of me. You see, Adele told me you'd had a name picked out and everything, and after that, I felt so unwanted. It sounds so ridiculous to say it but . . .'

Rose could have cried. 'Blast Adele,' she said vehemently. 'We had lots of names and when we thought you were going to be a boy, we liked Emlyn for some reason. God knows why, it's not a name I'd pick now, but, Holly, you must never imagine that we didn't want you. Please believe me. I went through post-natal depression, I wasn't myself. It was nothing to do with you.'

The waitress thumped two sandwiches and two glasses of water onto the table.

Rose was too distraught now to even say thank you, so Holly did. Then, she stared firmly at her mother. 'Now listen, Mum, stop getting upset. It was a bit of a mix-up and I should have known better than to listen to Adele.'

'I still can't believe that you spent years thinking we wanted a boy instead of you, Holly. That's terrible.' Bitterness at those wasted years welled up in Rose's heart. She had failed Holly. She should have seen what was wrong and fixed it instead of letting the misery fester like an open wound. 'Please forgive me, please tell me we can start again.'

'Of course we can.' This time, it was as if Holly was the mother, the one who nurtured and protected. 'I can't believe I ever thought that,' Holly said ruefully. 'I should have known better but I felt so insecure and that seemed like the reason. I suppose I wanted something to blame for how I felt.'

'And I was the one to blame all along,' said her mother sadly.

'You weren't,' insisted Holly. 'I wanted there to be a reason for me feeling insecure and shy, I wanted something to blame. It's easier to blame something or someone than to face up to yourself. I am what I am and changing that is down to me.'

'But I'm your mother and I should have helped, I should have understood your insecurity.'

'You did help and you're helping now.' Holly spoke so genuinely that Rose felt the first vestiges of comfort. 'I love you, Mum, and I know you love me, isn't that all that matters? Let's put everything else behind us?'

Tears fell onto Rose's sandwich but she didn't mind. Who needed food at such a moment?

'We've got to eat up,' Holly said apologetically. 'I've only got another fifteen minutes for lunch.'

Holly wolfed down her sandwich, while Rose nibbled hers. 'During Freddie's lecture, she told me I wasn't entirely blameless over the matter of your father's affairs,' she said.

Holly listened wide-eyed as she ate.

'I knew for years and I went along with it. I should have confronted him and told him he was damaging our marriage. I honestly don't think he knew what it would do to me. For him, it was diversion, a bit of fun.'

'He's sorry now,' Holly said. 'He's shattered that you left him, Mum, and he's so sorry. He'd do anything to turn back the clock.'

'You're a good daughter,' Rose smiled. 'You took care of him.'

'He needed looking after,' Holly said simply. 'It wasn't a matter of choosing sides. But he needed me most.' She hesitated before asking the question she most wanted to know the answer to. 'Do you think there's any hope you'll make it up?'

'I don't know. I needed to resolve this between us before I thought about your father,' Rose pointed out. 'This was more important.'

Despite her constant worry about Hugh, Holly felt a burst of pride at the knowledge that she was the most important thing on her mother's mind. 'He loves you,' she said quickly. She had to stand up for her dad.

'I know,' Rose said. 'I know. I just have to decide what to do. I've made such a mess of things, haven't I? Hurting you and not dealing with the problems in my marriage.'

'Nonsense,' said Holly, feeling guilty for having said the wrong thing. 'I'm the one with the disastrous love life,' she added.

'You never tell me about your boyfriends,' Rose said quietly.

'There's never been much to tell,' Holly joked. 'When I fell in love with Richie Murdoch, I started a long line of hopeless romances.'

'You never told me what went wrong with Richie, either.'

Holly winced. 'I wanted you to guess, to be honest. He dumped me and I didn't want anyone to know.'

'I knew what he'd done all right, the little pig, but I got the impression you didn't want sympathy from me. Your father told me that you'd talked to him about Richie. I felt like a terrible mother at that point, because it was clear that you preferred to talk to your father about having your heart broken. Stella and Tara both told me their problems and you didn't.'

'Oh, Mum,' Holly said sadly. 'I never knew. I thought you didn't have a clue about Richie.'

Rose shrugged gracefully. 'Your father and I did talk, you know,' she said. 'You confided more in him than in me.'

'I met Richie at the ruby wedding party,' Holly said, suddenly grinning.

'Sorry about that,' Rose interrupted. 'His mother begged, she had nobody else to drive her and I meant to warn you that he was coming . . .'

'It was OK, really,' Holly said. 'He was flirting like mad with me but I was very cool and collected. He even wanted my phone number.'

'I hope you didn't give it to him.' Rose was enraged at the cheek of him.

'I implied that I didn't believe in revisiting old ground,' Holly said proudly.

'What about new ground?' asked her mother shyly.

Holly waved at the waitress to ask for a coffee and then began the story of Tom.

'I'm over him,' she said at the end. 'It seemed a bit stupid to long for a man who was engaged to someone else.'

'He cheated on her with you?' said Rose dubiously.

Holly shook her head. 'Nothing so scandalous, I'm afraid. Ours was the most innocent relationship in the history of Windmill Terrace. The two little old ladies in the basement probably have wilder sex lives than I do. We talked, and laughed, and . . .' Holly closed her eyes and remembered all the things they'd done. Saying it out loud, her relationship with Tom sounded as thrilling as a one-person party, but it *had* been thrilling. Her entire being had come alive when she was with him. How did you put that into words? 'I could talk to him. I've never been much good at talking to men. Kenny doesn't count, but you know what I mean. Tom was my friend. Perhaps that was the problem.' Holly looked exasperated with herself. 'The first man I can talk to and I think it's the passion of the century.'

'He liked you too, though?'

Holly nodded. 'I suppose I was waiting for him to make the first move and he didn't, and then his girlfriend came on the scene. Tara says forget him.' She looked to her mother to see if Rose agreed with this piece of advice.

'Tara's Tara, and you're you, Holly. Is he worth fighting for?'

'There's no point any more,' Holly explained. 'He's engaged, Caroline has the wedding of the century planned, probably complete with the London Philharmonic playing something to symbolise her true love for Tom as she walks up the aisle in a wedding gown trimmed with a thousand rosebuds, with a dove in her hand.'

'That sounds a bit over the top,' said Rose, who was as romantic as the next person.

'Yeah, Caroline believes in romance with a big W. Womance.'

Rose screwed up her nose fastidiously. 'She sounds awful. You should save him from her.'

'That was Kenny's plan. He dragged in three beautiful male models to flirt with Caroline and let her see that the world was her oyster, and why tie herself down with marriage just yet.' Holly smiled. 'Kenny should never have got satellite television. He's been watching too many romantic comedies where that type of thing happens with great regularity.'

'Like where the Julia Roberts character gets Rupert Everett to pretend to be her boyfriend and it makes her ex jealous?'

'I *love* that film,' sighed Holly. 'Funnily enough, she

doesn't get the man at the end, either! But, she doesn't mind; she's happy without him. If only real life was as simple as it is in films.'

'It could be,' said her mother. 'You should tell Tom how you feel.'

Holly shook her head. 'Tom's the past. It's over. That's why I walked out of his engagement party. What was the point of driving myself insane by trying to remain friends with him? I don't want to be friends with him. I'm crazy about him. Was crazy about him,' she amended. 'I needed a clean break. You can't just be friends if you really fancy someone.'

'When Harry Met Sally!' smiled her mother.

'Exactly. So Tom is in the past and I have a good future ahead of me.' Holly spoke firmly. 'Secondly, I'm going for the job in the international fashion department. Gabriella's leaving and I know I can do it. I'm not afraid of it any more.'

'I'm so proud of you,' said Rose, her voice quivering with emotion.

Holly's smile was sweet as she leaned across the empty plates and stroked her mother's hand. 'I know,' she said.

CHAPTER THIRTY-SEVEN

'Oh Mummy, it was great and Daddy came too but he said he was scared! I wasn't.' Amelia was gleeful at the notion that she hadn't minded the scary bit of the Snow White train journey in Euro Disney, but her father had.

Stella smiled at the phone, happy that Amelia was enjoying her holiday but miserable because she'd have loved to have been the one taking darling Amelia to Disney. Well, her and Nick. They'd talked about it often enough but now, it was hardly an option. So when Glenn had suggested that he take their daughter to the theme park as part of his two-week holiday with her in June, Stella hadn't felt able to disagree. It was important that Glenn had a good relationship with Amelia and Stella now knew enough about fractured families to know that she didn't want to use Amelia in some sort of divorced parents' power struggle. Time spent with Glenn was for Amelia's good and Stella had told Glenn that it was vital he kept in touch with Amelia more regularly.

'She needs to grow up knowing you're a part of her life, and that she's a part of yours,' Stella had said.

'Yeah, I worry that she'll forget about me,' Glenn said. 'I try to keep in touch but you know what I'm like. I've never been good at birthdays and stuff.'

'I know,' Stella replied crisply. 'Don't worry, I won't let you forget in future. This is for Amelia.'

'Bye, Mummy, miss you,' said Amelia, sounding plaintive for the first time in her excited monologue about Disney.

'I miss you too, darling, but you'll be home soon and

you've got lots of exciting things to do,' Stella said cheerily, not wanting to upset Amelia by letting her know just how much she missed her.

' 'kay,' said Amelia. 'Bye.'

Stella hung up and went back into the kitchen where she was making cheese on toast for her dinner. With Amelia gone, and Nick more or less out of her life, Stella didn't feel like bothering with proper food.

It had been a week since the big row with Nick; a week in which they hadn't seen each other. For the first few days, Stella had steeled herself not to phone him. He could make the first move, she decided. Then, he'd phoned her on Friday morning to tell her that his mother was in hospital and that he was driving to visit her.

'She was in bed with flu and she fell trying to get up. She's broken her hip and she's very distressed,' he said. He sounded weary and miserable. 'She's always had a weak chest and my worry is that she'll get pneumonia, and she won't be strong enough to fight it. I'm sorry,' he said again. 'It's been a nightmare week. Jenna's in trouble in school again and that's not all. She and Wendy are at war; Jenna's being very rude to her mother. I've tried talking to her but she keeps saying "What do you care?" I can't get through to her and Wendy goes mad and says I'm not trying to sort it out. You can't imagine how awful it is.'

Stella thought she could picture the scene pretty well. A distraught Nick trying to keep the peace but somehow failing everyone: failing Jenna by not being her live-at-home dad any more and failing Wendy by not performing her undoable task. And it was undoable. Nick couldn't sort out Jenna's relationship with her mother. That was between Wendy and Jenna. No matter what the fallout from the divorce, Wendy shouldn't blame every difficulty on Nick. She'd destroy his relationship with Jenna if she did.

Even though she'd sworn to herself she wouldn't say too much about the Jenna/Wendy relationship, Stella had to say something.

'Nick, don't let Wendy manipulate you into a situation where the only times you talk to Jenna, it's to harangue her.'

'I don't harangue her,' protested Nick.

'That was the wrong word,' Stella said. 'But you end up talking firmly to Jenna every time you see her. I know,' she added, hearing Nick about to interrupt, 'she's been behaving badly at school and being awful to Wendy but they're two separate issues. You can't control Jenna to the extent that you tell her how to deal with her relationship with her mother. She's growing up, she's testing her boundaries.' Stella grinned to herself. Now she was standing up for Jenna's rights in all of this, instead of giving out about her.

There was silence on the other end of the phone. 'You're right, Stella. I'm sorry you're having to deal with the fall-out of all of this. I'm sorry about everything,' he added. 'I should have phoned you to tell you that, but I didn't. This morning, I decided that this had gone on long enough and I was going to drop round this evening and try to sort things out but now . . .'

'It's all right,' Stella interrupted. 'We can talk when you get back.'

She wasn't sure where that talk would get them, but what the hell. They'd talk.

He rang again on Sunday night, his voice hoarse with tiredness.

'She's turned a corner, the doctors think. In fact, she's just given out to me for looking as if I hadn't brushed my hair this morning, which is a sign that she's on the mend.'

'That's wonderful,' said Stella. She'd really liked Nick's feisty mother and had hated to think of that bright spark quenched with a painful, frightening illness.

'All going well, I'll be back in Dublin on Tuesday.' He paused. 'Could I take you out to dinner?'

Stella thought about it. If she and Nick were to solve their differences, they needed to have a frank discussion. Doing this in a crowded restaurant would probably be a mistake. 'I'll cook you dinner here,' she said.

For the first time in a week, Stella woke on Monday morning feeling happier. She was looking forward to seeing Nick in spite of everything. She was in work early and flew through her morning's appointments.

'How are things?' asked Vicki tentatively just before lunch. Stella shrugged. 'OK.'

'Good,' remarked Vicki. 'Are you in the mood for a girlie gossipy lunch?'

The previous week, Stella had worked at her desk during lunch, feeling too heartbroken to put on a convivial act. Today, lunch sounded great.

'I'd love lunch,' Stella said. 'But what about Craig?'

These days, Craig often joined their lunches. He and Vicki were getting increasingly serious about each other and Stella loved teasing Vicki about wedding bells.

'Craig knows his place,' said Vicki primly. 'In bed, behind the hoover, in the kitchen,' she recited. 'Never at girlie lunches.'

'So, tell all,' commanded Vicki when they were sitting at a cosy table in a jammed restaurant across the street, having ordered enough food for a regiment. Stella, who hadn't been hungry for a week, was suddenly ravenous.

'He's coming over for dinner tomorrow night and we're going to talk. About everything.'

'Be honest, tell him how you feel,' advised Vicki. 'And if he doesn't understand how much he upset you, dump him.' Vicki was very fond of Nick but she was fiercely protective of her friend. If Nick hurt Stella again, he'd have Vicki to contend with.

'If I phone you at midnight tomorrow, sobbing my heart out, will you come round and rescue me?' asked Stella.

'Promise.'

When Stella got back to her office, there was a message on her direct line voicemail.

'Hello, this is Mrs Winston, vice principal of The Harmon School. I'm trying to contact Mr Nick Cavaletto about his daughter, Jenna, and his office gave us this number. If you could help, Ms Miller, I'd be grateful.' She left a phone number, which Stella rapidly scribbled down before dialling.

'Hello, Mrs Winston, this is Stella Miller, I'm, er . . . a friend of Nick's.' She could hardly say she was anything else, could she? 'He's out of Dublin right now on family business, can I help? Is there a problem with Jenna?'

'Yes, and I'm afraid I can't reach Mrs Cavaletto either.'

'I can try to reach Nick on his mobile and tell him to ring you,' suggested Stella. Whatever the problem with Jenna was, she wasn't getting involved.

'I have tried his mobile but it's off,' pointed out Mrs Winston.

'Right,' said Stella. He wouldn't be able to keep the phone switched on in the hospital ward. 'I know where he is; it's just a matter of getting a message to him. I'll do my best.'

'Thank you. That would be a great help.'

'Jenna's not ill is she?' Stella asked, just to be sure that there wasn't anything seriously wrong.

Mrs Winston's snort of disapproval was quite audible.

'She's not ill; she's been suspended and we need somebody to take her home.'

It took a few minutes to track Nick down in the hospital and he sounded nervous when he heard Stella's voice. 'What's wrong, Stella?' he asked.

She explained briefly.

'Shit. That's all we need. What has she done?'

'Mrs Winston didn't tell me and I didn't ask. She can't get hold of Wendy and they want Jenna to go home.'

'Thank you, I'm really grateful to you for stepping in,' said Nick wearily. 'I'll phone later.'

But when he phoned back in fifteen minutes, it was to ask for Stella's help.

'Jenna's in deep trouble,' he said, sounding even more shattered than ever. 'She was caught bunking off maths and smoking with a friend in the showers and when they were caught and the teacher gave out to them, Jenna went ballistic and said something along the lines of "she could bloody well smoke if she felt like it". Bad language was a major feature of her tirade, apparently. Mrs Winston has just given me an earful about how they won't tolerate that type of behaviour in the school. Jenna's on a warning and if anything like this happens again, she could be expelled.'

Stella winced.

'The problem is, Wendy isn't at home and her mobile is turned off. The school insist that Jenna is picked up. I know this is asking you a huge favour what with all that's happened between us, and I know you're busy at work, but would you do it?'

'I can't imagine she'll even get in the car with me,' Stella pointed out.

'She will,' said Nick grimly. 'I just spoke to her on her mobile and she was very subdued.'

Stella couldn't imagine Jenna being subdued. She must ask Mrs Winston for the secret.

'Of course I'll do it,' she said with a confidence she didn't feel. Jenna would probably be as rude as hell to her, but despite their row, she couldn't let Nick down. If he'd been just another parent with a kid who needed picking up, she'd have helped.

'Thanks,' said Nick gratefully.

It was just after three in the afternoon when Stella drove into The Harmon School. A group of male and female students in grey tracksuits sloped back into the school to face the afternoon after sports.

'I'm looking for Mrs Winston's office,' Stella said to a couple of sweet kids who looked so young that they had to be first years.

Following their directions, she found herself in a modern corridor with signs pointing to various offices. At the principal and vice principal's office, the school secretary sat in an anteroom in front of a computer. She was a strikingly attractive girl and Stella imagined that all the male students had crushes on her.

566

'Can I help?'

'I'm Stella Miller and I'm here for Jenna Cavaletto.'

The girl's face dropped. 'Oh,' she said.

'Is she in very big trouble?' asked Stella.

'Pretty much,' said the girl. 'She's lucky the principal is away. He's tougher than Mrs Winston.'

Stella wondered what the principal could possibly be like because Mrs Winston had sounded quite stern on the phone. She turned out to be tall, lean woman with short grey hair and a grave, intelligent face.

'Ms Miller, thanks for coming. You're Jenna's stepmother, I believe.'

Stella sank into the proffered chair. 'Not precisely. I'm a friend of her father's. He'll be home tomorrow and I'm sure he and Mrs Cavaletto will come in to discuss things.'

'You were good to come and pick Jenna up. We have a policy of not allowing pupils to remain on the premises when something like this happens. If they spend the day in class, suddenly they've done this brave thing and stood up to the staff. That seriously undermines everything we stand for. We have found that sending the pupil home gives a firm message that this behaviour is not acceptable.'

'Of course it isn't,' Stella murmured.

Mrs Winston buzzed for Jenna to be brought in.

Stella wondered if she ought to let Mrs Winston in on the fact that Jenna might refuse point-blank to go home with her.

She decided not to.

Jenna came into the room, her face white. Her expression was minus the usual truculence she displayed whenever she met Stella.

'Hi, Jenna,' said Stella flatly. 'I've come to take you home.'

'OK,' said Jenna quietly, looking at the parquet floor.

'I hope you'll think about what I've said, Jenna,' said Mrs Winston. 'If you're not prepared to behave in a reasonable manner, then we don't want you in Harmon.'

'Yes,' mumbled Jenna.

Despite the fact that on many occasions, Stella would have done anything to see Jenna downcast and reprimanded, now that it had happened, she felt a surge of pity for the girl. Jenna didn't look like a tough, rebellious girl any more. In her school uniform with a biro stain on a cuff and her school bag dangling from one shoulder, she looked like a kid who needed a hug.

Still, she wouldn't appreciate one from Stella.

'Let's go,' Stella said. 'Thanks, Mrs Winston.'

Jenna led the way, seemingly anxious to be out of Mrs Winston's presence.

The two of them walked in silence to Stella's car.

When she switched the ignition on, the radio came on and Stella made no effort to turn the volume down. Given their past history she didn't want to talk to Jenna in case the girl started raging against her again.

'I suppose I'm going to get a lecture now,' snapped Jenna as they reached the school gates.

Stella, concentrating on getting out into a line of heavy traffic, shook her head.

'Not from me. That's between you and your parents.'

'But you're my stepmother.' The way Jenna said it, made the word sound like triple axe-murderer.

A month ago, Stella would have flared up at Jenna's tone of voice. Now, she'd learned her lesson. Jenna was a troubled kid and it wasn't Stella's job to sort her out. All Stella could do was be calm with her.

'No, Jenna, I'm not your stepmother. You're too old for a stepmother, you don't need my help. And I'm not getting into a fight with you. If that's what you want, phone your mother. I'm driving you to my home as a favour to your father, that's all. If you want to fight, I'll turn this car around and deliver you back to Mrs Winston.'

Jenna said nothing.

'Do you want to be dropped home or do you want to come to my house until we can reach your mother?'

'Your house,' Jenna said quickly.

568

'Why? You don't usually like being in my house.'

'Dad said I should go home with you until we can talk to Mum.'

The rest of the trip was silent. Stella thought about the possibility of Wendy arriving at her house in fury and engaging in a screaming fit. Strangely, the notion didn't upset her. Wendy could scream and rant all she wanted. Stella was out of the Cavaletto family loop. They could sort things out on their own. And they had better do it quickly before Jenna did something really outrageous. The poor kid was looking for attention and nobody seemed to realise it.

At home, Stella walked in, leaving Jenna to follow uncertainly. The message light on the answering machine was on, blinking furiously. Stella walked past it.

'You've got messages,' said Jenna.

'I'm not really in the mood for messages,' Stella said. 'I need a cup of tea first. Would you like some tea or a sandwich, Jenna?'

'No.'

The anger finally flared in Stella. 'You say no *thank you*,' she said fiercely.

'Says who?' Jenna's words were cheeky but there was a flicker of uncertainty in her face.

'I say so,' Stella rapped. 'Let's get one thing straight, there are different rules in operation now.'

Jenna blinked in surprise.

'This is my home and I was ready to share it with your father. I loved him. Because I loved him, I made a big effort with you and you threw it back in my face. That's your choice, you have the right to make it. Nobody can make you like me. But,' Stella glared at the girl, eyes flashing in anger, 'you do not have the choice to be rude to me in my own home. If you can't be civil, you won't be coming here. Simple. It's a bit like Mrs Winston and your school. Life has rules, Jenna, and if you keep breaking them, eventually people get fed up with you. Frankly, I have bigger worries than you right now.'

Stella went into the kitchen and boiled the kettle, feeling the fire in her veins cool down. She shouldn't have said that, she thought, leaning her head against the cool of the fridge. So much for being calm and controlled. The *Art Of Step* experts would be horrified if they'd heard her. She heard the television being switched on in the sitting room. When she'd made herself some camomile tea, she went in to Jenna and found her with a packet of cigarettes in her hand.

'Don't even think about smoking here.'

'I wasn't going to,' Jenna said quickly. 'Dad will kill me for smoking.'

Stella smiled for the first time in ages. 'My father went mad when my youngest sister started smoking. She was seventeen and he said he'd ground her for the rest of her life. She stopped, and started again when she left home.'

'What's she like?' asked Jenna, looking interested.

'Holly is beautiful; she's very tall and dark haired and she works in Lee's Department Store.'

'I love Lee's,' said Jenna enthusiastically. 'Does she get a discount? Can I meet her?'

'I don't think it would be a good idea for you to meet Holly,' Stella said. 'She's been going through a rough time lately and I know you're not too keen on members of the Miller family.'

'I like Amelia,' protested Jenna.

'It's only me you hate, right?' Stella said wryly.

'I don't hate you,' mumbled Jenna.

Silence reigned for a few moments.

'Where *is* Amelia?' asked Jenna.

'In Euro Disney with her father.'

'Oh. I thought Dad said you and he were going there with her.'

From the sad look on Jenna's face when she said this, Stella intuited that this had been another nail in the coffin. Jenna had been jealous as hell that her father loved Amelia.

'We were going to go to France,' Stella said quietly, 'but now that your father and I are ... well, the plans have changed. Amelia's father has taken her on holiday for two weeks and he said wanted to take her to Euro Disney.'

'What do you mean "the plans have changed"?' Jenna looked suspicious.

Stella debated telling Jenna the truth. It might be interesting to see how the girl reacted to the news of her father and Stella splitting up. She'd probably jump for joy, which would be final proof, if proof were needed, that Jenna hated the idea of another woman in her father's life.

'We're probably going to split up,' Stella said flatly. She waited for Jenna's reaction but instead of the satisfied smirk she'd expected, the girl's face fell.

The knowing adult expression had vanished. Jenna looked like a nervous kid who'd been caught out doing something wrong.

'What is it?' asked Stella curiously.

Jenna shook her head mutely.

'Fine.' Stella picked up the cup of camomile tea and walked to her bedroom door.

'I'm sorry.' Jenna's voice was small and full of remorse. 'I didn't mean it.'

'Didn't mean what?'

'Didn't mean you to split up. I never wanted to hurt Dad,' bleated Jenna tearfully. 'I love him. It's only because Mum said he'd forget about us if . . .' She broke off and rubbed her eyes roughly with her sleeve.

'He'd forget about you if . . .' prompted Stella gently.

'If he had a new family,' finished Jenna, and raised her chin at Stella as if to say 'you can't deny it'.

'Could you imagine your father forgetting about you under any circumstances?' Stella asked.

Jenna's pretty face was unsure.

'Because I can't. He loves you, adores you, Jenna.' Stella felt unbearably sorry for this mixed-up girl who could even imagine that her devoted father would neglect her. 'He'd never forget you and he wouldn't be much of a father if he did. And he's a good dad, isn't he?'

Jenna nodded tearfully.

'But you hate me,' she said suddenly.

Stella sighed, feeling guilty. 'I don't hate you, Jenna. And I'm really sorry if I've made you think that, honestly I'm sorry. I dislike the fact that you're rude to me and do your best to make my life difficult.'

Jenna had the grace to look ashamed.

'But disliking your behaviour isn't the same as disliking you. Whereas you haven't really given me a chance from the start, as if you blame me for the fact that your parents are divorced.' There, she'd said it. Stella held her breath. With Jenna being honest with Stella for the first time ever, it had seemed like a good idea to clear the air once and for all. But had that been a mistake?

'Mum said . . .' Jenna stopped.

Stella definitely didn't want to get into any conversations about what Wendy thought, so she swiftly moved the subject on. 'What does Sara think about your father and me?'

'Sara told me not to be stupid and that it was never going to happen: they weren't going to get back together again.'

Jenna looked sadly at the floor. She looked up to her big sister and had felt like some stupid kid when Sara had talked like that to her. 'What planet are you on?' Sara had said angrily. 'Mum and Dad are better off apart. Have you forgotten all the yelling and screaming? I haven't. It's nice to have a bit of peace and quiet. Just because Mum decides she wants Dad back doesn't mean he's going to go. And would it be any better? Grow up, Jenna.'

Jenna had always kept that hope alive in her heart, the hope that everything might work out and she'd have her mum and dad together again. Most of the time, she knew it was a childish dream, like when she looked into her snow globe from Disney and dreamed what it would be like to be inside it for a moment. She knew parents who split didn't magically get back together but Mum had made it sound as if it could happen.

'You want your Dad back, pet, don't you?' Mum had said

that day after she'd been out with Aunt Clarisse. Mum had been crying and she'd been drinking. Jenna hated Clarisse, stupid old bat, always talking in a put-on posh voice, except when she thought nobody could hear her.

Clarisse must have told Mum that Dad wasn't happy and that they could make him come home again, if only they tried.

'Clarisse says she knows you hate that woman and you've made it obvious from the start,' Mum said.

Jenna had felt ashamed then, to think that someone as horrible as Aunt Clarisse thought she'd been a bitch on purpose. I mean, hello? Jenna was angry because nobody told her anything, she was treated like this kid and expected to go along with everything. Dad had known Stella for ages before he'd told Jenna. Even Amelia, who was a kid, had known about it. And then when she'd met Stella, she'd behaved badly and Stella had looked so dismissive of her, like Stella couldn't imagine why anyone would be so awful. Jenna had felt like a worm. Worse than a worm, a maggot.

Stella was so calm and elegant, she looked like the sort of person you could tell stuff to but Jenna couldn't, not after that first time. She couldn't become Nice Jenna when she'd started out as Horrible Jenna.

Stella put her tea cup down on the coffee table and sat down beside Jenna. 'I wasn't trying to be your mum, Jenna,' she said. 'I love your dad and I only wanted to be friends with you. That's all.'

'I love my dad too,' said Jenna and burst into tears. She jumped up and rushed into the bathroom, slamming the door.

Stella sighed. Oh well, she'd tried.

When the door rang just before six, Stella knew who it would be.

Wendy Cavaletto was slim, with frosted blonde hair in a pageboy cut, light blue eyes expertly made up, and was dressed immaculately. Her skin was tanned and certainly showed her age, but what surprised Stella was how attractive she was. Somehow, the idea of Wendy had developed into a screaming harpy with claws out and a dissatisfied expression on her face. To be faced with this stylish woman in a black linen trouser suit was a surprise.

'Come in, Wendy,' Stella said. 'I'm Stella Miller.' She didn't hold her hand out, not knowing whether the gesture would be repudiated or not.

'I know, hello. Thank you for this.' Wendy managed a brief smile but she was tense too, Stella realised. The other woman's jaw was set firmly with unease despite the smile.

'This way.' Stella led the way into the room where Jenna stood anxiously waiting for her mother.

'Hi, Mum,' said Jenna.

'What was it this time?' demanded Wendy, glaring at her daughter, the cool persona gone. 'Who did you cheek today, madam?'

Stella's pity for Jenna went up another notch. It was easy to see how Jenna was a touchy child who flared with anger at the drop of a hat. She'd learned it from her mother. 'Would you like some water or coffee, Wendy?' she asked, keen to be out of the room for this confrontation.

'No thank you, we're going.' Wendy's voice was clipped. 'Thank you for picking her up. I was with a friend and hadn't bothered to turn my phone on but I know you had to leave work early. I just hope Jenna appreciates it, although she never appreciates anything I do for her.' This sounded like a familiar tirade.

'It wasn't a problem,' Stella replied quickly. She felt downright sorry for Jenna now. She couldn't imagine how she and Amelia would get on if she dressed Amelia down in public like Wendy did with her daughter. Shouting at Jenna wouldn't solve this problem.

'Bye.' Wendy whisked round and headed for the door, clearly just as uncomfortable as Stella was.

Jenna didn't move. 'Thanks, Stella,' she said quietly. She looked up and gave a grin, so small and quick that Stella wasn't sure if she'd imagined it or not. 'I'll see you soon,' Jenna added.

Stella didn't know how to reply but followed Jenna to the door. She probably wouldn't see Jenna again, not if she and Nick decided to finally end their relationship.

Wendy had already climbed into her car and Jenna swivelled on the doorstep to talk to Stella.

'Jenna!' called Wendy from the car, her tone impatient.

Jenna shrugged. 'Got to go, bye.'

'Goodbye,' Stella answered. Some impulse made her reach out and clasp Jenna's shoulder in encouragement. As soon as she'd made contact, she regretted it. How many times had Jenna spurned such a gesture. But Jenna didn't wrench herself away this time.

'Thanks,' she said in a small voice, and ran down the path to her mother's car.

Stella shut the door and wondered if she'd finally managed to break the ice with Nick's daughter – or if Jenna was merely happy because she thought Stella and her father were going to split up? Since Stella had mentioned the possibility, Jenna had been verging on the polite, which was possibly a sign that she was delirious. But, had there been a hint of something else, a sense that Jenna didn't mind Stella quite as much as she'd done before? No, probably not, Stella reflected. Jenna hated her far too much for that.

CHAPTER THIRTY-EIGHT

Holly waved at Bunny across a rail of tweenie denim jackets and sparkly T-shirts. Bunny, who looked fed up with spending the day getting ready for the launch of the summer sale, raised her eyes to heaven and then went back to checking that no toddler party dress went unpriced. The August sale proper would start tomorrow morning but this evening, at six, Lee's would be stampeded by the shoppers who had store credit cards and were being treated to a special twenty per cent pre-sale evening. Both Holly and Bunny were veterans of this pre-sale night and it was usually miles more frantic than the actual first day of the sale. The store card customers were zealous shoppers and would fight to the death for the chance to buy classic items at massive discounts. In anticipation of this deluge, Lee's had been closed all day while the staff marked everything up for the sale. The actual pricing of all the stock had been worked out painstakingly a week earlier, but making sure that every item was reticketed was exhausting and time-consuming work. It was now just five and Holly hoped that Bunny would be ready to grab a quick cup of coffee in anticipation of the caffeine-free three hours shopping to come.

She hunkered down beside her friend. 'Have you nearly finished?' she asked her friend.

'Five more minutes,' said Bunny. 'I should have been finished ages ago but the new girl, Meg, wasted an hour putting fifty per cent off stickers on all the Pretty Mama baby gear which is their new season stuff, so I had to de-sticker it all. I don't know what recreational pharmaceuticals Miss Jackson was on when she hired Meg. She's very sweet and everything, but mentally, she's away with the fairies. Ooh, here she comes.'

Holly watched her replacement with interest. Meg certainly looked the part of a children's department sales assistant, being in her early twenties and baby-faced with an engaging, lop-sided smile.

'Bunny, you're going to kill me but I forgot to take the box of flip-flops out of the stock room. There's hundreds of them and I haven't done them yet. Sorree!'

Bunny tried to glare at Meg and failed.

'We'll do them together,' she sighed. 'By the way, Meg, this is Holly who worked here before you.'

'Lovely to meet you,' said Meg. 'Bunny says you've gone to international fashion. I'd love to do that.'

Bunny shot Holly a look that said Meg wasn't likely to end up making the tea in international fashion if she mis-stickered things with incorrect fifty per cent discounts and left whole boxes of sale goods in the stockroom. It was one thing to do that with flip-flops and baby clothes, another thing entirely to do it with designer evening gowns where a fifty per cent mistake would pay most people's mortgage for two months.

'Get the flip-flops and we'll have them finished in ten minutes, right?' Bunny said to Meg. 'I'll join you in the canteen in fifteen minutes for a coffee,' she added to Holly. 'I've got to rush out to the car park for a ciggy first.'

'Don't talk about cigarettes,' pleaded Holly, who was trying to give up. Since she'd applied for – and got – Gabriella's job in international fashion, she'd cut down to five a day. It hadn't been easy. There were times when she longed for her usual twenty a day and only iron will kept her from rushing out at every break and chain smoking. If she could keep this up for another month, she planned to give up totally. She made her way up to the canteen, thinking that so much had changed in the past few weeks. Her transformation to a five-a-day smoker was only one. The other change was one that wasn't instantly obvious: it was in Holly herself. Somehow, Holly had discovered that most elusive quality of all: self-confidence. It wasn't a flood by any means, more of a slow, gentle trickle. But it made all the difference to her.

Finding out that she really was good at her new job also helped. She had an instinctive eye for what worked fashion-wise, an instinct that the department's customers appreciated. They also appreciated Holly's genuine kindness; she didn't differentiate between a wealthy chauffeur-driven matron who could afford to buy everything in the shop and an *In Style* addict who'd saved like mad to buy one beautiful designer piece.

In the canteen, Holly got herself some green tea and sat down beside Annmarie, one of her new colleagues in the fashion department.

Exquisitely groomed and outwardly self-composed, Annmarie was the sort of person Holly would have been utterly intimidated by before. But now that they were working together, Holly found that Annmarie was nothing like she'd imagined, was friendly, bubbly and possessed of a wicked sense of humour.

'Toffee?' said Annmarie, proffering a bag of sweets.

'I'd love one.' Holly reached into the bag.

'Take two,' suggested Annmarie. 'You'll need the sugar kick.'

She was right. By half eight, Holly had never been so tired in her life. The pre-sale night in children's wear had *nothing* on this crazed, handbag-jabbing frenzy where grown women rampaged through rails of designer clothes, wailing with rage when they found that the perfect Prada suit only came in an eight when they needed a twelve. And who did they blame for this mean-spirited turn of events? The sales staff.

The initial frenzy had calmed by now and the shoppers were more relaxed as they flicked through the rails. In their corner of international design, Holly and Annmarie allowed themselves to relax.

'Remind me never to wear these boots again,' said Annmarie, through gritted teeth. She held out a foot encased in a soft suede ankle boot with a heel like a dagger. 'They may look nice but they're not made for sale night.'

Holly was about to reply when she saw two customers approaching and she put on her professional and welcoming smile; a smile which slowly froze into a rictus. One of the customers was Caroline, the other a woman who could only have been Caroline's mother. She had the same petite frame, the same girlish blonde hair and the same pixie-ish sense of dress. Right now, they both also had the same slit-eyed expression on their faces.

'I hope you're happy,' hissed the older version at Holly, who recoiled at such naked rage.

Annmarie's perfectly waxed eyebrows arched.

'There's no point talking to her, Mother,' sneered Caroline, her face just as contorted with temper as her mother's. 'She's played a clever game after all. She thinks she's won, but she hasn't!'

'Excuse me, can I help?' said Annmarie smoothly, stepping in front of a shell-shocked Holly.

'You can't. Only she can help. She stole my fiancé!' shrieked Caroline.

'What are you talking about?' asked Holly, moving out from behind Annmarie. She wasn't going to hide; she had nothing to hide.

'You know!' hissed Caroline Snr. 'Don't go all coy on us. I told Caroline you were a Trojan horse all right. And Tom was taken in by you, well, I'll have you know that you'll never be happy with him . . .'

'I haven't seen Tom since the night of the engagement party,' protested Holly. What was going on here?

'Don't play games with me. You know what I'm talking about!' shrieked Caroline. 'You stole him from me! He moved out this morning. Just packed up and moved, said it wasn't working out. Can you believe that?'

Her mother glowered at Holly. 'Tell her what happened when you asked was there anyone else,' she urged.

'Oh yes, I was just coming to that,' Caroline snarled. 'I said that I wouldn't force him to stay if he didn't want to, but that I needed to know one thing, just one thing – was he going to *you*!' She almost spat the word '*you*' at Holly. 'At least he had the manners to look ashamed and he didn't lie to me, not like you, you . . . you cow! Lying to me that you haven't seen him when I know you have!'

Annmarie shot Holly an anguished look and was surprised to find that the beginning of a smile was spreading across her colleague's lovely face.

'Caroline, I think you should leave,' said Holly pleasantly. 'You're making a big mistake here. If Tom has left you, then it's your fault, not mine. I haven't seen him since your engagement party and that's the truth.'

For once, Caroline was speechless.

'Tom and I have never been anything but friends,' Holly added. She could say that with her hand on her heart. No matter what she'd felt about Tom, there had never been a moment between them where he'd betrayed Caroline or said anything untoward to Holly. For sure, she'd wished it was different, but what she'd wished didn't count.

'I don't believe you,' said Caroline. 'I've seen the way he looks at you, the way he talks to you.'

'Caroline, Tom and I have never done anything for you to be jealous of,' said Holly.

'Oh yes, well why did he say 'sorry, sorry,' when I asked was he leaving me for you?' shrieked Caroline. 'Why didn't he deny it?'

'I don't know,' said Holly, feeling the excitement singing in her heart. Tom had left Caroline that morning; for her. He was coming to her, she knew it.

'Liar,' hissed Caroline's mother.

Annmarie took charge. 'Madam,' she said in a voice that dripped with icy politeness. 'I'm afraid we do not allow our staff to be harangued by members of the public. This is clearly some sort of misunderstanding and if you don't calm down, I shall have to call security.'

The two women turned pink with fury at being out-manoeuvred but Caroline saw that Annmarie meant what she said.

'Come on,' she said to her mother. 'We've said all we wanted to say.' She shot one parting glance at Holly, a look that would curdle milk, then they stormed off.

'You're going to have to tell me what that's all about,' remarked Annmarie.

Holly's smile lit up her face. 'It's quite a story, all right,' she said.

Holly stopped at her favourite deli on the way home and stocked up. Definitely Italian tonight. As she carried her purchases to the bus stop, she sang to herself, not caring if anyone heard her or not.

'You look happy,' said the bus driver when she got off at the end of Windmill Terrace. 'Got a date?'

Holly beamed at him. 'A hot one,' she said.

There were two 'For Sale' signs on houses near theirs on Windmill Terrace, plus a planning permission application stuck onto the gate of number 65. The revamp starts here, Holly thought. The area was about to be upgraded and no doubt the landlord was already working out how to entice his tenants into leaving so he could sell the house to developers. It was what Holly, Kenny and Joan had been dreading for months, but it didn't worry Holly today. Everything was going to be fine.

At home, she started preparations on the Italian meat ball dish that Tom had once praised. When the raw meat balls were mixed and shaped, she put them into the fridge to be cooked later. They wouldn't take long and when Tom arrived, she wanted to be ready to offer him a gorgeous meal while he told her everything.

Next, she stepped into the shower and covered herself in her favourite shower gel, the Jo Malone one Kenny had bought her and which was used sparingly because it was expensive. Luxuriating in the glorious scent, Holly dried herself and then slathered on Fairy Cake body lotion, rubbing it into every inch of her body. Finally, she slipped on her most beautiful underwear and topped it all with a long vintage silk dress, high mules and a pink silk flower in her hair. She was ready.

With every candle in the flat lit, she turned off the lights, switched on the CD player and waited for Tom. He'd left Caroline. He'd left Caroline *for her*.

When ten came and went without so much as a twinge of the doorbell, Holly pulled the flower from her hair and went to the fridge where she ate cheese and crackers standing up. She switched off the CD player and tried to find something amusing on the TV. She could always switch it off later when Tom came.

By eleven, she'd realised he wasn't coming. Despondently, she switched off the TV, blew out the candles and went to bed. This time, the heartbreak was worse than before. Then, she hadn't actually believed that Tom was in love with her. She'd hoped, but she'd had no proof.

Now, thanks to Caroline's tirade that evening, Holly had allowed herself to believe that Tom did love her and that he'd come to her. Stupid, stupid Holly for believing that. Caroline's jealousy had made Holly the number one suspect. Tom was probably just fed up with Caroline and Holly had nothing to do with it. How could she have been so naive?

The following morning, the queue for the sale snaked right round the building and almost to the staff entrance at the back when Holly arrived at Lee's.

'Some of them have been waiting all night,' said the security man as he let her in.

'I know how they feel,' she muttered.

Misery emanated from Holly in waves but if Annmarie wondered why Holly was no longer the joyous woman she'd been the previous day, she was too kind to ask. Besides, they were all too busy to do anything so mundane as talk.

By evening, the department looked like a mild tornado

had flashed through, whipping every second garment and throwing it into the wrong corner, inside out into the bargain. Holly and Annmarie surveyed their portion of the kingdom with dismay. It was their job to stay late and sort the place out. Either that, or get in at seven in the morning and do it then.

'Tonight,' suggested Annmarie. 'That way we don't have to get up at the crack of dawn tomorrow.'

Holly nodded. She'd tried so hard all day to seem cheery and good humoured, and she was worn out with the effort.

The house was silent as the grave when she let herself in that night. It was just after ten and there was no music coming from Kenny and Joan's. They were probably out. Holly, who would have loved to have gone in to her neighbours for some comfort and consolation, opened her door wearily. She dumped her handbag down on the counter and worked out how many cigarettes she'd had that day. At least ten, which was awful. But she still felt like one now.

There was a peremptory rap on the door; not the sort of knock made by either Joan or Kenny. A businesslike knock. It could be the new tenant upstairs, a nervy man in his thirties who had thin red lips which he'd spent altogether too long licking on the day Holly had first met him. Creepy was the word that came to mind. She was not in the mood for creepy tonight. Grimly, Holly wrenched the door open. Standing there with an assortment of suitcases and an unpacked draughtsman's desk, was Tom.

'I never even heard you,' said Holly, looking in amazement at all the belongings strewn over the second-floor landing.

'Kenny helped,' said Tom.

'Remind me never to volunteer for anything ever again,' groaned Kenny, staggering up the last step with a cardboard packing case.

'I've moved out of the flat in Glasnevin,' said Tom.

'I know,' Holly replied.

'How . . . ?'

'I met Caroline and she . . . erm . . . told me you'd split

up.' Holly knew she sounded very formal but she didn't care. She was not going to be hurt again. No more jumping to conclusions for Holly Miller.

'Where did you meet Caroline?' inquired Kenny casually as he flicked imaginary dust from his oatmeal linen shirt.

'She came into Lee's. We bumped into each other,' Holly stammered.

Kenny shot her a look that spoke volumes.

Tom was staring at her, she knew, but she deliberately didn't look up at him. She wasn't going to make a fool of herself.

'What did Caroline say?' he asked.

'Nothing much,' Holly lied.

'Anyhow, Tom has no place to stay so I said he could bunk up with me when Joan goes,' Kenny continued.

Holly thought of Kenny and Joan's flat. It was bigger than hers, certainly, but still possessed only two miniature bedrooms. There was no space for a six foot two giant who could take up half of a three-seater couch when he sat down, and that was when he didn't stretch his legs out. Joan walked in her sleep and no matter where they put Tom, she'd keep falling over him in the night.

'Where's he going to put all this stuff and where's he going to sleep until Joan goes?' she asked.

Kenny's face assumed its 'placate difficult customer' expression. 'Well, you see, that's where you come in, Holls. Joan won't be going for two weeks and until then, to make things easier, Tom needs somewhere to store some of his stuff. Or, he could stay with you and store his stuff in our place.'

Kenny's face was so angelic, Holly thought. Even when he was matchmaking, he looked as though butter wouldn't melt. But Kenny was jumping to conclusions, just like she'd done. Just because Tom had left Caroline, it didn't automatically follow that he wanted to be with Holly.

'I don't think that's a very good idea,' she said quickly.

Kenny's look of surprise was almost comic, but Tom didn't look surprised at all. He knew what Kenny was up to, Holly realised, and he was embarrassed. He'd hoped that Kenny might help him with somewhere to stay and now he'd got roped into this saga of setting him up with Holly, *again*. Holly's face burned with the hurt and shame of it all.

'Sorry,' she said, and rushed back into her flat, slamming the door.

'He's gone,' shouted Kenny ten minutes later. 'Let me in.'

Holly leaned out from the bathroom where she was attempting to dry her tears, and she clicked the lock on the door so that it opened. With tissues jammed up to her eyes, she didn't wait for Kenny to come in. Back in the bathroom, she got out some cleanser and rubbed it under her eyes where her mascara had run down in sooty rivulets. She looked appalling; her eyes swollen fatly from crying.

'I'm sorry, Kenny,' she sniffled, 'but he isn't interested. I know you're doing your best for me but you can't make someone love you. He left Caroline yesterday, I know because she came into Lee's and screamed and yelled at me. She blamed me! Honestly, can you believe it?'

There was a clanking noise outside as Kenny filled up the kettle from the tap.

'And I thought that Tom had left because of me and I waited all last night for him to turn up and he didn't.' Holly splashed cold water on her face to see if that helped. 'He isn't interested, Kenny, and he was just embarrassed by the way everyone kept pushing me in his direction.'

She waited for Kenny's reaction. It was unlike him not to volunteer some opinion.

'I can't believe I was so stupid,' she went on. 'Stupid, stupid, stupid.' She stared at her reflection and saw a scarlet-faced dumb fat girl who'd been in love with a guy who'd been her friend and who'd run a mile from her now. Holly sighed. There wasn't a scrap of make-up left on her face, so she slathered on a decent coating of moisturiser. Might as well make some effort not to totally destroy her skin. Perhaps the tears would act like a home-made acid peel. Shiny-faced, red-eyed and full of self-loathing, she left the bathroom.

585

'Oh, Kenny, what am I going to do?'

But it wasn't Kenny who stood in her kitchenette dunking a teabag into two mugs. It was Tom.

'Bub.' Holly tried to speak but no intelligent words would come out. 'Wha . . .'

'Tea.' Tom handed her a mug and Holly took it.

Cradling the mug in her hands brought back some semblance of normality. 'You were here all along,' she said. 'I thought you were Kenny. You heard everything.' It was almost too much to bear. Why had he done this? Did he want to humiliate her totally?

'Have some tea, Holly, love,' he said softly.

'Is this wise?' she said. 'Giving a woman you've just absolutely humiliated a huge mug of boiling liquid?' Her hands began to shake.

'You're upset. I thought it would help,' he replied, reaching out for her mug.

'Help what?' she screeched, moving back jerkily so that tea sploshed around her shoes. 'Help me look more of a fool that I already am? What are you doing here, Tom? You can't stay here. I've told you that.' Her voice was high and furious, hurt making her lash out blindly. 'How many ways do I have to tell you?'

'I love you, Holly.' He said it quietly first, then more loudly. 'I love you, Holly Miller. Even if you don't love me, even if you think I'm stupid for even being here, I love you.'

She stared at him uncomprehending, listening to the words she'd longed to hear for so many months and yet, she couldn't quite believe them.

'Did you hear me?' he asked. He took the mug from Holly's hands and stood so close to her that she could feel the heat of his body and smell the scent of spicy cologne put on many hours before.

He placed his big hands on her hip bones, curling his fingers in wonderment around her contours. Somehow, the right thing to do was to move closer to Tom, so that their bodies were inches apart and her face was a hair's breadth away from his shoulder. And if she moved her head, she'd be looking up at his face, his mouth.

Holly had thought about kissing Tom all right, and she'd thought of his hands caressing her body, but now that she was standing nipple to nipple with him, she forgot all her imaginary kisses.

All she could think about was his nearness, his maleness, the fact that she wanted him more than anything else in the world.

'Did you mean it?' she whispered.

Just so she had no doubts, he said it again, 'I love you,' as his mouth moved down to hers and they were kissing deeply, drowning in the luxury of each other. Holly's hands were clinging to his head, pulling him closer to her, and his forearms were crushing her body against his. There were small whimpers of pleasure and Holly didn't recognise them as coming from her.

He moved his mouth from hers, just far enough so that he could see her face. 'Do you love me?'

Holly stroked his dear face, astonished that he couldn't feel the love flowing from her fingertips. 'Love you? Are you crazy? I love you so much it hurts.'

And then, Tom's arms grasped her tightly around the waist and lifted her from the ground. Holly wrapped her legs round him, her mouth locked with his, their tongues plunging deeply and sweetly. Gently and without knocking into anything, Tom carried her into her bedroom and laid her down on the bed.

In her whole life, Holly had never felt more desirable or more desired. Kissing and murmuring endearments, they pulled each other's clothes off, with Tom marvelling as each garment was removed.

'You're so beautiful,' he murmured as he unclipped Holly's bra and his fingers splayed over one dusky pink nipple, making her arch her back and gasp with pleasure. Holly felt beautiful. And tiny. Next to Tom's strong, muscular body, she was slender and delicate as a reed. Even more intoxicating was the effect she had on him. When they were both naked and Holly ran her fingers from the bulk of his chest down to the flat planes of his stomach and beyond, Tom groaned as if he couldn't quite take any more.

'I wanted this to last forever,' he said hoarsely, as he covered Holly's body with his own and she stretched languorously under him, loving the feel of his skin against hers. He began a slow trail of kisses from her collarbone down to the silky skin of her thighs, his hands caressing and stroking.

'It can take forever next time,' she said.

She hadn't known lovemaking could be so tender or so wild. And when Tom's hard body moved into hers and exquisite shards of the most intense sensations ever exploded inside her, she felt like an ancient fertility goddess filled with dazzling light as the earth, the sun, the moon and the sea streamed into her in some magical ceremony.

They lay curled together afterwards, Holly's head resting against Tom's big shoulder, their legs entwined companionably.

'I love you, Holly,' Tom said. 'I've loved you for so long, since I met you, practically. But that night at Joan's fashion show, when you were so brave and beautiful like a warrior queen striding down the catwalk, I knew then.'

Holly's fingers reached out and touched the contours of Tom's chest.

'I love you too,' she said. 'Love you, love you, love you.' She laughed softly and snuggled her head even closer to him. 'It's funny that you picked that night,' she added. 'I couldn't believe it when Caroline said you were engaged, I was waiting for you to tell me it was all a mistake.'

'Oh it was,' he groaned, rubbing his forehead with a hand. 'What Caroline wants, Caroline gets. We'd been treading water for a long time. That was partly why I moved away from Cork. Our relationship was dying a natural death and then Caroline came to Dublin, liked the idea of it, and that was that.'

Holly sat up in the bed. 'Did you ask her to marry you?'

Tom sat up too. 'No and yes,' he said apologetically. 'We'd talked about it a year or so ago. But we never decided that yes, we'd get married. And then Caroline was here the week-end before the fashion show and said, "Right, let's do it. Let's get married." I didn't know what to say.'

'No?' suggested Holly.

Tom gently pulled her into his arms, so that they were face to face. 'You're right, that's what I should have said, but I didn't. And by the time I'd worked out that I didn't love her, that I loved you, it was too late. We were on the wedding merry-go-round and I didn't know how to get off without breaking her heart.'

Holly kissed him gently. 'You're a kind man,' she said. 'You didn't want to hurt her.'

'True. The person I wanted to hurt was Vic. I wanted to rip him limb from limb for daring to touch you.'

Holly was amazed to see true fury in Tom's gentle face. His mouth was set in a grim line and his eyes were like flint.

'My big, handsome Corkman, fighting for my virtue,' she murmured, nuzzling his neck. 'There was nothing between Vic and me, well, not on my part,' she amended. 'I wanted Vic to be you.'

'Honestly?'

'Honestly. He tried to take me to bed.' She could feel Tom's whole body stiffen as she said this. 'But I couldn't do it. I wanted him to be you.'

'I'm so glad,' he said, burying his face in her shoulder. 'I know I've no right to be jealous but . . . I am.'

'Jealousy is all right in this context,' teased Holly. 'I was jealous of Caroline.'

'And she was jealous of you,' Tom pointed out. 'I met a friend for a drink two nights ago and Caroline went mental, accusing me of having been out with you. That did it, really. She was raging at me at one o'clock in the morning, scream-ing about you, and I had a sudden image of myself and Caroline together forever. Caroline and Tom. Not *Holly* and Tom. That's when I knew I'd have to be honest and leave.

I moved out the following morning, with her still screaming at me.'

'She came into the shop that evening and blamed it all on me,' Holly said.

'And that's when you came home and waited for me,' finished Tom. 'Sorry. I had to know if you were still going out with Vic, you see. I phoned Kenny but I couldn't get hold of him until this morning and he told me that Vic was off the scene. I also needed to know if you felt the same about me,' Tom said slowly.

'Dear Kenny, matchmaker extraordinaire,' laughed Holly. 'He's probably outside the flat with a glass jammed up against the door as we speak. He tried so hard to get us together.'

'I know. And every time Joan came up with another hare-brained scheme to set you up with a man, I was furious.'

'Were you?' Holly closed her eyes happily, luxuriating in the knowledge that Tom had been jealous of her.

The phone rang, blistering their peace with its loud tone.

'Hello?' said Holly.

'Hi,' said Kenny. 'We didn't like to knock but is everything OK?'

Holly grinned. 'Very OK.' She turned to Tom. 'Do you want Kenny to drop your stuff off?' she asked. He nodded. 'Come on over, Kenny,' she said.

Tom and Holly enjoyed a lingering kiss before getting up. While Tom pulled on his clothes, Holly wrapped herself in her dressing gown and went to open the door.

Kenny and Joan, wide-eyed with anticipation, stood outside.

Holly said nothing but her beaming smile gave her away.

'Ooooh,' said Kenny from the doorway. He beamed back at her, thrilled that Holly and Tom had finally found each other. 'Isn't true love wonderful. You owe me a tenner, Joan,' he added.

'Do not,' said Joan, just back from a night out. 'I always knew they'd get together in the end. The bet was about *when* not *if* and I can't remember what I said or what you . . .'

'Hi, guys,' said Tom, emerging from the bedroom with a parcel in his hands. 'I was looking for my socks and I found this under the bed. It's got my name on it, Holly.'

Holly looked at the carefully wrapped present which contained the birthday present she'd bought for Tom all those months ago and hadn't given to him. 'It's your Christmas present,' she said, deadpan, 'but you can open it now if you want.'

In reply, Tom leaned over and kissed her softly on the mouth.

'Christmas presents? Already?' said Joan, scandalised. 'Are you mad, Holly? I mean, holy shit. You are scaring me. It was my sister's birthday last week and I still haven't got her anything . . .'

Tom kissed Holly again when he saw the Le Corbusier book. He and Kenny admired it, while Joan went on about presents and honestly, she was broke right now. Holly made another pot of tea and couldn't keep the goofy smile from her face. Everything was just perfect.

CHAPTER THIRTY-NINE

Stella stood outside the Intensive Care Unit and leaned against the pale green hospital wall. She'd been there all night and yet the lack of sleep didn't really bother her. She'd heard that in times of trauma, people's bodies found the resources to survive from somewhere. And it was true. It was eight in the morning and all she'd had since the night before were three cups of coffee, a bottle of mineral water and no sleep. Not that she'd have been able to sleep even if she'd had a bed: she was too worried.

Angela's phone call at just after eleven the previous night had given her an enormous shock.

As soon as she'd heard her old friend's voice, Stella had feared the worst.

'Angela, I . . . what . . . Oh no, it's Dad, isn't it?' she'd said, holding onto the edge of the coffee table to steady herself.

'He's had a heart attack and he's in Kinvarra General, Stella. He's in intensive care. The doctors don't want to tell myself and Alastair too much because we're not family. I think you should come . . .' Angela's voice trailed off.

'How serious was it?'

Angela was grave. 'Very, I'm afraid. He was with us when he had the attack, or I don't know what would have happened. He was so distraught, Stella, but he kept saying not to tell your mother. I'm so sorry, I didn't know what to do.'

'You were right to phone me. I'll be there in an hour,' whispered Stella. 'I'll have my mobile phone with me. Phone at any time.' She left the number and hung up, rushing into her room to grab a few things which she stuffed into a small hold-all. Three minutes after Angela's phone call, Stella was in the car. She dialled Tara's number and the answering machine kicked in. 'Tara, if you're there, could you pick up?' said Stella.

Tara didn't pick up. Damn. Stella didn't want to leave a terrifying message on the tape but there was no option. 'Could you phone me on my mobile as soon as you get this, Tara. Bye.'

She tried Tara's mobile but got another machine, where she left the same message. Then she phoned Holly.

'Hiya, Stella,' said Holly, sounding sleepy.

'Hello, darling, I've got bad news, Holly. Dad's had a heart attack.'

'Oh no.' Holly was wide awake now.

'Angela has just phoned me and I've grabbed a few things and am in the car driving home. Do you want me to pick you up?'

'Yes. It should take you ten minutes, I'll be at the gate.'

A wan-faced Holly clutching a weekend case was waiting when Stella pulled up outside the house in Windmill Terrace.

The sisters hugged tearfully.

'Did Angela say anything else? Is he very bad?' asked Holly as she clicked on her seat belt.

Stella shook her head. 'She didn't know much. Luckily, he was with Angela and Alastair and they phoned an ambulance. I hate to imagine what would have happened if he'd been on his own . . .' She had to bite her lip to stop herself from crying.

Holly patted her sister's arm comfortingly. 'Come on, Stella, he's going to be fine, we've got to believe that. If we arrive at the hospital as if we expect the worst, Dad will pick up on that. We've got to be positive for his sake. And he's in the right place, he'll be safe there.'

'I know.' Stella wiped her eyes roughly and did her best to concentrate on the road.

'Did you phone Tara?'

'She's not at home and I didn't want to leave her a message and tell her what had happened.' Stella paused. 'Mum doesn't know either. Angela said that Dad begged her not to phone Mum.'

Holly groaned. 'Oh poor Dad. He thinks if Mum knows, she'll come home only because he's sick and he wants her to come home because she wants to be with him. We've got to tell her, Stella.'

'We can't phone her in the middle of the night, she'd only drive up and crash the car or something.'

'Well, we have to phone first thing in the morning, then. She loves him, you know,' Holly added. 'She really does.'

The gods were with them on the journey and they made it to Kinvarra in just over an hour. It was years since either of them had been in the hospital but the cardiac ICU was well signposted, and they sprinted up stairs and along corridors until they saw Angela and Alastair sitting quietly in a waiting area. They were holding hands and Angela was crying. Stella's gait slowed till she was moving like a person in quicksand. Angela could only be crying for one reason.

'No!' sobbed Stella, the word sounding like a wail.

'Oh, Stella, it's OK.' Alastair leapt to his feet and held both sisters close. 'He's not dead, it's OK, we're just a bit emotional . . .'

That was all they needed to hear. While Holly hugged Angela in thanks, Stella rushed off and found a nurse to take them in to see Hugh.

The ICU ward was quiet but for the hum and bird-like beeps of banks of monitors. Three of the four beds were occupied, with patients lying as still as mummies, swathed in thin hospital sheets, surrounded by the machines that registered their every heartbeat. Hugh was by the window.

The man in the bed didn't look like her father, was Stella's first thought. Her father was always healthy-looking, with a glow and a vibrancy emanating from him. Now he was frighteningly immobile and his skin was grey, as if he was already dead. He had oxygen tubes running into his nostrils, monitor sensors sticking to his chest and a drip attached to the back of one hand. The nurse made room for them to stand beside their father.

'Don't be alarmed. It always looks terrible,' she said calmly.

'How is he?' Stella asked, clasping Hugh's limp hand. On the other side of the bed, Holly pulled up a chair, sat down and stroked her father's forehead, her eyes clouded with unshed tears.

'He's doing all right,' the nurse said guardedly. 'He was lucky he was with people who could phone for an ambulance. I'll get a doctor to talk to you. Sit down.' She pulled another chair over and Stella sank onto it gratefully. Round them, nurses came and went, checking Hugh's progress, making notes, nodding hello at the sisters who sat in numbed silence.

Stella prayed like she'd never prayed before, asking God for forgiveness for how rarely she went into His house, but begging for his help.

Please, please save my father. He's a good man, he doesn't deserve to die.

It had been half an hour before they'd seen a doctor, a tiny Indian woman with the darkest, kindest eyes Stella had ever seen.

'Your father has had a massive heart attack. At the moment, the biggest risk is arrhythmia: abnormal heart rhythms. We're monitoring him and giving him drugs to try and control this but the next few hours are crucial.'

During the night, Stella and Holly had spent time sitting outside the ICU when the medical team were with their father. Stella sent Alastair and Angela home to get some rest.

'There's no point in us all being here,' she said. 'You need some sleep.'

Twice they'd got cups of milky weak coffee from the

machine in the corridor, yet the knot in Stella's stomach meant she hadn't been able to finish hers.

There didn't seem to be any change in Hugh's condition during the long lonely hours of the night. He'd woken briefly once and smiled a faltering smile at his daughters, who'd whispered that he was going to be all right and that they loved him and ... But he'd drifted off again, leaving them a little bit more hopeful.

At half seven, the nurses sent the sisters off to get some breakfast.

'We'll phone you if there's any change. The specialist will be around by half nine, so be back then.'

Holly said she'd just visit the loo first, so Stella waited for her, leaning wearily against the hospital wall, thinking back over the night.

It would soon be time to try Tara again.

'OK?' said Holly, coming back from the loo and putting an arm round her sister's shoulder.

Stella nodded.

Outside the calm, unreal atmosphere of the hospital, it was a bright sunny morning. It seemed odd to see the coming and going on the street: cars with tired commuters heading for work, people walking smartly to bus stops. In the ICU, it had felt as if time had been suspended somehow, and yet Stella could see that it hadn't.

The nurse had recommended an early-morning café across the road as the hospital canteen wouldn't be open for hours. The scent of frying mingled with the tang of strong coffee hit them as they walked into 'Sid's Caff: Good Food All Day'.

'I don't know if I could eat anything,' muttered Stella.

'Nonsense,' replied Holly firmly. 'We're having the full Irish breakfast and you're going to eat every mouthful if I have to shovel it in myself.'

Somehow Stella managed to eat half of her breakfast, and she did feel a lot better when she sat back to finish her coffee.

'I wish you'd give up,' she commented as Holly lit up.

'Don't nag,' begged Holly. 'I'm down to five a day.'

'Heart disease is genetic and if you keep smoking, you'll end up in a hospital bed like Dad one day,' Stella said. She was suddenly furious with Holly for smoking. How could she risk her life like that?

Holly watched the play of emotions on Stella's pale face and she knew her sister was right. Stella wasn't nagging, she just cared.

Holly opened her packet of cigarettes. There were nine left in the box. Nine and the one she was halfway through smoking. 'You're right,' she said, sighing. 'I promise never to buy a packet of fags again, deal? I'll smoke these and that's it.'

'You promise?'

'Cross my heart and hope to die.' Holly uttered the childish vow with her eyes shut.

'Not so much death, please,' said Stella, but she was smiling. 'Thank you, Holly. I know it'll be hard but you'll be doing yourself such a favour. And all of us.'

Holly took an extra long drag on her cigarette. 'I had to bite the bullet some time,' she said. 'Talking of the rest of the Millers, hadn't we better phone Tara?'

Tara lay immobile in her bed, listening to the radio and willing herself to wake up properly. Sleeping tablets were overrated, she decided. Even her previous state of insomnia was better than this. Last night was the second night she'd taken one and while she had actually slept, it had been more of the knocked-out-by-Mike-Tyson sort of sleep than anything refreshing. Isadora had mentioned that the tablets were strong but she hadn't said anything about the knock-out-punch capabilities.

'The doctor gave them to me when my father died,' Isadora had explained. She peered at the best-before date. 'No, they're still OK. But don't have a glass of wine or anything with them, or you'll feel dopey in the morning.'

There was no alcohol in Tara's apartment any more. She'd emptied every single bottle down the sink, even the tonic bottle she'd been surprised to discover was half full of vodka. She'd felt queasy even smelling the alcohol, and simply couldn't face the notion of so much as a white wine spritzer. Alcohol had no place in her life any more, not after what it had done to Finn.

So she'd taken her sleeping tablet with an abstemious glass of mineral water both nights, and had still woken up like a zombie.

She moved in the bed, her limbs leaden. Definitely no more sleeping tablets. A cool shower was the only option. The noise of the shower blocked out the sound of the phone the first time and Tara stood face-up under the streaming water, trying to invigorate herself with icy water. She was just towelling herself off when the phone rang again. It was only ten past eight, nobody but Finn would phone her at home at that hour of the morning. Tara lunged for the phone in the hall and was startled to see that she'd had two messages.

'Hello.'

'Tara, thank God.' It was Stella. 'Is Finn with you?'

Tara's mind ran rapidly through the possible answers to this. 'No, he's gone to work early,' she said quickly, then, 'why did you ask.'

'I didn't want you to be alone when I told you,' Stella explained. 'It's Dad. He's had a heart attack.'

Tara held the towel closer round her body and began to shake.

'Hello, girls,' said their father. He was sitting up in bed with a nurse beside him giving him several pills.

'Oh, Dad,' Stella beamed at him.

Holly kissed his forehead softly. 'You gave us all a fright, you bad boy,' she teased.

'Probably too much disco dancing,' joked the nurse. 'These tall, silver-haired fellows are all the same. Once they hit sixty, they go mad for dancing.'

Hugh laughed and both Holly and Stella relaxed as they saw the spark of humour in his tired eyes.

'Now, girls, we want your father to get some sleep, so we'll throw you out for a few hours. The night staff say you were here all night, so you might want to get a bit of a rest yourselves. We'll look after Mr Disco Dancer here and we'll phone you if he does anything wild.'

It was the right approach. Hugh hated being treated like an invalid and now his grin broadened naughtily, as if he really was capable of dancing, rather than being confined to bed after a massive heart attack.

Outside the unit, a different doctor filled them in on their father's condition.

'We need to find out how much his heart has been damaged and to discover if blocked arteries have contributed to the attack. We'll probably do an angiogram in a few days but we want to make sure he's stable first. These first few days are when he's most at risk.'

When the doctor had gone, Stella and Holly went back to sit with their father for a few minutes.

'We've been talking to Tara and she sends you her love. She's on her way here.'

Hugh nodded. 'About your mother . . .' he began.

'We're going to phone her,' Holly said firmly. 'Don't get upset, Dad. Mum needs to see you.'

'What if she doesn't want to come?' Hugh said weakly.

Stella crossed her fingers surreptitiously. 'She'll come.'

The sisters were both shocked at the state of their home in Kinvarra. The house was adequately clean, yet somehow cold and unlived in. The essence of Rose had gone and the rooms were bare and cold without her touch to liven them up.

'Go to bed, Holls,' said Stella. 'I'm going to wait up until Tara gets here. They said they'd let her in to see Dad but they won't let her stay if he's asleep, so I told her to come here and we'd go in together later.'

'You've got to phone Mum.'

Stella wondered if she was doing the right thing by phoning Rose. She didn't want to distress Hugh in his state, but she knew that her mother would never forgive her for leaving her out of this crisis.

Rose had spent the morning in the Albertine Residential Home, helping make beds. In fact there was a lot more to it than that, but making beds was what she was officially supposed to be doing.

'That's how we describe what our volunteers do to the health board,' explained Matron Jessica Arthur, who ran the home. 'If they thought we had people doing any more than that, they might cut some of our staffing allowance and we'd never cope.'

Rose didn't know how the home coped as it was. In the Marigold unit, which was where she was working, there were fourteen people in need of twenty-four-hour care and staffing problems meant there were often less than four nursing staff on hand. Freddie had her name down for helping out when her ankle was better, but the doctor had said she needed a few more days off it and she'd be fine, so Rose stepped in to help until Freddie was ready.

Which was how Rose came to be helping feed Violet, a tiny, frail old lady who was nearly blind and lived in a world of her own due to several strokes. Violet was ninety and when she was well, had taught piano and been an ardent grower of orchids. Now, she sat day by day in a cosy chair specially made for frail people, with a soft sheepskin rug underneath to keep her bones from hurting. A soft-as-rabbit-fur mohair blanket in pale lilac covered her because, as the ward sister, Ellen, had explained to Rose, 'Violet adores lilacs and pinks.' That was what Rose loved about The Albertine. In some homes, she felt that Violet's love of lilac and pink would be forgotten because keeping the blankets clean wasn't easy and it wasn't as if Violet could even see the pretty colours properly. But in The Albertine, dignity and love were of the utmost importance. Violet liked her blankets and she would have them.

While Rose gently spooned yoghurt into Violet's mouth

the rest of the staff were free to rush around doing their jobs, averting danger when eighty-three-year-old Gwen nearly walked into the door because her eyesight, even with thick glasses, was bad, dancing a bit with Mike, to the Glenn Miller music that was today's easy listening, and patiently escorting people to one of the unit's three bathrooms.

'Ooh, In The Mood,' said Ellen cheerily. She linked her arm through Mike's and he shone a toothless grin at her. 'Will we dance?' asked Ellen.

Mike didn't remember who he was or even who his only son was when he visited, but Mike loved Glenn Miller and was always ready to waltz.

'Well done,' Ellen added as the pair of them shuffled past Rose and she saw that Violet had taken nearly all the yoghurt. 'I think that you and Violet have definitely made friends for life, isn't that right, Violet, pet?'

The patients in the Marigold unit were all suffering from various forms of neural disability, from stroke damage and dementia to brain injuries. They weren't the easiest patients in the home to care for and, as Matron explained, it took a very special person to do so. But Rose loved working there. On her three mornings a week, she felt taken out of herself. This was what she should have been doing all her life: caring for others. Not sitting through endless committee meetings and discussing how many raffle tickets she could sell. No, this was what she was good at. Really helping people.

After her morning in The Albertine, Rose drove through Castletown and stopped outside Murphy's Grocery to pick up something for dinner that night. Murphy's sold everything from food to beach balls and during the summer months, was jammed with children queuing for ice creams, while sun-kissed holidaymakers who'd been sunbathing on the beach ambled slowly round the shop, their bare legs dusty with sand from the beach. At this time of year, there was always a fine layer of sand on the floor in Murphy's, Freddie said. Carrying her basket, Rose passed two little girls standing in front of the children's sunglasses and trying to make the vital decision as to whether sparkly silver or more girlie pink glasses looked better. They couldn't have been much more than eight or nine and they kept trying the glasses on, giggling at each other and then giggling even more when they saw their reflections.

They reminded Rose of Amelia and for a moment, she felt a pang of loss. During the summer, Amelia often spent weeks in Kinvarra with Hugh and Rose, and they had such wonderful times, going on adventures: taking trips to McDonald's; making Hugh go up in the roller coaster by himself when the funfair came to town, with Rose and Amelia on the ground waving up at him. Biting back the sudden rush of tears, Rose wriggled past a gaggle of customers deliberating over the sun creams. She threw a French stick into the basket, added some local Castletown cheddar, a jar of pickled onions from the organic farm down the road, and then picked tomatoes, lettuce, cucumber and peppers for a salad. It was nearly two by the time Rose parked outside Nettle Cottage and hoisted her shopping from the boot.

Mildred, Prinny and Pig ran out, panting, with Freddie following, still limping.

'Where's your crutch?' demanded Rose as she walked up the path with the dogs excitedly investigating the thrilling smells coming from her shopping bags. 'I'm shattered,' Rose went on. 'I had a marvellous morning but, wow, it's hard work . . .' She broke off because Freddie was looking at her strangely. A sort of working-out-how-to-break-bad-news strangely, Rose realised instantly. Her body began to shake and she had to put the bags down on the path.

'Come inside,' said Freddie, picking them up.

'No.' Rose stood still. 'I won't, not until you tell me. Is it the girls or Amelia? Tell me for God's sake, Freddie!'

'It's Hugh. He's had a heart attack. Stella phoned me this morning just after you'd left. She didn't want you to hear it over the phone and I felt the same, which was why I didn't phone the nursing home.'

'A heart attack.' Rose knew her face was as blank as her

mind. 'But how . . . And how is he? He's not dead, is he? You're not trying to break it to me gently, are you?'

'No, I'm not. He's alive but he's in Kinvarra Regional Hospital and Stella and Holly are there with him. Tara's on her way. Come on,' Freddie urged. 'Come inside and sit down. You've had a shock.'

Rose let Freddie lead her inside and she sat in front of the fireplace. She felt limp, drained, as if her life force had been sucked out and all that was left was a shell. The click of the kettle told her that Freddie was coming to the rescue with hot, sweet tea.

'When did it happen?'

'Last night.'

That was an even bigger shock. 'Yesterday? But why didn't they tell me sooner?'

Rose simply could not understand this. She and Freddie had been in all the previous evening because the poker classic, Freddie's absolute favourite form of evening entertainment, had been cancelled.

The dogs, sensing that Rose was upset, ranged themselves round her as comforters. She reached out and petted Prinny's soft head while Freddie silently continued with her tea preparations.

'Freddie, why didn't they tell me sooner?' asked Rose again before the answer popped into her head. 'Hugh didn't want me to know, did he?'

Freddie put the tea tray on the low table with a bang.

'I know you don't like sugar usually but when you've had shock . . .'

'Freddie, tell me,' warned Rose.

'He didn't want you to know. He didn't want Stella, Tara or Holly to know for that matter,' Freddie announced. 'But Angela Devon wouldn't listen to him and phoned Stella.'

'And not me,' said Rose quietly.

'Perhaps she thought that the girls should talk their father round on that one,' Freddie replied sensibly.

Rose took a sip of the tea and shuddered. It was too sweet

to drink. Rushing into her room, she found her mobile phone and turned it on. Quickly she dialled Stella's and then Holly's phones, but neither was switched on. Then she rang Tara.

'Oh, Mum,' said Tara tearfully. 'I'm driving down to Kinvarra now. Stella couldn't get hold of me until a little while ago. Poor Dad, I don't know how he is or anything . . .'

'Hush,' comforted Rose, 'Don't worry, darling, it's going to be fine. They're wonderful in Kinvarra hospital, they'll look after your Dad. You know he's as strong as an ox.'

'But he's not,' sobbed Tara. 'He's got so thin and he won't eat or anything. Stella said he'd lost loads of weight and he's just given up. I can't take any more, Mum. I can't take it. Not after Finn.'

'What about Finn?' asked Rose in horror.

'He left me,' sobbed Tara.

Rose closed her eyes and said a quick prayer for the safety of her family. This was her fault. She should have been looking after them and then none of this would have happened.

'Tara, love, it will be all right. Your Dad's going to be fine, he's a fighter, you know. I'll be there as soon as I can and I'll cheer him up. And as for Finn, he loves you, darling. He'll come back.'

'He won't, he's been gone for ages, I haven't heard from him,' Tara continued.

Rose felt as if she'd missed about ten episodes of a television series and was having trouble catching up. 'Don't worry,' she repeated. 'It will be all right.'

Tara snuffled goodbye and then Rose began to pack at high speed.

'Give Hugh my love,' said Freddie, hobbling into Rose's bedroom to help.

Rose nodded. She didn't want to think about love or she might cry.

'Give him your love too, Rose,' Freddie added. 'That's what you both need.'

*   *   *

Rose didn't know how she made the journey from Castletown to Kinvarra. She drove on automatic pilot, some unconscious part of her mind telling her which route to take and which bits of the road to be careful on. She wanted to drive like the wind, breaking the speed limit to reach Hugh before it was too late, but the sensible Rose knew she couldn't do that. It was bad enough that one of the Miller parents was in hospital.

As she drove, she tried to get her mind round the idea of healthy, robust Hugh in hospital. He'd never been sick in his life. Flu, bronchitis, tiredness: they were things that affected other people, but not Hugh. He was vital, with this life force thrusting through his veins.

'Good blood,' he used to joke and Rose had felt irritated because she felt he was implying that his wealthy, privileged background made him hardier than her dirt-poor peasant family. How stupid she'd been. He hadn't meant that at all. He was just proud, in that typically masculine way, that he was never ill. There had been no slur intended on Rose and her family.

Dammit it, she didn't care about the speed limit. She had to get there. If she got stopped by the police, she'd tell them she was racing to see her husband because he'd had a heart attack and she loved him and had to be with him. She loved him, she really did. Rose put her foot down on the accelerator. Please, please let her not be too late. She'd never forgive herself if she was.

'Stel, it's Glenn for you.' Holly called up the stairs and Stella rushed into her parents' room to pick up the extension.

'Glenn, hello.'

'I'm so sorry to hear about your Dad,' said Glenn.

'Thanks,' said Stella, bursting into tears.

'I didn't mean to upset you,' said Glenn awkwardly. 'I only wanted to phone and say I'd got your message and ask did you want me to fly Amelia home early.'

'Yes,' sobbed Stella.

When she'd finished talking to Glenn, she went into Holly's old bedroom and found her sister lying fully dressed on the bed.

'I don't feel like sleeping,' Holly sighed. 'I wish I could, I'm wrecked.'

'I keep crying and I don't know why,' sobbed Stella.

'Stella, Dad's in hospital, Mum's ripped apart with guilt for having left us all in our hour of need, why wouldn't you cry?'

Holly pulled Stella close and petted her the way she petted Amelia, stroking her sister's head and murmuring soothing noises. 'It'll be all right, darling, you know it will.'

'It's ridiculous. *I'm* supposed to be the oldest and the one who doesn't cry.' Stella sobbed into Holly's shoulder and was surprised to find the shoulder suddenly vibrate with laughter.

'You're hilarious, you know,' laughed Holly. 'Being the oldest doesn't mean anything, well, apart from the fact that you were the only one of us to get new school coats!'

Despite her tears, Stella giggled. 'Sorry about that.' As the oldest Miller girl, she'd had two new maroon coats over the years in Cardinal School, while Holly and Tara got them handed down.

'Have you been speaking to Nick yet?'

Stella began to cry even more loudly. 'It's not working out,' she said. 'I haven't seen him for over a week and I think it's over. I'm a mess.'

The sisters sat on the bed for a while, with Holly saying nothing, just stroking her sister's hair.

'You can work it out, you know,' Holly said finally, when the worst of Stella's sobs seemed to be over. 'Look at what happened with me and Tom. If we'd both said what we'd thought from the start, we'd have saved ourselves a lot of pain.'

Stella squeezed Holly's hand tightly. She'd been so happy to hear that Holly and Tom had worked things out. Her sister deserved the best.

'You love him, you can work around the problems,' Holly insisted.

Stella wiped her eyes. 'The positive part of me believes that, but I don't feel very positive right now.'

'Stella Miller,' said Holly sternly. 'You've never been a quitter. Get back with Nick and I know you can make it work. Jenna will come round, she just needs to get to know you first. You're the kindest, warmest, most wonderful person I know and I'm proud as hell of you. So have faith in that.'

Stella managed a teary smile. 'Thank you. Why don't you try and get some sleep. I'll phone Nick and see what happens.'

She felt ridiculously tearful on the phone to Nick and had to stop herself from blurting out that she wished he was with her.

'Your dad's going to be fine,' Nick comforted her when he'd heard about Hugh's heart attack. 'He's strong and healthy, you've got to believe that.'

'I know.' Stella reached for a tissue. 'That's what Holly says but it's just so frightening to see him lying there, hooked up to machines and everything. He looked frail and old in the hospital bed, I never thought of my father like that.'

'I felt the same about my mother.'

There was silence as they both thought about the pain they'd have to face one day. Nobody lived forever, Stella knew, not even Hugh and Rose.

'Do you realise we're being kept apart by parents?' said Nick softly to lighten the atmosphere. 'It's like we're a couple of teenagers and they're doing their best to stop us seeing each other so we can study.'

Stella laughed. 'I never looked at it that way.'

'I did. I miss you, Stella, so much. You have no idea.' Nick was fervent now. 'The only thing that's been keeping me going is the thought that I was going to see you again and that we'd sort it out.'

Stella had been standing at the window in the kitchen. Now, she sat down on the window ledge.

'Jenna said you'd told her we were probably going to split up.'

Stella winced. It sounded so cold when Nick said it and she hadn't meant it like that. 'I was feeling very down,' she said, 'and, to be frank, I thought she'd be happy to hear it.'

'Actually, she wasn't. I know she's been awful to you, Stella . . .'

Stella interrupted. 'She was very sweet that day, Nick. We actually talked for the first time ever.'

' 'She told me that too,' he said. 'She said sorry, sorry to both of us, that she didn't mean to split us up. And,' he added grimly, 'it sounds as if Clarisse has been meddling, making Wendy think that we should get back together for Jenna's sake.'

'Oh.' Another piece of the jigsaw fell into place for Stella. 'I told you Clarisse didn't like me.'

'Yeah well, I'll be having a word with her and Wendy.'

'Maybe you should leave it,' Stella advised. She felt suddenly protective of Jenna and didn't want either Wendy or Clarisse's wrath drawn down upon her. 'I'm sure it's been difficult for Wendy too, and nothing's going to improve if you blame her for Clarisse being a cow.'

'You're the boss,' teased Nick.

'Glad you know it,' she said back.

When Stella hung up she was smiling. If only Dad would get better, everything really could work out all right.

She was really hungry now and opened the fridge. No wonder her father had been ill. There was practically nothing in there, except for milk and some mouldy cheese.

'Right, I'm going to take a quick trip down to the shops,' she announced out loud. Leaving a note for Holly in case she woke up, Stella set off for the supermarket where she got one of the bigger trolleys and began stocking up. There probably wasn't anything in the freezer either, so she fired in all sorts of groceries. Fruit, vegetables, juice, bread, flour to make her own homemade bread, lots of chicken, fish. Whizzing around, Stella soon had a stacked trolley that was hard to push. Boy but she was hungry. Maybe she'd get some salads from the deli counter and eat on the way home. Picking up one of the plastic containers, Stella deliberated over the self-service tubs. Pickled onions, yes. And tuna in fatty, rich seafood sauce, definitely. She kept piling her container higher, bypassing the rice salad and some crisp greens in search of even more gloopy cholesterol goodies. Egg mayonnaise . . . Stella stopped with the spoon midway into the tub. She hated egg mayonnaise. Always had. Yet now she was suddenly overwhelmed with a craving for it. Cravings. The shock of hearing that her darling father was in hospital with a heart attack was only slightly more shocking than realising that she was pregnant. For the second time in twenty-four hours, Stella had to hold onto something to steady herself.

Rose could see Hugh through the glass doors of the Intensive Care Unit. He was asleep and he was alone. She pushed the door open and entered, walking noiselessly to her husband's bed.

Rose had been in many hospitals in her time and seen many ill people, yet even so, it was a shock to see Hugh lying there. He looked so still, as though the life was leaving his body even as she watched. The resolve that had kept Rose dry-eyed during her drive crumpled and she felt her throat constrict with a dull ache.

She should have come home sooner. If she had, this might not have happened. She sat cautiously on the edge of the bed and laid cool hands on Hugh's hot brow. He looked younger strangely. The weight loss made him resemble the man she'd fallen in love with all those years ago, even if he bore many more wrinkles.

They'd had so many dreams then. They were supposed to grow old together. That had been their plan and that could still happen. If she was lucky. She'd been kidding herself that she could cut Hugh out of her life: she couldn't. She needed him, despite everything.

His eyelids flickered and suddenly opened, eyes milky with sleep stared up at her.

'Rose,' he croaked. 'You came.'

'What did you think I'd do?' she said softly, stroking his brow. 'Leave you to the tender mercies of Adele?'

'She's been here but I sent her home,' he said. 'It's you I need.'

'You never did before,' she replied lightly.

'Oh, but I did, Rose, I did.' Hugh's eyes filled with tears and Rose bit her lip to stop herself doing the same. It had been a long time since she'd seen him cry. 'I didn't think you'd come,' he added, his voice a hoarse whisper. 'You said it was over.'

She leaned forward so he didn't have to try so hard to speak. 'I was wrong, Hugh. It's not over, not when you've shared as much as we have. I needed time on my own, now I'm back. To sort you out.'

He smiled weakly and closed his eyes briefly. 'I need sorting out,' he said. 'I'm lost without you.' Suddenly, he tried to sit up and Rose had to help him. 'I told them not to phone you,' he said anxiously. 'I didn't want you to come back because I'm dying.'

'Oh, Hugh.' Rose laid her head close to his. 'You're not dying, my love. I won't let you. And I was going to come home anyway. I had to stay with Freddie because she'd hurt her ankle. I was coming home when she was better.'

'Promise?'

She nodded.

'Dad, Mum!' They looked up to see Tara rushing into the unit, her face tear-streaked and white. She looked like a wraith. 'I thought I'd never see you again,' she said, burying her head against her father's on the pillow.

Hugh's eyes met Rose's.

'Don't cry, love,' he said. 'It's all fine now.'

Rose found a chair for her daughter to sit on. Tara looked so weak that Rose didn't want her standing.

'I'm sorry, love,' said Hugh, still stroking his middle daughter's spiky hair. 'I never meant to hurt your mother or you, love. I can't explain . . .'

Tara held a finger up to his lips. 'Shush,' she said gently. 'I understand.' And she did. She'd loved Finn and yet blindly gone off and betrayed him. At the time, she hadn't thought of how much it would hurt her husband. She'd just done it impulsively. It was only afterwards that she'd realised how much that unguarded moment had hurt him. She'd primly condemned her father for his infidelity, then she'd done the same thing herself. Under the circumstances, she understood what it was like all right.

The memory of Finn's bitter, hurt face that night came to her again and she couldn't smother the strangulated sob that emerged.

'Don't cry,' begged Hugh, thinking it was all his fault.

'It's not you,' cried Tara. She held his hand and cried.

'It's going to be all right,' Rose said, stroking both her husband and her daughter in comfort.

And for the first time in ages, Tara thought that perhaps it would be all right.

CHAPTER FORTY

The nursing staff were very keen on getting Hugh walking.

'I've done three laps of this floor already today,' he said indignantly to Rose when she arrived to visit him after lunch on Friday.

'They're trying to prepare you for the marathon,' Rose replied straight-faced as she put some bottled water and a bag of apples down on his hospital locker. It was four days since she'd raced from Castletown to the hospital and Hugh was vastly improved. The promised angiogram had shown remarkably little arterial clogging for a man of his age and there was talk of him coming out of hospital after the weekend. The doctors had prescribed a litany of pills for him and said he'd need regular checkups, plenty of exercise and no stress.

Hugh, never the best of patients, was getting antsy at being cooped up – and antsy at what had so far gone unsaid between him and Rose. There had been no time for long conversations about the future, partly because there was always somebody popping in and out of Hugh's room, and partly due to the fact that Tara had been spending a lot of time in the hospital. Stella and Holly had gone home on Wednesday evening but Tara had taken time off work to stay in Kinvarra. She hadn't wanted to but Rose had insisted. Shocked by Tara's gaunt face and lack of spirit, she'd wanted to keep her middle daughter close so she could take care of her. 'You never take all your holidays,' she said firmly. 'Take some now.'

Today, Tara had slept late and woken up looking a little better. There was a healthy colour to her cheeks and her eyes held some of their old sparkle.

'Do you mind if I don't come to the hospital this afternoon, Mum?' she said. 'I think I'll go into town and take a look round the shops, maybe spend some time in the library.'

'Good idea,' said Rose, relieved to see some signs of Tara returning to normal.

Which meant that Rose had Hugh all to herself on the afternoon visit. Adele, who'd been very shaken by her brother's illness, was due to visit that evening.

'Let's take another walk,' Rose said now.

Grumbling, Hugh allowed her to help him on with his dressing gown and they set off along the corridor, Rose linking Hugh's arm as they progressed slowly.

They'd turned the first corner when Rose spoke. 'We need to talk.'

She could feel Hugh tensing.

'Don't you want to talk?' she asked.

'I do,' he said, 'I'm just nervous of what you're going to say.'

'Why? What do you think I'm going to say?'

'That you came here to make sure I wasn't going to shuffle off this mortal coil and now that I'm getting better, you're going away again. I couldn't bear that.'

'Why didn't you say anything, then?' Rose inquired. 'No, don't tell me. You thought that if you said nothing, it would all go away.' She was fed up with Hugh's procrastination.

'Please, Rose,' he begged. 'Don't fight with me. I'm not able to fight. I'm sorry for everything, so sorry. I told you that before and I've had weeks to sit and think about it all. That's all I did, you know. Think about you and the girls and how I'd let you all down.'

They kept walking, but Hugh's head was bent now, as if in penance.

'Believe me, Rose, if I'd known what I was doing to you, I'd never have done it. I just didn't think. It was stupid,

stupid seeing those women, but they were no substitute for you. It just happened.'

'And how would you have felt if I'd done the same,' she said, her voice hard, 'if it had just *happened* for me? If I'd had a fling with Alastair, or run around with James from the bank? How would that have felt to you? You know exactly how it would have felt, you'd have been furious and devastated, Hugh.'

'I'd have wanted to kill them,' he said simply.

'It's no different for me. Except that I wanted to kill you too. How could you do that to me, Hugh?' That was the question that had haunted Rose for so long. How could a man cheat on a woman and think it meant nothing, and how could he cheat and still love her? Men and women were different, as modern psychology experts were always pointing out. Was that enough of an answer?

'Rose, I am sorry. I can't make up for what happened in the past, and it was the past. I haven't looked at another woman for years. She . . . she was part of the past and I was trying to be kind to her.'

Rose could imagine that all right. Hugh had never been much good at jettisoning people.

'Things are different now. If only you'd come home and stay, please . . .'

A nurse waved at them and Rose managed to wave politely back as they continued on their way.

'And you'll never, ever do it again,' she said.

'Never. I love you, I nearly lost you, Rose. I'm so sorry . . .'

Hugh leaned wearily against the padded handrail that lined all the corridors. He looked grey in the face again, making Rose realise that he had still a long way to go to recover. She felt a wave of compassion drift over her. She did love Hugh, despite everything.

'I should have said something a long time ago,' she said quietly. 'I knew you'd been involved with other women and I let it go on because I thought it was more important to keep the family together than to break it up over your affairs.'

'Rose, please forgive me.'

'I have,' she said dryly, 'or I wouldn't be here. I had to forgive myself first.'

'You did nothing wrong,' he interrupted.

'I allowed it to continue,' Rose said. 'We were living a lie, Hugh, and I won't do that again. Everyone thought we had it all, the marvellous Millers. Living that lie nearly destroyed us.'

He gripped her hands tightly. 'It hasn't, though, Rose, has it? We're not over, please.'

'We're not, but you have to promise that it will never happen again. You have to choose me, Hugh. Because if you betray me again, I'll leave you and I'll never see you again. Ever.'

'I know. I promise. I love you.'

She believed him. Hugh understood that she meant what she said.

There in the pale green corridor, they embraced, Rose holding the thin body of her husband close to her, careful not to squeeze too tightly.

'We're not over,' she whispered into his ear. 'But there can be no more lies or secrets.'

'Never,' he whispered back, holding her just as tightly.

'God, would you look at the pair of them,' said one of the catering staff as she wheeled along the afternoon tea trolley. 'They'll throw you out, love, if you keep at that!' she roared at Rose.

'She thinks I'm your fancy piece,' Rose said wryly.

Hugh smiled. 'Much better, you're my wife.'

Stella stood outside Austyn's Jewellers and admired the engagement rings. There were no prices visible on the fat velvet cushions. If you had to ask the price, Stella knew, you couldn't afford them. She tried to work out which one she liked best. The enormous diamond she'd seen being purchased the previous December had been replaced by something similar, another knuckle-duster that would need its own insurance broker and a hotline to the police station.

There was one ring she really liked; Art Deco-style with a square cut diamond surrounded by tiny emerald stones. She held out her hand and tried to imagine what it would look like. Her fingers had swelled up, she noticed. She'd been the same when she'd been pregnant with Amelia. Her actual bump had remained small and neat until the fifth month, but water retention meant she'd had to stop wearing her ring from the third month. If her calculations were correct, she'd be three months pregnant very soon and it looked as if the water retention aspect was repeating itself.

'Working out which one looks best?' said a voice.

'Nick!' Stella turned and Nick caught her in his arms.

'Sorry I'm late. It's a nightmare parking round here.'

Stella hugged him tightly, feeling the familiar waterworks spring into action. She cried at the drop of a hat. How the hell was she going to tell him she was pregnant without bursting into tears in the restaurant. Hormones were one thing but this was ridiculous.

In the four days she'd known she was pregnant, Stella had mentally gone through every permutation of the words 'I'm having our baby.'

She simply didn't know how to say them. She and Nick had never discussed the concept of having a child together. They had enough trouble with their offspring as it was.

'I've missed you, so much,' said Nick, still hugging her. 'If you hadn't been free for lunch today, I'd have marched into your office and pretended to be a client again. I couldn't have waited until tonight.'

Stella grinned. As it was, she'd rescheduled several appointments so she could meet Nick for lunch. When she'd driven up from Kinvarra the night before, she'd deliberately said it was too late to see Nick because she was too apprehensive about telling him the news. They walked up the street holding hands and stopped outside a Japanese restaurant they both liked. Next to it was an old-fashioned American restaurant which was famous for burgers, spicy potato wedges and a calorie-laden chocolate dessert that added an instantaneous five kilos onto anyone who ate it.

'Right, healthy noodle bar lunch or pig-out enormous platefuls of chips?' said Nick.

'Chips,' said Stella firmly.

'OK,' he replied, astonished.

'And chocolate cake for afters,' said Stella dreamily.

The rich scent of flame-grilled burgers made Stella salivate with hunger as they sat down in the restaurant. 'I'm ravenous,' she said, scanning the menu and wondering if she could have her burger with extra onions. Oh, yes, milkshake. She licked her lips. A huge glass of sludgy, creamy strawberry shake would be fabulous.

The waitress took their order without batting an eyelid. She was used to people coming in and ordering enormous meals. Nick, however, watched in stunned silence as Stella went for garlic mushrooms ('extra garlic, please'), the Mega-Byte Burger ('lots of onions'), a large plate of wedges, a deluxe strawberry milkshake and a side order of guacamole. Finished ordering, she smiled and looked at him.

'Er, medium burger with cheese, small order of wedges and a Coke,' he said.

'You can have some of my mushrooms,' Stella said kindly.

'Did you starve in Kinvarra?' teased Nick when the milkshake, a giant portion of garlic mushrooms and Stella's burger arrived and she attacked the meal as if she'd been on the Dr Atkins Diet for six months.

The waitress placed his burger in front of him; beside it, Stella's meal looked huge.

'There's enough there for two,' he laughed.

Stella's mouth fell open and Nick stopped laughing. His hand, on its way to pick up a potato wedge, dropped like a stone to the table.

Stella took a gulp of milkshake. 'I didn't know how to tell you,' she said, 'but I guess I have.'

'You're pregnant.' It was half question, half statement.

Stella suddenly didn't feel as if she could eat her lunch.

Her stomach felt the way it did when she was on a plane and it hit a pocket of turbulence.

And then Nick smiled, and the turbulence feeling vanished.

'That's incredible, our baby. How long?'

'Three months.'

His hands snaked past the mountain of food and found Stella's. 'I don't know what to say,' he said, still smiling idiotically. 'I'm thrilled, it's . . . we're . . .'

'I wasn't sure what you'd think,' Stella said, beaming back at him. 'We have enough excitement in our lives as it is.'

'Oh, Stella, I love you.' Holding hands like teenagers on a first date, they smiled dreamily at each other.

'I love you too.'

'So when are we having the baby?'

She giggled. '*We're* having the baby in December. I hope you're going to take your share of the contractions and all the other pain?'

'I'll expect an epidural,' Nick said. 'I'm no good with pain. And whale music, don't forget that. I love a bit of whale music.'

They both laughed at this silliness. Stella felt like laughing all day long. How had she ever felt worried about telling Nick the news? The only question now was how they were going to tell their respective children. Stella hoped that Amelia would be thrilled, but what about Jenna?

'Amelia has wanted a baby sister for years,' she said. 'I'm not so sure how she'd feel if we have a boy. What do you imagine Jenna and Sara will think?'

'Two months ago, I'd have groaned at the idea of telling Jenna this news,' Nick said. 'But now, I think it'll be fine. I had a long talk with her during the week; a talk I should have had months ago.'

Stella's stomach experienced a bit more turbulence and she drank some of her milkshake.

'Jenna's sorry, Stella. She told me that she'd said sorry to you last week.'

'She did,' put in Stella. 'I honestly thought we were getting somewhere and then she burst into tears and rushed into the loo.'

'Well, she is genuinely sorry. Saying you're sorry is a huge thing for Jenna, but she is. I'm to blame too. I made a mistake from the beginning by not telling her about us,' Nick admitted. 'She's not a kid but I treated her like one.'

'We'll have to tell her and Sara about the baby soon, then,' Stella pointed out. 'And you'll have to tell Wendy too.' She wondered how the other woman would take the news.

'Wendy will be fine,' Nick said. 'For the girls' sake. We talked about the whole Clarisse fiasco and Wendy's furious about the way Clarisse manipulated her; particularly how it affected Jenna. We were both tied up with how *we* were feeling and we didn't recognise how it was affecting her.'

Stella felt her waterworks spring to life again. Everything really could work out all right.

'There's no need to cry, darling,' said Nick, searching his pockets for his handkerchief. He found it and handed it over. 'Why don't we eat up. There's something I've remembered I've just got to do.'

Stella dried her eyes and looked at her meal. It was getting cool but she was hungry again, and it would be an awful shame to waste it. They talked babies all through lunch. Stella told him what it had been like when Amelia was small, and Nick remembered Sara as a naughty toddler who'd rush upstairs and turn on all the taps whenever Nick turned his back. Even when he talked about Wendy, saying that Jenna was such a good baby by comparison and how she'd sit on Wendy's lap and smile sunnily at everyone, Stella found that she didn't mind any more. Nick had a past and she had a past: feeling envious of it was a wasted emotion. What mattered was the present and the future, their future. And now, that future looked bright.

'Come on, Stella,' said Nick when they were finished eating. 'Let's pay the bill.'

They strolled happily down the street again, and Stella

laughed when Nick kept asking her if she was tired or if she needed a rest. 'I'm pregnant, not sick,' she teased.

'I know,' he said, 'but I want to take care of you.'

'You will,' she joked. 'I'm going to be a tyrant when I get bigger. Although, on second thoughts, maybe I do need to rest now. You can be my slave and carry me.'

'No problem. Will a fireman's lift do?' Nick supported Stella with one strong arm.

They were still laughing when they arrived where they'd met; outside Austyn's jewellers.

Nick gently steered Stella towards the window she'd been standing at when he'd arrived.

'Which one do you like?' he asked softly.

Stella turned round and stared at him.

'They make maternity wedding dresses, or so I believe,' Nick went on. 'Or we could wait till afterwards if you think your Aunt Adele might collapse with the shock of her niece walking down the aisle nine months pregnant.'

The image of Aunt Adele's face was so delicious that Stella exploded with laughter.

'Is that a no?' he asked, grinning.

'No, it's a yes,' she replied.

Holding hands, they walked into the shop.

An assistant shot out from behind the counter.

'Sir, madam, may I help?'

'We want to look at your engagement rings,' announced Nick with pride in his voice.

'Cushion number one,' added Stella.

The salesman smiled. God, he loved his job.

Mike Hammond's house sat in a small hollow in thirty acres of rolling hills. The house itself was a sprawling ranch-style building, and behind it were staff quarters, a stable block, a separate gym and garages for his collection of vintage cars. Tara knew this because the house and Mike's second wife, a limpid-eyed Portuguese model, had been featured in a magazine recently. At the front of the house were two huge paddocks and a couple of glossy-flanked chestnut horses grazed in one of them, raising their elegant heads to look inquisitively at Tara's car as she drove past.

This was real money, Tara thought ruefully, aware that she'd blown her chance to ever touch such real money. Working on Mike's friend's script had been her chance to shine and because of everything that had been going on, Tara had found it to be one of the hardest jobs she'd ever worked on. The words that usually streamed from her brain in a seamless rush didn't come. Instead, every rewrite was a painstaking effort with the result that Tara thought it was the worst work she'd ever done. Every line reminded her of the pain of Finn's drinking and the stupidity of her fling with Scott Irving. If they ever did make the script into a film, which she thought was highly unlikely, Tara knew she'd never be able to bear looking at it without remembering this awful time in her life.

Mike's assistant, Steve, took her through the house to a first-floor office with panoramic views of the countryside. With its rosewood furniture, exquisite Aubusson carpet and oil paintings on the walls, it wasn't the sort of office she was used to. But then, Mike was a big name in Hollywood. He would probably be stunned to know that Tara worked on a laptop that sat on a hideous and cheap computer desk by her living room window.

'Thanks for coming, Tara.' Mike came in. He looked more casual than he normally did, dressed in jeans and a sweat-shirt, as if he'd just been in the stables with his beloved horses. The Old Testament prophet image was less strong when he was out of his normal LA black ensembles.

He shook her hand. 'Would you like something to drink?'

'No.' Tara herself was surprised at how vehement she sounded. 'Sorry,' she added. 'Water would be lovely.'

'For me too,' he said to Steve.

'You've a beautiful house,' Tara said, recovering.

He grinned. 'Not bad for a country boy from Galway,' he said.

Tara grinned back. 'You could say that.'

He motioned to her to sit and they faced each other from two vast cream sofas.

'About the script,' Mike began.

'I'm really sorry,' interrupted Tara. 'I blew it, I know. This was a huge chance and I blew it. There's been so much going on . . .'

'What I was about to say was that I loved what you've done with the script,' Mike commented.

Tara gazed at him. 'You couldn't, it was terrible. The characterisation was weak and I couldn't manage to get it right.'

The door opened and Steve appeared silently. He laid a glass of water in front of each of them and went out again.

The nerves she'd managed to suppress up to now emerged and Tara took her glass and gulped back some water.

'The original script was a crock of shit,' Mike said. 'Unsalvageable, I'd have said, yet you managed to breathe real life into it. Yeah, sure there were places where it was flat but there were plenty of touches of sheer genius. You did that and I'm impressed.'

She gulped more water down.

'That's partly why I asked you here today. Some things have got to be done in person. Aaron tells me you've been having problems.'

'Aaron?' Tara felt as if her synapses were fried. What had Aaron to do with this?

Mike shrugged. 'We go way back. We worked together in New York years ago.'

So that was how Aaron had known she was working with Mike Hammond.

'I have a proposition for you but I need to know if you can take it on. I want you to come and work for me in LA.'

The only way Tara managed not to drop her glass was because she was holding it in a tight grip.

'But if you're having personal problems, you might not want to. I need to know and fast.'

'To work on what?'

'A movie script. It's historical, which may turn you off because you like working on modern stuff but . . .'

'No, I'd love it,' said Tara. She could barely believe this. It was all she'd ever dreamed of: being offered a chance to go to LA and become a screen writer. Yeah, she knew that writers could be the lowest creature on the totem pole, but she didn't care. This was the stuff of fairy tales.

'That's good but I need to know that you can handle it, that you're not still going through this bad time you mentioned,' Mike continued.

Tara wondered whether Aaron had a better idea of what was going on in her life than he pretended. He was astute enough to find out about the Scott Irving debacle; perhaps he knew about Finn too and had told Mike. Either way, she had to come clean.

'My husband and I have split up.' Saying it made her want to cry. Finn had disappeared, that was splitting up in every sense. She'd heard nothing from him for three weeks now.

'So a change of scene would be good, right?'

Tara nodded. 'A change of scene would be just what I need.' If Finn wasn't coming back, she might as well leave the country. Perhaps if she wasn't constantly reminded of him, she'd begin to mend her shattered heart.

'Congratulations.' Mike held his glass up. 'They say it's bad luck to toast with water but I don't drink, so what the hell.'

Tara held her glass up too and clinked it gently with Mike's. 'I don't drink either,' she said.

Tara stood at the door of the apartment complex and watched the storage lorry trundle off down the road. Her life was now boxed up and on its way to an anonymous lock-up somewhere until such time as Tara needed it again. She'd sent two big boxes off to Los Angeles and Mike promised that his people would make sure it all arrived in the condo they'd rented for her.

It still hadn't quite sunk in that she was leaving Ireland.

There was a definite feeling of unreality to the whole experience, even though she'd gone through all the fond farewell palaver. She'd been to the riotous leaving party with her *National Hospital* colleagues and had been deeply relieved when Scott Irving hadn't turned up. She'd driven out to Four Winds with the few remaining bits and bobs of Finn's that he hadn't taken that night when he left her.

Gloria had been noticeably absent, to Tara's relief. Even though her animosity towards her mother-in-law had shifted down a few gears to pity, it didn't mean that Tara actually wanted to meet her. Desmond had hugged her tightly and said he loved her, which made Tara feel worse than ever and she'd cried all the way home.

All that was left was the family get-together the following night in Kinvarra, and Tara hoped that she might feel excited about the trip by then. Rose was planning a beautiful dinner for the extended family, but Stella was worried that the celebration, complete with Tom and Nick, would upset Tara. 'Are you up to it? Tom will be there and Nick, so just tell me if you'd prefer if they weren't.'

'I can't mourn forever,' Tara replied. 'And I'd be one hell of a bitch if I was upset that my sisters had found love just because I haven't.'

'Oh, you know what I mean,' said Stella. 'You might prefer it to be just us.'

'No, the more the merrier.'

Tara hadn't been lying. She wasn't upset by the fact that she'd be alone at her special dinner. Finn's absence was something she had to get used to. After all, it was her fault. She deserved the penance.

She shut the door of the flat and looked around. It looked strangely empty without all the books, papers, CDs and assorted other junk. The rental company people were coming first thing in the morning to get the keys from Tara and they had prospective clients due in the afternoon. Renting the flat out was the only possible course of action because without Finn, she couldn't sell it.

She clicked the kettle on to boil, made herself some tea and sat on the couch flicking through the TV channels. She was idly watching a rival soap when she heard a noise in the hall. She froze with terror, casting round frantically for a weapon; something to use against the intruders. They were in the hall, coming into the living room . . .

Suddenly Finn was at the door, wearing his battered old jeans and an unsure expression. They both stared at each other wordlessly.

'Hi, Tara,' said Finn.

She couldn't move, she just kept staring at him, drinking him in after all this time. His hair was shorter and spikier and his face was thinner, like he'd been training too hard in the gym. And his eyes . . . she tried to work out what the look in his eyes said. Was he coming to collect the rest of his stuff and give her his lawyer's name? Or, dare she hope, was it something else?

'Say something,' he muttered,' don't keep looking at me like that.'

'Hello.' Tara got up from the couch but felt too unsure to move towards him. What if she went to hug him and he shoved her away? She couldn't bear that. A lone tear swelled up in one eye and she jabbed at it impatiently.

Finn stared around the room, taking in the bare shelves, the lack of photos and everyday detritus. 'What's happened to all the stuff?'

'I'm moving out,' Tara said, watching him carefully. 'I've arranged to have it rented out. I didn't know what else to do.'

Finn slumped against the wall. 'Moving out, huh? To live with him?'

Confusion reigned in Tara's mind. To live with whom? Mike Hammond? 'Don't be silly, he asked me to work on a script . . .' she began before suddenly she understood what Finn was asking. Was she moving out to live with whoever she'd slept with. Was she moving out to live with Scott Irving. It was so laughable, so utterly ridiculous, that Tara burst into laughter, a sort of high-pitched giggle that sounded odd even to her ears. 'No, don't be silly.'

'What's silly about thinking that?' he asked quietly.

Tara decided that one of them had to take the initiative. She moved closer to him, and leaned on the edge of the couch, just two feet away from where he stood.

'It's silly because that was a huge mistake when I was distraught about what was happening to us. I love you, Finn, there's never been anyone else for me, but I made a mistake. I'm moving out because I got a job offer abroad. I didn't know what else to do because I'm ... I'm ...' The words just wouldn't come. Tara wanted to tell Finn that there was nobody else and that she loved him with all her heart but it had happened again. Just when she needed to be able to pick the perfect words to tell him how she felt, her mind seized up and she felt tongue tied. Ironic for a woman who worked with words. 'Heartbroken,' she tried, hating saying it because it sounded like such a cliché. Yet clichés worked, if they were true. 'I'm heartbroken because you left me and I can't stop thinking about you and how we could do it differently if you came back.' She ran out of steam and words.

Finn was still watching her, his face unreadable, his eyes opaque.

'You talked to Fay,' he said.

She nodded.

'She said that you still loved me even though you told her about my alcoholism.'

Tara's breath stilled. Finn had never used that word before.

He smiled, a weak little smile. 'Yes, I said it. Alcoholism. I am an alcoholic.' His eyes were no longer opaque: blue and anxious, they found hers, spearing into her soul. 'Do you still love me?'

For her answer, Tara lunged at him, wrapped her arms round his body and clung on. 'Oh, Tara,' he cried, his face buried in her hair, then his lips were on hers and they were kissing wet kisses as tears ran down Tara's face. 'I love you.'

'I love you too,' she sobbed, 'but never, never leave me again.'

When their tears were spent, they sat hand in hand on the couch and Finn told her where he'd been. It wasn't a rehab clinic in the strictest sense of the word but a slightly New Age place run by a recovered alcoholic who wanted to give something back. You paid to stay in one of his rooms, you worked on the small organic farm he ran, and you went to AA meetings every day. Nobody was ever allowed to stay twice. It was a one-off deal. You cured yourself and there were no second chances.

When Finn had stormed off, he'd thought of going there but had been too angry. Only after a two-day bender, had he made the decision. 'I couldn't call you, I needed to see if I could stop,' he said, 'or it would have been wrong to come back. I couldn't ruin your life too.'

'You could have told me you were all right,' Tara said, remembering the pain of wondering where he was. 'I thought you were dead in a ditch somewhere.'

'I thought of e-mailing you but I was too much of a coward,' he admitted. 'I wouldn't have been able to face it if you'd replied and told me you didn't want to see me ever again.'

They talked long into the night. Finn sat with his fingers interlaced with Tara's, wanting her to understand but still scared at telling her his story.

'You'd sit there with your one gin and tonic, and I used to long to be like you. One was enough for you, you didn't care if you didn't have another one. But me . . .' Finn's face was suffused with sorrow. 'One wasn't enough. Or two. I wanted every drink in the bar. None of it would be enough, I wanted to blot everything out and not think.'

'Not think about *what*?' Tara desperately needed to understand.

'Me, what I felt about me, how much I hated me. It's hard to explain.'

627

She squeezed his fingers even more tightly. 'Do your best,' she said softly.

'I wasn't good enough, there was this hole inside me, this emptiness and I had to hide it.' Finn closed his eyes, as if he could see what he was talking about and only then could he describe it. 'You're a good person, Tara, and you don't understand what it's like not to be one.'

'Don't be silly, you're a wonderful person . . .'

'No, let me explain. That's what I see inside me: this gaping hole, this nothingness. And when I drink, that goes away a little bit. Or I can't feel it so much. I can like myself when I drink. The self-hatred goes woozy with that first hit of vodka. I feel that nice warmth and it's good, and that's the problem, I think that if I drink more, I'll feel more of that nice warmth. But it doesn't work like that, so I keep drinking to try and regain that first feeling and then, I get scared that the nice feeling will go away altogether and I have this compulsion to drink more. Even when I was drunk, I had to have more, just in case. I used to keep vodka in a tonic bottle in the kitchen.'

Tara nodded. 'I know, I found it.'

Finn opened his eyes and looked ashamed. 'Sorry,' he said. 'I do love you, you know that, don't you?'

'Yes, I know. Why didn't you tell me any of this? I could have helped.'

'That's the sixty-four-thousand-dollar question, isn't it?' he said wryly. 'No alcoholic wants to tell anyone because then, other people will know. It won't be a fear in your head any more, it will be real and you'll have to face it. And stop drinking.'

'And now?'

'Now it's over. I can't drink again, ever. A drink will never be just a drink for me, Tara. It'll be a drug, an anaesthetic. I can't drink any more. Not a glass of champagne on special occasions or the odd half bottle of wine with a meal. I'd love to be able to, I'd love to be able to control it but I can't. I'm an addict.'

'You're supposed to give up the people you drank with,' Tara said.

'Like Derry? I'm fired anyhow.'

'Good. What about a new start in a new country?'

'Do they have AA meetings there?'

Tara grinned. 'They have fabulous weather, glorious beaches, a fantastic standard of living and we've got a condo off Melrose.'

'A condo, huh?' said Finn. He pulled her onto his lap so that they were sitting curled round each other. 'That sounds fabulous. Let's do it, but do you know what I'd like to do first?'

She shook her head.

'Get into bed with you, curl close and sleep. I missed you so much, especially at night. I'd lie there and think of holding you close, sleeping with your body right beside mine, of waking up and feeling your back wedged against me, your skin naked next to mine. That's what I want to do now: sleep.'

Nothing had ever sounded better to Tara. They got to their feet, switched off the light, and walked hand in hand to the bedroom.

Their lovemaking was gentle and tender, as if the tenderness could make up for the pain of their separation. Afterwards, Finn curled up close to his wife and fell asleep. But Tara knew she wouldn't be able to sleep yet. There was so much to think about. She lay in the dark and thought about the future with Finn.

There were no happy endings in real life, she knew, no walking off into the sunset with violins playing a mystical gypsy tune. Their life together would be real, crude and perhaps painful: hard-edged reality instead of a sepia-tinted world as the credits rolled.

Finn wouldn't be able to sit at languorous dinner parties and trail his long, skilful fingers round the top of his wine glass any more. Tara used to love watching him do that, it was like a private prelude to sex, the implication that those fingers would soon be exploring Tara's body with the same subtlety of touch. His eyes would light up as they met hers, teasing her and sending that shiver of liquid excitement rushing through her.

No, their life would mean avoiding those sort of parties, of going home when everybody else was going out. They'd both smile tautly at grand occasions when people were hoovering up champagne, and there'd be a lifetime of people who didn't understand, innocently saying 'oh but you must have one glass. One won't hurt.'

Would Finn be able to cope with that? Would she? Could she be the gatekeeper of his sobriety, always watching, rewarding *good* behaviour like a mother with a naughty child? Tara didn't want to be anyone's keeper. She moved gently in the bed, and watched Finn as he slept. Still the same long lashes and the serene, unworried curve to his cheeks. In sleep, Finn looked as if nothing but good luck had ever touched his life.

She reached out and touched a strand of his golden hair. He looked golden still and he was there, with her. Tara closed her eyes for a minute to gauge how she felt. There it was: that little oasis of comfort in her heart, spreading its heat out into her whole body. She opened her eyes. It was still there. It was there because she was with Finn. He was the person who made her feel this way. They were in this together.

She rearranged her pillow until she'd squashed it into the desired shape, then she wriggled down the bed until her body was lying skin-to-skin with Finn's. In his sleep, he groaned and moved, edging closer to her, with one arm snaking around her. Tara arched herself closer and closed her eyes. There was only one option: they had to try. Now that she'd made her decision, she knew she'd sleep like a baby.

Rose stood in the garden beside the musk roses and shaded her eyes against the evening sun. From inside the house, she

ould hear the last few bars of the music at the start of the
ix o'clock news. Outside, the only sound was of the final
azy droning of bees exhausted after a day spent working
amid the blossoms in Rose's rambling garden. Rose felt tired
oo, but it was that pleasurable tiredness from an enjoyable
ay. She'd spent the morning with Minnie Wilson and it had
een worth spilling her heart out to see Minnie's dawning
omprehension that she wasn't the only person who'd ever
attled depression before. Minnie had been so touchingly
rateful for Rose's help that Rose felt hideously guilty for
ot doing more sooner. She'd hidden behind the facade of
er perfect life instead of being honest and trying to help
Minnie. That would never happen again, she vowed. The
olden Miller facade had been demolished. Rose wanted to
ve a real life, warts and all.

In the afternoon, she and Hugh had gone grocery shopping
o buy food for the family dinner that was to be Tara and
inn's going-away party.

Hugh had decided that it would be extra special if he
ooked the meal and Rose had said why ever not? The old
ose would have had her doubts and hovered around to
elp, waiting for the moment when her expertise was
quired. The new Rose was happy to let other people take
eir turn and she'd come into the garden to cut flowers for
e table.

Consequently, Hugh was labouring away inside, mutter-
g every few moments about how the vegetable peeler must
ave something wrong with it because it wasn't working
operly.

Rose picked up her secateurs and had soon filled the old
ardening trug with her favourite off-white old roses. She
cked some sprigs of lavender too to add to the scent of her
ouquet and was collecting a few more stalks of rosemary for
ugh's ambitious leg of lamb when he walked out into the
rden, wearing her old apron over his clothes. He still
dn't put on the weight he'd lost after the heart attack. It
ade him look older and more vulnerable. He wasn't the

golden boy any more, Rose knew. He was her husband and though he tried to hide it, he was still affected by the brush with his own mortality.

'Was I moaning?' he asked as he sank onto the old wooden seat beside Rose's prized rockery.

Rose pretended to think about it. 'Just a teeny bit,' she said. 'It *is* a useless vegetable peeler, though.'

'But you've managed with it for ages.'

'I'm an expert,' she reminded him, sitting beside him. ' picked some more rosemary for you.'

He took the wiry stalks and inhaled the scent. 'It's year since I cooked,' he said. 'I'd forgotten how much I enjoyed it. Despite moaning about the equipment,' he added wryly

'What was that dish you used to make when we were firs married? Something with baked beans and . . .'

'Mushrooms with an egg in the middle. It wasn't ver successful, was it?'

Rose closed her eyes against the sun. It was lovely sitting there, relaxing, not rushing. Just being. It had taken her tim in Nettle Cottage to appreciate that.

'The calm before the storm,' mused Hugh.

'I'm looking forward to meeting Tom,' remarked Rose. ' did say to Holly that we'd understand if he was a bit pu off by meeting the whole Miller clan in one go, but she sai he'd take it in his stride.'

'As long as Adele doesn't get the thumbscrews out an interrogate him,' Hugh said.

They both groaned at the thought of Adele's unsubtl probing of boyfriends she considered unsuitable. Adele ha certainly softened up in the past weeks, but a person coul only change so much. Hugh's heart attack had instantl healed the rift between Adele and her darling brother. She' been quietly thrilled that he and Rose were back togethe although she'd never say as much.

'Tom's an architect, so Adele will love him,' Rose decide 'I only hope she says nothing to poor Finn about the evi of drink. Will you have a word with her?'

'Yes, of course.' Hugh paused. 'I am worried about Tara and Finn. It's not going to be easy for them.'

Rose smiled. 'Nothing is simple, Hugh. I worry about her too. I worry about all of them. And you. But we've got to let them take care of themselves. Tara and Finn love each other very deeply, that's the best start. They've been honest with each other.'

Hugh's fingers found their way into hers and Rose squeezed back tightly.

'I'm sorry I wasn't always honest with you,' Hugh said.

'Hush,' she replied. 'That's the past. We're living in the future, remember?'

'Rose,' said a querulous voice from the kitchen door. 'Something's burning. The smell's terrible and it's giving me a headache.'

Husband and wife exchanged amused grins. 'Just a minute, Adele,' called Rose. 'How about you see to Adele and I see to the fatted calf,' she suggested.

Hugh's lips brushed her cheek tenderly and his fingers touched the soft curve of her jaw. 'Whatever you say, Rose.'

In the kitchen, Adele muttered to herself as she opened the oven door and peered in at whatever it was that Hugh had been cooking. Something smelled singed, that was for sure. She couldn't see what, so she hoisted the roasting dish out. On the shelf underneath was a dish of blackened vegetables. Broccoli. Clearly, Hugh had cooked it then put it in the oven to keep it warm. Idiot. But she smiled. They'd nearly lost the idiot and Adele couldn't have borne that.

Adele removed the offending vegetables and threw them in the bin. Really, she didn't know what Rose was doing by letting Hugh get involved in the kitchen. With a big family dinner, you'd think Rose would do it herself. Hugh couldn't boil an egg. Just as well she was here to help.

She washed some more broccoli and thought about the impending dinner. It would be interesting to meet Holly's young man. An architect, no less. Adele was impressed.

Holly had done well for herself. And Stella had too. Adele approved of that nice Nick, even though he was divorced. Still, you couldn't have everything. But as for Tara . . . That was another story. Adele would say nothing, of course. Nobody would accuse her of putting her oar in where it wasn't wanted, that was for sure. But, it was as plain as the nose on her face that Tara was heading for trouble with that young Finn. Lovely lad he might have been, but he was trouble. She'd seen it herself from the start.

Still, she supposed that it would all work out in the end. Luck, that's what it was. Wasn't it better to be born lucky than rich, Adele reflected.

Coming in Autumn 2003

Cathy Kelly

BEST OF FRIENDS

The warm and wonderful new novel from
the number one bestselling author of
Just Between Us.

BEST OF FRIENDS

Good times or bad, friends are always there . . .

Abby's TV career is taking off and now she and her husband, Tom, can have the life they've dreamed of in the lovely town of Dunmore. But after seventeen years of marriage, when you're feeling taken for granted, an old boyfriend can spell danger . . .

Abby's daughter, **Jess**, thinks being a teenager is the worst thing ever. While her classmates are blossoming into confident women she's too scared even to smile at the boy she likes. Is she ever going to catch up?

Lizzie has time for everybody: her friends in Dunmore, her grown-up children, even her ex-husband. Then Myles finds someone new and Lizzie starts to wonder if there's anyone out there for *her*.

Erin was happy to follow her husband home to Ireland from Chicago to help his career. But is she ready for small-town life?

Then someone else's tragedy touches the four women and, as they draw together in their sadness, they realize that life is for living, and they have to grab it in both hands . . .

00 715403 8

Someone Like You

Cathy Kelly

Emma, Leonie and Hannah all want just one thing in life and then they'll be truly happy.

For just-married Emma, happiness means escaping the control of her domineering father and conceiving a much longed for child with her beloved husband.

For Leonie, divorced mother of three teenagers, it means finding the true love that was missing from her ten-year marriage.

And for Hannah, striking out alone after the man she loved abandoned her, happiness means independence and security – something she doesn't think any man can provide.

As they work out their hopes, needs and desires, Emma, Leonie and Hannah come to rely more and more on one another's support in their battles to win through.

But sometimes when you wish with all your heart for a dream to come true, you risk destroying the happiness within your reach.

ISBN 0 00 651476 6